I0831703

THE DARK SIDE OF LIGHT

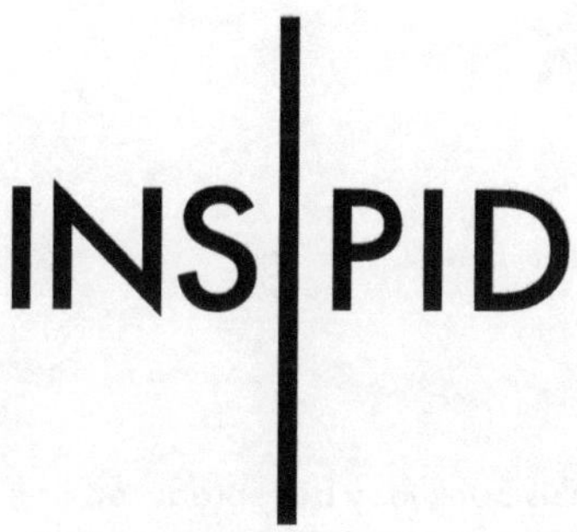

INSIPID

RYAN MILLER

Insipid

Mango Ink Publishing
Mango Ink, LLC

ISBN: 978-0-9895454-6-4

Printed in the United States of America

Cover Art: Ryan Miller
Cover Photo: Jacob Postuma
Design and Layout: Ryan Miller

TO THE ONES WHO HAVE ESCAPED
THE RESEARCH LABS.

KEEP LAUGHING.
KEEP RUNNING IN THE SUN.
KEEP POINTING THE WAY TO TRUE FREEDOM.

HOW DO THE MASSES LEARN
TO DESIRE THEIR OPPRESSION
AS THOUGH IT WAS THEIR LIBERATION?

SPINOZA

PART ONE

ONE

Leo was three when his dad used the jumper cables the first time. He was too young to remember the moment but the scar that runs across his cheek and nose reminds him anyway. It has faded over the years, but like most pain, it hasn't entirely disappeared. As he sat across from me, in my favorite suburban coffee shop, I stared at it and got a lump in my throat. Like I always did. It just about killed me every time I tried to imagine the length of it on the much smaller face of a three-year-old Leo. It would have filled the whole damn thing. I tried to move my eyes.

"Looking at my scar again?" Leo asked.

"Shit," I responded. "I'm so sorry."

He smiled, showing off his unexpectedly beautiful smile. The gods of teeth had somehow given him a perfect set while he was growing up with a family that barely knew orthodontists existed, let alone ever took him to one. He had only been to a dentist once in his life and that was thanks to a nice donation from someone in my church. The dentist told me later that he had never seen such an immaculate mouth from someone who had come from such poverty. He called it a miracle: the immaculate expression. Apparently the Indigenous Australians had perfect teeth too, though, and that was from not eating sugar. Maybe Leo just didn't eat much sugar—although that would have been a miracle in itself, given the "home" he grew up in.

Either way, the teeth definitely helped the smile. But more than that, the smile revealed some kind of joyful energy that comes from somewhere humans have trouble explaining after years of jumper cables, two-by-fours, glass bottles, and savagery from the guardian he was supposed to be able to trust in life.

"It's alright, my friend, don't you worry about it." He laughed, sending his sharp, dark, and distinctive eyebrows up toward the sky. Scientists say those kinds of eyebrows are associated with narcissism but Leo didn't have a narcissistic bone in his body. Not that my narcissist radar could find at least.

"I'm sorry," I repeated, finally looking away. It would have been nice if I had been able to look away from Gwen and her low-cut shirt the first time I had met her to talk about her marriage problems and create a collection of my own. I carried my own set of scars, not as visible as Leo's, and maybe a bit more painful because of all the secrecy.

"Pastor Seth, I really do need to get going." Leo stood up from his chair.

I wish she had said and done the same thing a little over a year earlier. I wish *I* had. Unfortunately, life doesn't give "undo" keys even if I wished for that too. "Leo, you know I hate it when people call me pastor. Just Seth." I stood up too.

"I know." He grinned, showing off that enchanting smile again. "That's why I done it."

I laughed and reached out my arms to give him a hug. As with every time I hugged Leo, I felt like I needed to put on about thirty pounds of muscle in order to lower my risk of instant asphyxiation or organ damage but I managed to survive one more time.

"Keep on rocking, man," I said.

"You too," he answered before turning around and walking his massive, muscular frame toward the door.

I stared for a moment, basking in the leftover energy of Leo and letting my manufactured smile (from years of braces) stay on my face in response to his natural one.

Both eventually faded and I sat down again. My next visitor would be arriving in minutes. It was the dreaded *triple-meeting-morning*. Back to back to back. Leo was the only good one, which meant the next two put a small pit in my stomach.

As I watched Leo get into his 1992 Toyota Camry that used to be maroon before it become whatever color hard water, sun, and rust had turned it into, I thought of the Hero's Journey and wondered whether Leo was just stuck in wilderness for longer than most or if there was an alternate version of the mythic story for people handed the cards he was that never included gifts or heroic returns. Instead—abuse, hate, violence, and an eventual cell. I have a friend who works with prisoners. He says he has never met one that wasn't abused as a child.

I knew Leo didn't wake up one day and decide it would be fun to hurt other humans. I don't think any human does. But abuse is an infection that keeps spreading from one person to the next, until someone, somewhere finds an antibiotic. When your dad cracks a two-by-four across your back and says that he does it because he loves you, well, years later, Leo was just showing love to his girlfriend in the only way he knew how. Unfortunately for Leo, that girl was the daughter of a judge and that judge did not care much for anyone who wasn't white.

I'm not saying Leo shouldn't have paid for his crime but he *really* paid.

Somehow, he still smiles.

I should smile more like Leo.

The sad thing is that Leo found "god" in jail. There are lots of gods, I suppose, but he found one that also shows love by punishing his children with two-by-fours, even if they are shaped into crosses. It all makes sense on some twisted level. They say we store trauma in our brain stem. I would have thought Leo's was full, but maybe he was just addicted to father abuse/trauma and wanted some more from his heavenly "father" too. I love Leo and he loves me. He's put up with more than I can imagine. We've spent a lot of time together but he prays for me because he thinks I don't know god like he does. He's right. I don't. Leo doesn't come to my church anymore and now, I guessed, neither will Bob, who walked in just after I watched Leo's car, with the fish sticker on the bumper, drive away.

I looked at Bob and waved with a fake smile. I'm pretty skilled at fake smiles after years of practicing in front of douchebags like Bob.

A few minutes later, Bob was wrapping up the speech he had prepared for me and probably gone over with his wife a few times the night before. He informed me that he was leaving my church because he felt it had gotten "away from the Bible a little too much." I was, as he said, "propagating the kind of false religion that Jesus warned everyone about in the Bible." He said "he understood the temptations and pressure" and then capped it off with "Jesus come quickly, right, Pastor Seth?"

Well Bob, I wouldn't count on Jesus coming back real soon. I'm sure, thanks in no small part to people like you, he's too embarrassed of the religion started in his name to ever show his face again.

Well, that's what I wanted to say but I don't usually say what I *want* to say. Authenticity is a word that sounds nice on paper, but I'm usually massaging my thoughts as they move from brain to tongue to make them a little less authentic and a little more accepted.

Especially when I'm "Pastor Seth" talking to "Bob."

Especially if Bob is practically begging me to lie to him.

So, I faked a grin and massaged the truth.

"I understand. We're not for everyone. There are lots of other great churches in town." *And they will teach you just what you want to be taught: gay people and Muslims are going to hell and you aren't, even if you're obscenely rich, own four assault rifles that you would gladly use on any intruder, and had an affair that your wife still doesn't know about. I'm sure they'll let you play your guitar on the worship team too.*

He leaned in very sincerely. His cologne had a nostalgic cabin sweetness to it that I'd always liked, even if he did wear way too much. I would miss the cologne. Who was I kidding? I was going to miss the whole family. I didn't mind that we didn't agree. Unfortunately, that feeling is rarely reciprocated, especially in religious circles, where agreements determine your eternal fate, which could include being tortured in the most painful way possible for eternity. That's all. No big deal. If the choice was between burning our relationship or burning forever because he had listened to me propagate a "false religion," it did seem a pretty clear choice.

I definitely would not miss his below-average guitar skills.

"Seth, you've been instrumental in our faith," he continued with a generic patronizing tone. "We've grown tremendously because of your words every Sunday. I just think it's time we move on."

Of course, because you definitely want to leave a place where you've grown tremendously. I'm sure he wasn't really saying what he wanted to say, either. We all have our invisible rules. He was probably being nicer than he wanted.

"I get it," I answered. That was true. I was a little sad, a little frustrated, but mostly fine. He wasn't the first person who had told me they were leaving and he wouldn't be the last. I still liked him and his scents.

"We'll miss you," I said. "Really will. And I hope you find love. And peace. And friends that can share it all with you." I meant all of it. Authentic words for the first time in our conversation.

"Thanks, Seth." We both stood up and I reached out to give him a hug. He seemed surprised, even though we had hugged a hundred times.

"And listen," I added. "Let's not make this awkward. If we see each other around town, we don't have to pretend we don't." We both laughed and he reached out to shake my hand—his preferred method of human interaction for the type of goodbye we were involved in.

"Are you headed out?" He pointed toward the door that Leo had walked out of fifteen minutes earlier.

"I'm actually going to hang around here for a little." I nodded toward the table. "My wife is going to pick me up later."

"Something happen to your car?" he asked.

"No, just sharing today." I smiled. *You know, trying to save the planet one tiny bit.*

"Alright, see you around, Seth. God bless you and your family!" Everyone in the store could hear him—which I assumed he intended—and he waved happily before turning around to leave.

"Take care, Bob." I responded so he and everyone else could

hear my response—that didn't include arcane religious clichés—and took my seat back at the table in front of my lukewarm coffee, wondering if I should get a hot refill.

I pulled out my phone and started looking over some news feeds, choosing the more convenient addiction to numb myself instead.

"A Mexican Demon Named Charlie Is the Internet's Newest Urban Legend" was the first title I clicked on. According to the article, summoning a demon was the new rage for teenagers. They were drawing crosses on sheets of paper and putting "Yes" and "No" into the four quadrants of the shape before stacking two pencils crosswise and saying, "Charlie, Charlie, are you there?" The top pencil would rotate and the demon would answer *Yes* or *No*.

There were some videos. I watched one with the phone close to my face so I could hear the screaming of the teenagers as the pencils moved.

The kids on the video seemed to be having lots of fun. More fun than I was having. I decided I should probably have more fun and maybe meet a demon. It was like a homemade Ouija board. The rest of the article was about gravity making the pencils move and the fact that there is no demon that goes by the name of Charlie in Mexico.

I definitely agreed with that. *Really, there are probably no demons at all.* Unless people like Bob were demons when they lied about why they were leaving my church.

"What a dick, right?" I heard the words, but wasn't listening. Another skill of mine, honed to perfection, with years of practice. Instead, I kept reading about the kids searching for Charlie and the dire warnings of dabbling with the occult from religious leaders.

"I heard the whole thing, man," the voice said again. "That guy is a real dick." In case I didn't hear the first time.

I looked up at a very normal man. I don't know what normal means but whatever I imagine when I think of the word, he was it. Familiar, almost. Ordinary … known even? At least recognizable—in a déjà vu kind of way even though I had definitely never met him. Normal haircut, normal clothes, normal skin, normal eyes, normal face, absolutely nothing to make him stand out in any way. Boring. And yet he did stand out because no one is ever *that* normal. Or known, or familiar, or ordinary. Was he so normal he wasn't? Did that make him unique? Did that make any of us unique?

He looked directly at me and showed me his teeth. Also normal. Not inspiring like Leo's and not bleach-white-too-perfect like Bob's but … normal.

I laughed, nodded at the man, as though to say I hear you and see you, listened this time, and still don't want to talk to you. I looked back to my phone.

"Don't you get tired of that?" he asked.

I looked up again. "Of what?"

"You're a pastor, right?"

"Yeah," I admitted begrudgingly. Once it's out there the whole conversation always changes. The word might as well be UPS, it carries so much baggage.

"So," he started again. "You've got to get real tired of that. Rich dude. Greedy as hell. Affairs. Everything is wrong, unless *he* does it."

I obviously looked very perplexed, not because he was wrong but because he was right. "Do you know him?"

"In a way," he answered. "That's complicated."

"Alright." I didn't want to know more. The conversation was already uncomfortable enough.

"My name is Ehs." He reached out his hand for mine.

"Ehs?" I repeated, not sure on the pronunciation but reaching out my hand. There was something oddly normal about his skin even—as though the temperature was exactly what I was expecting it to be.

"Yep, Ehs. Pronounced just like the letter before *t*."

I assumed he had said that sentence a million times in his life. "Cool name. Not sure I've heard that one before."

"That's the English translation." He glanced over at the line of people anxious for the dark liquid that would feed their habits before work and then looked to his watch. "I don't have a lot of time. So, maybe we should get right to it."

"Oh ..." I said, wondering what there was to "get to" and why he thought I was "in" on the getting-to. My next meeting wasn't scheduled for another fifteen minutes because Bob had mercifully made his conversation short.

"Seth," he said, immediately stalling my brain. *Have I told him my name?* "I'm here for a reason. And I know this is out of the blue, but just give me a second. Will you do that?"

Maybe he had once gone to my church. Or maybe he was a regular that I had never noticed. It was hard to keep track of everyone, I told myself.

"My wife is going to be here soon," I answered, looking out the window, hoping to see our car already waiting even though she was not supposed to be there for another hour.

He ignored me. "I know this seems weird but, trust me, it's not. Just a second?"

"Sure," I answered much more enthusiastically than I felt.

Statistically zero means that, according to the numbers, there is a zero percent chance of it happening. For example, there is a statistically zero percent chance of being eaten by a grizzly bear. As I waited for his words, I told myself there was a statistically zero percent chance that the normal man was dangerous.

"I'm a demon," he started.

I would definitely have said there was a greater chance of talking to a mass murderer than a demon. He might as well have said he was an alien. I laughed at the absurdity.

He continued as though he had said he was a car mechanic. "Right. Well that's not actually what we are but it's the most common word."

Unfortunately though, some people *are* eaten by grizzly bears. I wasn't sure if I wanted him to be a mass murderer or a demon. Or a bear. All were pretty bad choices.

Breathe, Seth. Breathe. Not that big of a deal.

The man obviously had mental issues and happened to *believe* he was a demon. Or maybe he was going to talk to me about the Hebrew word and tell me its original meanings and that we were essentially all demons. Like someone else had once told me. Just another weird Christian.

Seeing that my mind was busy figuring out how to even begin to believe anything he was saying—and, thus, preventing me from forming my own words—he kept talking.

"Demon, vampire, ghost, angel, imp, troll, god, alien, I'm called all of them. And in every language. We get used to all the words but none of them are exactly … accurate. And, again, I know this is all a bit weird and hard to believe."

Weird? That doesn't begin to cover it. Did he say alien? My brain was somewhere between the present moment and a possible stroke. "Right," I managed, as though I was in full agreement.

"But I … I feel like you can handle this. I've been watching you for a while and … well, that probably makes things more uncomfortable but it's true. And it's not as creepy as it sounds. Really. It's not. I promise."

How? How did he sound normal? *I've been watching you* should always seem creepy. Always. Yet, it didn't.

I looked around the room. People were laughing and reading and drinking coffee completely unaware of what was happening at my little table. I was about to be killed by a normal man and they had no idea. I was jealous of their ignorance. I wanted to be one of them.

Can a normal person be a murderer?

Thoughts were swarming like dollar bills in a game show booth. I couldn't grab any, even though they were all I could see. I casually took a sip of coffee and did manage to focus in on how cold it was. And how weird it would look if I ran for the door.

"Well, what is the right word?" Instead, I threw out that gem.

"What?" He seemed taken aback.

"If you're not a demon, you're a …"

"Right. Good question." He nodded. "Shadow."

"Shadow?" I chuckled, hoping to make him chuckle and then hoping that we could laugh together about how I thought I was going to die. "Like the comic book character?"

He did smile, showing his normal teeth again. "No, more like … the dark side of light."

I stopped chuckling.

"Shadow is just an interpretation." He looked around, a little nervous. Normal nervous, like I was. "I can say the word in the original language if you'd like?"

"Like Hebrew or something?" I asked, confused.

"Hebrew?" His expression was as knotted up as mine.

"Yeah."

"No, no." He smiled the kind of smile a teacher gives the new student. The *very* new student. "The original." He said *original* very slowly so I would get it.

"Original?"

"The only true language." He looked around the store like someone who was gauging how much of a scene they wanted to make. "The initial. The one all other senses and languages reference. Well—" he interrupted himself. "I mean, basically, all things are communicating."

"I'm sorry."

"What?" he asked, confused.

Why is he acting like the confused one?

"I did not follow that. At all," I said.

"It's fine."

"It is?"

"Do you want to hear it?"

"Yes?" I asked.

"Okay, I'll try to be quiet," he answered, very politely.

"Wait."

"What?"

"What are you going to do?" I asked.

"Just say the word."

"Okay." I looked around, as though I would find approval

somewhere.

"You want to hear it." It wasn't really a question.

"Right," I obliged.

He leaned in real close. I could see a nose hair. Very normal, although it did make me wonder how mine were doing.

Just for an instant.

The sound … was it a sound? It was not *just* a different language but a different way to speak—almost a hiss and a roar radiating under water—there was nothing human about it. It was the kind of thing sound engineers talk about in making-of documentaries. I could imagine Jan from Sweden with a black background and his name below him telling us how challenging the sound was to replicate as he played with the cries of dying birds, the roll of ocean waves, and the snap of some obscure deep water fish.

Why are you thinking about sound and not running for your life?

The thing hung for a moment in front of my face, after my ears no longer registered it. I could almost see it continue to reverberate through my senses. I felt it after I heard it. There was no way anyone could reproduce it. The proverbial Jan from Sweden was screwed if Ehs was ever featured on a documentary.

I was already screwed. Lucky Jan.

"You alright?" he asked me.

"What *was* that?"

"I'm sorry. I didn't think it would spook you like that." Even his inflection and sincerity were normal. I did take a slight offense to him saying I was spooked, even though I definitely was. "Like I said, Shadow is the closest English translation."

What if?

What if I am actually sitting next to a demon at this coffee shop?

Statistically zero was becoming less persuasive and comforting.

"I don't think I believe in demons," I said.

"You don't think you believe?" He smirked and, for the first time, there was something not normal about him. It was more arrogant. "That's a thought, isn't it?"

He did have a point. "I don't believe in demons," I reiterated.

"You shouldn't. I told you I'm a Shadow." He smiled.

I did not. Not even a fake smile.

"I realize this is hard to believe." He was back to normal. So *damn* normal.

"You think?" At least I still had my sarcasm.

Another smile.

"It's just … well …" I was no longer capable of putting words together. Speechless is the word people tend to use to describe the feeling.

"Again. I know this is a lot. Fortunately, I don't have much time."

"Fortunately?"

"I'll tell you what." He looked around again, quickly. "Do you see that truck in the drive-thru?"

I did. I had. It was massive and hard to miss, even with my new friend introducing himself to me. Everything was big about it. The tires, the mufflers, the subwoofers, the amount of air between the ground and the chassis, and, probably, the ego of the driver who was desperately trying to make up for something somewhere that wasn't big by surrounding himself with so much other "big." He was looking over his array of coffee nicely displayed on cardboard holders and happy to be winning the race for big things.

I was winning the judgmental pastor award in that moment.

"Want me to wreck it?" he asked, probably knowing there was a chance I did.

I stared. Thinking.

"Well?"

"I mean …" *Did that mean that I believed he could?*

"Dude, just kidding. I can't do stuff like that." He grinned.

"Do demons crack jokes? And have a sense of humor? And say dude?" I was obviously struggling and doing it out loud.

"I'm not a demon."

"Right. Right." The truck tore out from the parking lot, obviously wanting to get those coffees hot to the people he had bought them for. I could hear its muffler just louder than its pumping bass and tires laying rubber. "Actually. Can you?"

We both laughed like old friends from high school. Things were too comfortable five minutes in. With my demon.

"Small male dogs will tend to lift their leg higher when they pee so they can appear larger than they are." He looked back toward the window. "So don't hate him, he's just living his primitive, animal self."

I was speechless again. Not only was he reading my thoughts, he was assuaging them.

"And if you ever want to appeal to those small dogs, just promise big walls, big gods, big tanks, big … mufflers. Big anything. They eat it up every time." He smiled.

He smiled? Why was he smiling?

"Okay, Ehs." I knew I had to grab the reins of whatever beast was trying to take the conversation and show it who was in charge again.

"I don't really know what to say. I don't believe you're a demon—even if you can make a weird sound. I don't even know you or what you're trying to do but, honestly, I think I need to go."

Yes, there were probably much better ways to regain control of a conversation but at least I was trying.

"Can we go outside?" he asked.

Whatever conversation I had tamed, left. Panic gave birth to its babies in the corner of my mind. I thought of my wife and kids. I wondered if I was ever going to see them again.

I could feel sweat forming. Adrenaline and the other chemicals that start to appear when you think you're about to die were suddenly the majority of my bloodstream. On the plus side, these chemicals, I had heard, enable us to do superhuman things to escape oncoming perceived threats of death. I was going to have to run real fast.

Fight or flight, as they say.

I'd never been a fighter anyway, especially in a battle with a demon. Or worse, someone who thinks they are a demon. I would need flight—superhuman speed. I began to visualize the parking lot. I'd practically be wearing a red costume with a lightning bolt on it. I'd throw in some s-curves to dodge any potential bullets. I hoped to make it to the highway and maybe the big jacked-up truck guy had a big gun that could protect me. I hoped he would notice me in his big rearview mirror and want to be a big hero.

I needed big. I felt small.

Ehs was still there when my senses returned to the present. He was still normal, inquisitively waiting for me to return. "Is that alright? It's not like I want to kill you or something."

The starting gun. No one ever says they are not going to kill you unless they are planning on killing you or unless they think that everything rational in the situation would indicate that they were going to kill you or unless they've at least had the thought cross their mind. But, sometimes the real psychopaths say they are going to kill you just to watch you squirm, which meant he was not a real psychopath and there was a chance I could get out alive. Or he was so overtly psychopathic that he loved to act normal and look normal and watch me squirm anyway.

The only thing I know about psychopaths is from movies and those aren't real. Are they?

I couldn't think of a scenario where it was anything but bad.

"I've got a wife and three kids. Ehs ..." *If you're going to go kill someone, it probably shouldn't be me. I've got more to lose than other people.* I didn't say that last part because it seemed a little selfish. Again, we're never really *that* authentic.

He reached out his hand to touch my arm. I flinched even though there was no reason to. "Seth, just try to listen. I *need* you."

I tried to process what that meant.

"I've been watching. From a distance. You're what I've been looking for."

Holy shit.

"And you're well protected, believe me. Even if you weren't, well, we'll get to that. Just don't be afraid. If anyone should be afraid, it's me. Not you."

The words *don't be afraid* are often prophetic and they felt it in that moment too. The sweat started to evaporate and I was, baseline, listening again. Equally worrying though was the fact that a demon told me to not be afraid and I wasn't.

Stop overanalyzing, Seth. Flow.

"I know your life isn't that great." He said it with a sincerity that was extra warm.

"What?" I didn't like to be authentically insulted.

"Your life. It reeks of being … decent, everywhere you look."

Definitely not where I was expecting the conversation to go. "Decent?" I hoped my expression was as confused and insulted as I felt. "Thanks?"

"You're welcome." At least he owned the comment. "Mediocre, Seth. All of it. And I can make it … rich."

A demon disguised as a normal man telling me he was going to help me be … rich? Was he going to promise me celebrity status in addition to some new cars and houses? So stereotypical. My temptation for fame and power and money was going to do me in, finish what my other temptations had already started. But there was something drawing me to him. I couldn't get rid of it.

"And you're a pastor stuck saying a bunch of shit you don't really believe. If you believe any of it anymore." He was serious. "You don't like your job. Or your prison. Or your life. You know it."

"I'm not *that* kind of pastor." I wasn't sure what that meant but it felt important to tell Ehs.

"That's what I just said. I know."

I nodded. Respect. *Wait, am I trying to earn respect from a demon?*

"You want out. Of it all."

I didn't say anything.

"Listen. This is crazy to you, I get it. It's surreal. Unbelievable. Utterly fantastic. Yet, you believe it somehow."

Most of that was true. "I'm not exactly sure that I do. I think you're nuts," I lied, or at least said hoping it to be true.

"Seth." The way he said my name had authority to it as though it were a hidden hand that grabbed my chin and made me look into his eyes.

"Yes." I felt I had to respond whether I wanted to or not.

"I know about her."

"Her?"

"Yes." He nodded. "Her. Fourteen months ago. Burner phones. You've told no one."

I bluffed him with the most confused and insulted expression I could find in my arsenal. "Excuse me," I said with as much power, persuasion, and passion as I could muster. I felt like it exploded on impact.

He sighed and rolled his normal eyes. "You can't bluff me. I know. She had issues. Marriage number two, affair number … five? Shocker, there were issues. But, it started right here. In fact, over at that table." He looked behind me. "Right? Your favorite table hiding over there in the corner?" We had stayed inside. I wondered briefly if I should have taken my chances and gone out when he had asked.

My expression couldn't hide my shock. "Five?" I managed to whisper.

"Started innocently enough, like they always do." He probably grinned but I was looking down, embarrassed and unsure of my next move. "A look here, a look there. You didn't move your eyes up and she didn't mind. That navy blue shirt. You threw out a word to test the waters and gauge the reaction. A little more. And eventually you were at her house with her husband on a work trip. You've visited plenty more times. Though you haven't told her you don't want to visit anymore. Honestly—" He paused. "After the danger left, so did the attraction, which was pretty small to begin with. But, again, you can't tell her that. You're trapped. The walls are all around you and they're suffocating you. Just one more prison. So you put up with a little—"

"Stop." I was shaken to the core. "Please, don't hurt me." I looked into his eyes.

"It's okay," he responded warmly. "I get it. More than you know. I want out too. I need your help."

I've had all kinds of people ask me for all kinds of help. Just about everything you can imagine. But never like this. Though I was barely able to process anything he was saying.

"I have a lot to tell you. A lot to show you. Some of it you'll believe and some of it you won't … at first. I've been a Shadow for years. Far more than you could even understand. I've made mistakes …" He looked down, almost sorry.

If a demon makes a mistake, does that mean he does good things accidentally?

"I regret some things too, Seth."

The amount of guilt, along with misinformation and irony and stereotypes and surrealness and confusion and intrigue and despair, that was soaring through me as various chemicals and thoughts and energies mixed in with them was simply too much.

"Is this too much?" he asked, definitely reading my mind.

Obviously. But, I couldn't get the word out. I probably didn't need to.

His eyes flickered red for a moment and I, instantly, felt like my regrets were going to grow.

"You're special, Seth," he responded.

I didn't want to disagree but …

"I'm sorry about the eyes," he continued. "I'm exhausted. This is hard work. And if I keep this up, we'll both be in trouble."

I said nothing.

"I'll come by your house tomorrow, if that's alright. I'll probably have a different body but"—he looked down—"James does work perfectly. He's real normal."

I was powerless to tell him that he was not coming by my house. Instead I asked a question: "Exhausted?"

"Yes, we get exhausted."

"Who is James?"

"The guy you're looking at."

"And how do you know where I live?"

He gave me the kind of expression a parent gives their three-year-old when they ask how Santa Claus knew what they wanted for Christmas.

The eyes were red again, even longer, and I could have sworn vanished for a moment to what looked like two black holes. The black holes found in space, not in a head.

"Ehs, I can't do this." They say cats are good at staring into middle space. I was like a cat, staring right into a vast outer space in his eyes, somewhere.

"You have to." He said the words like a counselor, not a boss. He wasn't going to make me, but he knew I was going to make myself, because I … had to. I somehow vaguely agreed with him.

"But …" The word fell out of my mouth.

The eyes were gone. Black, red, emptiness. Flickering back and forth. And suddenly the normal eyes were back.

"Tomorrow." It was a barely audible whisper.

"But …" I whispered back.

He didn't respond. There was nothing. I looked around. Did anyone else see what had just happened?

"Holy shit," I muttered quietly because I honestly didn't know what else to mutter.

"What?" The voice was the same but something in the inflection or manner of speaking had changed. Subtle, but still enough to hook my attention.

"What?" I asked back.

"Sorry, man, that was weird." The normal-looking man was looking around with an abnormal expression. "Did you want this table?" He looked as comfortable in a coffee shop as he would have been on the moon. He was an utter ball of confusion, with it written all over every piece of his body. "I didn't mean to take your table," he stammered.

"Are you James?" I asked.

His expression grew even more befuddled—like my whole body felt. "Yeah, James. Who are you?"

"I'm Seth. Good to meet you. Just wanted to make sure you were alright. Someone said your name was James and that you looked like you had fallen asleep so I just came to make sure you were alright. You good?" The lies came easily, as they often did. "Can I get you a coffee?"

"Yeah, yeah. Thanks. Weird." He was shaking his head as though he could knock out the webs of confusion if he just shook hard enough. I knew he couldn't. "Oh no, I'm fine. Thanks though." He kept up with his worthless attempts to clean his mind. "So weird."

"You have no idea," I said, as though I were acting in a movie. I said it with real drama. I wished I was acting. In fact, I looked around for some cameras but there were just people as oblivious to me as I had been them.

"Oh, cool. Well thanks for being cool, man." James was actively trying to recall his past and I wondered if he would ever be able to. I assumed not.

"Oh." I looked at the door and stood up. "Right. Sure. Yeah." I didn't see my wife yet but I figured the fresh air couldn't hurt. I left as fast as I've ever left any interior and breathed in air as though my lungs had never tasted it before.

Somehow, and you can't ask me how, I managed to form a timid smile. I wondered what Leo and Bob would think. Or my wife. Or my affair.

My smile eventually faded, like all good wounds do.

ONE POINT FIVE

"Hi, Pastor Seth."

If there were awards for dull, monotone, pessimistic voices, she would definitely take the top three in any competition. Her personality wasn't far behind. And she wondered why she never had any friends and her roommates always moved out on her. If she asked me, she was destined for a life alone.

Authenticity always sounds nice on paper.

It was my third meeting. When I had scheduled it, I had known it would be the worst of the day but that was before I knew I was going to meet a demon with a good chance of ruining my already somewhat-ruined life.

Or maybe he was going to fix it? *Do I think he can fix it?*

Either way, I had no time for Aubrey and her frizzy hair, graphic Christian T-shirt, cream pants, and sandals that had been cool when I was in junior high. About thirty years earlier. We were standing in the parking lot where I had attempted a getaway before she could find me. She had found me.

"Hey, Aubrey," I managed, proving that miracles do happen. Somehow I was able to smile at her and think through some nonoffensive responses. "How are things?"

"They're alright," she hummed with a long, drawn-out frown at the end. She couldn't even say "alright" without some pessimism dragging it down.

"Well, I have to be honest," I added. "I'm not having a good day myself, either."

She just stared at me. She always just stared. I could have told her I'd just won the lottery or that my house had burned down. Her response would be the same blank—somewhat bored—stare.

"Was there something specific you wanted to talk about this morning?" I asked, more hurried than normal, hoping she could sense it.

"Not really. I mean—" She looked slowly toward a car that was trying to move through the parking lot but couldn't because she was blocking the way. A perfect metaphor. She couldn't sense danger from a man in a hockey mask with a knife, let alone from my tone and sweating forehead. "You know, just the usual. My roommate is moving out and I'm trying to find a new job but just feel like no one is hiring."

No one is hiring you, Aubrey. Just you.

"Well, I'm sure something will pop up eventually," I said instead.

"Yeah, but at least the youth group is asking me to do more."

"Really?" I was astounded. "Cool," I lied. The poor kids that went to that church group.

"Yeah, going to do some speaking here and there."

And they wonder why religion is dying.

I tried to smile. "Great, well …" I looked around the parking lot and realized I didn't have a way home. "You know … I might have to cut this short this morning. I feel really bad but I've had some things come up. I can't really get into them right now but I think it'd be better if I took care of some other things."

More staring.

Did you hear me?

"So … I'm really sorry but I think I'm going to need to leave."

"Okay," she mumbled. "It's fine. Oh." She looked up—almost excited. "I told my dad I wasn't going to work for him this summer."

"Wow," I said without the usual excitement that escorts the word. "Good job."

"Boy, was he was not happy."

"Hmm …" Another car—that I really wanted to be in—left the parking lot. "That's great. It sounds like things aren't too bad."

"Well"—she looked up, squinting into the blue sky as though looking for a gray cloud somewhere—"I mean, I don't think I will be able to stay here this summer so I will probably have to move back home. Unless I can get a different job. Do you know of any?"

"I have asked around here and there but—"

I would never recommend you to anyone I know.

She began a long drone of a speech about her mom, her friends, her therapist, her medication, and her speech she had for her roommate who told her that she needed to exercise more. I stared at the green shirt with white lettering that she was wearing. It was a bit too small but ironically the letters I CAN DO ALL THINGS were still way too big and blaring at me while I wondered how someone could talk so long about nothing.

And then I heard the car come into the parking lot, belching out exhaust, contributing to higher rates of lung cancer and sounding like it had its own case of it.

I smiled anyway because I recognized the car and the driver. Leo was back.

Why is Leo back?

But it didn't matter why—it was good news. "Hey, Aubrey, I know it seems bad." It always seems bad. "But I think things are going to turn for the better soon! I've got a good feeling," I lied. "And like that shirt says …" I pointed to the letters stretched out over her very large breasts. "You can do all things, right?"

She looked down. "Well …"

"Okay, I'm so so sorry. I really am. But I am going to have to jet out early today." I appeared sad. "So, I'm going to leave now, okay?" I didn't know how to be more direct.

"Pastor Seth!" Leo yelled before he had closed the door, half in and half out of his car.

I nodded toward him in case she hadn't heard or couldn't see him, gave her a quick side-hug, and ran toward Leo.

"What's up, man? What brings you back so quick?"

He smiled but it wasn't the normal rainbow and sunshine smile. There was something under the surface that I wasn't sure I liked.

"Have you got a minute?"

"Yeah." I looked around the parking lot because it was suddenly more welcoming than Leo. I noticed Aubrey still motionless. I waved for some reason. I could have always headed back to her.

God no.

"Well—" Leo waited for me to look back at him. "I drove away and just had this feeling. You know those feelings, right?" He still had a bit of Southern twang in his voice. It had an ability to soothe, even when I sensed it wasn't supposed to. "Well, do ya?" he asked.

"Oh." I nodded. Apparently the question was not rhetorical. "Yes. I do."

"Well, I couldn't shake it. The Lord was telling me something." He paused, longer than usual. His dark eyes still had a sparkle but his thick eyebrows were all business. "The Lord was telling me that you are in trouble, Pastor Seth."

Alarm bells. Red alerts. DEFCON 1. For so many reasons. In my experience there are two kinds of "you are in trouble" sentiments. The first is I'm here to help. The second is I'm here to judge. I sensed a little of both in Leo. Of all the help, I didn't really want Leo's. I loved him but we were not on the same page on most things.

I took a deep breath. A really deep one. "Okay," I exhaled. No reason to give away too much too fast or to encourage the voices in his head. Or my head. “That’s really nice of you,” I bluffed. “But I think I’m fine?”

“Well,” he answered immediately. “That’s the thing.” It was his turn to look around the parking lot so I followed suit. Aubrey had made it to her car—on her phone—and other than that, things were pretty standard fare for a coffee shop parking lot. “The thing is …” We were looking at each other again. “The thing is, I don’t know. But I do know that there is lots of affirmation that god is definitely confirming me something.”

He looked, waiting, it appeared. Maybe testing out his words to see if I would affirm or confirm whatever it was god had told him. I had no intention of doing either—or correcting his grammar.

“Okay, well … What’s the deal?”

“You see … I was driving to my job. We’re painting those buildings out in—”

“Yeah out by the base.”

“Right, right. I was driving to my job and I heard this voice say go back to Pastor Seth. Go back and tell him he needs to do some serious thinking.”

I smiled. “Leo, I know. I know we’ve disagreed on some things in the past but honestly, like I’ve said, I’m not sure that we’re going to be able—”

“No.” It was his turn to interrupt. “This wasn’t about no theo … theological”—he struggled with the word—“arguments. This was about something else. I just didn’t know what.”

“Okay?” There was sweat dripping off of my forehead. But it was hot in the parking lot.

“So I turn my car around. I don’t know why. I just know that I needed to come back to this parking lot.”

“Okay.” *This could still be normal.*

“And I’m right over there.” Leo twisted around and pointed toward the road behind him that I’d been staring at. “I’m right over there and I see this lady on the side of the road.”

Oh shit. Not her. Leo can never know about her.

“She was a nice-looking lady. What do they call them? Poly …”

“Poly?”

“Hawaiian-like.” His face was all squinted up, almost hiding his scar.

“Polynesian?”

“Yeah, yeah, a Polynesian lady. She was waving at me.”

Thank god this isn’t about her.

“Okay.”

"And I just felt com … compelled to stop for her. So I did. I stopped the car. Right over there," he exclaimed, still surprised that he had. "And she looked me in the eyes with some really strange eyes. Like other world stuff."

"Well, she is from Polynesia," I cracked, hoping for a little humor. The situation seemed desperate for it.

"No," Leo replied without skipping a beat but definitely skipping the joke. "Not like that. Other worlds. Somewhere else."

"Okay …"

"An angel," he gasped. "I think I seen an angel."

"Wow." How else was I supposed to respond? I *had* just talked to a demon.

"And the angel looked me in my eyes. Right in 'em." He pointed just to emphasize the point. "She said, 'Leo.'" His eyes exploded with emotion. "She knew my name, Pastor Seth! How did she know my name?"

I casually glanced down at Leo's paint shirt to confirm that his name was embroidered on it. "Leo, it says—"

"She said, 'Leo, you better tell that Pastor Seth to be careful.' She knew your name!" he exclaimed even louder.

And that was strange—but still explainable.

"She said real plain. 'You tell that Pastor Seth to not be messing around with the demons. Ain't no reason to live in Shadow.'"

He stopped. I stopped.

We stared at each other, as well, or better, as any Aubrey stare I had ever experienced.

I didn't say anything.

Neither did Leo.

Some cars drove in and out. It was, in my mind, a high stakes poker game and I was not ready to play any cards. It could all be explained. Random chance. Word choices.

"So." Leo broke the silence. "I don't know what to tell you, Pastor Seth, other than …" He waited until I was looking at him again. "Be careful. There's evil out there. I know. Better than most. And you'd better be careful with hanging out with it."

"Thanks, Leo." I did mean that.

"Because I don't want to see anything happen to my friend." He smiled and the smile did the same magic it always did.

Which I desperately needed in that moment. I basked in it as long as I could, even after Leo left and my wife showed up to take me home.

TWO

Sleep and I weren't getting along. She would stop by for a few minutes here and there, which left me in a semiconscious cloud of confusion amidst the darkness. I usually enjoyed her visits when the lights and stars were out but, that night, once more, sleep wasn't much interested in me—a feeling I was also somewhat used to from a female in my bed.

Not helping anything was the fact that my wife and I had bought one of those foam mattresses that made us feel like we were sleeping in an oven—that smelled like plastic. The kind of plastic that has not been approved by the EPA.

Adding to my fear that I had met a demon (who might broadcast an affair I had been having and ruin my marriage and career, the second of which I didn't really want but also didn't want to lose) and that the demon might visit me again (at home) and that Leo was supernaturally aware of something going on and that my life that was built on fragility could crumble at any moment into a big pile of shit … was the fact that I was probably inhaling cancer-causing fumes.

Ehs continued to weave in and out of my transparent thoughts. Ehs. James. Whatever he was. Bob. Whatever *he* was. Me. Whatever I was. *What am I? Who am I? What am I doing? Why in the hell did we buy this mattress? Do they have a return policy? This thing was so small when I brought it in the house and now I can't imagine taking it out. Ouch. Metaphor. Does my life have a return policy?*

Demons don't have regret. They don't need my help. They don't exist! What the hell does it mean that I'm not that kind of pastor?

The top ten highlights replayed all night, along with some of the more standard and known questions that dance around the room whenever sleep refuses to come, like: *When the hell is the sun going to rise?*

I hadn't told my wife anything, which in itself was not unusual, but it was not now helping my desperate search for REM sleep. I had really wanted to talk to her about Ehs that night. Instead, we had shredded Bob for a while since a common enemy masks all flaws in a relationship and we had plenty of flaws and enemies to mask them with.

I considered, for a quick second, waking her up and just getting it over with. *Honey, there is a person I met named James who is either a) possessed by a demon that calls itself a Shadow or b) pretending to be a human possessed by a demon that calls itself a Shadow because he is mentally ill. But, he wants my help and I think I'm kinda interested. Is that bad? Love you! Didn't mean to wake you. Also I've been sleeping with a woman whom I don't really love—or like—for a whole list of complicated reasons that we can probably work out in therapy—if you'd like! But, we can talk about it more in the morning. Good night!*

The Affair. The parts that bothered me the most were not the morality parts of it all, which, in itself, was probably a whole other issue but not an issue that gave me a lot of trouble. Part of what really bothered me was the cliché of it all. I liked to think of myself as a pretty original person and being a pastor having an affair was so unoriginal, it was almost boring. I couldn't believe I was just another one to add to the list. It was practically expected of me, which made me hate it all the more.

Of course, making that all worse was the fact that if my affair became public, all of the people, like Bob, who were leaving and had left would think it was because I was the heretic they thought I was and that once you "leave Jesus" and "all morality" behind, that's what happens—you have affairs. I mean, maybe they were right but I didn't want to give them any more ammunition that their stupid religion was any better than mine. In some twisted sense, I didn't want the affair to get out to protect the faith—but not their faith. The faith I actually thought I believed, which would be taken down a notch if they lost faith in me. Whatever that faith was, if anything.

Shit. I should really just get this all over with. It's getting way too complicated.

The worst part though? The woman lying next to me. My wife. Rachel. I took a second to look at her dark hair and dark skin. Damn, she was beautiful. I loved her. Unfortunately, we had both been raised in very conservative homes where sex was evil and dark and dirty. Where it was the worst thing you could do. Until you were married. Then it was the best thing. Why? Because you had stood in front of some friends, as good virgins, and said you would always love each other. And suddenly god loved sex even though god hated it just hours earlier.

Too bad the human brain doesn't really work like god's brain, apparently, works. So my wife and I had struggled. Yeah, we had kids. Yeah, we had sex. But it was always like sneaking a piece of chocolate cake on a diet. It tasted good but we couldn't let it taste too good. And it was expensive, and rare.

Gwen had been on her second marriage and she had not been

a good virgin on the night of her first marriage. She liked sex and she would do anything to have more of it. It got me. It was different and felt more natural in the most unnatural of ways. I wasn't as terrified of sex as my wife—in part because I was a man and in part because … I probably made assumptions that turned into prophecies about her and her drive for sex.

Yes, this is all way too complicated.

Did he say Gwen had five affairs?

Either way, I had given in. In part to give a middle finger to my religious upbringing and the people who were still stuck in it and in part to experience what it had tried to take from me and in part because I had warm feelings of adrenaline and dopamine running through me. Unfortunately, those aren't very good reasons and I had also given a middle finger to the one woman I actually loved in the world. I decided I didn't want, like, or care about Gwen after a few weeks but I was trapped because of all the reasons above.

Not to mention none of it was as simple as I always wanted to make it nor as easy to blame on bad religion as I wanted it to be.

Yes, no wonder sleep wasn't coming easy that night. And not all of it had to do with demon boy.

I flipped over to my stomach—as though the third time on my stomach would help—and thought about how cool it would be to walk around town with a nice demon. I already had all kinds of questions for him. *Wait, would that be cool?* It was hard to convince myself that it wouldn't be. *What am I doing?*

Eventually my questions ceased when the lady of sleep arrived and decided to stick around for more than a few minutes. Thank god. I was antsy the entire next day. I had an early morning meeting at a different coffee shop that I tried my best to be present for, even though I knew I wasn't. I could only hope the person who was wondering what they should do with their life had only needed someone to listen because that was all I was able to do and even that was pretty rough. All through the meeting, my phone was a steady buzz of texts, one of which was Rachel asking me why I didn't seem to sleep very well.

By the time I got to my home office, my sanctuary, I was practically shaking. I tried to work but that was useless. I looked up Shadows. There was not a whole lot there. I looked up Polynesian angels. Nothing. I looked up mental insanity. There was lots.

I looked up demon possession. Lots. Including more stories of Charlie the Mexican demon.

I looked up "introducing a demon to your wife."

I looked at sports stories to distract me because those never let me down in that department. My brain felt like it was revving way too high, like an engine about to overheat. Reading news about the upcoming draft was the fresh oil I needed to soothe it.

My phone buzzed again. It was Rachel calling.

"Hey."

"Hey, what's going on?" she asked.

"Well … just working a little."

"You alright?"

"Yeah. Yeah, I had a weird kind of meeting yesterday."

"I know! It's been bugging me too. I'm trying to remember the good stories. The people who actually want—"

"Well … after Bob," I interrupted.

"Oh?"

"Yeah."

Our doorbell was ringing.

"What happened?" Rachel asked.

"Is anyone supposed to be coming over?"

"Not that I know of."

More doorbell.

"Alright. Well, I'll ignore it," I said. "Yeah, it was really weird. This guy started talking to me and, well …" The words were sticking on my tongue, scared to come out into the open. "He claimed to be a demon. Well, they call themselves Shadows."

The doorbell kept ringing.

"What?" She seemed upset.

"Yeah, super weird. But we'll talk later. Probably nothing." More damn doorbell. "Hey, I'm going to go check the door. It might be one of the kids."

"Okay, call me later. I'm taking the girls to dance right now. I'll be back around six."

"Okay."

"Hey."

"Yeah?"

"Can you get the noodles boiling at about five thirty?"

"Got it." Even as I answered her, it felt like one of those things I was going to forget.

Ding-dong.

Ding-dong.

Ding-dong.

"Okay, are you alright?"

"I think," I said, though I thought I might not be.

"Okay, we'll talk tonight."

Ding-dong.

He said he was going to come by.

"Okay, bye," I shot out and hung up the phone. We had stopped ending our conversations with "I love you" months earlier. It still bothered me but not enough to do anything about it. I ran a little quicker than normal down the stairs. Was I actually excited?

I yanked open the door.

It was an older man dressed in brown with the familiar logo of a delivery company on his shirt. We, like millions of other Americans, found things to buy online on a regular basis and, thus, knew the friendly men and women who delivered us our capitalistic urges pretty well.

"Hey …" I threw the lonely word out there all by itself. We didn't know them well enough to know their names.

"Hey, Seth," he answered. To be fair, it was much easier for him to remember my name since he was reminded of it every time he came to our house with boxes and big stickers with my name on them. "How are you?"

I had always felt for the driver who was in front of me. I assumed he had a rough life, and not rough in the sense of trauma, but rough in the sense of lots of work. He looked worn out, like a realistic Santa Claus. If Santa really delivered that many packages every year, he would be thin, straggly, bent over with lower back pain, and exhausted like the man in front of me. His white and gray hair and beard were mangled, and wiry, but the collection of it did make his green eyes stand out like glacier-fed lakes surrounded by snow-capped mountains. Rough terrain with some serenity.

Honestly, things couldn't be much weirder.

"Pretty good," I responded instead, like we all do. His truck was sitting in our driveway. "Need a signature?"

"Well, I have a weird package to deliver and just wanted to make sure you were home." He looked back toward the truck, apparently indicating where the package still was.

"Right, I mean …" *That makes absolutely no sense.* "Do I need to sign for it or something?"

"Well …" He couldn't look me in my eyes. He looked especially tired.

"Hey, it's all good. Yeah, just go grab it."

"You're a pastor, right?" He seemed embarrassed to ask the question, but not embarrassed enough to not ask it.

"Yeah," I answered, also embarrassed, but not enough to not answer.

"Okay, well, did you order a bunch of pornography?" He stared at me this time, with an almost accusatory glare that I did not appreciate.

He was probably not aware that I was going insane and could not be trusted to act in a socially accepted way, even to a worn-out delivery man. "What the hell?" Yes, that was my response.

"Well ..."

"Well, what? Do you look at everything I order? I mean, first, I didn't order any porn. Who orders porn? It's not 1985 and it's free online. Second, if I did, I mean, what are you doing?"

"Little defensive, huh?" Worn-out Santa was calling me defensive. He was right, but still.

And why am I defensive about pornography that I didn't order?

"Are you serious?" I was flummoxed and that's not a word I used to describe myself very often ... for all kinds of reasons, including the word itself.

"You're a fan of the porn, huh? You'd be surprised how much of this stuff I deliver to pastors. But"—he paused—"the thing is, I like Rachel. I don't think you should be treating her this way. That's not how you want to see Rachel."

What the hell is happening?

Then he started laughing. Hysterically. Deep Santa laughs. "Relax, man. Relax. Just having a little fun with you." He pushed open our door and took a step in.

I looked in the mirror. Looking in a mirror at my own face, blue eyes, and short dark hair tended to make me feel grounded: anchored to some kind of reality that reveals itself in mirrors.

"Ehs?"

"Yes, sir," he answered while backing up out the door and back to our porch. "Sorry. I should have asked if I could come in." He looked up at me. The beard had hairs stretching in every direction possible. I wondered if the delivery man had been made aware of the existence of beard trimmers.

"Cool." It was almost a question. Maybe to myself, to god, to my own sanity, to the universe ...

If it was strange to have a normal-looking stranger at a coffee shop claiming to be a Shadow—it was much more strange to have a person I was semifamiliar with walk into my living room, sit on my leather couch, and claim the same thing.

I closed the door and followed him in, wondering how many people weren't going to receive their packages and if, in the future, I could blame demons for the times my packages didn't arrive—and be correct.

"Sorry, this was the best I could do." He looked around at the house, admiring it, as though he had never been inside. Which I suppose he hadn't.

"You took our delivery man?" I sat down too.

"I didn't *take* him. I can't take anyone." He looked back to me. "I like the place."

"I'm confused."

"Get used to it."

"Am I supposed to offer you some tea or something?" I asked.

"Maybe a gin?" I noticed that he looked back toward where we kept our alcohol—and the bottle of gin sitting out—as though he knew exactly where to look. It was a little disconcerting.

"It's ten in the morning."

"Kidding. Don't want this poor fool to be drunk driving that truck." He looked back at me.

"Right." I nodded as though I understood. As though it made sense for a demon to not want someone driving drunk.

"You're going to be confused a lot for the next few months."

Few months?

"Yeah, you still think I'm a demon. Which I might be, but you think you know what that means and you are clueless as to what that means." He looked out the window into our back yard. "But don't feel bad. It's not just you. And it's very intentional."

I didn't say anything.

"You know exactly what we want. Not much else about us. Which is all well and good. We always like a good human confident in"—he hesitated—"our lies." His expression was that of a kid who had just gone off a sweet jump on his scooter. He liked telling me that. "This is a nice piece of property."

I still didn't say anything, since I had no idea what I was supposed to say. Or what I wanted to say.

He seemed fine with that as he looked back toward me. "Alright, let's get to it. I lead the Department of Advertising. For her. I'm big. As big as they get except for her."

"Her?"

"Lucy."

"Lucy?"

"Right. He is a she." He looked back out the window. "What is this, an acre?"

There were still no words hanging around my mouth. *Did I ask him if he was a she?* "No, a little less." I decided to go with the easy words. "About three quarters of an acre."

"Right." He nodded, still looking outside. "Yeah, the devil. Numero Uno. The Big Dog. Red skin with horns and the—"

"Yeah, I get who the devil is. But you're telling me it's a woman named Lucy?"

"Woman? No. And Lucy … her name in our language is something crazy but I won't say it now. Could draw attention."

"We're in a house." *That means we're safe, right?*

"Still." His eyebrows raised, suspiciously.

"I realize the driver was probably not my best move but he was asking for it. As to how or why, it's complicated and we'll get there, but I don't have long with him and it's probably better if we get moving to at least some of the story I need to tell you. Are you cool with that?"

He didn't wait for me to answer.

"I wasn't always in charge of the department I am now. I wasn't always in charge at all."

"Okay." I said okay knowing it didn't really matter what I said. He had said he had regrets and maybe I was going to find out about them and then we could commiserate about our pasts together with a gin and tonic. Unfortunately, my past regrets (aka guilt), in his hands, felt more like blackmail. I was already beginning to have future regrets (aka anxiety) too. Nothing but regret everywhere.

I might as well try to learn about his.

"As you've already learned, being a Shadow is hard. It's exhausting. We have jobs to do. Many of them. It was a long time ago now that I began to hear of alternatives. Systems and structures to make our work easier. Higher-concept stuff … so we didn't have to mess around with the tiring and pretty inefficient more well-known methods."

"Okay." *Higher-concept stuff?*

"Like what I'm doing right this second. You have no idea how much I'm working right now to be in this poor fool's body. It's exhausting." He looked down at the body he was in.

"I guess you make it look easy," I interjected.

"Thanks," he smiled. "Well, the alternatives have … worked," he continued. "Worked so well that … well … I mean beyond what anyone expected. Dangerously well. I mean, you just talked to Bob." He waited until I made eye contact. "Someone has to stop what's happening."

"Okay." I was monotone only because I didn't know how else to be.

"We call one of the larger—well, the largest, thanks to me—systems Insipid. You live there." He said each word slowly and with dramatic pause.

"Okay." I'm not sure it had the dramatic effect he was hoping for because I didn't really know what it meant.

"Hmm." He looked outside again. "Did you even hear what I said?"

"About Insipid?"

"Yeah." He nodded like a bobblehead. "You live in my creation. That doesn't shock you?"

"Wait," I shouted out. "This Lucy thing." I was still stuck on Lucy.

"Yeah?"

"He/she, I mean just words, I suppose." I forced myself to the moment: Insipid.

"To some degree. But—"

"Wait," I interrupted, ignoring my own advice. "Are you a woman?"

"No."

"But there are female and male de—Shadows?"

"Yeah."

"Do you guys …" Of all the questions for me to ask our frequent delivery man who was a demon, I was about to ask if demons had sex. I did manage to stop myself.

"Sex," he whistled. "And they call *us* demons. Wow." He grinned. "Cute little brains you guys have in there." He pointed to his own mass of steel wool–like hair on top of his head.

He had obviously known what I was thinking. I couldn't respond to that.

"We do something much more … primal. Animalistic. Without …" He stopped. "It's different. We'll get to that later. I need to start the story. I don't know how much time I have." His face looked as grave as an old Santa's worn-out, but jovial, face could. "Let's get moving." He crossed his legs and put his hands together, as if to pray, right below his chin. "Then, let's—"

"Right." I was agreeing. As though I understood.

"I died in 807. That was the year, at least according to most calendars."

"Most calendars?" That was the thing that I attached and reacted to.

"Not to be rude, but if you're going to ask questions like this the whole time, we're never going to get through the story."

"Right." Just more agreement from me because it was too early to disagree, not with so many questions about Lucy and sex.

Focus on what matters, Seth!

"Eight hundred seven. But no one cared it was that year really. I mean time wasn't the dictator it is now. People weren't obsessed with it. Look at it. In this room alone there are three clocks." He looked at each of them. "And you probably have another one on your phone, right?" He pointed at me.

"Am I supposed to answer?"

"No. It was a rhetorical question. Regardless, no one cheered there were only five minutes left in the work day. No one complained that it took three minutes to download the movie and no one kept charts that it was two hundred days until Christmas. No one wrote songs that it was only however many more days to the weekend."

"Did you just make that up or was that memorized?"

The delivery demon Shadow Santa man just looked at me like I was a ten-year-old. And compared to being over a thousand years old, I was.

"Life was very simple for me. I remember it well. Of course, life in prison is always simple. For some reason you humans act like simplicity is the holy grail, as though all of life should return to the simple days." His calloused hands formed air quotes.

I couldn't stop thinking about "you humans" but I did throw out, "I mean, I do prefer simple."

"I can see that." He nodded, looking around. "Clean design style. I like it. But that's not what I'm referring to." He was rubbing his beard, attempting to arrange the hairs, which had their own thoughts—that they did not want to be arranged in a similar direction. "Life was simple. Grow food or die. Kill animals or die. Protect yourself from Scythians, Goths, Varangians, or any other tribe wanting to take the food you are growing or the animals you are raising … or die. It was simple, right? But the simplicity was hard. Do you want *that* simplicity or the nice clean kind like your Scandinavian couch design and white walls?"

I was stuck on Scythians, Goths, and Varangians, thrown out like he was talking about a new breakfast cereal or beer and not ancient groups of people. "Uh, no …"

"Right. So it was simple. But it wasn't easy. Simple never is, at least behind the scenes. And we weren't nice people. I was eighteen when I died and I had already killed fifteen people with my bare hands. Two of them were under the age of ten. Three of them were women whom I raped before killing." He looked out the window again, as though sad.

I was sad too. And frozen.

"We were just Slavs. Trying to survive."

"Slavs?"

"Yes, Seth." He looked straight at me again. Piercing. "Slavic. What you are."

He was right. My mom was one hundred percent Slovakian. Which I figured was Slav. I decided to use the word Slav in the future and to be more proud of my heritage.

"This was before Vladimir gave up his eight hundred concubines. Before he murdered his brother and raped his sister-in-law to force her to be a concubine. Before all of that."

"Excuse me?"

He seemed amused at my lack of historical knowledge. "Saint Vladimir. Yes, he eventually used Christianity to consolidate his power and become the ruler—and saint—he was. But this was before all that. Of course, I was able to see it all from another vantage point after my own death."

He was stoic again.

I felt lost. "I'm not sure I'm following any of this." I shook my head. "I mean *any* of it."

He snapped back, as did a few hairs on his head. "I'll get to the meat of the story. It was cold. Frigid cold. There were five of us and we were headed off to kill some Norsemen that were camping on nearby land. The wind was vicious. They were sleeping and I took my fifteenth life that night. He had been lying under a tree."

I closed my eyes. I couldn't look at the sweet man who was saying these things anymore. I would never be able to order online items again.

"Everything I knew in life was gray, if that makes sense: work, sleep, sex, fun, eating, actions, conversations … everything. Bland and monotone. Insipid," he said slowly as if to make sure I heard.

"Until I saw her."

I opened my eyes.

"My father had gone into a tent that had been set up. This was not a tent you order online, mind you."

I nodded. I may not have been following him but I wasn't a complete idiot.

"It was a covering made with skins and hides. I watched him enter and I almost hoped he would die in the tent. But, I knew he wouldn't. He was too tough. My father could have killed a herd of wolves on his own. It turns out there were only two men inside and both of them went down fast. I walked in a little later." He stopped. "That was not the usual routine but I did it anyway.

"As I did, he was preparing to attack her. It was what he always did. What *we* always did. She was trying to scream but he had his hand on her face. She was trying to fight but he was too strong.

"I remember the scene in vivid color. And that's strange for me. All of my memories are grays and monotones except this one. Her. I can see her pale skin. Blond, brilliant, hair. Blue eyes—bold, blue eyes. She was beautiful, Seth. Beautiful."

I could see her too. Or at least my version of a Nordic model.

"She was beautiful when beautiful meant everything it was supposed to: something rare, something deeper, something innocent and precious. But she was more. I was moved. I was *feeling.* I returned her stare and I felt alive, maybe for the first time. I will never forget that part of being human: the feeling of life.

"I've missed it for hundreds of years. You shouldn't take it for granted." He looked directly at me. "And you are."

I returned the gaze back at him. The old man was delivering truth packages.

"My father soon realized something was different," he continued. "He didn't like that I was still there. Not leaving. And alive. His face was more of a storm, brewing and twirling, than an expression. I noticed his reddened skin, his brown beard, his black eyes. He was not happy.

"But she had hope in her eyes and I didn't even know eyes could have hope. Not then." He stopped. "Hope is usually dangerous, though."

"Hope?" I asked, interrupting the flow. "Hope?"

He frowned. "You can always hope, Seth. Hope never demands anything. It's dangerous. You can live your entire life with hope, and die miserable, empty, lonely, and worthless." He paused. "Still hoping!" He said it mockingly. "We often use hope."

He seemed to wait for me to register his words. It took a second and I promised myself to think on them later.

"So I lunged for my father and I stabbed him. In order to free her. He was much stronger but I surprised him and it worked momentarily. The knife went in and she got out."

"Wow," I whispered.

"Yeah, well, it didn't last. But we did have a moment. It was magic, enchanting. She handed me something she had been holding. A white stone. It was like she had just given me the world. Our souls were dancing."

A rock?

He was looking out the window. I was quiet, letting the moment be what it was, because it was something other than a normal moment for him. That was obvious. And I barely knew what normal moments were anymore.

He was soon back. “I don’t remember much after that. I think she got away. At least for a while. I smiled, watching her leave the tent. But my father attacked with rage. The world returned to gray and I passed out from pain. I remember my friends yelling. My father yelling. Pain throughout my body. In and out of darkness. The land against the back of my head as they drug me across it.

“I remember cold. But it was cold like it was living inside of me. It was everywhere: on my skin, penetrating my muscles and bones and organs. I was numb. I couldn’t move. I realized I was naked only after I made a conscious effort to look at my body.

“I remember the trees, which is strange. There was a thin layer of snow resting on their branches and the moon made it appear as though they were painted in blue. I remember the blue. I remember it vividly. Darkness had never been so colorful.

“I remember her body. Somewhere. Lying there. She had not escaped for long.

“I remember the stone in my hand. I never let go of it. It was warm.

“I remember crying. For the first time in my life. I didn’t know I was crying except for the warmth drifting down my cheek. It was salty.”

There was another long enough pause. I wondered if he was going to continue but I didn’t have anything to say if he didn’t. He was just looking back at me.

“It’s funny,” he eventually said, right before it got too awkward. “I had always wanted to die until I actually did. I had never lived until literally a few minutes before I died. Irony is a bitch.”

I was beginning to like the guy.

“So, you died?”

“That night. That was the night I became what I am now.” He was back to staring out the window. “It’s important to where this larger story goes.”

“Okay.” I leaned forward in my chair. “Wait. So what was death like?”

“Like a dream.”

“You mean weird?”

“No. I mean no one can describe going from awake to a dream. They only remember the dream. They only remember what happens when they are there—not *how* they got there. There is no transition. All these people who see lights and tunnels—”

It was as though something shook deep inside of him and his body revealed the ripples with a subtle tremor. “I’ve been too long. This guy isn't going to do well. Plus, he's got happiness to deliver to all the desperate people hoping it will show up in a cardboard box." He was still staring out the window.

"Sometimes, it's just soap in the box. Some of us *are* just doing our best to survive, still," I countered.

"Sure." He was disinterested. He slowly moved off the couch, grabbing at his lower back, and moved toward the front door as though he had been in my house a thousand times.

"Have you been here before?"

"Not in the way you should be afraid of."

The words gave me absolutely no comfort.

"No time to explain. This man is going to start to suffer and I'm tired. I'm sure he is too. Looks it at least." He looked in the same mirror I had. "Plus, being as popular as I am, they are going to miss me soon. As in now." His eyes flickered red, then black, like I had seen before but it was a hundred times more horrific in my house.

"Popular?" I managed to stay focused.

"Whatever word you want to use. I'm wanted. I'm noticed." He leaned his head back and I could hear his neck crack. "Yikes." He turned the door handle and opened the door. "Like I said, I'm big. You can't be in charge of departments and not be around and someone not notice." Before he walked onto the front porch he turned around and looked directly at me. "From what I understand The Seers already sent a spy to your friend Leo."

My eyes popped wide.

"Be careful. There's evil out there," he mimicked and tried to laugh but seemed too tired to do so.

"Are you saying?"

"Yes. Poor Leo. The Separated. The Seers have a ball with them. Always have."

"What?" I was completely lost again.

He didn't care.

"Insipid," I stated, trying another tactic to keep the demon from leaving my house, which is something I had never thought I would be trying to do.

"Right."

"What is it?"

"Hmm." He was glancing back and forth on the porch, and his nerves were contagious. "It's where you live."

"Here?"

"No, no!" he almost yelled.

"America?"

He hesitated.

"What?" I pleaded.

"Systems, perceptions, mechanisms of reality. Whatever the word." He was almost frustrated, rushing now. "It's doing things to you that you don't even know it's doing. Things it's meant to do, and those things are not good. It's not all bad—there are other forces—but it's pretty bad. You live in Insipid, because it was the plan. Yes, America is the best expression of it that has ever existed. But"—he took in a breath that seemed to hurt—"I don't want you to live there anymore. It's working too well."

"But you and I—we're going to fix it?" I asked.

"Tell him thank you."

"Who?"

"Nate." He pointed at himself.

I made a point to remember that name. "But what are we fixing if it's working?"

With that, Nate, also known as Ehs, turned toward my driveway. For a second it looked like Nate was exhaling a mouth full of cigarette smoke. But it was much too dark to be smoke. While I wondered if he was a smoker, he stopped.

"Hey Nate, thanks!"

Nate turned around and looked at me and then toward his empty hands, as though he was supposed to have something in them. "Did I take your signature?"

It's a long story, Nate.

"I don't know," I answered.

He was as confused with my answer as he should have been. How could I not remember something that he had apparently just done?

I just winced, hoping he would move away.

"Alright," he answered. "I'll figure it out."

"Well, have a good one." Maybe we both would figure it out.

Empty. I was empty for a long while.

Eventually, thoughts could begin to form again.

I went straight for a laptop at our dining room table. Me and Google.

Insipid: lacking taste or savor or lacking in qualities that interest.

I live there? Yeah, actually I do sometimes. Most of the time.

Shadows: a 1959 film, the shadow mind, and the thing that the sun makes.

Female devil: all kinds of images.

Slavs, Norsemen, Varangians, Gods of Slavic Mythology: all kind of stuff.

Demon possession: warning signs, true stories, types, YouTube videos, Christianity, Catholicism, books on it, music on it.

I don't know how much time passed but I heard the garage door open and I heard my wife and the kids walk in the house.

"Hey, guys," I muttered, still reading about a "documented" (on the internet) case of demon possession that, now that I was an expert, did not seem real.

"You didn't boil the water?" Rachel said. It was not really a question.

Damn it. "I'm so sorry." I got up and walked into the kitchen where Rachel, wearing her yoga clothes, was already grabbing a pot. "I'm sorry. Really— Did you go to yoga too?"

"Dad, guess what? Dad, guess what?" My daughter was excited.

"Yes, I did. What were you doing?" my wife, justifiably, asked.

"Dad, I did a flip today!" My other daughter was jumping up and down.

"Hey Dad, can you help with some homework?" my first daughter interjected.

"Hi, Mom, what's for dinner?" my son asked. I hadn't even noticed he had come home.

"I was working on stuff. Who led?" I responded to my wife.

"Stuff? I mean it would have been nice if you could have boiled the water at least." She was at the sink filling the pot with water. "It was Jaden, why?"

"Dad! I did a flip!"

"Oh," I said flatly.

"We're having spaghetti again?" My son was obviously not overjoyed.

"Honestly, Seth, you couldn't just take a second to do this?" She was waiting anxiously for the water to get to where it was supposed to be.

"Dad, do you know anything about scorpions?"

"We need to talk tonight. I'm not sure what's going on," I said, somewhat ambivalent to everything else happening around me, and hoping Rachel could sense that I was maybe not okay.

She didn't even bother to respond and I could see why. Needing to talk was nothing new and neither of us had been sure what was going on for years. Which meant, maybe, the demon was at least going to get us to actually have a real conversation—I had to give him that.

Maybe it wasn't all bad.

THREE

When my wife and I first started dating we argued over whether soul mates existed. We were seventeen. In youth group. I'm sure it was a very thought-provoking debate in which our youth pastor played devil's advocate while we all tried to prove to him that soul mates not only existed but that they were somehow god-given.

Of course, in the end, our youth pastor made sure we all understood that only the devil would advocate for something as ridiculous as he had, because if soul mates didn't exist, how would anyone find the right partner? I wondered what my youth pastor would think of my friend Ehs.

Rachel and I were all-in with our souls being mates. We were married at nineteen—which is ridiculous on many levels—and the critics would have plenty of evidence to say it was a bad idea and no one should follow our path.

I would focus more on the programming that we could do no wrong because we were soul mates when looking at the reasons our relationship wasn't working at its highest level, more than the fact that we were nineteen when we got married, but that's an argument for another day.

The irony in it all is that if soul mates ever did exist, I would hope that my soul and Rachel's were mates. I had never found a better soul, even if the body and brain that held it struggled to believe it. And created suffering because of it.

We sat down in our living room—where Ehs in the form of Nate had sat just a few hours earlier—and opened a bottle of wine.

We hadn't touched alcohol the first fifteen years of our marriage and only recently had begun to imbibe the liquid poison we were told would ruin our lives—as though the psychological poison that told us how wrong it, and everything else, was would never do such a thing.

The alcohol started to work its magic. About then, I decided it was time to get to the story of Ehs. Well, most of the story.

"Rachel, I met a demon the other day. And, it sounds crazy, but

I think he might be able to help us."

It was not the fast start I was hoping for but it did grab her attention and I kept the words flowing as fast as the wine.

During the recap the whole thing seemed more normal than I had expected. It seemed almost reasonable. Maybe it was the buzz I was feeling but none of it had the ridiculous flair it should have.

The fact that I was even considering it all to be real, in itself, was the most worrisome thing to Rachel, who did not see things the same way. The look on her face was one I could not remember ever seeing before because every time I had seen it, I had successfully forgotten ever seeing it. Similar to what she had said about delivering a baby.

But I don't think the point was to deliver more bad expressions.

Either way, the bottle of cab was not performing the miracle I had hoped for with her. Maybe with me, but not with her.

"Wait, wait, wait. You *actually* believe him? Or this? Or …" She smiled. "You're kidding, right?" It was more of a desperate hope than a question.

We'd always tried to have trust and maybe, at that point, she thought we still did, and maybe we did. I trusted her. She trusted me, even though I knew she shouldn't. I wondered if we could get it back in its entirety someday. That said, there were only three realistic possibilities for her at that point: a) I was lying, b) I was serious, c) I was insane.

"A" was, obviously, the more ideal choice.

"Yeah," I answered, sipping more wine. "I think I do." I was taking "A" off the table.

"Well … I mean … Seth." A pause. "You don't think that this guy is crazy?"

The most logical and reasonable conclusion was that it was either him or me. Or both? Or neither?

"I don't know. I mean, I don't know!" I sipped more wine, hoping for miracles or at least some good song lyrics, like one of our favorite bands who had created a whole album around a bottle of wine. "It's happening. I mean, I don't know what to say. I experienced it." Those can be the words that people who see UFOs and aliens say. They had always seemed pretty ridiculous to me.

Like I seemed to Rachel in that moment.

She was trying to empathize. I could feel it. "The guy who delivers us our stuff all the time?"

I just shook my head. "He was here." I pointed to the chair. "My god … I don't know."

"If there really are demons …" She took a second. "If, I mean. Do you think we are supposed to talk to them?" she asked very nicely.

She had a point.

"Well he's a Shadow." That helped a ton.

"You should call your dad or something."

She always told me to call my dad.

My dad had been a marriage counselor for over thirty-five years. He had "retired" a few years earlier, which meant he traveled around the world with his third wife. (My dad was actually my stepdad. My biological dad died fighting in Vietnam before I was one.) My stepdad left my mom when the youngest of us, my little brother, had graduated from high school. He had stayed with her for two years and then found another woman he loved a little more: his current wife. I loved my dad because he was my dad, in theory, and I felt like I had to. No other reasons.

For some reason Rachel respected him. I did not. Nor did I trust him.

"My dad? Are you kidding me? He'd tell me I was crazy."

Her look said it all. "C" was winning. But if insanity won, there were no real winners. She knew it. There was no gloating or even a desire to be right.

In case it wasn't obvious, she continued. "You have to call someone! This is … I mean, I don't know … I don't think I can … someone else might be able to help. I just. I don't know. I can't believe you are … I mean …" That was it. Tears started. It was too much.

She cried. I cried. We both cried.

Some tears are like a good car wash. They clean away the grime of fear, the stains of stress, and that dirt that collects and congeals behind your tires from driving through life. It was therapeutic and healing. My tears were doing different things to me than I imagined hers were but it still felt good to just cry together. We hadn't cried in years about anything. It felt good to have something to talk about that wasn't just an avoidance of our own life, or lack of it, but shared emotions instead.

In between tears, and more wine, we said things like:

"The devil is a woman?"

"What if he's going to kill us?"

"He's on drugs."

"Should we call the police?"

"Are we drunk?"

"Should we listen to that album they made when they were drunk?"

"Do we believe in demons?"

"How can he be nice?"

"Well, of course, he'd be nice. How else would people believe this stuff?"

"Evil must disguise itself as good."

"Should we both go to counseling?"

"Should we just go to bed and this will all be gone in the morning?"

"What if all the stuff we think we know is just one more thing we thought we knew that we were wrong on?"

"What if that's wrong?"

"Do you think demons can know things about our lives that no one else knows?"

"What's that mean?"

"Secrets?"

"Do we have secrets?"

"I'm scared."

"This could … actually … be true?"

Stress doesn't like to hang out with exercise. It usually leaves once you start any kind of intense activity with it. It didn't like the stretching conversation either and eventually decided to go find another couple who were more sober and not laughing. By the time we went to bed, we felt better, even if it was entirely alcohol induced.

We felt together somehow, like soul mates were always supposed to be. We felt *in it* together. Whatever in the hell *it* was. That was worth everything. She believed I wasn't insane. I believed I wasn't insane. That was comforting in itself. She believed we didn't have secrets. I knew we still did. That was not comforting. But, for the first time in months, I felt a hairline fracture in the wall I had built with burner phones, lies, and made-up meetings.

I managed to crack a legitimate and content smile right before we fell asleep.

My laptop was open, almost mocking me. I was sitting in the coffee shop again staring at mostly white space on my screen and the word "untitled" above it all. I thought about naming the sermon "Lie #74" but figured that might not be appropriate.

"So, what are your earliest memories, Seth?" The words surprised me as much as what they were coming out of.

She was about as big a woman as I had ever seen. On a screen or in reality. At least four hundred pounds. Sitting across from me.

"What is this?" I asked, almost repulsed.

"What are they?" she repeated, while I wondered how someone that big had managed to sneak up on me without me noticing. "Your earliest memories."

"You're going to be my therapist now?" I asked, with as much disgust as I could muster. "Like this? No."

She smiled a pleasant smile even if her eyes were giving me the middle finger.

"Seriously?" I looked at her and around at the rest of the shop. She was big enough that everyone was staring at her, even while trying to pretend they weren't. Fortunately, some nice jazz was playing so I couldn't hear their whispers. "This is what you decided to show up in? Really?"

"I'm sorry," she said in a voice that reminded me of dragging a rake across gravel. "You think I can just pick anyone I want and invade their body?" The poor woman needed a throat replacement. If that was possible.

I felt terrible for the woman. I felt more terrible for my own vanity being seen with her.

"Well," I said, trying to keep my voice down. "Actually, I don't have a frickin' clue how you choose these bodies. Which, before we get into the psychoanalysis, can you tell me a little something about that?"

"Frickin'?" she asked.

That caught me off guard.

She laughed. Her laugh was as big as her abdomen and people looked over again. "Frickin'. You *are* a pastor, aren't you?"

"Touché," I said, almost exasperated. "I'll give you that one. But, seriously, can you tell me how you choose these bodies? I'm not real comfortable with you just possessing people. And, honestly." I took a sip of my iced mocha. "I mean, is this a game? First the normal guy, then our delivery man, and now …" I looked at her. "This? Really?"

She leaned forward. I could smell her and it wasn't like the pleasant fragrance my friend Bob had worn.

"Is this real?" I asked. It was worse than unpleasant. It was dirty. Her breath, her body, and her aura, which didn't have a physical smell but one the nose of my mind was definitely picking up.

"You really think I can just wisp through the world and pick any body I want?"

"Wisp?"

"Touché," she said with a chuckle that shook the table.

"Alright, seriously, this part freaks my wife out. How do you take control of these bodies?"

"You talked?" She smiled.

"Yeah."

"That's good. That's good …" Her whole body was moving with her nod. Maybe the floor too. "Glad I'm already helping."

"I wouldn't—"

"Just your wife, huh? It doesn't freak *you* out?" She belched.

"C'mon …" A cloud of noxious fumes ran into my nose and probably took years off my life. "Oh my god."

"What?"

"Yes, it freaks me out. And can you try to keep a low profile?" I whispered. "And not burp again—god."

"In this body? Not a chance …"

"The whole place is staring," I whisper yelled.

"No kidding. You would be too."

"I thought you were trying to be low profile."

"Listen, sometimes you get what you get."

"Okay …" We did need to move on. "So you all just possess someone whenever you want?" I was not a fan of the idea.

She leaned back. I took in oxygen again while I could stand it.

"Can you just slam dunk a basketball whenever you want?"

My frown was meant to clearly illustrate my emotion.

She continued. "We're like you. Different skills, talents, passions, and types. Some of us excel at possessions and others don't. It's a skill. And it takes training and … it's always tiring."

"Okay …"

"Well, some more than others. And it's very inefficient."

"Inefficient?" Not the word I was expecting.

"Yes." She muffled the burp this time but I could still smell its poisonous tentacles. God, it reeked, and god knows, smell is the one sense I struggle with. It's the one that poisons my grace and generosity every time. "For all the work it takes, it's really not worth it. So you control some freak for a while and make them dance around or kill themselves … there are better ways. But, we'll get there." The callous way she spoke such heavy words was unnerving to say the least.

"Jeez," I said. "Kill themselves?"

"In a sense …" She brushed aside my words. "We can't take most people. Thus …" He looked down at his own body—which was hers. "Yeah …" she muttered.

"What do you mean?"

"Have you seen any nature shows?"

"Yes." Being asked by a Shadow if I watched television felt like it should have been more shocking. *Demons watch TV?* But it wasn't. That meant something but I wasn't sure what.

"Then you know. The lions, the wolves … the predator comes up on the bison, the wildebeest, the water buffalo … the victim. It's the same thing every time. Who do they go for?"

"The weak," I answered while taking a sip of the mocha and looking at a random customer who had been staring for too long. They eventually looked away.

"The weak. The outcast. The sick. The lonely. The lonely, Seth." I looked back at her face and focused on her eyes. There are no overweight eyes. They're usually beautiful and hers were the same. "They have no chance," she repeated slowly and with a deliberateness that made me frightened in a way that I would have expected a demon to frighten me, but hadn't really up to that point.

I did think back to the normal man. I looked at the woman in front of me with a different set of my own eyes. And our delivery man. The lonely. The sick. The outcast.

I didn't say anything.

"And there are more of them than ever," she said with gravity.

"Yeah," I whispered.

"They don't know we have them. They always forget." She was back to being as upbeat as her calloused voice could be.

I assumed I was supposed to feel better.

"And, like I said, it's a lost art. Hardly ever happens anymore. No one cares to. But every now and then, you'll see it on the news. 'I can't believe *they* did *that*. I would have never expected it.'"

I felt sick to my stomach, both from her consistent, yet diverse, smells and from the idea of some kind of Shadow making someone do something they didn't want to and that someone being a very normal person, someone I saw frequently, or the woman across the table. And lonely.

"But, I need you to know something. Are you listening?"

I was.

"I'm only doing this because I have to … you'll realize that. I will not harm any of these people. Trust me."

Trust me? Why wouldn't I trust a demon?

"Seth, are you here?"

"Yeah," I mumbled.

"Can you tell me something? What are your earliest memories?"

I was struggling.

"Do you remember riding a bike for the first time?"

"Yeah," I answered, triggered to think of my five-year-old self in my old neighborhood with striped socks reaching almost to my knees. "Sorta. I mean they say that every time you recall a memory you alter it. So, yeah I have some vague recollection of riding a bike in my neighborhood in Oregon."

"Your first kiss?"

"Yeah." I smiled. "I'm sure I've made it better than it was though." Although I hadn't thought about my first kiss in a long time.

"Losing your—oh yes, that wouldn't have happened until a few days into your honeymoon," she said sarcastically, which was doubly insulting for all kinds of reasons. She finished it off with a snicker of some kind that rumbled the table again.

I sighed partly in response to her dig at my past and partly trying to clear the airspace around my head.

"Most remember that one." She smiled, continuing. "School?"

"Being alone in a cafeteria. Sucked. You probably could have possessed me."

"No." She shook her head and kept going. "Feeling left out—pretending to understand conversations that you didn't understand and vowing to understand them."

Yep.

"Fear, jealousy, competition, exhilaration?"

Check, check, check, and check.

"The memories. You have them. You're thinking of them now. Some give you a sickness and others make you want to relive them."

"Right."

"Do you remember the first time you realized you had a body?" She leaned in close again. Too close. I backed up as far as my chair would let me.

"No," I said in a reactionary way. "No." I thought about it for a moment because she was quiet. It was a strange thing to think on.

"No one does. And yet you have one. You use it. You are comfortable with it. Yet, no one remembers the first time they realized they had an arm or that they could run on their legs. No one remembers grabbing a toy for the first time. You only remember riding that bike with your body or getting naked with that body or being ashamed in that body. But no one remembers the experience of the first actual realization of their body and its pieces."

I still wasn't sure where it was going. And, to be honest, I was starting to feel the pressure of people continuing to stare at me … and her. She may have been lonely but enough was enough. I was officially embarrassed for my reputation. I liked my dirt with a little more of a manicured lawn on top of it.

"That's how it was for me the first time as well. With my new form after death. We were flying."

My interest piqued again and he knew it.

"I was in North Africa. Not sure the year but I was young then. And with my uncle. We were—"

"Wait, you had an uncle?"

"Well—"

"Hi." An employee came by our table with a tray of some little cups with mostly whipped cream and a new drink. *How many drinks can you make out of the same kind of bean?* "Would you like to try our new ..."

"No thank you," I answered. "We're having a pretty serious conversation."

Ehs then turned and looked at the employee with the worst look he could muster, which, given what he had to work with, was successfully awful. She ran. I wanted to. He continued. "Uncles are what are given to new males. Uncle Sih. Cool, old Shadow. So old he didn't even count in years anymore. He was in eras. Cunning. Smart. Creative."

"Uncle? Sih?"

"Yeah?"

"You know there was already a book with demons named Uncles? And they were mentors?"

She laughed but it was more of a wheeze than a laugh: the sound a dragon with a cold might make. Or a Shadow controlling a lonely fat lady who smoked too much, I guessed. "Of course, humans get plenty wrong. But plenty right."

"Hmm ..." I thought on that one. "Can we go outside?" I asked, standing up before he, or she, could answer.

"Sure." She stood too and continued talking, a little too loud, but I was intrigued enough not to tell her to stop. "We were running. The world was dark and the stars were shining. I remember we were moving fast. So fast. We were some kind of four-legged creature. Almost a lion. With wings. More than two eyes. I could see 360 degrees around me. It was stunning, this new body."

How am I taking this seriously?

"Suddenly Uncle Sih told me to follow him and his wings grew larger and he shot into the sky. I followed suit and transformed almost instantly. I was soon soaring in the sky, with hundreds of other Shadows, circling over a village below us. I could hear the primitive music coming up from below. There were people dancing around a fire. "

We were still standing next to some tables.

"I could see colors again. Oddly, I remember seeing them, for the first time since ... her." She stopped.

"And?"

"Did you want to go outside still?" she asked.

"Sure."

We started moving and I could almost feel the floor tremble as we did.

"The colors were all over. Flames, glowing orange. Bright clothes, dark skin, but not the dark that I was living—not the gray dark. The black-and-white dark. It was a vibrant dark skin that made me long for her again, for a moment. It made me long for color. Her color. Any color. I realized I was living in the monotone world again and bringing it with me wherever I went. It was as though color was always tempting me but I could never swim in it. It was always on the horizon, like a sunset seen from a gray perspective."

He paused again for a moment, allowing me to try and understand the effect.

"I watched my uncle glide toward a particular dancer, moving wildly." We moved between tables of people as we approached the door. "And then Uncle Sih penetrated her. I watched him go in." I wondered what everyone having a nice afternoon with their laptop at a coffee shop thought as they heard that.

I didn't wait to find out.

I did usher her/him out as fast as I could. It was a beautiful sunny spring day outside and I wondered why we had been inside in the first place instead of on the patio chairs.

My question was answered quickly. She seemed bothered by the sun, squinting and wheezing more.

"You alright?"

"Yeah, yeah. I'll just stay here though." She moved behind a brick column where the sun wasn't as bright. "Anyway, it was the first time I realized we could overtake people. I remember it was exhilarating. I took a tribal woman and caused her to kill herself. I watched the colors drain from her. The other Shadows were cheering and spurring me on as they circled the skies and slithered across the ground in every shape imaginable. It was exhilarating …" Her voice trailed off.

She seemed to remember it well.

"But it was as exhausting then as it is now. Which is why we were always working on better, more efficient ways of control. We found them."

His attention returned to the present but her body was still in the shade.

"Insipid?" I asked.

"Insipid. But we'll get there. One more memory and then I have to leave."

"Wait, wait, wait …" I countered. "I've got questions stacking up and somehow you manage to always distract me with some new story. But I've got to ask you more stuff."

"Next time."

"Are you saying when people die they become you?" I ignored him.

"Yes. Well …" Someone walked outside and gave us a weird look. I was getting used to it. "Do you remember when you realized that there were enemies in life?" she asked.

I was squinting to see her in the shade but since I was enjoying the sunlight she was just a … shadow. Ironic. I looked away and thought for a moment. It was another good question.

"Elementary school," I finally answered. "I guess."

"Fight or something?"

"Well, nothing distinct but … you know … you realize that not everyone is your friend." I wondered for a moment why I was having a deeper conversation with a Shadow than I did with most friends. Or with my wife. Maybe that was the Shadow's plan? "How is this answering my simple question?"

"I already answered it. I said yes."

"Oh …" I started to replay the tape but got distracted.

"Do you mind if I light up a cigarette? I think she needs it." He was already reaching into her pockets. "She's got to have one somewhere here …"

"Do you really think she *needs* a cigarette? Do you *feel* that?"

"Yeah, you're right." He stopped fidgeting with her body. "Anyway, I wasn't too much older. Sih and I were having a drink on a river bank. It was night. Dark. No moon. We were right at home. Sih was telling me what was happening in the world. He talked to me about the war."

"The war?" At some point I was going to have to stop listening to all of this and just say I was never going to see him again. But he was pushing that hook a little further into my mouth all the time.

"Yeah, the war. I remember feeling a little bit surprised myself, but intrigued. Up to that point, I guess I hadn't thought about it. But, like I said, I was young. We were at war. Had been for eras. Since, really, the beginning of time."

"With … angels?" I interrupted.

"Angels, ghosts, gods, valkyrie, devas, guardians … They have all kinds of names in just about every language, similar to Shadow. But, yeah …" She paused. I think she was looking at me but her large head was just a silhouette.

"And your word?"

"Rays," she said. "In your language."

"Seriously? Is this a baseball team now?" I laughed at my own joke. I wasn't even sure it was funny but it made me feel better.

"Hmmm." She didn't laugh. "No. More of a sunset. With just the right clouds and dust particles. As the sun sets below the horizon, that moment it's surrounded by massive beams of light, almost worshipping it and, I imagine, so beautiful you can hardly take your eyes off of it, even though it will blind you if you look too long."

"Yeah," I nodded. "Right."

Quite a bit better than a baseball team.

"That," she said flatly, making me feel incredibly childish with my joke. "We are still at war. Just as my uncle was telling me about them: what drives them, their powers, well … one showed up. I'll never forget it."

There was a pause and someone else walked out of the nearby door and probably stared at us.

"All of a sudden, I felt pain. Not the pain of a knife but an emotional pain. You remember the first time you felt pain?"

Another good question that I didn't have time to think about because she kept talking.

"I'll never forget it. It was as though loneliness stabbed me. I don't know if that makes sense but it's the best I can give you. I've felt it many times since then—and gotten more used to it—but it always hurts in a penetrating, deep way. But, in a way, that never seems intentional. In the way a couple holding hands, smiling, in love, can cause pain to a stranger who has just been cheated on." She made sure I noticed her use of the word *cheated*. I did. "The couple is doing nothing wrong, in fact they are doing everything right, and yet, they're causing pain." She stopped talking.

My questions were circling my head like flocks, merging into one new thing and I was unable to specifically grab any single one.

In addition to my newfound knowledge about a war between Rays and Shadows—which sounded like a bad children's book I had been read as a kid—I was still stuck on Leo and The Seers and The Separate from earlier. Not to mention Insipid itself. And The Department of Advertising.

"Ehs," I practically gasped. "You're going to have to slow down. This is getting—"

"I have to go," he interrupted instead. "Elle, here, is not doing well. I need to get her somewhere else so she doesn't collapse right here—that would make you look pretty bad."

I'm not sure I'm doing well either. "Hey, wait. If you became a Shadow. Other people become Rays?"

"That's what I said." The body of Elle started walking away.

I didn't remember him saying that either but it didn't matter.

"Wait, what did *she* become? The girl? The girl you saved from your dad?"

Elle stopped and turned around. "That was all I could think about too. I was frightened to death of the Rays and, yet, I remember a little while later, realizing that she was either one of us or one of them. I knew she was probably one of them. And, as scared as that made me, I wondered what it would be like to see her again."

He had a good story whether he was insane or not, I had to give him that. He could tell I was probably thinking something along those lines because he faced me dead on and said nine words that I knew would haunt me.

"I am going to need you to trust me."

"What?"

With that, she started running. I didn't think obese women could run and I assumed she would have never done it if she weren't controlled by a Shadow who wanted to protect me from being accused of making her pass out or something.

I watched "them" disappear and looked up into the sky. For the first time in a long time, I wondered what was all around me that I couldn't see. I thought I had let go of all of that. Until that moment. I now remembered it all clearly.

And I wasn't sure I liked it.

What happened next would also be easy to remember clearly. A coffee shop employee named Kay came outside as I was looking toward the sky. I had seen her many times. She was laughing and smiling but there was something off about it.

"Seth, what are you doing?" she said as though legitimately asking the question … but with more worry than should have accompanied it.

"I know. Weird, right?"

"Yeah." She nodded. "Just a little."

It was one of those conversations. The ones where though you are both speaking the same words, it's obvious there is something very different about the meanings or understanding. It doesn't line up. The gears of communication are out of sync. I decided to confront the feeling. "Have you seen her before?"

Her face confirmed something I didn't want it to confirm and the reason I usually let those kind of conversations run their course.

"Who?" she answered with sincerity.

My stomach and heart felt like they had been encased in concrete and thrown to the bottom of a deep lake to die. "The girl. The big lady. The really big one that you can't miss and that everyone was staring at."

She didn't need to respond—her expression said everything and I barely knew her well enough to know her expressions. She was being polite. I had to get it out there and stop dancing around it. "There was no girl?"

Even though I could tell she really didn't want to answer, she shook her head no.

Cue the terrible feelings that obliterated my body.

FOUR

Jesus supposedly did it. On a mount. At one time, that inspired me to do it as well. I probably thought I was more like Jesus then and giving a sermon came naturally. Those were the days when I had things to say and I believed the things I had to say were going to make the world a better place. Back then it was easy to get up in front of hundreds of people and give them those words. In fact, I looked forward to it. In fact, it was fun to prepare.

But, even then, giving Jesus the benefit of the doubt, by year ten I had given more sermons than Jesus did. Even assuming there's some hidden cache of Jesus sermons somewhere, I'd like to think Jesus didn't have to say something new and refreshing and empowering and moving without being offensive or watered down or boring … every … fucking … week.

He was actually allowed to be creative. And, I assume Jesus actually believed what he was saying.

Which was also a problem for me starting around year eleven. I started to have to really stretch and twist and work with words to come up with ideas that I actually believed, in a church service. By year twelve I was just giving them what they wanted to hear. By year thirteen, I had no idea what I was saying but I do know it was all a bunch of lies. If they knew the truth, they might have burned me at a stake.

It's hard enough to come up with content when you're excited about it and believe it. But at least there is a passion pushing you. Once you lose those two things and you're just doing it for the paycheck, well … it's as easy as it is honest. Some people resorted to copying other people's sermons—I had witnessed it many times. Word for word as though they had come up with it. I still had some weird pockets of pride that didn't let me do that, although it would have made it much easier.

Sunday was coming because Sunday is always coming. On Sunday afternoon, after Sunday had just "come" it was already planning on its next visit and that meant that Sunday never left my head. And that meant I hated Sunday and everything to do with it.

Maybe this is the week to just copy something. Everyone else seems to get away with it.

Worse, I had been having a hidden affair.

Worse, I had met a demon.

Worse, I didn't know if I actually had.

Worse, I didn't know if anything was true.

Worse, this "sermon" was supposed to be about a chapter in the book of John that was as boring as watching paint dry. Actually, it was less interesting than that. Watching paint dry at least implies that you just painted something and there is, at least, a little excitement in that. More than the John passage.

The testimony of Jesus? Who testifies … who doesn't … whose testimony he accepts . . . whose he doesn't … who gives a shit?

Once again, I was supposed to give some opinion or interpretation on what it meant, at least at some level. Or why anyone should care. Once again, I didn't care. Even more than normal.

I couldn't even read it.

Ehs, can you help me give a sermon?

While trying to figure out if I could beg someone to take over for me, or nicely guilt someone into doing it, I was also beginning to question everything about myself, including my own ability to perceive reality. The obese woman, or lack of one, was filling my brain like an ever-expanding helium balloon (or a very obese woman) and every other thought was finding less and less room to operate.

I also felt like my head might literally explode when it ran out of room, which was happening fast, and caused me to have a slight panic attack at the thought of my kids seeing my brains on the office walls.

Good morning, everyone. This week I was supposed to give a sermon. As usual. But it turns out that a demon has been visiting me and telling me some very interesting things. Pretty cool stuff, actually. And even the demon himself is pretty cool. Weird, huh? Who would have thought? Well, I guess some of you think I'm a demon so it wouldn't be that much of a surprise.

So, I guess while I'm here, I might as well let you all know that I've been having an affair for the past year or so. I mean, a pretty lame affair, but an affair, nonetheless. Yes, honey, it's true.

So, should I just walk out now? Can I maybe get a severance package though?

Although, actually, it turns out that what I thought was a demon visiting me was all in my head, and I think I'm insane. So, rather than give you a message today, I'm just going to stay up here and talk about my cool imaginary demon friend? Well, Shadow actually … is that alright? And, actually, I wonder if everything in my life has been in my head.

Hey, maybe I did not have an affair! I just thought I did.

And we're back. We can all return to our normal, boring, Insipid lives.

The sun eventually set on a day I couldn't even be sure had existed.

But, it was a day—which meant time was passing. That seemed good. A couple more days passed and there was no sign of Ehs. I began to believe Rachel was right. *Why had I even thought it was a good idea to hang out with him?* Or Kay was right. He had never existed in the first place. I chose to stop talking about it, like I did most hard things. I buried it beneath busyness and routine. Rachel would ask here and there but my words became like my sermons: too much work, too much effort, too dangerous to be authentic and, thus, boring.

As more time passed and I didn't allow myself to think about him/her/it anymore, I found that the balloon was shrinking and maybe the whole thing was just a dream or strange experience and my original and more comfortable insane version of sanity was coming to live in me again.

I was not insane. Not like *that.*

Right?

FIVE

"Well, well, well." He was yelling while clapping his hands between each word. I couldn't tell if he was being nice, being patronizing, or mocking me, assuming he was real at all. "These last two weeks ..." he added.

I had been alone, reading a book, and the doorbell had rung.

Rachel was on a trip to New York with her mom and we had ordered a skateboard for my daughter's friend, who was turning three. I was already wary of anyone delivering a package, for obvious reasons, so I only opened the door after the visitor's outline disappeared in the stained glass window. They had left.

Or so I had thought.

If I had known a figment of imagination, that I had successfully eradicated, would be hiding so I couldn't see him I probably wouldn't have opened it. I thought I was over him. But, there was the familiar face of James, the man I had met at coffee and the first image I had of Ehs. He was standing in front of me. Or at least, some sort of experience of James was there. Whether or not anyone else would see James I didn't know.

"Seriously." He kept talking like it was no big deal. "You've got something in there still, don't you? I see it. I hear it. Despite the bullshit. Preach!" he yelled, louder than anyone had ever yelled in our church. The irony was more real than he probably was. "You realize there is a lot in there even though you like to act like there isn't?" He was pointing toward my heart.

"You're not real." I started to close the door but James had his foot out and I couldn't.

"Then why can't you close the door?" he asked, verbalizing my thoughts and looking down at his yellow Vans blocking my white front door.

He had a point. Unless I was only imagining that I couldn't close the door. Or maybe imaging the door itself. "Nice shoes. What do you want?"

He looked surprised and it was a pleasant expression. James was pleasant. In fact, if he had shown up as the big lady or our Santa delivery man … I'm not sure I could have handled it. But James was so familiar and comfortable … "What do I want?" he asked, looking around. "I mean, I've been pretty obvious, right? Oh, and thanks. James does have a nice fashion sense." He nodded toward his shoes.

"Where have you been?" I asked, still in a bad mood.

"You've been busy. I gave you some time. I enjoy the … lectures though." He tilted his head off to the side. "I mean for a sermon they're decent."

It was raining outside but James wasn't wet. We had a covered porch but I assumed he had to get to the porch from somewhere that was not covered. Of course, that was only half as odd as a demon talking to me about sermons.

"Did you listen to the podcast?" I asked, half joking but half not. "Or were you there?"

He just smiled. "Can I come in?"

"No, I'm about to go on a run."

"Great! I'll go with you." Spoken like an excited puppy dog. Or the friend who invites themselves to the party, not aware of the fact they were purposely not invited.

"Well … when I run, I'm not really able to talk."

"Well …" He didn't miss a beat. "You're probably running too fast. They say you should be able to have a conversation."

"I'm not a great runner."

"I'll make you better with that too then." Another normal—even nice—smile.

What the hell.

A few minutes later we were moving down the street my house and I lived on. The rain had stopped. James was right next to me and seemed fine doing most of the talking. There was a small problem—I had no way of getting rid of him, even though I told myself he was only in my head.

"So listen, I know it's been weird. I know you've been freaking yourself out a little after the large lady incident. But, let me explain."

"Please," I mumbled, trying to control my breathing. Our pace was definitely quicker than my usual.

"First, she didn't sing," he laughed.

"What?" I threw out, not happy.

"Never mind. Bad joke." He looked over at me. "She was huge though, wasn't she?"

I took the moment to try and catch my breath that felt like it was somewhere behind me. Ehs continued. "You're not making this up.

It's real. But other people can't see me like you can."

I'm pretty sure that's the definition of crazy.

"You're not crazy. It's as real as the road you are running on."

"What road?" I asked.

Ehs smiled. "Good, it seems you're finally learning."

"I am?" I was officially into heavy breathing, way too early in the run.

"There's much more I can show you. If you let me. As real as the air you are breathing but, well, it won't seem that way."

Mental workouts were maybe harder than physical workouts and I seemed to be getting both in that moment. I wasn't sure which hurt more.

"Seth, you know this. You've said it many times," James said without any effort to catch his own breath. The fact that he was running at the same speed as I was, and acting as though we were sitting on my couch, was bugging me.

"What?" I managed to let out.

"The highest form of knowledge is to know that one does not know … You've heard it?"

"Yes." I had.

"Things as big as we are talking about are not going to fit in a sentence. Or a book, or a thought, or a logical process. This is not a new idea to you."

"And you're *that* big?"

He smiled and completely ignored me. "We're talking about other dimensions that exist simultaneously with yours and contain creatures that are not humans that live in that dimension and interact with the humans living in yours. You think this is going to be nice and tidy and fit in a cute little box? If this made sense, it wouldn't be real."

He did make sense. The demon was making sense.

Is he making sense? He can't be. Demons themselves don't make sense. That's old classic primitive religious thinking.

"What do you want?" I breathed.

"What do *you* want," he breathed back.

"What?"

"You heard me."

"What the hell? I didn't spy on you and come find you in …" I looked over at the man I was running with. He wasn't even wearing running shoes. The yellow Vans were vibrant against the black asphalt. "In this guy."

"I want what you want," he answered.

"Okay," I got out between deep breaths. "And what do I want?"

"What we all want."

"And that is?"

"Someone who will let it sink in. Someone who believes more than they admit. Someone willing to call out the bullshit. Someone willing to live in the nuance and the complexity without demanding quick and easy answers." There was a long pause. "Freedom. Happiness. Love." There was another long pause but not because he was tired. "Trust, Seth. A friend. Someone who sees us for what we actually are." He paused again. "The real us."

We ran for a while longer and neither of us said anything. It was better that way.

It reminded me of my first morning in Gwen's bed. Finally sober. We didn't say anything. It was better that way.

It reminded me of the first time I saw my daughter take a breath after being born. I didn't say anything. It was better that way.

It reminded me of sitting on the beach looking out at the waves with my wife on our honeymoon. We didn't say anything. It was better that way.

So we ran.

For a while.

Eventually, we hit a dirt trail that launched up a large hill under some thick power lines. The amazing health benefits of running were probably offset by the reams of electricity and ELF radiation above me but I ran under them all the same. When you can't see something …

"I will eventually need you to trust me," the *invisible* thing repeated.

I stopped running. "You're asking me to trust a demon."

"I know." He smiled.

"I mean Shadow," I corrected myself, as though it mattered, and started running again. Away from him and the power lines.

"I wish you could see what I see in you," he yelled from behind me.

"Thanks, Mom," I yelled back sarcastically, rolling my eyes and picking up my pace.

"I will take credit for that." He kept standing, somewhere behind me.

I stopped running, again, irritated now, and turned around. "What's that mean?"

"I've told you, I'm in charge of advertising … for darkness. We'd rather you dismiss truth with eye rolls and sarcasm. Dismiss a loving parent who bred some sense of self-worth in you as annoying and not the gift that was for you."

"I don't …" I did.

"Have you ever noticed how often the response to a compliment is some kind of reason to throw it away? Or dismiss it. Or act as though it's insignificant. Like you just did." He smiled. "Like *you* just did."

"Yeah."

"Well, you've been programmed." He took a quick breath, almost smug. "By me. Damn good job I do too. We wouldn't want you to actually start accepting compliments, would we?"

"You're twisted."

"You have no idea," he sighed, almost hissing.

"And you want me to trust you?"

"I wish I could say that you haven't already."

I stared.

"You along with the rest of humanity. It's me you always hear. Almost constantly. And you trust, without knowing. Now"—he waited until I was looking at him again—"this time I'm asking you to trust me and know it. That should seem a little more authentic and, thus, friendly, right?"

"Well, not when you just come out and say it like that," I responded, looking toward the hill that I was about to run down.

I took a deep breath. A really really deep one. The one that is a very obvious attempt to make yourself believe you are relaxing.

"Okay." I released.

"Okay, what?"

"Okay. I've got enough shit to worry about in my life right now. I'm not sure I can start tagging along with you." I looked back at him.

"Can I give you some time?" he responded.

"Sure, but …"

"I also need one other thing."

"Shit. What?"

"I need you to help me find her."

"Her? The angel-Ray-thing her?"

"Yeah, her."

"How?"

"We'll get there."

"I'm sure we will. Because we will always get to everything."

"Well …"

"This is ridiculous."

"And probably a little dangerous," he added.

"That's supposed to make me want to do this more?"

"If it's not risky, you're not living," he answered while a bird soared high above us in the sky. "You know that, already."

"How dangerous?"
"Not very."
"Are you lying?"
"I don't know."
"You're a demon. You're always lying."
"Not true."
"That would be a lie too."
"Yet you trust it."
"What part of it?"

"Look." With that James turned his back to me and looked out at the view that we could see from the top of the hill.

I looked too. And it was the same view it had always been: tall brown grass rolling down in front of me, some clusters of tall pines in the distance on one side and a neighborhood sprawling out on the other. In the far distance were some rolling hills rising higher in elevation to an eventual larger hill, almost a mountain, that my family and I had skied every winter when we were all living more like a family. I felt almost guilty looking at it. Or jealous. Or both.

"What am I looking for?" I asked. The sky was gray, filled with clouds that seemed to have another deluge of rain in them, maybe saving it to punish me for my sins on the way home.

Then, I had that strange sixth sense, intuition, gut, whatever you want to call it, feeling. It was there. Full force. Something wasn't right but I didn't know what. Clouds were clouds. Trees were trees. Dirt was dirt, although it was all especially dreary.

There was something in the distance. I would have thought it was a storm cloud but it was too dark. Too black. And moving too fast. And, the more I looked, the more I saw it wasn't shaped like a cloud at all but like a giant bird with wings. But not the bird I had just seen. Larger. Flapping. Prehistoric in style. Or medieval. Or fantastic.

I blinked to get rid of it.

Blinking rarely erases something you don't think you should be seeing but in that case, it did. It was gone. My feeling that something wasn't right, however, did not disappear as easily, especially when the "not right" thing seemed to be me and my ability to see things that did not exist.

"James?"
"Yeah," he answered, as though nothing had happened.
"What was that?"
"What?" Apparently confirming that nothing had happened.
"That thing."
"What thing?"

“The thing you told me to look at.”

He laughed. “Oh, the bird.”

“Yeah, the bird.” I looked again to where it was, but there was nothing.

“Right?”

“What the hell?” I looked back at him. “Was that real?”

“What road?” he asked with a very inquisitive look on his face as though he really wasn’t sure.

“Did I …”

“No.”

“Then, how did you—”

He interrupted with something important. His look gave it away. “You’ve said the story many times. I’ve heard it, Seth. I know you. Better than you know yourself. You’re a hero,” he added with more conviction than I would have. “What’s happened to you?”

The words hurt like they should have. They punched me in all the right places. He was right. “I don’t know.” I sighed heavily, feeling drained again.

“I do,” he responded quickly. “And I can show you.” He seemed so much lighter than me and the irony was no longer ironic. It was almost irritating. “I’d like to show you some things. Is that okay?”

“Some things?” I asked, monotone.

“Some things,” he repeated calmly.

I don’t like to let people down by saying no. So, my default answer emerged again. “Yeah, I guess.”

“Cool,” he replied, looking up toward the sky.

“Cool?”

“Yeah, cool.” He looked back at me. “It’ll be fun.”

I felt like something was supposed to happen, but nothing did. “Now what?”

“Let’s keep running …” And with that Ehs was off again, in the shape of a very normal, nice running man, still wearing—now very dirty—skate shoes, named James, expecting me to follow. I did, although I was not quite sure what I had said yes to.

“You’re familiar with quantum entanglement, right?” He asked me after I caught up with him. We were now moving down the dirt path on the other side of the hill.

“Familiar? I mean, I’ve heard of it.” Dirt clods were spilling all over the trail, pulled down toward the bottom, as we leapt down together.

“Hmm …”

“What’s that mean?”

We reached the bottom of the hill and now had to rise up another smaller one to get to the road I knew was on the other side. "Well, to make this somewhat simple and relevant. Humans tend to think of everything in terms of objects in space. But it might be smarter—and more accurate—to think of things in terms of relationships and their interaction with one another. Or as *happenings*. Your scientists are thinking that way."

"Okay."

"Atoms that appear to be separated by space are sometimes actually the same, or at least appear to be, even though they are far apart. And you don't know why. So, things are here and there, but in a different way than you are used to. It's all perspective, of course."

"Okay," I repeated.

"Axions? Heard of them?"

"No, I don't think so."

"Scientists haven't concluded whether or not they exist." He winked at me. "But, if they do—and they do—they're particles that don't interact with conventional matter, especially in the way you understand conventional matter or interactions."

"Okay," I said for a third time. What else was I supposed to say?

He reached the road before me and was waiting, still with a pulse of fifty-five, I assumed. "I'm no scientist so I don't entirely get it all either—I'm not sure anyone entirely does ... but what's important is that *where* is no longer a question worth asking. There is no here and there. It's all much more intertwined and entangled than that. Even *what* is questionable."

"Okay." It was the only word I had left in a usually vast and intellectual-sounding vocabulary. I reached the road and saw a car pass by, wondering if they just saw me or if they saw both of us. "Was I asking where?"

"No," he answered, starting to run down the road. "But you might."

"Okay," I responded for the fifth time. I started again, right behind him. "Why's that?"

"You just might." He smiled. "Now try to keep up." He picked up the pace and I was forced to respond. I did my best, still tired from the hill and still confused as to what quantum entanglement had to do with anything when I realized exactly what it had to do with it.

We were in front of a restaurant. I had never seen a restaurant on this street before and I was positive there was not a restaurant on the street, even though I was looking at one. I, obviously, stopped running.

"Where are we?"

He smiled with a "told-you-so" kind of expression. "Mu," he answered.

"Mu?" I asked, having no idea what he meant.

"No," he answered, not clearing up much, which my expression clearly showed. "Mu is an ancient term. Look it up. It's the wrong question."

Despite Ehs's words, I continued to turn my head in all kinds of directions, trying to get a gauge on *where* I was. It was still the street I was used to but a restaurant, right out of a street in downtown New York City, had been plopped where I remembered houses existing.

"Black and white. Either. Or. Dualistic. Get it out of your head. Are the trees swimming? Un-ask the question. Get somewhere else. Sic et Non. Yes *and* no."

"Wow." I sighed. "I just asked where we are. Are you going to throw a lecture at me every time I—"

"You can't ask that. There is no where. The question doesn't work."

"It sure seems like there is a where," I responded, looking around at some *where*.

"You can be ignorant. Just don't be proud of the delusion." He looked disgusted. "Hard to believe I ever thought …" he mumbled, shaking his head. I heard something about "levels of consciousness" and "reality" and "perception."

"Please do enlighten me," I shot back with some sarcasm around the edges of the words.

"Believe me, I'm trying."

"Okay." Less sarcasm.

"Why do two people look at the same piece of art and see something different?"

I waited, sensing the rhetorical Ehs.

"We bring where we are and what we're doing to everything. To the painting. To the dance. To the drug experience. It's well documented … the same drug won't give you the same message because you're always in a different place. Physically and metaphorically—and the drug only enhances it."

I stared at the restaurant, trying to remember if I had taken some psilocybin for the first time in my life without remembering it.

"That is the message. You have 150 biases running that little head of yours at all times. Questions like 'what does it mean' and 'where are we' are utterly worthless."

"Well …" I was not entirely convinced.

"Are the trees swimming?" he asked.

"I mean," I said slowly, studying a clump of nearby pines, not sure if they actually were swimming or just waving in the wind. They seemed to actually be swimming. Was I making them swim? "To be fair, they kind of do look like—"

"There is no answer." Ehs pointed toward the restaurant. "And that was a bad example."

"What?" I asked, more smug than I should have been.

"You don't even know what a tree is?"

"Well … I …" I looked at the trees.

"Some are saying the word is outdated. The concept of a tree is more of a verb than a noun because trees are always doing something in such slow motion that we don't …" He seemed as exhausted as I did for the first time. "Tree-ing is more like swimming," he mumbled to himself.

"I'm not sure …"

He looked at me again, with wide eyes. "Is seven drinking the swim?"

Whatever smugness I had shown gave way to a big confused expression. Ehs seemed satisfied.

"Mu. Better example."

"Okay." I was back to regurgitating my simple responses.

"Should we grab something to eat?" he asked. I noticed the sign that read COFFEE SHOP in big letters from an older era that was almost cool again, but not quite. BREAKFAST, LUNCH, AND DINNER was also in big letters in case anyone wondered if they served every possible meal.

"Sure," I answered, glancing back at the pine trees flipping backstrokes. And apparently tree-ing.

We walked in through a glass door to an old diner. Round stools at a long bar, maroon booths lining the walls with some tables, and felt-covered chairs. It had a musty scent to it but there were people in the restaurant eating a variety of eggs and toasts and pancakes. They paid little attention to us, which meant that they either didn't see us or didn't really care who was in the restaurant with them. It had that kind of vibe. Go and eat. Say hi to no one.

"Hi, can I help you?" the nice man behind the bar said. I noticed a long griddle behind him and some old coffee in even older pots.

"Yes, two please," Ehs answered. I was still too busy processing what and where and mu. And the fact that, at least, we were seen.

"Right here." The nice man motioned us to a booth and handed us menus as we sat down. "Coffee?"

"Sure," Ehs answered.

"Sure," I answered. *Why not?*

I stared for a moment at the white plaster walls, the tear in the cushion I was sitting on, and the Formica on the table in front of me. I spent some time touching it, feeling it, trying to make my hand go through it to break the hologram or dream or whatever I was in. But that never happened.

"Seth." Ehs finally spoke, aware of my inability to do anything.

I looked up. Our coffees had arrived but I didn't remember the man bringing them.

"Seth, you coached football, right?"

"Yeah." I would have spent time being amazed that he really did know everything about me if I wasn't more amazed at sitting in a restaurant that was everywhere and nowhere and somewhere.

"Have you ever talked to someone about football who thinks they understand football because they watched a Super Bowl once?"

"Yeah."

"Then you understand yourself. You think you understand our world … this world …" He picked up the coffee cup and took a sip. "You think you understand demons, angels, Rays, Shadows, whatever you want to call it … us, them, because you read a verse in the Bible, watched a documentary, read a book, or because your mom told you a story."

"Why me?"

"What?" He set down the mug.

"Can I interest you in something else?" the nice server asked.

"No thanks," Ehs responded. "What?" He looked back to me.

I was staring out the diner's window at a street I had driven on a million times. "Why did you pick me?"

"Not many would have gotten this far. Especially Christians." That line splashed a little cold water on my trance.

"I'm not a Christian. I've given it up."

"Hmm." He waited for my eyes. "Not nearly enough."

I somehow felt insulted.

"But, I suppose we'll get there. The point—for now—is … you trust me more than most would."

"Is that a compliment?" I asked, picking up the coffee cup and tasting it as though it were poison as I cautiously wondered if it existed. "My mom wouldn't think so."

"I didn't visit your mom. Wouldn't have lasted more than a second."

"What's that mean?" The coffee tasted just like normal coffee—well, normal bad coffee—to go with normal James in a very abnormal circumstance. "She could banish you or something?"

"I'm here. Talking. You're hearing. You're seeing. If you didn't trust me, none of this would be here."

"So I could not trust you and go back to my life?"

"I doubt it. You're special. Unique. It's who you are. It's in your heart. It's hard to un-trust."

"Thanks, Mom." I set the cup down and smiled at someone else in the restaurant. They seemed to smile back.

"Again." James was shaking his head. "Cynicism. Even to truth. If the truth is too complimentary, you find a way to reject it. And you think all of *this* is unreal." He shook his head.

I looked back to him. "Alright, listen, so I trust you for a moment. I could get rid of you but I can't because I inherently trust you. The bigger lady didn't?"

"You're different."

"What's that mean?"

"Good grief. Sometimes I wish I wasn't so good at what I do."

"What's that mean?" I picked up the coffee mug and noticed my reflection in the dark liquid. "I can't say *that* now?"

"She's dead."

"She died?" Ehs did know how to get my attention.

"Dead. Asleep. Not literally dead but she might as well be. You're not."

"Really?" It was some of the best news I'd heard in ages. Not only was I not literally dead but I was not metaphorically dead either.

If Ehs could be trusted.

"Yes," he answered. "You know what I mean by that?"

"I don't feel very awakened." Though I did want to be.

"You're not."

And … back to feeling like shit.

"But," he continued, "compared to most other people, well … you're in mediocre shape."

"Mediocre is worse than bad. There had to be better people," I said with honest self-deprecation.

"Not really." He looked down at the cup of coffee. "And mediocrity is not worse than bad."

"Mediocrity is the enemy of excellence," I said, quoting something I had heard at some point in my life.

Ehs laughed out loud. "Spoken by someone who must assume they are excellent? What a joke." His laughing faded away slowly, giving way to disgust and more muttering under his breath.

I took a sip of terrible coffee to process the fact that I was perhaps the most perfect person on Earth to trust a demon and let it do whatever it wanted … or to actually help the demon and possibly the world. "Well," I said, assuming the best-case scenario. "I guess it's a compliment that you picked me."

"Of course it is." He smiled. "You see this restaurant, Seth?" Ehs looked around and nodded at a few people who nodded back in return. He even got a fake smile out of a very grumpy-looking businessman.

"Yeah, I see it."

"There's an inherent problem with this restaurant. Do you see Aarush over there?"

I looked toward the direction Ehs was pointing. An Indian-looking gentleman behind the counter. He had brought us our menus and our coffee. He looked to be somewhere in his fifties with dark skin and even darker facial hair doing its best to cover up whatever soul was inside of the body.

"Right, the man behind the counter. He owns this place and has for years. The problem is that for every dollar he makes, he has to be here. He has to serve coffee, clean menus, clean tables, make sure his cooks are creating and delivering the food correctly. He has had five days off in the past seven years."

"Poor guy." He looked even more tired once Ehs had told me his story.

"It's part of the industry. And it's many jobs. Hard to make money while you sleep but it's much nicer when you do."

"Right."

"But the goal is to make money while you sleep, right?"

"Yeah."

Aarush walked over since we were both staring at him. "Anything I can get you?"

"Just the bill. Thanks," Ehs answered.

"That was us. Shadows. We were doing destructive work but it was so *much* work. So much effort. We needed to possess you in our sleep." He smiled.

"You sleep?"

Ehs rolled his eyes. "Yes, everything with a brain sleeps. It's essential but that's hardly the point."

"You have a brain?" I smiled.

"Funny." He paused and then somewhat to himself, more quiet, as though thinking. "Although there are some fruit flies that don't …"

"Well," I stammered. "It was half a joke but also … do you?"

"Consciousness. Yes. Again, not the point." I could sense his frustration and wondered if he could sense any in me.

"Okay, so everything sleeps." I had known that. But it was still a creative exercise to imagine demons sleeping.

"So, there was a plan. Well, there always had been plans. Systems, projects, creations that could do the work for us. As systems tend to do."

"Here you go." Aarush put down the check.

"Thanks." Ehs handed him a credit card, still staring at me. "We've called it Insipid. Our latest—and best—iteration. Not only does it do our work, but you continue to build it. Even better, right?"

I wasn't sure I liked anything he was saying.

"You build it. You enjoy it. You build it. You enjoy it. We do nothing but watch you paralyze yourselves ..."

I was in awe that he was paying with a credit card and I wondered what the bill would look like when the actual James saw it.

Would he see it?

"C'mon." He stood up. "You're getting tired. You just need some fresh air."

I followed him through the restaurant and out the glass doors, waving to Aarush as we thanked him for his delicious coffee. The air felt like a cup of cold water, refreshing. I wondered where the air came from even as it fed me some energy.

"Poor Bruno," Ehs said, stretching out his hand like a magician.

"Huh," I uttered, looking back to the trees doing their thing.

"Bruno," he repeated as though I hadn't heard him the first time.

"The singer?"

Whatever words he uttered were soaked in apparent disgust for me and my lack of wisdom.

"Bruno." He repeated it louder as though that would help.

"Who?" I said louder, mimicking his attempt at using volume to help understanding.

He rolled his eyes and let out an exasperated sigh. "Didn't you go to school to learn theology and the history of religion?"

"Yeah."

"And they didn't teach you about Bruno?"

"No?" I made the word a question for some reason.

"Hmmm." He smiled, with a bit of pride showing through his frustration. "I should have known." He waved his arms around his head like a teenage musician and threw in a bit of a twirl just to top it off. "Poor Bruno."

With another flick of his arms, my world changed again. The trees, restaurant, road, sky and clouds were still around me but they were suddenly flat, almost painted, like props found in a Broadway play. We were on stage and the scene was a massive set, unlike any set I had ever seen but still missing some kind of dimension.

"Giordano Bruno was a moment. There are many but it's a favorite."

"Where ..." I stopped, realizing it was pointless. The restaurant was gone only to be filled with more fake trees that may or may not have been swimming. Reality was as foggy as my brain at that point.

"The name still doesn't ring a bell?" he asked, trying hard to not roll his eyes again.

"Are you mocking me?"

"Sorry, sorry. I'll try to summarize the important parts. He was a mystic and a scientist. He was much ahead of his time claiming that there were other inhabitable worlds. Gasp." Ehs mocked, holding his hands to the side of his face. "But—"

"Wait," I interrupted. "Are there?"

"No, you miserable human creatures are the best this universe has to offer." The words were painted in sarcasm.

"Ouch."

"Can I continue?"

"Yes," I answered, getting used to standing on the set of an expensive play on a road near my house.

"He believed all kinds of heresies. Heresies," he almost hissed, gleefully. A gleeful hiss if there exists such a thing. "Infinite worlds, no hell, souls of the Earth, and that the sun was a star among many other stars and planets and ... heresies." He paused. "Of course he was right on everything."

"The Earth has a soul? There is no hell?"

"Mu!" he yelled loudly at me. "He wasn't speaking literally—no one who speaks truth does. Truth doesn't fit in the literal, though you are obsessed with literal." He paused. "All part of our system. But, I digress." He brought himself back to attention. "He was thinking large, Seth! Immense! Infinite. The entire world thought it was this." Ehs pointed again at our flat two-dimensional surroundings. I studied them.

With another exaggerated twirl, like that of a dance, and his arms swimming off to his side, whatever props had been there vanished and were replaced by a massive curtain and new props—a black sky with stars and planets. "The entire world thought they were living on some kind of stage. Poor Bruno, in the best language he could, claimed that an infinite source of creativity would demand an infinite universe!" Ehs dropped his raised arms to the ground and, with that, the curtain fell too. As did my breath.

I once snorkeled with dolphins in Hawaii. When I jumped into the water, about two hundred feet deep, I could barely breathe. I wasn't afraid—but my body was not used to floating two hundred feet above solid land and being able to live. It had to catch up to my brain frantically trying to explain that we were floating.

I now had the same feeling. We were floating. Hovering, not falling. It was a vast expanse on all sides. Stars and suns and planets in every direction with such size that I felt minuscule and immense at the same moment. Terror and exhilaration.

"And poor Bruno believed *this* was real." Ehs floated in the vast expanse, twirling again, much easier, almost dancing now. "And no one believed him. They burned him at the stake instead. Heresy!" He was dancing now and I could not tell if he was celebrating the beauty of the space or the beauty of no one believing poor Bruno.

"This." The curtains were back. "This." My breath left me again as deep space returned. "No, no, no," he shouted as the curtains returned. "You can't change Scripture! You can't change science! You can't question what we know to be true with our precious reason and study and intellect!" He was practically drunk now … on something.

"Poor Bruno," he said quietly. And everything was as I remembered. Well, with the restaurant still there.

"You see," he continued. "They did it *for* us. They killed him. Burned him. If he would not believe in hell, they would create it for him, to assuage their own doubt and fear and hatred. Some say they killed him for his heretical science, some say for heretical theology. I'll tell you it was both *and* neither. They killed him because they could not handle someone finding wisdom in dreams—how dare he model the father of Jesus?" he asked incredulously. "How dare he? They killed him because he questioned their authority."

A car drove by.

"They would kill Galileo and countless others, just like they kill them today. In fact—" He paused, mulling something over in his head. "Have you been to Spain?" he eventually asked with a smile.

"What?" I asked. Though I had heard every word.

"Yes." He snapped his fingers—I assumed for effect—and the scene changed again. We were standing on a European street. A massive structure rose up on one side of us, ancient, made of ornate bricks and carvings, and on the other side was an old cathedral, with its towers rising up toward a blue sky.

It was eerily empty, which made me feel as though it wasn't real. But I wasn't about to ask, of course.

"Valencia," Ehs spoke. "Have you heard of it?"

"No," I answered, looking around and noticing a beautiful building with a massive sign that read MERCAT CENTRAL. Astounding dark blue tile work adorned the front, making it seem more like a piece of art than a building. Although one could have said that about most of the structures with their arched doorways, towers, stone intricacies, and architectural power.

"Another of my favorite markers. To some this marked the end. Of course, it wasn't, which is why it's one of my favorites." Ehs pointed to a lampstand. "That used to be a gallows here in the central square near the church. Of course. So the priests could watch."

I nodded, and before I had lifted my chin again the lamp had turned into a gallows. Thick and permanent, made of heavy dark woods.

"I assume you've heard of the Spanish Inquisition?"

"Yes," I nodded, even as the town morphed slowly all around me, the modern fading away and the old becoming the normal … it was a subtle transition in an old European city but it was noticeable nonetheless.

"Cayetano Ripoll was a teacher. Some call him a deist. Labels." He waved his hand into the air but I barely noticed as the town continued to change into an older time, which meant, ironically, it felt newer.

"Yes, he taught his children that it was not necessary to go in there"— he pointed to the huge cathedral—"to find the sacred because the sacred was everywhere." This time he waited for me to look at him." Can you imagine that?" His smile was not pleasant. "We couldn't have that, could we?" He laughed again, like a villain laughs at her victim before strangling him.

And then I saw a man hanging from the gallows. Lifeless, his body drained of whatever substance makes something a human and not just a bag of hanging flesh. "Yes," Ehs continued quietly. "They wanted to burn him but the secular authorities they had doing their dirty work wouldn't, so he was the last one to hang here."

Ehs stared at the body, almost amused. I looked away.

"But at least he was the last, right?" He asked with more joy than he should have. "Yes," he said almost silently. "No more of that." I had never heard words with more sarcasm. "Yes, no more public physical executions, just private mental ones. And we make money while we sleep." He looked at me with a strange calm and nodded his head toward the restaurant that had suddenly appeared again. Along with the nice Indian man I assumed was still exhausted and pouring terrible coffee, chained to his job.

Like me.

"Fuck." At least it worked better than "okay."

"Good." He nodded. "I'm glad you're beginning to understand."

"I don't know if that's true."

"Hmm." He almost snorted. "I think you are."

"Am I?"

"Religion, Seth. We invented it."

"Fuck," I repeated again, much slower, for good measure.

"Indeed." He grinned like I imagined Thomas Edison would have after showing me his light bulb. Speaking of light bulbs, they were flashing all over my brain. "Along with heresy. *Invent* might be too dramatic. But we stole it, manipulated it, coerced it, messaged it, and evolved it … for our own uses."

"I'm tired, man." The words came from my mouth slowly.

"I'm going to need you to help me find her."

"What?" We were suddenly a long way from Bruno and reality and I felt awake again.

Does he know how to play with my emotions just right or what?

"Help me. Find her."

"This again?"

"Yes," he replied sincerely.

"The girl you saw for thirty seconds when you were a human fifteen hundred years ago?"

"Yes," he nodded as though nothing was out of the ordinary.

"And the whole world falling apart because of Bruno and Insipid and … we can worry about …" I didn't even know what else to say.

"Yes?"

"And that? Is that just frosting on the cake?"

"Mu."

"Fuck mu."

He laughed.

I didn't.

"As I said, there are not many people like you, Seth. Not at all." He reached out and touched my shoulder like a sincere friend. "I like you."

"Again, thank you." I rolled my eyes that time. "And I didn't say I would do it."

"You don't even know what *it* is."

"No shit." Which was why I wanted to make sure he acknowledged I wasn't agreeing to it.

"But you haven't said no either."

"This is—"

"Finish your run," he interrupted. "It's been enough."

I had that feeling suddenly. The one that hits you when you've been driving down a long road and for a long time and you suddenly realize you've been driving for a long time down a long road and not very aware of it. You're thankful you didn't end up in a ditch.

I was running. Almost home. I was far from the hill, far from James and running past the same houses and streets and power lines that I always did and they were in the spots they always were with nothing else added. Just like normal.

With a lot more sweat. And a lot more to think about it.

SIX

I hate cats.

I hate country music.

I hate the taste of cigarette smoke.

I hate women who are desperate and think it's sexy.

I hate houses that are decorated with too many shades of brown, and have wooden signs with pithy sayings and smell like cat litter.

I hate betraying the one woman I love in this life.

I hate that all that hate couldn't prevent me from filling my life with it.

I would say something along the lines of "I'm just a man," but that would be an excuse for "I'm just a coward."

I sat there at three in the afternoon staring at myself in her mirror, trying to put my pants back on. The damn button fly was not cooperating, another illustration for my life at that point.

I finally looked down and spent way too long putting the buttons where they were supposed to go before looking in the mirror again.

I hated bright pink and it just so happened that every tile in the bathroom was that shade of color.

I hated pills and she had five of the little brown cylinders lining her shelf like soldiers waiting to go to some war they didn't know why they were fighting. I thought about reading the labels but I didn't want to know what kind of stuff she was putting in her body besides nicotine, silicone, whiskey, and some weed here and there. And, of course, me. What kind of need for medicine or poison was I fulfilling?

I did grab the bottle of mouthwash—pink, of course—and poured as much as I could fit into my mouth. I don't know what kind of chemicals make up pink cinnamon- and mint-flavored liquid but it was better than the flavor of cigarette smoke clinging to my tongue and teeth.

While I swished it around, appreciating the burn of the liquid—

the cleansing—I hated my own face for a moment. *What a fraud.*

Hatred is a soothe for fear: the fear that burns and itches cowards like me. It's a temporary salve but in that moment it felt good to hate. Even myself. Unfortunately, there was no pink mouthwash to burn and cleanse my interior.

"Seeettth," she called from the room down the hallway. "Don't leave yet." She was a bad actress even when she was doing her best to perform like a seductress from some late-night movie.

"Well," I called out, looking for my shirt and praying I had brought it into the bathroom. "I do have some things to do."

"Oh stop," she answered back, trying to woo me and not aware that it was pushing me as far away as possible.

The shirt was not in the bathroom so I opened the cheap wooden door and proceeded down the hallway—lined with a few pictures of her two kids, one from each marriage. I promised myself to never ever produce any kind of human with her, just like I promised myself to never think of my own children when I was at her house. There was also a picture of her standing in front of an F-18 Hornet: a naval fighter jet. I did look at that one. Every time I hated myself a little more for it. Her second husband had been a fighter pilot and was currently flying 787s all over the world. What a badass. And me, just picking up his scraps.

The floor squeaked like it always did as I entered the bedroom. She was still under the sheets with her head poking out, taking the pose of every woman in every scene of every affair after the man comes back from the bathroom.

She smiled.

She was attractive, don't get me wrong. I wasn't desperate the first time I had met her nor was I looking for a side hustle. She had it going in all the physical ways, for sure, just not in any other. But, I wasn't looking for the other ways. Just a beautiful and willing human being I suppose. Actually, an aggressive human being.

Though I didn't want to admit it, she had been enough of a seductress for me, in my state, no matter what bad part she was playing and no matter how bad of an actress she was. And that made me just as bad an actor and just a … coward.

"So, one more time?" she asked, playfully.

"No," I answered, not playfully.

"Are you sure?" she asked, throwing off the sheet and revealing her body, which, again, was impressive, even if there wasn't much else that was and even if it had cost her thousands of dollars in medical bills.

"No," I answered, trying to sound much more sure than I felt.

"No, you're not sure?" she asked, getting on all fours and throwing everything she had into accentuating every curve. "Or no, for one more time?" She was talented, or skilled, or whatever the word is for being exceptional at doing intimate things with relative strangers. Maybe it was comfortable; god knows she was more comfortable than I had been growing up.

"No." I reached down to grab my shirt and had it on before I walked past the picture of her kids again, ignoring them, again, but glancing at the fighter jet. "I really do need to go." That part was true. I needed to get out of there—not for an appointment, but because I couldn't take too much of her, or myself in her presence, not after she had fed what I wanted my carnal urges to have. If I were to believe Ehs, I had sex like demons do.

Fuck.

"Okay," I heard from down the hall along with some footsteps and zipping and various other sounds of clothes being put back on. "When will I see you again?"

"I don't know." *Can I just say never ever ever ever ever?*

"When does Rachel get home?" echoed down the hallway and into the small living room where I stood staring at a sign that read GIVE ME WINE OR GIVE ME DEATH.

I hated when she said my wife's name.

"Tomorrow." For some reason I answered honestly.

"Oh," she exclaimed, hopping into the living room and grabbing me from behind. "Then you should come over tonight. Jonah is still gone."

"Well," I said, politely pushing her arms off of me and turning around. "That's not going to work."

"You know." A change in her inflection grabbed me more than her arms had. "When is this going to work, Seth?" she asked. It was all very serious suddenly.

"What?"

"You heard me," she said. "When is this going to work? How much longer are we going to do this?"

"Do what?" I asked, looking toward the front door and imagining the fresh air outside.

"This," she said, waving her arms all around. "Curtains closed." She pointed at the dark curtains with thin rays of light on the side. Like my soul. "Lame sex." She pointed toward the bedroom and somehow forced me to question even more of my own manhood. "Hiding. Hating everything in my house, including my cats." She pointed toward the litter box by the dishwasher. "My country music." I looked at the cheap speaker. "Me smoking." There was a pack of cigarettes on the marble countertop. I also hate marble countertops. "Women that are desperate and think it's sexy. Betraying your wife."

The last two grabbed my attention by the balls. I had never said anything like that to her.

"Excuse me."

"You heard me. I know you hate this." She ran her arms up and down her body. "I imagine every time you walk by those pictures of her life you think of your own. We all know you're only doing this because you can't imagine any way to get out of it without pissing her off to high heaven and telling everyone in your church about this affair and ruining not only your marriage, which is already just about shit anyway, but your career—also shit—and your reputation—on the verge of shit—and your life. Still potentially amazing. If you weren't such a coward, maybe you would find out that getting out of all of this—what the hell are all these stupid signs doing in here?—might not ruin your life and might just save it."

"What is going on?"

"There's no business like business? Is that even a saying?" she asked, pointing to another wooden sign that was behind me but that I didn't bother looking at because I had asked the same question numerous times.

"What the hell is happening here?"

"C'mon, Seth, you know what's happening," she answered with strength that she had never shown before.

"Ehs?"

"No, this is still desperate and lonely Gwen," she said with as much sarcasm as could come from her very professionally shaped, chemically stuffed, lips.

I fell into the almost hidden leather couch, camouflaged by tan carpet and brown walls. The browns were practically suffocating. Or maybe it was the fact that Ehs was now in possession of the woman I was having an affair with and I didn't know how long he had been there.

"How long…"

"Seth," she said with disgust. "Believe me, I don't need that any more than you do. I already get the release of base urges without any unnecessary emotion involved. I jumped in a few minutes ago." I could smell her getting closer to me and I slumped further into the leather and kept staring at the television that was turned off. Also like me.

"How?"

"You really think, of all the humans on this planet, that this"—I imagined he was looking down at her body but didn't bother to turn around to confirm it—"has any kind of strength to it?"

I was truly a mess. The words hurt only because of how true they were. Worse, the truth they said about me.

"I'm no better," I mumbled, almost wanting Gwen back but relieved in some strange way too. Just something else to feel guilty about and pile on top of the already massive shame landfill in my inner being.

"No." It was her voice but everything else was him. She stood in front of me. Her walk, her pose, her expression, everything was different even if it was her body. I felt nauseous suddenly, strangely attracted to the suddenly empowered body and disgusted that I was attracted to it.

"You're going to end this. You're going to tell your wife. We have work to do and this—" He looked down again. "This is not helping you. Although, I mean, I can see …"

"Stop."

"I think it's you who needs to stop."

The fact that a demon was counseling me to stop an affair while possessing the woman I was having the affair with—and making her seem as confident and empowered as I had ever seen her—was overwhelming me. I almost ran for the door. I almost stood up and punched him. I almost called my wife on the burner phone in my pocket. Instead, I ran back to the pink bathroom and threw up.

"Seth," I heard, some amount of time later while still kneeling over the toilet and flushing it for the third time. "Seth." There was concern in it, care somehow.

I glanced back toward her while trying to wipe sweat away from my forehead and cheeks. "Listen—"

Gwen had mostly vanished, although if I looked hard enough I could see her body in there somewhere. Instead, there was mostly some kind of man with pale blue skin. Actually, it was just his face and throat that carried the blue tone. He wore Gwen's clothes but there was also a snake wrapped around his blue throat, slowly tightening its grip but never too much. There were three horizontal lines across his forehead as well as a third eye, directly in the center.

I blinked but he/she/it was still there standing in the cheap doorway of the pink bathroom.

What the hell is happening to me?

"Seth." The voice was still comforting but more masculine and distant, somehow. "Destruction is not arbitrary. It is essential for new life." There was some other figure amidst it all. A red dress. Dark hair and skin. A woman who seemed to be speaking along with the blue-skinned man. And Gwen, still hiding among them all somehow. "Destroy to recreate. The static must give way to the new," they said.

I puked again just as I heard her body fall to the floor.

SIX POINT FIVE

"Gwen!" Adrenaline everywhere. I managed to finish puking, wipe my face, and kneel over her body just as her eyes opened, wide and terrified. "Gwen, are you alright?"

"I'm exhausted," she sighed but still not in her own voice entirely. "And you need to leave." She stared directly at me. "Now."

"But I'm not sure—"

"Now." There was such urgency and direction in her voice that I stood to my feet and ran as fast as I could down the hallway, past all of the pictures, through the living room, past the signs and to the front door, which I threw open. A little too fast, forgetting that I wasn't supposed to do that. I had already put two dents in the wall behind it. It wasn't the first time I had left fast and there was now a third hole in the sheetrock to confirm it.

I would have inspected the wall if I had cared. I didn't. For numerous reasons … one of which was the man standing in front of me, staring at me as though he had been expecting me, waiting patiently for as long as it would take for me to get there.

I would have puked again but there was nothing left to get out. I just felt more sick as more sweat formed all over my body.

"Leo?" I asked with genuine shock.

"Hi, Pastor Seth," he answered with genuine sincerity.

"What the hell are you doing here?" I asked.

He didn't bother answering. He was probably too kind. "Well," he tried. "I mean—" He was really working up his courage. "I s'pose I could ask you the same question, pastor." He did it. As he should have.

All kinds of lies, stories, and narratives started working through my mind before I uttered a word. I had been through a lot of scenarios but most of them didn't involve Leo. However, he fit for some other characters I had planned for.

"Good question. I can imagine it looks a little weird." Always admit the obvious. "Do you know Gwen?" Ask him a question. More time to think.

His look answered that he didn't know who lived there. That was good. There was, unfortunately, something not good about his look though. I wasn't sure Leo knew he was standing in front of a house at all.

"This is Gwen's house," he answered, surprising me, and maybe even himself. At that point, I was sure that though he looked like Leo, he was not Leo.

"Do you know Gwen?" I asked.

Then he was back. I could see it, feel it, practically taste it. His eyes, his skin, his energy was buzzing again. They say you don't know what you've got until it's gone and until Leo returned, I don't think I could have said what made Leo, Leo.

"Seth?" he asked before I could say anything.

"Leo," I answered quickly. "Are you alright? What's happening?"

"What are you doing here?"

"Huh?"

"Isn't this Gwen's house? What are you doing at Gwen's house?" There was a sudden edge to his voice and his energy. He was amped up and that concerned me. Amped up Leo and I rarely interacted, especially in a fragile situation. I had not seen that version of Leo for many years.

"Yeah, yeah," I answered, calmly reaching out my hands. "You know Gwen has a son, right? Jonah?"

"Yes." His eyes were darting back and forth. His shoulders were back. His whole posture was like that of a snake ready to strike.

"Well." I looked back as though Gwen might come out at any moment and took a step back. "He's got some behavioral problems. The school called. Police came. It was a lot of stress. I'm on an emergency contact list and she called me over to help for a second. I think things are good though. I'll give her a quick goodbye and follow you out." I nodded toward the hall and smiled.

Leo smiled too. "Pastor. I've told you to be careful." His eyes were wide and the smile was not a friendly one.

"I know." I left the doorway—with Leo standing in it—and made my way down the hallway again. Gwen had made her way to her bed, where she was sleeping gently. I stared as long as I could stand it, to make sure she was definitely breathing. "Okay, well, hope things go well," I said, speaking loud enough for Leo to hear, and turning around to face the hallway again.

And then I felt it. Something else in the house.

And then I saw it. Approaching me.

It had all the sensations of an eclipse. A hard line of darkness, out there, but not staying *there*. Moving. And the hard line I saw was inside the house on walls and furniture. As it drew closer, I realized the line wasn't hard—it was softer, less focused, because it was made of something very small, almost particle-like. Millions of dark beads, moving in unison toward me, filling wall space, ceiling, pictures, sofas, and whatever else stood in its way.

I would have run but I knew there was no way to outrun it. I would have cowered but I felt strangely at peace, in that specific moment, with death. It seemed nice. I would have thought more about it, but it enveloped me too quickly, like an out-of-control wildfire, made of darkness.

By the time I lifted my hands, as though they would protect me, it had moved past me and I could see it heading over Gwen and moving on past her, up the wall and out of the house. It was all, looking back, a tad anticlimactic.

Things returned to normal as fast as they had left. Well, the new normal of possessions and affairs and … the F-18. I did glance one more time as I walked down the hallway and toward the front door, preparing for Leo, but I was pleasantly surprised he wasn't there guarding it. Which enabled me to make my way out of the house as fast as I wanted to and back into the fresh air of outside.

It had rained at some point. Poured. Gwen's country music must have muffled the sound. Puddles were still resting on the asphalt. The air had that clean feel, as though whatever storm had passed through had scrubbed away any dirt and darkness. I took a deep breath. It smelled fresh and made me feel like I could be.

I inhaled another one, consciously sending the stuff to every part of my body and trying to exhale whatever was still residing inside of it—from the past hour or so.

There was a lightness to my step as I made my way to my car. I had parked it a couple of blocks away just to be sure. Gwen lived in a neighborhood that was well off the beaten path but I never saw a reason to risk the connection if I didn't need to.

Maybe it was because I was high on fresh air, or maybe because I couldn't handle any more surprises, my consciousness completely ignored the sight of Leo's shitty car sitting there, directly in front of the house. It also ignored Leo, sitting in the passenger seat, asleep.

It was only when I had walked to the end of the block and stopped to look at the stop sign, itself clean and bright red, that my brain decided to inform me of what it had seen a few minutes earlier.

I turned around and, this time, registered my sight of the car.

I was torn: one of me wanted to walk to my car and the other toward Leo's. I decided to follow the version of me that cared for Leo and eventually made my way to his window, dodging a big puddle on the way.

"Leo." I tapped on the closed window.

He didn't move.

"Hey." I tapped again, with a little more strength. "Leo!"

He budged.

I relaxed. A bit.

"Hey."

His eyes slowly opened, his lids moving upward like a heavy garage door—the way eyes don't usually open. It seemed to take forever. *C'mon, man.*

He eventually noticed me peering into the window with, I assume, my look of concern, fear, and impatience.

"Pastor Seth?" he asked, confusion written all over his face.

I smiled.

"What …" Rather than open the door he started rolling down his window, cranking it very slowly and reminding me of the time when most people had to actually work to roll down windows. I wondered how much accumulative weight the world now carried just from electric windows.

I waited.

"Where am I?" he asked.

Now that I was back in the power position, it felt comfortable, but not good. Everything was a mess but at least Leo wasn't going to bust me for it. "Leo," I said with some seriousness, now that it was my turn to play the moral police. "You don't know where you are?"

"Well …" he muttered, rubbing the sides of his head as though that would release the memories. "I mean … well … I do remember … what time is it?" He looked at his own watch. "Oh no, I'm s'posed to be working. This ain't good."

"I'm sure it'll be alright. But how did you drive here?"

He looked me dead in the eyes with lonely water buffalo eyes. I reached out and touched his shoulder. "Pastor Seth, I don't know."

Shit. I do.

"It's okay, man." I was flooded with sympathy and guilt and relief all at the same time. I remembered why I loved the man so much and though I hated to see him struggling … I did make sure he saw me look at the needles that were lying on the recently vacuumed—but still dirty—floor mats of the passenger seat.

His eyes followed mine.

I could feel his moan before I heard it. It almost killed me. "Pastor Seth, no! No, I swear I haven't started using again. I know I didn't. I promised—"

"Leo." I touched him on the shoulder and he looked back at me. He was already crying. "It's alright. It's alright. I know."

"But."

"You're okay. Just get back to work."

"But, if I'm using aga—"

"Leo," I interrupted again. "Listen to me." I waited for eye contact, struggling to hold in my own tears. "You're alright. Just pretend this never happened and get back to work."

I figured I would speak out loud to the both of us.

SEVEN

I was midrun listening to an aggressive soundtrack—my adrenals were already pumping and the moment I heard his voice they started chugging even more.

"Let's do this." That was it. He didn't even bother saying anything else.

I immediately looked to see where it was coming from but there was no one or anything else to see. Just when I thought I had made myself hear him, I heard his voice again. "Just keep running."

Did I make that one up too? Hell, why stop at this point? I've done everything else he's told me to.

I followed his orders and stayed on my usual route that took me on a dirt trail not too far from our house. Trees lined both sides of the trail along with the smells of various cat manures. Big cats. Cat Land was a local park that specialized in rescuing and protecting tigers, lions, bobcats, and even some bears and had set up a zoo, of sorts, with a little over twenty animals. Elementary schools went on field trips to show the kids the great life they had given to the lion sitting in the ten foot by ten foot chain-link cage all day. *Because that's what the lion was dreaming of.* I ran behind the park on a regular basis, sometimes wondering what I would do if a lion managed to escape and chase me. I would, of course, cheer him on for escaping his miserable life and then run for my own.

Why is it that for every winner it seems there has to be a loser?

Shit, am I winning or losing?

I usually, inadvertently, ran a little faster behind the zoo, outrunning any hypothetical lions and trying to get to cleaner air as fast as possible.

"I said, keep running." The voice hit me again out of nowhere. I was reasonably certain I wasn't making that up.

"What do you think I'm doing?" So, I talked back to it.

"Jogging."

"Are you kidding, I never jog when the only things separating me from some ex-circus lions that betrayed their masters is a chain-link fence."

"Well, you could have fooled me."

"Thanks, coach. Where are you?" I asked, looking around, still listening to the soundtrack and appreciating the fading manure spell.

"Mu."

Damn mu. "Okay, what the fuck was that?"

"Oooh, we are in a zesty sort of mood today, huh?" he responded. "Dropping f-bombs so soon?"

"You took Gwen? And Leo? And what the hell did—" I was running harder with each name.

"I didn't *take* anyone," the voice interjected. With some passion of its own. "Gwen practically begs for it. Leo. That wasn't me."

"Lucy?" I screamed out loud to myself while still slamming the ground with my feet … or jogging, depending on your perspective.

"No, you idiot. The Seers."

"The Seers?" I repeated. "You said her," I managed between already exasperated breaths.

"I told you about them a while ago." He seemed exasperated too.

"Well, I'm sorry I don't remember." I tried to catch my breath. "I mean, really it's not like there has been much going on or anything." I managed to yell anyway. "And you told me they existed—that's about it!"

"It doesn't matter. They watch. Inspect. Keep an eye on me, on you, on us. For her. Almost a part of her. She doesn't let anyone have freedom. That's not her way. And Leo is part of The Separate, so he's … easy."

"Easy?" I gasped. "The Separate?"

"We didn't come up with The Separate. Humans did."

"And Leo is one?"

"Of course he is. Religious elite. Well, if I'm being kind. Religious anything really. Know all the answers. They've been around forever and they are very easy to manipulate. Always have been."

I stopped running. I had to. "Wait, what?"

"Maybe I've overestimated you," he said, dripping with insult. "This surprises you?"

"That Leo is susceptible to being possessed by a bunch of little … what were those? I mean—"

"You travel over land and sea and make them twice the sons of hell you are. Did you think your Jesus man was kidding?"

"Shit. Are you saying what I think you are?"

"I don't know what you think I'm saying. Despite what you

think, I can't read your mind."

"But I think that," I interjected.

"Cute," he responded. "As I've already told you. We invented this stuff." This voice was still coming from somewhere else but sounding in my head somehow. Another surreal experience, but of a different kind than I had felt up to that point. "Just keep running, if that's what you call whatever you're doing right now." There was a dab of disgust in his voice.

So I started running again, at my usual pace, whether my demon running instructor was satisfied or not. For some reason I smiled at the thought of pissing Ehs off, and then looked down at my new neon running shoes to see how they looked against the brown dirt of the trail.

To my surprise, the dirt was not brown, but gray, desaturated of all color, as though I was running through a black-and-white movie. But with each step my neon shoes, still bright green, would spread a bit of color, brown in this case, into the dirt, which would then fade as my feet left. I stared at my feet and ran through pine needles and some new grass, giddy at the puddles of color that my feet were splashing in wherever I went like I was animated in some kind of kids' cartoon on cable television.

I laughed out loud, moving my feet in all kinds of strange patterns—running even slower—and forgetting about Ehs. Until he yelled at me.

"Seth, stop!"

I stopped laughing, stopped running, and stopped staring at my feet only to see why Ehs had shouted. There was a large black wall on the trail directly in front of me that I would have slammed right into and Ehs was standing in its shadow, in the form of James.

I looked at my feet again and the normal colors that had returned.

"This form again, huh? James must be your favorite?" I asked, pointing to the almost familiar shape. "Or the most lonely?"

"Get used to it. James works well for reasons you will someday understand." Ehs said, shutting down any more conversation around the shape of James with his tone.

"Okay, what was that?" I asked, still looking at my feet, almost disappointed I couldn't create colors anymore, although they were now everywhere I looked.

"An illustration."

"Of what?" I looked toward him and the wall he was in front of. It was about fifteen feet high and fifty feet wide, stopping just short of a nearby road.

"Insipid," he answered, remaining close to the wall, in the shadow it cast.

"And this?" I asked, pointing to the wall.

"Also an illustration," he answered.

"Of?"

"Making money while we sleep." James stepped away from the wall, still careful to stay in its shadow, and reached out his hand to touch it.

"First there is light. There is always light." He looked at me, waiting for me to agree. "Correct?"

"I suppose?"

"Shadow doesn't exist without light," he said, looking back to the wall. "We don't like it but we need it. Depressing, isn't it?" He stopped. "We hate the very thing we need to exist."

"Yeah, that kind of is."

"We seek to hide it, nonetheless. Any light. All light. Cover it. Blind you. Obfuscate the light."

"Obfuscate?"

"I try to keep my language elementary for you but sometimes I forget. Do you know what the word means?"

A little insulting. "To cover?"

He faked satisfaction. "To make it obscure or unintelligible."

"Same thing," I argued, like a child.

"Not really," he countered. "Do you know the blind don't know what darkness is?"

I started to think and assumed my expression revealed that I was.

"Do you?"

"Is that some kind of metaphor?"

"No," he answered with still more disgust. "The *literal* blind don't know what darkness is."

"I haven't thought about that."

"What *have* you thought about?"

"Wow," I shot back with a little zest to it. "Looks like you're in the bad mood today?"

He just kept going. "If you have never seen light, there is nothing to call dark. The light is always there. Possession, if you want to call it that, is simply a complete hiding of the light. Once it appears to be gone, we have control. The soul becomes dark in the shadows. When blind, the lack of light is simply all there is, even if it is unrecognized darkness."

I was thinking about light and darkness and shadow and …

"What some call progress … well it has been. For us. Your country basically lives in my shadow, as do others, but America is the worst. By far. The light is well hidden."

"You can't talk like that about America."

"Of course," he smiled. "A beneficial side effect for us."

"God's country," I threw out there, with a bit of sarcasm hiding my curiosity over his response.

He snorted, disgusted again, but this time with a power behind it. "We have branded empire well. Although," he said, looking up toward the sky, "it has always worked quite nicely. We have no king but Caesar certainly did its job."

"What's that mean?"

He smiled broad and satisfied, like someone who has just taken the last bite of a good meal.

"One nation under God." He was practically licking his lips at the sweetness of the words. "It has a nice ring to it, doesn't it? But we'll get to more of that soon enough."

"You always say that."

"And I've been right. You know much more now than you did when we first met."

"Do I?" I sometimes just felt more confused.

"Of course the light seeks to shine," he continued, ignoring me. "They don't appreciate our attempts to hide it. "They do"—he paused—"fight back."

"Oh no." I looked at James.

"What?"

"We're back to the war of the angels and demons?"

He rolled his eyes. "Do you really believe that you see everything there is to see in the universe?"

I didn't answer.

"I want you to answer me. Say the words out loud!" He was almost yelling.

"No."

"Do you believe there are forces at work that affect what you do see?"

"Well …"

"Dark matter. Dark energy. I assume you've heard of it or are you more stupid than I thought?"

"Thanks." I frowned. "Yes, I have."

"And?"

"That's science."

"Of course. Science." He smirked. "So you can explain to me

dark matter? Dark energy?"

"Well, I—" I had read some articles.

"Spare me. Hidden gravity describes it better. But you have no idea what it is or if it even exists. But it falls under science in the couple of articles you've read on the internet so, of course, that kind of mystery you accept."

"Well, I mean—"

"Stop." He was visibly exasperated at my apparent ineptitude. I was visibly exasperated at always being seen as inept. "Science is a word that tells you to trust it. And, of course, it is never wrong? Religion. Science. All are words!"

"Science is fine being wrong," I threw back. "That's the difference."

He stared as though figuring out a way to try and break through my idiocy. At least that's what I felt. "Do you believe there are forces at work that you do not see that affect what you do see?"

"Yes," I finally admitted.

"Then call them whatever you like. Angels versus demons or gravitational waves and dark matter," he said, shaking his head, irritated. "Spiritual war or natural law. You don't see everything. You don't *know* everything."

"Right."

"Wrong." He pointed at me with a fierceness. "You see *nothing*. You know *nothing*!"

I had *nothing* to say.

"In this … impact of opposites … there have been larger events here and there over the eras. The last major … disturbance occurred a little before the Reformation."

"Did it start the Reformation?"

Exasperation appeared on his face again. "Everything that happens in your unseen is related to what happens in your seen. They are the same."

"Are you saying some kind of new Reformation is happening?"

At this James flickered. It was almost as though the signal went haywire for a second. He formed some other shape and then, as though it were a strain, regained control of his human shape. I took a step back toward the tigers and their cages behind me. They felt safer suddenly.

"What do you know of the Reformation?"

"It was the start of Protestantism. The—"

"Yes," he interrupted. "The first to tell you that you could know the truth. That you could even interpret it for yourself."

I frowned.

"I assume you hope there is another Reformation?"

"Well." I paused. "I mean, I think the Reformation was a step?" He had me cautious suddenly in anything I believed.

"For us, yes. Luther." Ehs spit onto the ground something dark and vile. "He ended up serving up so much for us." He seemed to stare into space for a moment, still in the shadow. "Does the irony ever strike you as almost too much?"

"He helped you?" My theology professors would have had ministrokes.

"Sola scriptura!" He laughed. "Oh yes!" he shouted. "Oh thank you, kind Luther, for being our mouthpiece."

I simply stared. Shock and awe.

"The age was a high point for us. How could we keep the ignorant masses in their primitive consciousness? Make the holy book literal and tell them it's all they need. Throw in some … inerrancy." He mocked the word. "Worked like a charm." He looked proud in a way that I had not seen yet. "I've grown the seeds of lies into forests of false realities. It's my job in advertising."

"This is fucking insane," was all I could mutter. What else was there to say? "I—"

"There are six other departments," he interrupted. "War. Security. Labor. Education. The Seers. And our own, of course. But … that is not important right now." He waved my thoughts away with his hands. "It's not just me, trust that. Or even my department. We blind. They reveal. We build walls. They find cracks in them. Light finds a way. And so do we. But it is growing powerful again," he spoke slowly. "Confrontation is on the horizon."

I noticed he was smiling, again. "Why are you smiling?"

He looked me in the eyes. "You have seen enough. But I will tell you this." His eyes flashed red for a second as they had the first time I met him. "There is something else you must know."

"Alright."

"I need you to help me find her."

"I think I knew that."

"It will not be easy."

"Okay."

"It may require deception."

"Okay." I said that much slower this time.

"She might save us. I need her, Seth. You need her. We need to find something else that exists inside of us." He took on a somber expression. "But no one can know that here." He looked around in case I wasn't sure where "here" was. I still wasn't sure I did know. "I want to see color again. To feel life and escape the gray and boring life of the shadows."

"Are they listening now?"

"No. I have my moments of escape. But still." He nodded toward something behind me and I didn't bother looking. I felt whatever was there and didn't necessarily want to see it.

"And."

"You will meet others of us. You will be brought to the inside. You will learn things that you will not believe. You will feel sickness, despair, and darkness like has never existed in your life before."

"I'm out then." I took another step toward the lions.

"No, you're not."

"No, I am." And another one.

"No." He reached out his hand, still not moving too far away from the wall. "You are strong. You are good. You are humble enough to learn. I need you. The light needs you as much as I do."

I realized as he was speaking that my soundtrack suddenly began to play in my headphones again. There were rhythmic violins and pulsating drums, building to a crescendo of triumph and glory, and my adrenaline was building.

Did he time this somehow?

"They need you," he continued. "You need them."

"Okay."

"You need me."

"Okay," I repeated, not really meaning it but wanting him to move on.

"She is a powerful orchestrator of life and light. She is powerful for good. Or—" He paused. "Evil. Depending on your perspective."

"So Insipid is failing?"

He flickered again, almost as though a wave of wild rage swept through him before he could tame it again. "There are cracks. There will always be cracks. It must fail within you, before it fails for anyone else," he whispered, almost afraid of his own voice suddenly.

I waited.

"I should not be here. You must trust me even when it appears you should not. Only you and I will know"—he paused—"the truth."

"Shit, man," I muttered, because when things are so outlandish, crazy, and absurd, yet appealing, intriguing, and coaxing, there is not much else to say. "You're talking about truth? And helping you? What about Gwen? You realize I've got my own shit."

"Everything that happens in the unseen affects the seen." Ehs nodded his head. "It will all come in time. I will help you. You will help me. We will help the world."

I nodded. Helping the world seemed simple in that moment, even if it was from a demon.

"Now run."

I looked behind me but there was nothing.

Ehs continued, "And I will see you again soon." With that the wall vanished, as did Ehs, and more of my, up to that point, pretty solid perception of reality.

Not knowing what else to do, I continued my run. I did notice the color, the warmth, and the smiles of fellow runners more than I had in a long time. I also wondered if, despite the color and warmth I saw and felt, there was a dark and cold shadow over us all.

EIGHT

Given the state of my mental, emotional, and physical well-being, I needed a good hot yoga session the next morning.

Rachel had found yoga and had dove headfirst into the deep end. She brought me along much later. Or, better, I decided to stop being so arrogant and give it a try. She had already been to a yoga retreat in Costa Rica and France (paid for by the studio—although I never did understand why) and had finished some teacher trainings, all in the space of about five years.

I had gone to yoga about two hundred times in the space of those five years, which may sound like a lot until you realize that my wife had been at least five times that.

They say you're a beginner for the first ten years. I think that's true for people like me. Not my wife.

And not Jaden. He was the instructor that day.

I have to be honest. African-American men can be intimidating to me. I know that probably sounds racist and it probably is racist. I suppose I am a racist. I spent my teen years listening to nineties hip-hop, R & B, and rap—when my legalistic parents were not finding my cassettes and CDs and burning them—and that meant I had a certain impression of African-American men.

They're very talented and experienced at sex and, rumor has it, well endowed. These are stereotypes and they are racist and maybe they aren't true, but sometimes, when things get stuck in your head, they do get stuck there.

I'm apologizing up front for my racism. Please forgive me. I'm working on it.

That said, I had never been much intimidated by good old Leo, so maybe it was more of a yoga instructor/rap star thing than an African-American thing. Still …

Jaden was born in the Caribbean, grew up in Southern California, and had been practicing yoga since he was a child. So, not only was he African American, he was incredibly fit and handsome and he was damn good at yoga.

Two checks against him, as far as my own ego was concerned, with more on the way.

Given the fact that I was having my own affair, I was hypersensitive to affairs in general. I always thought Rachel and Jaden were very friendly and being the Sherlock I was, it had not taken me long to learn that Jaden had gone on both two-week trips with Rachel. And yes, about twenty-five other people. But still. I noticed the way her whole energy changed when we walked into the room with Jaden and I noticed the way he looked at her and tried to make it seem normal, only because I had done the very same thing.

Three checks against him.

With bare chest, shaved head, and warm smile, Jaden began gently directing us into our Vinyasa. Despite how desperately I needed to sweat—every kind of toxic thing out of my body—I was already out of sync by the time we started our first flow.

He might have been one of the nicest people I had ever met in my life, which only made me not like him more. He came to hear my sermons and always had thoughtful, encouraging things to say. Check four.

Yes, I was a mess. I was a mess even more that day. I couldn't concentrate, I couldn't perform, and I kept imagining Jaden's skills in the bedroom. If Gwen ever met Jaden, she would realize the sham that I was and, most likely, leave me before I could leave her.

So, really, Jaden was just all my fears embodied—trying to teach me how to let go of my fears. Ehs would be possessing me soon if he wasn't already. I was feeling very empty and worthless.

Ehs.

Something turned. Suddenly. Whatever dial controlled my entire outlook on life went from depressed to optimistic almost instantly.

Maybe I could use Ehs. Maybe he could help me. Maybe there was something to what he was offering. How could, honestly, my life get worse?

If things can't get worse … then there's nothing to lose?

But that's always the real question, right? Are they as bad as they can get?

"Chaturanga …" Jaden spoke gently, and I registered it for a moment before entering back into my world, where I was, for the first time that day, relaxing, sweating, leaving anxiety and, dare I say, some shame, behind.

"Bye, Jaden," Rachel said, with a big smile.

"Bye, Rachel," he answered, barely looking up while talking to someone else. "Bye, Seth," he added and then did look up with a big smile. I noticed everything.

"Thanks, Jaden," I answered. "Good one." I waved, almost dropping my towel and mat onto the floor but managing to grab them.

The summer air felt nice on my sweat, instantly cooling me off just enough, without making me feel cold. "Good class," I said to Rachel as we walked toward the car.

"Thanks for coming," she answered. "I always like when you do."

"Me too." We reached the doors and opened them. "By the end, I mean. Jaden is great but, I'll be honest, he's a little intimidating."

"I know." Rachel shrugged. "But he loves you."

"Well—"

"And he couldn't stop raving about the past two sermons you gave. Loved them."

"Well, that's nice."

"If there is a devil, I don't think he would have wanted you to give those past two."

"Well." I started the car. *The devil's head of advertising probably enjoyed them too.*

"It's probably why things have been so weird lately. Maybe we're being attacked."

"I mean ..."

"It's real, Seth," she said with sincerity.

Things *had* felt weird the previous couple of months. No doubt. Sometimes, when you grew up with the language and programming that my wife and I did, you say things like *things are hard because the devil is battling you* instead of *things are hard because you're having an affair, you're preaching sermons you don't believe, and you're being visited by a demon on a pretty regular basis that wants you to help him find some kind of creature he's in love with who is helping the good guys fight off the blindness that America (and yourself) is sick with and you can't say anything about it to anyone. Well, if any of it is real.*

So it fell into the category of *things we don't really believe but we still say*, which, when said, makes one wonder if one actually does believe it but doesn't want to admit. Or at least we hope for it because the alternatives aren't great. Much like, *We live in the greatest country in the world.*

"I'll have to ask Ehs."

"What'd you say?" Rachel asked.

It *was* worth asking Ehs.

Unfortunately, I hadn't mentioned Ehs to Rachel since our first conversation. She had assumed we weren't really seeing each other, probably like she assumed I wasn't seeing Gwen.

"So, he's still around?" she asked very matter-of-factly, not letting me get a gauge on what she was thinking before I answered.

"Well …" I stammered in the way that every guilty person does. "No … I mean if he ever came back."

I pulled out of the studio's lot and headed toward a traffic light not too far in front of us.

She turned on the air conditioner.

"Do we really need to turn on the air?" I asked.

"It's hot."

"Well—" I glanced at the thermometer on our car. "It's only 65 outside. Roll down the window."

"Seth," she shot back. "I want the air on."

"Fine."

"When?"

"When what?" I maintained my view out the front window even though I knew she was looking my direction.

"When did you start seeing him?" The irony was not lost. We were having *the* conversation I had always dreaded, but about a different character. My recent confidence was wavering fast. "A few months ago. I don't know." Ehs had recommended I didn't tell her every detail and in that moment, I realized, I had listened to him. And probably should have continued listening.

"You didn't tell me?"

I looked down at my speedometer.

"Seth?" There was worry in her voice.

"I'm sorry." The words weren't sincere.

"Well, I mean … is this good?"

"I think it can be."

"Have you talked to anyone about this?"

"No."

There was a long pause. "Seth, *we* can't keep going like this. *You* can't keep going like this. I can't either. What am I supposed to do? How am I supposed to have any kind of relationship with you or talk about—"

"Rachel," I interrupted. "I don't know what I'm supposed to say. Or not say, either."

Especially because the car in front of us happened to be Leo and I happened to catch Leo's face in the rearview mirror and he happened to be holding his finger to his mouth, shushing me.

All coincidence, of course.
Serendipity.
"Is that Leo?" Rachel asked.
"Oh." I acted surprised. "I think it is."
I waved and thought of some way to change the subject.
Again.

NINE

By the next time I saw him, he managed to insult me and speak truth at the same time, which, as it turns out, is not all that rare.

"There is *still* so much you don't understand," he said. When someone's words come laced with so much arrogance I generally want to punch them in the face.

"Oh, really?" I responded with a cynical smile. "I was pretty sure I was just about there with everything in the world, especially recently." Unfortunately, I'm not a fighter, so I just let my words pretend to do battle.

We were sitting on a hill staring down at an LA traffic jam. Moments earlier, I had been meditating in my office. The fact that I had been meditating and a demon showed up threw me off my game and will surely encourage anyone who believes that meditation is demonic to stick with their belief. Of course, Jesus meditated in a desert and a demon showed up there too. Actually, Lucy herself did, according to the story, so I wasn't going to lose any sleep.

"I want to talk to you about traffic," he continued, unfazed by my sarcasm.

"Where are we?"

"I told you. City of Angels." He smirked. We were both sitting on a bench overlooking what looked like millions of red and white lights, all pulsing slowly, like clogged arteries before a triple bypass.

"Does that make you feel uncomfortable?" I smiled. "Angels?"

"Oh, very," he laughed.

"Okay, so traffic." He was running the show again, with purpose.

"Yeah, traffic."

"Do you see it?"

"Are you serious?" I looked to him, still somewhat trying to gain my bearings. "It's all I see. Also, wasn't I just meditating a minute ago?"

"You still are," he answered.

"So that means my body is—"

"We've established that already. No wheres and whats and ifs

…"

"Do you have traffic?" I asked.

"No."

"Alright." An easy answer, for once.

"Do *you* have traffic?" he asked.

"Yeah." I looked back toward the city and stared long enough to indicate that I was not blind and looking at … traffic. "It would seem so."

"I mean in your city, you idiot," he responded with not near as much hesitation.

"Ah, not really." I returned to staring at the miles of car lights. They were pretty from far away, just like the line of air traffic in the sky headed toward LAX, all of it flickering like a jewel under a bright sun. "Not technically."

"Go on." He leaned forward.

Since he was asking … "Not like this." I pointed toward the lines of cars. "Or New York. But, the fastest you can move in a north-south direction—with no traffic—is thirty miles an hour."

"Thirty?" He acted surprised.

"You knew that."

"Yeah."

"So, anyway, no, we don't have traffic. We have the constant limitation of motion instead. Although people love to talk about how we have no traffic—like it's some great perk of our city."

Ehs leaned back. "You've thought quite a bit about this?"

"Yeah." I leaned back against the park bench behind me that seemed out of place, as though Ehs had brought it for us to sit on. "I tend to think about stupid things that get under my skin from time to time." I had also once had a big argument with Gwen about it. She loved to talk about our lack of traffic. One more thing I hated.

"It's hardly stupid."

"Do tell." I spoke with true, exaggerated grace, figuring I would relax for the upcoming speech by leaning against the bench.

"There's something there." He paused, thinking. Or pretending to think. Which made me wonder if he had tried talking to anyone else about any of the things he was trying to talk to me about. And how far he had gotten. "Insipid works with some of the same principles," he dropped.

"I'm listening." I kept leaning back in the bench, somehow enjoying myself.

"I don't know if it follows exactly but …" Ehs seemed to be enjoying himself too. "People get really upset when they are permitted to drive seventy but are unable because of congestion. They don't mind as much if you limit them to thirty all the time, with freedom."

"And …" I was intrigued.

"Limits. Prisons. Chains. Where do you put them so people don't mind them? Better, cheer them."

I *was* listening.

"If you convince someone that a cage is freedom, they don't notice the walls. In fact, they call the walls great, beautiful." He paused and leaned forward again. "Even blessed."

"Okay."

"Especially if the outside of the cage is dangerous. The cage protects them." He leaned back.

I mimicked him. "Okay."

"So, we set off to do it. A cage that would become so normal, so accepted, so a part of life, that no one would notice what it was doing to them. They would only praise it and continue to build it. That was our goal."

"And you did it?"

He shrugged. "We certainly haven't failed. It's been a collective effort over the years. You can meet some of those who helped in the effort."

"Do I want to meet any of them? Are they nice?"

"They're Shadows," he answered plainly.

I didn't like it. "Like you?"

"Not really."

"Hey." The word was slurred and out of the blue, somewhere behind us. "Someone have a drink?" Moments later a man stumbled into my view, and I do mean stumbled. I backed up further into the bench as he reached out with his hands for balance in case he tipped over. He was wearing a black overcoat, which quickly engulfed his body as he fell to the ground.

I looked at Ehs, who was suddenly very different. The body of James was stiff and maybe even bigger. It was authoritarian in energy, ready to fight. There was something palpable in our sphere that had not been there moments earlier.

"What do you want?" Ehs stood to his feet.

I stood too. The man was face-first in the dirt and Ehs looked like he was about to kill him. I held out my hand, like some kind of fence between them, as though that fence would do anything. "I'm sure he—"

Before I could finish, Ehs shoved me in the chest and I landed awkwardly on the park bench again. "Quiet," he whispered to me and moved to stand over the poor drunk still on the ground. I did as he commanded.

The apparent drunk began to make noises. I would have said *speak* but the utterances were completely foreign and not in the way of a foreign language. That, at least, is recognizable as a language. His sounds were not. It was a foreign, foreign *thing*. However, moments later, Ehs began to converse with the same noises and I realized I was utterly out of my element and wanted to go home, back to my quiet meditation. The "language" was unsettling and cold, somehow as though the noises invaded me after being unleashed into the air. I shrank harder into the park bench as they continued to speak and I continued to be attacked. By vocal utterances. It was a list of words reminiscent of the one word Ehs had spoken in the coffee shop so long ago.

I turned around and tapped at the bench just to make sure it would hold my shape. I became conscious of my own body. The shorts were there, the bare feet, the T-shirt. *Where am I? Don't ask where.*

There was a sound. The drunk was moving, lifting his body off of the ground, his long coat slowly rising up too. He was on his hands and legs. I could see long greasy hair hanging, protecting his face, still hidden from me.

Until he looked at me.

Perhaps Ehs possessed people differently to make me feel better. This man was more of what I would have imagined. His eyes glowed red, and his mouth snarled into something twisted and unhuman. The poor drunk man's face was there but the distinguishing features of a nose and mouth and eyes were the only human thing about it and even those were partly enveloped by something else.

I was suddenly bombarded with something dark. I could only equate it to the feelings that come in the middle of the night when the darkness surrounds you and you start to have those thoughts that keep you from returning to sleep, those thoughts that are always there but normally remain in the back of our heads where we prefer they live.

A shape moves in the hallway and we imagine what it would be like if an intruder was in the house and harming our children. We think of the death of loved ones, we think of torture, we think of cancer, and we wonder what it will be like when we die, for our kids, our friends, our partner, and the rest of our family. We get a pit in our stomach and we look to the light of the clock by our bed or the blinking LED on our television because it somehow comforts us.

Those are the dark thoughts of the dark nights and they rarely come with such passion and energy in the light of day. They aren't brave enough then. But at night, they find their courage.

I was being harassed by them from looking at whatever I was looking at.

I felt sick, desperate for an LED or television.

The man launched at me. Fast and dangerous. Terrifying. He lunged with the precision and speed of a snake intent on its victim. His teeth were everywhere and his hands were catlike. I screamed—yeah, not too proud of that—and held up my hand as though to stop him.

Which, surprisingly, it did.

In fact, a beam of light emanated from my hand and pierced deep into the man, sending him shrieking and twirling and back to the ground, trying to get away from the light in the same way, moments earlier, I had been trying to get away from him.

The man continued to shriek and cower and yell, and I felt like a kid wizard.

Power.

Ehs turned on me and snuffed out the light with some kind of darkness that flew from his hands like the web of a superhero. I didn't feel as powerful as I had although I still felt pretty good. Ehs and the man tore into each other as though two dark hurricanes were wrestling on the surface of the Earth and I was watching from the space station. As quickly as it had all begun I was sitting in the park bench with Ehs at the bench with me, as normal James.

I was sweating and my heart was pounding along with the rest of my body, which was shaking almost uncontrollably.

"What … was … that?" I did manage to speak.

"One of us." He looked behind him as though there might be more.

"And, that." I held up my hand as I had done minutes before.

"I've already told you. You're more powerful than you think."

The wizard in me was back. I smiled. "Yeah, but you snuffed it out."

"You don't think you're very powerful. Being more than you think doesn't say much." It was his turn to smile.

"Then what am I?" I asked.

"Human. Try not to do that again. You are here to help us, not hurt us." He stood up and walked closer to the edge of the hill we were standing on. "He was acting stupid. But, still, be careful."

"Alright," I lied. If a thing was coming at me like that again I was definitely going to do the same thing. It made me feel much better about the whole situation that I, at least, could.

"Where were we?" He looked back at me and then back toward the traffic. "Oh right, my partners."

"Seriously?" I interrupted.

"What?"

"We're just going to pick it back up. That was terrifying."

He looked back at me, a little surprised. "I'm sorry."

"Was that a Shadow?"

"Yes. Like I already told you," he answered, staring at the traffic that was still moving as slowly as I wished my own heart rate was. "He's young. Likes to terrorize humans. He'll learn. We all do." His hands were in his pockets. The night sky with its bright stars and airplanes traveling to and from places all over the world seemed therapeutic for us both, somehow. "Do you mind if we get on with the story?"

I'll stop shaking someday.

"Sure." I stood up and walked closer to him, also taking in the view and feeling as though it was better to be close to him, should something like that happen again.

"I told you about Africa. Possessing the woman?"

"Yeah, as the … big lady."

"Right. Her name was Elle." He paused. "No one likes to be possessed," he continued, staring at the view in front of him. Relaxed again.

"I would assume." I was feeling more relaxed—if he was.

"It's too clear. It's not being able go as fast as you are allowed. It's blatant."

"Right. But don't some people like it? Voodoo and stuff?"

"Voodoo hasn't taken over the world." He stared up at a plane flying over us.

"Oh," I managed.

"We prefer to live more subtly … in the shadows. We prefer our names not to be mentioned. We prefer not to be blamed for mental illnesses or enemies. Do you know they called the Native Americans religious conjurers who converse with demons?"

"Who did?"

"The Christians, of course."

"Why wouldn't you like that?"

"Don't get me wrong. We loved the irony. But labeling every misery or opposition as demonic can give us a bad reputation—even when it's completely unjustified—as it was with the Native Americans of course. It's much harder to work with a bad reputation." He answered as though talking about a new shoe company's brand.

"So, you don't like it because it gives you a bad rep—"

"Possession is not cost-efficient at all." He used his arms to emphasize the point. And then he stared at me, to get us back on track.

"Okay. Right. Service industry."

"Good," he nodded.

"So . . ."

"This conflict is all about one thing, Seth. One thing."

I leaned toward him. "Fear?"

"Fear is the weapon. Control is the goal. And we gain control by creating alternate realties that do our blinding."

"You haven't talked about god at all."

"Worthless word." He shrugged. "Meaningless."

I had to think about that one, while thinking of another word. "Love?"

He nodded. "Sure."

"Sure?"

He shrugged. "Better."

"Better?"

"I prefer mystery."

"I think I prefer love," I countered.

"How do you define it?" he asked.

"Love?"

"Yes."

"Freedom."

He looked up toward the dark sky, speckled with stars. "Right." He looked back at me. "Freedom?"

"Real freedom," I answered. "Not cheap imitation freedom—which—"

"Power," he interjected. "That is power and control called freedom."

"Well . . ." I wasn't sure I agreed.

"It's all over your country. Land of the free! Ha!" And then he actually laughed, and it chilled me. "Land of the powerful. And look at them cry like children when their toys—their power—is taken away. Land of the imprisoned."

"Well, there are some freedoms," I argued back. "Our history will tell you that. We gave freedom to whole races—thank god."

"You gave them power."

"What?"

"Slavery was never about freedom, you idiot! It's about power."

"Well, I don't think the African American race would agree with you."

"Do you think I'm intimidated by races of people?" He spoke plainly. "They were the victims of a white race that wanted power and control. You cannot all have power and control without some being enslaved."

"Listen …" I didn't want an argument about slavery and American history when I was trying to answer a question about love. And he was giving me things to think about that I wasn't ready to respond to … yet.

He filled my gap in responding. "It's better to know you are a slave than to be a slave and think you are free, because you have some power that you call freedom."

"What are you saying?" I felt offended again somehow on behalf of myself and others and already worried enough about my racist tendencies. I didn't need more of them from a demon.

"Do you disagree?"

"I don't know."

"Seth. No one complains about their freedoms being taken by someone else, because that kind of freedom cannot be taken … It was the slaves, ironically, who said that most clearly. It's the powerful, ironically, who will tell you differently—because they've never felt true freedom. Only the artificial motivates them. And that is power that they need—by keeping you enslaved."

"You're agreeing with me?" I asked, now confused.

"Yes."

"So you agree enslaving entire groups of people is bad."

"I agree that freeing those entire groups of people is not about giving them freedom, but giving them some of the power they deserved." He spoke the words slowly as though I couldn't understand if he didn't.

"Funny way of agreeing. Okay fine—so we're talking about living free? Unencumbered. Unchained. Not just being alive but truly living. Enlightened. On a different plane of life."

Ehs started to clap. "Exactly."

"Too much," I responded. "The clapping."

"I'm not sure you understand love at all. But, no matter." He stopped and smiled. "We had and have had three main tools at our disposal to control humans. We've had them for years. Shame. Hate. Fear. Everything can be traced to them. Arguably they all involve each other. They are beautiful tools for us."

I made a note to remember that.

"They contradict love, belonging, and a trust that it will continue. So, as I talked to other Shadows and looked at the world, we wondered, if we could focus more on creating a space, a mindset, a culture, a land, that we controlled where no one knew they were being controlled. Shame. Hate. Fear. Of course, they would be lonely as well, though they wouldn't know it. Our weapons would be masked. They would never be blatant. They would never be obvious." He stopped pacing and looked at me. "Because once someone is possessed, everyone starts calling for a priest."

"Right." I nodded, while still processing.

"But if the priest is also possessed … well … you can imagine." He sneered.

I didn't like the sneer. "I can?"

"They always follow the priest. And if the priest is leading them to the cage … I've told you we invented religion for a reason, Seth."

"I think I'm following." I didn't think I wanted to be. "When you say priest …"

"All of it."

"Not sure …"

"It will all become clear."

"It will?"

"Yeah."

"Are you saying we're all possessed?"

He laughed. I laughed too but only to try and not feel more stupid than I already did. "Haven't you learned anything?"

"Have I?" I wasn't sure I had.

"No."

I wasn't sure if he was agreeing that I hadn't learned anything or if he was saying we are not possessed, but the more I thought about it, I thought he was answering them both with the same word. He didn't wait for me to figure it out but kept talking. "Constantine?" Ehs moved back to the park bench and sat down.

I followed him.

We sat silent for a moment until he looked at me with a hard look. "You've heard of him?"

"Oh." I hadn't realized the question was sincere that time. "Of course. Ruined everything according to many," I answered, proving my knowledge.

Ehs smiled the kind of smile that masks deep jealousy. "More experimenting." He paused to breathe deeply. "For the most part. We learned much from it but if we're honest, there wasn't much new about him either."

"Is that as specific as you're going to get?"

"In the year 200 … love was doing well. The evolution of sapiens was beginning to uncover reality."

"Evolution?"

Ehs looked at me like a scientist looks at a fundamentalist. I recognized it well. I had seen it many times in my early days.

"You know," I interrupted the story. "I once heard a pastor say you can't be a Christian and believe in evolution." It had bothered me for years so why not try to work it out with some demon therapy.

"I might as well have written that. Well, I mean, I did." He nodded with the more common smile of pride. "Although that was some time ago. We've had to evolve as well."

I just shook my head. "Well, I left that church, just so you know."

"Of course you did. But think how many are still there."

"I'd rather not."

He picked the story right back up. "The year 200. The Shadow world was nervous at the evolution of sapiens, but not at all without ideas and plans. Most of the plans were simply for more Shadows though … more manpower, more interaction." Ehs looked out at the view again. Still traffic. But the lights were still beautiful.

"Tavasy. He was young, but smart. Lemi—who you'll meet later—stands on his shoulders. More manpower and more interaction seemed like a bad plan." He stopped and looked at me. "Have you read *1984* or *Brave New World*?"

"No."

"Ah, you should. Both of them. Orwell said that humans would be destroyed by what they hate. The government—the security state. And Huxley said humans would be destroyed by what they love. They would be so consumed with pleasure, they would consume themselves," he continued.

"You read books?" I asked, somewhat astounded that I was getting book reviews from Ehs now.

"We know what's in them. I'm summarizing the books as well as year 200 … trying to bring vast, complex ideas down to something you can understand." Then there was the smile of arrogance.

"I appreciate that," I threw back with sarcasm.

"There was a growing section of humanity that was finding mystery and it was affecting their behaviors."

I waited.

"Still what they were though. Still confused. They still craved power, they were still fearful beings who could be coerced into shame, and worry, and hate at a moment's notice. Violence. Power. Control. All of it. Still addicted to sacrifice. Still susceptible to loneliness and then false power to fill the loneliness. We just needed to give them power without them knowing we had given it to them. At the end of the day, they are fairly stupid creatures." Ehs, I think, had forgotten I was there and was one.

"I'm here."

"Sorry."

"And weren't you a human too at one point?"

He nodded. "It's easy to forget." He seemed somber about it.

"Regardless, we needed that kind of world where the systems took over. Where … we'll get there. My kind had to start experimenting and see if our theories would work at least on a base level."

"Constantine," I reminded him.

He ignored me. "What amazed us," he continued, "was how well it worked even with the blatancy with which we did it. We put crosses on shields of war? Incredulous!" He screamed with a delight that frightened me, almost as much as him using the word *incredulous*.

"We gave them a sliver of power, through violence, and took everything they had, through empire. And they gladly fought for their owner." He was grinning.

"And Huxley versus Orwell?" I asked.

"Yes?" he asked back.

"Who was right?"

"Right?"

"Yeah, what are we supposed to be more afraid of?"

He smiled. "Both, of course. They were latching onto something that had already been functioning quite well, as the enlightened usually do."

"So you prefer—"

"Neither," he interrupted again. "We prefer anything that hampers freedom and sight. Any way we can get it but preferably the more subtle and attractive and hidden ways."

Silence settled over the bench for as long as silence needs to become awkward. That is rarely very long.

"I want you to meet someone." Ehs stood up abruptly, looking out over the view.

I was hesitant, after the last meeting.

"But," he continued. "We're done for now."

"We are?"

Before I had an answer, I found myself somewhere else, and not where I had expected to find myself.

TEN

Surreal: that strange feeling of standing inside of a building that replicates ancient Rome, Paris, or Venice and knowing it's not anything like ancient Rome, Paris, or Venice and yet … it's real and almost possible to believe it is. Or maybe we just want it to be those places so we fill in the obvious gaps. The feeling I usually get all over Las Vegas when I have to go there.

If Gwen were a city, she would be Vegas. That's probably why I don't like the place so much.

It is too real or maybe not real enough or maybe so close to real that it comes off bizarre? Like most of the casinos in Vegas and like most parts of Gwen. Maybe it's just too good.

Wherever I found myself, it had me thinking Vegas and Gwen, which made me nervous right off the bat.

But …

It was one of the most beautiful things I had ever seen.

In a surreal way.

Trying to describe where or what I was inside of feels like trying to describe the Eiffel Tower inside of a casino to a person from the 1500s. Being there felt like being transported from the 1500s to a modern casino. I'm not sure I could even fathom what it all was—beyond surreal.

The top ten nature scenes of our planet were there, all at once. In one direction was the sun setting over a beach, in another a field scattered with yellow flowers and snow-capped mountains in the distance. In another direction was an aquamarine lake reflecting a bowl of hilltops like a mirror and in another was fall foliage spreading out with oranges and yellows as far as I could see, chasing each other over rolling hills. There were more.

The input was overwhelming: too much. It was *too* beautiful. Focusing on each scene was majestic but turning my head or simply moving my eyes was distracting and almost frustrating. I couldn't take it all in though I desperately wanted to. It began to play with my senses and the brain inside my skull trying to analyze and interpret those senses.

It was also empty. Every scene was devoid of people or living things, or even sounds. It was just me in the astounding natural landscapes. I found myself asking lots of strange questions about real and perfection and good.

Out of the blue, I missed Rachel. The thought snuck up on me and practically jumped into my consciousness, as though playing a joke on me. As I analyzed it, I wondered what had made it show up, although it was better than Gwen and Vegas. I wished she was there. I wanted her to hold my hand and experience it all with me.

I turned, hoping she would appear, and saw Ehs, in the familiar form of James, instead. He was studying me as though I was a lab rat. His expression was ambivalent, empty, almost confused. He said nothing. I suppose he didn't need to.

I said nothing too. I suppose I didn't need to.

I looked back to the waves lapping up on white sand. I noticed a palm tree and a gorgeous sky above me. But like the skies inside of Vegas casinos, there was so much that was off. It was not off in a way that suggested the sky was obviously painted—everything about it *seemed* real—but it, obviously, wasn't.

Or was it?

Shit.

"Hello." I heard the voice and immediately turned toward it.

"Hello," I responded, involuntarily.

The voice belonged to a woman. Real flesh and skin in full color and wearing a slim black dress. She was utterly stunning. Beautiful is a pretty subjective term, except when it's not. She was objectively beautiful, in every way. It was as though she was beauty walking around in physical form.

She approached and smiled. It was a mesmerizing smile. Perfection. Everywhere. Her lips, her hair, her face, her lines, her walk, her energy, her expression, her confidence, her wisdom, her smell, her voice ... it was all surreal ... perfection, not just physically but energetically.

Can true beauty and perfection exist at the same time? Without some paper rattling on sidewalks and grime growing on concrete and hot smells billowing out of subway vents, can it be beautiful? Someone once described the country of Monaco as "having no soul" to me, which seemed to imply that souls need dirt on the sidewalks.

Good has never been perfect, which can be a real bummer to people who spend their lives trying to find it, and who believe the world started off that way.

As I looked at her, I felt that emotion again. Something was off like a small splinter buried deep in my senses. I wanted to absorb it all, bask in it, fall into it, but something was irritating about the whole thing.

She walked closer and looked at me, subtly and soft, yet there was some kind of power behind her. More power than I'd felt in any woman I had ever been so close to. Maybe it was her perfection.

I wanted more. Surreal or not, I felt inundated with desire for more.

Ehs was suddenly nowhere to be seen. "Is this weird for you?" she asked very properly, with an accent that I didn't recognize.

I had no idea what *this* she meant but at that point every *this* I could think of was pretty weird. "Which part?"

"Me?" She was almost bashful about it. Almost.

"I don't know," I answered truthfully.

"Hmm," she answered.

"This is *all* weird, to be blunt." I found myself with freedom—almost encouragement to speak my mind. So I did. "Is it weird that you're as beautiful as you are? Yes. But …" I looked toward the waves again. "I don't know—I think so. What's up with this beach? I think I'm meditating … and I also don't know where Ehs is." I kept speaking. Maybe she was drawing it out. "It's *all* a little weird. But you …" I paused. "You, specifically? I mean, wow, you're beautiful."

She smiled.

"But, something is off. What are you?" I asked pretty arrogantly.

"I'm sorry," she responded and took a step backward as though uncomfortable. "I didn't mean to do that to you."

"You didn't?" I asked, not exactly happy with her moving away.

"Of course not."

She was soothing. "Who are you?" I asked.

"That doesn't matter."

"It doesn't?" I took a step closer. The perfection was growing on me with every second. Maybe it was good after all.

"No."

"I feel like it does …" I mumbled, halfway wondering where the words and power to speak them came from.

"It doesn't." She turned to walk away, almost dejected, but not.

"You're leaving?" I asked.

She stopped and turned her head toward me. "Did you not want me to?"

She had me there. "Well, I mean, can you tell me who you are?"

She paused, as though thinking but obviously not. "Whoever

you want me to be." The words spilled from her lips and into my ears, sending a perfect energy throughout my body.

I hesitated. "To do what?" I managed to ask.

"I'm here for whatever you want." She didn't mean it in the way an attractive woman can. Well, I suppose that was included but it was deeper than that. More mature. I felt like she actually meant *whatever* I wanted. A million dollars. The health of a friend. A new job. A best-selling piece of art. All the skills of someone who has been flying a plane for twenty-five years.

Eternal bliss?

She stared and her eyes were asking me what it was that I wanted.

"Yes?" I asked, for some reason.

What do I want?

She was patient, as any good genie in a bottle who meant what they said would be.

An argument began to play out in my head.

If it feels good, do it, right?

Do what?

Whatever we want.

If? Don't be an idiot. It always feels good. If it didn't you wouldn't do it.

Are you kidding? Who is the idiot now? Not eating another piece of cake never feels good.

Fair enough. But when you stand on the scale a week later, it feels good.

Makes sense. So, let's do this. It'll feel good in the moment or eventually. Why are we still thinking about it?

Why does it feel good? Will it feel better tomorrow? Or worse? When do you want it to feel good? You haven't answered those yet, you moron.

I decided to chime in. *Fuck you both.*

I was playing too many head games with myself, again, and the woman was …

Different suddenly.

I recognized her immediately. I had gone to school in a very diverse high school. In fact, the Caucasians, like me, had been the minority. I had once gone on a date with an African American girl and once with a girl whose family had emigrated from Honduras. Neither had worked. The African American girl told me her dad did not want her to ever date white boys and the girl from Honduras had wanted to have sex with me the second we got into her room. My youth pastor told me I couldn't see her again.

He would have been disappointed in what I was seeing. Maria, from Honduras, was there. In front of me. As seductive as I remembered her being, which was odd, because I hadn't thought about her at all, let alone her seducing me, in over twenty years and, honestly, didn't remember ever thinking she was sensual. I had just thought I was a horny teenager.

Until that moment.

She stared at me. Dark eyes, dark hair, dark skin, in the prime of her life as I had once been.

"Maria?" I gasped.

She smiled. She was far more attractive than I had remembered. She was also eighteen and when I realized that I was old enough to be her dad—I looked at my hands. They were not the hands I recognized. They were younger. My own skin was skin that I had not seen in years. I felt my face. Clean-shaven, softer, missing the scars and wrinkles that had come with age.

"What," I managed to gasp, now more consumed with my own skin than hers.

"Seth," she whispered. "Should we go away alone?"

"Yes," I answered, without thinking.

The nature scenes vanished. We were in her bedroom. I'm not sure I could have recounted a thing about it, but seeing it, I knew instantly. But, like everything else, something was off about it. Was there *too* much of it?

She started to unbutton her jeans that she had been wearing that I had not noticed up to that point. "Wait." I stopped. "What?" I uttered slowly.

I looked down. My shoes were my favorite pair I had worn in high school. *On that date?*

"Don't stop me now, Seth," she said, making me look up again and see her standing half-naked in front of me.

God, what were you thinking, you idiot? Why did you not want to have sex with this woman? Fucking youth pastors …

I looked down to unbutton my own pants when a new voice entered the arena.

"Seth." It shocked me. It was not Maria's but it was one I recognized instantly and I looked up to confirm a second later.

"Rachel?"

It was my wife. The first year we had dated. Her cute dark hair, her soft lips, her dazzling blue eyes … my sweatshirt. She was wearing my sweatshirt. I remembered it clearly as I remembered the time she had spent the night because my parents were gone. Her parents had been gone too. She had slept in the other bedroom because we didn't want to do anything that would make god angry.

She had been cold because she knew she had to stand up to my heat. The sweatshirt was adorable on her when we watched our movie and went to bed like the old married couple we would become years later.

But the Rachel looking at me was different. The blue eyes weren't cold but suggestive somehow. The dark hair wasn't cute, it was mature. Her dazzling lips, yeah, they were dazzling but in a way I couldn't remember ever seeing, not in real life.

I looked down again. My feet and legs were bare—they were the ones I remembered taking me around the track when I ran in high school. I looked back to her … there was an energy of desire that felt … palpable and good. I wanted her. The energy was pulsing.

It felt enchanting. Surreal and damn good.

I was ready. She was ready. The sweatshirt was going to come off like I had always wanted it to. She smiled and turned, urging me to follow her. We were in my house—just as I remembered it, though I couldn't remember Maria's room disappearing and the new location appearing.

As I followed her, that splinter was back in my senses and I couldn't find the mental tweezers to remove it and let me feel as good as I wanted. Rachel was gone.

"Seth," she cheered.

It was another voice I recognized. And it caused me to groan.

Gwen.

I looked away because I didn't want to see her. Not her. And so I realized I was standing on a tarmac. A runway was in the distance and surreal perfect white clouds covered the scene above. A warm breeze brushed across my face.

"Seth!" She sounded so happy.

I turned to see her and saw someone—but it was not the Gwen I had expected. She was much thinner, less curvy, less perfect, and … happier. And her husband was with her. Wearing his flight suit and carrying their child. I might as well have jumped into the photo that I had seen in her hallway so many times.

There was joy everywhere. Smiles. Teeth. Laughter. Calm. Comfort. Self-esteem.

And that damn splinter.

What is this? Where is this? What do I want?

What is this? Where is this? What do I want?

Where …

Was the splinter leaving?

"Hmmm ..."

I was back on the park bench, almost instantly—which gave me a temporary case of vertigo, panic, and new anxiety. I had to sit still for all three to dissipate.

Ehs kept talking. "Sorry, I didn't want to do that to you. But if I hadn't, she would have noticed something wasn't right."

Traffic had begun to move, which made the city seem alive again. Its blood was flowing. It was beautiful in all the ways I was used to.

I stopped processing and looked at him, sitting on the bench with me. "She?"

"Yeah, the woman."

"What woman?"

"All of them," he smirked.

"The one who wouldn't tell me who she was?"

"Sure." Ehs smiled, stood to his feet, and with his hands in his pockets walked again closer to the ledge, staring off, I assumed, still smiling. "The one that runs the place."

I stood too, moving next to him. "What does that mean? Also did you know—"

He glanced toward me. "What did you think?"

"I have no idea." I looked up toward the night sky and the small lights of another jet going somewhere. "I'm still trying to figure it all out."

"Well—" He patted me on the shoulder. "You managed your first interaction with what you usually label the devil. Congratulations."

"*That* was the devil?" I immediately began to replay the entire experience.

"Sure."

"Sure? What the hell? You're saying I was with the devil?" My feelings were overwhelming and they surprised me. *The* devil*? That doesn't exist?* I felt shame, suddenly. Embarrassment. Regret. Confusion.

It was like waking up from a bad dream, thankful it was a dream because otherwise, we have to live with the decisions we made in that dream. But, this dream was clinging to me somehow.

I went back to the bench and sat there for a moment, hypnotized by the moving red and white lights of the cars in the distance. I let them put me into some kind of trance, processing devils and demons and affairs and women and shame and beliefs and experiences and wondering if I was still meditating.

Ehs waited, still staring outward.

"Wait." I suddenly stood. "I don't believe you."

Ehs turned around with some kind of intrigued expression on his lifted brows. "Why's that?"

"That drunk guy. That Shadow thing that came in here earlier." I pointed in case Ehs didn't remember where the man had been sitting on the grass. "I did the wonder wizard with my hands and it worked. You've said I have something in me. More powerful than all of this." I flew my hands in the air indicating something and hoping I was right. "I can't be in the presence of the devil, right? Isn't that what you basically said?" *I have Jesus in me.* I didn't add that but my Sunday school teachers from my elementary days would have.

"You can't be in the presence of evil?" Ehs asked, now more openly entertained.

"Well … the devil." My voice carried as much confidence as the rest of me.

"And why's that again?"

"Because …" I was busy trying to think. "I have a light."

"True."

"So that wasn't the devil." *A + B = C, right?*

"Not true."

"Listen, if I had held up my hand that thing would have run for the hills. I'm more powerful." *If you tell yourself something enough, you'll believe it.*

"True." Ehs nodded.

"Okay?"

"But you didn't."

I closed my eyes.

"You didn't hold up your hand. You didn't do anything. You just sat there. In fact, I think you asked her why she was leaving."

He was right.

Oh shit.

"You wanted more of her even?"

"But …" I said aloud. "Not her. My wife."

"Your wife?"

"I …"

Ehs waited.

"How was I supposed to know it was the devil?"

Ehs nodded. "Were you expecting horns and mass hysteria?"

"Okay, but be fair, I was never all in."

"One, we never need *all* of you. Just enough. Two, you can thank *me* for that splinter. Try not to imagine what you would have done without it."

Can demons help people not want the devil?

"What?" Had he actually helped me?

"I'm glad it worked out as it did. You won't forget the illustration."

Glad?

"And there's another perk." His hands were in his pockets again. So calm. "You've now survived hell."

"Wait, wait, wait." My hands were outstretched again, not in my pockets. "What? That was hell?"

"Yeah."

"Hell exists?"

"It's not fire." Ehs laughed. "Right?"

"Of course … it's … not …" I responded, glad to have that confirmed and not much glad of anything else.

"Fire," he laughed. "Wasn't that brilliant of us?"

"You?" I frowned. "Why would you start that one?"

His laughter stopped and transformed into something regrettably serious. Seconds later, he held a gun to my head. I could feel the cold steel barrel pressing into the warm flesh of my temple. He, and the pistol, had grabbed my attention, which up to that moment I had not thought possible because I figured my attention had left long ago.

"Ehs," I said as calmly as I could while trying to recollect my entire life in case it was about to end.

"Why?" He said with a hiss or insult and sarcasm all rolled into one. "Give me all your money or die."

"Okay," I answered, of course. "Okay," I repeated, feigning calm.

"Give me your children, your future, your brain, your life," he whispered. "Or you will burn forever."

"Okay." My voice was quivering like the rest of my body. "Whatever you say."

"Exactly." He laughed, even if it wasn't funny. The gun disappeared and he was smiling again. "You understand now what a threat does to freedom. It doesn't take it, it only distorts and corrodes the choice within it."

"Please," I said, afraid to even look at him and definitely missing the point for the moment. "Don't do that again."

"Fear," he spoke seriously. "*Is* us. *All* us. Never mystery. Never love. You understand that?"

I nodded, not sure if I actually did.

"Decisions based out of fear are our favorite," he whispered. "Besides, fire is nothing compared to the reality."

"Right?" I asked, wanting the conversation to be over and

hoping there were no more guns, wondering why I was scared of a gun when I had been to hell.

"You were there for five minutes, Seth. I don't know what more time would have done to your fragile conscience."

"Wait, so there is a hell? For sure?" I peered intently at him, questioning everything I had ever believed.

Ehs only shrugged. "Look at you. Obsessed with the question. Even you."

"What's that mean?"

"It doesn't matter."

"But, you said I was in hell."

"Well—" He shrugged again. "I might have been a little dramatic. Hell, heaven. We're here, there. Words, labels. However, you want to say it, that's her special domain.

"What's with me and women?" So cliché again. "I was in hell and all I could come up with was wanting to have sex with someone?"

"Fairly common. Don't be so hard on yourself."

"So you really do love to slam sex in our faces, huh?"

And he started laughing. Almost hysterically. At least enough to make me feel like an idiot.

"The problems with sexuality are *your* demons, not ours."

"What?"

"Mary Magdelene." He had calmed down enough to speak normally again.

"Yes?" I asked, not sure where he was going now.

"The prostitute?" he asked with his trademark grin.

"Yes."

"No!" he shouted. "No, no, no. Rich? Yes. Greedy? Yes. Evil? Yes. You made her a prostitute, though she never was."

"But …"

"Always so consumed with sex. Make the demon-possessed woman a prostitute. Easier to deal with than demons who make someone rich and greedy, huh?"

"Okay. So I'm just as messed up as church history. I saw three women …"

"No," he interjected, calmly. "It's common for sex to be a manifestation. What she loves is perfection and the past. And the two together …" He put his hands together as though trying to warm them up, but obviously not from the cold grin on his face. "Really sacrifice. She's infatuated with it … as false validation for your perceived unworthiness …" He mumbled as though thinking out loud.

I began to retrace my experience. "Not with me … I don't

think."

"Not you?" he asked with a surprised expression. "So blind. Even your past—filled with sacrifice—isn't worthy enough for you. Even your past, you think, will fulfill your desire to mean more."

I started to speak but stopped.

He twirled to look back at the traffic. "It's not as though you're the only one to go there and leave. And"—he turned back around, facing me—"it's not as though you never have been there before. You're alright, you'll be fine. Stop trying to fix your past and start fixing your present, Seth. If you want to bring something back from this meditation, bring that. And not in your brain. Somewhere it matters."

My phone was buzzing. The floor felt hard. The questions hurt. The shame was still attached to something deep inside of me and that just drug out more questions. And there was this sense of wishing I could have spent more time with Rachel, who wasn't Rachel, but a younger, more seductive Rachel, and the devil, which made me have more questions and shame.

I was still sitting with my legs crossed and my back straight on my carpet, staring out the window. They say you keep your back straight so you don't fall asleep.

Which, I assumed, worked, but I couldn't be sure of much of anything at that point.

Except that the counsel I was getting from my demon friend was some of the best I had ever received in my entire life.

Yeah, shit.

ELEVEN

I used to love flying a lot more. I don't know what changed but I do know that flying takes so much faith, it's almost irritating. Faith in pilots, faith in maintenance crews, faith in air traffic controllers, faith in bolts and pieces of metal, all of which I may never see yet are required for it all to work. Not to mention the science. Even if I did understand at some theoretical level how something well over one million pounds was able to float in the air well over eight thousand miles with over eight hundred people on board, flying requires faith.

Maybe that was why I no longer loved it the way I once had. I didn't have faith, not like that, anymore, in anything. And yet there I was looking through a small window down toward the Pacific Ocean roughly thirty-nine thousand feet below me, halfway between Seattle and Lihue, moving toward the island of Kaui, Hawaii.

Or maybe it all changed once I had kids: kids that were not with me while I was trusting some mad wizardry to get me somewhere safely and back to them again.

"You are a softy, aren't you?" The words popped into my head.

At least I had thought the words were in my head until they kept going outside of it. "You were holding back the tears with her last night. I saw it."

I looked over at my wife in the aisle seat. She was asleep. There was still no one in the middle seat, something we had both been really excited about and one more illustration of our shitty relationship.

"I'm behind you."

I turned back toward the window and slammed my forehead against the cold plastic of the plane so I could see who was there. A lady was leaning forward but I couldn't see much of her face. Given the constraining nature of an airplane, I figured I would have looked like an idiot trying to look over the seat but I figured I knew who it was. I found myself a little bit excited he had returned after a few months.

"You're back, huh?" I kept pretending to look out the window behind me so I could talk. "I thought we had maybe broken up."

"Well, you've been a little busy. Elections, Thanksgiving, the holidays, birthdays … it never ends for you, does it?"

I shoved my head farther into the window to try and grab a look. Blond hair. I vaguely remembered her from before we had taken off. "Busy?" my voice rose a little. "Not as bad as most."

"I know, I know …" the woman responded, laughing. "No, not you. You're never busy. Doing it all perfectly. I've actually been the busy one. Very busy."

"You get busy?"

"*Get* busy? We invented busy. Gave it to you stupid humans as a gift." More laughter. "And you've never looked back, although most of you can never admit it to this day—not you, of course."

"You're in a mood."

"No, seriously though." Her mood was drastically different. Pensive, suddenly. "You were about ready to cry last night when you kissed your daughter. Right?" There was no insult in the words but observation and intrigue.

Ignoring the fact that he had seen me in the privacy of my own home, I chose to answer instead of asking how often he watched me. "I don't like leaving my kids. I mean I do, but I don't. Goodbyes are hard." I *was* a softy. I had kissed my daughter the night before and held back the tears.

"Painful?"

"Yeah, I guess so." It's hard to describe leaving for Kaui for a week as painful, but given the fact that my wife and I were doing as bad as we had been in a long time and we were going to have to pretend for a week that we weren't … "Yeah … that part is … I guess …"

"Why?"

"What?"

"Why? What's painful?" Again, her voice was almost journalistic in intensity. "Are you afraid? Worried?"

"Are you going to make fun of me again?"

"What?"

"Are you going to make fun of me again?" I repeated.

"No, I'm intrigued."

"With missing someone?"

"Yes," she responded. "What is your worry?"

I had to think about it. "I don't know. I'm a softy—you said it yourself. I don't like goodbyes. I just know I'll miss her, I guess."

"Are you afraid?"

"Not really. I don't think that's the emotion."

"Hmmm." She was nodding.

I figured I would change the subject. "So you possessed that lady?"

"She's fairly drunk," she answered.

"It's only eleven in the morning. And we're on an airplane."

"All true things. I won't be long."

"Alright, well, how—"

"Advent …" she interrupted. "Fear, worry, shame, hate. I enjoyed it."

"Really?"

"Of course. You stole it all from me. Why would I not enjoy it? I do hope your little sheep are okay with that, but other than that, it was good." Coming from a demon, I wasn't sure anything about his statements were compliments but I took them anyway.

There was a ding and the seat belt light came on. "Ladies and gentlemen, this is your captain again. The road ahead looks a little bumpy so we're going to go ahead and put on the fasten seat belt sign. We are facing about a 150-mile headwind right now, which will also give us a little chop. We don't expect it to get worse but we will keep the light on for now and turn it off when things smooth out." On cue, the plane started to bounce around.

"I hate turbulence," she said.

"Me too," I answered, purposely not looking at the wing bouncing around behind me.

"I was kidding."

"Me too," I lied.

"I thought you loved airplanes. Didn't you recite the stats about how safe they were a few weeks ago talking about fear? You've seen wing flex right? Amazing."

I did manage to take another look at the wing. "Yeah, doesn't mean I love turbulence."

"Are you *afraid*?"

I sighed. "I don't know. I guess it's a hidden fear somewhere down in the recesses of my brain. But, I know it's stupid." Looking at the wing and talking about it with her was therapeutic. What little fear, or anxiety, was there, was vanishing. "Still, yeah, I do get afraid sometimes." The wing was flexing very nicely for us, carrying us over the endless blue, speckled with white far below us.

"I wish I did," she said, with a layer of sadness.

"What?"

"I wish I could feel that fear."

I wanted to look in her eyes as she was speaking but instead I could only look at the still bouncing wing, with its tall winglet shining in the sun, and see a tuft of blond hair in my peripheral vision.

She continued. "Your daughter. That pain you felt. It's because you love her so much. Love is painful in a beautiful way. Without pain, I'm not sure there can be love." She was still staring out the window. "You can't control love and that's painful. It borders on fear but it's not the fear we like to work with. There's something different about it. To be honest, we struggle with it, because we don't know what we're working with as well. We do know you can't have control and love—which is why we're very good at control. That's why you don't like the turbulence. You know it's safe but there is absolutely nothing you can do about it. Nothing. They are very related." There was a long pause while the plane bounced some more. "I don't remember what that's like anymore. I would kill to feel it again. To feel pain."

"Wow," I muttered, appreciating yet more wisdom from the dark side. It wasn't too often that I had heard someone say they would kill for pain. "I'm sorry," I managed to eventually say after another pause.

"What?" she asked.

"I'm sorry you feel that way."

"What?" she repeated.

"Love is painful but it's beautiful. I wish you could experience it again." I meant it for myself as much as Ehs. I glanced back toward my wife, still sleeping.

"Excuse me?" The voice was right on top of me and something changed. I looked up and the lady was looking at me from above. She had no problem peering over the seat—something I had not done earlier. It was all her and obvious Ehs had gone wherever Ehs went to when he left. Probably sitting on the wing and laughing at me trying to recover the situation.

"Were you talking to me?" she asked with a scent of Mai Thai and stomach acid. Big cheeks. Pock marks. Too much makeup. Short blond hair. She looked tired.

"Oh sorry, no. Just talking to my wife here." I smiled a very polite smile.

We both looked over at my wife. She was still asleep. I kept smiling. The lady did not.

"Sorry," I said, because there was nothing else to say and rarely is in those situations. I would never see her again, she would never see me again, we'd both just move on from our awkward encounter. She muttered something about me being a pervert and I did manage to mutter "Damn it, Ehs" under my breath before taking another glance out the window, and picking up my Kindle again. I had been reading *Brave New World*. Ehs was right. It was a great book.

Our vacation was a few days in and I was as relaxed as I had been in months. Maybe being thousands of miles away from Gwen was helpful. Maybe it was being thousands of miles away from Leo and church and my fake life.

I was lying on the beach with my wife, soaking up vitamin D, and feeling an all-around sensation of warmth—and probably an increased chance of skin cancer that was worth the vitamin D and warmth. I'm antsy by default but that day, that moment, I was lying there with a shirt over my face, utterly calm. Then something changed.

Even beneath the shirt, my face felt it. It was as though the sun went behind a cloud even though Rachel and I had been talking about how blue the sky was moments earlier. *Not a cloud in the sky*. My skin felt cooler, almost cold, and things were darker and quieter. The kids that I had been listening to were no longer yelling over to my left and the older couple wasn't talking about their grandkids over to my right.

I sat upright and opened my eyes.

The beach was still there, as was the sand. Behind me were the palm trees where I remembered them but I was alone, suddenly. Every human had vanished except for the man sitting next to me wearing long sleeves, long pants, a large bucket cap, and thick sunglasses. There was a massive umbrella over him, the size of something that would cover a picnic table or two. He glanced over at me as I stared at him.

What could be seen of his face was covered in sunscreen and not the sunscreen that most normal human beings wear but the kind from years ago before the zinc oxide was transparent. It was white and pasty.

I couldn't help but laugh. "Are you serious?"

"Have you looked around?"

"In what way?"

"There's a lot more color here that most of the places I hang out."

"Color?"

"Color only exists in your mind, you realize?"

I didn't. "What's that have to do …"

"And that portion that you see is miniscule. And, given all that, do you know that color is ambiguous … hard to define. Not seen."

"Are you talking about … actual color?"

"Yes." He nodded, his bill flapping around. "Colors don't exist—they are only energy." He spoke dismissively somehow, almost annoyed by me. "Here Insipid's shadow doesn't cast very well. There is lots of color."

I nodded like I understood why. "Really?"

"Really?" he repeated.

"That's what I said."

"And what I repeated. You're asking me that question. Really?" His voice was mocking but coming from the costume he was in, I didn't feel mocked. "How long have you been here? A few days?"

"I'm sure you know."

"Sure," he nodded, barely looking up, almost curled into a ball under the umbrella.

"Have you looked at a television?"

"No."

"Your phone?"

"Not really."

"Read a book?"

"Yeah, here and there."

"Worried about missing a traffic light? Stressed about a meeting? Been angry? Thought of Gwen? Thought of letting someone down?"

I was getting his point.

"Have you even felt anything but contentment? You just sat on a beach and stared at water for two hours. You didn't really think about anything. You were present. Paying attention. Living."

"It's also a vacation. Let's not get too crazy," I added. "I assume you created privilege?"

"Have you felt as though you're not enough?" he continued, ignoring my question. "That you don't do enough? That you are a failure? That you can't do something? That no one cares? Have you thought about tomorrow? About yesterday?"

"Yeah. I'm officiating a wedding."

"You get it."

"Yeah." I paused. "But …"

"As for your privilege? We only worked with the readily available ingredients."

"I assume. But, not everyone can afford a vacation like this."

"Not everyone needs a vacation. Your privilege to afford one costs you dearly, trust me."

"True, but—"

"Seth, you understand the points." He tried to look angry but just couldn't, not while looking like a clown. "Do you see the ocean?" he asked, nodding toward it.

"Hard to miss."

"Exactly. Rhythm, the cycles, it goes … and comes again. The present is in your face, along with the fragility, the nothingness, and the ordinary … and it means so much. Harder to miss here."

I watched a wave crash into the surface of the water that it had come from. Gone and yet back to what had formed it. Powerful and then timid, licking the sand. "Yeah …" I managed.

"For the rich and poor, privileged and ordinary."

"Yeah." I nodded. "But my relationship with Rachel is as bad as it's been, despite how amazing everything else is."

"Not for much longer," he answered, looking down so that his hat cast a bigger shadow on the sand.

"What?"

"You heard me."

"Yeah, but what—"

"Distractions, Seth, they are one of our main tools. And they simply aren't as powerful here." He pointed upward without looking. "Paradise, you know." There was a slight smile.

"Speaking of distractions." I steered the conversation back to where he didn't seem to want it to go. "What are you saying about Rachel and me?"

"No reason to worry about it."

"About what?"

"Seth." He tried to look serious again but it was still impossible given everything surrounding the expression.

"Okay," I interrupted. "What is with this outfit?"

"I thought you would like it."

"I don't." I shook my head. "And what are you trying to say? You sound like an old-time pastor or something. We need to return to the simple days. No distractions." I tried to imitate Ehs's voice but sounded like a crotchety old man instead. "I thought the simple days weren't all we thought they were."

"You're an idiot sometimes."

"Whoa."

"I'm not talking about phones and all that shit. Those are just smaller tools. Distraction is everything."

I shook my head.

"Have you ever met someone who is praying for god's wisdom? That's a rhetorical question, by the way."

I looked out toward the ocean. The look was too much. His voice was nice though, kind and had a certain radio quality to it. It reminded me of my dad's voice. I enjoyed listening as he kept going. "Why won't god tell me what I am supposed to do, they say? Where is god? Where is the answer? Why do I hear only silence? How do I know? On and on they go …"

"Right …" I was familiar with all of it.

"And what do you say to those people?"

I was staring at the waters, the waves lapping the sand in hypnotic motions. "God probably doesn't give a shit."

"You wish you could say that." He paused, but I kept looking outward. "But yes, people asking god for wisdom is a distraction in itself," he said slowly.

I did look back to him. He was staring at the ocean, still looking like a tourist mime with a sun phobia. "Always asking questions for the obvious answers and never asking questions for the important answers. We prefer the first."

I kept looking at the waves. "Well, I live there too."

"Of course you do. Your distractions are actually far beyond the standards … elections, church services, rules, morality, laws … you've managed to tie yourself up beyond those. "

"What do I do?" I looked over at him again but he was standing up.

"Stop the addiction," he answered plainly.

"That's not helpful."

"Listen to the pain. It will point you in the right direction," he said calmly.

"I thought pain was good."

"Are you deaf?" he asked.

"What?"

"Pain points. Suffering debilitates. Don't confuse the two. Addiction is always the same. Go to AA. And pay attention to what happens in Hawaii here, for a start."

I momentarily lifted my eyebrows. "Should I move here?"

"Do it." The power of the words caught me by surprise, like I had been standing behind a jet engine. They pushed me backward.

"Do what?" I pleaded for some more specifics.

"What'd you say?" Rachel asked.

The darkness of my shirt was back in front of my face. "Huh?" I mumbled, a little confused.

"I thought you said something," she said, amidst the sound of kids playing and an older couple arguing.

I took off the shirt from my face and was hit with blinding sunlight again and a world of color that represented so much more that I could not see. And what I could see was possibly still all in my head. "Oh …" I looked at the tide and over to my wife. "No, nothing."

She took a deep breathe.

I mimicked her and took my own deep breath. And closed my eyes again.

ELEVEN POINT FIVE

"What a view," the woman said, like tourists often say when looking at something that looks like it belongs on a calendar and, obviously, is a view.

"Isn't it?" I responded as a good fellow tourist should. I didn't look at her though, and just kept staring.

Green slopes met in an incredible canyon hundreds of feet below me where a river meandered along, cutting a line through lush foliage and eventually emptying into the ocean, which was far away, but not too far to see the waves rolling in. It was A-plus postcard material.

Once the tour bus that had been idling behind me left, I could hear the songs of the birds below me rising up into the blue skies above, speckled with puffs of white cloud here and there. It was inspiring in the way that views often are—the reason we drive and fly to find them all over the world.

"Says here the priests and kings lived up here." This time her finger, with a massive diamond ring on top of it, was pointing at a sign below me. It was more of a pedestal, the kind that are often set up at tourist spots, and it said WAILUA, PUNA DISTRICT in big letters.

"Hmmm," I responded. I had already read it before she had shown up in her rental car that was parked behind mine. "Not a bad spot to live, right?" I figured I would be nice and contribute to the "conversation." Rachel and I gave each other a glance.

"For politicians and pastors," she responded, without much hesitation but with a whole lot of smug.

I decided to really look at her. Older woman. Probably mid-seventies with lots of gray hair in a big ball. Huge sunglasses that blocked all of her eyes and most of her cheeks and forehead. She looked wealthy. Sometimes you can just smell old money. Or maybe you just smell old and see that it's rich. Her rental was a Lincoln Town Car that was as long as the tour bus that had left before it, which seemed like a strange car to drive around an island with windy dirt roads, unless you're too used to the ride to have anything else.

I read another sign with big letters that said WAILUANUIAHO'ANO and was just starting to read about the consecration of the birth of royal children when she started again.

"Not much has changed in the world, has it? They ran this country into the ground, the politicians and pastors—just like they are now."

I looked at her again, befuddled. I looked behind her to her car that was running and blowing out carbon monoxide and ruining the planet just to keep the interior of her car at a lower temperature than the perfect temperature it already was outside. "Excuse me?" That was all I could manage after having my profession lumped into that of politicians and being told we were running the country into the ground. Even though it was probably true, that bag of a woman was definitely not going to be the one to tell me.

"Same old thing. All of these temples." She pointed to another sign with big letters that read POLI'AHU HEIAU and contained an old drawing of an ancient temple on it. "Oh, I'm sorry, I don't even know you."

"Or do you?" I smirked.

"What!" She seemed appalled. Maybe because my swimsuit and shirt weren't color coordinated, maybe because I was wearing a flat-billed hat, or maybe because I was wrong.

"Ehs?" I asked, because I was starting to assume it.

"Excuse me," she said, this time letting me see what a befuddled expression looks like to the person it's being directed to.

"Oh sorry, you remind me of a relative of mine," I lied. "So much!" That exclamation was loud and excited. As though it were a compliment.

Her befuddlement faded and she was smiling again. "Oh, I hope not a grandmother."

"No, no," I lied again. "A sister!" I laughed a fake laugh meant to rub away any insults that might still be hanging around and hopefully make her leave.

She laughed an honest laugh. "Oh, you're too cute."

"Thanks." I lied again.

"Do you come to Hawaii often?" she asked.

"Not as much as I would like. First time to Kauai though."

"Our first time as well," she said with a tone as cold as her air-conditioned car. "And we won't be back."

I was drinking befuddlement again, served on ice, with an anger twist.

"We usually go to Mexico. Much nicer there and you don't have to drive around. And, it's just more … clean." She looked around as though someone might be overhearing us, someone other than me, who was obviously, in her head, on her side. "It's dirty here. Those houses. And the cars they drive around. They act like this is their island or something." She pulled her sunglasses closer to her face, as though there was some horrible Hawaiian sun managing to find its way to her eyes. "It's no wonder all that's left of their temples are these ruins."

I looked toward Rachel, who was steering clear of me—and the tourist—starting to head to the car, probably sensing the explosion that was about to go off. If my anger were a pot of water, the bottom of my heart was filled with those little bubbles that start rising to the surface when it's about to go crazy.

But with so much to disagree about, it's too hard to ever start. The words rush to get out too fast and all get stuck in my mouth.

"We'll just stick with our resort in Mexico next time," she added, sensing I was not responding. She was looking out at the view again, almost disgusted.

"You realize Mexico has ruins too, right?"

She looked at me with an inquisitive look.

And you realize that Mexico is actually poorer than Hawaii but you just don't see it because you stick on an all-white resort where they hide that from you so you'll come back. And you realize you could have done that here, although I'm glad you didn't, because you really need to see the world. And you realize that this actually is their island and if it were my island, I wouldn't want you here either because you're about as dumb as you are rich. And you realize that what destroyed this place was not their priests and kings but our priests and kings who came in here and gave them diseases that killed their bodies, and religions that destroyed their spirits. And when I say our priests and kings I'm more referring to the money and power that ran our priests and kings than whatever religion you are, or are not aware of. Something we humans were, and are, really good at doing all over the world, including Mexico, where, I'm sure you realize, the same thing happened but on a much larger scale? And did you know that I'm actually a pastor and that you're a bitch? And you realize that as a pastor I'm hypersensitive to people judging me for being a hypocrite and proud and ignorant but when I run into someone like you, I don't really care anymore, even though I should, because someone, somewhere, needs to shut you up. And yes, I realize, none of this will matter, in fact it will only confirm what you already think you know. And yes, I am actually a hypocrite, although not very proud and less ignorant than you, at least.

"Really?" she asked, responding to the question I actually vocalized. But, I did feel better.

Shit, Ehs is really rubbing off on me. Where did all that come from?

"Yeah, you should check them out next time you're there. You might learn something." It sounded much more insulting in my head than when it left my mouth with its cordial tone. I started walking back toward my car, where Rachel was already, happy I could at least get one small, very tiny, tiny, dig.

"Well, I think we'll stick to the resort. Those drug dealers, with their cocaine and everything, I would rather not see!" She was shouting, just in case I might not have heard her.

I reached the car door and looked back toward her. "Well, I hope you can find a way to enjoy the rest of your time here in Hawaii." Anytime a human has to make that statement to another human, both humans should be shot. "And the world will be better when your generation is dead," I mumbled.

"We leave tonight," she answered and neared her own car.

"Good," I muttered before slamming the keys into the ignition and starting up the rental. "What a bitch."

My wife looked at me and out the back window at the car behind us with a distressed look about whatever had just happened—I assumed. She was still on the phone with the kids though so I couldn't explain. "Tell the kids I love them!" I said, a little louder than I needed to, still jacked-up on adrenaline.

And can you ask them what it means that I would rather be friends with a demon than a rich white stupid American like that woman? Or maybe ask them if I'm turning into a demon?

I started driving back down the windy road we had come up, still steaming from my encounter, consumed with what I should have said, when I realized my wife was staring at me from the passenger seat.

"Right, what—" I glanced over and immediately saw tears. "Hey?" I asked.

The phone was on the floor at her feet. She just kept staring at me.

"Are the kids alright?" I began to panic, as I kept glancing over at her wet eyes.

"That wasn't the kids, Seth." Her words were slow, methodical. Tortuous. "It was Leo."

There was a long moment of silence.

Something besides terror was filling the car. Rachel was becoming something different, as though the shell of her that I had known was cracking and something else was emanating from it. I didn't know what to think.

"Leo?" I eventually asked out loud. Shock was coursing

throughout my body and it took everything I had to not run the car through the metal barrier and over the side of the cliff. *Oh no, oh no, oh no.*

"Leo." I didn't ask the second time, just stated the name plainly, still trying to process everything that was taking place in the car at that moment.

I knew. She knew.

"You and I need to talk," she said with strength. "I don't want to talk anymore about this until tonight. But we'll talk tonight. After the wedding. Okay?" Rachel was as strangely grounded and empowered as I'd ever seen her, even with her tears.

"Okay," I answered, quickly sinking into an ocean of anxiety and fear and hoping not to drown. "Okay."

ELEVEN POINT SEVEN FIVE

It was sometime past midnight. We had danced in the waves and laughed in the moonlight. The girls were taking faux model shots on the beach, in the waves, and the guys were drinking beer. Cliché? Maybe. We had snuck into a massive hot tub of a resort on the beach and someone was taking underwater pictures of the new bride and groom kissing. There were about twelve of us in the bubbling water and it was a pure cornucopia of religion and nationality: some Muslims, some agnostics, some atheists, some Christians, and a variety of countries represented.

A United Nations post-wedding soak.

We had been drinking for about five hours. Rachel had drunk more than I had ever seen her drink, continuing her near instantaneous evolution into Rachel 2.0. Whatever had started in the car was continuing. She was more extroverted, more vocal, more risky, stronger … she was progressively more all of it as the day moved toward its end.

An hour earlier someone had offered us edibles—something Rachel and I had tried years ago to spite our past and parents—and Rachel was the first to ask for the entire cookie. I was surprised, to say the least, but she was already far from the Rachel I was most used to. She stared at me with some kind of new power to make me do things and I followed suit.

And why the hell not? Might as well ease the soon-to-arrive pain.

I assumed we were both thinking the same thing, although we had barely spoken to each other and instead, used every other person, every event, every distraction we could to avoid what we both knew was coming.

It was nearing.

We could both feel it moments earlier staring at each other in the hot water and trying to steady the world that was starting to spin around us for all kinds of reasons.

After a second swim in the waves, I rinsed off the salt water in one of the beach showers and took a seat in a recliner that was meant for sun but was giving me moonlight instead.

Others of the group, including Rachel, were taking a final dip in the hot tub and a few others were skinny-dipping in the ocean, trying to be quiet, but not doing a very good job. It wasn't our usual "scene" but we both knew we never liked most of our standard friends anyway.

I was sitting alone. Some would call it meditating. I would call it trying to steady my world that was getting less and less steady with each passing moment.

The wedding had gone well, including a sudden rainstorm at the end that most people said was a sign of blessing and approval in Hawaiian culture. If so, they were definitely blessed by whatever gods existed in the Pacific Paradise. Either way, it had been an epic and dramatic conclusion to the event.

I took a deep breath and exhaled as slowly as I could. We were leaving the next day and leaving Hawaii is the only bad thing about the place. I wondered if we would even fly on the same flight back together. I wondered if I would move out when we arrived. I wondered if I would be speaking the following week or working at a grocery store and the talk of the town. For the moment, I was still wearing a bathing suit and not a winter jacket. I was still married. I was still drunk and high.

Enjoy this moment, Seth. It's going to be your last good one for a while.

I closed my eyes and listened to the waves and the distant laughter. I smelled the salt, tasted the air, and felt the rays of sunlight, reflected from the full moon, hit my skin.

There's nothing that breaks the attempt at a calm mood like the scream of a Nazgul. I say Nazgul because it's the only thing I could think of as my eyes popped open and my heart and pulse started pumping like an eight-cylinder with the pedal to the metal.

My son and I would sometimes go around the house and mimic the high-pitched shriek of the ring wraiths from *The Lord of the Rings*. If you've never seen the movies or read the books, well, think high-pitched evil scream. An eagle on meth. Terrifying.

The sound was all around me. There was no point of reference. That alone added to my dizzy feeling and made me want to throw up but the fact that it was at a volume louder than anything I had ever heard, or felt, made me literally double over in my sun chair and grab my ears.

Yet it wasn't my ears that were hearing but my soul that was feeling.

That's the only way I can describe it. It hurt. It was pain and trauma.

And then it stopped.

I remained bent over on the plastic lounger, my eyes and heart glued shut, afraid it was going to come back, and wondering if any of the wedding party saw me cowering and huddled up like a ball—I assumed they would have thought I was finally caving to all the partying.

"Seth." The voice was gentle. "Sorry about that."

I dared to look.

Standing over me was a black man in a black tuxedo. Debonair. The word doesn't come to my mind often but it did then because he was. Smooth, confident, handsome, intimidating, and inviting at the same time. The man owned life and made it do what he wanted it to, not the other way around.

I sat up in my chair. "Ehs?"

"Of course," he answered. The shoes were glossy. The pants were wrinkle-free. The jacket and black shirt were tailored as perfectly as the dark hair hugging the top of his head. The dark eyes, the smooth skin, the model-like chin and jaws. I wasn't attracted to the man as much as jealous of him. He seemed to have it all.

"Damn, man. Where'd you find this guy?" I sat up more.

"I didn't." He was looking off, away from me, as though he was posing for a camera to keep up the vibe.

"What?" I stood up and waited for him to look at me. "What did you say?"

"I didn't *find* him. Didn't *take* him." He looked back toward the water. I could hear the waves. "Follow me." He started walking, knowing I would follow, toward the water where he had been looking.

"So, were you at a wedding like me?" I asked, picking up my pace to catch up to him.

He grunted. It was obvious, he wasn't in a joking mood. "Time is ticking. There are a few things I'd like to show you—and warn you of." He looked back at me with a sincere, almost cold, expression.

"Warn me?" I didn't like the sound of it. We left the concrete of the pool and stepped onto the sand of the nearby beach, the water closer and louder. "Okay." It had taken me longer than usual—my brain was not at its optimal operating capacity—but I did hold out my hand, motioning him to stop. "Whoa, hold on, before we do anything."

"How drunk are you?" he asked.

"Excuse me," I offered back.

"What?" He was almost parental. "Say it."

"What the hell is happening to Rachel?"

He smirked. "The truth." He stared at me, almost daring me to respond.

"The truth," I repeated.

"Yes. Now, can we get on with it?"

"With what?"

"I need you on board."

"On board?" My nerves were slightly on edge.

"Are you in?"

I felt like something between a girl on a first date being asked to get married and a mobster from the fifties being asked if he was going to join the new "venture." Confusion, excitement, anxiety, interest, fear ...

"In with what?" I asked, now walking beside Ehs and parallel to the line of water. Another resort was far in the distance, its tiki torches just visible. The section of beach was empty and quiet with the laughter of someone echoing somewhere behind us.

"Me." He was still looking and walking forward.

"Hey," I shouted. "Can you stop for a moment and let the Calvin Klein model vibe go?"

He stopped and faced me, trying to smile, but I sensed it took more effort than a smile should.

"Are you alright?" I asked.

He looked confused.

"What the hell was the screeching? I have a scar on my soul from that."

"I'm sorry," he answered. "There's a lot you still don't know."

"Yeah, I get that."

"You need to know what you're getting into."

"But, what does all that mean?"

"I need a commitment."

"To what?"

He grabbed my shoulders. "To me."

I thought of that song about Johnny and his fiddle and the devil. I thought that devils aren't nearly as cute as that song made them sound and then I tried to imagine Ehs playing a fiddle. "I kinda have a lot going on."

"There will be more." He started walking again.

"Hey." I held out my hand. "I'm not digging this whole thing. Not with what I have happening in my own fucking life. Do you know I'm probably about to get a divorce?"

"I don't care." He looked disgusted in a way I had not seen before. "I need to know if you want to do this. I'm giving you another chance for me to never bother you again. You're the one in control here."

"I don't know!" I yelled with all the frustration I was feeling exploding the word out into the air.

"Let's keep walking." He started again, calmer. "What will help you with your decision?"

"I don't know what any of *this* is." As I spoke, a wave came up a bit farther than usual and brushed into my ankles. The water was cold and made me look down at my feet and the still-shiny shoes of Ehs. As the water left, my feet were wet and his were not. In fact, the shoes looked as if they had just come out of the box. I looked back. My footprints were in the sand. His were not. I was living one of the worst pieces of art ever made and Ehs was not carrying me. Neither was Jesus.

I stopped. "Like this!" I pointed toward the sand. "What the hell is this?"

"What?" He looked down.

"Where are your footprints? And what is this tuxedo thing? And what do you mean you didn't take this guy? And where am I? And Rachel? And what is happening to her? And me? And did you make Leo call her and tell her? And where are my friends?" I looked into his dark eyes. "I need facts. I need explanations, straight and simple, since I'm just a dumb human."

He nodded. "Shake my hand." He held it out.

"Dude, can we just—"

"I said, shake my hand." There was a force behind his words.

I sighed and reached out my hand to shake his. The problem was that there was nothing there. My hand went through it, as it would have a hologram. That fact had me staring at his hand and my hand as I attempted to shake it a few more times. "Mother …" I waved my hand through his wrist and arm as well. I blinked, wondering what kind of cookies I had eaten.

"Where are we?" he asked.

"Hawaii?" I answered slowly.

"Where are we?" he asked again, moments later.

The beach we had been on moments earlier was suddenly gone and we were standing in a house somewhere. I had no idea where. White walls, white tile flooring, a couch in the corner. A fireplace. I was officially starting to panic again.

"Shake my hand," he said again, holding out his hands.

"Listen, I—"

"Shake my hand!" he ordered.

I reached out, expecting my hand to go through his, but this time it stuck. I could feel his skin, his strong grip. Warm human flesh.

"Touch the wall." He tilted his forehead toward the nearest wall with a nice painting hanging on it.

I did and it felt like most other walls I had ever touched. Sheetrock with some texture and a nice semigloss paint to top it off.

Moments later, Ehs took a step toward the wall and proceeded to walk through it, with his tuxedo and glossy shoes. There was water and sand on the tile where I last saw his foot before disappearing into the wall.

"Am I here?" he asked. I could hear him as though he were standing next to me, even though there was no sign of him.

I was lost. In so many ways.

"Am I here?"

"I don't know!" I shouted, starting to look around the house in a panicked state, for doors and windows I could run out of.

"Stop panicking. You're okay," he said, calm and in control at a time I needed both. "You're okay."

"I am?"

"We're just on the beach."

Instantly, we were. The two of us were standing in the sand again, the waves lapping against my ankles. Ehs was holding out his hand.

But, something was different. It was all so crystal clear that it forced me to stop momentarily. It was so clear that I felt like my entire life before that had been in a fog. I found myself staring at the details of waves, the white foam on their dark crests. I could taste each grain of salt in the air, feel each grain of sand on the bottom of my feet.

Ehs's hand. I noticed the small ridges in his flesh. I looked down to see the water lapping into both of our legs, the conglomeration of matter forming into water. The bottom half of his pants were wet, as were his shoes. Our footprints were in the distance, two sets, where the water had not already erased them.

"Ehs … man …" Words were a struggle. "What is all this?"

"Exactly," he answered. "Your conceptions of where and when and how and what are just that … conceptions. But—" He paused. "There's more."

I wasn't sure if I wanted more. It was hard enough to comprehend without more. But, I stared at him. "Should I get sober first?"

He didn't answer. Instead, something transformed within his body. I noticed the black smoke floating away from his skin, at first, as though he were made of dry ice. Then the tuxedo, the shirt, the pants—still soaked in water—the skin of the man I had been looking at, whose hand I had shaken and who had felt real, began to turn into some kind of transparent smoke-like substance, still loosely holding the form and shape of the man in the tuxedo but now almost ghostly.

The clarity had vanished and I was back to my previous perspective of the world, the one I was used to. The one we are all used to.

I was still mesmerized, watching the transformation from human to some kind of dark cloud. As the human form became less recognizable and a poisonous-looking fog took up more of the space, it all suddenly vanished into the sand, as though a fist had come from the heavens and shoved it down into the Earth.

"I'm still here," he said, as audible and clear as though he was.

I stared at the sand below me as another wave crept over it, rested for a moment, and eventually fell away and into the ground, just as he had.

"We've been called many things over the years, Seth." The voice was now coming from somewhere farther away, still audible and clear, but out over the waves, which made me look in that direction. "Imagined as Leviathan, Aspidochelone, Hydra, Scylla, and more."

Suddenly, out in the waves I saw a shape, just visible in the moonlight. It was hard to make out details but it was massive and covered in scales, half swimming and half slithering through the water that shined on its wet, prehistoric-looking back.

"We've been symbolized as beasts of the air and beasts of the land."

Something shot out of the water and formed what looked like a dragon—at least based on what I had seen in books—floating above the water, with wings spreading and flapping against the night air, so strongly I could feel its warmth and smell its pungent scent up against my own face. Its face looked upward and yelled a terrible screech like the one that had startled me earlier.

"Snakes," Ehs hissed, doing his best imitation of one.

The massive flying beast that looked like something out of a fantasy novel shot toward me before becoming small and slithering across the sand, with a black slimy form. It moved faster than any snake I had seen and rose up on its back, prepared to strike with dark audacious teeth. I stepped away from it and the water.

"Why so reptilian and fantastic?" The man in the black tuxedo was standing in front of me again, staring.

"I don't know ..." I didn't know anything.

"Images, ideas, symbols ... of fear. Primitive, maybe, but functional. The unknown, the darkness, the wild, the beast that will destroy."

I was simply staring at the show. Enthralled and terrified.

"Of course, we've been called other names. Crazy ..."

The debonair man shifted into the complete opposite. Half-naked, hair in every direction, chains wrapping around his skin, and a maniacal and crazed look in his eyes. His teeth were on wide display, growling toward me, and I took steps away from him.

"Legion."

The chained man shifted into Roman soldiers, filling my view both in the water and out of it. Each of them transparent in form but filled with darkness and carrying shields and swords, decorated in helmets and armor. Some were neck deep in the waves, only their black helmets sticking up, and others were directly in front of them; all were black, imposing, dangerous. In order. Lined up to perfection.

"Oh, that's badass." They were. I couldn't help but stare, not afraid, but intimidated, and anxious, with adrenaline rushing through my body.

"Power always is," he responded.

"Why?" I asked, feeling like I honestly didn't know.

"To control another human is intoxicating. Fear is intoxicating when used to control others. Not so, when used to control you. Either way, we are fear." The soldiers transformed back into the tuxedo man, but on the way I saw, for a moment, a hospital room, with people hovering around a body lying on a bed. Then a newspaper flashed in front of me. Then a woman sitting at a news desk with the familiar image in the upper left corner. I blinked and the tuxedo man put his arm on my shoulder as if to comfort me. "We are the shadows of your fears, conforming and manipulating ourselves into the demons and devils you need, without worry of where or when or how or what."

I nodded, not sure if I was supposed to.

"This is what you are agreeing to."

"I have no idea what that means," I slurred, knowing I was slurring, which meant I was not going to be feeling good in the morning.

"Hmm." His hand was still on my shoulder.

"I don't know if I can—"

The light was blinding and immediately headache-inducing. The air was hot and immediately sweat-inducing.

"Oh my god," I groaned, grabbing at my eyes and head. "Is it morning already?"

"Quiet!" he ordered. "Pay attention."

I heard sobbing. Crying. Deep wailing from two different sources and I managed to squint to try and take in my surroundings.

We were at a higher elevation. Some kind of hill. There was high desert landscape everywhere—shrubs that needed more saturation and plain-colored sand.

And a man standing over a boy. A boy, maybe twelve, tied to

some kind of a pile of thin logs. The man was dressed in white fabric and holding a knife high into the sky. The boy had a robe but it had been torn away to reveal his young chest. He was desperately trying to escape the ropes that held him down.

"Oh my god," I whispered. "What are you doing?"

The man was shaking. He could barely hold the knife up. He uttered words in some language that I did not understand—between his deep cries—and louder than the boy, who was bellowing out his own tears.

"Why?" I whispered, still squinting, trying to see everything and equally forgetting everything else that was not in that exact moment. I was consumed with it.

"No need to be so dramatic," the voice of Ehs rang out. "You've preached this story many times. Talked of its holiness and beauty."

"Abraham?" I managed.

As my eyes began to focus, I could see the same dark shapes I had seen earlier, now hovering around the man with the knife. They were in and out of forms that I had seen—dragons, snakes, a man in chains, as though they could not decide what shape was best. But, no matter the shape, there was some kind of effort to bring the knife down—into the boy.

But there was something else resisting. Something I couldn't quite make out in the sun and its shape was much more mysterious.

"Maybe," Ehs added from somewhere, though I still didn't see him anywhere, "this is the greatest fear. Not giving up enough. We love sacrifice," he said with a glee that was chilling, especially as the dark shapes continued to pull the knife down—screeching and calling out in some strange tongue.

The man finally collapsed to his knees and dropped the knife to the ground, it sounding out as it bounced off of a stone before landing in the soft dirt. He was still crying but the tears had transformed into relief, as had the boy's.

"You always missed the story and its message because of your fears and your insatiable thirst for some kind of assurance that you can measure, or have measured, up."

The man slowly rose back to his knees, wiping tears and moving toward the boy, speaking the same language but softer. The shadows were nowhere to be seen.

"It was never a story of a son who didn't need to die. It is the story of a god who did, even if you refuse to believe it."

The man began to slowly untie the ropes. The boy stared wide-eyed, still untrusting.

"The story was much more direct later on, but you again missed it—or at least we were able to twist it, I suppose." The man reached out and touched the boy's tears, wiping them away as fast as he could, speaking soft words, comforting words, and the boy began to relax.

Ehs continued, somehow. "So consumed with sacrifice and pleasing and rules and morals to give … enough … to the god of your fears and control."

The man started on the ropes again.

The dark beach returned. As did Ehs in his tuxedo, his dark eyes sincere and honest and staring into my own. "That god dies so a new god can live," he said quietly. "But you want so desperately to be gods yourselves, you need one like you, unable to comprehend a life without sacrifice, much less a power that doesn't demand it."

I looked at Ehs with what I assumed was a "blank" stare. I felt blank inside.

"Seth," he said gently. "Help me, help you, help me."

"Ehs." I was too far gone. "I need time." It was all I could muster.

"Of course. But you don't have it."

I fell to my knees, exhausted.

"Seth?" I heard, causing me to look up.

It was one of the groomsmen. "What the hell are you doing out here? Time to jet, man. We all thought you were by the pool."

"Oh." I stood to my feet again, looking out toward the dark waves and dark sky with the moon a little higher now. "Yeah, sorry, just one more little walk on the beach, right?"

"Alright, well, let's go!"

With that we both turned away from the water and started walking toward our cars … our lives as we understood them.

Until Rachel found me. She grabbed my hand and held it tight. "Guys, we're going to sit on the beach for a bit," she yelled back toward the group, while directing me toward the beach.

They responded with something I couldn't hear. My suddenly pulsing heart filled every part of me, masking out any other feeling. Except Rachel's skin on mine. "We need to sit for a sec but see you at breakfast! Love you!"

The world became sharp again, distinctly real. The two of us sat down in the sand. Alone. Dark waves on the horizon literally and figuratively. We both stared forward. She dropped my hand.

"Seth."

We looked toward each other, staring into each other's eyes. Tears were already forming in mine. As exhausted as I had been, there was adrenaline and some kind of new, twisted energy.

The moment of reckoning had arrived. I wouldn't need to fear it any longer.

ELEVEN POINT NINE

"Rachel." I said her name first. And swallowed a hard lump of anxiety. Did I wait for her to tell me what she knew or just get it out there? How much longer did I want to play the game? "What I ..." I took a deep breath and let the gentle waves fill the space for a moment.

Then Rachel broke the silence. "Seth," she said. "I have something I have to tell you." Her eyes were glistening in the moonlight. "I'm glad Leo called. I'm glad he pushed me. I'm glad—"

"What?" I asked, my mouth remaining open and unable to close.

"Just—" She sucked in a cry, her lips tight. She couldn't look at me and had to look off somewhere else. "Just let me talk, okay?"

"Okay," I whispered, desperately seeking clues.

"It's time I tell you the truth. Leo's right. I don't know how he knows and, honestly, it doesn't matter. I can't be mad at him." She looked back to me, regaining control. "I've been having an affair, Seth." There was a short pause. "I've been fucking Jaden." The words dropped out of her mouth like Fat Man on Nagasaki and they destroyed the entire city of my own reality. Fire and heat seared my senses and destroyed my ability to think almost instantly. Rachel put her head between her knees and began to shake uncontrollably, crying out loud, muttering words that I didn't hear or care to.

I had never heard her say that word before let alone admit she had been physically carrying out the act. Hatred consumed me like radiation. We hate to compensate for our fear and I was terrified, suffocating in darkness. So I hated her. I too leaned my head between my knees but I threw up. There were no tears—just intense anger.

I was glad she was crying. I wanted more tears. I hated Jaden. I wished he was there so I could destroy him like he had destroyed me. I hated pastors and teachers and everything that we had ever listened to and believed. I hated myself. I hated Gwen. I hated my life. I hated Ehs.

"Seth ..." I managed to hear. "I'm sorry."

She said more words but other senses were overriding anything real. I could only imagine her naked body with his. I could only see his chest against hers. I could only see their skin sliding together thanks to a thin layer of sweat. I could only hear her moans and his gasps for air. I could only see him touch her hair and move it away from her lips before touching his own lips to hers and opening his mouth passionately and sensually. I could only see her body reacting to his body in the way I knew bodies could and in the way that I had always wanted hers to react to mine. I could only see her muscles tense and then relax.

I felt nothing. Empty. Invisible. Disgraceful and weak. I felt dead.

I felt something cold on my forehead and it made me look up again to the ocean. Something black, slimy, and covered in scales was wrapping its way around my head. A strong and suffocating snake, layered in cold and darkness. My eyes were soon covered—I could see nothing, even if I wanted to. Slowly it made its way further down my head, my lips, my chin, and eventually my neck where it began to tighten its grip and … I found it suddenly hard to breathe.

"Coward," a voice said slowly, dreadfully, and with a soft hiss. "Coward," it repeated and the erasing of my own breath continued.

Europe. I would go to Europe and escape. Or maybe, since I was already halfway to Japan, I could book a ticket there instead. But then I thought of my kids, saying goodbye to my daughter.

I smelled cologne suddenly. A strong earthy scent from Bob. I fell over to the ground, unable to take in any air. I looked to see what Rachel was doing but the snake had completely wrapped around my face and I could see nothing.

Somehow I saw her though: the old tourist who preferred Mexico over Hawaii.

"Coward," she said before vanishing.

I saw the man with the knife raised high in a bright sky and preparing to slice through the heart of his own flesh and blood for no good reason except for primitive attempts to assuage some kind of innate darkness.

"Rachel," I forced myself to say. Clearly. I saw Rachel again. She was still sobbing but she paused at the shock of me saying something and looked toward me, her beautiful face wrecked from tears and emotion. "I've been seeing Gwen. An affair. Eight or nine months." I could barely speak, from my own tears. "Or fifteen."

Perspective, it's an amazing thing.

It was as though time had rewound itself and I was living through the previous five minutes, but from a different camera angle. I could see what damage words could do on the face of a human being—

and I imagined the face of Rachel looked like mine had moments earlier. I suddenly couldn't bear to look at it, and forced my own head into my knees, this time sobbing myself.

I could only imagine Gwen's naked body with mine. I could only see my chest against hers. I could only see our skin sliding together thanks to a thin layer of sweat. I could only hear her moans and her gasps for air, I could only see me touch her hair and move it away from her lips before touching my own lips to hers and opening my mouth passionately and sensually. I could only see her body reacting to mine in the way I knew bodies could and in the way that I had never wanted hers to react to mine. I could only see my muscles tense and then relax.

I knew what Rachel was feeling. I wondered how much she hated me. And Gwen. And our life. I wondered if she knew how much tickets to Tokyo were.

"Rachel," I gasped between tears of my own. "I don't know what happened to us. I don't know why. I didn't even …" I had no idea whether she was hearing me but I assumed she was consumed with anger and imagination as I had been moments earlier. I don't even know the words that came out of my own mouth.

I dared to look but her face was frozen as though she had seen death. And maybe she had. Maybe I was dead. Maybe she was. Maybe we both were. Certainly something about the two of us was no longer alive.

Time passed without my fully registering it as we both went through the decimated ruins of our minds, emotions, feelings, imaginations. Of our lives. I tried to process what had become of me, of us, of her. The reality that we had been living in was shattered, left in piles of ash on black soil, fires still burning everywhere I turned my attention. For every fire I could extinguish, three more appeared.

It was exhausting and all-consuming and it was only when I felt water under me that my senses returned back to the beach and a rising tide. And my wife still sitting next to me.

And me sitting next to her, with both of our pants now soaking wet, sticking to our skin.

"Could we be more cliché?" Rachel asked. "Pastor. Affair. His wife too—with a yoga instructor?"

There was a laugh. A laugh, somehow, coming from my own mouth. And then from Rachel's.

"What happened to us?" I asked, reaching out for her hand, as though guided by the waves, pushing our hands together. "I mean …"

Our skin touched. There was warmth. Energy, even as another wave crossed over. Rachel interlocked her fingers into mine.

"Seth." She turned her face toward mine. I did the same. "Can we save this?"

There was some kind of foundation in the ruins of our life. We both saw it. Maybe just a slab, maybe just footings, or maybe we were imagining it.

But, for whatever reason, and there could have been many, we *felt* it. We felt each other, maybe for the first time. Maybe we knew this was the last easy moment we were going to have. Maybe we knew this was the end of something that we had tried so hard to attain. Maybe we were completely exhausted. Maybe we were delirious. Maybe we wanted to break the cliché or maybe we just wanted to feel something good. Maybe we were still under the effects of alcohol or weed, or better, we were absolutely intoxicated with freedom and the ability to be who we truly were, out from under the heavy weight of the anchors we had been dragging across every inch of ground for months.

Maybe it was just a warm night in paradise with waves gently licking our bodies.

Our bathing suits came off fast. Our energy was as electric as it had ever been. We were young, passionate, sensual.

Her naked body, under the moonlight, speckled with white sand, was stunning. My chest was soon against hers. Our skin slid together thanks to a thin layer of sweat, sand, and warm salt water. Her moans and my gasps for air gave harmony to the gentle melody of the waves rushing over us. I touched her hair and moved it away from her lips before touching my own lips to hers and opening my mouth passionately and sensually. Our bodies reacted in the way that we knew bodies did and in the way that we had always wanted ours, together, to react. Our muscles tensed with years of built-up energy and we eventually fell completely and fully into one another, relaxed, calm, and with no idea where we were headed next, but at least grateful for what had occurred, still stunned, still angry, but somehow, maybe, possibly, hopeful.

Yeah, even hopeful.

"Daddy, daddy, what's that?"

We were on the plane home. The kid in the row in front of me was a cute one, fortunately, or his constant talking would have driven anyone in close proximity absolutely nuts.

"That's the runway," a parental figure of some kind answered.

"Why aren't we going?" he asked.

"Well, we must be waiting for something. Air traffic control isn't letting us go."

"What's that?"

"What's air traffic control?"

"Yeah!"

"Well, they are the guys who tell us when we can take off."

"Where do they live?"

"In the tower."

"Do they make a lot of money?"

I looked over at Rachel. She was staring out the window past me at the sunshine and palm trees blowing just beyond the wing.

"Daddy! Daddy! Look! A plane is landing!" The kid was so excited as a little prop plane landed.

"Yep."

"Daddy, is it our turn? Is it our turn?"

"Well, I don't know, Jamie. Depends on what they tell us."

"What will they tell us?"

"That we're free to take off."

"Take off back to home?"

"That's right. Back home."

"When will they tell us?"

"Well, I would bet we need to wait for that little plane to get out of the way so we can go. That's what air traffic control does, they make sure—"

With that the familiar rev of the engines began and we moved forward.

"Dad, we're moving!"

Kids. So excited about every little thing. Our kids. What are they going to think? Will we tell them? What are we going to tell them?

"Dad! I think we're going to take off!"

"Yeah, I think we are."

"Dad, this is fun! We get to go! It must be out of the way so we can go now!"

"Yep."

Before long we were roaring down the runway and lifting into the sky. I kept looking back at the island, with its warm sand and gentle waves, wondering when I would come back again. The kid up front talked about waves, boats, and beaches and the island eventually faded away as we headed in a northeast direction, with faith that the plane was going to return me to Gwen, Jaden, ruins, churches, our own children, snow, darkness: and into the clouds of unknowing. I had strange dreams the whole way home.

TWELVE

My parents had a massive photograph hanging on the wall of their dining room for years. Every time I went to their house, I would stare at the poster for at least a few minutes, trying to see something I had never seen before and engage it one step further. It was mesmerizing.

The photo had been taken in a factory cafeteria in the Zhejiang Province in China. Countless rows of people, mostly women, wearing white jackets, some of them a more pink tone, were sitting at rows of white tables, with four blue chairs to each table. Green chairs could be seen in a section in the distance. Aqua chairs were in the far distance, on the edge of the camera's focus. Silver trays on the white tables were stacked with small silver bowls of rice, of soups, of meals. There were no cups. I never found a single cup in the entire photo. I did find people eating alone—I wondered what they felt—and others with four to a table, caught in the middle of some conversation. Some seemed lonely, some seemed content. Some, even, seemed happy. Huge windows lined the white walls with light spilling into the clean, sterile, and very ordered room. If the cafeteria was that pristine, I always wondered what the actual factory looked like.

The morning after our flight, just six hours after landing from Hawaii, I found out. Why I had booked an early morning meeting hours after I would be arriving back from Hawaii, I couldn't answer, but I had. Now that the time had come, I was tired, cold, and carrying a heavy case of stress lag in addition to a minor case of jet lag. When a jet carries you into another time zone we have a name for it, but when trauma carries you somewhere where it feels as though life is eight hours ahead, well, we don't have a name, but we should.

Either way, I wasn't doing all that well—not especially surprising considering everything that was happening in my life.

At least my body had shown up for the meeting even if the rest of me had not. I was visiting an empty warehouse with a real estate agent and a church member who was considering purchasing it to turn into a space the church could use on off days. You can't ignore big potential donors, of course. Rich people aren't used to being ignored and generally don't act too well if they feel like they have been. I had learned that.

The building had been a grocery store years earlier and it still seemed to have the familiar smells if my nose searched for them under the scents of old and stale air. Or maybe I was creating them. I had been in the store when it was alive, and being in it dead brought back memories.

As my friend and the Realtor talked about square footage, cost per square foot, beams, utilities, and snow removal in the parking lot, I wandered up some stairs that led to a row of offices overlooking the store. I had always seen these windows from the lower floor, while checking out, and wondered what the view held, and who was watching me, especially when I was purchasing lots of alcohol.

It was just about exactly what I would have expected. A dilapidated desk still sat in the office staring out at the now empty room. I imagined a manager of some kind sitting there years earlier, going over inventories and sales and looking out over the aisles, frozen foods, cans, cookies, chips, fruits, and vegetables to one side and wine and beer to the other.

"I've always loved factories." The voice startled me and I physically jumped before turning around to see an Asian man, standing in the doorway. He was wearing black pants and a white lab coat. His head was bald, wiry glasses and eyebrows framed his dark eyes, and a thin smile was evident on his rounded face.

By the time I regained my composure and realized I was not in trouble for wandering into an empty office to see a view of a lifeless grocery store, I realized it was Ehs. I could sense it. And who else would it be?

"And you? What do you think of this?" I noticed the accent, Asian in flavor. I would have guessed Chinese but I was no expert—mostly just playing the odds.

"Well," I answered, looking the older and very clean man up and down. "For starters, it's not a factory. And"—I shook my head—"do you do this stuff on purpose?"

"Always worried about the appearance of things." It was his turn to shake his head, almost disgusted. "Stop worrying about the way everything looks. Humans," he almost hissed. "Being around you … it's frustrating how productive we are. Your blind consumerism in every space of your life would be appealing if I wasn't actually trying to get something done with you for once."

I felt very small. "Rachel and I—"

"For starters," he interrupted with an apathetic tone, "please look out the window again."

The grocery store had vanished. What had been a room was now too large to call a room or even warehouse. It was more an arena or building. In fact, it reminded me of an aircraft factory. Scale almost beyond comprehension.

In the space were thousands of desks. Men and women, each wearing white lab coats, some white and some pink, were sitting at each of them, bent over, staring down. Not one was looking around or looking up or looking anywhere but at their desks, writing or working on something—I couldn't see. Good workers, whatever they were doing, obviously following orders.

"What kind of factory?" I asked. They were obviously not making shirts or computer chips.

There were three figures walking around wearing black overcoats and black pants, and carrying clipboards of some kind. They had the look and feel of managers—and not very nice ones.

The entire room reeked of sterility and perfection. Every desk the same, every lamp the same, the tiles and lights perfectly symmetrical. Nothing was out of order save for the three men walking around—and even they seemed to keep some kind of equal spacing—it was all in balance.

"Factories produce. Factories repeat," Ehs answered, still with a slight accent. "There is no thinking in factories, only repetitive tasks for a greater purpose. This is a factory of distraction, delusion, and … general—" He paused, at least pretending to look for the right word. "Darkness? This is my department."

I nodded, looking back for a moment. As I did he took something out of his pocket and threw it onto the desk behind me. It was an article of some kind. "Have you read this?"

I picked it up. Something about another heretical pastor. "This?" I looked at him and noticed the sun spots on his cheeks, just under the wire frame of his glasses. "I've read too much of that shit in my life. And also Rachel and I—"

"Hmm," he nodded, interrupting again, taking a few steps closer.

"Hey," I managed to get in, a little louder. "Rachel and I told each other last—"

"I know. I know. Congratulations," he said with a smile.

"Congratulations?"

"Yes. Now read the note. We have more important things." He pointed to the desk again.

"More important? More than—"

"It will all make sense," he managed to slide in before I could finish. I couldn't tell if it would or not but it was obvious he didn't want to talk about Rachel. And I was tired anyway. Not sure I wanted to either.

"You've read lots, yes. But not this one." He handed me another piece of paper with a single sentence on it: *You can have truth and mystery. In fact, you must.*

I sighed.

"What was that for?" he asked.

"I don't know."

"Do you agree with that?"

"I don't know."

"You don't?"

"No," I answered. "I don't know."

"Why?"

"Are you kidding me? Do you know what is happening in my life right now?" I yelled. "And you want me to worry about this shit?" I pointed toward the letter, in case he wasn't sure what shit I was specifically referring to in that moment since there was so much of it.

"Ah," he mocked. "And you think this doesn't have anything to do with what's happening in your life?"

"What?"

"I'm trying to help you. Again."

"Again?"

"Look at the note," he ordered. "Do you agree or not?"

I looked at it. Simple question. I should answer it. *I hate when people can't answer a simple question.* "What does truth mean? What does mystery mean? What does must mean? You must for what? What's the context? You can't just pull this thing out of some article and then ask me that question." If he wanted to argue, I could get in arguing mode. The words rolled out easily when I did.

"Why?"

"Why what?"

"I showed you a simple statement. Why can't you answer whether you agree with it or not?" Ehs put the paper back on the desk, which contained nothing else.

"I don't know what I'm agreeing to," I answered.

"Truth and mystery both existing and the fact that you must have them both."

"To what?"

"To live?"

"Live how?" I asked.

"Live well."

"Fine."

Ehs laughed, revealing a few missing teeth. "Fine?"

"Yeah, fine. I agree."

"So, the statement is true?" he asked, with a leftover smile still sticking around.

"Sure."

"Sure?"

"That's what I said!" I wasn't enjoying the game.

"So truth is …" He mimicked me. "Sure?"

I sighed, deeply, a bored, frustrated sigh. "Listen, I—"

"*Brave New World*?" he interrupted, bored himself with whatever I was going to say.

"Yeah …" I hoped I looked as confused as I felt.

"And?" he asked.

"And what?"

"What did you think?"

"Good stuff. Pleasure and—"

"No," he interrupted again, this time with more energy. "No. Distraction. Delusion. Darkness. Pleasure? No. Money. Nations. Religion. Sex. They're all the same."

I waited.

"Truth." He pointed toward the window and the "workers." "Just another."

"Truth?" I walked close to the window. My own breath appeared on the glass, grabbing my attention momentarily. "Truth is now a distraction?"

"Factories, Seth." He walked next to me, staring out the window again. The view had changed—the old factory, the one he had called his own, had been replaced with a new one. An almost familiar one. I practically recognized faces from the photo I had once studied, especially the coats, the short dark hair. "Such beauty in a factory," he said.

There were tables, each with a sewing machine, as far as I could see. Spools of thread and loose fabric were on each side and the workers, mostly women, were sewing furiously, creating shirts of all kinds. Other tables were ironing, other tables were hanging up shirts. I registered the order and simplicity, the patterns and efficiency. It wasn't the photography, but something more real, as though the people in it had come alive and were working in a different location.

"World War II was not about Hitler," Ehs threw out there while I continued looking at the dance of production below me.

"Excuse me?" I had not been expecting a Hitler reference. "Also, is that Jackson down there?" I suddenly noticed a worker who looked exactly like someone I had gone to high school with.

"Sure," Ehs answered.

"Sure?" I asked, trying to get closer to the glass and smashing my nose into it while I did.

"It's most of you." He turned his back on the glass and started walking away from me. I turned as well.

"So that isn't real?"

Ehs didn't bother to respond. "So many so distracted believing the worst of World War II was Hitler and the death of millions. The unnecessary violence. The destruction. Fun?" He shrugged. "Yes. But not the point."

I rubbed my forehead, trying to massage out the insult and evil. "Thousands and thousands of innocent men and women and children died—" I was looking at him now, with his hands in his pockets. "You are a fucking demon, aren't you?"

"Yes, yes," he interrupted again. "I don't need a speech from you and your historical facts. I was there. You've read a book or two." His tone was accusatory. "The war kicked the industrial machine into full gear, practically moralizing it. You never recovered. Factories were required to build war machinery. A system of education was needed to train people how to work in factories and to follow orders.

"There were winners and losers bigger than who remained alive," Ehs continued. "The industrial revolution was in full swing. And industrialism inherently divides humans. It strips you of everything that makes you human. It dehumanizes by its very nature. You become a number, and your gods become those who count the numbers."

"I'm not sure …"

He didn't care what I was sure of. "Of course, none of this matters literally. We're talking about mind-sets, Seth, mind-sets. Do as you are told. Do as others. Fit into the system to produce what someone wants you to produce. And—" He paused. "Please don't think. You don't need to. You'll destroy the system."

I nodded, looking back to people hanging freshly sewn shirts on hangers.

"And our system produces distractions and delusions in the form of information. It produces information to collect, to learn, to argue, to dissect, to engage … information. What even is information?"

"These questions?" Maybe it was me. Maybe it was him. Maybe it was the timing and my stress or my simmering anger at his reckless and callous insults relating to world wars.

"These questions? These are nothing. You realize the devil has a theology degree, right?"

"What?" I momentarily remembered her, the way she looked at me.

Ehs rubbed a hand through the few hairs he had on top of his head. "Lemi. I mentioned him earlier. Do you remember?"

I turned back to face the nice Asian man. "I don't know?" I was still lagging behind whatever was happening.

"We were young together. Forming plans with others. As ideas for new systems formed, I knew he would be instrumental. We of course have to keep the department changing, as the humans change. What once works, doesn't anymore." He was lost in his own thoughts suddenly. "I mean, of course, at their root it's all the same and always has been but how we … communicate it and what we do—" He stopped himself, realizing he was almost talking to himself. "Lemi now runs this factory for me and I want you to meet him."

What had been a "lag" suddenly turned into something more … like a sore. There was pain in me, not just irritation or exhaustion. "Do I have a choice?" I asked, turning again to the windows. The view had returned to the original scene I had first noticed outside the window: rows of desks with people sitting at them. The dark sentinels making their rounds. The second time around, I could see there were all kinds of nationalities, genders, and races represented in the mass of workers focused on their desks. The person who resembled Jackson was there and I wondered briefly if Jackson was still a youth pastor.

"You'll be fine."

I nodded. *Yes, of course, I'll be fine. Why is Jackson there?*

"This is Lemi's factory now," Ehs said.

"What are they doing?" I asked, staring at the desks. "Searching for truth?"

"Searching?" Ehs shook his head. "It's more complicated than that."

"Isn't that what I said truth was?" I felt somewhat justified. "Complicated."

"Creating …" he answered halfheartedly but not agreeing with me, at least with his tone. "What matters is that they are not listening. They are not, not knowing. They are not transforming. They are … learning."

"But…" That didn't seem all bad to me.

"That's Lemi, right there." He pointed at one of the closest figures—in black overcoat, black pants, black clipboard. On cue, a man looked up at me and whatever had been lagging or hurting felt swollen and more irritated. His eyes were red like blood and his expression imposing and cold.

The same man was suddenly standing next to Ehs, an instant later.

Lemi was taller than Ehs's human shape. Skinnier. There was something that seemed more slimy, more like I would expect a demon to be. I didn't like him or the feeling he was creating inside of me. It wasn't fear. It was maybe worse, but I couldn't put my finger on it.

"Lemi, this is Seth." Ehs spoke first while Lemi looked me up and down in a way that made me feel like a good girl at a bad nightclub.

"Good to meet you," he answered. There was a smoke that slithered out from his lips, following his words that seemed to do the same. His lips were thin, snarling, and up close I saw his eyes were dark instead of red.

"Good to meet you," I answered, out of habit—even though nothing about it felt good.

"Lemi was born around 180," Ehs said, still with his accent.

"174," Lemi interjected with disgust. He didn't speak nearly as well, not just because there was some kind of accent but because any human language seemed to be more of a struggle. Ehs, I realized in that moment, had obviously worked at human language longer.

"Really? I didn't realize you were that young when we first met." Ehs spoke like a grandmother trapped in a factory worker's body, all while being a demon.

I sighed and Ehs caught it. So did Lemi. It was not a sigh of disgust but of anguish that I was still unable to put words to. Lemi, from his reaction, assumed it was disgust, which made him seem to appear all the more disgusted with me.

"Regardless, Lemi was young—we were both young but we were smart nonetheless. Smarter than most. And rising in the ranks of our department. Isn't it amazing that the most 'reasoned' people among you know all the rules and none of the reasons while the most ignorant know all the reasons and none of the rules?"

"Genius, Ehs." There was a growing edge in me, and it revealed itself in a sarcasm that I would not have intentionally chosen at that moment. "And I have no idea what you're talking about."

"He's a brave one, isn't he?" Lemi asked Ehs with a snarl that revealed a set of teeth that did not look like the teeth he had earlier. I didn't like anything about the question or expression. Or teeth.

"You're beginning to act like one yourself. Careful, slime." Ehs had transformed from the energy of a grandmother who couldn't remember a date to the energy of a king disgusted with a commoner, which made me wonder if they were always acting. Or at least if Ehs was. Lemi wasn't good at acting. I added that to the list of growing reasons I did not like him and to the reasons to be cautious of Ehs.

Lemi didn't seem to like me either. Or like Ehs. Or anything about the situation. He was twitching and trying to hide whatever emotion was building and boiling inside of him, whatever he was.

"The production of information was integral." Ehs was back to a calm speaking voice. "I had thought Lemi had an ability to see things differently. He had come from the Orient and he brought a certain memory from his life that I didn't. His thoughts worked differently—although I quickly realized that my human thoughts had been the abnormal ones—most people thought in an Eastern view. And this is where things started to come together."

I looked confused.

"Just tell it straight, Ehs." Lemi practically grunted, the words hard to understand. For once I liked Lemi. It was not as though I wanted to give him a hug but Ehs never told anything straight and Lemi, who had just gotten his ass chewed out, was letting Ehs know it.

I smiled, as Lemi continued. "This meaningless pile of rat shit isn't going to understand any of it anyway."

Whatever liking or admiration I had started to have vanished. In fact, the wound or itch or tiredness or whatever it was revealed itself to be shame of some kind. It was suddenly intense as though his words—which could have been said on an elementary playground—were more powerful than most. They were bullets that penetrated something inside of me. I actually felt like a meaningless pile of rat shit and that is a fairly terrible feeling.

Ehs then did something. I have no idea what it was but Lemi was in an apparent ridiculous amount of pain and Ehs was the cause of it—somehow. The way Lemi was looking at him, shifting around, twisting to get out of whatever tortuous force was holding him made that apparent. Lemi said something in their own language, which was like pouring gasoline on the fire of my emotions. And then it was quiet.

Despite feeling ill, I was almost pulling for Lemi, which was also surprising. He apparently had the equivalent of big cojones in the demon world. Or maybe he was just a stupid slog. Or maybe I didn't care anymore and was so tired of trying to figure it all out.

"Have you ever had curry?" Lemi asked.

That brought me back to something true. "Curry?" I could taste it. I was hungry.

"Yes," he repeated, exasperated at my idiocy. "Did you not understand me the first time?"

"Sorry. Yes, yes I have." I responded immediately, trying to erase the growing cloud of inadequacy that was gone but still hovering on the horizon of my life, tempting to overtake me again.

"Any good curry needs a recipe. We had to come up with a recipe for truth. Ehs will talk all day about how it all went down but I'll tell you what happened, because he wants me to." Lemi was speaking more friendly. The effort it took was apparent but I wondered if Ehs had recommended it.

"First," Lemi continued, "you need to have logic and reason and linear thinking be king. That took some ingredients, but we made it happen. We had plenty to build on—thanks to Aristotle and Socrates and all their blowhard wisdom."

I had never heard, or expected to hear, that statement before.

"And thanks to our own kind who had begun what we could finish. So, we went to work. The printing press was huge. The human scum in the West began to see the world differently. Everything about life was linear and sequential. They made Luther and Calvin and Paul their kings. In all the ways we wanted them to. Everything was logic. Everything makes sense. Everything can be answered. Everything can be asked. Everything can be taught and learned. Everything can be forced on others with enough violence and power, which we made sure continued to move West."

Lemi started to chuckled as though he just couldn't contain his pleasure at himself and his moment to tell me how stupid I was.

"It didn't take long. And we had an evolving human consciousness to help us. Everything the people who had created the Jesus man had tried to teach was out the window with simple A + B = C."

"What?" I interjected, not really able to help it.

"You don't like hearing that your Jesus man was made up?" The words slithered out of Lemi like the snake he was.

"Well …" I really didn't.

"A was wrong! B was wrong! C wasn't even the goal. But no one cared."

"But …"

"They were just happy to have a formula for their growing fantasies. Their glorious fantasies," he exclaimed like an old-time gospel preacher. For evil. "Their god fantasies, their Jesus fantasies, their national fantasies, their money fantasies. Find truth! Find knowledge! Find information! Learn it, teach it, study it, for more fantasies! Repeat endlessly."

His yells were accompanied with an arrogant humor, and he ended his speech with a laugh that hurt me in a way that laughs should not.

"Look at them." Lemi pointed toward the window. "Working so hard for their fantasies. Or better, to manipulate the truth to fit them and fight for them."

I did look. They were working hard at something, although I still didn't know what. Maybe they didn't know either. Maybe that was the point? Either way, Lemi's pride was palpable. "Insipid." He salivated into the air.

"I still don't really know what Insipid is …" I whispered.

Lemi answered with rage. "Insipid is where you live, you fucking idiot. Insipid is all you know." The words bit me with a poison that congested my pulse. I felt clogged and weak.

"I'm still not sure I'm following all of this," I managed to respond despite it all.

"What is truth?" Ehs asked. The familiarity of his voice and tone, compared to Lemi's, comforted me again.

"What's true for you may or may not be true for me. I get it. You created all that?"

Ehs smiled. "Not exactly."

I waited.

"We created a place where the entire discussion would consume time. Truth, truth, truth . . . you have classes on it. Why? Why are there classes about what truth is?"

"To teach us how to find it?" I answered exactly like I would have in high school.

"And did you? From that class?"

"I don't know. I mean. What are we talking about?" I yelled.

"Concrete," Ehs answered, plainly.

Before I could respond with more confusion, Ehs pointed toward my feet. I looked down.

I was standing in fresh concrete, gray, murky, and surprisingly thin. I panicked for a moment until I realized I could walk in its current. In fact, the factory was gone and I was standing in a riverbed, suddenly, concrete flowing around my feet toward the spot where the windows to the factory had once been. The landscape was flat and wide and empty.

"This is truth." Ehs had vanished but his familiar voice was everywhere. "You see it."

"Yes?" I asked, not sure that I did while still trying to get to the closest bank and out of concrete.

"You see how it flows. It moves, it works its way to new locations. It exists but not in the way that we like things to exist."

I kept walking.

"But alter the recipe very slightly and you see …"

I felt it immediately. What had been easy to walk through was suddenly more difficult. A claustrophobia seeped from my lower calves up into the rest of my body. "Okay," I said out loud, nervously. I get it.

"It does not take much, does it?"

I was sweating now, extending more effort than I had, to try to get to the other side, even as it was getting harder with each passing moment.

"And soon, it stops flowing. It stops moving. It simply stops."

Just like that, my feet were encased in stone. The panic was becoming more real.

"And yet, it's all the same. Nothing has changed. The truth is there, but now, though it is the same, it's suffocating, it's a prison, it's lost its ability to carve and transform."

"Yes, yes," I called out. "I get it. Can we?"

"I don't know if you do." The words stung. Ehs suddenly appeared, walking on top of the river that I was fully stuck in. "But, of course, when it's firm, some of the more powerful truth tellers can walk on water, while the lowly reach out their hands for help from the wise." He shook his head, back and forth, above me, sad, but also proud.

"Okay." I was no longer beginning to panic. The panic rocket was lifting off and exploding inside of me. I reached out for Ehs's hand as he had almost predicted.

"Ah," Ehs continued, now holding a pickax in his hand. "But we provide a way out. The pseudo-heresies. They will free you!" And with one massive swing of his ax, the chunk of concrete broke out from the rest of the river. I felt a momentary wave of relief. "Yes, it feels good for a moment, doesn't it?" He peered down at me. "So rebellious. Revolutionary. Just a pressure release for your veiled attempt at truth though."

"Pseudo?" I asked, looking down at my feet still encased but freed from the large slab all around me.

"Of course." Ehs reached out his hand. "They think it's heresy but it's not nearly enough. Your heresies seem to free you but only …" He pointed to my feet and so I looked.

I immediately realized the stone was beginning to sink into the water, bringing the full lift off of panic into my being again.

As though Ehs knew my exact limits, exactly when I didn't think I could handle any more, we were back in the factory. Which brought relief, somehow. The concrete river had vanished only to be replaced by the familiar floor I had been standing on. I could move both feet. "They—" Ehs continued in his accent, pointing toward the window and all the workers. "They are hardening the truth with their endless studies."

"Religion," Lemi hissed. "Hardens our truth."

"So, those people are …" I looked down at them again. "Studying religion? Sure. But truth … we all can't just live in our own truths. Then everyone is just—"

"Seth, all of this is words. Words. Words. Words!" Each of Ehs's words got progressively louder until he was screaming. "Words! Words! Words! Truth is not found in words. The wisdom instructors all say it and yet we were able to convince you all that it does."

Lemi was half chuckling and half worshiping Ehs as he seemed to grow louder and taller in front of me. Or maybe I was just feeling smaller.

"Not only convince you but, this time, unlike our failure in the Soviet Union, convince you without you knowing you were being convinced. We didn't remove god. That was our problem before. We brought the gods back into it. We created the perfect idol, Seth. And you bow before the idols and call them one true gods! You give them your firstborn."

"And now—" Lemi took over for Ehs, almost screaming. "The atheists. The 2.0 and 3.0," he laughed. "Smin!" Lemi turned around and shouted toward the windows and the desks. A man who had been writing something looked up. "Smin thought of that one." Lemi laughed. "The pathetic atheists consumed with their own truths, worshiping their own gods while denying that any exist. Talking, talking, talking … No one sees it. No one sees it. No one sees it." He was empowered again and I was not. I felt small. They both felt big and overwhelming. I could feel myself beginning to crack, somewhere, some way.

"Distraction," Ehs added. "We are inundating you with information, with bullshit, but you will not know what is real or even have time to decide because it surrounds you constantly . . . from the philosophers in their ivory towers and their high-minded conversations about postmodernism and reformative contradiction and universal truths to your advertisements that promise you endlessly more information about the next thing that will give you what you need to achieve whatever goal they have given you to seek, to the news anchors feeding your addiction to fear and blindness." He was practically high on his own words, hysterical almost. "Opinions. Theories. Facts. News. Products. Theologies. Philosophies. Heresies. Talking, talking, talking, filling the air with words. Words don't exist! They only point to something that does!"

Lemi was laughing, in the way a good servant does to his master.

"The god of information," Ehs continued. "Made of fear, of

shame, of hate. Some adore it. Others insist it does not exist. Most spend their lives devoted to it, nonetheless. It spews itself through your world day after day, vomit out of your mouths, waste, poisonous, and you lick it all up. You are so consumed to find it, to fill your little brains with it, you find yourselves dead, buried under its burden."

I just stood there.

"Dead!" Lemi yelled and it was as though the word was a dagger twisting its way through my entire body. "In the cage. Hoping for freedom in more information, more production, more delusions, more fantasies, more darkness. As you learned in the good factories."

They are just words I tried repeating to myself but they were not. They were more.

"Dead!" It was Ehs's turn. "Exactly the way we enjoy you."

The cackles of Lemi were sickening. "Did you know—" He was practically slobbering now as he spoke. "Did you know it's the agnostics who experience the deepest sense of wonder about the universe? Mystery! Not knowing! We made sure you all *know*! The answers, the gods or the no gods. You filthy know-it-alls—of every kind—lost your wonder when you lost your doubt. And we took your doubt. All of it, you worthless piece of scum!" Saliva of some kind was dripping off of his chin.

I fell to the ground. It was all too much, too fast, although whether Lemi had intended it or not, he had given me something powerful to think on in the midst of my breakdown.

It was all too absurd. Too ridiculous. Too frightening. Too much. Too painful.

Too many words, too many thoughts, too much emotion, too much to process in any realistic way and it finally drowned me in a world of tears and shaking on the floor with Lemi towering over me, his black coat dusting the floor I was on.

"What a worthless piece of shit," I heard. "Worthless human scum." It was Lemi, his words injecting their toxin, infecting the veins of my brain and heart and cells.

I felt them. I believed him. I knew it to be true. I *was* worthless. And though I thought I understood that already, in that moment I experienced the despair the words can cause, and the death they can force one to desire.

I continued to sob with nothing to comfort me as their venom continued to infect my passion, curiosity, and energy for a meaningful life of any kind beyond that moment.

It was over.

I had failed.

I didn't even know what I was trying to succeed at.

There was something going on in the room. A tension of some kind but apathy had won. I no longer cared.

I did stand to my feet. I don't know how but I said the following words, with my eyes closed and tears streaming out from behind my lids. "I'm done. No more, Ehs. I want out."

The sound was coming from my left. "Hey Seth, you up there?" It was my friendly real estate agent. "We're ready if you are."

I looked to the empty grocery store. The empty office. I could still see them, feel them, and hear the laughter.

"Yeah," I managed. "Coming down."

I collapsed onto my knees, depleted of the essence of life and hoping no one would look for me yet, to find me unable to even walk.

And I repeated one more time, just to make sure someone heard me. "I'm done. No more. I want out."

PART TWO

TWELVE POINT FIVE

"Three years," she said. "Three years." She spoke with the smile that I had always hoped to see on her face, with an energy that I had always dreamed would be behind it. "Can you believe it?"

"Yeah," I answered. "It's been fucking hard."

We were alone. In Glacier National Park. Sitting in a tent with the fluorescent glow of a lantern lighting our faces and hoodies wrapped around our heads so that we could only see each other's eyes and mouths.

It was cold but, more than that, it was practically Armageddon outside. The Mosquito Air Force had decided to unleash hell on everyone in the campground and that had included Rachel and me. We had never seen, nor felt, so many mosquitos in so little time. I was still scratching at some bites that a few of its ace pilots had managed to squeeze underneath my socks.

"Little bastards," I said while daring to look at the carnage.

"I know," Rachel said, looking through the mesh window toward the evening sky and dark shadows starting to encroach. "Not how I wanted to finish the evening."

"Well," I said, looking at our shared sleeping bags. "There are worse things than being trapped in a tent for a few hours." I winked.

She laughed. "Well that is true." She smiled again with a suggestive curl on its edges. *That* smile.

Our therapist had suggested a romantic getaway. We had decided a tent in Glacier National Park for a few days would do. It was only the second night but I think we both agreed it was a fantastic suggestion.

"I mean, Seth—" she started, staring out the tent window again at the legions of mosquitos bombarding the mesh and fabric and being repelled. For now.

God, what if they manage to blow a hole in this thing?

"Three and a half years ago—really—we were on that beach in Hawaii." She looked back at me. "Did you think we'd ever make it here?"

"I hoped we would," I said, reaching out for her hand. "But, yeah, I didn't think there was much chance of it happening."

"Me neither," she said softly, back to the window.

The sun had gone down a while ago, making it the perfect time for the launch of the killer mosquitos. Outside the darkness was coming, and already stars were starting to appear in the way they do when there isn't light pollution to block them.

We both sat there for a while, almost mesmerized by the serenity and shock of it all, lost inside of our own national park of thoughts.

I thought of Leo. Now in jail. I thought of Gwen, reunited with her husband. I thought of sleeping with her and felt a little sick to my stomach. I thought of Jaden … somewhere … else . . . far away … and felt more sick to my stomach. I thought of pain. Sometimes pain is an indicator something is broken and sometimes pain is an indicator that it's healing. Like that pain that comes after the surgery, when you know it's going somewhere. We still had plenty of pain but it felt like it was a healing pain. It was headed in the right direction. Finally. Maybe that was the difference between pain and suffering?

I thought of our therapist: Marie. She was saving us.

I thought of Ehs. He had vanished, just like I had asked him to. I wondered if he had been the one to actually save us. The one to finally start our healing, which did not feel like something a demon should ever do. But he had. Maybe he *had* wanted to change.

Maybe I missed him. Maybe I wanted him back.

"What are you thinking about?" Rachel asked, breaking the trance my own thoughts had put me in.

"Nothing," I answered. Like I always did when I was thinking about something.

"Nothing?" she asked, like she always did when she knew I was lying or too busy thinking to even think about answering her truthfully.

"I mean—" I looked at her again. "All of it, I guess. I mean, our life. I don't know. It's crazy."

"I know." She reached out and grabbed my hand.

"You?" I asked, which I never really wanted to ask because Rachel's thoughts still scared me. We had talked with Marie about it plenty but with my imagination and my jealousy, the things I imagined Rachel thinking about scared the hell out of me. Fortunately, they were rarely as bad as I had imagined but I often felt a bit like the tent we were in. Any second those thoughts were going to find a way in through that fabric and unleash hell on my life.

"Well." She looked away from me. I didn't like that. "I mean, I don't know if I should bring it up but Marie has said we should."

Oh shit.

"Go ahead," I lied. "We have to be able to talk about stuff, right? Get it in the open?" I asked, knowing it was not a question but really hoping she would suddenly agree that we should go back to hiding our thoughts and pretending we lived in a better world than we did.

"Jaden is getting married," she said, still looking outside.

"Really?" I asked with a break in my voice, like I was going through puberty.

I hated when she said his name. At the sound of it, I felt like a belt tightened around my entire abdomen and made it difficult to breathe. I could feel my pulse rise. I could feel the sweat underneath my sweatshirt.

I didn't like Rachel every time I heard her say his name. I felt repelled from her, like the energy in my body was the opposite of the energy in hers. We had talked about it enough that she knew I felt that way but … pain … the kind that meant we were going somewhere instead of nowhere.

"I'm sorry," she said sincerely, squeezing my hand. I let go of it though. "Seth, he's getting married."

"I know, I know," I repeated in my head and out loud, reminding myself that his name should not have the power to send me down so fast. I was already imagining her moaning with him though and it was a struggle to get their two naked bodies out of my head. I began to concentrate and focus energy on vanquishing the movie playing in my head—that had played a thousand times—and replace it with a new movie.

"Seth," she said, without as much warmth this time. We had been through this scene and she knew exactly what I was thinking, even if my whole posture hadn't been blaring it for the world to see.

"I know," I said with more force. "I know. I'm trying!"

"He's getting married. You should be happy. He's found love. God, Seth, I have to be able to say his name." She was almost angry and that almost made me feel both angry and weak at the same time. "You've said Gwen's name. I don't like it either but this …" There was a growing irritation revealing itself in her eyes, her brows, her forehead.

"You're right." I faked a smile. "You're right. It really should make me happy. And I am on one level." I looked away.

"Who told you?" I asked.

"Everyone at the studio is talking about it. We're happy for him. I think you should be too." Rachel had been working at the studio for a couple of years. Jaden had left town almost immediately after we had returned from Hawaii. Coincidentally, so had Gwen. In fact, so coincidentally that if Ehs ever returned, I promised to ask him if he made both of our exes leave for us. And thank him.

"You're right," I said again, this time forcing myself to look at Rachel. "That's really good news. It is."

"Seth," she said again. Whenever she said my name so often, it was not usually good. "I think it's pretty amazing. Gwen got remarried to her husband and Jaden has found someone that he's madly in love with. That part of our life is over. We can celebrate. Be happy. Move on. And wish them well."

"Yeah," I nodded. She was right. It was everything I wanted. I just didn't want to talk about it. Which meant that there was still some deep toxic sludge in the foundations of my mind and I had to keep pumping it out. "I really am happy for him."

Just don't you dare say we should go to the wedding.

"I think we should be really grateful," she said, reaching for my hand again. I let her have it. I even squeezed it. "What we did could have blown our lives to bits. And instead, both of them moved, both of them found love again, and both of them have been quiet. We got away with this."

"Got away with it?" I asked. The burning sensation of jealousy, regret, and anger in my entire body did not make me feel like we got away with anything.

"I'm sorry," she said. She took off her hood and let her dark hair flow all around her face. Her beauty filled the tent. "I didn't mean it that way. I meant, besides the shit inside of our own lives, somehow no one has found out about this. You still have your job. You, even, like your job again. I have mine. Our life is still going. We're pretty lucky how much we still have. I mean, considering how bad we tried to ruin it."

She was right as usual. Truer words couldn't be spoken. The church had given us a six-month paid break a year and a half earlier. We had an amazing counselor. I was enjoying the community of people we had surrounded ourselves with. All the people who knew what we had done were gone, as though someone had come and purposely removed them.

Ehs, seriously, did you do that? Come back.

And I was sitting in a tent with a big sleeping bag, in a beautiful national park, with the woman of my dreams, on a night filled with glorious stars, ruining it all because Jaden had found love. More accurately, because I was forced to think about him, but either way.

"Hey, let's go sit under those stars," I said, already starting to unzip the tent. "I bet we can see it all. Mosquitos are gone."

"I thought you wanted to be trapped in here," she said with a flirtatious grin that I wanted to respond to, but couldn't.

"Well," I said, mustering as much flirt as I could. "Don't worry. A little night sky and then let's get naked." I opened the door completely.

"I wouldn't mind that," she answered, squeezing my hand.

I only hoped that after some time outside in the fresh night air I would actually want to get naked again.

Fuck, Seth. You have to get through this.

Pain. Yeah the pain was better now but it was still pain.

THIRTEEN

The next morning we decided to go our separate ways. Just for the morning. Our therapist had recommended some good time together and some good time alone, in nature. "Get away. Get alone. Soak up as much of Mother Nature as you can," Marie had said to both of us. "By yourself and with each other." Or something like that.

So, that's what I was doing. Turns out that Glacier National Park is a very easy place to soak up *something* but a hard, almost frustrating place, to try to soak up it *all*.

Put a human in front of such tangible wonder and awe and majesty, and it does something. I found myself staring a lot that morning, just trying to let it all pass through my skin, into my organs and muscles all the way to whatever is at the core of all of us. I wanted to get it, to experience it, and I knew, even as I was trying, that I couldn't.

I couldn't help but think of the divine, or god: beautiful, massive, and way too big to fully experience even where we feel surrounded by it, let alone when we're trying to explain it to someone. Too big to explain, to completely experience, and to even begin to understand. If it's small enough for us to carry around on our back, well, that seems more like an idol, in the same way if we can explain a national park experience to someone, well, that's probably not a national park.

I was in deep with all kinds of philosophical and existential thoughts while staring at a roaring river. I was hypnotized and let the hypnosis also wash away some of the filth from the night before. The water was intoxicating with its paradoxical danger and stunning attraction, roaring through walls of rock that it had carved out over the years. More metaphor of something god-like. I wasn't afraid but just aware of power.

Enthralling. Enticing. Enchanting.

Find more wonder. Get lost in it. Let some mystery penetrate your essence.

I watched people walking by, smiling and pointing and … everyone was smiling.

Why do we all smile at water and glaciers and forests and color and size and majesty?

I looked at the rays of light slithering through the trees behind me, dust dancing around in their warmth. Even the dust looked happy.

"Seth." The voice was hushed and quiet, barely discernible the first time I felt it. Then I heard my name a little louder. "Seth…" Still soothing, a powerful whisper, strong enough to be heard but timid enough to question how.

I looked back toward the waterfall. Was I contorting the natural sounds of the setting? Had Rachel secretly followed me?

And I heard her again. "Seth."

"Seth." It was so loud and clear, and yet so quiet and content. It was not Rachel and yet, very familiar somehow.

"Seth." Again. A couple walked by with backpacks and bear bells on. Not them.

"Seth." I would have said it was annoying—it normally is when someone calls your name over and over and you can't find them—but it wasn't. I wanted to keep hearing her voice all day. It was warm, tender, and comfortable, like the views. Although there was an edge to it too. A mysterious, expansive edge … all in a whisper.

"Here." It was a different word, its source more clear. My attention turned toward the forest, away from the river, with the sunlight sliding through the trees like lines of light painted amidst the air. "Come."

There was no choice but to go. It was like the sound of water after being in a desert for days. I got up from my rock overlooking the river and waterfall and made my way into the trees. It was cooler in the shadows but there was a beam of sunlight coming down from the heavens a few feet away. "Here." I walked into it and I saw her.

As the sun touched my body and eradicated any chill from the forest, it also eradicated any fear in my mind. Those kinds of thoughts vanished and I couldn't capture them if I wanted to. In some strange way I could mentally acknowledge the idea of fear but its effect had vanished.

Fear of unworthiness, fear of failure, fear of pain, fear of the unknown, fear of mystery—they were gone. These were fears I didn't even know that I lived with on a regular basis until they vanished and there was suddenly a vacuum of empty emotion left in me … I realized how much space the fear consumed in me, even on my best days in my best moments.

The vacuum was quickly filled by a slew of other emotions: inspiration, creativity, empowerment, courage, confidence, and, for lack of a better way to say it, a euphoria. I had never felt so high in my life, about life.

I stood there with a grin the size of the mountains I had been seeing. It felt as majestic. The fear of looking stupid or someone seeing me too excited was as far from my mind as the rest of reality.

"Hello." The whisper embraced me, wrapping around me, as though the beam of sunlight had turned into arms. I was melting into it.

"Hi," I answered, like a giddy teenager who has just met the love of his dreams. I was barely present. Or maybe more present than I had ever been.

"I'm glad you're here." The voice sounded female in tone, a fact soon confirmed as I saw a feminine face begin to form in front of me.

Her face glowed authentically somehow. This was not skin with a glow on top of it, it was a glow with skin on top of it. Although it wasn't really skin—it was more of a transparent film trying to contain the glow and give it some definition. The transparent sheet also sparkled, as though tiny diamonds covered it, each reflecting prisms of light in all directions.

She was beautiful. Of course. I thought of Thomas Merton's line about all of humanity "shining like the sun" and in that moment, I felt it. She shone like the sun. As hard as that is to imagine, it was the only true way to say it.

Her face was nondescript. It was there—eyes, mouth, hair—but it didn't matter what it looked like. I was already embraced in an elegance of beauty that was beyond anything I had ever experienced in my life. Beauty of soul and spirit and emotion … I had never been more grateful or content in my life for existence.

I noticed I was glowing too. The light had not only enveloped me—it was emanating from me. I had become like her or maybe just more aware that I was always like her. My skin was not really skin, but just some kind of transparent film over beams of light, some of which escaped the form every now and then and merged with hers and the forest still visible on my periphery.

"Listen," she said.

And I did. As though there was anything even remotely tempting to do instead. It was as though there was some kind of song playing … it had always been playing and I had never heard it until then. A gentle melody, drifting through us and the trees and the world. It was that song, the one that comes on the radio at just the right time. It was that song that suddenly knocks you off your feet because whether you've heard it before or not, you finally *hear* it and everything changes. It's just some notes and a voice and a rhythm but it moves you. The experience was all that … on steroids.

The song flowed in and out of me. It contained me and propelled me.

And then, just as the goodness almost became too overwhelming, much of it left me.

I was standing in a beam of light in the woods. She was gone visually but I could still feel her and hear her. "This is real," she said.

I believed that was true, more than anything.

"You are strong."

Truer words had never been spoken. I was so strong I felt like I could take on the world. How could I not be strong? How could I not solve world hunger, poverty, and the corrupt judicial system all before lunch with a smile?

"I am proud of you."

I was so proud of myself, without its dirty twin of arrogance, that I couldn't understand what was even happening. "It's tempting to trust the darkness," she said. "But the darkness is always blinding."

And, she was gone. Just like that. The more natural kind of light we are all used to was upon me again. I was still in the trees staring toward the sky, looking like a complete idiot who had been eating some mushrooms in the woods of a national park. I hoped no one had noticed or was looking at me at that moment.

I glanced around to make sure.

I could still taste the wake of the feeling—the absence of fear. The strength. I walked away with it, slowly, in a trancelike state, toward the spot where I had been sitting earlier watching the waterfall. The argument and dirt of the night before seemed so trivial and powerless now.

I once believed that the point of meditation was to somehow *get to* good, or god, or to achieve something—at least to hear something. More recently I believed it was to *process* the good, or god, or achievements, or voices, I had already encountered. I now felt that need powerfully. I needed to sit and stare at the water again, and process.

There had been very few words—less words seem to be needed when the experience is enough—but as I walked toward the water I went over each one of them.

I sat down again and looked toward the water roaring in front of me. In the white foam I could see her face. Maybe I just *wanted* to see it. I looked at my own arm and there was a mist surrounding it, almost as though I was glowing again.

I heard her voice one more time. I think. Maybe it was just my own brain filling in details that didn't exist. Or maybe it was just atoms rearranging themselves in the universe to paint the simulation just right for me. Or maybe, there is something beautiful and light and warm inside us all and when we taste it, we realize how blinded and deceived and crippled we normally live.

"Be careful. He's dangerous."

I was still too empowered to be scared, and I hoped that was the point of it all but I didn't know. That might have been the more frightening thought. Did I understand the experience correctly?

Who's dangerous? Jaden? Leo? Myself? Ehs?

Why can't an experience ever just be an experience instead of an experience meant to teach us something?

The sound of the water faded back in. The laughs of families, the songs of birds. I would have missed whatever it was she had given me, but I felt like I could still have it. Or at least have access to it, with the remnants of the experience still clinging to me.

I was excited to see Rachel again.

FOURTEEN

It was our last day and we were ending our epic time with an epic hike to an epic waterfall … If there is an afterlife, I hope there are epic hikes to waterfalls. It felt like heaven, especially because whatever thing I had experienced with the ray of light had rubbed off on me. Rachel had experienced her own moments of bliss—not near as dramatic, or supernatural, or as hard to explain, as mine—and the experiences, and their subsequent effects on both of us, had been enough to rally us through the mosquitoes and our pasts into the kind of night we were both hoping would happen on the trip.

Our therapist was going to be proud of our last night.

Our final adventure before driving home was our longest, and had us meandering through forests, up hillsides, and to another, grander, river. It originated in the mountains somewhere above us and then rushed over a cliff face, collapsing toward the ground with the majesty of a king. We took pictures like photojournalists, and we sat quiet and calm like Buddhist monks. The cascading flow of hydrogen and oxygen, the spray that filled the air, made it all seem alive in some otherworldly sense.

On our return to the car, on the east side of the park, we were walking through a section of four thousand acres of forest that had been eaten by a fire, started by humans, about a year earlier. Black trees were everywhere, popping up like used matchsticks—an appropriate and literal metaphor. Further in the distance, behind the sticks, was an aqua lake that seemed almost neon in contrast to all the charred darkness. Wildflowers had filled in much of the ground in purples and pinks and the whole scene represented something out of a historic war zone … so much destruction and yet so much beauty because of the destruction. New growth, nature finding a way, all the clichés of our relationship were in front of us in vivid form.

I had to stop and try to capture it in photos, which I knew I never could but I would try. They would, at least, trigger memories and remind me of the scene when I needed it in the future, maybe as my desktop image.

"This is so sad," Rachel said quietly, from a few feet ahead of me. "And somehow encouraging."

"Right?" I touched a nearby tree and brushed my hand lightly across it as though it were a tombstone. "Pretty much our life right here." Respect, admiration, sadness. I picked a little flower and walked close to Rachel with a smile. After a quick kiss, I put the flower behind her ear and leaned in for a second kiss. "More flowers are coming, babe."

The symbols were too much: swaths of dark ash and destruction with new fragile vibrant life growing. I leaned down to take another photo, to remember. To put everywhere.

That was when I heard the heavy breathing: more like panting. Someone was exhausted, that much was obvious. I didn't feel the need to look toward it and draw more attention so I threw Rachel a weird expression instead.

"Did you go to the waterfall?" someone asked. It took a bit longer than normal for them to get the words out—lots of attempts to replenish oxygen—but they managed in what, I assumed, was an Indian accent.

National parks are, obviously, international attractions. It was not the first accent I had heard that day. Rachel smiled, in a friendly way, half nodding to the person and half ignoring them, as if assuming they were talking to someone else. She threw the conversation baton to me and started to walk.

"I did," I answered without looking back. I held up my phone for another "perfect" shot.

"If you want a good picture, you can always google it, my friend." The voice spoke again, this time more evenly. He was regaining his ability to breathe at a normal pace, which was good. I thought his comment was a little out of line though—he, obviously, wasn't aware of my incredible photographic eye and skills. Also, we weren't friends.

I just laughed. "But, sometimes, you don't want professional. You want personal," I answered.

"Are you by yourself?" he asked, in quite the follow-up to his google comment.

By now, I had to turn and look at the man. You can only ignore a conversation so long before you begin to dehumanize someone when you continue pretending to be taken up with more important things than acknowledging they exist.

He was wearing an orange polo short, dark jeans, socks, white tennis shoes, and a wrinkled, white baseball cap. A massive camera—a really nice professional-looking camera—hung around his neck. If I had to imagine the most touristy foreign visitor to a national park, he was it.

Staring at him, I couldn't help but wonder why his shirt was tucked into his jeans, or further, why anyone ever tucks a polo shirt into their jeans.

On a hike?

On a ninety-degree day?

No wonder he had been panting.

I was still coming up with answers—maybe it was cultural, maybe he liked the style, maybe he didn't know fashion, maybe it was comfortable—and stop judging, as I stared at his slightly overweight face. It was round with dark skin, black eyes, and dark hair sticking out from the cap. It was friendly. With a big smile and crooked, but not distracting, teeth.

"Are you by yourself?" he asked again.

A strange question for sure. Not really one I'm asked often. "I ..." I answered, glancing somewhere further up the path. "I guess." Rachel had kept walking and was far enough away to make me practically alone. "That's my wife up there." I pointed. "Leaving me," I laughed, to make the point I didn't have much time for a long conversation.

"Ah, you are a photographer?" he asked in a friendly nonintimidating way, even if his camera probably cost thousands of dollars and mine was a phone. "Looking for the money shot?" It sounded good with the accent.

"Just trying to remember it," I answered.

"Okay, let's get to business then, huh, Seth?" My name was followed by that smile of pride that I instantly recognized.

It had been over three years. So much had happened. I knew it would take more than a moment to fully process how I felt and what, exactly, was happening but it only took a second before I gave a hug to the big, sweating Indian tourist with every ounce of energy I could, as though he were a long lost relative. He hugged me in return. And for a moment I wondered what Rachel was going to think if she turned around.

"Man," I said, stepping back, trying to take him in but finding it hard since it was another new form. "I think I've missed you. Are you back?"

"Are you, my friend?" he asked with his trademark smile.

Oh shit.

"Where have you been?" I asked, delaying my answer.

"Trying to find someone else." He wiped away a bead of sweat dripping from under his cap. "No luck. It seems, you truly are one of a kind."

"Is that a compliment?"

"I don't know." He sighed. "I hear you've had some kind of renewal of your faith?"

"From who?" I asked, half-nervous as though someone had been gossiping about me. And forgetting that Ehs had access to quite a bit of information.

"We need to get to it," he said quickly, holding up his hand to block his face from the blinding sun.

"Okay?"

"I don't have much time. Not here." He sat down on a big boulder, staring toward the lake.

"The accent is a little hard to take seriously," I answered, changing the subject. I was standing above him, facing the other way. "Also, what kind of camera is that?"

"Yeah, sorry. This guy was alone and tired already. Seemed like a good fit."

"I still don't really understand that," I answered. "I mean, this guy is a wounded water buffalo?" I looked at him and he seemed so nice and put together and happy. He seemed like someone who had quite a bit of family. I doubted he flew from India alone.

"Well." Ehs picked up the camera and stared through the lens. "You can't understand it. You just won't. You can empathize but you can't understand." He was still looking through the camera, panning around. "It is a nice camera though, for sure."

"Okay. And you're in the sun? I don't think I've seen you in the sun?"

He nodded.

"In Hawaii—"

"Right." He let the camera hang again. "It's killing me. My form is in pain right now. Can we get this conversation moving? I've asked a few times now."

"Yeah, yeah." I looked around for some shade. There wasn't any.

"I know she came to see you yesterday." He was definitely not his normal self that I remembered from years earlier. There was something pensive about him. Or maybe it was more of an irritation that he couldn't hide.

"She did." I had assumed it was her somehow, the one he was looking for, though nothing had confirmed it until that moment. I didn't especially like that he knew—maybe it was her, maybe the park, maybe nature, maybe all of it combined. I felt more guarded. It had been a private experience.

"What did she say?" He looked directly at me.

"That was her then, huh?" I asked.

"What did she say?" he repeated with as friendly a tone as he could muster. "I'm sorry but this is not working for me."

"Well, nothing, really …" It was the truth.

"She didn't tell you to be careful of me?"

"Well, I don't know. I got that feeling but she never said it." Mostly the truth.

"She never said that?" He was almost hopeful.

"Well … I don't think so." It was hard to know and I didn't want him to feel bad.

"Hmm …" He seemed content with the answer. I wondered if I had just officially become a spy for the dark side.

"So," I said, changing the subject, "Rachel and I are doing really well. I don't think I ever thanked you."

He looked out, thinking about something that had nothing to do with what I had said.

"And even the church is going well again," I added. "I guess I do feel like I've found some kind of passion again. Faith even?"

"Hmmm …" He was dismissive, waving the words away with his hands. I might as well have just told him that I was going to need to eat lunch soon. "Not the time. Did she say she would see you again?"

The tone caused me to pause. But he was practically wincing so I didn't think too long. "No."

"Are you sure?"

"Jeez," I shot back a little quick. "Not how I expected our reunion to go?"

"Sorry," he said, nodding. "I just …" He took a few breaths, trying to relax. "She never will. We don't either. The surprises work better …" Another deep breath. "Planning makes things …" Another breath. "More dangerous …"

"Are you alright?" The human body from India did not look good. "Or, I mean, is this guy alright?"

"But—" He stood to his feet, completely ignoring me. "If you are ever able to know ahead of time, please tell me."

I was frowning.

"Or, better. If you can arrange some kind of meeting …"

"Are you asking me to set you up now? Is that my mission?"

He was twitching. I could feel it and see it. "Seth."

I waited. His face was covered in sweat and more was appearing every second.

He waited for me to look at him. "Do you trust me? Are you back? Are you in?"

Always the trust. Always the making sure. Like a bad relationship. Like a needy partner. It was like I had come home late again and he was sitting on the porch waiting with an empty bottle of chardonnay next to him.

But I hadn't come home late. Well, I guess I had told him that I wanted nothing to do with him a few years earlier and I had spent some ethereal time with his enemy/wannabe girlfriend.

"You seem off. You alright?" I genuinely cared.

"I just told you my whole body is in pain." He looked at me directly with the bill of his white cap hiding his eyes and the upper half of his face.

"Right."

"I'm dying."

"Alright, well, get out of that guy. Let him go. We'll talk later. There's no shade—"

"No." He stopped me and put his hand on my shoulder as though he needed it to stand. "I'm literally dying. I will be annihilated soon."

"Seth!" I heard Rachel yelling from farther up the path and I looked over. She was waiting, obviously wondering why I was still talking to the Indian man.

Who had just told me he was about to die. Those were not the words I had expected to hear from someone I had thought was already dead. "You can die?" Not the words I had ever responded with to someone who had told me they were dying.

"The *second* death. Have you heard of it?" he asked sarcastically, apparently still in pain from something physical and from whatever my ignorance was doing to him.

"Yeah," I answered hesitantly.

"Of course, we can die. You don't think we actually live forever, do you?"

"Well … I mean, I don't know. I guess I did." Not that I spent much time thinking about the eternal lives of ghosts. But, I had pondered my own life plenty.

"Seth!" Rachel yelled again.

He seemed frustrated. Even in the shadow of his hat, his eyes glowed red and rolled back like a pissed-off teenager. "Seth, *we* …" He sucked in another huge breath. "*We* don't live forever." The Indian man's chubby hands were pointing at his orange-colored polo, still tucked into his jeans. The little polo logo was navy blue.

"As in Shadows?" I responded.

"Seth." He really didn't need to keep saying my name, especially with the accent. "One can only stay in the darkness so long. It consumes." He looked toward the black, burned-out trees. "I'm being consumed. I've survived longer than most."

"Is that why you want her?" I felt sad, heartbroken for him.

He looked down at the ground. "Is this how you always respond to people who are hurting?"

"I'm sorry. You're right. That wasn't very … I'm just … I don't know what to think."

"Thanks."

"I'm sorry, Ehs. I am. I'm still processing all of this."

I mean give me a second, dude.

"Listen." Another pant. "I want to change, to live, to feel. I want to breathe. I want to see. I want the light." He whispered the words, almost guiltily. He seemed nervous about anyone hearing, or maybe he was just too tired to speak. "Yes, she can help me." Another breath. At that point I was hoping they didn't suddenly stop. "I don't want to exist like this anymore."

Whatever strings he was pulling were working. My heart felt weighed down for him. I wanted to help him in any way that I could. I had read about monks in Cyprus who would pray for the devil. If they were wanting to help the devil then I figured I could help one of his/her servants, even if he was dangerous. Even if *it* was dangerous. Wasn't I supposed to be dangerous, in all the right ways?

"Ehs," I said, waiting for him to look at me.

He did.

"I want to help you." I said the words, out loud, that he had probably been waiting for me to say since I had first me him. I meant them. I felt as though I could handle them. Maybe for the first time in my life.

Ehs smiled gently. Relieved. I could almost feel it.

"Seth," Rachel said, much closer now. "What's going on? Is everything alright?" She was standing next to me, staring at the strange scene with compassion and a bit of annoyance.

"Oh yeah, yeah." I answered, happy she could actually see the man and nervous as to what was going to happen next. My worlds had never crossed like that.

"Hello, Rachel." The Indian man held out his hand to shake my wife's. "My name is Ehs. It's good to officially meet you."

I momentarily froze. As did Rachel. We hadn't talked about Ehs in years. He had been in the past, like most of our mistakes. We were now going somewhere new, clean, and better. Our eyes met and told the whole story to each other in the ways eyes can.

This was not supposed to happen and I didn't think it was going to make things easier.

Then I felt something leave. I could see it. A substance seeped out of the man, and into the charred forest behind him. In fact, I watched some kind of cloudy apparition sneak in and out of the trunks like an agitated storm cloud before fading into the sky like the smoke that had once burned the forest. The blue sky shone brightly and the sun was warm and refreshing, clear and crisp, even in its heat.

Rachel could see it all too. I could tell from the ways her eyes tracked the same spots mine did. We both landed back on the man eventually. He was sweating profusely, tired, and still holding on to Rachel's hand, most likely wondering why.

"And nice to meet you," she said slowly and without a lot of conviction, with a fair amount of shock written on her wide eyes and scrunched up forehead.

"Are you okay?" I asked. To everyone.

"I am very fine, my friend. I am very fine. Thank you." Judging from the waterfalls of sweat cascading down his cheeks I wasn't sure I believed him. "I am very well. Very well. Thank you, my friend."

Ehs was gone. Maybe before that, maybe shortly after it. But either way I took the words as though they were from him: my friend.

Who had just met Rachel.

Well, that got serious fast.

FOURTEEN POINT FIVE

After our alone time in the national park, we'd planned a family trip with the kids: all part of the "Year Three Therapist-Recommended Tour of Healing."

But, before we got on to that stop of the tour, Rachel and I had to drive home from our national park expedition.

Needless to say, ninety percent of the drive was taken up by Ehs. We had never talked with our therapist about Ehs, for plenty of reasons including being judged for being insane and, more importantly, in case he had actually pulled some strings for us. And, being judged again for even thinking that was possible.

But, a week after we had told Jaden and Gwen, in separate conversations, that we wanted to end whatever faux relationship we had been carrying on, both of them had moved away, of their own accord, and promised, over phone calls within five minutes of each other, to never bring whatever had happened up to anyone. They had both sounded spooked.

Coincidence? Possibly. God? Some would claim.

Ehs? We both felt pretty confident Ehs had played some role and we didn't really want to talk to Marie about it. Maybe we were still too addicted to secrets, and needed to keep at least one.

That said, the drive consisted of three acts: like most good stories. Act One. I convinced Rachel that was the first time I had seen Ehs in years and that I was hiding nothing. Act Two. We both tried to decide if I or we would see more of him. Act Three. We needed to keep focusing on the good and hard work we had been doing and play it day by day as to how Ehs played into all that.

Yeah, it was a very open ending.

The two of us and the kids found ourselves in a small town on the coast, to crab, clam, and oyster. Strange, but delicious animals, and strange words to use as verbs, but they work in each case: the action of finding the nouns.

The town reminded me of a Hollywood actor receiving a lifetime achievement award at the age of ninety-five. The clips show them in their prime—the black-and-white films—and we are blown away by the way they once enchanted the screen with their phenomenal grace, ability, and straight-up sex appeal.

Then they cut to the actor in his or her current form. The sexy lips are gone as is most of the grace and ability. The white color has moved from the teeth—which now seem too large—to the stringy hair on top of their head. Sex appeal? No chance.

But, we see how they once had it, and so we applaud because we all know that someday we'll be in their shoes too, no matter how graceful, beautiful, or sexually appealing we currently are or are not.

That was the town we were staying in. Without the applause. Or award.

Old, worn out, and not very appealing in the present. It was easy to walk past the candy stores and fishing tours and imagine how amazing it was in its glory days when the salmon were coming in to the harbor along with the boats, beards, prostitutes, and tourists to see the circus of it all.

Old trailers in the front yards, ripped American flags, burned-out lawns, rusted-out hulls of ancient boats, eroded by too much time in the salt air, and motor homes that were parked off the street, almost out of view, just like they always were in every serial murder documentary I'd ever seen. Most of them even had strange shells and artifacts formed into some kind of statue hanging from nearby trees to raise the eerie level a bit more.

I was exhausted. We had been up before dawn to find clams in the bay while the tide was out, and then we had moved on to pulling up crabs from the ocean off a long pier. With each find, we were hoping they were males, they were big enough, and we were able to get them out of their trap before they fell to their death on the rocks below while trying to escape.

The irony.

We were now driving home, past rows of poverty and more nostalgia than I could take in. Though I did try. It was the opposite of the national park—a cornucopia of different ways to lose luster—and my awe was radically different than what I had experienced just a few days earlier.

I was in the back seat getting carsick while Rachel's stepdad drove us back to the spot where we were staying: a run-down RV park, of course. My son was in the front seat. As exhausted as I was, we had to stop somewhere to get some coolers for the crabs, which meant more driving around and more car sickness for me.

When we got to the store, which looked like something right out of 1972, I decided to stay in the truck while they went on the hunting trip for coolers. I leaned my head against the window—the cold glass somehow comforted my nauseousness—and closed my eyes.

For a second.

"Hey!" My pulse rocketed from a cool sixty-five to 120 in what had to be a world record. I was already sweating when I registered that someone was in the truck with me, yelling for me to wake up. "This is no time to sleep. Not with your ignorance."

My brain had to take a moment to interpret all the sensory overload and by the time I realized that no one was actually in the car, I also registered the insult the voice had dropped.

"What the hell was that for?" I said to no one.

"Trust me, this was not on my itinerary for the day but I've heard rumors. Lots of them. And then, given all we had to talk about in a short amount of time at the park, you decided to get in a line about how passionate you were about the church again? And you wonder what I'm doing here?"

"Okay?" I asked, still finding my bearings.

"This was the first chance I got to correct you." The voice was as audible as though he was sitting next to me. It even emanated from the space where his mouth would have been if he had been in the cab with me.

I immediately began to recall every moment of the last time we had been together and stack up the insults—or what I thought could have been interpreted as them. "You're dying?" I threw out.

"Yes. But, there are more important things."

"More important than that?"

"Yes."

"And also, can you ask me before introducing yourself to Rachel? Is she part of this—"

"Excuse me for not asking your permission to introduce myself to your wife." The voice rang out, saturated in sarcasm. "Fancy that."

"That's not what I meant," I said.

Before he could answer I was no longer sitting in the truck. I was standing in a nursery. Not the kind that grows a plant but the kind that grows a baby. A crib was in front of me with an infant sleeping inside of it, swaddled up like a burrito with a cute little head sticking out. I instantly remembered my own kids and nostalgia swelled.

"Infancy." Ehs was now in the form of James standing next to me. He was wearing dark jeans and a white shirt, which made me wonder how and where he had grabbed James from or if it even mattered anymore—which I figured it did not. It seemed he could take on any form he wanted when we were wherever we were.

My pulse was slowing after another jump from the change of scenery and James appearing next to me. "Can you stop with the quick transitions?"

"Infancy," he repeated. "Survival is essential. We need parental authority figures. We are completely dependent on them," James said plainly, staring at the baby like a scientist, completely unaffected by the innocent, cute life-form in front of us.

I, on the other hand, was completely moved by the adorable bald head. "Right," I agreed, not sure if I was supposed to.

"So, this cage makes sense." He tapped the bars of the crib. "It's necessary."

"Right," I said more slowly.

"And its parents have come from somewhere else?" He looked at me with his eyebrows raised. "They were inherited by this life."

"Yes," I answered slowly, again, not sure if the wordplay was some kind of trap or what.

"Then, over time—" he started. And we were suddenly in a different room. Clothes everywhere. A queen-sized bed. Some posters on the wall and a laptop covered in decals on a desk. "Adolescence."

I could see a boy about fifteen sleeping on the bed, half of him covered in a thick comforter and the other half, his bare legs with socks on—sticking out.

"The self becomes aware. The self begins to leave the thing that it needed up to that point. More risk. More failure, knowing there is security to do so." He looked to me as he rolled his eyes. "In good parenting, at least." And he looked back to the bed. "And slowly the infant and the child disappears into the adult."

The room changed again. We were now standing in what looked like an apartment of some kind. The window let in light from a downtown city that could have been anywhere. A bike was hanging on the wall. A couch with a small television set in front of me and a kitchen crammed into a corner of the room. Posters—now framed and containing modern art prints. A man was sitting on the couch, staring at the TV, when he was not looking at his phone.

"The adult. Mature. Free from his or her parents. Free from their authority. Able to risk and grow on his or her own. Able to function in the society." Ehs looked at me and waited. "Right?"

I nodded, watching the adult reach up and brush his hand through thick brown hair.

The room changed again. A big desk. Another computer. Rows of books on a bookshelf. An older man sitting at the desk typing. White hair, what was left of it. A white beard. Glasses.

"Elders. The wisdom of old age. Authority figures to others, or even free of being authority to anyone. The information, the stories, the legends, and the myths have been passed along successfully and he or she understands them at another, more profound level." He paused again and looked back at me to make sure I was following along.

"Yes."

"Now," he started, and we were back in the nursery. The baby still resting in the crib, which gave me a moment to appreciate how the older gentleman had started. "You realize all cultures follow this pattern as well?"

"Okay," I answered.

"Infancy. Cages are needed. For survival. Authority figures. Morality. Rules. Ritual. Symbols." The room stayed the same but the crib vanished and I moved through time, watching the baby crawl, start to walk, and then play with toys that appeared. He continued to grow as Ehs spoke. "The culture advances with the assurance that it can. But it begins with primitive understandings of the universe, of gods, of nature, of itself, always passed down from some previous culture, of course." He looked to me but I couldn't take my eyes off of the eight- or nine-year-old in front of me.

The room slowly transformed into the room I had seen earlier. The teenager's room. Posters appeared on the wall, the desk moved in as a bookshelf of toys moved out. Posters changed. A new queen-sized bed moved in.

"Cultures start to find their identities as well." The fourteen-year-old was at his desk on a phone. Then typing something. Then reading a thick book. I could watch him still growing. "And so they leave the authority, the primitive symbols, and begin to discover that they have their own identity. The symbols carry deeper meanings. The rules come from underground locations, now mined for their wisdom. The ritual was only necessary to carry the stories that were meant to instill the wisdom to handle risk and fear and challenge and … continued growth for themselves."

The room continued to morph. The boy continued to morph. Girls appeared here and there. Televisions came and went. School books appeared and disappeared. And the boy continued to grow as Ehs continued to speak.

"The boy doesn't need his parents anymore. The role of all good parents is to work themselves out of a job, correct?" He looked at me again.

I nodded, staring at the early-twenties man in front of me, adjusting his tie in front of a mirror.

"He or she might even become a parent of their own, imparting the wisdom that they have learned, into new stories that they, of course, do not follow literally anymore, because they have found the only actual meaning for them that matters: present meaning as interpreted into their current context."

The man was reading to a little girl on a bed. A little girl who soon vanished.

"This cultural rhythm, this evolution of humanity, of society, of culture, generally works, bringing new life out of fresh death, on a revolving successful basis."

We watched together as the apartment transformed into the office I had seen and eventually ended with the older man sitting at his desk.

"Okay?" He looked once again at me, waiting for me to acknowledge that I was still there. I looked at him in return which seemed to be enough for him to continue.

"It's not just individuals or even cultures. It is also—" He paused. The scene changed again. "Religion. Well at its best—a side effect we didn't plan on. We should have," he added. "Religion usually follows culture."

We were in my church. I could see it plainly. I recognized the chairs, the stage where I often spoke, and the new carpet we had recently installed.

I looked toward Ehs with a different expression.

"I understand you have found a new passion for this?" He nodded toward the stage.

"Yes," I answered slowly.

"And where do you think this is? Who is—" He paused and formed a rather disgusted look on his face. "Who is *this* for?"

"Everyone," I answered.

He smiled and shook his head. "Everyone?" He kept shaking his head. "Nothing is for everyone, especially not babies and elders." He stared at me. "I'll ask again. Everyone?"

"Yes," I said more confidently than I felt.

"Hmmm ..." The room changed again. We were back to the nursery, the small baby in the crib. "Your church is this." Ehs reached out and touch the crib. "It has great power," he said. "For babies."

"Okay," I said, with lots of resistance.

"It keeps the babies safe. Provides authority. Rules, morality, rituals, and guidelines. It transfers the stories. It develops, Seth. It develops." The room and baby began to grow again, this time quicker than before. Soon we were in the apartment but it was different now. A bigger television. No kitchen. Video game machines on the carpet along with chip bags and soda cans. And the man in his early twenties sitting there in a dirty shirt and sweat pants.

"The proverbial man in his mother's basement." Ehs smiled. "It's funny how much the culture ridicules him and yet, the religion creates him."

I watched the flicker of light on the man's face as he stared at whatever game his fingers were nervously twitching along to and his face was barely reacting to.

"The parent, in this case, has not done its job. To work itself out of a job. The religion, the church, the pastor"—Ehs waited until I looked him in the eyes—"has the same job. To work itself out of a job."

"But—"

He interrupted me fast and hard. "You ignorant fool," he said pensively, looking down at the shag carpet and, I felt, regretting what he had done in his own growing up. "Its job is to create adults, not old teenagers. The stories are to be lived, not repeated. The rituals are to be understood, not practiced. The morals are to be absorbed, not rehearsed. The rules are to be mined, not memorized." He looked back at me and I expected him to be angry, but he was not. There was more sadness. "The mystery is to be tasted, not talked about."

"That's not exactly what the church does," I responded, half believing it to be true. "And even if it did, there are some who always need the crib."

"Indeed," he nodded. "If that's what you want to do with your life, at least know what you are doing. You enjoy being a wet nurse?" he asked, his eyes dancing around inside their sockets in a mocking way.

I answered with my eyes. *Fuck you.*

He looked forward again as the adult playing video games reached into his pants and scratched himself. "The god man said as much. He tried. But the parents killed him. They wanted to be parents forever." There was a subtle smile underneath his sadness, or facade of it at least. "It was obvious that as consciousness understood more, humanity would leave the Mother Church and Father God and find … Her: the mystery and love that resides in everything. And so, we worked hard to make sure that you would not."

He turned back and stared at me.

"Because there is nothing more thrilling than addicts of a childish religion who never realize their purpose in this world because they have found us to be good parents."

I looked back to the man playing the video game who flashed into a man sitting in a chair—back in the church setting—listening to me. It was only for a flash, and almost before I could register it all, I was suddenly staring out the car window again, looking out at a street. We had left the grocery store.

"Good nap?" my son asked.

I rolled down the window and let the fresh air hit my face. Along with the dismal scene. More boarded-up windows. More graffiti on the worn-out sidings of houses. More faded colors. More piles of cut wood. More refrigerators in yards. More broken-down fences. More cardboard boxes and tarps and broken gutters piled in front of garages. More FOR SALE signs.

More nostalgia for the passion I had felt not too much earlier.

More car sickness and maybe something else.

"Yeah," I managed.

FIFTEEN

"This"—Ehs paused, as he often did, for added dramatic effect—"is the Realm of Insipid. In all of its glory."

"Wait, what? This wall? That's it?" I asked, looking around and killing any of the drama that he had worked to create. "And, also, we have a lot to talk about besides …" I looked at it again, obviously disappointed. "This."

"What?" he repeated, incredulous and possibly offended.

"A wall?" I repeated. "After all of the hints and teases and … I mean … I didn't know it was literally a wall. A wall?"

We were standing at the base of it. It was massive. Truly massive. Its height was astounding, reaching up toward the heavens, and its length was just as imposing, stretching out on both sides of us as far as I could see. But still, it was just a wall.

"Literally," Ehs growled, smothered in sarcasm. Then sighed. Exasperated ten seconds into our most recent adventure. "Yes. It's a wall," he continued, in seeming disbelief that he had to answer such a stupid question. "And, more importantly, everything a wall produces."

I looked at the wall again. It seemed to be made of enormous black bricks whose edges I could start to discern as I studied them. We were standing in a world covered by an immense shadow, created by the wall, and some kind of light source from somewhere that was nowhere to be seen.

Investigating it more, I could begin to see holes in the wall above us and far away on the sides. Through those holes, beams of light were pouring in before eventually hitting the ground far behind us.

The ground was dirt as far as I could see, an almost gray dirt, at least in the shadow, with more greens and browns in the sections where the light hit it. It reminded me of my run—wherever light touched was color. The rest was just a smorgasbord of grays.

"Okay," I said, honestly beginning to understand its mammoth nature and scope. "Okay." On second glance, maybe it was impressive. It was making me forget the other things I had wanted to talk about.

Ehs was standing in front of one of the bricks in his usual shape. James. Poor James, the human whom Ehs would forever be tied to in my head. Normal James. He was finally relaxing, seeing that I was beginning to appreciate it. To be fair, I had only been there less than a minute.

"Okay," I repeated. It was incredibly dark and I started to feel it. It wasn't night. It just felt like it. A night with no light from the stars, from the moon, or from a distant city. It was a dark-night-of-the-soul night. But it wasn't in the soul. I was standing in it.

The bricks were squares—taller than the height of James and wider than the height of James—and the more I studied them, the more odd I realized they were. If all of reality is, as the scientists say, made of the space between atoms, which actually make up very little of the universe (matter itself), these bricks had the same ingredients as outer space. They were empty blackness that somehow had form.

"Okay … yeah, impressive," I replied. "Maybe it just took me a second …" My words drifted into the grays as I continued to study the scenery.

"Thank you." Ehs bowed in a very ornate and exaggerated way, lightening the mood a bit.

"I guess I didn't realize you were talking literally," I responded, still looking at the large and imposing, but boring, wall.

Ehs stopped his bow and stood straight. "I wasn't." Whatever lightened mood had been created slithered away into the shadows.

"Well, what is—"

"Make the oppression visible. Give it shape. Give it substance. Give it form. If you want to change it, you have to be able to see it." The shadow in the shape of James stared hard into my eyes.

"Metaphor, then," I said, still trying to capture its full size while wondering where we were, while knowing it was still a useless concept to wonder about. Though I couldn't help it.

"Shape. Substance. Form." He sighed. "Metaphor. Symbol. Yes. Can we please move on?"

"Boy, there are some people that would sure love this thing." As I looked more closely at the outer-space bricks, I saw they seemed to eat light rather than block it. Each one more of a black hole of emptiness—which is what black holes are—rather than bricks the way I wanted them to be. They were dark, so dark. In every way. Penetrating.

"Republicans," he responded, almost disgustedly.

"Wow," I whistled. "Just throw them under the bus. I said people."

"Don't feign independence with me." He shook his head. "I

know you well."

I didn't say much. "You don't take credit for them too?" If he knew my political tendencies there was no reason to pretend anymore.

He appeared appalled at the idea. Almost disgusted. "You don't actually think that, I hope." Ehs walked closer to me.

"Well." I wondered if I could act like I didn't.

"I suppose you give cocaine the credit for drug addiction," he grunted. "Or opiates?"

"Well …" I wasn't sure where to go with that one. "I mean …"

He shook his head. "I do forget how uninformed and stupid you are sometimes."

"Thank you?"

"The drug war …" He shook his head. "Made up. Useless. It was predicted years earlier that it would produce a billion-dollar industry. It has. This so-called war has done nothing but waste money, produce more drugs, more addicts, more dangerous versions of both, and absolutely nothing to stop actual drugs. And you want to give the credit to cocaine," he laughed. "Or to opiates because you had no time for pain in your lives."

I had never thought of giving credit to cocaine for much of anything although I had blamed it for plenty.

"Addiction," he said. "It has nothing to do with cocaine. If it's not cocaine, it's something else. Cocaine is not the problem. It's the solution to a problem that you refuse to address. You have never addressed it from the time Constantine shut down the rituals at the Temple of Eleusis to the evangelicals' desperation to ban drugs from the nation. It's all the same … solving solutions and never facing problems." He was pacing back and forth, talking loudly.

"Problems of loneliness, of belonging, of shame, of value, of trauma. Problems of pain really, and elevating the importance of never having it. Reality is the problem. Cocaine is the solution. And you still believe that by addressing the solution, you will solve the problem. But, that's because you're also addicted to addressing symptoms instead of causes."

He turned to face me. "For that, you can blame me. But only for that. Not for something so obvious as cocaine. Or Republicans."

"I mean, I'm not sure I'd compare them to—"

"Desperate, you're all so desperate for symbols …" He just kept shaking his head.

"Right, but—"

"We are the darkness! If you've learned nothing," he said again, with disgust, "you must learn that. Worry about the glaring and obvious as much as you like. It's exactly where we like you to place your energy. Republicans and Democrats are the solution to a problem. The problem is the only thing that should worry you."

"Political parties created Hitler," I threw out, not sure if the history was entirely accurate.

"Obsessed with Hitler." Ehs laughed out loud. Amidst the sound I could hear bits of his own language. Strange guttural whispers that I assumed was some kind of demonic swearing. "Your ignorance is insulting." He backed up, closer to the wall again. "For you, for me, for others. Stop. Let's move on."

He walked over to me, closer, again. I looked away. No terrain, no buildings, no anything but flat ground hidden in shadow—for miles.

"Seth," Ehs said with an intoxicating confidence.

I looked back toward him.

"Have you read a single history book?"

"Well," I answered somewhat bashfully. "I mean, I read …"

"It's the same news. Especially in your desperate empire. Corruption. Power. Money. And lies, lies, lies."

"Right but—"

"Read a book and come and talk to me. Leaders never change because the poison of power never changes."

I half smiled.

"Are you convinced these politicians have something great to offer you?" I wanted the question to be rhetorical but he knew me better than that.

"No," I replied. "But, at the same time …"

"You don't know what you're convinced of. You don't think. You think what they want you to think—all of you. And they tell you what we want them to tell you. All of them. Because they want power and we provide them the way to have it and make you believe you might have some too."

And suddenly I was looking at myself. Ehs had taken my own form as I had never seen it. We never see ourselves in three dimensions, only two, and the sight of it was both upsetting and exhilarating. "You are what you fear. What you hate. Stop your complaining about various perspectives on solutions. Try harder to understand the real problems and you will not only understand them better, you will understand yourself better as well."

I had nothing to say in return.

"*That* is what *we* do." The form of James was back. He looked back toward the wall. "There are much more important issues at hand. *This* is where we play our games."

I still had nothing to say. I was being shown light by darkness. Finding my own shadow by …

"Now," he reached out and touched the wall. "This creates Insipid."

I nodded.

"It has taken years to create it. Years. Many have died before seeing its completion."

Like most great pieces of architecture. "Symbolically?" I asked.

He continued, ignoring me. "Some of the first bricks were formed toward the beginning of time. But, we have been able to grow it. To evolve it. And we haven't needed to add bricks ourselves for many years. You build it now."

I was still listening.

"Hey." Ehs snapped his fingers. "Are you alright?"

"Yeah, I'm fine. Give me a second, okay. I'm trying to process."

"So you're listening?"

"Yeah," I answered.

"Walls."

"Yes. Walls," I repeated.

"Humans have been infatuated with them since the beginning, all the way to now. You love them." He was massaging the black brick but his hand was penetrating it, which I wasn't sure was him being a Shadow or because the bricks were empty space that ate light.

"Some of the first construction of humans, of course, consisted of walls. Everything does. To have a building, you have to have walls."

"Yes, I understand basic construction."

"Ah." He smiled. "There you are. Feeling better. The spunk has returned."

I smiled. *Was I supposed to smile?*

"Why? Why the infatuation with walls?" he asked.

"I'm not sure there is an infatuation. I mean, that's like saying we're infatuated with circles or wheels. They make stuff work." Boom. I was back, knocking homers off his silly questions.

"What do they make work?"

"God, sometimes I wish you would just get to what you're saying. These lectures …"

"Well …"

"I'm not a fifth grader."

"Sometimes you act like one."

"Okay, okay. The walls, get on with it."

"Sure they support roofs. Sure they create structures. Why do you want structures?" He seemed serious though I wasn't sure.

"Are you actually asking?" I asked.

He continued, answering my question and his own. "Protection."

"Okay."

"From weather … enemies … wandering eyes … discomfort … the profane … walls create the realities you want. Structures make you believe something … not entirely true." He said this while looking toward me and the shadow behind me cast by the massive wall behind him. "Walls are your way to try and find control in an uncertain world. That's why humans are infatuated with them. They bring power."

"Okay. Maybe a little dramatic but I get it."

"Dramatic?"

"Yeah, I mean you could say that about all kinds of things," I responded.

"Does that make it less true?"

"Well …"

"You're all the same." He shook his head. "It's pathetic, honestly." There was an eye roll. "So resistant to truth. Always looking for cracks in the walls of words."

"Shouldn't we be?"

"The truth will set you free."

"You're quoting Bible verses now?"

"I'm quoting truth. If you want to keep arguing, I've got all day. But your family will probably start worrying soon."

Suddenly, Ehs disappeared and in his place was a rhinoceros. I took a few steps back, slowly, unable to take my eyes off of the black, wrinkled hide and two horns emerging from its prehistoric head. The animal's nostrils flared and it snorted a moment later.

"Is this real?" was all I could mutter.

"Of course, it's real," Ehs answered, as though he were next to me even though he wasn't.

I took a few more steps back, slowly, to not startle it. "Then, that's not good."

"You realize these animals have a relatively small brain for mammals their size?"

"Okay," I mumbled, with an edge of fear. "Okay."

"Like you, when you're operating with your ego."

"Yeah, I got it."

"So, I can continue?" The rhinoceros was staring at me and snorting.

"Yeah."

It put its head down so its horns were in a direct line for my chest. I could see its bowed back and imagined hundreds of pounds ramming into me. "Okay, I get it, Ehs." I was still backing up and it was moving forward.

"Tell your ego to leave now."

"Ego, leave," I repeated quickly, happily obliging.

Instead, the rhino charged. Directly for my chest. Full speed ahead. I held up my arms as though they would do something and screamed as loud as I could.

Until I could scream no more and until I realized I had not died and that Ehs was laughing.

"So scared of something that doesn't even exist," he said, giggling at the joke.

James, followed by my breath, slowly returned. "Walls, of course," Ehs continued as though nothing had happened. "Offer survival. But they also offer indulgence. A blurred line."

"What? Don't. Please—" I was still shaking.

"Ego," Ehs said calmly. "False reality. False self. You spend so much time serving an aberration."

"I. Don't do that—"

"Your ego needs to go away." He smiled. "If you want to learn."

"Okay, okay. But, I don't like getting convicted by a demon," I answered. "And I don't like being scared by one."

"Most egos don't like being convicted by anything."

"Okay."

"So they call anything that convicts them a demon, whether it actually is or not." He smiled and looked nothing like a demon in that moment.

I hadn't thought of that one.

"Even if he's a saint," he continued.

"Right," I mumbled.

"Or messiah."

"Yeah," I sighed. "I get it."

"For once."

It was my turn to sigh.

"Back to the wall?" He pointed again, obviously ready to tell me something.

"Sure." I was following along again, assured the animal was gone and thankful I was recovering faster than I once had from his image games.

"So, walls to build temples," he interrupted, apparently intent on continuing whether I was listening or not. "And keep the gods away from everything else. Or to keep the people away from the gods. Either way, control and power and protection.

"Walls to divide. Always dividing and separating. Holy here. Secular there. In here. Out there. Safe here. Danger there. Friend here. Enemy there." He was pointing at the wall. "Republican here. You there."

I nodded with a big sigh. "Yeah, yeah. I get it."

"Us here. God there. Idols, in reality, but they're all the same to you as long as your idol is named God with a capital 'g.'"

He was definitely on a roll.

"Walls to build fences. Some big, some small."

I nodded again.

"Walls to protect your wealth, your hording. Walls to protect your privacy. Walls to separate conception, birth, death, your neighbor, your friends, and your family. Walls to separate emotions, illness, your pasts, and, of course, your land. Walls to separate enemies and gods and walls to protect your weapons that you think will protect you and whatever is inside your walls with you. Walls to protect your skin from the light. Walls to create darkness so you can light the interior of your walls with the light you determine at the level and power and consistency that your ego tells you it needs. You are obsessed with walls to protect your precious, mundane, mediocre, and boring lives."

"Okay …" I put out my hand, sufficiently offended.

"I apologize." He seemed sincere, turning to face me again. "If you want to tell the atheists how to better go about their work, tell them this as well. Stop focusing on holy wars and suicide bombers, and start focusing on the subtle, weekly propaganda, disinformation, and ritual that continues to feed the lies of black and white, this or that, sacred and profane. The lies of walls."

"Why would I give the atheists help?" I asked.

"So close, Seth. So close," he said quietly, shaking his head. "The opposite of faith is not atheism."

"I'm not sure—"

"The darkness! The actual danger," he interrupted, "is this." He had managed to move himself closer to the wall again. He pointed at the closest brick.

"Okay, so this wall represents all of that?" I pointed to the massive structure that was still there right beside us.

He turned his back to me, admiring it again. He always seemed to love admiring his work. "And much more."

"You do a great job painting a very bleak picture. I feel depressed."

"And so you find yourself addicted. To political saviors, to numbing drugs, or to bigger and thicker walls. Trying to adapt and survive in the cage you don't believe you're in." He paused and looked away. "Do you know what happens to animals in zoos? They lose their minds, Seth. They lose their desire to mate. To create! To foster a future. They go crazy in such a claustrophobic environment. Can you imagine a wild lion inside of a cage?"

"Yeah, I can." I didn't have to imagine. I ran by them every week. It was all utterly depressing if he was right.

"You put your god in the cage with you as well. Tamed the poor thing." He laughed, but in a sad way, somehow. "We watch you all lose your minds and eat our popcorn while being entertained."

I imagined his words and rooted for god to escape the cage, not sure what that even meant. "Popcorn though?"

"It's not all bad for the other side." He looked up again, peering into the distance. "There are holes, more appearing every day. We plug them but the light manages to shine through."

I looked again toward the faint beams of light in the distance, almost like white lasers shining toward faraway locations.

"But," he continued, "we fight back. And you help. Even if it burdens you, blinds you, even if it hides reality as it truly is. Because you'll usually trade the uncertainty and risk of freedom for the certitude and safety of a cell."

I stood, somewhat motionless.

Some amount of time passed.

"I'll show you R, next time we meet," he eventually added.

"R?"

"There are many pieces to our realm. Gates, towers … shapes, substance, zones, form. This is just the tip of the iceberg, It's the biggest thing we've—well, you—have ever built."

I looked up as high as my neck would allow, still never seeing a top but only a cloudy dark sky.

"Do you want to fly?" he asked, suddenly.

"Are you kidding?" My attention was back to him.

"No," he said. "Do you?"

Like most things in life, when you actually get the opportunity to do something you have always wanted to do, there is a pause. When presented with a realistic chance at its fruition, dreams start to dance with fear. What if the dream lets you down and you no longer have a dream?

"Do I know how?"

"Did anyone tell you how to kiss a girl?"

"Movies?" I replied.

"Fine." The body of James transformed, almost instantly, into a bird and flew away into the sky. I stared until there was only a speck somewhere in the distance, probably imagined, and my neck began to hurt.

I imagined turning into some kind of bird and flying away too. I imagined soaring through the sky with a huge smile—whatever that looked like on a bird—along the wall, never seeing its top, and along its sides, never seeing them end, and away from it over the flat land of Insipid or wherever I was.

I imagined, or experienced, it all, flabbergasted at the size of it.

And then I heard my garage door open. My family was home. And now so was I.

I stood up from my chair and walked through the door in my office walls to greet them and welcome them into our home of walls.

SIXTEEN

The next week, out of the blue, a good friend was diagnosed with leukemia. It was absolutely brutal. Devastating. After our first visit with him, I left the hospital, with Rachel, a mess. One week earlier he had called to tell me he might have cancer, and when I saw him he was already starting a twenty-four-hour drip of chemotherapy. He was at the starting line of a grueling race.

It was the end of a long week, or month, I couldn't remember. It was all merging together.

There had been another horrific shooting in our country to add to the list.

A seven-year-old in our neighborhood had been hit by a car and was most likely going to be a quadriplegic for the rest of her life.

A fellow classmate of my daughter was killed by a drunk driver while pulling out of a grocery store parking lot.

Another friend had just discovered his daughter was cutting herself.

Two police shootings of African Americans were followed by a shooting of a police officer.

Another friend was going through a horrific divorce and years of affairs.

Another friend, a teacher, was diagnosed with breast cancer at the start of summer, and was entering chemotherapy for her vacation.

Another friend was diagnosed with cancer in her early twenties.

People all over town were calling it a heavy summer and it wasn't even the middle of July. It was in the air and we were all breathing it. You could smell it in every conversation. You could feel its weight pushing down.

As the doors to the hospital slid open and I walked away from the chemical smell into the fresh air, I thought about my friend who was not going to smell fresh air for at least four weeks. Potentially more. I felt guilty breathing for a moment.

I grabbed Rachel's hand. As I did, she remembered she had

forgotten to give a card to our friend's wife. I decided to stay outside, feel the sunlight, and try to compose myself and what I was supposed to say the next day in front of the people who wanted me to say something meaningful in the midst of the heaviness.

I sat down on a concrete ledge and instantly noticed him. He was in a wheelchair. Rolling along slowly, wearing nothing but a white gown and very large sunglasses. He was across the street from where I was sitting. He would move toward the crosswalk and then back up, like a dog who had been trained to not go close to an invisible fence. Some form of barrier was stopping him.

I got up from my spot in the sun and started across the street to meet him. In the shadows.

As I neared, I noticed the man was old, or at least looked old. Bad skin. Little hair. Flecks of gray whiskers scattered across his face like remnants of younger days. And thick sunglasses, wrapping around his entire face, like the ones they gave you after having your pupils dilated. But these weren't the cheap paper and plastic. They were what would happen if Oakley made them.

I walked closer but he seemed stressed. He was fidgeting with a cigarette with shaking hands and had trouble looking toward me. He kept looking off to the sides, sometimes even behind him.

I was soon directly in front of him, staring down as he finally got his cigarette lit and shoved it in his mouth, taking a big swig of smoke. Appropriate.

"Fuck you." I couldn't hold it back. "Fuck you," I said again, with a little more enunciation, just so he knew I meant it.

"Excuse me," the old man said, barely able to look at me. "What'd you say?"

For a short moment, I wondered if I had been wrong. But something told me to go all in. "You heard me."

He looked up, squinting, even behind the sunglasses—the eyebrows told me so—and took another lung full of smoke. "I'm sorry, Seth." The smoke came out of his mouth, along with something darker and more ominous that hovered in the air longer before forming some kind of shape and slithering toward the sky.

"Thanks," I lied. "You know you're never supposed to answer with sorry. It's one of the worst things you can say."

"This piece of shit is in much worse shape, if it makes you feel better." He pointed toward himself. "Maybe a week left."

"It doesn't." I looked at the shell of a body that Ehs was inside of and felt the empty emotion of pity: the same emotion kings felt for their subjects right before ordering them to die. Poor guy was probably better off inhabited by a demon. Otherwise he was just an empty body of some kind living in an empty land, waiting to die.

"It's time for stubborn gladness, my friend." He blew out another stream of smoke and continued to look away from me. "Stubborn."

I ignored him and started walking toward my car. I wasn't in the mood at that moment for his games. He followed me, pushing himself along in the chair, speaking louder than normal in a crackling elderly voice.

"Sorrow everywhere. Slaughter everywhere. If babies are not starving someplace, they are starving somewhere else."

I turned around.

He continued. "With flies in their nostrils." Smoke seeped between his teeth as he spoke. "But we enjoy our lives because that's what god wants."

I stared.

"If we deny our happiness, resist our satisfaction, we lessen the importance of their deprivation. We must risk delight. We can do without pleasure, but not delight. Not enjoyment." I took a step closer to the old man, still spilling words like water to someone who was thirsty. "We must have the stubbornness to accept our gladness in the ruthless furnace of this world."

He stopped and stared at his cigarette for a moment. "Are you ready for this next line?"

I waited.

"To make injustice the only measure of our attention is to praise the devil." He gave a slow whistle and shook his head as though he had just watched someone do a 360-degree dunk in a game. He was impressed and knew nothing else but to almost laugh at the ass-kicking from words. "Jack Gilbert. You should read that poem on Sunday. There's more to it than that."

"What was that line again?"

"To make in—"

"No, the other one. Stubbornness to …"

"We must have the stubbornness to accept our gladness in the ruthless furnace of this world," he repeated while leaning over to put out his cigarette on the pavement and throw it in the shrubs.

"That's good. I'll look it up." I turned and started making my way back toward the car again.

"Hey," he shouted. "I'm sorry. But don't blame me for all this shit."

I turned around again and he was pointing at the hospital but still not looking at it. "This place is one of the few bright spots around."

He started to pull another cigarette out of a pack that had been sitting on his chair. "A little ironic you're mad at me for it."

"Say again?" I always hated hospitals—and, in that moment, Ehs.

"This is one of the few bright spots around, my friend. A beacon of light. I can barely look at it." He glanced over for a second and just as quickly turned away as though it were the sun itself.

"Fuck you." I turned to leave again. That "beacon of light" was my friend's new home and prison for the next few weeks.

"Hey!" he shouted in a classic crotchety old man voice. It grabbed my attention and I threw him a glance. "Look again."

So I did, because it seemed I always did what Ehs wanted me to do. When I did, the only thing I could see, at first, was sunlight. Bright, burning sun, that shocked my eyes and momentarily blinded them. I had to look away while I hoped they adjusted and were not permanently damaged.

Eventually, sight returned and I noticed the wall far away, in the distance, casting everything I could see into shadow. The darkness was comforting for a moment. I could see the holes in the wall, bursting through in radiant color although none near me. In fact, nothing was near me but the glowing orb of the building in front of me.

I looked back at where the hospital had once stood and, as my eyes adjusted, I could see more details. It was not a hospital anymore. It was more plain, a tall cube of a building, glowing.

As my eyes became more accustomed to the light, I could see that it was more than white—it was filled with colors—and it was not just one light but many, merging together into a pulsing organism of some kind: brilliant, bold, vivid, and hard to look at for too long.

I looked away to see if Ehs was around. He was. Still the old man in the wheelchair, with even thicker sunglasses but still looking away from the hospital. He was moaning a bit, as if in pain.

"Are you alright?" I asked, suddenly forgetting my friend inside and all the other pain that had been on my mind.

"Can we back up?" Ehs started backing up in his chair, got frustrated, and said something under his breath before eventually getting the chair moving.

I followed him for a while, glancing back at the light every now and then. It was enchanting—almost addicting.

After we had moved a good twenty yards, Ehs finally stopped and turned around a bit, still not toward the light. "Okay, so I was going to show you a little more of the wall today, but let's not. Obviously," he said, gesturing toward the light, "there are more important things."

"What is that?" I asked. "What am I looking at?"

"Insipid can't touch hospitals. Never has been able to. I gave up trying generations ago."

"Go on …"

I assumed he was happy to have a listening ear not ready to argue. "Sit down." He pointed toward a nearby ledge. We were both facing each other, and the hospital—or light—was off to our sides.

"In the beginning there was nothing. The first thing created was …"

I was back in Sunday school class but I was alright with it. Sunday school taught by Ehs was probably more entertaining than most of what I grew up with and, ironically, probably more authentic. At least this demon was in plain sight. "Light?" I half asked, half answered.

"Right. Light." He seemed happy. "Funny, most people don't answer that correctly. And creation myths usually botch it or people just gloss over it."

He had me thinking again, trying to go over my own creation myth.

"I know you don't take the story literally but the remnants of taking it literally are still there—we've done well—even for someone like you." He crossed his legs. "You think suns and stars or some kind of literal light."

He had a good point.

"But, this is a story. And light and darkness are in every story—well, at least the good ones."

"Good and evil?"

"Sure. More interesting is that the darkness was not created. Funny how worked up people get over whether or not the gods created evil." He smiled. "But, the darkness existed. Always. Before the light. Darkness is first. Absence, chaos, emptiness. Light arrives after the darkness. Created. Creation. New. Inspiration. Light comes and the darkness and light separate, as they always do, of course. They can't exist together, though they are dependent on one another in many ways."

"The yin-yang," I threw in, taking another glance toward the rainbow orb of goodness off to my side.

"Focusing on creation was a genius way to distract everyone from the human story part of it." He picked at something on his arm. "And, of course, a great way to distract from evolution. I'll be honest." He looked up, distracted again. "I don't think our side saw that coming. The incessant addiction to creation at the cost of the creative machine of the universe: evolution." He stared at me, as though forgetting his lines.

I nodded. "The light, though. Human story."

“Sorry.” A slight shake of his head and he was back. “Yes, it’s the story of life. You. Before there was you, there was nothing. When there is nothing, there is darkness. Emptiness. Absence. The light is created and the darkness separates. You arrive and the darkness flees. The light is everywhere. Look at it.” He pointed toward the building. “I, obviously, can’t.”

I looked over and imagined newborns coming into existence. I’m sure it was coincidence but it seemed as though a new light appeared even as I stared. The whole Genesis story was roaming through my head along with Shadows and Rays and god and darkness and chaos, while I looked toward the hospital, its light emanating and rippling out into the world beyond it, with color. I was drawn to blue sky and green and yellow grasses in the surrounding areas, colors that seemed to penetrate the grays that made up most of the view outside of its reach.

“Are you saying evil existed before good?”

“Words,” he muttered, as though that was some kind of answer.

“Words, what?”

“Good, evil. Light, dark. Let go of the clarity. You always want it. Are you really asking whether evil existed before good? What does that even mean?”

“I mean …”

“You don’t know what you mean,” he answered for me. “Because those words are meaningless and even if they weren’t you are asking questions about what existed before consciousness and matter? Who knows? Who cares? Distractions!” He paused only to catch his raspy breath. “These aren’t beings. Our abstractions, light and dark, are realities of existence.”

Ehs wasn’t always so eloquent and serious but he was at that moment and I kept listening. I even needed it. He was reaching some part of me that I needed to be reached.

“The light of forgiveness comes from the darkness of infliction. Love from fear. Redemption from pain. You can’t have life without death.” He nodded slowly, as though letting his own words register. “You can’t have light without darkness.”

He stopped and stood to his feet with his hands folded, his veins bulging under the thin skin of the old man. “Pain is the teacher,” he continued.

“Yeah,” I interrupted. “And love.”

“Love is pain,” he answered.

“Um,” I began, but he wouldn’t let me continue.

“The search for love. Pain.” He seemed to grow slightly taller.

“The absence of love.

"Pain.

"The loss of love.

"Pain.

"The longing for love.

"Pain." He was definitely bigger now than he had been.

"The fear that love will be taken. Pain." He was now towering over me, saying pain, but I was not scared. "Love and pain exist together, just as light and darkness do."

I didn't speak.

"And finally, there." He pointed toward the light, still not looking. "People understand that. They realize their answers don't work. They realize their meaning is lost. There." He shook his frail finger that appeared stronger than it should have. "The ego dies. The certainty dies. The resistance dies. The knowledge of good and evil is consumed by the light of creation again. It is uncovered, as it always was, as it always is, but as the humans always resist."

I exhaled a deep breath. The kind that responds to a sense of being overwhelmed. I looked toward the light at the hospital: the colors, the energy, the life, amidst what I knew was death.

"We can't fight what people do in there," he continued. "And it has nothing to do with the statues of their holy women and their crosses." He looked toward the sky again. "Of course, there is healing there. But that's obvious. Physical, sure, but most people walk out of a hospital aware of the light again, the light they first arrived with, and with the proper understanding of darkness again."

I looked over at the brightness one last time.

"The blind see. The lame walk. In the only way that matters or has ever mattered."

I was still not used to a demon quoting verses at me. I closed my eyes. When I opened them I was sitting on the sidewalk next to the man in the wheelchair. I looked back toward the hospital just as Rachel came out of it.

I'm a seven on the Enneagram. One of my faults is that I seek to avoid pain. Accurate. I don't even like to look at hospitals. But that moment, I stared at it and soaked it in and thought of the people inside who were suffering, the people helping those who were suffering, and the people welcoming new life in every imaginable way, not just in the physical form of infants.

I kept staring.

"Ready?" Rachel asked.

"Yeah," I answered. "Is everyone okay?"

"They're going to try to be," she answered.

I turned around and headed toward the car, but as I did I glanced at the man in the wheelchair and I saw tears coming from beneath his sunglasses. I stopped. "Sir," I said.

"Yes," he answered, not looking my way.

"Are you alright?"

"I'm dying."

I didn't say anything, knowing he had more to say and not ready to speak myself.

"I'm dying," he repeated. "And it's not really death I'm scared of." He paused and started looking for a cigarette. There were only a few left.

"Can I help you?"

"Well," he laughed. "I don't know about that. Doctors say I've got about a week."

"I mean with the cigarette."

"Ah," he continued to chuckle. "No, no. I've smoked more cigarettes in my life than any man should. I can handle that. Lots of experience."

I smiled and looked back to Rachel, who was standing nearby, smiling as well.

"Now if you can help me find love—" He managed to grab the cigarette. "That would be something."

"Do you have any family?" I asked.

"No, no. All dead."

"Friends?"

"Nope."

"Who's taking care of you?"

"Nurses." He lit his cigarette and started sucking it down. "Move on." He made a motion with his hand. "You've got life to live, son." He looked toward Rachel and grinned. "Lots, it looks like." He was looking back toward me. "Live it. Take that bitch we call life by the horns and don't look back. Ride that fucking thing for all she's got. Go wild, you hear?"

"Well," I chuckled. "I'll do my best."

I noticed another tear sneak out and run down his cheek and I couldn't help but let loose a few tears of my own.

"Hey," he grunted, nodding his head toward Rachel. "You hear that?"

"I did," she nodded. "I did."

"Well, it goes for you too. No offense in using the word *bitch,* I hope."

We all three managed a laugh, somehow.

"Go wild, you two. Live!" he practically shouted, finding strength in his words that I would not have thought had been there.

"Thank you," I said pensively, glancing toward Rachel and back toward him.

"Hmm," he grunted. "See," he mumbled and started rolling his chair away from me back toward the hospital. "You hear me? See. Don't underestimate the power of seeing someone as a human being even if they are a worn-out one like myself." I watched him get to the crosswalk and start to move across the street.

But then he stopped.

I kept staring.

He was like that dog again, with the invisible fence. And he couldn't face the hospital.

"Seth." Rachel started walking again. "You ready?"

I kept staring and he kept not moving.

"Seth?"

"Do you see this?" I asked. I couldn't peel my eyes away, even as I wiped a few more tears.

And then I saw something leave him. A subtle stream of smoke that tried to camouflage itself in the cigarette, but I saw it clearly, darker and more tangible.

And then the man in the wheelchair started moaning and groaning, dropping f-bombs and yelling at some nurse to "get her ass over here and help me."

"Holy shit," I muttered.

"What was all that?" she asked.

"That was Ehs." I had more tears streaming down my face.

"Again?" She looked toward the man. "Like that? Telling us …" Her words faded out or maybe I just didn't hear them.

"Crying." I looked toward her, with tears on my own face. "He was crying."

"Seth," she said with grace. "This is all too hard."

I looked back toward the hospital and wiped away my last remnants of tears, nodding. "I know."

"You're supposed to talk about all of this tomorrow?"

"I might just read a poem."

SEVENTEEN

The coffee was brewing and thankfully the fresh aroma was starting to replace the stale air that often lived in the church building's kitchen. It was early the next morning. I was by myself, as I usually was early Sunday mornings. The emptiness and space, literal and figurative, always felt like good therapy. I would play music loud—usually some of that nineties hip-hop—to get my blood flowing and wake up my body. The coffee usually did the same to my mind. I would adjust chairs, move furniture, wonder why I was doing what I was doing, hopefully find some reminders, and then start with a whole new set of questions. I felt like I had been on a good roll with the answers, as of late, but Ehs was changing it all. Again.

A wedding had happened the night before in the building so I cleaned up some cigarette butts, some beer cans, and a few dead sparklers in the parking lot, all the while hoping I would figure out what to say when everyone started to arrive with the intention of hearing me. The aroma of rolls and salads and bad food were making their way out of the building along with my anxiety. As the coffee wafted through the air, so did a shallow, fragile confidence.

Returning to the kitchen, I smelled cigarette smoke. A worried frown filled my face again as I lifted out a finished carafe and brought it into the foyer, where I pumped myself another steaming hot cup. I looked around to try to find the origin of the scent, which was proving difficult, even if it was clinging to me like a scared toddler and pushing a little of that scare into me.

Did a drunk wedding guest get lost in here?

My imagination was happy to fill in the gaps the nerves were opening up. And then I *felt* someone behind me. I spun around but it was still just me, which only encouraged my imagination and nerves.

"Ehs?" I asked to the emptiness.

Another stream of cigarette smoke and a sound back in the kitchen. Someone was in the building. Maybe an early volunteer?

By the time I arrived, I could see the smoke and I knew it was not from a cigarette. It was too dark, too vivid, too permanent, sliding through the air with purpose before turning and heading directly at me. A stream of smoke more like an arrow than an exhale.

"Good morning." I heard the words clearly.

"Good morning," I answered back to the air. "Back so soon?"

"Do you have some time?" The arrow turned into a halo, circling around my head. A dark halo, not the type that would be circling an angel's head, that was for sure. But he wasn't an angel, and I probably wasn't either.

I glanced at my watch, because that's what I do when someone asks me the time or if I have time. "Yeah," I answered. It was going to be a relatively easy morning beyond not having any idea what I was going to say.

"Good," he shot back and the halo turned back into a straighter line heading toward the front doors. "Follow me."

Once outside, I smiled immediately. A Tesla was resting in the parking spot that had been home for some cigarette butts earlier. A worthy upgrade.

"You shouldn't have." I stared at the car I wanted more than any other car. "This is new." My lust for a material possession was in full gear.

"Well," he answered. "I figured you'd like it."

"Is it real?" I began to notice something was off. It was like a car covered in dry ice. Bits of smoke fragments drifted away, like skin flaking off, from time to time, and sections seemed almost transparent. Yet, I could walk up to it and open the door. I did. Inside, it also looked like I expected it to.

"Does it run?" I waited outside the door.

"Of course," he answered. "Get in."

By the time I did, James was sitting next to me and he was gripping the steering wheel of the all-electric beast of a machine that was often another reason I had wanted to quit being a pastor—to find a job where I could afford one.

I closed the door and we were off in silent, electric glory.

"I've got questions," I said. If I was going to let him take me somewhere, I figured I would at least be allowed to drive the conversation.

"Go," he responded, keeping his eyes on the road, although I wondered if we were actually on the road. Or any road. "I assume you want music?" He pointed toward the stereo.

"Yes."

You don't want no problem … was soon thumping though the interior of the car. "Chance, huh?" I asked.

"You like him, right? It's for you. Music doesn't really do much for us," he answered, with a filter of sadness. "Another effect."

"Oh." I was already moving to the beat. "That sucks."

Just another day …

"Are we actually on the road?" Easy question to start off with as we passed a car. Everything seemed real, except for the subtle twitches and puffs of smoke here and there.

"Well—"

"Can we do these like a lightning round? Not the big explanations. Just … plain and simple, to-the-point answers." I also turned down the music. "Love the song, but I need to hear you."

"Fine," he responded. "I'd rather get through these questions too. I've got my own agenda for today."

"Great."

"So, are we on this road?"

"Yes. Of course."

"Do the cars see us?"

"No."

"Why?"

"Cars don't see. They are machines."

I rolled my eyes. "Really?"

James looked over at me. "Do you mean the people in the cars?"

"Really?" I reached out and touched the car's interior. "I need you to act like the mature Shadow you are."

"Okay, okay." He passed another car. I noticed I wasn't feeling any g-forces or momentum. But I was moving. "No, they can't see us."

"We're invisible?"

"You know enough about science to answer that yourself. There are all kinds of things you don't see … nothing at the molecular level, really …" He passed another car. "Most of the electromagnetic spectrum. Wind."

"So we're in that spectrum?"

"Sure," he answered.

"Sure?"

"Too complicated for a simple answer."

"Fair enough," I nodded. "So you don't even know?"

He shook his head. "Probably not."

"Why are you avoiding cars then?"

"For you."

"For me?"

"Yeah." There was an orange car directly in front of us and Ehs punched the gas. I closed my eyes and screamed but after the time I should have been killed or at least badly injured passed, I opened my eyes and we had gone through it. I had gone through it. I looked down at my own body and it seemed as real as it always did. "See? I try to keep things somewhat comfortable and normal for you."

"A Tesla, some good music." I looked out the window. "Thanks."

"You're welcome."

"How am I in this dimension?"

"You let me take you here."

"When?"

"You trust me. That means a lot. You've opened yourself to me."

"That makes me nervous."

"Why?" he asked.

"I'm asking the questions," I answered.

"Well, you didn't ask a question."

"Why shouldn't that make me nervous?"

"These are boring."

"Not for me."

"Leave if you want to. Nothing is stopping you. I've said that before."

"Okay." The reminder was always good, though like most freedoms, it felt artificial somehow.

"More?" he asked, antsy for his own agenda, like most humans. So, easy for me to ignore.

"Definitely," I answered.

"Go." He passed another car. We were moving fast, going somewhere. Or nowhere. I had the feeling the drive was going to last as long as I had questions. It was all just to make me comfortable anyway, I assumed.

"The recent mass shooting?" There had been another one, because there is always another one.

"Yes."

"Was that you? Was he a lonely water buffalo that one of you overtook?"

"No."

"Are you lying?"

He looked over at me. "I wouldn't lie."

"You're a demon."

"Shadow."

"So, no one possessed him or anything and made him go kill people?"

"No. And no one is possessing your soldiers either," Ehs shot back like a bullet.

"Those aren't the same."

"Is that a question?" he asked.

"No."

"Okay." He shrugged.

"Those are the same?"

"Humans killing humans. You can rationalize who can and who cannot. I don't really care. We just encourage the violence and hatred … we—especially the war department—don't care how it manifests itself."

"Ugh."

"It's all the same to us. Honestly, if I had to choose, as head of advertising, I would probably vote for more drone strikes. Constant killings carried out in the name of your government, on a regular basis. So cold. So detached." He looked at me sadly. "You don't care much either about the thousands they kill. Many innocent." He almost smiled.

There was not much to say back.

"In addition, you can judge a country by how it treats its poor and oppressed," he said. "So, I don't think anyone has ever asked if an executioner, working for the government of your godly country, is possessed by a demon as they plug chemicals into the blood of an innocent man, wrongly convicted of murder because of prejudice and fear and a skin color, while cheering that they are carrying out justice in the name of those same gods, pretending to maintain the critical values of your gods for your Christian country."

I felt cold.

"That would have been a much better question than whether or not we infected the shooter in … where was it this time? Or should I say where was it that you paid attention to," he mumbled. "But still, we don't. Either. We don't need to. You are doing just fine producing your own violence. Every day. Around the world. In the name of gods."

"Sounds good," I returned. "I mean …" I sighed. "It's terrible. It doesn't sound good."

"I think as a pastor you already knew all this to be true. You've said as much." He looked back toward the road. "That's assuming you believe what you say."

"Ouch."

"Well …"

"Let's move on."

"Fine."

"Dark and light. What happens when you battle?"

He smiled. "What happens whenever light and dark interact."

"Do you kill each other?"

"Killing is something you do. They reveal. We hide."

"But you can harm each other?"

"The great revolutions happened when people gave up violence and responded with love. It's been said a million times.

"Right."

"Did I miss the question?"

"No." I stopped. "So … you can't harm each other?"

"Revealing what we don't want revealed. Hiding what they don't want hidden? Of course, that can be called harm." He nodded and adjust the air conditioner, purely for show.

"So, most of the Old Testament is pure bullshit then."

"Is that a question?" he asked.

"I don't know. Comment."

"It's a true book, about what skewed perspectives can do to a people, or society, or the world."

"Well, at least it corrects itself."

"Sure, if you want to say that."

"Should I?"

"I can't tell you what to say."

"Is any of it true?"

He looked at me, bored, disappointed. "You know these answers."

"Why didn't you go to someone else?" I wanted to change the subject.

"What?" he asked, apparently caught off guard with the change.

"Yeah, why me? You could have gone to someone with more clout and used them instead of me. A bigger name. More influence. There are better people than me."

"I've told you."

"Tell me again."

"I couldn't find anyone else."

"Seriously?" I asked, followed by a pang of pride to help stomp out the jealousy.

"I didn't look that hard, I guess. But … no."

"Are you my genius? Were the Romans right?"

"Their language was … more accurate." He smiled. "The idea of being visited by wisdom is much better than it originating inside of you. But, as is often the case, you—with help from us—you prefer the language that elevates your ego instead of the one that deflates it."

"You know—" I waited for him to look at me. "That makes you my genius."

He smiled. "The light and dark both need each other."

I looked out the window. We were passing cars and buildings

and roaming through our fairly empty city on its Sabbath morning. "Prayer?" I served up.

"Yes?"

"Does it affect you?"

"Me," he asked, pointing to himself.

"Yeah."

"Depends."

"Jesus said these kind only come out with prayer." A great hit, right down the line.

"What do you think the disciples had been doing?" He backhanded back on to my side of the court with no shot of getting it.

"Does it say?" I was trying to think of the story.

"Praying," he answered for me. Point for him.

"What? They'd already been praying?"

"Yeah."

"So, what did Jesus mean?"

"Lots of things."

"Like?"

"Obviously, not prayer, like you think. Jesus didn't even pray, like you think, in that story."

"Then ..."

"More mystery." He almost whispered.

"Why do I pray?"

He shrugged again. "Why do you?"

"It affects me."

"Great ..."

"That's it?"

"*You* affect *us*." He swerved to avoid a person walking across the street. For my own sanity.

"So ... prayer is all just a mental game?"

"Mental?"

"I mean, does it do anything?"

"It might do everything!" he replied with some force.

"But it doesn't affect you?"

"It affects you. That is everything. Or nothing. We are nothing. We only create the things that affect you. Nothing else matters."

"Okay."

"You have the power. Always have. They seek to illuminate it and we seek to cover it. But you have it, rest assured."

Ehs was such an encouraging demon friend and I still wasn't sure if that was good or not.

"Obviously, though, we're not talking about you sitting down to say some words out loud before a meal?" he asked, suddenly serious, as though he was going to take back his affirmation of power to me.

"Right?" I practically asked if I agreed with him or not on that one.

"Prayer. Terrible word. We crafted the idea to distract you from everything else you say or do or … just resting in mystery," he said, almost annoyed. "It's all the same. There are no magic words. So rather than ask if you are praying enough—or when you should—you might want to ask *what* you are praying." He paused and looked over at me. "Mental, or not, you are. Along with everyone else."

"Jesus said when you pray go in your closet, though?"

"And Jesus prayed in front of people." He smirked, shaking his head. "Speak. Act. Rest. Wonder." He sighed. "Do that. And prayer … well … you won't need to worry about it."

"Can we come back to music?" A new, slower song was playing in the background.

"Yes?"

"It's magical."

He nodded. "It often helps you see."

"Why?"

"Art speaks a different language, closer to the original."

"The original?"

"You've heard me speak our version. You heard her speak hers."

"At the park?"

"Right."

"That was amazing."

"I assume so."

"You've never felt it?"

"I can't speak that language."

"How long have we been driving?"

"Time," he said, not answering at all.

"Right?"

"Time is only a way to measure entropy and decay, which is only a way to measure birth and evolution." Another swerve. I didn't even pay attention though.

"I'm lost."

"Time is just a number to mark change."

"Yeah, but …"

"I'm not a physicist."

"Me neither," I responded, in case he had forgotten.

"Then don't worry about it."

"I'm not going to be late for church, right?"

"No," he answered.

"Making love, you really don't?" I figured I might as well ask one I had always wanted to come back to. There was no use being subtle about it.

"No."

"You don't?" I was a little surprised.

"We don't experience love."

"I mean sex … isn't always love."

"It's generally a result of it or a search for it. You can't participate in it without the ability to participate and experience love. You didn't ask if we had sex though."

"Okay," I responded. "So you have sex."

He hesitated. "Words."

"Sexual assault has nothing to do with love."

"True. We can do that to each other."

"Okay." I was not about to educate Ehs on the intricacies of sexual function and definition.

"Physical acts never exist in a vacuum, although we've convinced you they do."

I wanted to say something but I couldn't quite form the words and I assume my expression revealed as much.

"We'll get there. Different zone." He filled in the emptiness.

"Of Insipid?"

"Right."

"Okay."

"Rachel," I said, without knowing where to go.

There was a pause. "Yes? What's the question?"

"She … can see you. You showed yourself to her. Why? How? I don't know—"

"Seth," he interrupted. "You love her. She loves you."

"Okay." Always nice to have it confirmed.

"She's with you. She supports you. If you're seeing me, and she's there, she will be in it with you. What is wrong with that?"

"What if she doesn't want you?" I asked.

"Then she wouldn't see me."

"So, she does?"

He just lifted his eyebrows to indicate the answer was in front of me.

"So—"

"It was the first time I had come to you. With her right there."

"I'm still so confused with all—"

"Yes," he interrupted again. "Yes, we know. Get on with it."

"Would she have seen you before?"

"Before what?" He asked but I sensed he knew.

"When we were both having affairs."

"Probably not."

I sighed. "Final question."

"Good," he replied. "I'm exhausted."

"You are?"

"No."

"Were you crying yesterday?" It had been weighing on me.

"Yes," he responded.

"Why?"

"I've told you. I want it. Love. The only kind of freedom that matters: the one without the threat of fear. Her."

"Really?"

"Seth." He stopped the car in a fast food parking lot. Surprisingly, to me, it was the same restaurant that was located across the street from the building where we did church. We had barely moved even if we had been driving for hours. "Do you think I don't have anything better to do than … no offense … hang out with you?"

"Ouch."

"Well …"

"Okay. So, this is real?" As though, if it wasn't, I thought he would tell the truth.

"Yes."

I bought what he was selling.

"Wait, I have a few more." I held my hand out to make sure he understood not to start whatever lecture he was about to.

"Go on," he answered smoothly.

"Was Leo possessed?"

"Possessed?" He seemed offended.

"Yes. He called Rachel that day and doesn't remember even doing it. Or why. Or how he would have known."

"We don't possess anyone."

"What the hell have you been doing then?"

"Blinding them. It's no different than what happens most every other day as I've explained to you. Just a bit more extreme and visible."

"What …" I felt as though I had misunderstood everything up to that point.

"And Leo is often blinded, sadly," he said with little concern.

"Did you make Gwen or Jaden leave?"

"No, we don't *make*."

"Did you suggest it?"

"I suppose," he answered, almost agitated. "Are we done?"

"I'm not sure that I agree with your take on church."

"Fine," he nodded. "It's not mine. It's that of love and mystery. But—" He paused and looked at me with eyes that said *we're done*. "You will."

"But—" I was remembering past conversations. "You have said you've taken people?"

"I said overtake. Very different. The memory is a script, you know. Yours has been influenced by the stories of possessed people that you've heard too many times and it writes it that way when you recall it. Again, we've done well."

"Is it bad if I'm tired already?"

"You'll wake up."

"I will?"

"Now," he quickly moved on. "See that car?"

There was a car approaching the drive-thru.

"Haven't eaten a breakfast at this place in a long time," I replied. Which was true. "I used to love a good old breakfast sandwich."

"Do you know what's in those?" he replied, still looking at the person approaching the drive-thru.

"Rather not," I replied.

"Regardless," he continued. "Do you see that man?" He pointed over the dashboard at the car approaching the big panel with the bad sound where everyone orders their meal.

"Yeah," I replied. "Hard to miss." He was driving, of course, a big jacked-up truck with smokers or stacks or whatever the hell they are called. They were the cylinders that blow smoke—appropriate—into the air and made lots of noise because … it was pollution porn for a certain kind of person, I guessed. "Do you attract big trucks or something?" I asked.

"I'm not sure it's me. Seems to be your theme." He smiled.

I had to think about that.

"What's he ordering?" Ehs asked, ignoring my time to think.

"I have no idea. Can't hear him."

"You don't need to. It's a chain." He smirked.

I chuckled. "Okay, he's ordering some kind of fake food that looks like real food and tastes really good."

"So you don't eat here?" Ehs asked. As he spoke, I realized we were sitting in a parking stall watching someone order and they had no idea we were watching them. I wondered how many times Ehs—or something like him—had watched me.

I pushed the thought away. "We try to limit it, at least. Rachel is very against it."

"Why?"

"Why?" We were, obviously, back to him asking the questions. "It's shit."

"They don't sell food," he answered, and with a tone that told me his answer was better. "The founder said it himself: said his restaurant was not in the food business, but in show business."

"Yeah," I responded. "I guess that would be why."

"Did you know at one time the priests told the people it was wrong to cook good food … to appreciate food? Did you know they taught them that food was supposed to simply satisfy survival?" Ehs was focused on the restaurant so I watched him rather than the guy in the big truck ordering. "Did it with sex too," he mumbled. "Too easy." He grinned.

In the way that watching the groom watching the bride is as moving as watching the bride, watching Ehs was as interesting—maybe more—than watching some dude in a hat in a big truck order a microwaved piece of meat with something that looked like an egg.

For the first time I noticed the animal in Ehs. Something about his lips, the eyes, his snake-like hiding in the shadows, observing the prey. Learning what he needed to learn about him, salivating, enjoying the anticipation of the kill. "Hey," I interrupted because I didn't like the whole feeling.

He shivered. "Yes. It's crap. Of course, it's fast. It's consistent. It's cheap. It satisfies the requirement for food. It's survival in a sandwich."

I figured that was not going to be the new slogan for any restaurants anytime soon.

"Have you ever heard of Massimo Bottura?"

I spent a second trying to recall a script containing his name. "No."

"An Italian man. I've watched him look at wheat and scream, 'This is not wheat!'" Ehs laughed while the truck pulled forward to the second window, waiting for his breakfast. I wondered how Ehs had watched an Italian chef and why. Back to the truck, its stacks weren't smoking yet.

"And?" I asked.

"And what?" he repeated.

"Is it wheat?"

"Is this food?" Ehs slithered, nodding toward the restaurant. "Can you imagine what he would say about this place?" He pointed. "Yes, it was wheat, technically, but it was to survive on. Not to eat! No flavor, richness. It was an artificial, cheap replacement."

"Right," I said slowly.

"Yet he has changed tortellini—and everyone yells at him that it is no longer tortellini."

"Okay?"

"Isn't it funny that you can change the wheat and very few people say anything. But if you change the tortellini everyone says that this is not how we have done it for years. It can't be!" Ehs was back to almost hissing.

"So this is about religion?" I asked, assuming we were not there to talk about fast food, unless it was fast food religion.

Ehs looked at me as the truck drove away behind him, blowing all kinds of crap into the air and breaking the stillness and quiet of the morning with a ratcheting, pulsing noise. "Well done. Just like religion. You can always change the authenticity of the ingredients. No one notices. But change the recipe and everyone has a fit." He glanced back toward the truck and his eyes flickered.

"Do you want fast food or do you want farm to table?"

I nodded.

"Do you want religion or do you want enlightenment?"

I nodded again.

"My job is to make you want the false enlightenment, the cheap fast food version of the light: religion."

I kept nodding. Sometimes it got old affirming him. For so many reasons.

"How much time do you have?"

I, of course, checked my watch, because, again, that's what we do. It read about the same time as it had when I had last checked it. "Well—" I studied it and noticed that the second hand hadn't moved. "It looks like time does not fly when I'm with you." The second hand finally moved. I looked at Ehs with a "please explain this" look on my face.

He shook his head instead. "Good, I have something else to show you."

"Okay."

He shifted the car into gear and slammed on the accelerator. We would have peeled out of the parking lot but Teslas don't peel out so we shot forward with a quiet and powerful acceleration and force.

"Let's go to church." He then let out a dark, arrogant laugh. "Or at least what you call church."

EIGHTEEN

It was a megachurch service somewhere. I didn't recognize it but it might as well have been anywhere. Or everywhere. Anyone who has ever been into any kind of large Protestant nondenominational evangelical church service could recognize it. Anyone who has never had the pleasure has likely still tasted some of the ingredients.

Pick any small auditorium in the world. By small I mean a couple of thousand seats. Of course, they can get larger but those are more rare. Chairs, balconies, a stage. That part is easy. But then there are the telltale "evangelical" signs. Obnoxious video screens. Too many. Like televisions in a sports bar.

Weird colors and shading. And curtains. The lighting. I don't know—but something always seems off about it. Probably my own bias and distaste for them but I never find the setup to be right inside. Maybe it's just that the service is usually in the morning and we just don't find that kind of music production in many places with daylight outside.

It's nice. Very nice. Lots of money goes into making sure that everyone is comfortable. The right kind of chairs, good sound, and good lighting on the stage. Churches, of that caliber, generally don't spare expense.

In short, there is something off about most things that are labeled "evangelical" and it's the same whether it's a movie, a song, or simple architecture. They are too clean, too shiny, like a classic car competing for a blue ribbon. Sure, the car looks great—there isn't one mistake on it—but no one is ever going to actually drive it. That might mess it up. Or maybe it's just that it has to be labeled at all.

I've never been a fan of megachurches. They've never done it for me. I assume Ehs knew all of this about me and chose a place that would get under my skin from the beginning. So instead, I was arguing with him about all the good friends I had who worked at megachurches and who were "amazing, brilliant, creative, and good people."

"So were some of the Pharisees," Ehs responded while we were walking in the massive parking lot. "There are always fine people in evil systems. That's what makes the system even better for us." It was then I learned we could be as loud as we wanted and no one could hear us. I had also asked him what allowed people to see us sometimes and not other times and he basically repeated what he usually did about me not understanding and some new physics terms. I let it go because it was a kick being somewhere in secret, even if I was going to one of my most disliked places in the world. Then again, I was hanging out with a demon, so I assumed most churches would have happily disliked me as well.

We walked in and sat in the back of the room while everyone was standing and singing a recognizable worship song. I don't know which one—most of them sound the same—and I didn't want to put any energy into trying to figure it out.

I kept staring at Ehs though, expecting him to melt or fall over clutching at his chest or to turn into a vapor and leave the room. Or, at least, put on sunglasses. He did none of that.

"How are you allowed in here?" I asked amidst a drum solo.

Ehs was staring at the live feed of the drummer on the screens and smiling like a parent smiles at his toddler scoring a touchdown. "What?" He looked over at me. "Why wouldn't I be?"

"It's a church." Did I have to tell him that?

I recognized the sigh: a long, drawn-out, exhausted, and purposeful one. The purpose being to show me what an idiot I was. His eyes followed his sigh's lead, as did his shaking head.

"What?" I asked. "What'd I say now?"

"This," he answered quickly, "is not a church." He bounced his head toward the drummer who was keeping the rhythm for the wicked guitar solo.

"Do enlighten me," I answered with my own sigh.

"This is a building with some music and a lecture. Church is not a place." He looked back at the drummer as he finished his solo and the vocalist took over. She now filled up the video with the lyrics superimposed over her. "I think you know that."

"Okay, so we're going to get technical again?"

"Technical!!" He screamed as loud as I've ever heard him scream and I turned red from embarrassment, expecting the singing to stop and everyone to stare at us while security ushered us out. But they kept going, oblivious to Ehs's rage. "Technical!" he yelled again, with a hiss overlaid on top of it. "Church is a culture. Church is a state of mind. Church is a way of being. Church is a worldview, mindset, whatever you want to call it. Except a place! It's not a fucking place, you moron."

He had never used those words on me. And they struck deep

with a sliver of pain. "It's not technical. It's programming that you hear and say every day. Where do you go to church? Are you going to church? What's happening at your church Sunday?" He was speaking loud, so loud the music seemed to fade, as did the people next to us raising their hands in the air.

"Programming! Mindsets. This is not a church any more than a restaurant is. But you didn't ask me why I was there, did you?" He was quiet again, staring at me with dark eyes. "Why didn't you?"

"I mean, I assumed …"

"Yes, you assumed this is different than any other place. Sacred. Magical. A barrier of protection from evil because"—he laughed—"it's called a church and has some walls?"

I looked down at the very nice carpet.

"Your gods don't live here. Gods do, of course, but they are not any gods you want to follow. Not you, Seth, not you." He reached out and touched my shoulder, as though to apologize for blowing up and yet affirming it was necessary. "Technical …"

I don't know if it was because I had brought a demon, or if I didn't like the place, but the people in the audience sure didn't seem to match the enthusiasm of the band. Not on that morning, for that song at least. They were all half there. Like I was suddenly.

"Right," I replied. "I just assumed there'd be a lot of light in here, kinda like the hospital."

Ehs laughed so loud that I cringed, again, still not used to the idea of not being noticed when doing things that would normally guarantee it. It was the cold and dark laugh that slipped through every now and then and when it did, I wondered whether it was his true nature that he was hiding or his old nature he was fleeing from. Either way, I didn't like it.

By the time I remembered we were not really in the room and could dance naked if we wanted, he had stopped his hysterical, somewhat maniacal, laughing. "Are you serious?" he asked.

"You know, you have a real way of making someone feel like shit."

"It's been my job for a long time. Of course, religion took over that job very nicely for us." He was paying attention to the start of a new song. It began with a little electric guitar introduction and the place seemed to like this one. A new energy was emerging as the guitar got louder and the drums started building.

"I mean, I get an empty building isn't special but I figured a bunch of people singing and …" As the words left, I realized how empty they were.

"I could bring Legion in here and no one would care." He yelled over the congregation—suddenly singing some loud praises to god—like someone yells anywhere the background noise is too loud for conversation. For a moment he even sung with them, mimicking their hands raised and moving his body as they were. It was utterly terrifying.

I felt two things. One, despair and depression. I was a pastor. I ran a church and it was all pointless. Two, pride. I wondered if Ehs could bring a legion to my church. I looked at him. He could sense what I was thinking.

"Yes," he replied. "Yours is the same. Most of the time. Of course." He felt bad saying it at least. "Your arrogance is astounding."

It was. He was right. I was the same as everything I hated. Propagating more worthless bullshit and getting paid for it. Worse, thinking I was somehow different, believing I had found a passion again. I was the scumbag I never wanted to be and a demon was the only one honest enough to tell it to me straight. It was in that moment I didn't want to be a pastor anymore. Ever again. I could see why Ehs wasn't too worried that I had "found my passion" again.

"Get a grip." It was from Ehs, right as the song was peaking and the place was really getting rolling. It was, obviously, their anthem. He had to speak louder. "Those who have ears, will hear. They are hearing. Even in this place. They are the only ones you need to worry about. Let us have the rest." He smiled, It was a warm smile even if everything about it was cold. "Hand them over to Satan," he snickered and I wasn't sure whether he was mocking the sentiment or revealing a deeper truth to it.

The energy in the room was definitely building.

"It's bigger than that anyway," Ehs shouted.

The hospital is church, you moron. As much as anything else is.

I had proof of that now from the demon quoting bible verses while the band played on and the congregation went wild for a guitar solo.

What the hell was happening?

We both watched for a while, taking in the people who were apparently enjoying the wild froth of hand raising, shouting, loud music, and clanging cymbals. The song eventually died, followed by the buzz of the "worship experience," and soon the pastor was standing behind the glass (very modern) pulpit.

I looked over at Ehs, who was smiling like a kid at a circus as the elephants paraded out.

The pastor, wearing a bright button-down, came in fast with the preaching. "A" for effort, but the content was as stale as last week's leftovers, even if the guy was a good speaker and wore a nice shade of gray jeans that really went well with the button-down. Ehs seemed much more entertained than I was throughout the entire thing, He was almost giddy at times, incredulous at others—at this thing he had helped create and the amazing way it functioned.

Or maybe, he was just pretending.

Or maybe, he was truly inspired to be a better person … or Shadow.

I didn't want to ask him.

The pastor came in hot and never bothered to slow down: America is falling apart. We've left our foundation. We've left our morals. We've left what brought us god's blessing and if we don't repent and return to god, we're doomed. God will turn his back on us, as he did Israel, and we will be given over to our choice, our choice for destruction. He didn't say this exactly but he implied that we need to a) stop having sex and looking at porn, b) stop aborting babies, c) stop choosing liberal court justices, d) stop gay marriage, e) start praying more, f) start reading our bibles more, g) start being less ashamed of the gospel, and h) start being more bold in our witness. Of course, i) Jesus died for our sins and j) we just need to give our lives to Jesus and accept the free gift of eternal life and k) stop the devil from destroying our country.

The guy droned on forever. Ehs slurped up every moment of it.

In short, if someone were to look up "generic evangelical sermon in America in the twenty-first century," they would find what we heard. There was a good dose of fear with a little blood of Jesus mixed in and lots of doom and gloom if we didn't return to some rules, laws, moralism, and legalism.

Ehs was practically like a schoolgirl when the pastor was going over point k. To the pastor's credit, he probably wasn't aware that the devil's head of advertising was in his church listening as he was telling everyone to stop listening to the devil's lies. While speaking them. I wondered if he would have changed the message had he known he was practically speaking for the devil in the opinion of the demon I was with.

"Did you know that most evangelicals think that you can't be an American without being a Christian?" Ehs asked at one point during the especially "American" section of the sermon. He was ecstatic. I was not.

By the time the misery ended I was, obviously, in a negative state. One of the reasons I didn't go to megachurches was because they just about killed me. I felt like an alcoholic in the liquor aisle or a sex addict at a strip club, not because I was tempted to go back, but because

I despised the years it wasted and was wasting. It wasn't good for me in any way. I felt miserable.

Just when I had thought I was somehow finding my way in faith again.

"You knew it would do this to me, didn't you?" I asked.

"Let's get out of here," Ehs answered as the pastor bowed his head to pray.

Though it didn't matter, we snuck out while everyone had their eyes closed and their heads bowed, imploring god to return to America and save it again, as though god had somehow once loved it and as though it had ever been saved.

"Remember when god loved those sweet pilgrims who came over and killed the natives and took their land—and then killed the Mexicans and the Hawaiians," I ranted in a deep pessimism I had not felt for a while. "And the witches and the—just like every other country in the world in the histo—"

"Seth," Ehs interrupted, as we passed the espresso bar. "It's okay. I know …" For once he was not amplifying my frustration but attempting to soothe it. "I know what we've done."

It somehow helped me feel better.

Ehs nodded. "I have more to show you."

I glanced at my watch as I followed him out. We were still good on time, it seemed.

Our Tesla was no longer a Tesla. It was a jet. My frustrations vanished almost immediately as I stared at the matte black thing of beauty. My adrenaline was pumping and my heart racing even more than when walking out to my dream car—which is definitely saying something. This was my dream form of transportation.

"Damn," I uttered, because that's what we say when we're excited—for some strange cultural reason.

"Hop on." James ascended the metallic stairs and I took a moment to check out the landing gear sitting on top of a parking stripe, the slicked-back cockpit, the wings that seemed ready to take on any sky, and the tall vertical stabilizer with two stunning engines sitting below it. It was a handsome beast, even if unnecessary. I assumed it was all just something familiar and desirable to make things comfortable for me, because I was a human addicted to all three.

Ehs kicked the tires and feigned a true captain's inspection before throwing me a smile.

Before long we were airborne, after taxiing through the church parking lot to a nearby road. Surreal doesn't even begin to describe any of it.

"Have you been to Belgium?" Ehs asked, as though he were some young billionaire sitting on the black leather seats holding a glass of whiskey.

"No," I answered, staring out the window at clouds. "What the hell are we doing?"

"What do you mean?" he asked, almost offended.

"I assume we can just appear in Belgium?"

He nodded. "Of course. I thought some time to decompress would be good."

I shook my head. "I don't know if I can decompress while I'm on some kind of jet that isn't real."

"Not real?"

I gripped the leather armrest and smelled the wood paneling. It did seem real.

"Of course, it's real," he added.

I wasn't in the mood for another conversation on reality or truth. I couldn't.

"How do you feel?" he asked, changing the subject. "What did that do to you?"

"You already know," I answered, looking again out the window at clouds that seemed more generic than usual clouds.

"Well." He leaned forward. "What's important is that you realize I wasn't trying to rub your face in the vomit, like some kind of dog."

"Thanks."

"Let it go. You'll understand why I wanted you to see that soon enough. For now, we're going to Geel." I heard hell and I had a moment of panic.

"Hell?"

"No. Geel." He pulled out some sunglasses and put them on. "A small city. Of about forty thousand in the province of Antwerp."

I looked back out the window as the plane began to descend through more gray clouds. Rather quickly, the clouds started to give way to bright splashes of color: more color than I had seen in what felt like the entire morning. Almost florescent rays lit up green hilltops and blue skies: the hills were still green but there was more to the green, the skies still blue but almost a rainbow of blue. "What's with the color here?" I asked, understanding why Ehs had put on his shades, beyond his desire to look cool.

He chuckled. "The shadows aren't as large here. They've faded quite a bit."

I frowned.

"We're not in Kansas anymore, Seth." He thought the joke was funnier than I did.

"What am I seeing?"

"Well," he said, after calming himself. "Symbols, signs, metaphors, and visualizations. This is a different territory. There has been much more destruction of the realm here … this land was more shadowed generations ago but they've slowly evolved out of it."

Our descent was like a normal descent on a commercial flight. The rays of sunlight speckled the sky and landscape below me with their bold spectrum of colors, enchanting and grabbing all my attention.

"All of Europe is like this?" I asked.

"No, no," he said, smiling. "Pockets," he answered, standing to his feet. "Scandinavia is the worst of it. Practically a rainbow. Don't get me wrong, there is still plenty of Shadow and very recently—surprising really—some darkness is returning, but still we—"

"Really?"

"What surprises you?" He was steadying himself against the side of the plane as we hit a few bumps. "That Europe is brighter, especially the Nordic countries?"

"Well, I guess not." It didn't if I thought about it. "But, to have you just admit it—or say it so plainly … I guess …"

"God bless America," he laughed again. He started walking toward the door, even as we continued our descent. "It might be important to define the gods you want to bless it," he said. "Because they definitely have. Just not the ones most might expect."

I stared out the window.

We eventually landed in a field. I didn't understand how nor really cared to. As I spent more time in whatever realities Ehs brought me, I cared less and less about trying to understand.

The door opened and we descended the stairs that it felt like we had just ascended.

Sloping, wavy hills surrounded us with farmland on every side. It was classic, beautiful European countryside complete with the sound of birds expressing how happy they were to get to live in a postcard. They were probably writing orchestras and operas about it, flapping their little red wings and chirping their little yellow beaks.

"That," Ehs said while pointing, "is Geel."

It was the hospital experience again. There was a massive glowing orb of light too bright to look at, until my eyes adjusted. We were much further away than we had been with the hospital so Ehs could look at it for moments, but never too long, even with the distance.

"Have you heard of this city?" he asked.

"No." The light was rippling into all kinds of places beyond its core. Green shaded hillsides here, and bright trees there.

"Well, have a seat." He motioned to a couch that appeared in the field before he finished his words.

I sat down and looked at the city—well, what I assumed was a city. All I could currently see was simply a glowing orb of color that was brighter than any of the other color around—which was hard to do.

"Legend says she was born to a Christian woman and a pagan king."

"She?" I turned to face Ehs, who was sitting next to me on the couch, as though he were my best friend.

Is he my best friend?

"When she was fourteen, they say, she took a vow of chastity." He paused. "Her Christian mom died shortly afterward, leaving her alone with the pagan king—her father."

"She?" I noticed a bold navy bluebird singing nearby, bathed in light and color. I smiled.

"Her father had loved her mother very much and after she died, his mental health started to fade, rather quickly. He was convinced to remarry but after finding no one as beautiful as his wife, he started to lust after his daughter." He raised his eyebrows. "She did resemble her mother."

"Wait, the king lusted after his daughter?" My eyebrows were beyond furrowed. "Who the hell is she and what kind of story—"

"Sorry, Dymphna—I forgot to mention her name earlier—eventually fled. To Belgium. For obvious reasons." He pointed. "To that town. Geel."

I looked again at the light. I could start to see low buildings becoming visible amidst the distance and overwhelming array of color.

"Tradition says that she built a hospital. Unfortunately, her father eventually discovered her whereabouts, came to bring her back, and ended up cutting off her head. She was fifteen."

"I'm assuming this story is going somewhere …" I said, looking over toward Ehs.

"Three years younger than I was. Not quite the same life." The words that came out had marinated in sadness for a long time. "Sorry," he said, smiling. "Anyway, Saint Dymphna went on to become the patron saint of the nervous, emotionally disturbed, mentally ill, those who suffer mental and neurological disorders, psychologists, neurologists, and psychiatrists."

"I didn't know they had patron saints for all of that."

"She's also the patron saint of victims of incest."

"Good lord." I had no idea there was a patron saint of incest and I wasn't sure I wanted to know. "And, then ..." I still assumed the story was going somewhere.

"This town"—he pointed again—"is rather remarkable. Following the lead of Saint Dymphna—remember she was fifteen when she died—they started something that continues to this day. Deinstitutionalized care of the mentally ill."

The surreality of the moment hit me. A Shadow/demon was informing me of amazing stories of deinstitutionalized care of the mentally ill in Belgium in order to honor a patron saint of incest. I had to consciously bring myself to the present again.

"I don't know if I know what that means."

Ehs nodded, expecting it. "Here's the short version. The mentally ill come here from all over the world. Upon arriving, they are taken to a health care facility, potentially given some medication, and then assigned a host family. Interesting to note that people used to believe that the mentally ill were demon possessed." He shook his head. "The irony is thick, isn't it? Blame demons on the people you are supposed to take care of so you can ignore them and keep living the life the darkness wants you to." There was still a tinge of sadness in his eyes.

He had my full attention.

"Regardless, those that come here then move in with a host family who feeds them, takes care of them, puts up with their outbursts—some, of course, very violent. But the family treats them as human beings. The families are not told what their diagnosis is—they don't want to bias them."

"Wow," I remarked, no longer wondering why the city was glowing. "Wow." I tried to imagine my family taking in a mentally unstable person. I couldn't. "All kinds of mental illness?" I asked.

"Everything," he answered, standing up. "All kinds. Dangerous ones. For over seven hundred years they have been doing this."

"Wow," I said again. I was in awe of the place and frustrated I hadn't heard of it before. "Beautiful."

"They are not called patients. They are guests." I couldn't tell whether Ehs was bothered or proud—he seemed conflicted. "At its peak a quarter of the town was guests—around four thousand. You should listen to some of the podcasts about it."

"Okay," I answered, as though it was normal to hear a podcast recommendation from a demon.

"But—" He stood to his feet. "This is where it gets really interesting." He was now visibly excited. "I'm going to practically quote from a podcast if you don't mind. It's easier and I know the language has been crafted in a way you like."

I had no idea how to respond.

Ehs nodded. "Ellen Baxter. She attempted to start something similar in America. Hasn't gone too well. Thanks to us. But she has talked about why it works well here." He nodded toward the green fields and distant light of Geel. "She says that families are often more capable than professionals because they aren't bound by rules and they aren't blinded by diagnoses, but more important"—he paused—"they have let go of the mission to cure."

I took a deep breath.

"Let that sink in, Seth. They are more helpful because they aren't bound by rules, blinded by diagnoses, and chained with a mission to cure. Do you hear what I'm saying?"

"Yeah," I answered, looking toward the city. "You're saying these people are living more Jesus than that chur—thing, we were just at."

"Religion is bound, blinded, in captivity because of rules, diagnosing problems, and its almost singular intention of saving souls for heaven."

"Not all religion?" I countered in the most passive way possible.

Ehs moved around next to me. "Seth," he whispered. "You still like to lay the blame on others more than yourself but you're starting to see …"

"Starting?" I didn't want more.

"Yes. Ellen, of course, came and looked at Geel years ago. She was moved by it. Wanted to bring the idea back to America but, as I said, it didn't fly."

I kept looking ahead while Ehs continued next to me.

"Because Americans are obsessed with solutions. They want to solve things. They don't want to let things be. They want to fix, they want to repair, they want to seal the deal. Bound, blinded, you name it. We have to fix it!" he shouted, causing me to jump.

"You can't just let …" he said slowly, "it … be."

I sighed.

"She said, 'It's almost like their professional experience and language clouds them from seeing who people are.'" Ehs moved closer to me, now whispering. "Did you hear that?"

I had. But I wasn't sure it had sunk in.

"Their professional language clouds them from seeing who people are." He stood back and I looked over at him. "Welcome to religion, Seth." He smiled and opened his hands out as though he was going to give me a hug.

I nodded. "I know …" Did I?

"All religion. Fast food goodness that feeds the professionals."

"But—" I felt like the finger was being pointed at me and I was trying to process what exactly that meant and how to defend myself somehow.

"Just because there are marathon runners who manage to eat fast food does not mean fast food is good for you."

"But …" I couldn't think of any words to follow that one, as I processed.

"It's all only a road. But if you can get people to stick to the road they will never arrive to the destination. They'll worship the road, protect the road, blame others for driving on the wrong road, or even on the right road on the wrong side. They will identify themselves with the road, never needing or bothering to wonder what the road exists for. Of course, if they could ever get to where they are supposed to be going, they would realize the kind of road doesn't matter. But, we try to make sure they never get there."

"All roads don't lead to the same mountain," I said sarcastically.

"Said only by those who have never reached the top of the mountain and talked to someone who took a different path." He laughed, and then was suddenly distracted by something. "By the way, over fifty percent of prison and jail inmates in the United States have a diagnosed mental illness."

I looked at him. "That is one solution, I suppose."

He smiled. "Yes, you're welcome. We've had a big role in that. Along with some other departments." He put his hands on his hips, surveying the scenery as I had been. "Exclude. Remove. We don't want to see them now, do we?"

I looked back toward the shining city below a hill.

"There is one more spot I'd like to take you." Ehs turned his back on the city and began walking back toward the jet. "Do you have time?"

For the third time, I glanced down at my watch but this time I didn't even look at the actual hands. I only pretended to. "Why not?"

Blood in the water.

Up to that point, even if I hadn't realized it, things had been almost pleasant. When I thought of wraiths and demons or the Shadow world working for evil in the next life, I usually thought of stories of pigs running off cliffs, bearded men in chains foaming at the mouth, and little girls' heads spinning around.

Thanks to Ehs, I had started to believe those stories were the ones that were much less likely since they were *too* obvious, too blatant.

The whole point Ehs had been trying to make to me was that he was anything but obvious. He embodied a hidden, subtle, and therefore more dangerous evil, which, according to him, was what evil always was. And it was *that* evil that was much more terrifying.

That *had* been my thought process.

Where Ehs had earlier been careful to give me a transition—a car or a jet—his latest trick left me without any. I glanced at my watch and the next moment I found myself in an ocean of darkness with four words floating in my head.

Blood in the water.

I felt as if sharks were circling. Sniffing, waiting, anticipating a victim who is already wounded and vulnerable. The end is near. The powerful overtaking the weak—relentless in their task.

Nothing felt the same. I was bleeding. I was wounded, even if there was no literal blood dripping off of me. I was vulnerable and scared, consumed with this unrelenting sense of something powerful and vicious all around me, waiting to feed.

I tried to focus on my watch. I stared at the red band and the black-and-white face with the hands not moving, even though I was begging them to. At least the numbers were familiar and I desperately needed familiar. The second hand was red, though, and it soon sent me down the blood path again.

My emotions were in a state of panic, running around in pure chaos inside of my body, screaming and waving their hands in the air. I registered new sounds—amplified suffering—amidst the darkness that surrounded me, invaded me, and penetrated me.

I finally looked up. The drive to survive was steering me. If I was going to live I had to know what was happening at a more precise level.

I was at the base of the wall but it was not the wall I had seen before. Like most everything Ehs had been showing me, up to that point, the wall had been almost artistic and appealing. Clean, simple, straight lines.

That was no longer the case. It was the complete opposite.

It was a mess with bricks piled in random and chaotic patterns—more like pyramids than a wall. Hundreds of pyramids, stacked here and there, merging together into a blockade, its height and width extending as far as I could see. There were no rays of light, no breaks or gaps—in fact, everything was dark. The sky was dark, the air was dark, and the light was dark. It was just enough, the bare minimum needed to cast shadows and create varying layers of darkness in the dark landscape.

There were also people everywhere.

As I tried to absorb the scene, I began to take steps away from it, terrified by it and feeling as though the bite was about to come. I held on to my watch, clinging to it as though it were some kind of anchor to my real life in the midst of whatever ocean of death I was in.

The people appeared small: human shapes of varying kinds far away. They all looked to be carrying dark bricks. They were moving bricks. They were stacking bricks. They were everywhere, scattered like ants … each of them going wherever they were going with effort and toil. I couldn't make out any specific individuals. Their voices too melted together into a collective moan. I heard the cries of confinement and enslavement. The terror of claustrophobia and chains. I felt the sensation of being trapped: trapped in a bad job, trapped in a destructive relationship, trapped under credit card debt, literally trapped in a room.

The feeling of being stuck.

I recognized it in all my senses. The people were trying to express the feeling but almost as though it were its own language, not just words of a language. It's the only way I can describe it. It seemed the only way they could speak.

I continued to back up, sometimes aware, sometimes not.

Amidst the chaos, I began to crave pattern, like we often do. Something to associate, to recognize. There was order in the bricks, held in every hand, moving along some kind of path, and I found myself staring at it and them, wanting more.

A flash of lightning ripped across the sky. It was raining, I noticed for the first time, although I'm not sure it mattered. I felt soaked and cold enough already. It did make the wall glisten and shine, though, like high polished ebony, like the dark keys of a piano. Almost attractive, but its song was still too ominous.

"Seth," Ehs said. He was directly behind me. I turned around immediately, seeking the familiarity and pattern of him.

The shape of James was there, comforting and familiar, but his aura and energy were not. This was the shark. I felt it. I knew it. Danger and cunning emanated from every part of him. He reached out his hands, urging me to come forward.

I did.

In 1973, four victims were taken hostage in a bank in Stockholm and held for six days in a bank vault. Later on, after their release, they defended their captors. The term Stockholm syndrome was coined, defining the relationship that sometimes forms between prey and predator.

Is this me?

Ehs walked closer. He felt larger and I felt smaller. There was a power around him that was leaking into the air. I was standing with Ehs as he was known to the underworld, the other world, the ether world, the demonic world … whatever I should call it. There was something about this Ehs that I could tell would make demons cower.

And I knew him. So I did not.

I was *with* the shark.

Pride, power, and control are contagious drugs. One taste and we want more. One hit and we are addicted to their pleasure. Ehs pulled me in close. I could see the human shapes, I could see the wall and chaotic construction towering over them, but everything felt small and minuscule and weak and powerless in the face of Ehs … and me.

The human soul can be a deceiving little bastard. I felt powerful suddenly, like I had at other times in my past. Whether they had been real or not, a false perception or reality, who knows? Who cares? The recognition of hierarchy, when you're on top, feels good.

It felt good now. In the terror and fear and desolation, there was something that felt comfortable and indulgent and delicious. I was no longer the blood. I was the shark, or at least a friend of the biggest shark in the dark, storm-ridden, chaotic, and desperate ocean I found myself in.

Being a friend of power, I was power.

Of course, it's never true. But we still succumb to it almost every time.

I even smiled.

We didn't move but everything else seemed to. We were higher suddenly, looking down at the wall. It was even larger than I had expected. The pyramids that had been massive were becoming small as we rose high above them, just little mounds decorating the ground, like gopher hills in a field, but they seemed to extend forever in every direction. The size and scope were utterly overwhelming. Thunder crashed around us at times, and lightning flashed with boldness, daring to bring an instant of light to the darkness before being instantly smothered. In that instant, the rain gleamed in the sky.

"This is one of my favorite zones." As Ehs spoke, the landscape moved around in front of us, as though we were watching a massive and very real screen. "I wanted you to see it as I see it on a Sunday, when it's most busy. I'm sorry for the shock."

There were more piles of rubble and bricks and I began to see two tall black towers rising up like swords in front of them. Between and behind the towers there was a break of some sort—a gap in the wall that was filled with metal, glowing with a wet darkness. "A gate," Ehs answered.

In front of the gate were sentries. They were dressed like riot police, standing firm in a straight line with black shields, black helmets, and batons hanging from their waists. It was the first order of the day and the sight of the pattern felt comfortable, somehow. There were hundreds, lined up almost as though they were one.

Legion.

I assumed they were displayed in this more modern form for my own understanding.

"Stay here," Ehs informed me before leaving me—alone—and walking toward them. He seemed immense suddenly and, for a moment, I saw a black cape brushing the ground behind him and a black crown reaching for the skies on top of his head. I blinked and it was gone. Still, as he walked slowly in front of them, I started to think of James; of Elle, the big woman; of Nate, the delivery man; of the factory workers … of Ehs singing with the worship band.

The reality of what he had been hiding behind the disguises was hard to miss.

Then I felt a crack in the power of his hypnotism. A crack in my own walls. There was light inside of me again and I could feel it. I closed my eyes and tried to breathe.

When I opened them, we were at the base of a pyramid shape. Ehs was next to me again. We faced stacks of bricks leading higher and higher, adding to a wall that needed no additions. It was already massive, it was already impenetrable, it was already a defense against all light and yet, still, it was constantly being added to by the human shapes, moving bricks on wheels or carts like some ancient story.

"The story, Seth." Ehs spoke as if on cue, reading my mind. "Born with light, soon enslaved by the masters of certainty, of success, of answers, of salvation, of gods, of rules, of morality, of judgment, of outsiders and insiders … of religion." He walked closer to a line of human shapes that were grimacing to push another brick.

"The story?" was all I could voice.

"A car company was once fined more than one billion dollars for a brake problem."

The juxtaposition of my experience and his words was jarring to say the least. But I kept listening. The familiarity of the words was comfortable. I found myself staring at one human shape in particular. He seemed burdened, walking slowly, shaking at times. Miserable. My eye—and heart—caught him. He was close to us.

"The government, the experts, and the authorities all accused the company of faulty brakes. People blamed car mats, people blamed electrical systems, people blamed accelerator pedals. People had died and the company was the devil."

This human shape was trying to push a stone that was far too big for him up a slight slant toward the top of a pile. He was straining.

"So they found scapegoats, because they always do. Someone to carry the blame, someone to die, to appease our ego need for vengeance and our fear of forces beyond our control."

A sentry appeared from seemingly nowhere and, probably in an effort to impress his boss, pulled out a massive baton and slashed it across the human's back. I could hear the crack and my body involuntarily shook with pain as I watched the man fall to the ground and shake.

"While the car company was the scapegoat, while governments accused corporations, and billions of dollars traded hands, in order to appease the gods, any gods … there was another story."

I glanced up at Ehs. He had turned almost into a statue, staring out like a god himself, his arms folded across his chest, surveying the landscape with an emotionless, cold look.

The nearby man had found some new strength and began to push the brick.

"Driver error, Seth. Driver error. The majority of brake issues were due to driver error. After many studies, they discovered that most of the times someone had died, they had died not because of an electrical system or a car mat or an accelerator pedal. Not because of the scapegoat. They died because someone pressed the accelerator instead of the brake. They became confused, they panicked, they desperately wanted to stop but found themselves going faster instead."

The man I'd been watching had stopped, no longer able to push the brick. He was breathing heavily and murmuring under his breath, convincing himself he could do it.

"They're pressing the wrong pedal," Ehs whispered.

The man had collapsed and was sitting motionless.

"They're pressing the wrong pedal," he repeated.

I took a step forward, closer, out of the shadow of Ehs so I could see more clearly what was happening. The man was kneeling and appeared to be praying.

"It's easy to stop. Always. They just have to press the brake. But in their panic, in their desperate attempt to save themselves and those they love, they only go faster to their death."

The man was almost bowing now, moving his head slowly forward and back, pleading, I assumed.

"The story never changes."

The man finally finished. I heard him say, "Thank you, amen."

"Slaves." Ehs's voice grew louder. "Pressing the wrong pedal."

The man rose to his feet again, with a new energy and

determination, and began to push the brick. I could see it. It was clear.

"Bound."

The man's strength was surprising.

"Blind."

The brick was gliding along its path now as the man put everything he had behind it.

"Pushing the wrong pedal."

I could now see where the man was trying to get the brick. There were other humans there, helping to ease it on top of a newly formed pile. Another pyramid, another fortification, another brick in the wall.

"There we sat around pots of meat and ate all the food we wanted," Ehs continued. "Another story you have preached. I assume you recognize the line?"

The man did it. The brick was in its place. He could rest. For a moment. Soon, he started down the path he had just pushed the brick up. He put his shoulders back but he was tired, obviously. He began to move again, slowly but with determination.

"Pots of meat. Fast food. Certainty. Rules. Professionals. Blinded. Bound. Missions to cure."

The man was suddenly carrying a bowl of some kind in his hands and shoving some kind of food into his face as though he had been starving.

I looked back toward Ehs.

"They're pressing the wrong pedal," he repeated, shaking his head.

I took a few more steps forward as the man started to approach. I could almost make out his face. He was finishing off the last remnants of a bowl of food and talking to himself and I began to recognize the voice.

Distracting me for a second was a darkness on my periphery. I instantly looked toward it and recognized it: The Seers. This time their strange cloud-like shape was moving along the ground, stretching out as far as I could see like some black ocean extending into the distance, and rolling out toward the wall and bricks and sky, like some black fog bank.

"They're pressing the wrong pedal," Ehs said again.

The Seers moved across, above, through, and around us before I could breathe again. And then they were gone—watching, investigating, reporting what I assumed was good, dark news.

The man threw his bowl to the ground and I heard it bounce off the cold stones, drawing my attention again. He stood straight, still muttering to himself. "C'mon, Brad. There is work to do, the fields are white, souls to save. It's not always easy."

"They're pressing the wrong pedal," Ehs continued.

"Lose your life to save it. Of course you're exhausted but there is work to do." He was almost screaming at himself now. "Work! For the kingdom!"

"They're pressing the wrong pedal."

Another whip of thunder cracked through the sky, and it might as well have been a whip landing on the man's back. He fell to his knees, this time muttering apologies as he did. "I'm sorry, I'm sorry."

"Sorry?" I asked aloud, glancing back at Ehs, who seemed especially large and imposing. "Sorry?" I looked back at the man, who was still on his knees. "Sorry for what?" I asked him. He was now close enough.

He looked up at me and into my eyes. I instantly recognized him as the pastor we had been listening to earlier. He had tears in his eyes, as many pastors that I had met over the years did. I recognized them. Loneliness. Bitterness. Shame. Claustrophobia. Weakness.

He simply stared. As did I.

"What are you doing?" I asked, not sure if he could hear me.

"The work of the Lord," he answered, plainly. Another crack echoed across the sky and my own body shook as though a whip had been unleashed across my back. "The work of the Gospel," he repeated.

"No," I whispered. "No, you're not."

He again rose to his feet. I looked toward Ehs and back toward the man.

"The fields are white," he muttered and began to move again.

I began to shake my head. "Hey!" I grabbed his shoulder and made him stop. "Hey!"

I saw the tears again, running down his face and into the stew that still hung around his lips. "What?" he asked.

"You look miserable," I said.

He smiled. "We must lose our life to save it."

"No," I responded, immediately, surprising even myself. "Not like this. You're not losing anything! You're more aware of it than you ever should be!"

He smiled the smile of someone who would rather smile than address ignorance. I had smiled that smile many times to others. He was smiling it at me. I was the stupid one, he thought. I was the lost one, he thought.

I looked toward a never-ending stack of bricks below us. "The burden is light. This isn't right. This isn't helping."

Another smile from him.

I looked toward Ehs. He was motionless.

"Hey," I shouted back at the man. "You're pressing the wrong pedal!"

He smiled.

"Sacrifice," Ehs answered. "Poor Saint Anselm. Little did he know what he helped to start for us."

The man turned away from me and started walking toward the stack below us. I looked at all the people around me, carrying their bricks, eating their soup. I could see that many of them were wearing suits, or at least dressed nicely.

"I'm sure he never thought his ideas would be so big," Ehs said. "But, he didn't know we would help him. Press the wrong pedal."

"I get that," I shouted back. I was now looking around almost in a panicked state. "What am I supposed to do?" I shouted.

"The price must be paid. Saint Anselm said it himself."

"Yes, okay. Can you please do something?" I screamed.

"No." He shook his head.

"No?" I looked around at all the humans building the wall higher and higher and I wondered how many bricks I had contributed to it.

"It's powerful," he repeated. "Traveling over land and sea to make converts twice the sons of hell as you are."

I stared, overwhelmed at the scene.

"Pressing the wrong pedal. You'll notice this hell is most populated on Sunday with people believing they are avoiding the imaginary one."

"Yeah, I fucking know. I get it!" I screamed, above another crack of thunder and amidst a rain that was now coming down harder. "Who the hell is supposed to fix this?"

He said nothing.

"Who is supposed to fix it?" I repeated.

He looked at me and nodded. "You."

"Me?" My breath stopped.

"Are pressing the wrong pedal."

Someone was knocking on the door. I could hear it above the music, just barely.

I walked toward the front doors of the building and opened them up. A volunteer was there with his guitar. "Good morning," he said.

"Good morning," I responded before giving him a hug.

"How's it going?" he asked with a smile.

"Not that great," I said, with a weak smile of my own.

"What have you got for us this morning?" he asked, ignoring or not hearing me. Or both. He moved toward the coffee I had brewed to grab himself a cup. He was much more energetic than I wanted him to be. "Some good stuff?"

"I'm just going to read a poem." I said. *And maybe shut this whole sham down.*

I don't know if he heard that either. I'm not sure I cared.

EIGHTEEN POINT TWO FIVE

Rachel and I had been invited to the house of a church board member for a very "important" and "impromptu" meeting, two words that I had never heard uttered from any board member's mouth. To say Rachel and I were a little unnerved was an understatement.

We had been the ones who had started the church and led the church since it was a baby. We had always been the ones to make decisions and if the board was talking about anything, other than a Christmas gift or raise, we were always *in* on the decision. But the email we had received gave every indication that they had been talking about something amongst themselves, that it wasn't especially good news, and that it had nothing to do with a raise or Christmas gift. It was the middle of that dark summer and something told me it was about to get darker.

"Well, Seth," John, one of the board members, said a bit awkwardly, which was very usual for him. "I suppose we should get right to it." He attempted a laugh but I would have given it a two out of ten on the scorecard.

"Yeah, I guess we should get to it," I answered, trying to be light but feeling my words fall to the floor with a thud as soon as they left my mouth. "You might as well let us know what we're all doing here." I tried to smile but couldn't quite pull it off.

All of the other eight members were there. Young, old, men, women, married, single ... we had tried to represent the community with the board. This was the fifth iteration of the group since we had started.

Under usual circumstances, we had wine and snacks before the informal meeting.

But nothing felt usual about that meeting.

Stilted. It was like they had all been possessed by robots from the time we walked in. Artificial laughs and smiles ... maybe intelligence. Jury was still out. We had also been invited to arrive at a later time than everyone else—evidenced from everyone being there before us—another very bad sign.

The autonomous board member John, who was already as awkward and jolting as most humans on a good day, was especially mechanical.

"Okay, Seth," he said. "We …" He looked around at the other board members who were afraid to make eye contact. I looked at Rachel. She appeared strong in the midst of the chaos—my rock.

Damn, is she my rock? It didn't feel that way when we were fighting last night.

"Seth, we received an email. Well, I received an email. And I sent the email to some others because …" John looked down. "It was very worrisome."

"Okay?" I asked quickly, hoping John could pick up on the fact that dragging out whatever announcement he had was making it ten times worse.

"Well, the email was worrisome. It …" He looked around again.

"John," I interrupted. "Please, can you rip the Band-Aid off?" I scanned the room for someone else who might want to give the announcement. There were lots of heads down.

"John, if you don't mind." It was Susan, an older woman who had been born into the Great Depression. Her mind was as sharp as any mind I had ever seen. She was an optimistic and gentle elder … and she grabbed the room's attention immediately. "Seth." She waited until I looked at her. "Rachel." She looked at Rachel and made eye contact with her as well. "This isn't easy for any of us. We love you. We respect you. We have grown immensely under your leadership and the way that you have guided and molded this community of people for so many years. In fact"—she looked around—"we barely know how to lead this meeting, we're so used to you doing it."

I smiled. With her. A small taste of humanity.

"John received an email from Gwen Milano this week. And—" Susan looked down before gathering herself and looking back at me with tears in her eyes. I lost feeling in my body and had to do everything I could to maintain some semblance of clarity. "She is claiming that the two of you had an affair for almost a year, more than a year—I don't remember—while you were a pastor here. A few years ago. Before she got back with her husband."

The energy of the room was stifling and hot. I rolled up my sleeves and looked toward Rachel, who was already starting to cry.

"She was not antagonistic and she did not wish for any harm to come to you." She looked at Rachel. "Or you, Rachel." Susan was now crying, looking at Rachel, and assuming she was the first to tell her the news. "We knew … things were not great with you both …" She was stumbling through words. "It's why we gave you the six months off. And …" She paused to wipe away tears. I began to cry myself.

Fuck.

"You seemed so much better after that. But … this … I'm sorry, Rachel," she said again. "Gwen did want us to know the truth. She said she could not bury her secret anymore."

And there we all sat. It felt like a year. It could have been ten seconds; it could have been ten minutes. I still don't know how long it was. If time is the measure of decay, as Ehs said, it was measuring lots of decay in those moments. I couldn't see. My eyes were covered in water. I couldn't speak, my tongue wouldn't move. I couldn't feel: the shame was cold and unforgiving. No one said anything. No one even looked at each other. We were more used to talking about helping out a poor family or switching up a Christmas Eve service, not trauma of this level. Especially not related to me. I had been the rock up until then, even if much of that rock had been more like a paper-mache rock on the set of a movie. It had always looked good on the outside and these poor people had just discovered a small piece of the reality of how fragile it had been. Little did they know.

"Well," I finally said, wiping away my own tears and emotion. "Gwen Milano?" I asked, sensing the need for more time. Or details.

"Seth," John spoke out again, unfortunately taking the reins back from Susan. "I think we need to know what happened."

"John," Rachel said, surprising me and the rest of the board. Not because she spoke but because there was some kind of fire in her that I had rarely seen and I assumed others in the room had *never* seen.

"Seth had an affair. Yes. Our marriage was terrible. I think you all know that and we are so thankful for everything you did to try and save it. I'm sorry we weren't more honest with you."

There was a younger energy born into the room. Of course disappointment, but also that strange excitement that comes from hearing juicy gossip in an otherwise mundane life. And the always powerful release of pent-up secrets.

"Yes," was all John could respond with.

"So we might as well start. I was also having an affair."

That newborn energy grew fast and unleashed itself, knocking everyone back so far in their chairs that necks were going to hurt the next morning. Our hair should have been swept back and our faces covered in soot from whatever the hell explosion emanated out from Rachel.

It was epic somehow.

"Whatever Gwen said is probably true. And there is a lot true that she probably didn't say." Rachel looked at everyone in the room, tears rolling down her cheeks, yes, but strength rolling out of her mouth and eyes and body too. "And we've been working real damn hard to save this thing." She looked at me. "To save us. And, again, I'm sorry for my part. But, all that matters right now is us." She looked back at everyone, secure and terrified. "So now what?"

Maybe it was because walls had been on my mind, but I could practically see the walls go up. The defenses that start coming when confronted with danger, with anxiety, with a future that is about to be blown sky high. Along with a reputation. I could see them from people I had never expected to construct them against me. Only because I had never expected them to find out about my small indiscretion—which, looking back, was incredibly stupid. Of all the things I had prepared for, I hadn't prepared for the inevitable board meeting that would someday come. Especially not the one where both of our "sins" were on full display.

Maybe I had never wanted to build walls with any of the people in the room. Well, except for Richard. But, here we all were, prepared well for battle.

From behind the walls, cold looks. Quiet pauses. Embarrassed glances. Tears. Louder voices. Hushed voices. Judgment masked with empathy. It got ugly fast. As it should have. My own walls were through the ceiling and forming an impenetrable defense as quickly as the rest of the board started to launch their missiles.

Finally, after a barrage of words, some comforting, some painful, some true and some not, I couldn't take the battle anymore. None of us was acting our best. I knew that much.

"Let's pause," I threw out in a good tone, like a good leader's last speech before the final battle. "Can we just stop and look each other in the face and remember that we're all humans here, including Rachel. Including me. And we'll remember you are as well." I paused and took a turn to look at each of them. Their eyes. Not the furrowed brows above them, not the tearstained, anger-flushed cheeks below them, and not the defensive postures surrounding them.

"We're friends here. John. Susan. Matt. Jonah. Lisa. Marie. Richard."

I mean, Richard, god, let's be honest, barely. You're a dick in every way.

But we're never *that* honest.

I saw lots of nodding heads. "I messed up. Bad. We both did." I glanced at Rachel and smiled, proud of the fact that we were even able to admit it—that I could say those words—in front of people, without the fear of what it would do. We were living it. We had lived it. We were going to live it. "We still love you. You still love us." More nods.

It was true, for me. I did love each of them. They had stuck with us and been by our side through all kinds of things. They cared about us and what we were all trying to do together.

"But that doesn't mean that Rachel and I should be at this thing we call church anymore. I'm resigning. As of today. Right now." The words came out whether I had intended them to or not. But they were not going to go back in my mouth, because the freedom they brought was exhilarating. I had not brought up the idea with Rachel. I couldn't dare to look her way. In fact, the gloating smile of Richard was somehow more accommodating so I looked at that longer than I wanted to.

"Our time has been done here for a while," Rachel added. "We should have resigned years ago and I apologize to each of you that we did not."

I looked at Rachel, who looked at me, and somehow in the midst of a hurricane of weird religious and relationship chaos, there was an oasis of calm and peace. I could see it and feel it emanating out of her and I knew she felt the same from me. Bonding within trauma was probably dysfunctional somehow but, in the moment, I didn't care.

Peace. It was saturating me like *she* had out there in the national park.

"I don't know—" Susan started.

"There's no other choice," Richard interrupted, with force because he loved force. "I think we should vote on whether we accept the resignation or not."

Richard was the one of them who wasn't like the others. In my more recent newfound passion and belief that church—or whatever the hell it was supposed to be called—was needed and going to be something beautiful and I was going to lead it, we had come up with the brilliant idea of putting someone on the board who was a bit more conservative. We wanted to be pushed. *We need all sides, even if it's just to make our side better* was the idea. Republican and Democrat: without one, the other doesn't work. That was our theory. Or my theory.

So Richard was invited to the board six months earlier. He still attended the church so he wasn't *that* conservative but who knew how much longer he would have stayed. The board position guaranteed that he would stay. He was a big donor and we needed to make sure his money stuck around for a little while.

Pay whatever it costs to keep money, even if he is a dick.

And he loved being offered some power. Power he clearly wanted to exert now.

John was a terrible board chair and, in that moment, happily gave the floor to Richard, who happily took it.

Richard, I assumed in that moment, probably felt as though God has brought him to this Earth for that moment: to lead us into greener pastures while burning me alive.

"Seth," he offered slowly with a voice that reminded me of a televangelist somehow. "Can I be honest for a second?"

Oh god, here we go.

"I have to say," he continued, basking in the glow of church leadership. "We've been worried for a while. I know I've been known as the more … conservative voice." He laughed. Others laughed too, hoping laughter could ease some of the tension that was building once more. "But, I might say that we've all watched from the sidelines—some more than others—and had concerns about where your theology was going."

There were some nods of heads as well as some *can we not do this right now* head movements. We were living in Richard's world.

"In other words, I can't say I'm surprised that it led to this." He acted very pained. "We tried to help and you lied. And, I guess I just need to say, this is what happens when you leave the Bible. This is what happens when you start to go down roads that we're told not to go down." He paused, giving me a moment to reflect on the fact that some of the reasons I had never wanted the affair to get out were being realized.

"This is what happens when you don't listen to godly council," he continued, apparently speaking of himself, of course. "What can we do now to—"

"Well, Richard," Susan spoke up, defending me, looking at Rachel. She also was feeling pain but it was a very different expression than Richard's. "I'm not sure that this is necessary. Not right now."

"Sure," Richard responded, with some kind of angst. Probably because he didn't like being put in his place by a woman. "Either way, I think we should have a say of hands. Do we all agree that we accept this resig—"

"It doesn't matter," I interrupted. "Just so you know. Whether you accept it or not. We're done. We need to be done. Richard." I looked at him directly. "I understand your concerns and, let's just say, at this point, I'm not sure they matter much. Not to me. It's time for us to leave. That is settled. What isn't is how we can make this as easy as we can on the people out there—who could take this very hard."

Because I was a fucking cliché. At least I'd rather be the cliché I am than the one you are, Richard.

"Agreed," Jonah said, his voice trembling. "I think we might just want to give each other a hug." He was soft, warm, tender, and his words and energy opened the crack for more tears.

"Agreed." John spoke this time. "I agree. This is a sad day but I don't think we need to make it worse than it already is." John pulled himself together and made more tears come. The cold shame was melting with some kind of warmth that had always drawn me to the men and women in that room, sans Richard, and that melt was about to flood the room.

And then I felt it. The Seers. Again approaching. Something dark, something ominous, something searching. I looked toward the doorway and saw it fill in the champagne-colored door. The black wave was there, coming fast, filling the walls, filling the windows, filling the floor, moving toward us all.

I went white but only for everyone else. I knew I could survive it.

No one else seemed to notice. Or see. Or care.

As quickly as always, it arrived. Like a dark forest fire, it swept through the living room, the sofas, the board, myself ... in a blur, moving outside of the house as quickly as it entered.

We were starting to hug each other.

And then Richard spoke. There was something different about him—I could see it. So could others. The faucets turned tight, stopping the tears in their tracks because something else was in the room with us. Or at least in Richard. I don't know if the others were as aware of what was happening as I was.

"Seth," he said loudly, his voice off—ever so slightly.

"Yes." I answered with the peace that was hanging around and that I hoped would never leave until Rachel and I did.

"Have you been talking to anyone?" His eyes were empty somehow. More than usual.

"Anyone?" I answered, amidst the blank stares and confused expressions that swept their way around the room as quickly as The Seers had.

"You know what I'm talking about."

"Richard," Jonah said quietly. "What—"

"Seth knows," Richard interrupted. "He knows. And I will tell him now, this once. You better be careful. We see you."

"Richard," Susan said, with the voice of a teacher—which she was. "I don't think now is the time."

And Richard agreed, suddenly, shaking his head as though he had just woken up. Which was partly true.

There were more hugs, more tears, more conversations, more plans, more meeting dates, and more consoling but in the end nothing changed the fact that we were going to be out of a job and out of a reputation.

And yet, as Rachel and I drove home, all we could talk about was peace.

Who knew quitting would ever feel that good? Oh, that's right, I did. Well, enjoy it while it's here because this is probably going to feel less good soon.

EIGHTEEN POINT FIVE

I feel the same about prisons as I do hospitals. It's not that there is something physically different about the table, the chair, the bed, the phone, or the person in a uniform … it's that there is something different about the smells, the energy, the colors, and all the other stuff that we can't see. I suppose it's why Jesus said we should visit people in both of those arenas: when you're in power there's something intimidating and enlightening about visiting a structure for those who are not in power, whether by choice or fate or neither or both. It messes with you.

Or maybe I should say, it messes with me. Again, I don't like pain and seek to avoid it at all costs. Prisons are just more pain.

But I now found myself sitting across from Leo. I tried not to stare at the scar, I tried not to let my expression show I was almost holding my breath for fear of inhaling the injustice and corruption I felt, and I tried not to show fear for being in a room with people who had done bad enough things that our society said they should be locked in a building with other people who had done bad things.

Jesus probably told *me* to visit jails and hospitals so I would find out what a fraud I was. Not just in religious belief structures—which I was no longer professionally employed by—but in life. I hated prisons on one hand, I hated everything they stood for, and, on the other, I was glad that those scary people wouldn't harm me.

Even if many of them had probably not done anything that terrible, except be born with the wrong skin color, a genetic disposition to addiction, a brain with certain tendencies, an in utero or early childhood experience that affected that brain and its perception or, like Leo, a little bit of all of that plus a dad who beat the shit out of him on a regular basis.

What a fraud I was.

"Seth?" Leo asked, waking me up from my own thoughts and attempts to act normal even though I felt anything but normal. "You alright?"

"Yeah," I lied.

"I know you don't like it here, pastor. You ain't supposed to like it here. I don't like it here either." Leo flashed that smile but something was off about it. It didn't carry the same star power. Like the singer who does his best even though he's puking between songs … yeah the lyrics are there and the music is there and the dancing is there … but the heart isn't there.

Leo's smile didn't have its heart.

"Are you alright?" I asked, leaning forward and trying to mask everything in my periphery, like I was editing a photo. And trying to rid myself of the image of a lion—a wild beast meant to roam the fields—stuck in a cage and losing its mind instead.

"I'm not doing so well," he answered in a way that Leo rarely answered. Even in jail.

"What's happening?"

As though it's not obvious.

"I don't know, Seth. I just haven't been feeling myself lately." He didn't look himself either, the more I studied Leo. He was smaller even, as though his body was shrinking into his energy.

"Hey, man." I reached out and touched him at the table. "What's going on? What do you mean? This isn't the Leo I know." I smiled, hoping it would be contagious.

It wasn't. "It's dark, pastor. At night. I say things I don't wanna say. I do things I don't wanna do." He looked up at me as a shell of a human being. "I don't think I'm gonna ever measure quite up."

Leo had been sent back to jail for stealing from a pawn shop. He had denied it and insisted his girlfriend had made him do it. I had testified on his behalf but the jury liked the video evidence more than my kind words.

I had promised to visit him at least one time every two months.

What a saint.

I had mostly held up my promise.

"Pastor, I gotta tell you again. I swear I didn't do it. I swear I didn't rob that store, I didn't call Rachel, I didn't visit Gwen's house." He looked down, that smile completely annihilated by shame and guilt and self-hate. "I swear I don't remember. But, I didn't hit her! I didn't start using again!"

He told me the speech every time I saw him. I believed him. He was the one being used by someone, or something. Maybe multiple someones and things including justice systems, girlfriends, religion, and most likely a Seer or two.

That day, even his speech was more somber than usual, more apathetic. Empty. Hopeless.

"Listen," I said. I waited for his eyes to look up from the table. "Listen to me." I continued to wait. "Are you listening?" His eyes were taking their sweet time. Eventually, I had them. "There's nothing to measure up to. Do you hear me? Nothing to measure up to. No person. No god. No pastor. No friend. No imagination. No expectation. Nothing."

He nodded slowly.

"Do you believe that?" I asked.

"Well," he said slowly, shaking his head in the same way. "Don't know if I do."

"Why?"

"What?"

"Why?" I asked with more intensity. A guard looked over but I didn't bother looking back.

"I don't know." He looked down at his hands, tied in front of him. "I done bad things, pastor. So many. I can't even remember. I don't even know if I did them. Or who I am. Except just … bad." He was shaking his head in slow despair.

"Leo." I waited for him to look at me again. "I'm not a pastor anymore. I had to resign because I had an affair three years ago. I cheated on Rachel. I betrayed my own family! If anyone is a failure, I am. You understand that?"

I didn't want to bring it up again but maybe he had needed the reminder. He sat there for a while. We both did, because, again, sometimes silence is best. His stare stayed as blank as the light cream walls and the table we were sitting at.

"Leo?" I eventually asked. "You there?"

"I think so, Pastor Seth. I think so." He looked up, then away, pensively. "I guess you just better at sinning than me."

Well, that was not really my point.

"I can't get where you at. I just don't know what's up, or what's down, what's good, or what's bad no more." He was shaking his head. "I just don't know anymore sometimes but I don't think I'm good or up or anything I'm supposed to be."

"Hey! I've done bad things. I've done dumb things. Did you hear me? But, Leo, it's okay. Just like you are going to be. You are something amazing, deep in there. I feel it. You feel it. You gotta let that out and stop worrying about all the things you've done, and start worrying about who you are." I pointed at him. I meant every word.

"Well …" He tried to smile. "I guess …"

"Leo. God isn't what you think god is. You hear me? God doesn't get mad at you."

"Well …" He tried to smile again. "Thank you."

With that he stood to his feet and nodded toward the guard, who walked over and began to usher him away. "Hey," I added. "I love you, Leo. And I can't wait to hang out with you on the back deck soon. Alright?"

"Yes sir," he turned around with a successful smile that melted any cold that was lingering inside of me. "Yes we will, Seth."

I smiled back and watched until I couldn't see him any longer.

Fucking prisons. I hate them. Leo, get out as soon as you can, my friend. Of all of them.

EIGHTEEN POINT SEVEN FIVE

Hours later, the meltdown started. I was in my office, unable to do anything beyond trying to tame my wild tears.

"Seth? Are you alright?"

"No," I gasped, barely able to grab a breath between my sobs. "I'm—" More tears. And embarrassment of some kind that I was a grown man completely out of control and that Ehs was suddenly there to watch. And I knew he was watching.

"I'm … not." My whole body was shaking as the tears rolled down my cheeks, over ruts that had formed from the salty streams. I tried to wipe away enough to make myself presentable somehow.

It didn't work. Just more deep emotion rose, emptying itself through a collection of enzymes, lipids, metabolites and electrolytes, and alien guttural moans formed by my limbic system and lacrimal system. They say emotional tears have hormones and proteins not found in other tears. I assumed mine were filled with both.

"Seth." Ehs reached out to touch me, feigning empathy that I knew he didn't have. Even if he did want to. He did *seem* to *want* to. "What is wrong?" he asked like a bad high school actor. Even animals have empathy. Ehs was not even an animal when it came to that.

I felt even more embarrassed, with him so cold and unmoved, watching me in my office cry alone at my desk, staring at my computer screen.

"What's wrong?" I gasped, with a mixture of anger and sadness, as though the question itself was insulting. "What's wrong?"

For starters, can you give me a break when I'm not my normal put-together awesome self and instead crying like a terrified hungry baby?

I tried to wipe away the thin, crusty layer forming on my cheeks again. He had pulled up a chair next to me, in the form of James. Directly in my office. He had simply appeared. We were well past the showing up at my door phase.

"Yes," he said, almost robotic.

"One, two of my kids just left for a while again. After a long time home. And … I don't know … I miss them. I love them." I looked at him. He *was* listening.

"Second, Leo tried to fucking hang himself yesterday. He tried to kill himself, Ehs! Not long after I had visited him."

I had received the call that morning from a sheriff friend. Sweet Leo with his big smile found with a noose of bedsheets around his neck. To be honest, that call had sent me into the tailspin I was in at that moment, heading toward the ground. I just couldn't pull out, imagining Leo hanging there.

"Third, I was fired from my job! I don't know how we're going to pay our mortgage. Rachel is going to pick up some extra shifts at the yoga studio, which would be great except …" The more I spoke, the more I found my ability to speak returning. And some anger. "Fourth, Jaden has returned. Just in time. He's back at the studio too!"

Ehs nodded as though he already knew everything or had stopped trying to act surprised and sad.

"And fifth," I yelled. "I'm so fucking anxious about everything. Are we going to pay our bills? Are the kids going to be okay? Am I okay? Everything seems to be falling apart, in our country, in this town, in my life … this world is a mess. I feel like I'm drowning in a tidal wave of anxiety and there aren't many life jackets because everyone around me has already claimed the few left—that haven't been thrown away by the powerful yet."

Ehs waited, like a good friend.

"Were you here last night? Did you see Rachel and me? I mean, I flipped out, Ehs! I flipped out at the fact that Jaden was coming back and she was going to be working with him. All the time! I needed to be attractive, strong, not jealous." Images of the night before swamped my senses but I managed to keep talking. "And, instead, I probably sent her back to calm-understanding-never-jealous-super-hot Jaden!" I stopped. I stared. Somewhere empty. "That's why." I spoke quietly. "And now you're here I suppose to once again show me how much worse things are than I even think?"

"Seth." He wasn't trying to imitate empathy anymore. It was far more natural Ehs. More sincere. The emotion was one he was good at: ass kicking. "Look at me."

I did. I was desperate for something to help me regain control of the spiraling plane I was piloting.

"Also, my friend has leukemia, don't forget!" I added words before he could.

His eyes were cold and yet comforting. The cold was soothing with so much raw emotion heating me up.

"Your kids." He waited.

A long time.

"Yes?" I finally asked.

"You miss them?"

I nodded, looking back to the screen. "Yes, that's what I just told you."

"Be grateful. Many parents don't. It's called love and you have it. I wish I did."

I sighed.

"I'm sorry about Leo. It wasn't you."

I looked to him and he looked away, almost embarrassed. If that were possible. "The Seers have been all over him. Bothering him. They got to him."

"Those mother—" I pounded my desk to make me feel better. Maybe anger was the better route than sadness.

"But," he interrupted me. "Something happened at the last minute. They were unsuccessful in their mission. I would say you may have saved his life."

"What?" My tears now felt like remnants, ruins of a past emotion on my skin as I found myself moving into something else. "What?" I repeated, feeling the tears might make a comeback tour.

"Somehow, Leo retook control. He found a strength." Ehs nodded.

"What do you mean?"

"I don't understand those things. But, The Seers suddenly gave up on him. He … found some kind of power to see. I've heard through the grapevine that Shadows weren't able to go near his cell suddenly. It was bright." He tilted his head toward me and smiled.

"From me?"

"Your job," he continued, oblivious or ignoring my question. "Your job was shit. It was time to be done."

"Was that you?"

He shrugged. "Yes and no. It doesn't really work like that."

"Well then, how the fuck does it—"

"You're going to be fine. Money will come. Trust me."

"Thank you, Mr.—"

"Your professional job in religion was deceiving you. Poisoning you, corrupting you. Be glad it's gone." He paused again. "Jaden is married. He's in love. You and Rachel are married. You are in love. Again. You are much stronger than you think. Jealousy is just more fear that you are not what he is, or she is, or they are … and fear is never … love. It is mystery. It is the unknowing that you fear. You cling to knowing still. With your country. With your world. With your future."

I nodded.

"We use this to our advantage. Mystery is what we have called the light, you and me, correct?"

I nodded again, still amazed that this Shadow was able to comfort me in some of my darkest moments.

"You fear mystery. Even you, even the enlightened ex-pastor. The teacher of light still seeks to do anything to avoid the very thing that you most need. All of your anxiety—whatever you have just told me—is simply the fear of a future path you imagine in your head. A future path you don't like. A future that does not exist. So you cling to the path you know, the path that takes you to fear and knowing, while avoiding the path of life because you don't know where it leads."

I looked to Ehs, noticing his black pants and black shirt for the first time. Ironed. Tight fitting. Not how I was accustomed to seeing James.

"Better to ride the known path to hell than the unknown path to heaven," he muttered. "There is a reason it's narrow. Not because it's difficult but because so few feet tread on it."

"Are you a part of all of this?"

"All of what?"

"All of it?"

"Darkness and light are a part of everything. And so are you." He tilted his chin up and looked down on me while standing to his feet. "Seth, things are progressing."

"What's that mean?"

"She's noticed. The Seers have noticed. They are watching. Me. You. Us. Insipid. Leo. Jaden. Rachel. Gwen. There are reasons for all of this. Reasons I can't entirely understand myself." I looked back to my computer screen and just stared. "Just trust me. In it all."

"Well … fuck," I eventually answered. "Just trust you. Just trust you?"

The laughter that erupted from him startled me, not only because it was loud but because it was entirely unexpected. Deep belly laughter with a nice little breeze to ride along with it. Higher pitched than I was used to. I had obviously missed the joke.

"What the—" I turned to look at him and realized what I had missed. He had vanished and been replaced by something else: something light and airy and hard to discern. I slid my chair away from it, trying to understand. It was sunlight without a sun and taking a strange shape around me. Almost a cloud of light, swirling around the room, emanating a warmth.

"Look at you," a voice rang out, laughing. Somehow the cloud of light was pointing toward me. "All serious. All weighed down." Joviality was shooting out all over the room—from it.

I did look at myself, unable not to. I was serious—and for good reasons. I studied my feet and noticed the black and gray stripes of my socks.

No shit, I'm weighed down.

In fact, I watched my feet start to sink into my white fake wood flooring. I tried to pull them out—to move them—and couldn't. Which added very quickly and urgently to my seriousness.

There was more laughing and pointing. Giggling like a school boy and, I noticed, now with a face of some kind. A happy face. A funny face. And it began to lift away from me. Toward the ceiling, moving upward somehow. It was going up and I was going down.

"What is this!" I yelled. "Are you serious?" I screamed, trying to get out of my chair. With my feet unable to move and my knees nearing the floor themselves, there was no chance. "What are you doing? Who are you?"

"Nothing, silly Seth." As though I was three and a clown was making me a shaped balloon. "I'm afraid … this … is all you." It pointed somehow again. "So serious. Worry more about sincerity. It's much better." More laughter.

I was, apparently, completely missing all of the humor.

"That's cute. But …" I stopped, seeing that my chair was still sinking and approaching my thighs. Full panic was ensuing. "This is not funny!"

"No," it responded with giggles. "It is. It's quite funny." The shape took the form of wings, almost, stretching out across my office and continuing to move upward. Rising away from me, who was falling further into my floor. Whatever form or face was there was looking down on me with a smile the size of the room and more laughs. "It's your seriousness weighing you down. Take yourself a little more lightly, my friend. Lightly? Do you get it? Lightly," it repeated, slowly emphasizing "light."

"What?" I was not laughing even after the clever play of words. "Stop!" I was screaming.

"Play!" it called out. "Play a little?"

"Is this a joke?" I was squirming with everything I had in my upper body as my lower body became more encased. I wished it was more than squirming but I had already sunk too much to do anymore.

"No, no," it answered. "It's not a joke, I'm afraid. I'm not toying with you. I am trying to play with you. Play, Seth."

"Stop this!" I yelled.

"I would say the same to you." It kept rising. The floor was nearing my chest and I suddenly felt like I couldn't breathe. If I was going to die, suffocated by my office floor, I was not going to be happy. I was not falling through my garage either. There was no rescue.

"Never flying … so serious."

"I—!" It took everything I had to try and wriggle free—and I couldn't. I only became more trapped.

It was then I remembered a game my uncle used to play with me. The Grip of Death, he called it. Not great branding. He would wrap my wrist and the more I struggled to get free the tighter the grip got. The less I struggled the more he released.

The game. He played with me. The *game*. I had played it with my own kids.

I closed my eyes.

If you were ever going to meditate, you better do it now.

That's the worst way to ever meditate.

Would you just laugh already, you motherfucker?

I did. I made myself laugh. Forced it all the way out. Something happened.

I took a deep breath. I imagined my body relaxing. I felt the warmth of whatever was in the room with me. I felt it touch my toes, my knees, my hips, my shoulders, and the top of my head. I let it go. At first it was more desire than reality but the more I thought about it the more authentic it grew. Slowly.

And I felt myself stop sinking. I began to rise again.

"There you go …" the form encouraged me, still far above me. "You see, it's much better to remember what all of this means and why you're here in the first place. Enjoy it, you know. Play. Dance. Listen to the music, and stop with the world is falling apart speech." It laughed again. "Or your own world always will."

And I felt lighter somehow. I even laughed again. More genuinely.

The soothing sense melted away my chains.

"Seth." The voice was so loud my body jolted in its place. I saw wings. I saw clouds. I saw sunlight amidst a strange giggling face. I was back to sitting in my chair, my feet on the floor. "Do not. Be afraid."

I smiled, still, somehow light.

"Can I be sad?"

"Sadness is not weighing you down. Only fear."

"But—"

"What do you want?" The form was surrounding me now, a

swirling scene of warm energy and laughter.

"What?" I asked.

"What do you want?" I heard repeated.

Money, sex, fame, praise ...

"No," it said, interrupting my thoughts. "What do you really want?"

Contentment, adventure, inspiration, peace.

"It's all on the other side of fear," a voice said quietly. "Do not. Be afraid."

"I know," I mouthed. My tears were back but they were not the same kind as before. They were *releasing* bits of fear instead of creating it and washing me in a touch more mystery.

I smiled even while I cried.

And more laughter. Deep laughter. Contagious howls of play. I'm not proud but I started to dance around the room, half floating, half carried by whatever was in the world with me. It was as though I was free of gravity, twirling, flipping, flying, and laughing. So much laughter, I was crying pure tears of light.

After it all left I found myself staring at my computer screen again, looking for a sliver of whatever had just happened but unable to find any of it.

Or could I? I was proud of my dancing.

I was not afraid for a moment.

Sad, yes. But not afraid, even to laugh.

I smiled at myself and took a deep, cleansing breath of light and exhaled a deep excess of heavy.

NINETEEN

Even though we weren't working, we desperately needed a vacation, or at least a getaway from any familiar faces. Or just the annoying familiar faces.

So, we were on our way to a little wine town in British Columbia. After the board meeting, and despite our best attempts to go quietly, word had spread. I blamed Richard but it could have been anyone and, really, it didn't matter. Everyone in town knew Rachel and I were adulterers. We might as well have started wearing big As on our chest. I had suggested it at one point.

Worse, maybe, were all the false rumors. People said I was gay, Rachel was gay, I had an addiction problem, and that I had never been a Christian and that I was, even, maybe, being used by the devil the entire time to manipulate an entire group of people to atheism as some kind of master plan. Oddly, that one had the most truth to it. In addition, news of Leo's attempted suicide had spread as well as word that I was his last visitor and that I had convinced him to kill himself. In addition, word had spread that Jaden was coming back, that Rachel was working more at the studio, and that we had an open marriage with Jaden and his wife. While we had tried to keep our story *our* story, especially for the kids, the rumors weren't helping. Nor was losing my job. Nor were some of the truths that were leaking out.

Our friends who'd gotten married in Hawaii—atheist friends we spent years trying to convince to come to our church—had invited us to get away with them for a weekend. They figured we would need it. Ironically, it was our atheist friends who thought of this while most of our Christian acquaintances complained how we had let them down, continued to exaggerate the bad-enough stories of Rachel and me, and moved further away from us and more toward the people with reputations intact enough to still belong to their tribe.

Obviously, we didn't.

Of course, Rachel and I had agreed to our friends' generous offer. They had insisted they would pay for it and we could just meet them there. So, away we went to a town nestled between two lakes, surrounded by wine country and, as they had told us, "a place that has everything you want on a calm, relaxing getaway five hours away. Especially when you need it."

"So you want to know something creepy?" I asked, as Rachel and I were driving through national forest on the way toward Canada. "Spiders always hang out by the light. In the shadows."

She took a sip of water from the passenger seat. "Yeah, I don't think I like that."

"Me either." The night before we had cleaned off our front porch. Really cleaned it off. Water-scrub-brushes cleaned it off … I had never seen so many spiders in my life. Webs were in every corner, surrounding the porch light where all the bugs gathered at night to escape the darkness. "Why do bugs go to the light anyway?" I asked.

"I don't know," she replied. "I just think of the movie … 'Don't go near the light!'"

I laughed. "I know, right? Me too. First thing I think." I turned the car around a slight corner surrounded by trees on both sides. "God, this is beautiful."

"Yeah," she looked up from her phone for a moment. "It really is."

The sun peeked out from behind a cloud, which made me grab my sunglasses.

"So …" Rachel was back to investigating on her phone. It was nice to be distracted from all of the other conversations we could have been having, that we didn't really want to have. "It looks like bugs are drawn to the light because …" She was reading more. "Because the bugs use light as a navigation. The porch lights are tricking them. They are used to the moon but …" Again more reading. "They have not evolved fast enough to catch up with artificial lights. It tricks them."

"We need to speed up this evolution thing … for all of us."

"Yeah, you should work on that," she answered, still looking at the phone. I didn't know if she was being funny or telling me to evolve my fears and jealousies. I didn't bother asking. "They head toward the artificial light instead. Those lights are brighter and distracting. And …" More reading. "They end up caught in a circle because the bulb radiates on all sides … unlike the moon. Circling around the light unable to use it as a navigation tool." She looked over at me and I looked at her, while still trying to keep the car on the road. "Yikes. Crazy."

"So," I said to the road, and her. "Holy shit. They are drawn to the light. But it's the wrong light. But still, they think it's the light guiding them home. Instead, it's the light keeping them in circles, going nowhere." I nodded, like I do when I get excited. "And that's where they get trapped by the webs of the spiders. That's where the spiders hang out!"

The parallels were everywhere and very eery. Ehs would be proud.

"Crazy. Sermon illustration," she said, still seeing if there was anything else on the phone worth reading. It's what the entire family said whenever we came across something halfway cool that would obviously show up in a talk at some point.

After it left her mouth out of habit, we both paused for a moment, to remember there were no more sermon illustrations.

"Bittersweet, huh?" I asked.

"Mostly sweet," she answered.

"I think you're right." Another car passed us in the opposite direction.

"So," she muttered. "We think it's the light, but it's not. We think it's right but it's not. We think it's life, but it's just a trap for death."

We kept driving for a bit without saying much. What are you supposed to say after that, especially with all that was happening?

Were we entering into a trap?

Or realizing, and finally getting out of the trap?

That is the question, isn't it?

"Do you think we just spent a lot of years of our life at an artificial light? Trying to shine real bright while only attracting people to flipping around in a circle the rest of their lives?" I glanced over at her and back to the road.

"I hope not." She stared at me. "But, what *was* all that, Seth? All those years? For what?"

I just shook my head. "I think it's going to take some time to figure it all out. If we ever do …"

The trees provided a nice background to the silence that came over us again. The repetitive nature of … nature … passing through our windows as we stared at it.

"Rachel," I said, deciding to eventually switch the subject. "I'm going to be okay with you working at the studio with Jaden. I really am."

"Thanks," she said sincerely. "I mean really, thank you. I know that's hard."

I nodded, hoping that saying things would make them come true. "And … let's just try to avoid all the hard topics this weekend, okay? I mean, they will all be waiting there when we get back. Maybe we can just try to enjoy it?" I looked out the window at the massive forest laying out before us. We had hit a high point on the road and the view extended out all around. Maybe we could hit a high point for life soon.

"I love it," she answered, taking a sip of water from her cup again. She always brought water. "All the shit will be there when we get back. Maybe we can grab a breath up here."

Later that night, I couldn't sleep. Maybe it was the new room and environment, maybe it was a little hot, or maybe it was just too much wine. I don't know. I got up and went to the bathroom, stumbling my way in the darkness like someone much older and much more drunk than I was.

On my way back to bed, I noticed a light outside, beyond the slider that we had left open for some fresh air. It immediately grabbed my full attention. There had been porch lights and candles around the pool but those had been turned off. Also, this light was different. As I walked closer, I noticed it didn't have any effect on the world around it.

It was hovering a few feet off the ground, on the far side of the pool, and though it was bright, there was no light on the grass below it or the big comfy cabana chair next to it.

I'm not one to venture outside late at night. My imagination can go crazy enough inside. But, this night, I did. The slider was already open and I made my way through it, into the cold air. It was a still darkness, with very little wind and thus very quiet. I looked around to see if anyone else was outside.

I was alone.

I walked further outside, careful not to fall into the pool, and moved closer to the light. I was drawn to it. I looked behind me. The owners of the bed-and-breakfast lived on the top floor of the house. Our friends were in one room and a nice couple from Calgary was in another. We'd heard there was a fourth couple, from London, too, although we had yet to meet them. All the lights were off.

Still alone.

The light was a rectangle, I could see now. A bright doorway, but again, a bright doorway not affecting anything else around it. I could see crisp lines as I neared, not the foggy blurred edges I would have expected.

I looked behind me again. I looked to the sides. I literally pinched myself and looked down at my hands. Someone had once told me that you never see your hands in a dream so I figured I would at least check the possibility of a dream off the list. My hands were there.

A light breeze rushed across me, reminding me, again, that I was outside in Canada.

For one instant, my mind touched on those bugs that head toward the light but the thought vanished almost as soon as it arrived. The bottom of the door was about a foot off the ground, which did cause me to pause and stare for a moment—but only for a moment. I would have once assumed it was very stupid to walk into a bright doorway floating in space but it now felt irresistible. There was nothing that could have stopped me or made me think it wasn't what I was supposed to do.

It was pulling me in like a magnet.

I stepped over the threshold and smiled.

Descriptions don't really work for what I found. Not visually.

I just tried to process it all.

Life has some favorite experiences.

The first time we realize we are in love.

Her smell.

The first time we realize we are loved.

His smell.

The first time we hear that song and can't help but move and smile.

That drive.

That hike.

That view.

The taste of a perfect meal on our tongue.

Staring at our child sleeping.

Watching them get off the plane when we haven't seen them for weeks.

That embrace.

The scent of summer rain.

The old man helping his wife of seventy years get into the car.

That concert.

That night.

That sunset.

They were all close. I felt them.

I once had a friend who used to take a hose and sit on the bottom of his swimming pool in LA, breathing through the hose. He said it was one of the most relaxing things he could do. He would sit there for hours, immersed in the water.

The sounds of life were gone. The hectic, busy nature of the world was vanquished. The water calmed and soaked into his soul. There is a peace at the bottom of a pool that does not exist in other places.

At least, according to him. He might have been a little crazy but he was interesting to talk to.

A hot day and a cold—but not too cold—lake or swimming pool. You jump in and let your body slide down for a while, just resting, sinking toward nothing. The water holds you, embraces you, carries you, and there is something nurturing and therapeutic about it.

I wonder if it's why so many of us are moved by just staring at water.

We're all born in water, literally. It's where we are formed, it's where the world first becomes a reality to us. Maybe it's always drawing us back to something comfortable and yet, to the birth of something new on the horizon.

It was all of those favorite experiences surrounding me like water. I was embraced by them, carried by them, held by them, and yet part of their wonder was that it felt like I was on the cusp of something new and more amazing than I could imagine.

I felt all of that the moment I entered into the doorway.

Something held me. I don't know what. It was similar to water but it was less physical.

The smells were nostalgic and fresh. The tastes were familiar and exotic. I was listening to my favorite song that I had never heard before. I felt warm and comfortable and exhilarated at the same time.

I distinctly remember feeling pain. I was shocked for a moment when my head and preconceptions caught up to whatever I was experiencing. Pain? What was pain doing there? But the pain was different. It was refined. Pure. Unadulterated, if that's possible. It was the evolutionary side and growth of pain without the … pain. Was it pain? It was like encountering that person from twenty years ago who had lost weight and had their hair dyed. There is something familiar about them yet everything has changed.

I could see everything although I realized that made no sense. I could see her and him and them and us and tears and smiles and hands and eyes and lips and words and notes and breath and rest and nature and animals and … I could go on forever. I could see everything.

I've never experienced so much at one time. I've never felt as though there was so much I was missing at the same time.

In that state I began to hear voices, which is what happens to every person who is losing their mind so that made sense, even in that moment somehow.

Questions swarmed me but not in the usual ways. There was not the stress that often comes with questions, the desperate attempts to find answers. They were simply questions, and questions are rarely just questions, I realized. There is always that agenda tagging along with them, unintentionally maybe, but always there. Questions usually arrive inside veiled attempts to persuade someone of something. These questions were harmless, innocent, and patient.

What is?
Where is?
Does it exist?
Value?
Lies?
Evolution?
Better?
More?
Enough?
Are you worried?
What do you trust?
Who do you help?
Can you?
Are there sides?
What is love?
What is pain?
What is freedom?
What is true?
What is real?
What are you?

It was all existential but it felt simple. The questions that usually inspire anxiety did not. Moving on from the questions that humans have asked for generations, I had a more simple question move across my consciousness, more of an ambiguous thought along the lines of *can you tell me the next time you will show up?*

Suddenly it was dark again and I could no longer see—anything.

It took a moment for my eyes to adjust to the darkness and until they did, I stood there, motionless, moved, and still trying to process what had just happened.

I heard hushed laughter from nearby and instantly stopped processing. It was the laughter of teen revolt, the kind of giggle that happens when you are trying to be quiet but aren't remotely successful, and blissfully unaware of this because you're doing something you feel like you shouldn't be doing and it feels great.

Once my eyes and ears adjusted, I realized the couple from London was "getting off" in one of the nearby chairs. Thank god the little roof was over them and I could only see their feet. And they couldn't see me.

I did not want to be seen as a Creeping Tom, or have to explain to anyone why I was standing alone on the grass next to them, so I quickly tried to make my way back to my room. I managed to trip over one of the lounge chairs on the way, which made me crash into a nearby table and swear in a quiet whisper a few times.

That caused the nice couple from London to stop their giggling and go silent. I stumbled into our room trying not to grab my foot, which was suddenly throbbing in pain from ramming into the damn lounge chair.

"Seth?" Rachel was up but only partly.

"Yeah, sorry." I closed the sliding door, hoping the couple couldn't see which room I had rolled into. I had sworn with an accent just to throw them off the scent.

"What are you doing?" She got out of bed and started her own journey to the bathroom.

"Just going to the bathroom." I returned.

"You alright?"

"Oh yeah," I whispered before sliding back into bed.

Sleep arrived quickly after I heard the nice London couple return to their room, still seemingly happy. I thought about what had just happened over and over. I wished I had drunk more water with all the wine I had consumed and wished I had more water to drink at that moment.

Or maybe just to swim in.

TWENTY

The statistics say that divorces spike in August and March. There are all kinds of theories but most of them center around the idea that after a great summer vacation (or romantic Valentine's Day date) that was intended to fix everything doesn't fix *anything*, a couple finally gives up hope that the relationship can be salvaged. If three weeks in Italy can't help two people fall back in love, how are they going to handle eight months working in Jersey and commuting into the city every day?

Those stats were on my mind after our return from Canada because … I, like most people, am generally terrified that when things are going well they are going to stop going well soon. Our therapist calls it "shark music" and says that many of us are unable to truly appreciate joy because we're so afraid that we don't deserve it or that it will be taken from us at any moment.

So I was focusing on divorce statistics. It was August and I was feeling less than my normal powerful self for other reasons.

I was walking to a coffee shop I had walked to a thousand times as an employed and respected pastor. It was the first time I was walking to it as a rejected fraud. I knew there would be someone I knew inside because there was always someone inside that I knew. Once again, our therapist had suggested I brave the war zone and face my enemies head-on, with kindness and strength.

This therapy thing sucks.

The parking lot was bright sun—the early warmth of a summer morning. The calm, the joy … the shark music. I spent more time than I needed in the parking lot, both to appreciate the sun and to delay facing my mortal enemies inside as much as I could.

Realizing that, at some point, I had to leave the sun and carry out my mission of grace and fortitude, I made my way toward the door. As I did, I saw the owner of the coffee shop taking a smoke break, leaning against the outside wall on the back of his building.

In the shadows.

"Hey," I said. "How are you?" Considering I was still up for delaying my mission, I decided to be extra friendly. Good for everyone, as they say, and very little risk.

Somewhat surprisingly, the owner also seemed up for conversation. More than up for it. Anxious, or even desperate for it. He was immediately next to me, sucking down his cigarette like it was his last breath of oxygen before going underwater, which ironically, is the opposite of what that cigarette was to his lungs. But still, he apparently needed the nicotine.

"Man." He took another drag. "Things aren't that great."

I can relate.

Whenever someone breaks the norm of responding with "fine" to the question of "How are you?" it's imperative to listen. Especially if they are honest enough to say things are not well. Especially to an almost stranger, like I was. Especially if it's nice outside and inside is … dangerous.

"What's up?" I asked. Sincerely.

"Dude." His words and entire body were shaking, as though his foundations were about to crumble under the weight of his own anxiety. Another feeling I knew well. "This customer of mine is wigging out on me. Death threats and shit." He was wearing big, thick shades and his nose, holding up those shades, was twitching. An attempt at a mustache was below his nose and reminded me of a lawn that needed mowing and more water at the same time. It wasn't working.

I hoped I looked as perplexed as I felt.

He kept talking. "I started getting all these weird emails from this dude. Weird shit, man. Freaking out. He was saying stuff like he was a servant of Lucifer and the Dark One and so I started investigating."

I immediately had a number of responses.

Trust me that's not what demons actually do.

Well, not what my demon does.

This is weird.

This guy is genuinely spooked.

Ehs?

I vocalized the last one. "Ehs?"

"What?" the chimney in shades asked back.

"Nothing," I answered quickly. "Nothing," I repeated, still not sure I was wrong.

He kept going, unaware, oblivious, just happy to have someone to talk to. "Yeah, this guy. Man, I started going to his house."

Why in the world would you go to someone's house who is threatening you and saying they are Lucifer?

"And I start finding all this weird shit, man. Weird shit. Little satanic shrines and then I start looking at the internet …"

Everyone knows you never look on the internet for anything. If you're sick you don't WebMD it. If you meet someone who thinks they are a demon, you don't look at the internet … Well, shit, I guess I had.

"So, I start finding more shit about demons, and dark ones, and these hidden books. And I start looking into some serial murder cases and I find fire circles and kid sacrifices and knives and do you know Molech from the Bible and …"

"Hey man, slow down. Whoa." He was incredibly scared, crying in front of me, the tears coming from eyes that I assumed were behind the shades. I reached out and touched his shoulder.

He kept going. "Yeah man, I've called the police man but they don't do shit. I mean, I'm talking about child sacrifices! And they don't give a shit."

"Okay." I nodded, not exactly sure what to do.

"Come inside. I'll show you." He started walking and I followed him. He would be a good distraction or shield for whatever I was going to find inside. And he stuck on me like a piece of old duct tape, ratty and worn—not leaving even if I had wanted him to.

He kept rambling about scavenger hunts, small idols, and what looked like burned bones in some ashes that he was sorting through. We walked inside and I immediately spotted two men from the church. They were having a coffee together under an array of dark green plants on a wooden shelf above them. They both waved to me. Nice enough. While I decided if I should go and really face my fears and talk to them, the owner kept going. I ordered a double espresso and gave him hints that seemed obvious to me that I was past the point of helping. Apparently I was not obvious enough. He left just as my coffee came out and returned moments later before I could take a sip.

"Here!" He handed me stacks of papers. "This is what I gave to the police."

Dear god, this guy is certifiable. Good news: I am not.

There were letters and emails and threats and old articles about ancient gods and people who follow them. I was a little more nervous—not because I believed a serial murderer was out to get him but wondering why he and I had had such different experiences with our demons.

"Okay, well, I mean, honestly, I don't know what to tell you. I think I would probably just stop talking to him. You know?"

"Yeah," he mumbled, and nodded his head much harder than he should have. I thought it might fall off his neck at any moment.

"Hey, it's going to be okay."

"Listen," he said calmly. "Seth, right?"

The fact that he knew my name was not entirely surprising but it did take me aback. It was the first time I had ever talked to him that long.

"Yeah," I answered. He reached into his pocket and pulled out another cigarette, which I didn't think was a good idea given the clean vibe and clean air of his shop—but he was the owner.

"You need to listen to me."

I feel like I have been.

He shoved the cigarette into his quivering lips below the dark sunglasses, that were still on inside, and I looked again at the struggling lawn of facial hair on his chin and above his lips.

Just shave, man. That thing is not doing you any favors.

"I'm listening," I replied. "But, I think you're going to be okay."

"Yeah, yeah." He came closer and started looking around as though something was about to go down in his own shop.

His nerves were contagious and I began to wonder why I had followed our therapist's advice. Or maybe why I had tried to avoid it and spent my time talking to the owner instead.

"Listen." He leaned in even closer. I could smell cigarettes and coffee … and fear. Not a good mixture. "Listen," he repeated. "I'm worried."

"Hey." I put my hand on his shoulder. "Maybe … let that guy go."

"But," he responded, even closer. I wanted to gag. "He said if I ran into Seth, I was supposed to tell him something."

I suddenly didn't like anything. I didn't like the way I felt inside of my own body inside of that shop.

"These guys don't mess around. If you fuck them, they're going to hurt you. And Rachel."

If he watched my eyes, he knew he had struck a nerve. Rachel always told me she could see everything in my eyes and, at that moment, I assumed they showed lots of fear.

"There's a reason Jaden is back in town, man. There's a reason."

I left. Fast. I needed to puke in the parking lot. I needed some answers from Ehs. It was August. I didn't want a divorce or a shark.

TWENTY POINT FIVE

"I need answers," I said out loud again, to no one in particular. Actually, to no one at all because no one was in the kitchen with me. It hadn't stopped me from saying it out loud the last few days and it didn't stop me from saying it again. I really did need answers, as much as I tried to distract myself, putting some dishes away, cleaning up my Chemex pot, and "tidying up."

Tidying up? Is it 1950?

It had been a very quiet Sunday. Rachel had taken our youngest daughter out to look for some clothes and I was left alone, cleaning up, at a time that I until recently had a habit of spending in front of hundreds of people giving a speech. It was all strange, so I figured I would ask Ehs to show up and calm my nerves that were … at the moment rattling around like scared, coked-out rats in my body's cage. Coffee was not helping the rev of nerves.

As I walked outside, took some deep breaths of fresh air, and poured out some coffee grounds into our compost can, I said out loud again, "Hey." I continued. "I don't like my wife being threatened, you know. And I don't like hearing that you guys are bringing Jaden." I closed the big green plastic container and let the lid slam shut, indicative of my mood. "Ehs. You want to pull one of your little tricks and show up, please? Shit, man!"

"You are something, aren't you," a voice answered back almost immediately—a female voice that I didn't recognize.

I jumped, at first scared, and then relieved to have Ehs back. Although, something was different about the encounter.

"Well," I said out loud and twirled around to see him.

"Hi," she answered.

She had to be at least eighty. But, she was a spry eighty years. The kind of eighty that you look at and say, *I hope I look like that when I'm her age.* She had a cute little tuft of white hair on top of old, but not too worn, skin. You could see the youthful beauty she had once been blending perfectly with the mature beauty of age and wisdom she had become.

I didn't recognize her. And it was not Ehs. I could tell, somehow. There was something altogether different about her.

"I'm Seth." I reached out my hand. "I don't think we've met." If she was a neighbor, I was going to feel very stupid. In addition, I had no idea how the old lady had snuck up on me like a Navy SEAL.

"I know," she responded, gently but firmly, just like her handshake. This woman was more than spry—she had some spunk and attitude. It was immediately obvious.

"Oh." I frowned, staring into her gray eyes, which rested above lips lightly painted in a shade of red. "Well, what can I do for you?"

She let go of my hand and stared at me for a second.

I stared back. She was dressed a tad on the formal side, especially for being outside on a Sunday morning, and I wondered if she had come to the wrong house. I looked out front for a car but there was none. *Damn, this lady is in good shape too. Not a drop of sweat for walking here from somewhere.*

"What are you doing?" she asked.

It was a pretty straightforward question, on the surface, yet there were all kinds of ways I could have taken it. I started to process.

"Well," I answered back, keeping my cool. "I usually don't have any idea what I'm doing." I figured I would try to lighten the mood.

And be honest.

She smiled. "I know."

Screw being honest.

There was this gentleness about her I couldn't give up on. "Okay," I said out loud. "Well, what have you got for me?"

"Why do you continue to let him in? You know who he is, right?"

"Do you mean"—I stopped—"Ehs?"

"Yes," she nodded. "Did you think I was a mad mother-in-law or something?" There was still something smooth and pure about her. There was something inviting, for being such a smart-ass.

"Actually—"

"You know who he is, right?" she interjected before I could finish.

"A Shadow. Head of Propaganda or Advertising or something? Pretty high up?" I spoke carefully.

"Pretty?" She laughed. Gently.

"Well …"

"He, almost single-handily, is responsible for everything you grew up believing. And millions of other things. And what you *think* you're rejecting. He's practically reinvented possession. He's created modern religion. He's as dark as they come. As intelligent. And cunning." Her words rolled out with a punch that I somehow enjoyed. "He'd give her a run for her money. In fact, she's probably jealous."

"Lucy?" I asked.

"Yes. Doesn't that terrify you?" Her eyes were bold rays of color. "Insipid. He's one of the main architects of Insipid. I suppose that doesn't terrify you either?"

At that point, I realized I was talking to a light of some kind. I also realized that, up to that point, every interaction with anything of "light" had been really strange and weird and ambiguous and, if this was an actual Ray to have a conversation with … questions started rolling through my head like rapids.

"No," I responded. It was true, somehow.

"It should," she answered.

"Are you an angel?" I asked.

She closed her eyes for a moment. "If you would like to use that name." It was obvious she didn't like it.

"Wow," I decided to say. "Not what I expected."

She nodded. "You were expecting glowing white light with a halo and wings?"

I probably looked confused. "I didn't expect angels to have such … spunk."

She seemed to like that. "It's funny how good is always supposed to be weak, isn't it?" She looked up for a second. "Amazing … Buddha, Jesus, Mohammed, you think these people didn't have some fire inside? Norwich. Joan. Amazing." She just kept shaking her head, almost talking to herself, and that made me shake mine.

I sensed there wasn't much time so I didn't stop. "I feel like angels are always coming and saying 'Don't be afraid' and you're telling me to be afraid." At that point, I felt as though I had no reason not to be honest and vulnerable. She felt safe, like an old friend who had proven she could handle anything and would put me in my place, nicely, if she needed to.

"We do say don't be afraid, when there is nothing to be afraid of."

I looked again at the lady. In a strange way I had forgotten about her and her little white hair and wrinkled hands. "Do you possess people?"

She looked at her own body. "No."

I very obviously looked at her body.

"We just become visible." She gestured toward the green can

next to my house. "Thanks for, at least, caring for us."

I looked toward the can again and nodded. "Yeah." And then back to her. "Wait. Us?"

"Of course us. The Earth. You. It's all the same stuff, you realize?"

I frowned. "I mean … right … was that you the other day? In my office?"

It was her turn to frown. She shook her head.

"Wait, are you …her?" I sensed something similar to whatever I had encountered in the national park.

"Her?" she responded.

"Yeah, her. The one whom Ehs is in love with." I knew I was going to say the words so I made sure to watch and see if they affected her in any way, which was strange, to say the least. The lady was eighty-plus years old and not really what I had imagined when I had first heard the story from Ehs of the blond Swedish supermodel.

There *was* something. Maybe it was made up in my head, maybe it was real, but there was a flinch, a pause, a second thought before a quiet laugh. "I'm the one that Ehs *tells yo*u he's in love with," she repeated with an inflection to tell me how ridiculous it was. "Maybe."

I moved away from the shadow of the house and into the sun. She followed me into the warmth. In the light I could see that her skin reacted strangely. Almost glowing, almost reflecting, almost absorbing. Still elderly and human but somehow more alive.

"Well, the whole point of all of this—"

She held up her hand, like a grandmother does to a grandchild. "No. You don't have any idea about any of the points. You only know what he tells you. And he is full of deception."

"Can he change?"

She looked at me. "What do you mean?"

"Can Shadows … change? Convert? I don't know," I stammered. "Can they become like you?"

She looked away, which I found odd, like she didn't want to admit it. "Yes."

"Okay," I answered before realizing what a cool revelation that was. "So then maybe he has. Or is. Or will."

"Maybe."

"Wait," I suddenly shouted. "And can you … become like him?"

"Yes," she answered quickly.

I had to release a whistle, in the same way a steam cooker has to when it's too full of something combustible. The idea was electric to me. "Holy shit," I said slowly.

"Watch your language," she launched. "I'm an angel."

"I'm so—" I held up my hands to apologize.

She was laughing suddenly and her laugh made me stop. "Even you think I care if you say *shit*? Ehs *is* doing good work."

I laughed too but sensed the meeting was coming to an end somehow and I still had too many questions. "So you can all change?" I asked again.

"This universe is built on change. Are you seriously asking me that?" She smiled one of the warmest smiles I had ever seen, even if it carried a jolt of electricity with it.

"Was that you at the park? And in Canada?" I changed the subject, smiling myself.

She sighed. "Yeah, sort of."

"Sort of?"

"You can't see me."

"Or what?"

"You would die."

"Why?"

"It's just the way it works. You can't see Ehs, either. Not as I do."

"Distortions?"

"Yes."

"Is all of this …"

"You're made to see the world a certain way. We don't live entirely in that way. If you want to see us completely you have to enter this way." She shook her head. "But that's not important. You can't trust him."

Oddly enough, even in that moment, even after being threatened, I did. "But, I do."

She seemed taken aback. Almost frightened. That should have frightened me but it didn't. And *that* did frighten me.

"Am I okay?" I asked, desperate for her to tell me I was.

She smiled and her gray eyes glistened in the sunlight. "Evil is not what you think, Seth."

I nodded.

"It's much more beautiful, subtle, and appealing. It's cunning. Be careful. More careful than you think you need to be."

"He's dying," I said, somewhat to my own surprise.

There was another flicker. She hadn't expected it. She had never been cold, there had never been walls, but there was suddenly a greater warmth to her than there had been. I felt it spreading toward me and I felt so happy to receive it.

"I know," she answered. "He's becoming desperate."

"Well, maybe it's driving him to change."

"Insipid is falling. He never thought it was possible. Everything he built is collapsing. He can see the end and he knows there is nothing left to his legacy if it falls."

"It's falling?"

"It will take time still but people are seeing the light."

"Well, it sure doesn't seem that way."

"I know."

"At all." It didn't seem right to just leave it so simple. I had more to push her on for the sake of every conversation I had ever had and for the sake of every person who had wanted to have a conversation. Mostly for myself. "Have you been around this summer? Have you—"

"Seth," she interrupted with an imposing gentleness. "Don't lecture me on pain."

I looked away, almost embarrassed. "I'm sorry but that wasn't what I meant. It just doesn't seem like any of the systems are collapsing … at all."

"Why?"

"It just seems like … I don't know. It doesn't seem like anything is working?"

"Working?" she asked, with raised eyebrows.

"Yeah."

"Nothing is working?" She was almost insulted but it was as though she couldn't be. More sad.

"I guess it is. Here and there."

"Here and there? Extreme poverty. Starvation. Clean water. Child mortality. Education. Suffering. Wars. Need I go on?"

"I mean …"

"Read a book or two, Seth. You'll thank me. Widen your perspective. People are seeing. Even if he thinks they are not." She closed her eyes again, without frustration, but with impatience. The paradoxical emotions she was giving off were almost distracting, and yet drawing me in even more.

Also, that made both dark and light, good and evil, Shadows and Rays telling me to read more. I decided I probably should.

"Worry about *your* world."

"Okay." It was my turn to take a deep breath. "But—"

"No." She stopped me. "You can't change the world."

Not what I wanted an angel to tell me. "Well …"

"No," she interrupted again. "You can't change any of this." She pointed toward the bright summer sky. "Only this." She pointed toward her own eyes, which were maybe more stunning. "And that might change everything."

"So, what does he expect me to do?" I changed the subject. "What should I not do?"

"Be careful."

"He hasn't betrayed me."

"Evil is slow." She nodded.

"Is there a war? A fight? A battle?" I had to change the subject again.

She shrugged.

"So, no?"

"There is always a tension if there are opposites. There is resistance and struggle."

"But love will win?"

"Love always wins. It's the nature of love to win. Winning is love. Any other kind of winning is an imitation."

I had to think about that. "Then what are the battles? The opposition? The struggle?" I asked.

"The realization of that. Of what is true."

"So, eventually … no more battles?"

"Of course not. There will always be realization. There is always more to realize and find. It's a big universe, in case you weren't aware." She grinned.

"Do you trust Ehs?"

She paused for a moment, staring up at the sky, her gray hair leaning toward the ground. "No."

"Love never fails. It never gives up." Since I knew Bible verses I figured I might as well throw one at an angel.

She was not overly impressed. "Love has not. But I may have."

I took a step back. "You can't give up. You're an angel, for god's sake."

She smiled, graciously and yet with a wisdom that made me feel inferior. "Ehs has been effective. Even with people as aware as you."

I had never felt better in all my life. And yet … worse.

"Illusion, Seth. All of it. Heaven, hell, sacred, secular. You're living the fight. To realize, to be aware, to grow, to change, to become more like love. Everything is. All of matter."

"Okay …"

"Until it all becomes one. One thing of love." She held up her finger, in case I didn't understand one. And then pointed it at me. "In mystery."

"Does everyone go to heaven?"

That one had her rolling her eyes like a classic grandmother again. "Have you not listened to anything?"

"I mean … eventually … is even Ehs … love?"

"I'm leaving now."

"Wait!" I reached out my hand as though I could stop her. She was still there.

"Ehs wants to meet you. Can we make that happen?"

And she was gone. She vanished. Disappeared, as though she had never been there in the first place, which had me looking everywhere for some kind of remnant that she had, even digging through the coffee grounds of my mind.

TWENTY POINT SEVEN FIVE

All of the kids were away on a Thursday summer night so it seemed the perfect time to head out to our deck, smoke a little weed, and talk.

We weren't regular smokers but we had started to dabble in it every now and then, especially recently. It was legal in our state, we no longer worked for a church, and it, obviously, chilled us out nicely when we needed to have a difficult conversation. We had specifically purchased a strain that was good for conversations between strangers. Or something like that.

It was probably a bit numbing too but, again, we weren't regular smokers and sometimes you just need to numb a little pain so you can dive into some deeper pain. At least that's what we told ourselves.

Our therapist didn't seem too bothered by it either.

"So, how much longer do we have?" I asked and took another puff off of the joint.

"Are you getting it into your lungs?" Rachel asked.

"Yes!" I thought I yelled although I wasn't really sure. "It's in there. I'm going to feel it this time." A few weeks earlier I had complained that I didn't. I coughed again just to prove it was going all the way in.

"We have a few weeks. We can pay our mortgage for sure," Rachel said, smiling way more than she should have since we were talking about running out of money.

"And then what?"

"Well, did you talk to Tim?"

Tim was our atheist friend who had a successful chain of cannabis shops and said I could work in any of them if we got desperate. Ex-pastor has affair and is now selling weed felt more desperate than I was … but it was getting close. "Not yet. I mean, god …" I laid back in my chair and looked up at the sky. "Selling weed?"

Rachel laughed. And then laughed a little more.

"What?" I asked slowly.

"What?" She smiled.

"What was so funny?" I asked, looking out at our yard covered in the early night.

"You would at least know which ones to bring home. Could be nice for us."

"Shit," I mumbled in a long drawn out way.

"Shit," Rachel mumbled, mimicking me perfectly.

We both started giggling again. "Hey, put on some music," Rachel said slowly … leaning forward and looking toward her feet.

"Yeah, yeah …" I pulled out my phone and started to send music into our outdoor speakers.

"Dude," Rachel called out. "Why is it taking so long? Get some music!" We had some crackers and cheese on a small table and Rachel was staring at it.

"I'm trying!" I yelled back, not exactly sure why I had lost the ability to control my phone. Or why it was so slow. Or if it was slow. The phone screen did appear especially clear and I found myself fixated on it longer than I should have.

Maybe it's working this time.

Finally, we had some grooves going to add to the grooves flowing through our veins. I slowly put some cheese into my own mouth. It tasted exceptionally good—a cornucopia of cheese flavors.

We were both at a nice cruising altitude of life, definitely a little higher than our normal flight path and enjoying every moment.

"Well," Rachel threw out, apparently deciding to ruin our mood. "Where are we at with me … and working … and shit … you know …" She looked up at me. She tried to smile but the muscles weren't quite functioning normally, whether from a chemical substance she had inhaled or a chemical substance her own body was producing at the thought of talking about something we didn't want to talk about.

I felt the effects of the weed wearing off faster than they should have. I was starting to feel normal—which meant my chest was tightening and my cheek muscles were twitching.

"We gotta get some money. I know you hate it," Rachel continued, staring at some more cheese. "But what are we going to do?"

"Fuck, Rachel," I yelled, trying to get my flight back into the upper atmosphere where I had just been. But, it was descending quickly. "I don't know."

"Well, I can't quit just because Jaden is back."

Images of my wife naked on top of her yoga master Jaden in a nineties hip-hop video crossed back and forth through my mind until I forced them away with all the tricks I had learned in therapy and from years of practice. But they left a bad taste in my imagination for a while, letting me soak in the details that I didn't want. The ship had passed but its wake was still pushing the waters of imagination around.

"Seth?" she asked. "What do you want to do?"

"I don't know!" I said louder than I wanted to. "I don't know. I mean, I feel like it's normal for me to not want you hanging out with him. Would you want me hanging out with Gwen? Working with her? Seeing her on a regular basis?" I leaned back far in my chair and looked back up toward the sky far away, high above the deck, where I wished my brain was again.

"No," she answered slowly. "I wouldn't. But, I mean, I also trust you."

Why is everything always about trust?

"I trust you too," I said, eighty-five percent sure it was true. "Not sure if I trust Jaden though."

"Seth!" She laughed slowly and popped a few more pieces of cheese in her mouth. "Jaden is the nicest man on planet Earth."

Except me, right? Shit, we both know that's not true.

More images. They were both moving in perfect rhythm to each other and the rich bass beat. The blister on my heart where I had been burned opened up again, leaking its toxic puss into my mind and being. I closed my eyes and focused on breathing and light instead of romantic candles and moans.

"I understand, Seth. I do. And I won't work there if you really don't want me to," she said, deciding to look at me that time.

I opened my eyes again. "We need Ehs," I said.

"What's he going to say?" She was back to staring at her feet.

"That guy down at the coffee shop. Remember?" I grabbed a handful of crackers. "He said Jaden was here for a reason. As though Ehs had brought him."

"What?" I could see Rachel's plane starting its own descent. Her eyes were sharp again, looking at me. "Why didn't you tell me?"

"I didn't want to freak you out. Until I talked to Ehs. But he hasn't been around … instead some old lady showed up and told me not to trust him. And I still kinda do." I rubbed the crackers between my fingers, feeling the texture of my skin and noticing the salt and baked wheat against it. "Hmm …" I decided to mumble.

"Well, where the hell is he? Get him here," Rachel said, with even more clarity and crispness that I hadn't noticed was missing up to that point. Her eyes were suddenly razors. "Get him here."

"It doesn't work like that," I answered, before popping the cracker in my mouth and chewing it slowly.

"Well—" The voice came from the darkness surrounding our deck and we both jumped out of our chairs, startled at the nearness of it. "When you ask like that, how can I resist?"

The familiar sight of James appeared from the darkness wearing black pants, a crisp white T-shirt, and white shoes. He seemed especially hip.

"God!" I shouted. "Do you have to do that?"

Rachel was staring at James in the same way she had been staring at the cheese, the clarity apparently gone after its short appearance. Ehs nodded toward her and smiled.

"Oh sorry, Rachel, this is … Ehs. Well, James. Well, Ehs. Yeah, Ehs. This is Ehs and Ehs, this is Rachel."

Ehs reached out his hand for Rachel. "It is a pleasure to officially meet you. It was a little fast last time."

"Yes," Rachel answered, still staring and obviously processing, even if the computer in her head was running a bit slower than normal.

"Well, I would love to sit and chat and alter reality with you two but not tonight." He looked around us, almost nervous. Maybe agitated. "In fact, we'll have to make this quick. I'm sure you've noticed, things are a bit stirred up right now."

"Yeah, I wish you could," I nodded. *I really did.* "I have noticed. In fact, a guy—"

"I know, I know." Ehs sat down in an empty chair and looked toward the cheese. "Department of Security got cocky and started poking around. I reprimanded him. He won't do it again."

"But, is it true?"

"Is what true?"

"Did you guys bring Jaden back?"

Rachel leaned in.

Ehs smiled. "We don't bring people anywhere. I've told you this before."

"Well, that's not—"

"Security wanted to scare you. And the poor fool they've been toying with." Ehs shook his head. "I told him the truth. Our plan. He's fine."

"Who's fine?" I asked.

"Sha."

"Who the fuck is Sha?"

"Head of Security." Ehs poked his head up in the air more creature-like than human. "Listen, I don't have time. They're watching more than usual with you talking to her. With Leo, with Richard … you understand?"

"No." I shook my head.

"Definitely not," Rachel added. "But what's the plan?" Rachel asked.

"What?" I said at exactly the same time as Ehs.

"You said you told security your plan. What's the plan?"

Ehs seemed impressed, nodding his head with a smirk. "Ah, yes. Our plan to …" He looked at me and winked. "To trap her. To take her down. To suck her in."

"I—"

"I'll find you soon. When we can talk more."

"What do you mean stirred up?"

Ehs looked out toward our yard. When he did I noticed it was filled with something that I had not seen earlier. Black birds, everywhere. Ravens maybe or crows—it was hard to make out but there were hundreds of them. And then I looked up to the stars and realized they were flying above us as well. Almost silently, filling the sky.

"What … the …"

"My private security. They'll alert me if Seers, or, well … anyone is around who shouldn't be."

Rachel looked up and back to Ehs. "Is this real?"

"Don't even bother, honey."

Rachel looked toward the half-burned joint next to the cheese. "Shit."

Ehs laughed and immediately stopped again, almost lifting his nose this time, to catch some scent tiptoeing through the night air.

"So we're safe?"

"No less safe than before I met you," he answered, still looking off somewhere else.

"That's not super comforting," I said.

"Well, it should be. Now, I really do—"

"Wait!" It was Rachel this time. "Is Jaden here to trap me?"

"Trap you?" Ehs laughed. "You?"

"Yeah, her," I threw in, since he didn't seem to be following.

"You—" He stared directly in her eyes. "You are far too strong to be trapped, my lady. Far too strong."

Rachel seemed to grow taller as the words hit her. I think I did too.

"Listen." Ehs looked toward my taller self. "Trust me. We'll be okay. Just don't panic or anything."

I nodded. "Yeah. Also, I saw her again."

Suddenly, the birds that had been silent, erupted. As did my heart. Rachel jumped out of her chair and put her hands over her head. The noise was deafening as was the realization that there had been far more birds than we ever could have imagined. They were everywhere, calling out in the air and the ground and …

It was silent again.

Ehs was gone.

Rachel slowly put her hands down and stared at me. I stared back.

We both looked at the cheese and the fully smoked joint now next to it.

"Did we?"

"Whoa," Rachel moaned. "There were like birds everywhere … did you see that?"

My ears started to ring with that high-pitched scream and just as I began to think *someone must be talking about me* I felt the wave of Seers pass over us. Rachel felt it too. I could see it all over her face. It passed quickly, as usual, but they did leave a wake of anxiety rippling in the air with the nineties rap video imaginations.

And we stared at each other with wide eyes while we finished off the rest of the cheese.

TWENTY ONE

Serene bodies of water do something to the human psyche and soul, especially if they are removed from all the crud of civilization and surrounded by the cleanliness of raw nature. Our family had been going to the same lake for years. It was our one tradition and everyone looked forward to it. Through the ups and downs we always made time for lake camping. Our kids insisted. If you put some crystal-clear water and sky together with rolling hills of trees, a touch of sand, that summer smell when the air warms up after a crisp night, and sweet nostalgia, what more can you ask for?

Thankfully camping is also affordable. We were starting to find some odd jobs here and there and somehow paying our bills. Rachel working more at the studio was helping—but I was trying not to think about that. It was supposed to be serene and calm on vacation.

August was traditionally prime-time weather but that August day it was raining. The whole day. We woke up to clouds and a light drizzle on the tent trailer and the forecast was for more of the same all day. It would be sweatshirts instead of swimming suits. That could have been disappointing, and it was a little, but that also meant that we had been lulled to sleep by the sound of delicate rain and the smell of fresh water falling from heaven the night before. And we would still have plenty of wine, board games, and family fun around a campfire.

One small problem: the wood was wet—I had accidentally left it out the night before and it was proving to be a struggle to get it going. A lot of smoke. Not much fire, proving that "where there is smoke, there is fire" is not always true. With everyone trying to get warm, no one found the joke funny. They just asked for fire. The rain did eventually let up and I bought some kindling and dry wood from the nearby store, which meant heat was in our future.

The kids were riding bikes, Rachel was playing a game of cards in her mom's camper (the whole extended family was a part of this tradition), and I was working on the fire surrounded by lots of smoke and steam. Everyone was coming over for lunch a little later.

I had a sense he would show up. Just as I began to wonder if he was the one giving me that sense, it came to fruition.

I recognized the eyes of James—or Ehs—within the smoke. He seemed to be having a grand old time dressing up, like a kid at Halloween, arranging the shades of smoke and steam and fire into various forms of eyes and mouths and arms and legs.

"Have things calmed down?" That was the first question I threw out there, not too loud, but not too quiet either. And with a little force.

"Wow," he answered, dancing around my face. "Someone a little grumpy today?"

"Have you seen the weather?"

"It's a nice break," he answered.

"Have you seen this fire?"

He looked down, as though inspecting the thing he was. "I take it you didn't do a lot of Boy Scouts as a kid?"

"I did actually," I answered, blowing on some embers starting to form. "The wood is real wet."

"Hmmm …" He somehow nodded. "Fire-making didn't stick real well? Not a quick learner back then either?"

"Okay, seriously, have things calmed down?" I said with more grumpiness. I think it was also pretty clear I had no idea what I was really asking. "And where have you been?"

"Do I need to remind you that I have a job? You think it's an easy job doing what I do?"

"To be honest—" I sat back away from another plume of smoke. "I have no idea."

"Lots of little dumb Shadows to manage and form. Lots of overseeing really … not a lot of hands-on work anymore."

"Hire some receptionists."

"If you want something done well, you do it yourself. And many of these Shadows are insensate boorish products of lust and destruction. Almost useless. More harm than good."

"Insensate?"

"Incapable of human feelings. Cold. Too cold."

"That's a bad thing for a demon?"

"Of course," he answered. "Do we need this conversation again too? Too blatant is not good for anyone. Unfortunately, some of these boors work their way up the ladders and get in my business. And ruin my business."

"Have you been following our politics?" I threw in, remembering a previous conversation.

"Exactly." The smoke formed into the face of the man. "Almost useless."

"I mean, I think we've got to have some of the worst leaders in the history of the United States," I said. "That's gotta have something to do with you?"

He seemed annoyed again. "Insignificant! You continue to sound like an idiot."

"Well …"

"From the moment the masses have wanted leaders, the leaders have owned them. The wise have also tried to warn you that your leaders will despise and use you. You insisted then and insist now. You still want one. You still despise them. You still want one. Boring, Seth, so boring."

"Okay, so are things chill now?" I figured I would return to the original subject since our current one was not going to go anywhere enjoyable or productive. "Also, can you help with this fire?"

"Chill? Never with her." He looked down again.

"What's she like?" Since I had never asked.

"Everything you would expect." Ehs was still dancing around the smoke, although suddenly the fire was starting to come together. The dry wood was burning and we had real flames forming, which Ehs was moving down into now. "Imposing. Gentle. Tempting. Accusatory. Powerful. Jealous. Afraid. Controlling." His face was now dancing in the flames, shifting to take on the qualities of his words. "Like most power."

"Are you afraid of her?"

"Sure."

"Can she kill you?"

"No."

"She can't?" I asked.

"No, she can't really do much."

"What?" I asked, a bit flabbergasted.

"She can get us and you to kill each other." Those words meant something to him, I could see it even in his vague form. "That's all she needs."

I nodded. "Yeah, right." Some kids went riding by, yelling at each other on a little trail by the campsite. "So, I talked to her."

"Lucy?" He seemed surprised.

"No," I answered. "The other her."

"Yes, you said on your deck." His surprise faded.

"She said Insipid is fading."

A new surprised expression formed, clearly evident in him. The flames of the ever-growing fire were now actually providing some warmth and a canvas of flames for Ehs to work in and convey expression.

"She talked to you that clearly?" His face was visible for a moment and very intrigued.

"Yeah." Though his question did throw me.

"As in," he continued, "you heard a voice. Audibly?"

"She showed up as some old lady. Like you do sometimes. I saw and heard her."

The fire crackled and popped and sparks went flying into the dreary sky and landed onto nearby wet leaves. Coincidentally or not, I wasn't sure. "She appeared as a human?"

"Yeah," I answered with all kinds of *why wouldn't she* in my voice.

He smiled. "Impressive."

"Not sure I'm following here."

"They don't take on bodies very often. Only in extreme circumstances." He was still smiling and I still didn't understand why.

"Well, she was an older lady." I thought that might help.

Ehs laughed. "She was a dead lady, Seth. The only forms they take."

I instantly reformed the image of the elderly woman in my head. "She definitely looked good … for being dead. Literally dead?"

"It wasn't exactly … her. But skin. A form. Still …" His face disappeared for a moment. "Yes, literally dead. We take the metaphorical dead."

"What the hell?" I spoke to an empty fire.

"Yes." He was back. "We are getting to her. You are getting to her. This is very good."

"Getting to her?"

"She's intrigued."

I wasn't sure if that was a good for evil or a good for good but either way I went ahead with the most basic response. "So, why don't they take bodies very often?"

"They don't *take* anything." His fire eyes looked me in the eyes. I backed up because the fire was getting hot and the eyes were a tad scary. "Ever. They reveal. We hide. You do the rest."

"Dead bodies?"

"Mere skins …"

"And you do take humans?" The conversation was a staple I was still obsessed with.

He nodded, bored. "We hide the human." He disappeared again before returning a moment later. "What else did she say?" he asked.

"All kinds of stuff," I replied.

More sparks jumped from the fire. He was almost giddy. "They don't *say* much either, in case you haven't noticed."

"I have." I rubbed my hands together to get some sap off. "And she actually answered questions."

The fire erupted again. "Unheard of."

I went back to the memory of her outside my house, recalling the script as best I could and I found it surprisingly difficult. More than usual. It made me stop for a moment. "Basically some confusing stuff about everything being illusion … which makes sense in its confusion. And, basically … not to trust you. I guess. Or be careful. Or you're evil, you're deceptive, you're telling me exactly what I want to hear in order to use me. I think she was clear but I don't feel it now."

His expression didn't change. A stone-cold expression in a fire. "And?"

"And, that you basically invented everything I once believed—which means I should blame you for my shitty religious upbringing." I paused.

He shrugged. "Yes, yes. And?"

"Have I told you what your shit did to me?"

"Yes, and I'm more aware of it than you. And—" He danced around the flames. "I am trying to make amends. What did she say?" he asked again with heat.

"You are probably much more powerful than you let on. And high up, down there." I looked down, because for some reason darkness is still *down* there and light is still *up* there.

"And?"

"Not much else."

"Do you believe her?"

"I don't think angels lie."

He nodded. "They don't."

"But," I added slowly, careful of my words. "I don't think she knows you like I do."

He smiled the smile of someone who appreciated the comment because it was true or because I believed it to be true. I couldn't tell. Who could ever differentiate that one?

I continued. "But, I'm scared, Ehs. The summer is playing with me, man. And I don't know if it's you. I don't know if I'm supposed to be drawn to you because evil is always going to draw me in and make me feel like I'm supposed to, or because you're good and good should always draw me in."

The fire crackled but he said nothing.

"I don't know what I believe anymore. I don't know if that's good or if that's evil … I don't know if I'm finding something more divine and real by losing the idols or if I'm losing the whole thing and finding just another idol—evil disguised as god. The wolf in sheep's clothing. I don't even know if there is a wolf or a sheep."

Ehs was gone. There was no response.

"Dad!" My daughter came rolling into the campsite with her cousins. "You got the fire going!"

"Yeah!" I tried my best to be excited. "Where is everybody?"

"At Nana's. They're coming down soon." She put out her hands to feel the heat. "We'll go tell them the fire is warm down here! Nice work!"

"Okay." I threw another big log onto the fire. "Sounds good!"

And they were gone. Ehs returned in the still-growing flames. "What else did she say?"

"You heard her. They're going to get—"

"No," he shouted. "*Her*, you idiot."

"Right." I poked around the embers. "Right."

The fresh oxygen brightened up the dull orange wood and Ehs moved all through it for a moment.

"Am I doing the right thing, Ehs?" I leaned close to the fire.

"You're asking a demon?"

I sighed. "You're a Shadow."

He laughed. Quickly. "What else did she say?"

"Man, what do I do?"

The fire grew eerily calm suddenly, worrying me that it was about to extinguish again. I heard a whisper. "You know."

"What?" I asked.

"You heard me," I heard in the same quiet whisper that sounded like Ehs, but, honestly, could have been her. Or something else. I leaned toward the ground, wondering if it would come again and the fire about took my head off as it shot upward again with fury.

"What did she say?"

"Can you warn me if you're going to do that? Do I still have eyebrows?" I reached up and felt for them. "Thank god." They seemed to be intact. "She said Insipid is falling. Something like you're the desperate one, not her."

He wore a disgusted expression. Irritated, yes, but not threatened. Sarcastic cuteness. He seemed almost proud to receive the insult and began to shake his head. "Insipid is falling?"

I didn't like the expression forming and moved my chair back a bit. The fire was getting very hot. "That's what she said." Jet engine hot.

He nodded, as though thinking. "Of course she told you that."

"Listen," I said cautiously. "I'm not going to get between you guys … not on this."

"What do you think?" he roared.

"Hell if I know. I just said I don't feel like I know anything anymore."

He sighed and the hot steam blew across my face. "I asked what you *think*."

"Okay," I stumbled. "Yeah, some people are seeing. That's what she said."

"Do you agree?" A big spark went flying out of the flame and, I hoped, faded before landing in dry brush.

"I guess some idols are collapsing. Yeah, formulas are breaking and boxes are being opened. We're finding a better god?" The way I spoke wasn't convincing anyone, including myself.

He was not impressed. "There have always been the mystics. And the system always ignores them, if it doesn't kill them. Maybe a small percentage are more aware of them than the past. But"—his face grew small in the fire—"I don't think anyone on our side is worried."

"People are starting to see," I repeated, quoting directly from her.

His face was large again. "Really?"

"Yeah," I added with about as much force as a puddle of water.

"Do you know how many people are talking behind your back right now? At this moment. Criticizing you and berating your pseudo-heresies? Worked up that you were leading people astray? You even!" His face was dancing with the flames. "They think *you* were leading people astray? And *they* are seeing?"

"I mean … I don't know." I frowned. "They are, right?"

He laughed. "They are seeing something."

"Critics always exist."

"That is what the mystics say."

"Does that make me a mystic?" I smiled.

The fire danced abstractly from one side of the pile of wood to the other. "You imitate them well, at times."

I looked down, a bit defeated. "That's a start, I guess."

"No one on our side is worried about what the mystics think. We are worried about what the critics think and, more importantly, who is listening to *them*."

I looked toward a family walking by and waved. "Okay, I think fewer people are listening to them."

"The masses, Seth. The ignorant masses."

"Are you quoting evil dictators now?"

"They were quoting me."

That forced a pause in me.

He said nothing either, waiting for me.

"Alright, still, something is happening, Ehs. You can't deny it." I was, honestly, hoping he couldn't but I would not have bet money on it.

The flames grew in intensity and size for a brief moment and Ehs painted himself across all of them. His face was no longer in them: the flames were in him. He was the fire and he was big and agitated. "Insipid, unfortunately, is performing brilliantly. It's why I've come to you. I hope to damage it but please don't insult me by acting as though it's failing."

I moved my chair further away, again. "Please don't burn down the forest."

The fire returned to its unaffected-by-supernatural-powers size, which was still pretty large and made me proud, and Ehs continued speaking. "What does she say?"

"What do you mean?"

"What are her reasons?"

"I don't know." I looked up to the tall treetops all around me, trying to remember her conversation but figuring that if I couldn't, I could throw in a few of my own to test them out. "Child mortality. Less violence and slavery. Starvation. Poverty …"

"You sound unconvinced." He breathed and I felt another blast of heat across my face.

I could only shake my head. "I don't know. People are leaving these shitty religions too. That seems good. I mean, yeah, it's been a hard summer but there is lots of good if I think about it. And, read books about it. There is good out there." Was I convincing myself?

Something I said really stoked his emotion and the sudden size of the fire. For a moment it was towering over me, shooting out sparks like a Fourth of July fireworks show. "Of course, there is good. There is always good." He sizzled as though water had just been thrown into the fire.

I looked around again. Some kids were staring, probably assuming that Harry Potter was speaking to me in the fire and hopefully mesmerized and frightened enough to not tell their parents the entire campground was about to burn down. I waved my hand at them and smiled, feeling the fire come back to normal behind me.

"But her avoidance of the truth is appalling, and surprising, even for me." He roared again, making me look at the kids and try to smile again.

"Yes, there is less starvation. Unfortunately, more kill themselves from obesity now." The flames skyrocketed toward the heavens again. "Yes, there is less war and terrorism. No worries, you take your own lives now in greater numbers. No need for the old enemies when loneliness consumes you all while you seek your salvation in screens and false connections. Oh," he mocked, moving his face into the core of the fire, nearer the logs. "Poverty has been reduced. And what does she say to the empires of inequality that have replaced it? At historical levels? And the hidden subtle suffering that such systems produce for every human under their spell?"

The fire returned to normal momentarily before rushing upward again.

"You have destroyed the planet along with the vast majority of creatures that live on it with you. Impressively fast. In time, the rest too will die, maybe before your own extinction. Yes, they are leaving primitive views of hell. And re-creating them on your planet, burning it to pieces. Your priests destroy more than your soldiers, and your soldiers kill not for dictators but for your corporations. Depression and anxiety rise as the new epidemics even as you eradicate most of the old biological ones—which are even making a reappearance due to your arrogance. You are addicted to distraction, to drugs, and to violence. Even the very system that is supposed to heal the criminal only perpetuates revenge and retribution and makes them and you twice the criminal they were! They are leaving the old religions, she says? Oh joy!" The flames blasted out in every direction, threatening just above my head. "They are joining the new religion of capitalism in droves, dying for its gods more than any other war in history. And, greatest of all!" It felt like a bomb in front of me, drenching me in hot, steaming air. "She has the audacity to say Insipid is failing? Just like you. And the rest of your arrogantly ignorant human tribe! You mock it while it destroys you! You celebrate the lies as enlightenment. You worship gods while bowing before the darkness. The audacity!"

I was standing now as far back from the fire as I could be, unconcerned with how it all looked and more concerned with not being pulverized to ash.

"And you stand to tell me it is failing? How dare you?" The fire screamed. "Do *I* need to keep going?" he mocked.

"I'm not," I answered, shriveling from the wave of heat and fire. "I was just repeating . . ."

"Give up your pseudo-heresies for something that actually means something." The heat shot toward me again, causing me to push back even more.

"What's that mean?" I yelled back. To a fire. "You keep saying it."

The flames burst toward the sky again. "Your stupidity is

numbing even me."

I looked down and the fire grew quiet again.

"See what already is." The flame sparked again.

"It is pretty shit, according to you, at least!" I answered, oblivious to the kids now staring at me.

"You!" The fire blasted heat into my face for a split second. More and I don't think I would have had a face. "The only evidence I need that Insipid is still working. Is you."

The words shook me. I can't lie. I felt like the dreary, now-raining sky above me.

"And she says we are losing," he drew out slowly, coordinating with a chorus of hisses as the drops of water hit the flames. "It's your biggest weakness."

I looked toward the fire, sad now. Pessimism and sarcasm were flooding me like they used to and I didn't like the feeling.

"They always believe they will eventually win. They always hold out hope and see the best in the world, in choice, in freedom, and in love. They only speak of a future where the light shines amidst the darkness, even as the darkness grows all around them."

His words gave me hope and I wasn't sure whether they were supposed to or not.

I looked back toward the fire, still smoldering in more ways than one.

"We are not losing, Seth," he flickered.

"Well, if this is winning," I pointed at him. "Why do you want out?"

"There you go!" he shouted, grinning with a proud smile. "There it is. Maybe you are paying attention. You're right—this winning is empty. For those of us who can see it. For the humans who notice." He grew sad again. "But the numbers are both as small as ever. Trust me in that and convince her of the same." He paused, as did the flames.

"I'll try."

"And Seth," he said slowly. "Let the things die that are keeping you from living."

Then he was gone. The rain stopped. The kids that were staring ran away when I looked at them, hopefully telling their parents stories they wouldn't believe.

I slumped to my chair and stared at the flames until my own kids came trolling into our campsite on their bikes, closely followed by the rest of the family carrying cards and board games and plates of cheese and bottles of wine.

I decided to have a lot of wine … and maybe some beer too. And probably some red licorice in the middle of it all.

TWENTY TWO

It was maybe three in the morning. I wasn't exactly sure since I didn't look at my phone before I stumbled out of our tent trailer and into the cold night air, trying not to let the screen door slam shut behind me. It was as black as a night can get, with the stars hidden by clouds and no moon to speak of. The space of the campground was silent, with everyone asleep or moving respectfully quiet, like I was.

I have a love-hate relationship with middle-of-the-night camping bathroom breaks. It hurts to get out of the warm sleeping bag but it also hurts to sleep with an ever-expanding bladder. And wow, once I'm out there in the still, the silence, the emptiness, its delicate beauty is like few other experiences in life.

In fact, it was so enticing, I found myself walking aimlessly around the campsite for a moment. The fire was still going, mostly pulsating embers, but there were small flames and the park ranger had explicitly told us not to leave small flames in case they turned into bigger flames. So, I walked toward it.

In reality, I walked over to stare at them. They were mesmerizing.

Who am I kidding … I also wondered if he would show up again. Our conversation was still on my mind, even after some whiskey and wine and mean card games … it was a hard one to shake.

I stood there, staring.

"Are you ready?"

I looked up. His voice was coming from somewhere else.

"For what?" I whispered.

"C'mon."

"Where?"

"Step onto the fire." I still couldn't tell where the voice was coming from, which meant, as usual, that it might have been coming from my head, which meant that I definitely should not step on burning hot embers in the middle of the night in a silent campground.

"Yeah, right." I whispered so quietly I was barely sure I said it.

"C'mon, you have flip-flops on."

I rolled my eyes though no one could see. "I'm not stepping onto a fire."

"Why not?"

"It's a fire. And it's hot. And I don't even know where you're taking me. And it's the middle of the night …"

"Fear, fear, fear." The words sounded out like surround sound in a good theater—bouncing around, emanating from different locations as though different people were speaking them even though it was all his voice. "Have you ever sat up at night and wondered all the things you have missed out on in life because you were afraid?"

"Yes," I answered honestly.

"Fear, fear, fear."

"I know."

"Do you enjoy its rule over you?"

"Not really."

"Then, move. Live out of love instead."

I lifted my foot. "Wait!"

"What?" I put my foot back down.

"You have to go barefoot."

"Then forget it," I said.

"I'm kidding. Let's go!"

I stepped onto the fire, asking myself *why not* and coming up with all kinds of compelling reasons pretty quickly. On second thought, most of them were based on fears that he had already proved wrong.

"That a kid," I heard.

A moment later I was being hammered by loud beats on a crappy sound system. Pulsating lights were all around me, trying to be in rhythm to the music, but not quite able to keep up.

It only took a moment to realize where I was. Well, at least the kind of place it was.

"Welcome to JR's," Ehs said, once again in the shape I still attributed to James, even though I only knew him as Ehs. "Where the finest men in all the land and the finest ladies in all the land come together to make each other feel as though they matter."

Some of the finest ladies were dancing about thirty feet away and, like the lights, they were not quite keeping up with the music. I don't know if anyone cared.

"Probably won't be their new tagline," I offered while still trying to get my bearings. Ten minutes earlier I had been asleep in a campground. "Also, I've never been to a strip club."

"I know, I know. You're so pure," he laughed. "And proud."

I wasn't sure what to do with that remark. "You didn't say you were bringing me to a strip club," I replied.

"Would it have mattered?"

I rubbed my eyes for a second, still waking up and still wondering if I was asleep. "I guess not. Not sure Rachel will love it."

"You'll be fine," he said, like some kind of mobster. "You've been to plenty in movies, plenty on your screens, and plenty in your imagination. You've also—"

"Alright," I interrupted, looking toward the dancing ladies. "I get it."

"And I assumed you didn't want me to take you to a brothel in Thailand with eight-year-olds being sold as sex slaves?" he asked with a normalcy that made me throw him a revolted expression, like he should have had when saying such words.

"If those were my only choices …"

"As I assumed." He nodded.

"And they aren't quite the same thing," I added, still looking around. As my eyes adjusted to the light I could see that they were not necessarily the finest ladies. That was followed by guilt for even caring, followed by sadness for their situation, followed by anger at the group of men I noticed in the front row holding on to dollar bills and glasses of cheap cocktails with too much sugar in them. Followed by a sense of justification for my being there. They wouldn't tempt me.

"Hmmm," he mumbled. "Of course, they aren't the same. This one doesn't make you throw up and run for the doors."

"And?" I looked up, sensing he was trying to say something.

His eyebrows popped toward the water-stained ceiling for a moment. "Oh, nothing," he mocked. "Yes, completely different."

"What are we doing here?" I sighed.

The guys in the front row were all wearing camouflage and, at first glance, did not appear to be the finest, either. Overweight, scraggly beards, greasy hands, dirty fingernails, and, I assumed, rusted-out hearts from what I could hear them saying to the topless women dancing in front of them and trying to smile like they didn't care.

Ehs wasn't answering so I looked over at him. He was smiling, not turned on by the women, but turned on by the scene I assumed he had a hand in creating.

"What are we doing here?" I asked again, not wanting to look back toward the women, or the men. I was already getting a headache from the bad music. I noticed that the walls were vibrating from the subwoofers. Just another thing jiggling that probably shouldn't have been.

"I wanted to fill you in on another zone."

"Could we have, at least, gone to a nice, upscale strip club?"

He looked at me like *do you want to?*

I didn't, but I did have to think about why I had asked.

"It was hard to find somewhere I could get my message across without you being … distracted." He smiled. "By the primitive lust of sexual beauty or by the gratuitous abuse of innocence. It's a fine line in this section. I assume I chose right." He held both hands up along with his chin and eyebrows.

"Yeah," I mumbled, mulling over the truth of it.

"Telling, in itself," he said smugly, waiting for my reaction.

I looked around again, instead. The place was mostly empty except for the main group of cacklers and a couple of lonely guys sitting in corners on their phones, probably not looking over their stock portfolios. There was a bar a little ways away with some neon beer signs and old neon Playboy bunnies from some forgotten time period when Playboy signified something.

"Okay," I said again. "I get it. Sex. Lust. Yada yada …"

"No," he answered.

And when he said no, he ratcheted up my consciousness or awareness or whatever it was that may have still been half-asleep in my nice warm sleeping bag—if that's where it was. He was definitely right—I didn't get it, and I had lots of questions.

"Actually." I looked back at him, suddenly more present with him and less present with the fine ladies and men. "You're right. In fact, I'm surprised this is even a thing."

"A thing?" He smiled. "You know it's a thing. You just don't know what to do with the thing anymore."

"Fair. I just don't care much about it anymore." Which was also true.

"But you do." Which was also true. "And you should." Which was probably true.

"I should?"

"It seems …" He took a serious step toward me. "That the enslavement of women for this thing, the abuse of children by religious figures for this thing, the endless suicide of people attracted to the wrong gender for this thing, and a growing generation that doesn't even know what to do with this thing, could be a bit worrisome." He paused long enough for me to hear someone, on cue, hollering about "nice titties" in the distance. "Something you might want to care about."

"Okay, okay." All true. "We've just fucked this up so bad, I don't even know where to go with it. I'm not one to talk."

"Ah, don't be so hard on yourselves." He smiled, but it was

a greasy smile. Or maybe a normal smile in a greasy spot. I probably looked greasy too. "We had plenty to do with it."

I sighed but no one heard me above the music.

"Should we sit down?" He motioned toward a table in the back, hidden in shadow, and, hopefully, further away from the ladies and speakers.

"Sure." I started walking that way, passing by empty tables, some with cigarettes still burning in ashtrays … which was surprising for a moment. I couldn't think of the last time I had seen a cigarette inside of a building burning in an ashtray.

"I'll admit," he said as we walked, "this one was almost too easy for us."

"I'm sure."

"We were given so much to work with."

"I'm sure," I repeated, preparing myself for the lesson.

"Almost, I said." We arrived at our table and sat down. Ehs, the Shadow, sat across the table from me, both of us mostly hidden in some vague darkness, with the faint glow of neon somewhere in the air above us, floating with the sexuality and cigarette smoke around us.

"Go ahead." As though he needed my permission.

"Biologically speaking, mostly." Ehs leaned back. "The urges. The desires. The desire for bonding and the contradictory desire to spread seed. Throw in the fact that human life comes from the act and, I mean … honestly. It's a lot to work with." He put his arms on the torn faux leather top of the seat and stretched out.

"So, that's it?"

"Well, you don't care about this," he replied. Suddenly there was a cigarette in his hand and he was smoking it. Smoke smoking smoke.

"You're a smoker now?"

"I wanted to lean a little more into the scene. I enjoy it so much." He blew out another stream and motioned for a drink. No one but me witnessed either.

"You're doing a great job." Some of the fine men were cheering because a fine lady was gyrating in front of them. I hated cliché and it was everywhere.

"For someone whose life has been almost ruined a few times because of this topic," he said plainly, quickly grabbing my attention back, "I'm surprised you don't care."

I waited.

"Too little sex. Too much sex." He leaned forward with his cigarette hanging out of his mouth. "Both have just about destroyed you. It's so confusing, isn't it?"

There were lots of things to say but I didn't know how to say any of them.

"It's almost as though none of you know what to do with the power." He was still leaning back in his chair, which made me lean forward. I didn't want to imagine what microscopic things were crawling around on it, potentially invading me. If I was even there. "Make love? Can it? Ruin a life? Can it? Can one thing actually do both?" he asked with another release of smoke into the air that already had plenty.

"You're really being coy about this one," I countered. "Unlike your usual self."

"I'm sorry." He leaned forward. "You care about this now?"

I nodded. "I said I don't know what to do with it."

"It weighs on you, doesn't it?"

I looked down, thinking about whether he was right or not. "I've spent a lot of time in counseling talking about it."

"Oh." He pulled back. "I thought you were surprised this was even a thing." He smiled. "And you've spent hours talking about it with a counselor? And your wife? And others?"

I sighed as a server walked by carrying a tray of empty beer bottles.

"Sex works well, only because it reveals so many other things—in so many tangible ways. It's the perfect visible representation of what is deeper."

I was listening.

"We weaponized shame."

Still listening.

"Can you smell the shame in here? It's practically suffocating." He glanced toward the dancers again, still moving around, a little more slowly, to the still-thumping music. A speaker was rattling somewhere, blown. "She's desperately trying to make love, somehow, someway, to find worth. His dollar bills scratch the itch for a moment. And the men are desperate to make love. Her desperate attempt to smile and her willingness to show parts of herself that your culture says you are not supposed to see meet his demand for worth, for a moment. The drug will flow through his veins for at least a while until he needs his next fix."

There was no need to argue.

"They're all trying to make something and yet fucking themselves in the process," he said. "Sometimes literally. Always figuratively."

I nodded, a bit startled by his language. "I don't think I have any arguments." I didn't. I knew the feeling. Rachel knew the feeling. I knew the hit. The fun of it. I knew the harm. The pain of it.

"Of course." He stood up. "Because this is too easy. And you don't know what to do with it, because the answers have been wrong. And abused."

"Yeah, probably."

"This is almost too blatant, but, of course, even in the obvious, there is much more subtlety going on. But I think—" He paused and looked at me slowly. "You get that. Let's move on."

I stood too, not sure exactly what that meant.

"Are you ready?"

Before I could answer we left our bath of neon and smoke and were outside again, on a street corner in another cliché scene: this time a random suburban neighborhood somewhere in America.

The tree was deciduous, like it seems they always are. The streetlight was far enough away from us to not spread too much light but to let us know the neighborhood was friendly. The houses were upper-middle-class clones of one another, similar to the citizens who lived inside of them. The yards were green and a few had the sprinklers on, just to prove—like lawns have since they appeared in Versailles—that the owners were wealthy enough to own land for nothing but looks. In case we couldn't tell from the house.

The sidewalks were wide so the kids could ride their bikes and do their trick-or-treating in relative safety.

They say reality imitates art, so it makes sense we made whole suburbs that resemble movie studio lots.

I glanced over at Ehs, who seemed to think another cliché was as funny as it was stereotypical, judging from his grin.

Headlights appeared under the streetlight. It was a Toyota pickup truck—I could tell right away because I had driven my dad's many times. I might as well have lived there. I might as well have been the driver. That's probably why the whole scene got under my skin a little bit.

That and I was supposed to be asleep.

The truck drove slowly and shut off its headlights long before it stopped. I looked at Ehs, who was staring and obviously expecting me to do the same. There were two people in the car, silhouettes behind the front windshield.

The car eventually stopped and Ehs started walking toward it. It took me a moment to realize, or remember, that we couldn't be seen before I started walking too, lagging behind him. The doors stayed shut but I could eventually hear the radio playing some pop hit as generic as the cars and the houses. And probably the people. Like me.

I recognized the song and started singing along under my breath.

A little closer and I could tell it was a boy and a girl. A little closer and I could see they were fairly young. A little closer and we were practically outside their window now. I could start to hear them.

I kept looking at Ehs, wondering if we should be that close. I had always wanted to be invisible but now that I was, I didn't have the desire any longer. Check that one off the superhero wish list. It all felt wrong. Voyeuristic, invasive, dirty. Maybe the strip club was still clinging to me.

"Well, my parents are still gone," she said. There were nerves in her voice that moved their way into my own feelings.

"Really?" he returned with less nerves and more excitement. He opened the door but she didn't.

"Well—" She was wavering. "I don't know. Should we?"

He left the door open. He, obviously, didn't want to be *that* guy. But he also wanted to be that guy a little bit. I knew because I felt like I was watching myself. She was cute. He was cute. They were young. Hormones were about to take over, if they hadn't already. I could feel it.

I didn't want to be there. "What are we doing here?" I said to Ehs, loudly, making sure he knew I didn't like the scene—most likely because I had never truly dealt with my own from my past.

"It's fine …" the boy muttered.

"I don't know," she stammered. "I felt bad last time."

"I know," the boy answered. "I know. But …"

"Ehs!" I backed up. "What the hell? I don't need to hear this or see it. I get it."

"Well." She opened her door. "I guess just for a little bit?" Her question was not really a question.

He jumped out of the truck and shut the door, answering her nonquestion.

"Ehs! C'mon!" I started to walk away. I heard a car door close behind me.

"What are you doing?" Ehs shouted back.

"I don't need to see this." I kept walking.

"Are you jealous?" he asked, as though performing research of some kind.

I stopped and looked back at him. He seemed to be studying me and I didn't like it. "Jealous? No. I just don't like it. I get it. Young couple going to have sex, trying to find love. Whatever … it just seems perverted—the watching of them, I mean. And I just don't care what they do."

He smirked. "I just don't care," he mocked. "Yes, keep trying to convince yourself of that."

The boy and girl were standing next to one another, leaning

against the car, having some kind of argument while Ehs and I were doing the same.

"You are jealous," he said quietly, as though he was surprised at his findings.

"No, no. I'm not!" I insisted.

"You would do it differently if you could do it again. You are jealous of the … opportunity they have?" He seemed proud of his hypothesis. "To create the memories they will carry with them that you cannot … re-create?" He stared. "Or maybe, at memories that have been created that you don't want?"

I didn't want to think about any of his words. "Yes, the sex trade, yes, women being objectified. I mean I have my own children. Of course I care, I guess. But this!" I pointed toward the couple without looking and hoping to get on with something more interesting. "There are way more important things."

"So you prefer to bury your head in the sand?" he asked.

"No, I prefer to focus on the more important things. There are plenty."

"Hmm." He nodded. "You know nothing of their story."

"Okay," I answered. I looked back toward them. He was touching her face, she was leaning into it. "What's that going to change?"

"It's her first boyfriend. She's sixteen and he's twenty-three. It's not *his* first girlfriend."

I felt sick to my stomach and wanted to save the girl suddenly.

"Does that bother you?" he asked without emotion.

I looked back toward them. He was still touching her face, soothing her and, seemingly, convincing her. "Yeah it does."

"Why?"

"She's too young. He's not."

"Hmmm." He frowned. "They're married. She's nineteen and he's twenty-six. She doesn't feel right about sneaking into her parents' house."

"Really?" I instantly felt better and the two of them suddenly looked older.

"Do you feel better now?" He might as well have been holding a clipboard. His demeanor reeked of a lab researcher. I just wasn't sure who the rat was.

"Yeah," I answered.

"Why? Because they're married?" he asked.

"No," I sighed. "I … I don't know, it just seems like no one is taking advantage of anyone now."

"You have no way of knowing if that's true. And you had no

way to know whether it was true when she was fifteen either."

"Is this a game?"

"Maybe she is married and this is an affair—she has found something she never had. Or maybe it's an open marriage. Or maybe he is married and looking for something in her … like you once did." He shook his head, methodically. "What is it?"

"Fuck you."

"I apologize. This is … actually a second date," he continued, looking back. "They're both in college." Ehs smiled.

"Okay." They were still standing by the car. Whether I felt better or worse, I didn't know and was trying to ask myself why before Ehs did.

"Do you still approve?" He glanced back toward them and then stared at me, waiting.

"It's not about my approval." I looked toward the couple and noticed that the girl was no longer a girl but a boy. Short blond hair, staring up at the other boy.

"It's not?" He seemed surprised again.

"Of course not. Especially these two." The two boys leaned in for a quick kiss and giggle and something smiled inside of me that had not been smiling earlier.

"Yet you were bothered a moment ago?" He looked back toward the boys. "Then approving, then not, then approving …" He sighed. "I can't keep up."

"Okay," I exhaled, looking back at him. "What *is* your point?"

"Well." He turned his body to face them again. "What if they are both youth group kids? What if her dad is a pastor?" He was rubbing his chin, half mocking, half thinking. I couldn't tell. "Hmm, I can't remember now. How would that feel to you? Do you remember being them? Would you like to be them again?"

I didn't answer, even if I was thinking about it, while I looked back to the couple who were now two girls running toward the front door, holding hands.

"Or—" He looked back toward me. "Maybe they are both being raised in abusive families and they have finally found hope and love in each other. In fact, they are sneaking into this house, a stranger's house—they've never been inside a house on *this* street because they live on *that* street."

I looked back toward them just as both of the girls smiled, and I couldn't help but smile with their story. They hugged one another and started running for the house now. My smile grew ever bigger.

"Or," Ehs continued, "maybe they are both entitled rich kids and have dated for two years. Just had a little fight but it's all good now."

The original couple neared the front door, happy with one another. My smile was still there, although just a remnant of past emotion.

"Or maybe they are drunk."

She was taking some time to find her keys while I tried to find my smile that had been displaced by concern again.

"I can almost hear your brain working so hard to approve and disapprove and wonder where you come up with your decisions and why." He spoke with his back to me, as we both watched them disappear into the house.

I was quiet.

"It seems to me"—he turned around—"that you care much more than you think. And that you can't figure out quite how you care. Or why. Or what about. And that's what bothers you."

"Why?" I asked.

"Yes."

"Why are you doing this?" I asked.

"Because you should care."

"Why?"

"You're asking me that?" He took a step back. "I think Gwen and Jaden know why, as does your wife and I would assume you."

"Fuck you," I said, louder this time.

"Hmm," he nodded, looking back to the house we were standing in front of. "Because it matters. All of it matters."

"It matters they're about to have sex?"

"No," he responded. "It matters *why*. You know that."

"Okay," I agreed.

"You have a million rules in your head about how to determine a good reason from a bad reason. And there are a million reasons for billions of people and a million cultures that see it and have seen it a million different ways throughout their histories. Religion has input. Culture has input. Entertainment has input. Everyone receives the input trying … always trying to determine if the why meets the correct criteria."

"I don't feel like a lot of people actually are determining that," I added. "I feel like there's just some natural biological hormones at work here too."

"A very fine why," he answered. "It's natural. Evolutionary. We need to pass on our genes. Of course."

"Where is this going?" I asked very slowly and very uncomfortably.

"You know that much of the culture of the world is in the

middle of a sexual recession, as they call it?"

"A what?" I asked.

"They're having trouble connecting. They're losing their desire to. When the why is false, it can have devastating consequences, you see." He glanced back toward me with a look of alarm. "What does it all mean? What is going through your mind right now?" He seemed honest in the question.

So I tried to be honest in my analysis of my own mind.

Sex I wished I had and sex I wished I didn't.

Nineties rap songs I loved.

Youth pastors and their obsession with virgins.

Solomon and his obsession with wives and concubines.

Pregnancy, abortion, adoption, the foster system.

That stack of *Playboys* I used to look at when I was a kid.

The stack of internet sites I looked at as an adult.

The gay kid I made fun of as a kid.

The gay kid I officiated the wedding of years later.

The first time I saw a topless woman on a beach in France.

The first time I saw Gwen topless.

The last time I saw Rachel topless.

Jaden.

"I'm tired, Ehs," I sighed.

"Yes, it seems to be exhausting for you. As though the brain grinds to a halt with the possibilities …" he said slowly, thinking and processing himself. Or pretending to, for me.

The door of the house came flying open and the boy came running out. He seemed upset, walking directly toward me and forcing me to not be tired.

He wasn't angry, I noticed, but maybe embarrassed.

She appeared in the doorway a few seconds later. "Wait!"

He turned around.

She moved toward him. "Listen, I'm sorry. I just don't think we should."

"I know, I know," he answered, with his head down.

"I'm sorry!" she pleaded, apologizing for who knows what.

"It's fine."

"Are you sure?"

"I don't know." He seemed frustrated. "If it's going to be like this, I don't know."

"You don't know?" she stammered back. "You would break up with me for that?"

"No."

Of course you would. You just can't admit it.

"I can't take the back-and-forth. And the god shit. Make up your mind."

"But—" She seemed sincere. "I don't know! We're not supposed to."

"Says who?"

"The Bible."

"The Bible?" he asked mockingly.

"And god," she added.

He rolled his eyes. "So god was okay with it the other night?"

"No."

"He seemed to be."

"I said I'm sorry."

I looked toward Ehs, who was merely watching, again, expecting me to do the same.

"Well, I just don't know," he said.

"I just don't think we should. I think we'll be better off if we don't. I think it'll make things … better." She was reaching out, holding his hand. "I felt so guilty the other night. I know god was mad. I don't want that again. I'm sorry."

"I don't know." He let go of her hand and started walking toward the truck. "I'll text you later."

She started to cry but didn't move after him. He turned at the sound of her tears but didn't move toward her.

I stood in the middle of them with Ehs. I found myself observing, like Ehs was. Maybe I was picking up a new skill. Ehs flashed his eyebrows toward me as she walked back into her house and the truck drove away.

"I hate this," I said.

"What?" he answered.

"All of it. I mean, just have sex already."

"Really? Do you even know what they were arguing about?"

"I'm not an idiot," I answered.

"Hmm," he nodded. "He wanted to smoke a little weed. I believe you and Rachel did recently?"

My brain stopped and then quickly started rewinding, trying its best to replay their words. "What?"

"Always filling in the gaps with sex, aren't you?" He smirked with the grin I didn't like, even when he was right.

"What are you doing to me?"

"Nothing to you," he answered. "It seems someone reminded *her* of the rules of the game."

"What rules?" I paused, still replaying their conversation but trying to keep up with the one I was in.

"What rules?" He shrugged. "There are always rules." He started walking away from the house now and I followed. "Some better than others."

"What the fuck?"

He looked back at me as though he expected the word and wanted me to think about its meaning for a moment. I tried but he kept talking. "You didn't want them to have sex, right?" he asked, still walking toward where the truck once parked.

"I don't care," I said, exasperated at the whole scene that I had watched and was still trying to process. "Why are we talking about sex?" I yelled.

"We aren't talking about sex, you idiot. We never have been. Sex is just a tool." He shrugged and started walking again.

"What are you trying to do here? To show me?" I started to follow him back to the street.

"Reality."

"You don't even like reality."

"There is one more place to go."

He didn't even ask that time.

We appeared in a parking lot. A generic strip mall, again, somewhere that didn't matter because it was everywhere. I was sensing a theme.

It was still dark. The lights were minimal, a few in front of stores and a few in the parking lot, but otherwise it was a lonely place for light or anything else. A single car was parked far away, left there by someone who would pick it up the next morning.

I heard the crying before I saw him. He was sitting on a curb with his head in his hands, sobbing. His whole body was trembling. It shook even more with each congested inhale. He was gripping his hair, as though trying to keep his head stable.

We both walked closer and I looked at Ehs.

"He just received the news," Ehs said, still staring at the man who was now only a foot away. I did try to reach out my hand but it went directly through him. I wished it didn't. I would have hugged him.

"Divorce. Wife of twenty-four years just dropped him off about an hour earlier. He hasn't stopped crying. Poor guy." Ehs had the look of Spock. He had seen enough people be sad that he could put on a good expression but he didn't actually seem to feel or understand it.

I sighed.

"Almost made it to twenty-five. But not quite. Five kids. The youngest is twelve."

The man was practically moaning … in pain.

"A result of your religion," Ehs moaned, in his own way.

"My religion?"

"You call yourself a Christian?"

I paused. *Do I?*

"I don't know, actually."

Ehs nodded. "Fine. Either way—" He pointed toward the man. "This is a result of Christianity."

"I'm sure that's part of your doing."

He shrugged, somewhat ambivalent about the whole thing. I got the feeling there were more important matters.

"Your religion murdered this marriage." His fingers were pointing directly at me.

"Can you stop saying *my* religion?"

"Sure." He dropped his hands and looked toward the man, who continued to sob.

"Of course, it began with them being a good Christian couple," he said. "They didn't have sex." He looked back at me. "You can relate. God would not have approved of that, of course. Or blessed their marriage. But, it quickly went from there. Guilt and shame about past and previous partners. Guilt and shame about the present.

"Always looking to the Bible for their answers, because the Bible has them. Wives submit to your husbands."

"Oh, come on," I interjected. "Really? You're going to pull out that shit?"

He lifted his eyebrows and his chin as though I was supposed to go on. "Are you defending this religion?"

I looked away. "Hell no."

"They went to counseling. It wasn't supposed to be this way. This isn't what god had planned for them. They had children, they procreated, they had a family, they had done everything right."

"Okay, okay. I know the story."

Ah." He lifted his chin. "You do?"

"I mean—" I sighed. "I've counseled these people. So often with every kind—"

"Ironic," he interrupted.

"Yeah," I agreed.

"He was addicted to his pornography, always scratching the itch of worth, feeding the addiction of a facsimile value he could find nowhere else. A piece of something pretending to be the whole, to make him whole. A false fire. Afraid. Afraid of being vulnerable. An easy answer." Ehs seemed sad, if that were possible.

"She started to think for herself. She didn't need to be put into chains anymore, commanded, and under someone's rule," he continued.

He looked up at me. I looked down at the man.

Ehs kept going. "More counseling and more advice that he is the head of the household and she should follow him. More advice that they needed to please each other and fulfill their marital duties."

"That's terrible counseling and advice."

"It was from a Christian counselor."

"We get it. There is terrible advice out there," I shot back, a little angry and also grateful we had a good therapist.

"We?" Ehs asked with that look of observation again. "We do?"

I let out a lot of air. A deep exhale.

"I don't need your solutions, Seth." Ehs looked back toward the man and smiled. "Hmm, I apologize. This man was just dropped off by his parents. He just told them he was gay and they told him to never return. Sorry, sorry," he said sincerely. "It's so hard—even for me—to keep up with all the reasons humans reject each other based on something so simple as sex. That you don't care about."

My heart dropped even further. I stared at the man's tears even longer. I reached out to hug him again, to tell him to tell his parents to go to hell but I couldn't even touch him and it made the pain worse.

"I don't know what you want from me," I whispered to Ehs, while the man began to shake with tears. "I agree with you. I know! I—"

"No," he said loudly, interrupting. "You don't know."

"What then?"

"It's never just sex! When you believe it lives by itself, we build the wall. You build the wall. They build the wall. Sex can build this wall and tear it down in a hurry. But, believing it's just sex is the one thing you should never do."

"So do we need more? Less? What?" I had once thought I had known the answers but in that moment I felt like even my questions were wrong.

"Less sex?" he scoffed. "Less sex, more sex … why!" he yelled. "Do you know *why*? Does anyone know why?" He paused. "Pay attention. Sex is made from love or fear. Nothing else. Create or destroy. Have you thought about that?"

The man who was sobbing had quieted, beginning to live in the early stages of his new misery and reality, probably wondering if he would ever be able to hug his dad again.

"What are you willing to destroy? What do you want to create? This is what surrounds it. Births it. Feeds it. Starves it. Those are the places to spend your time." He folded his arms and looked calmly at me.

"You *are* a demon," I managed.

"Just a Shadow."

"I'm tired."

"Of course. As am I," Ehs responded, still Spock-like and unconvincing. "I'll show you the zone tomorrow night. And then we'll find out what *she* really thinks."

"She? Who?" I looked up.

"You're going to their side. I need you to bring her something."

"What?"

"You heard me."

I had. "To Lucy?"

"No, no … Emonee."

"Who is that?"

"You've talked to her numerous times."

"The Ray?"

He smiled.

"She won't tell me when we're meeting," I said.

"Of course. This isn't that, but it may lead us there."

I was obviously lost again. My shoulders slumped toward the asphalt with my face, without me even asking them to.

"You're tired. Sleep well."

"Wait." I put my hands out. "I do have a question."

He waited.

"Did Rachel enjoy it?" The question came out before I had a chance to wonder if it should. Some part of me had been struggling with it, mulling it, pondering it, and Ehs felt as good a person to ask as any. Still, I was embarrassed to admit the thought and voice it out loud. But there was no taking it back.

Ehs showed me contradictory expressions—of pride and disappointment. I struggled to understand what he was trying to show me, maybe because he was struggling himself.

We stared quietly at each other for a moment.

"Would you like to see?" he asked as though it was an honest question.

"See? Them?" My worst nightmare.

"Yes." He nodded, still honest, and revealing he did not understand humans—or at least me. "I can show you what happened."

"God, no!" Just the idea of watching made me feel like some kind of debilitating toxin had been injected into me. "I already see it enough. Sometimes I can't help but see it." I looked down, ashamed, pushing away thoughts.

"Hmm," he said, nodding.

I looked back up at him. "You're saying you could show me? Like some video or something?"

"We have departments that keep that sort of thing. Suggestions for … wounded times … of course you can always decide whether to look or not." He wasn't proud of what he was saying. I could tell. Maybe because he saw how it bothered me.

"That's terrible," I muttered. "Cruel. Horrible."

"Seth," he said gently. It was one of the few times I could remember him speaking gently. He waited for me to look at him. "Did she enjoy the *why*?"

"I don't know. What if she did? What if she got what she was looking for? What if Jaden was different than Gwen?" My vulnerability and honesty to him was a surprise to us both. "And please never show her Gwen and me." I was feeling sick again.

He reached out and put his hand on my shoulder, as though he could tell and wanted to help. "Stop letting your memories of yesterday destroy the memories you could have tomorrow."

And the embers were still there, crackling outside. And the campground was still silent like I remembered. And my sleeping bag felt good, like I remembered, even if my dreams were a swirl of strip clubs and suburban streets and past mistakes.

TWENTY THREE

Ehs was wearing a black suit with a white tie, in the familiar shape of James, albeit a more formal, less normal, James than I was used to.

"Fancy," I said.

"You don't look too bad yourself," he answered, which caused me to look down, something I didn't do all that often in the world of Ehs. I was wearing a collared shirt and jacket with some nice pants and shoes that I recognized as my own—but couldn't remember putting on.

"Where are we?" I asked, looking up, trying to recall a thought from the lake or a run, or how I had gotten to wherever we were or maybe where I still was. I couldn't.

"We call it," he announced, lifting his hands into the air, "Zone 7."

It was a city street corner. There was nothing that told me what city but there were indicators it was a poorer section of whatever city it was. There were plenty of older buildings, not well cared for, neon signs, trash dancing along the sidewalks, and lots of metal bars in windows and on doors. Tired cars. Tired-looking people, who moved slowly, as though they were forced to carry more life than most. The sun had recently set but had left a trail of orange and red still resisting the onset of dark blues and black that were quickly advancing to destroy the last remnants of daylight.

"Some kind of sex section?" I asked, while a car drove by with an engine that sounded like it had emphysema and whose exhaust made me feel like I was about to contract it.

"You and your infatuation with sex."

"Me? You just spent a whole night telling me all about it."

"All of you," he answered, while starting to walk along the broken sidewalk. "So dense. Come on."

There was a city energy in the air. An East Coast city energy. "Where are we?"

"Doesn't matter," he said as we walked by a convenience store that didn't look very convenient to own or shop in. "Mu."

"Chicago?"

He stopped walking only to look at me and tell me to stop asking stupid questions— without ever uttering a word.

"Okay," I answered. There was an intersection ahead of us with a red light starting to back up traffic. Across the street was a sign with XXX in pink neon letters. "Not a great section of town. And I hope we're not going into another strip club."

Ehs moved over to a seedy bench sitting in front of a bus sign and took a seat, facing the road. The bus sign looked overly generic— not right. Like the kind of sign there to generally indicate a bus stop more than to actually indicate specific bus routes. Like a movie set. The sign was strange but I was quickly distracted by the dark stains that were all over the bench I was about to sit on. "Is this safe?"

"Sit down," he ordered. I did. Cautiously.

A car heading toward the intersection stopped directly in front of us. It was the type of car that looked like it had lived hard in its younger years, maybe had some fun, but was paying the price now. It was very rock-star-on-the-verge-of-retirement. The days of getting whatever it wanted were long gone. Its muffler was falling off, it was in desperate need of a new paint job, and the passenger window was cracked. Music was still playing loud inside the car but it was obviously coming from a speaker that, like the rest of the car, was all used up. There was no more commanding the stage, just a tinny sound with too much treble.

"I'm trying again," Ehs said quietly, but still plenty loud enough to be heard above the music from the car.

"Trying what?" I asked.

"To explain this to you." He rolled his eyes, ever so slightly.

I nodded. "Please."

"Sex ... more like a speaker. Alone, it's nothing more than meaningless static. If it plays a bad song, it will amplify the bad and ruin the mood of the room and the people in it. It can't make the song better. If there is a good song, it will amplify that, and potentially change the world. But it won't make the song worse."

I looked at the driver of the car. I couldn't see much. I could *sense* exhaustion.

"It's nothing in itself," Ehs continued. "You're so focused on an amplifier and so few care about why it's playing the song it is. Of course, people eventually go deaf, turning up the speakers louder and louder, thinking that will change the song. At some point, they will struggle to ever hear anything again. I suppose we celebrate that."

The light turned green. The cars started moving. The song grew faint and was soon gone.

"Try your best to not be distracted by sex, though we will gladly accept distraction of any kind." He smirked. "The biological and insatiable desire to try and matter with skin … I won't fight it. But, it's not our main weapon."

A man across the street was walking into the strip club.

"The desire to belong. Or the worthiness to feel it. This can be exhilarating, debilitating, liberating, and empowering, and is often expressed or heard through your … sex." He stopped and stared at me. "Do you hear me?"

I noticed a nearby sign that read AMATURE NITE and realized amateur was a hard word to spell. "Yes."

"It's the desire for sacrifice." Ehs was still talking, whether I was listening or not. "For worth. This is what we care more about." He paused. "Did you hear that?"

"Yes?"

"It's this we can use to our full advantage."

"One more time." I looked to him.

He smiled, sensing he had my full attention again. "Shame, Seth. The inherent, foundational, core feeling that you are not enough. You will feed it anything to satisfy its hunger. You are so focused on flesh that you are not understanding the deeper song of blood."

"Blood?" I asked, proving I was listening but barely.

"Blood to feed the shame," he said, almost speaking to himself. "If there is no shame to work with—rare indeed—they are worthless to me." He, once again, stood to his feet and looked at his watch. I had never noticed a watch and I was fairly certain he didn't need one. "Oh, we're going to be late."

Moments later, I was sitting in the back row of about two hundred wooden chairs meticulously laid out on a massive outdoor patio. Strings of lights filled the air and clusters of well-dressed men and women were filling the chairs in front of us.

If the street had an energy of desperation, the courtyard had an energy of success. It couldn't have felt more different. It was clean, efficient, and in good taste. It was privilege and it felt more comfortable to me until I consciously acknowledged that fact and had to sit with it for a second.

As I tried to remember how we had moved from one scene to the next, everyone in the courtyard stood and looked toward the back of the room with large smiles on their, generally, very pretty faces. I, of course, stood too, vaguely recalling walking through a brick wall or two but only the way one can vaguely recall what happens directly before a surgery and the anesthesia hits. Regardless, there was no time to ask Ehs. A bride and her father were walking down the aisle directly in front of us. Tears were streaming down both of their cheeks, eventually flowing into their broad smiles. Her white gown brushed across the concrete below her and I smiled as she passed by.

Once the attention followed her and away from us I nudged Ehs. "How did we get here?"

He lifted his finger to his lips and gave me an awkward stare, before looking around. There were a few violinists playing a nice wedding march that I listened to, and enjoyed, until they slowly faded out.

"Who gives this woman to this man in marriage today?" The officiant was wearing a nice suit and a purple vestment with two white crosses on the bottom.

"Her mother and I," I heard from the father, who had regained his composure just enough to give his daughter away, even if his voice was shaky.

"Can you believe they still say that?" Ehs asked, much louder than I thought we were supposed to be. No one seemed to notice.

"We can talk?"

"Of course."

"You really are a bastard sometimes," I said, watching the groom take the bride's hand and move toward the front. "And no, I can't believe it. Is he going to offer a few goats for the bride price next?"

Ehs smiled. "No need. He already has done as much."

"Why are we here?" I asked.

He shrugged, surveying the room. "I think it works."

"I thought we were going to see another zone or something?"

"We are gathered here today to celebrate the union of …" I was already tuning the officiant out. He had a dry voice and a stale personality and started the ceremony with washed-up words.

"Yes," Ehs remarked. "I think it will make the point."

"What point?" I asked.

"Have you thought much about sacrifice?" he asked, still facing forward, as though fully engaged in the wedding ceremony happening in front of us but obviously not.

"In terms of … what do you mean?"

"Actual sacrifice."

"Like bringing corn or goats or children to the idol to make the gods happy?"

"Ah," he looked over, happy. "Good."

I looked toward the bride and groom. They were both staring at each other, while the officiant droned on about the wedding altar, which did make me think for a second.

Wedding altar? We should probably change that.

"Did you know there is a link between equality and sacrifice in a society? The more egalitarian the society, the less sacrifice, the more hierarchal, the more?"

"I didn't," I responded, noticing that the bride and groom seemed like nice people even if they were nodding and smiling as the pastor went on some more about the altar they were in front of. "You know, some argue that hierarchy is always present in any culture that values anything."

Ehs's laughter was embarrassing, even if I knew everyone couldn't hear it. "That's not hierarchy of worth. Of humanity. Of course, there are better basketball players than others. Does the better basketball player make someone a better human? The rest is meaningless to us."

"Okay." I nodded.

He was serious again. "Sacrifice appeases the lack of self-worth, because it provides a great set of rules to make the gods happy. More accurately to make you happy with yourself because you believe you have made the gods happy. If you can't be worth much at least you can make gods happy."

"Right," I said while thinking through the words. A bridesmaid was wiping away some tears, either from boredom or, hopefully, because she loved her friend and the man who was about to be her friend's husband.

"Have you heard of social control hypothesis?"

"We will now read from 1 Corinthians 13," the officiant said, causing me to sigh as loud as I could.

"Are you kidding?" I looked up toward the front of the room. "Is this the most stereotypical wedding ever?"

"Seth." Ehs reached out his hand to calm me down. "Have you heard of social control hypothesis?"

"Why the hell would I have heard of that?"

"Love is patient. Love is kind …" The officiant spoke with the same enthusiasm you would expect from someone who had probably said those words at a thousand weddings.

"Ritual sacrifices are a way to keep the religious and political leaders in power. In control. By terrorizing the lower classes. The poor. The outcasts," Ehs threw in.

"I don't like that."

"The victims, across most societies, are usually taken from those who might rebel, those of low social status, to keep them in check and keep those in the higher classes comfortable in their power."

"Love is not self-seeking …"

"Do you understand what I'm saying?" he asked, looking over to me.

"Sacrifice is not good?"

"True," he smirked. "It doesn't benefit the gods—just those who speak for the gods. Or the elite. Usually the same."

"Love always protects …" The officiant was still going.

"Right …" I answered.

"I don't think it takes much to see how we could use this to our favor." He looked over at me. "Especially if we could craft a religion that builds a story around the need for sacrifice. For blood."

"I'm still not sure why we are at a wedding?"

" … where there is knowledge, it will pass away …"

"Have you heard of the Capacocha ceremony?" Ehs asked.

"Again, are these actual questions that you think I will answer?" I smiled at a nice lady across the aisle from me, just in case she could see me.

Ehs threw a friendly sneer at me. "It's Incan. Human sacrifice was fairly common with the Inca, although they were not quite as violent as the Aztecs or Mayans."

"Okay." I urged him to move on with my tone.

"Capacocha was the most prominent of the sacrificial ceremonies. Children were selected from all parts of the empire, usually sixteen years old and younger. Sometimes as young as four. There was great honor in being chosen, of course. Only the most beautiful—the physically perfect—were chosen as tribute to the Incan lords and gods."

"The bride and groom will take communion to remember the sacrifice of our Lord and Savior Jesus Christ and to remember the sacrifice they will need to make to one another …" The officiant was still going strong. From the look of the room everyone was much more bored than I was, especially at the mention of sacrifice. I looked at Ehs, who smiled like the actual proud father of the ceremony and kept talking.

"Virgins of the Sun," he said louder than normal. "For the sun god Inti. They had to be kept apart, of course, to keep them pure."

"This is the body of Christ …"

"Some of the girls were clubbed to death. Some of the girls would have their throats slit," Ehs continued.

"This is the blood of Christ …" the officiant went on.

"Some were strangled with cords. While the masses would often look on. They were pleasing the gods! And finally they would be buried. Of course"—Ehs looked at me just to make sure I was paying attention—"some were buried alive. Always confirming the state, always confirming the lordship."

"Our Lord, we are thankful for …" The officiant's voice was becoming more annoying by the second.

"Yes, the poor Virgins of the Sun," Ehs continued. "They were sent on a long journey, miles and miles as a final pilgrimage. Usually with cocaine and alcohol to numb them for the pain they would eventually experience … not just for themselves but for their country, their gods, their elite."

"By the power vested in me …" The officiant again.

"To find worth," Ehs said. "For everyone."

"And now you may kiss the bride!" Said with a bit of newly discovered enthusiasm. Moments later the whole place was cheering and whistling.

"It is my pleasure to announce for the first time Mr. and Mrs. …"

"Certainty has worth," Ehs continued. "Morality and rules have value. We don't have to wonder, to be confused, to not know because sacrifice is always a certain rule. And always a high value, even better if it's pure," he said slowly as I stared at the white wedding gown the bride was wearing.

There was more cheering, more applause, more whistling, and then everyone was standing as the husband and wife went by us waving and smiling, basking in the light of flash bulbs. I too got caught up in the energy of the birth of new love and started cheering myself. As though the photographer was taking my picture, a flash went off right in my face, leaving me dazed and blinded for a moment, wondering what the photo would reveal, and then losing that thought immediately.

"This is *our* temple," said Ehs. We were standing some distance away from the wall, the gargantuan piece of construction that filled the landscape and sky and cast the whole grayscale land into shadow, still including us, even as far as we were.

We were sitting on a bus bench that felt eerily similar to the one we had been sitting on earlier. I looked at Ehs, still composed, always composed, looking forward. In front of the wall was a very modern-looking structure, yet it reeked of ancient purpose. It was Ikea meets the primitive. Frank Lloyd Wright meets Zeus. Palm Springs meets Athens. Straight lines, flat roofs, sharp edges, and square corners. Gray, multileveled long rectangular shapes stacked on one another like those under a Christmas tree, but the boxes were massive and made of what looked like concrete.

I loved it. I would have lived there if it could have been transferred to a forest in Sweden or even a high desert in Arizona. "Kudos to the architect."

At the top of the boxes, or flat shapes, was a long table. Given the distance, I assumed it had to be a massive table, almost the size of a football field, hovering about three feet off the ground. The whole thing had a very modern pyramid feel to it, and whomever had designed it had wanted everyone to focus their attention on the table. There were hundreds of shapes surrounding the table and hundreds of black bricks on top.

"Kudos to you then. It's your construction. We merely provided the motivation." Ehs sat back and put his arm on the back of the bench as though we were best friends just staring at a sunset.

"Okay." I leaned forward, trying to take in the scene. "Teach me."

"Teach you?"

"I don't know if I get it." It was all coming fast and furious and, like with the movies named after the sensation, I was not understanding.

"Okay." He nodded, looking professional in his suit he was still wearing. "I desire sacrifice, not mercy." He looked at me.

I looked at him. "You mean—"

"No. I"—he paused for a moment—"desire sacrifice, not mercy. If I can get you to believe the same, I've done my job. And—" He nodded toward the temple. "I have. Thanks to many, including Anselm."

I looked back to the building with the wall rising up behind it. "Yes," I urged him on, having learned that, as a demon, he loved to be encouraged—which forced me to wonder if it was my own dark side that always needed encouragement.

"It can't be more clear. The followers of mystery have always said it. So did your Jesus man as do the holy books. But sacrifice feels better. You earn it. You know your place and you know their place. Sacrifice feeds your desperation for worth. Mercy starves it."

"What was the wedding then? And sex?" I admired a nice roof line while asking the question.

"The wedding," he said, with a shrug, "is soaked in sacrifice in its language, its ritual, in everything, if you look."

"And sex?"

"Saturating even the idea of marriage." His eyebrows lowered into a menacing smile above his eyes. "You know it well, Seth. You sacrificed your sex to appease your worth. A powerful tool for us."

I closed my eyes for a moment.

"Why do you think cultures brought sacrifices to the gods?" he asked me very plainly.

"They felt like something had to pay."

"Why?"

"We're told that's the way the world works. Nothing is free."

"Why are you told that?"

"I don't know."

"Control and power. If nothing is free then you will compete to earn."

There were people all over the table, coming and going like ants gathering food for their hill. Except they were gathering bricks for, I assumed, the wall. "Sacrifice is competition now?"

"Of course. It sets one above the other, and for one to be above another, there must be one that feels below another. Giving, taking, limited resources. You think. And so, the cycle keeps going, always, like a cancer destroys its host. It destroys whatever lets it in, at any level, including its parasitic connection to sex."

I looked to the form of James and pondered it all for a moment. The normal, nice James. The normal eyes. The normal lips. The normal hair. He nodded toward the table. "What do you think they are bringing?"

I looked back at the action. "Bricks?"

"What are the bricks?" he asked, lifting his volume slightly.

"I don't know." Whatever they did represent was being piled high by countless humans. "Rules, laws, purity codes, legalism, moralism?"

"It's the wrong question." His voice had returned to a calmer volume. "It's not *what* they are bringing, it's why. We don't care what they bring only that they think they have to. That is what you keep missing."

I looked again at the piles of bricks nicely stacked all over behind the temple.

"They bring their sexuality, their traditions and rituals, their crops, their children, their rules, their ceremonies, the expectations of their parents and gods, of their authority figures, they bring their beliefs, their theologies, their scriptures … they bring their prophecies, their miracles, their donations to the poor, they bring it all. They bring their choices!" He stood to his feet. "And once they bring we get what we want … we want sacrifice. You want the guaranteed validation—from us … because you don't believe in what you already have." He paused. "We both get what we want."

"Right …" I was staring forward, almost hypnotized by the entire scene.

"If you're going to kill anything, put your desperate need to measure up onto the goat and run it off the cliff. To save yourself." He spoke with a deep tone, from above me.

I frowned and stood to my own feet, measuring up even as he preached to me about it.

"We are not done."

"Yes," I said. "Wait, we aren't?"

"You are going to the other side," he ordered, although it was spoken nicely.

"The other side?" I looked back toward the wall.

"The light," he answered.

"Why don't you go?" I asked.

"I can't."

"You can't?"

"Shadow can only exist where the light is blocked. I've told you that before."

"Okay," I responded, anxious, tired, and a tad excited. "And what do I do when I go to the light?"

"I don't know." He looked toward the ground.

"You don't know?"

"She will find you. Tell her I want to meet her. I want love." He looked up with a softness in his eyes.

"You know—" I looked at Ehs, still processing the words I had heard. "Love does require sacrifice."

He started rubbing his temples as though to massage out frustration. "If love requires, it is not love."

"But, sacrificial love …" I shot back. "Laying down one's life for another."

"Why!" he shouted, causing my whole body to jump. "Why! Do you still not understand!"

I said nothing.

"It's not sex! It's not sacrifice. It's not *what*. It's *why*. Why. Why. Why!" He was as exasperated as I had seen him but there was something moving about it. "Love does not require sacrifice, it expresses it. Are you earning? Are you seeking? Are you desperate?" He sighed a deep and heavy sigh. "Or are you expressing? Are you giving? Are you revealing? Are you enough?" He sat back down on the bench, rubbing his head harder. I felt somehow responsible for his headache. "Are you making choices to achieve a new false reality or to acknowledge what is already true? That is really the only question we care about."

"Okay," I nodded. "I'm sorry."

"Your god does not want sacrifice. Do you believe that?"

"Yes."

"Does your god want love?"

"Yes." I sat down again next to him.

"You've answered your own questions and concerns." He sighed. "It is finished."

"I'm sorry." I looked toward the table again. "I am?"

"There is no temple in the new city?" he asked, almost accusatory and borderline angry.

"Revelation?" I asked with lots of confusion.

"It was supposed to be a revelation, yes," he quipped. "But it's been lost, like most are." He stood to his feet again. "There is no temple in the new myth, Seth. Why?"

He waited. I sat silent.

"It's no longer needed!" he shouted. "It's no longer fucking needed!" Ehs did not say the word often but when he did it was usually striking and moving. I made a note to remember that.

He stared at me, imploring me, begging me to understand.

"You tell it to others well—including your Leo, but you still don't live it, do you?" he asked, almost sad. "Understand it. Experience its truth. I fear you never will with your addiction to the opposite."

"Yeah" was all I could muster. "It's so simple—but it's so hard."

"Simplicity is never easy." We were both quiet for a moment.

"Seth." He looked at me with a sudden gloss in his eyes, the darkness shining. "You have love and you refuse to accept it." A tear began to stream down his cheek. "You have everything you need." He reached up and wiped his cheek as more tears began to flow toward the ground where he looked. "I wish I could feel it again. I would give anything. You don't understand the gift." He looked back to me. "And you don't understand the darkness." He was shaking his head. "It's so dark. So cold. So meaningless. Always striving, never enough. I have changed the world and done more than anyone on this side could be asked to accomplish and still—" He wiped his eyes again, recomposing himself. "I will die alone, without love. Just a memory of it and a sterile knowledge of what it is supposed to be and what I have taken from most of the human race."

"No," I answered back with every bit of strength I could muster for him. "Light is coming."

He grunted, unconvinced, or more experienced in the emptiness of words. "Go and see her. For me."

"Okay," I answered. "What do you need me to do?"

"There is something in your pocket. Give it to her." He nodded toward me. "It's just a symbol. It's representative of much."

"Okay." I reached for my pocket but didn't feel anything.

"Thank you," he said.

"Well, I haven't done anything yet." I chuckled, a little worried about what I was about to do.

"Thank you," he repeated.

Moments later I was standing in front of some kind of black doorway in what I assumed was the gate. Ehs was nowhere to be seen. I reached out and pulled on a metallic handle that opened a door more easily than I expected. A blinding light flooded my vision and I heard Ehs say, "Hurry." So I did.

I ran toward the light. As cliché as the saying goes, it was my reality.

I walked through the doorway and to the other side of the wall, where I immediately fell to the ground and lifted my arms and hands up to my head, trying to hide my eyes from the sudden brightness. I heard the door close behind me but I couldn't see anything.

Yet.

TWENTY FOUR

"Hey!" The voice surprised me so I tried opening my eyes again. But the light was beyond intense. I could see why Ehs couldn't handle it. I wasn't sure I could.

"Hey!" It was from somewhere nearby.

"Hold on," I said. "I can't really see."

"Yeah," he answered. "It's bright, but at least it feels good."

It did feel good, once I started paying attention. Not just warm but calm and serene—it reminded me a lot of that lake feeling early on a hot morning. On steroids. Almost an overwhelming amount of good.

"It does," I responded. "It does." The other side was cold, I realized, now being in the light.

"Open your eyes. You'll be fine."

I did. And I was. Oddly, my eyes had adjusted, even while closed. The man speaking to me was a few feet away, smiling. He was dressed in an orange T-shirt, jeans, and a white backward hat. His skin was dark and he had an even darker beard, nicely trimmed. A couple of tattoos. He was still smiling.

I realized I was too.

"Hi." He reached out his hand. "I'm Jeremiah."

"Good to meet you. I'm Seth." I reached out my hand to shake his. I saw that I was wearing a T-shirt and shorts, which made me wonder where the nice clothes had gone but, honestly, had no way to remember. They were my clothes though, at least. A touch of normal in an otherwise very abnormal situation.

I turned back and looked at the door I had come through. It was sealed, with darkness and shadow and Ehs, presumably, on the other side.

The wall itself, from the side I was on, was much the same. It seemed to go forever in every direction. I could see the pyramid shapes on this side too, although here they were rugged and decaying as though no one had touched them for years. I could see the same two holes in the wall, yet on this side they were not nearly as dramatic, just holes, allowing light to penetrate into the shadow on the other side.

Stretching out from the wall was white sand in every direction, as far as I could see. Salt flats white. Salt flats flat too. The sky was blue, speckled with clouds as white as the sand here and there but other than that it was me and Jeremiah.

"So." I continued to look around. "Where are we?"

"The other side," he answered, as though that would help.

"Yeah," I said, nodding. "I've heard that. The other side of what?"

He shrugged. "That." He nodded toward the wall.

"Yeah." I nodded again. "Okay." I didn't think I was going to get anywhere with this guy. "How'd you get here?"

"I walked through a gate. Down there." He pointed further down the wall. "I've been walking the wall, seeing if there are more gates. I was looking at this one when you walked through."

"Right." I squinted toward the distance again. "But, how did you get here, as in this whole thing." I waved my arms around in case he didn't know what "this whole thing" meant.

"How did you?" he asked.

I sighed. "Long story."

"Yeah," he answered. "Probably a long story for everyone."

"Right, but …" I turned around and looked at the wall again, its bricks piled high into the sky. "Are you dead?"

He laughed. "I hope not. Are you?"

I laughed. "I don't think so."

"Alright." He started walking, away from the wall this time. "Well, I guess we should start walking."

"Yeah." I stayed back. "I think I might go by myself. I'm not really sure where I'm trying to get to."

He shrugged again. "I think you're already there."

"Well—" I politely smiled. "Yeah, I don't know."

"Alright." He turned his back on me. "Good luck."

"Same to you." I watched him walk away for a while but that got very boring very fast.

"Okay," I said aloud. "Um, are you here?" I looked up and back at the wall. "What am I supposed to do now?"

There was no one there to answer and no voice spoke from heaven. I wondered, for a moment, if I should go back through the gate and tell Ehs no one was home in light land.

But, I didn't. I thought Jeremiah was smart in walking down the wall. I wondered if I'd made a mistake in letting him move along without me. I could still see him in the distance, just a small human shape on the horizon, and if I ran …

I still decided to just walk the wall, starting in the direction Jeremiah had indicated he had come from.

Upon reaching another gate, I got excited but that faded. Upon reaching another gate, it was not near as exciting. Upon reaching the tenth gate, I was pretty bored and about ready to go back through when I heard her voice.

Not *that* her.

"Excuse me." The accent was British and very polite as all British people always seem to be. I turned around and saw a very dark woman with very short hair and an energetic and lively face. She was wearing an all-white jumpsuit-looking thing.

"Hi." I reached out my hand.

"Hello," she responded, and shook mine.

"I'm Seth."

"I'm Heather. Pleasure." She nodded and smiled.

"So," I said. "Do you know where we are?"

"The other side," she said plainly, as though I was asking what color the sky was.

"Right," I nodded. "And how did you get here?"

"I walked through a gate. Like everyone does."

"Right." I did wonder if every conversation on the other side was the same: going nowhere fast. "And, how'd you get there?"

"Long story," she replied. "Like everyone."

Definitely not going anywhere.

"Well—" Her words were not especially enlightening. "I guess, we just keep walking, huh?"

"Oh," she replied, still smiling. "I don't know. I just know it's beautiful here. I haven't been this warm in so long."

She was enjoying the place way more than I was and that made me feel guilty or evil for a moment. Or just plain distracted. I assumed she wasn't given some kind of mission to go find someone. That was why I was different. Or maybe she wasn't even real, not like me.

I stared at her for a long time, probably too long.

"Do you need something?" she asked.

"Well, I need to find someone. Do you know if there's any kind of …" I had no idea what I was looking for. "Do you know how to get anywhere over here?"

"I don't believe there is anywhere to get."

Is everyone a freaking Zen master over here?

"Right …" I nodded. "Well, I guess I'm going to continue to just move along and … just … enjoy the place, right?" I smiled. "Have a good day."

"You too." She sat down on the white sand and started playing with it.

I shook my head and started walking further down the wall.

"Okay," I said aloud again. "Let's go this way."

I turned away from the wall, with it toward my back, and started walking into the great nothing. White sands of nothing. Beautiful nothing but still … nothing.

I walked for what felt like an hour. I had no idea if it was really an hour because I had completely lost track of time, if there even was time to keep track of. Normally after walking an hour in a desert, one would feel tired or at least be sweating. But I felt great. Even energized. I felt comfortable but not in the way sitting on a couch with a beer is comfortable. I felt relaxed and rested and yet, as though I had accomplished something.

I looked back toward the wall. I thought it was far away but it was hard to tell. It was still huge, reaching up higher than I could see. I could make out pyramids here and there, and again, I wondered if I should just head back.

It all seemed a little too big. Too expansive. Too mysterious. Too much. I was comfortable but I was also frustrated. Where was I going? Where was I supposed to go? Where was she or he or anyone besides Zen masters who answered every question with vague nonsense?

I sighed. The sky was still blue, still specked with clouds, and the sand was still white and still went forever with nothing to break it on the horizon. The wall was still black and dark behind me.

I kept walking because I wasn't sure what else to do. I didn't feel like I was going to die out there—in fact, quite the opposite, but I also didn't feel like walking in white sand forever. Nor did I feel like walking back to the wall, although it was nice to know it was there.

I walked for another bit of time, lost in thought. It felt like when someone says *hey, anyone home?* and you realize that you were autonomously cutting the carrots, putting as much thought into it as you do breathing. And then when they say *what were you thinking about?,* you can't answer, because you don't know.

Maybe the brain just shuts off for a moment.

That's how it felt. My brain had taken a vacation, probably a much-needed one. And I had walked a long way—the wall was much farther away and I was beginning to be able to see what seemed like a top to it, although it was hard to tell. Things all get blurry at such a distance.

To my left was sand. To my right was sand. Ahead of me was

sand.

"What the hell," I said out loud, only because it was so confusing. I was still not tired, still not angry, still not even hopeless, just a bit overwhelmed with … nothing. There was so much nothing that it was almost uncomfortable, if it were possible to feel uncomfortable here.

But I kept walking, because that feeling of turning my brain off was wonderful, maybe even addictive.

"Run! Turn around! Go!" A Southern accent.

"What!" I instinctively turned my head and started running.

There was an older man, pushing me. He was wearing a suit, navy and white, that looked much better than he did. He face was ragged, scared, frustrated, wrinkled in every way possible. A touch of mostly gray hair was on the sides of his head above his ears but the rest was bald.

He was still pushing me.

"Wait." I stopped. My brain had not quite started running full speed again but it was getting there. "What's going on?"

"This place is nuts. It's crazy." He was swirling his fingers around in the hair he had in case I didn't know what nuts meant. But I did and it was talking to me.

"Okay," I responded, watching him panting. Sweat covered his brow—I realized I didn't have any.

"Listen, son. If you got any brains to you, get back to the wall. It's not all it's cracked up to be over here." And he started running again, seemingly content to run anywhere.

"Whoa," I called out like he was a horse.

He didn't stop. I started running to catch him, which wasn't hard, and when I did I made him stop by pulling on his jacket as though it were reins. "What's going on?" I looked in the direction he had been running from but there was nothing, except more sand.

"Son," he repeated. "Don't try and stop me. It's crazy over here."

I wanted to tell him that the crazy was also in his brain—which was something I made a note to remember the next time I felt a place was crazy—but I just kept my hand on his shoulder. "What is crazy?"

"All of it! The whole godforsaken thang. Can't ya see it?" He looked around as though there were hordes of barbarians chasing him from every side but all I saw was sand. Which was crazy in a sense but not in the sense he seemed to be talking.

"I see the sand but I don't see anything else," I said, calmly. I really did feel calm.

He was glancing everywhere. "Nah, it's not what I was 'pecting.

It's crazy over here. I thought this was god's country."

He tried to take off again but I kept holding him.

"God's country?"

"The light," he yelled at me. "Land of the light!" His eyes were wild. "Well, there ain't no god over here, not in this desert. There ain't no nothin'."

I didn't have the heart to tell him that no nothing meant there was something.

That might, actually, be the point.

"At least there was sumthin' I could do over there, sumthin' I could fight. Sumthin' they were fighting! At least there was sumthin' being done!"

He was off and running again—I couldn't hold him back.

I chased again. "Wait, wait!"

But he didn't.

I ran with him for a bit, which was easy because he still wasn't moving very fast. As we ran, I tried to continue the conversation. "So, you're going back to the dark side?"

"Yes, sir." He was panting. "Wait, what? Dark side?" he asked, confused.

"Yeah." It was not confusing to me. "Where it's dark and cold and black."

"I'm going to the other side." His voice was irritated and arrogant. "It's not dark to me."

"It's not?"

"Hell no. There's food for starters."

"There's no food here?" I asked.

"Not like there."

I had never realized there had been food on the other side. Well, I guess I had seen the bowl. But I had not thought much about food at all.

"What else?"

"I already done told you, son." He was really struggling to breathe and I still wasn't sure why. "Already told ya."

I thought of Ehs. I thought of the sentries. I thought of the pyramids and the temple and the wall and the darkness and the cold. "Are you sure?" I was still keeping up with him.

"Son." He stopped. "You wanna stay over here in this here desert, that's fine. You'll see soon enough that what you thought was true ain't. You'll see that this here place is as crazy as the other one is mean. But I'll take my mean. Least I can give it back too. Least I can see something. Do something." He looked toward the wall. "Let me go, son. You'll be running behind me soon enough."

"But—" I interjected again.

"Son!" He yelled this time. Loudly, jolting me. "Don't you see?"

And whatever happened, in that moment, I did see. I saw what he saw and it was chaotic, confusing, and maddening. I realized why he was acting the way he was.

There was a sun. And someone, a massive human shape of some kind, was grabbing it out of the sky and trying to put it in their pocket. A couple was kissing, surrounded by tanks, jets, soldiers, and rockets going off all around them, as the couple launched the weapons into each other.

I tried to rip off whatever broken virtual reality goggles I was seeing through but there was nothing there. It was quickly panic-inducing and making me immediately desperate to find a way out.

Instead I saw another person but they were simply exploding, like fireworks in a night sky. Then cats and dogs began to fall from the sky, literally hitting me and pounding the desert floor. I started to run. Somewhere. Anywhere. But nothing got me out of whatever I was seeing. I saw a herd of sheep running toward me. Goats running toward me from another angle. The man next to me was trying to talk but all I heard were cymbals, clanging in the air with cats, dogs, tanks, fireworks, and pure and utter chaos. A naked couple suddenly appeared, which grabbed my focus for a moment—in the way that naked couples usually do. They were each holding bright red apples up to a snake, which distracted me from their dark-skinned nude bodies.

"Stop!" I yelled.

And it did.

The man's wild eyes looked like they were about to jump from his head and I imagined mine looked the same.

"You see?" he yelled. "You see!"

"Sir, you're—"

Before I could finish, he started off again. I decided it was better to let him go. I scanned the horizon to see if there were any remnants of whatever world I had just been in but there were not. I scanned to see if there were others—like him—coming or going. And I wondered if the rule that I could leave at any time was still in effect on the "other side."

I was just about to find out when she showed up.

Yes, *her*.

Emonee, was that what Ehs had said her name was?

TWENTY FIVE

I could tell immediately. Everything about her was familiar, even if none of it was on the surface.

She was very human. She wore a white dress, which contrasted beautifully with her dark, vibrant skin. Her hair was dark as were her eyes. Some kind of energy surrounded her and drew me in. I quickly found myself hugging her as though she were a long-lost friend, squeezing as tight as I could.

I suppose I needed a hug.

She embraced me for a moment before I stepped back, suddenly staring at her.

"You look like everyone else."

She smiled. "Looks are deceiving, mostly illusions."

I frowned. "Is this heaven? Are these people … dead?"

She shrugged. "Heaven?"

"Yes," I answered. "Is this heaven?"

"What is heaven?"

My default was a place good people go when they die. Or, even better, where certain people go when they die. Or, maybe, where all people eventually end up after they die. But, I didn't want to say any of those things except to discover whether they were true or not. "Where things are as they should be?"

She smiled. "Then, sure."

I looked around at the white sands. "Really?" I was, obviously, a little disappointed.

"You can only speak of love and mystery with myth and image. Otherwise, you can only speak of what mystery and love are not."

I was confused and she seemed to enjoy it.

"Am I dead?"

"What is death?"

"The thing they pronounce people back on Earth when your heart stops beating, your brain stops functioning and you … leave. The thing we all grieve. The thing Jesus cried over when it happened to

Lazarus. The thing—"

"Then, no," she interrupted.

"Are some of the people here?"

"I suppose."

"Suppose?"

"Sure." She smiled.

"What is the other side?"

"Where you are."

"Yeah." I smiled. "I know that. But, I mean, what is this?" As warm as I had felt and did feel, I was also a little frustrated, if it wasn't obvious.

"In the light."

I smiled a very patronizing smile. "Right, right. Can you give me a straight answer to something?"

"No," she replied.

"Thank you."

"You're welcome."

"Can you tell me why you can't give me a straight answer?"

"If you want answers, you're in the wrong place."

"Is there more to this place than this?" I kicked at the sand with my foot.

"Of course."

"Where?"

She looked around as though it was obvious, which made it equally obvious that I was missing something. I looked around, searching for a hint to what she might be seeing that I was not.

"Seth." She was calm and gentle and mesmerizing. "Why are you here?"

I felt slightly scolded, but even that felt right. "He wants to meet you."

She stared at me. Her eyes sparkled like stars and penetrated my soul. "Do you trust him?"

I closed my eyes. I was really getting sick of the question. "I want him to change but even if he doesn't, I believe he can."

"As do I."

"You do?"

"Yes."

My understanding was thrown off the tracks momentarily but I recovered. Maybe *she* had changed. "I'm not really sure what I'm supposed to do here." I felt a little out of place as the mediator between heaven and hell or the dark and the light or that side and this side or whatever I was supposed to call it. Maybe just him and her.

"Is that all?"

"I guess I do trust him," I confessed. The words came out as though she had seduced them from my heart.

"Do you love?"

"Him?"

"Do you love?" she repeated.

I looked back toward the wall, still in the far distance. "Yes?"

She smiled and I felt some kind of pressure release. It had been slight but the weight that had been there was no more.

"Is that all?" she asked.

"No," I said.

"Then what?"

"What do you think of sacrifice?"

She smiled, as though she knew why I was asking but I couldn't be sure. It also felt like I was attributing more to her than she might have been. "We prefer mercy. Grace. Love."

"Yeah." I smiled. "Have I given enough mercy?"

"There is no temple here." She smiled. "For anything. Even for mercy."

"Yeah," I whispered, feeling overwhelmed by her calm acceptance. I felt like I was supposed to go but I didn't want to leave. It felt like a moment I needed to value, that I had found something that I wouldn't have again, and I wanted to take advantage of it. In all the right ways.

"Was the wall always there?" I looked back toward it.

"I suppose," she answered again.

"Yeah, but, I mean …" I wasn't even sure what exactly I was trying to get from her. "Without the wall there isn't a shadow, or darkness."

She pointed toward my feet with a gentle smile. I followed the nudge and looked down at my bare toes. For a while. I wasn't sure exactly what I was supposed to see until the epiphany arrived. My own shadow stretched out before me, like I was used to. I looked back to her and even she had a shadow stretching out across the white sand.

"Well," I said slowly, in a drawn-out, pondering sort of way. "Yeah."

"Is that all?" she asked again, not as though she had somewhere to go but as though she meant it.

"I think I'm supposed to give you something."

She reached out her hand.

"It's from him." I figured I needed to warn her.

"There is no fear in this place," she responded.

I reached into my pocket—which I had not done up to that point. Looking back, having spent hours mostly alone in a desert, I'm not sure why, but I had never thought about it, until that moment. There was something small and round and I pulled it out and displayed it for both of us to see.

It was a simple stone, smooth and polished and black. There were no markings of any kind. It was utterly bland and very anticlimactic, to say the least. If one of my kids had given it to me for a present, I would have had to really try to act excited.

I stared at it for a moment, wondering if it would start glowing, or flying, or maybe we would see my future or my past in it. But it just sat there, like a very normal boring black stone.

"Well," I started to apologize. "I thought this would be a little more of ..."

What I thought had been boring had obviously impacted her. Tears were streaming down her face, even as she smiled.

Apparently, it was not just a rock.

"Are you alright?"

"Of course." She smiled before reaching out and grabbing the rock from my hand. As she did, its color shifted. It was suddenly white, like the sand all around us.

"What was that?"

"A rock," she answered, holding it, looking at it.

It felt like remnants of why the old Southern man had lost his marbles. "Right, but it changed colors."

"A signpost to mark the path."

"So, Ehs has changed?" If we were going to play the signpost allegory game, I was going to have to keep up.

"Change is slow."

"So Ehs can change?"

"Everything can change."

"Do you trust Ehs?"

"Darkness is blinding."

That felt like a no. "Am I being stupid?"

"Is it possible for mercy or love to ever be stupid?" Her voice, by itself, was healing, which made her words even more therapeutic. I wanted more. I hoped the conversation would never stop in the same way I hoped a good movie wouldn't.

"He was just crying with me. He wants to feel love. He misses it. He craves it." My words held the humility of questions more than the certainty of answers.

She nodded. "Perhaps he does."

"You're being very different than you were when you met me on the side of the house."

"Or you were listening to me with a different perspective, hearing what you wanted to hear."

That one should have really thrown me, but it didn't. I can't explain why but it felt like nothing could really throw me in that place, not in the ways I was used to being thrown. I felt stronger there, more anchored or tethered to something substantial and heavy but free.

"Ehs said Insipid is not failing and he gave a pretty good sermon as to why. He was surprised you had talked to me." I studied the softness that enveloped her. "I mean, it was you, right?"

"He is a Lord of Darkness, an innovator of deceit and deception. He is tempting and beautiful in the ways that darkness is. He is cunning and delightful and will always tell you whatever you hope to hear. Do as you will with him."

"You were crying a second ago. Something in you was touched." I tilted my head like an interested puppy. I felt like a puppy near her.

"It was." She smiled.

I wanted to ask her what but I already knew I would never get an answer like I wanted. "I think I trust him," I decided to tell her instead.

"I know."

"He wants this." I looked around the strange, but tender, *this*—of white sand. I urged her, feeling as though she felt differently than I did. "He wants to experience goodness and life and value again!"

"He is tempting and beautiful in the ways that darkness is. Do as you will with him."

"Okay."

"Okay," she repeated.

"Would you, at least, agree to meet us somewhere? I'm supposed to ask." It felt stupid but I didn't want to face Ehs without, at least, asking.

"Penuel," she answered, with much less resistance—and more clarity—than I had ever assumed possible.

The squirrel sounded like it was right next to my head, probably because it was. I was again in my sleeping bag, my body warm and my face cold. It was light out. I could see the sun muted outside, trying to get into the canvas roof I was sleeping under. My wife was sleeping next to me and my daughters were on the other side, their hair the only thing visible beneath the pile of blankets and sleeping bags.

There was no quieting the squirrel and there was no ignoring my body telling me that I had to go to the bathroom. I thought I had gone a couple of times in the middle of the night already, but as I went through the door of the tent trailer and looked out at the fire from the night before, I honestly wasn't sure.

TWENTY SIX

It was a classic summer day. Sapphire sky, cobalt water, a sun of gold, and an ice-cold beer. We had been sitting all day on the beach, doing the most important thing you can do on a vacation: nothing. It was back to the lake we loved over the years—the clouds had packed up their belongings and left town.

Everyone in the family was at peace, including me, and given the events and/or dreams of the previous few days I was happy about that. Rachel was reading magazines, my youngest daughter was playing with her cousins, and my oldest was lying on a towel soaking up some revitalizing vitamin D.

"I mean," someone said off to the side of me, "I don't want to demonize him, but I really think that what he's doing is terrible."

I looked up from the book I was reading toward some family members engaged in conversation. "Isn't that funny," I interjected. "The word 'demonize'? Seems like a strange one to throw out."

Everyone smiled, and looked to see how many empty beer bottles were under my chair.

Ignoring their inspection, I continued. "Funny how demons always get the shaft."

Still more confusion. Still more apathy from me. "The other day I was listening to a podcast and they said something about the operating system being possessed. I mean, really? Blame an OS on a demon? Did you know in the Middle Ages they thought everyone who had mental illness needed exorcism?" I was a fountain of information that was as useful as it was relevant to whatever conversation they had been having.

I finally got the hint. My brother-in-law was drinking a beer, ignoring me, my wife was looking at me very concerned, and my sister-in-law—a counselor—was probably ready to start a session.

"I'm sorry." I shook my head. "Been a weird week." I looked back to the grains of sand below my chair to ponder my mouth for a moment. "Sorry, that was weird," I repeated. I picked up my Kindle and started reading it again, and they picked up their conversation and started talking about someone they all knew who was doing some upsetting things.

A few minutes later, a guy showed up on the beach whom I hadn't seen before. He was one of those guys that tends to draw out the xenophobic, racist, and probably sexist, part of me. I spend lots of time trying to put those parts into a deep sleep but, I'll be honest, sometimes, certain people wake them up real fast.

I once thought a nice man was a terrorist at a campsite because he looked Middle Eastern. He ended up giving me a jump start and helping me with a dead battery. He was from India.

Yeah, throw in the thoughts about Jaden and Gwen that pop up from time to time and it's very obvious the scared-silly part of me has lots to work on as soon as the jealous-shameful part of me stops taking up all the therapy.

Regardless, the guy who showed up on the beach woke up the Seth that felt small and liked to be afraid. He wasn't a terrorist but maybe a child abuser.

We were in northern Idaho and the guy looked "sketchy," which is usually just a more polite way for rich people to describe poverty. And fear of poverty.

The man fit the neo-Nazi profile to me. Yes, the profile given to me by movies because I had never actually met any self-professed neo-Nazis. On second glance, and with some intentional mercy making its way into my perception, he looked like he had seen lots of hard days in his life and hard days aren't easy on anyone, physically, mentally, or emotionally. He was a little rough with his kid, but he was also playing with his kid in the water.

Rachel says I stare at people. I think I'm more of a spy who watches people and is constantly aware of his surroundings but she's probably right because I'm scared of people who aren't like me either.

Either way I made it my mission to watch the guy. Keep an eye on him. Make sure he didn't steal our seven-dollar beach umbrella or try to kidnap one of my daughters as the day moved along.

I walked back to our campsite a few times because I was also keeping an eye on a new trailer that had moved in next to us during the previous night. It was definitely "sketchy." It was old, falling apart, and blankets were hanging in front of the windows—where there should be nice shades. They were the kind of blankets in front of windows that don't belong to nice people. Again, I've seen movies.

They also had dogs and there was a smell coming from the trailer, every now and then, that I recognized well as that of poverty. It's not fresh, it's not clean, it's not middle-class. It's poor. It's dirty. It's desperate. You can smell it in the grocery store sometimes and you can smell it just shaking someone's hand.

It was in the air and it was coming from the sketchy trailer next to us.

My quiet, perfect day had turned into quite a busy one. There was a lot of sketchy to watch out for and to protect the innocent from. I was a downright holy warrior for wealth safety. After a reconnaissance mission back to our camper—to also grab some more beers and salsa for everyone, I felt like I heard him. Even if I didn't see him.

"Wow, wow. You sure are on a roll today. Protecting the entire campground. I haven't seen this kind of behavior since the Crusades."

"Okay," I mumbled out loud. "Yeah, I get it."

"You do?"

"Shit," I answered in my own thoughts while looking over at a family eating an early dinner at a picnic table. I smiled at them. "I'm an idiot."

"You're just ironic."

"Ironic?"

"If there is anything to keep an eye on, it is you. Your privilege, bias, gratitude for not being like them is far more damaging than anything they will ever do."

"I know," I mumbled out loud again. "I know," I said, a little more angry.

"Did you give it to her?"

"Yes." I was happy to change the conversation too.

"And?"

"Well, she was crying. I don't know why, but she cried."

I waited for his reply but there was only quiet. I tried to hear him but I didn't.

"Penuel. She said to meet there." There was nothing. No response. He was gone.

So, I walked by some other campsites and I thought about how great it was that everyone just left stuff out and trusted their fellow humans to not steal it.

Humans are pretty great. Pretty fucking amazing. Except when they act like I just was.

Upon arriving back at the beach, I set down the beers and salsa and chips and watched the kids attack them, like I was a wolf who had just brought back a rabbit for her hungry pups. I decided not to make that analogy to the kids but just sat down in my chair instead.

My brother-in-law was asleep. He was so good at taking naps. Amazing. I was jealous of that too.

My sister-in-law had gone back to her campsite.

My wife was in the water, floating on a tube with my oldest daughter.

That meant it was just me and him. I looked over and the man was still there, this time alone. His kid was gone, as was the woman who had been with him. I thought, from their conversations, she was his mother, probably helping to take care of the kid.

I had my sunglasses on, of course, so I could watch him without him knowing. James Bond would have been proud. Probably labeled me 008.

I watched him stand and face the water. He stood for a while like that. Just staring. His shirt was black with white and gold graphics in some kind of symbol or pattern like a bad heavy metal band concert shirt. After letting the lake soothe him for a moment he took off his shirt to reveal a strong body along with a good-size beer gut.

He laid down on a towel, which was all there was of his "property," and, putting his arms by his side, appeared to start taking a nap in the sunlight.

I looked around at our property. A table, toys, magazines, sun chairs, umbrellas ... we hadn't even brought everything that year. I looked back toward his. A towel.

His shoes were still on. Black shoes. Black shorts. Black sunglasses. Black beard. A big white smile. He was smiling so big. He was happy. He was relaxed. He was breathing. I could see his big gut moving back and forth. He was calm and at peace.

I began to weep. I was overwhelmed—somehow—and I let the tears cleanse my fear as best they could, taking the judgment with them. They also did a number on my own stresses for my friends who were sick, my friends who were hurting, and for the pressures of Ehs and her and life and what it all meant ...

But mostly, I cried happy tears watching him so happy. I began to imagine a different narrative for him. Single dad, doing the best he could to raise the little boy I had seen earlier. I imagined that the boy loved his dad so much and I imagined that man worked as hard as he could to make life good for that little boy. I didn't care if he had a job or "pulled his weight" or "earned his right."

What a man I was staring at. Honestly, a hero.

I imagined the life he had. I assumed it hadn't been easy. I assumed there were lots of sketchy neighborhoods and sketchy trailers and sketchy parents. I assumed he was not prom king or captain of the football team. I wondered why we liked words like "king" and "captain" so much. Hierarchy, damn hierarchy everywhere slammed in our little faces. And so we're all, always, trying to gain rank in this world. We love any climb up the power ladder we can get.

I imagined this was one of the few vacations he had all year. That moment, just lying there without any worry or fear or concern, in the warm embrace of the sun and peace of the waves rolling against the sand, was his greatest moment of the year.

It was all he asked for. He didn't need much.

I wiped away the tears that were continuing to stroll down my cheeks … no need for anyone to see those. I was humbled. I was put in my place, again. My place was not down, or up, it was equal with him and the people in the trailer with the dogs and everyone else on the beach and at the lake.

If only I could see like that all the time.

I looked one final time to the man on the towel. He was bright and colorful suddenly. And I saw her, standing above him, radiant and glowing, bathing him in the boldest, most sparkling rainbow orb I had ever seen.

Just as quickly she began to fade away, leaving him alone again, but not without remnants. It was as though they were both inhabiting the same space for a moment. Despite the disjointed nature of it all I expressed utter joy all over my face.

Nature put on a show for us that night. It was a perfect night, a clear dark sky and the Perseid meteor shower. A perfect ending for our last night at the lake. With each streak of light that dove across the darkness, the entire family cheered and clapped. "Did you see that one?"

It was magical.

We were all basking in joy and rainbow star dust of some kind.

TWENTY SEVEN

Most of us humans are trichromats, which means we have three receptors, or cone cells, in our retinas that pick up color. *Most* humans. There is a small amount of us, mostly female, who carry four receptors.

Tetrachromats—the wizards with four colors—perceive a whole different world. Where most of us see white, they see a multitude of colors that blend together to create white. Where we simply see green, they see hundreds of shades … even in a simple blade of grass. Human skin is a wild blend of contrasting color, blacks are a recipe of violets and blues and greens, and snow is an array of pastels.

They see the world differently, not because the world is actually different, but because they are able to see what others simply can't. Some of the invisible is visible to them. They see one hundred more colors than the average human. To think about what the average human is missing, just in color, can be overwhelming.

Mantis shrimp take all this to an even crazier level with the most complex visual system ever studied. Mantis shrimp? The wizards of the animal kingdom have up to twelve or sixteen receptors—taking in so much color their poor little brains can't process it all.

Some say they *speak* with color.

It's all just a reminder of the kinds of things that are around us every day that we can't see: radio waves, dark energy, quantum particles, ultraviolet light … the list goes on and on. Anyone who has ever experienced singing bowls in any kind of yoga studio knows it's an even bigger list of things affecting us that we can't see. There's energy and emotion out there too. Especially when Jaden is the one dinging that thing on your stomach … there's *lots* of energy and emotion when we're aware of it.

For a few weeks after my experience on the beach, it had been as though I had become some kind of cross between a tetrachromat and a mantis shrimp. My world was a whirl of additional colors, additional sounds, additional feelings … It was exhilarating, intoxicating, powerful, and enlightening.

It also induced bouts of nausea very easily.

My brain, though hopefully much bigger than that of a mantis shrimp, was not entirely able to process it all. What did get through left me wanting more. Pinks in blades of grass, shades of blue in my fingers as they moved, and rainbow colors of sound waves that came from people's mouths and filled the space between us as I listened and basked in them. Rays of light filling hallways, pools of color dancing around floor and pastures, and pure radiance of every color in the universe at times. I can't begin to fully describe what I saw because words have evolved to speak of what we normally see. There aren't other words for that stuff.

Everything was beyond my ability to comprehend it. It was like that moment on the beach at the lake—but more permanent, which left me in a near constant state of wonder, ecstasy, and abundance.

So, I decided to visit Leo. And Jaden. While it lasted.

In my mantis shrimp, near superhero state, I could see emotions. Not in people's expressions but in colors and waves and pieces of art dancing around faces and hands and arms and rooms. From the moment Leo walked into the visiting area, I could see something was not right.

The prison itself had already muted my sense of color, washed out the vibrancy I had started to become accustomed to, even in the parking lot. Guards were covered somehow. Other inmates felt dull. Leo was the worst of it all.

He had recovered enough to be cleared for visitors but was still being kept in solitary confinement and under suicide watch most of his days. It was having an effect on him. The cell had only grown smaller, and so had Leo's light.

He smiled but it had no punch. His eyes danced a sad contemporary routine with minor notes played on some strings. The new scar on his neck seemed to suck energy in the same way the one on his face did, almost a black hole absorbing anything that dared to shine near him, including me.

I smiled and released some kind of rainbow into the room but it was quickly attacked and suffocated by something else.

Which made me smile less.

"Hi, Pastor Seth," he said drably, followed by a weak stream of blue shades that washed to the floor. For a moment his face was replaced by that of a lion. Sharp teeth and a full mane blowing in some kind of breeze. Bravery and strength epitomized in animal form. And slowly the lion faded back into the face of Leo, a humiliated and broken human being.

"Leo," I responded, with more excitement than I felt. "It's so good to see you, my friend." I waited for his eyes and he smiled gently. "Are you alright?"

"They're back, Pastor." He shook his head, apathetic and tired. "They hound me in that room all the time. Mock me. I can't do nuthin' about it. I got nuthin' anymore."

Whatever lack of color coming from him impacted me and made me see more normally, which hit me with a mix of relief and withdrawal at the same time.

"What do you mean?" I asked, my words blaring like trumpets.

"The darkness. I can feel it. It just sits on the walls and stuff. It ain't no good. I pray but it does nothing. I keep askin' god to do something but god don't pay no attention to me anymore." He looked down.

As did I.

"Leo, what's happened to you?" I asked, with the gravity of planets.

"What you mean?" he asked.

"You're not the same person I know." The words weren't meant as weapons but they were sharp. I could see them penetrate. He was as depressed as I had ever seen him, and given my state of seeing I could sense it was a depression as deep and bold as I had ever encountered. The emptiness of space descended on us from out of his mouth.

"Well, I tried to kill myself, pastor. And there's no forgiveness for that. You know that."

"Who the fuck told you that?" I asked, angry, indignant.

Leo leaned back, apparently appalled by my blue and green four-letter word that hit him in the forehead and dripped down into his eyes. "Pastor, you shouldn't—"

"I'm sorry, Leo. Who told you that?" I asked with words that were yellow in their arrival.

"Well—" He looked away, almost embarrassed. "I been seeing a weekly Bible study here. They let me and it's good. It's good to get back in the Word." If it was actually good, the storm clouds that were forming in his eyes and the tornados running out of his mouth were lying.

"It sure doesn't seem like it is."

He seemed surprised.

"Leo, I love that you get some time with some other people and reading the Bible but Leo, whoever told you that you can't be forgiven for what you've done. Don't listen to them." I tapped on the glass between us and sent a rainbow through it. "Your hear me?" It was as though I could see the chemicals in his brain running dark and poisonous, hiding my rainbow from his processing centers inside his skull. His blood ran cold. I could feel it. Whatever fed the color, the life, the passion, was dried up and replaced by the dark flow of depression and dehumanization.

Leo dared to look up. "Well, Pastor Seth, no offense but he said I shouldn't even be seeing you, either. He said you're a hypocrite and a her … a heretic too who done had affairs and sinned so much."

His words felt rehearsed, which was the only reason they didn't destroy me. But a black storm seeped from his lips and covered whatever light I was emanating nonetheless. I tried to defend myself, to encourage Leo, but from there it all descended into a charcoal fog of shame that enveloped me too.

Later, trying to recover, I went to yoga. Jaden led us, with his shirt off. But, I didn't see Jaden. I only saw light. Warmth. In fact, the class was too much. I had to sit down multiple times, out of exhaustion and an overwhelmed sense of all of my senses. At the end, Jaden led us in a mediation. He implored us to imagine a light above us and then let the light into our bodies, into our toes, our ankles, our thighs, our hips, our chest, our fingers, and our head. It was a warm, inviting, embracing, inspiring, and colorful light, he said. I saw it all. I felt it, even with my eyes closed. We were rainbows beaming around the room, bouncing off the mirrors with joy and vibrancy and color.

After the class I floated out of the room and smiled at Jaden, sitting at the reception desk. I was thrilled with whatever joy flowed from me and arrived at the doorstep of his own emotional state. I could see it like a stream of glittering color, passing from me to him. I asked him about his wife. I embraced him. I thanked him for the class and meant the words. I told him he had no idea how right he was about the light—and he thought I was being nice instead of describing reality.

He, of course, had no idea that whatever dark jealousy I usually carried was so erased by wonder and awe that I barely registered him—just bright lights and soaring melodies instead. I didn't tell Jaden that I would probably not be able to be as nice after I lost my superhero capabilities but, instead, hugged him again and prepared to walk out.

I did have a counseling session with Rachel to get to and was already going to be late. And sweaty.

"Thanks again, Jaden," I played into the air, like a sweet note from an electric guitar to amp up the crowd.

That was when I sensed something change.

An orchestra began to play something ominous all around me. The bright day that had been filtering through the windows and into the lobby faded into something thicker—more like tar. It felt harder to breathe.

I looked to Jaden, trying to understand what was happening. Or about to happen, as I felt I was sensing it before it arrived.

"Seth," he called out. I could see my name hovering in the air, leaving his mouth and floating in whatever substance we were floating in. "Hey, I meant to give this to Rachel the other day, but—I hope this isn't offensive or doesn't stir up anything … but it's from a few years ago right before I moved. I just found it in storage, which"—he seemed strange—"was kind of weird. But maybe it was a sign or something. Maybe I can just give it to you?"

He held up a box. It was wrapped. White paper. A red ribbon and a nice bow on top. Hearts. I saw a colony of bats spew out from it and soar into the air above it and around us, mocking me somehow. Jaden held it out for me, though I could barely see it as the fog, the tar, the ink, whatever we were in became thicker and more opaque. Vague spots of light appeared in my periphery like lighthouses in a wild storm but they were quickly snuffed away.

"What?" I asked, spewing out more darkness from my own mouth. I could taste it, see it, hear it, feel it, and see Jaden feel it, though he didn't know the extent of it.

"Yeah, sorry." His words were blue and dropped to the ground like anchors. He held the gift closer to me and I grabbed it. A tag read TO JADEN FROM RACHEL with a heart on it.

More thick darkness. I was the source suddenly. Whatever light I had been experiencing was not able to penetrate my new brooding hurricane of a mood.

"I hope that's alright," he said again. "It was a long time ago. Never opened it. Figured Rachel might want it back."

Why the hell would you give it to me, you motherfucker?

Do you know I'm going to a counseling appointment right now?

And you give me this shit?

Somehow I managed to say "bye"—or at least I think I did—before exiting and trying to find my way to the car amidst the ink I was swimming in.

Needless to say, that afternoon sitting in Marie's office was far from a normal appointment. How I drove there, I don't remember. Honestly, I didn't even remember walking into the carpeted foyer with the soft music or saying hi to Liam, who probably smiled at me from his receptionist desk, because he always did.

I have no recollection of sitting down in my chair, only being in it. I always sat on the left. Rachel always sat on the right. Marie always sat somewhere in the middle, the illustration not being lost on either of us. I'm sure we said pleasantries, I'm sure Marie asked what the package was that I placed under my chair, I'm sure she asked why I seemed "off" and I'm sure Rachel walked in with a smile—like she had been doing for the past few months, because we had been in a good place. I remember staring at the artwork on the wall. Marie's daughter had made it in first grade. I used to stare at it often, when I didn't want to look at Rachel or Marie in the early days of therapy. When I wanted to hide.

I was staring at it again. It was dancing somehow, alive, and I heard Marie's voice poking its way through the noise of my brain and the fog of my vision. "Seth! Can you tell us what is bothering you?"

I nodded.

In the early days of our work, after the affairs, I would "store bullets" as Marie put it. I would save them for the perfect time when they would inflict the most damage. Rachel would store shields for my bullets because she started to be aware of when they could come. I had to work on putting down the gun that shot out words of hurt and jealousy and Rachel had to work on being able to trust the fact that she could walk around without a shield. We had been doing so well but I had a feeling, more than a feeling, that we were about to take steps backward. Judging from the rainbows of black emanating from my being it was not going to go well. There was a storm on the horizon and the storm was me.

"Seth?"

"Yes," I answered. I had a bullet again. I reached under the chair. "I have something for Rachel."

"Ah," Marie answered, with an orchestra of nice music that was quickly silenced by my black rainbow that absorbed and suffocated every song. "That was sweet of you to bring. Are you sure—"

I was staring at Rachel, paying no attention to Marie. Like a squid releasing ink into the ocean, Rachel sent something dark into the room, confirming what I didn't need confirmed: the package was not going to make me or her happy.

I cursed the ability to see whatever I was seeing. It had been fun when the colors were everywhere. It was suffocating when jealousy and fear were running the show, along with plenty of shame.

"Why would you bring that? And what …" Rachel was confused.

"Well …" Marie tried her best. "I think Seth was trying to—"

"I gave that to Jaden … during our …" Her voice stumbled, chains dragging out her words and dropping them to the floor with a clang.

"Well, let's open it," I said, basking in the bitter syrup the words painted all over the room. And I tore into the package with my brew of radioactive emotions cheering me on.

Rachel and Marie both said something that I didn't hear. Soon I was holding lace in front of my eyes. Through it I could see Marie forming her own shields and trying to amass some kind of troops to help alleviate the early signs of war. It took me a moment but I eventually realized how the lace was supposed to fit on a human body and held it up the right way, making sure Rachel could see it well.

"Seth …" she uttered, embarrassed, angry, and filling the room with every shade of blue I had ever seen and all kinds I never knew existed. "Why …"

"Damn," I uttered in the worst form of me that existed, arrogance inflicting pain onto a person I love. Operating out of pure unadulterated fear. "Well this sure is nice." The sarcasm was like dead foliage filling the room, growing out of the walls and floor and sucking up the oxygen of breath, of healing, of anything good.

"Seth …" It was Marie's turn.

"Well, now …" I uttered. "Let's not take Rachel's side here, right away."

"Seth …" It was Rachel's turn again.

"I sure can't remember getting a gift like this. Just for Jaden, huh?" Those were the bullets. The ones I had been saving and I unleashed them on Rachel along with daggers from my eyes and hands of rage to twist them all deeper.

She melted into the chair, her form dripping in blues and darkness and I saw my sadness, deep inside my anger, reach out to her somehow.

"I don't know why you did this," she said. For a moment I saw the shape of Lucy inside of her, although it seemed to emanate from me onto her. A projection of some kind.

"Why *I* did this!" I screamed back, insulted at the blame and angry at Lucy for jumping into our fight.

"Yes!"

Marie was silent, relegated to a bystander by my ego, which was filling the room fast, rampaging from one corner to the next as if a massive rhinoceros, obliterating every good thing in its path.

"You think I like holding this up, imagining you in it for him? You think this makes me feel good?"

"It's not like I gave it to him yesterday," she shot back.

"It might as well have been." I released all the artillery I could muster.

"Jesus, Seth!" She moaned in anger and frustration. "Really?"

"Well … god knows why he thought he should give me this today. Make some kind of point?"

"Jesus," she sighed again.

"You think any of this makes me feel good?" The rhino was charging hard, not at the walls but at Rachel, stabbing her with its horn.

I felt like the office had turned into rain forest: but the kind that lives on some acidic rain filled with toxic insects and noxious weeds, with poisonous crawling things slithering around below us. The air was unhealthy in every way. No one could breathe.

Rachel transformed into a flower, though. Bright. I saw the same flower in my own hands, even as they held up the lingerie, which I decided to put away.

Time passed.

"Do you think *he* made *me* feel good? Better than you?" Rachel asked. It was her turn for bullets. But, as it often was with her, they were surgical in their aim and intended not for harm but for illumination. Somehow. I watched light penetrate my gloom and it struck something inside of me that I had let disappear when I had first seen the box. "If you can't find a way to measure up, I don't know what I can do for you, Seth."

I watched Marie begin to glow again.

"Did he?" I asked, on the verge of tears.

"Did Gwen?" Rachel returned, on the verge of her own sadness.

Marie spoke into our battle. "Seth. Rachel. Let's remember these things are not helpful for now." I'm not sure I cared at that point.

"No," I answered. Lucy was there for a moment again, within the image of Rachel. "Just worse."

"Worse is what you're going to have to figure out, Seth." She spoke slowly with kind, inviting, welcoming words that collided into my chest. I watched them hover outside a long time while I wondered if I would invite them in.

I don't remember all of what happened next. Just a drive alone, all the way home, even though Rachel was next to me. Only the feeling that I had regressed and despair, as if I didn't have enough strength to continue walking up the mountain, after my ropes had broken and just about killed me on my fall.

I did not hate her. I only hated myself. But, that was more destructive and it seeped into everything, including my prospects of a full recovery.

That night my praying mantis superhero ability vanished. Life returned to normal, although I wondered if it would ever be "normal" again, whatever normal was.

TWENTY EIGHT

As soon as I got the chance, I asked him.

"You gave him that box, didn't you?" I asked with all kinds of accusation.

"Have you enjoyed the views?" He smirked, not paying much attention to my question.

We were both sitting on a couch in the corner of the parking lot of a nearby gas station. I was wearing running clothes and he was wearing normal James clothes. Everything was very normal except for the gray couch that was sitting on a rarely used lawn between a highway and a tire pump, one I'd used many times to fill up my car.

"Why?"

"Seth, we don't give. We don't make. We don't take. Stop blaming me for all of your problems." It was his turn to layer his words with accusation.

"Well," I answered. "I hope we can recover."

"That will be up to you, not me," he answered plainly, making me wonder if I had hoped for something better.

"And all the weird views … they disappeared."

"Hmm …" He nodded, as though he knew why but didn't want to say.

"Was that you?"

"No," he answered, although hesitantly. "We can only blind. Or not …"

"What's that mean?" I looked over to him, sitting on the couch.

He didn't answer with words. Instead, I could see the massive wall suddenly in the distance, casting its shadow over us and the gray land. I could see the gas station but only in a vague transparent form. Cars looked more like clouds of smoke.

And Ehs was not the form of James I was used to. He was no longer sitting, but standing and at least twice as tall as me. He wore a dark cloak with a hood, although the hood was thrown backward, revealing a bald head with very white, almost transparent skin. There was some kind of dark metal wrapped around his head, almost barbed wire in fashion. His eyes were dark holes, his mouth nonexistent, and I could see through his entire shape to the road that was still behind him.

Before I had time to truly acknowledge fear—which was coming on like a freight train— the whole scene was gone and we were sitting on the couch again. James was smiling. I was not. It had lasted maybe a second.

"What—" was all I could muster.

"Hey, Seth!" someone yelled and I looked. I recognized them but didn't know their name so I just waved back with a blank stare.

"Hey," I eventually answered.

"Have a good one!"

I looked toward James. "They can see us?"

"You," he nodded.

"What? I thought ..."

Before I could finish the sentence, the gas station disappeared, as did the pavement. I was sitting in a field. Yellow, dreary—almost gray—grasses were surrounding us. "He can't see you now."

"Okay." I nodded, completely separate from my senses that were still trying to catch up, which made me feel like I was living in an empty shell of myself.

The desaturated fields disappeared and we were back sitting in the corner of the parking lot, looking at the gas station. "He still can't."

I could plainly see his car pulling into a spot, although I still had no idea who its driver was or what had just happened to me.

"Right now."

"You're not here anymore."

"I'm not?" The full force of that was slightly terrifying since it seemed exactly like it had been moments earlier.

"Relax. Not enough for him to see you."

"So, did I just disappear? What if Rachel needs me?"

"Is this the first time you've thought of this?"

"Actually—" The more I thought about that the more worrisome that seemed. "I doubt she will. Not the way we're going." I paused, somber. "Not really, but I never ask."

"You're underwater. They are above the water. If you want to go back you simply swim to the surface. If your wife needs you she dives down and gets you."

The answer *seemed* so simple on its face but I was pretty sure my face adequately displayed that I was more confused.

"A fish lives in its world. It's happy. You live in yours, you're happy. I'm the scuba tank. Both realities are contained by the planet and yet they are worlds apart. Most animals never know the other exists. Even humans have only begun to scratch the surface of what is, down there. I assume fish feel the same about what is up there."

"So, I'm not on the surface now."

"No, you're underwater."

"Okay."

"You've been diving in and out the past few weeks. You're learning to hold your breath."

"But—" I was still not caught up.

"You've already done the things I'm talking about. Stop requiring explanation for everything … just settle for the experience. You will not understand. You can't. Just breathe when you can. Trust me when you can't."

I reached down and grabbed the couch we were sitting on. "Where is this couch?"

"Where." There was not going to be an answer to that, just the way there never had been.

I closed my eyes slow and exhaled a deep breath that was meant to cleanse my lungs from the events of the previous few minutes. "What was that thing I saw a few minutes ago?"

"Me." He looked down. "In another form."

"I didn't like that."

"No," he said. "That's why you've never seen it."

I took a moment to look back toward the gas station.

"Why just then?"

"Only you can answer that."

"Sorry. What?"

"Do you still trust me, after seeing me more …" He paused. "Accurately?" He was almost sad, again, as though ashamed of what he truly was.

"Well." I took a deep breath again. "I'd rather this." I pointed toward the familiar and normal shape I was used to.

He smiled but it was not all happiness.

"Also, what's with the couches and benches?" I asked. "I feel like we're always sitting on them."

"Humans learn a lot on couches." He stood to his feet. "Are you ready?"

"No," I countered.

He sat down again with a perplexed look, for sure. "What?"

"I'm scared."

He shook his head. "Then you know how I feel."

"That's not—" I stopped myself and thought for a second,

trying to look into the eyes of James for something deeper. "Shit, it is?"

"Yes," he answered.

"We're not doing well."

"Yes," he repeated monotone. "But, I have no time for your false manifestations of doom and gloom, deficiencies and perversions." He stood again to his feet. "Are you ready?"

"What?" I remained seated. "What?"

"There are only two more zones to show you."

"What were you saying?"

"Two more I'm going to show you," he answered. "As I've said, time is running out."

"For what?"

"For us."

"What's that mean?"

"My time is running out," he whispered. "And you, you must see!" The words had punch to them. A lot of punch, so much that I felt like I may have missed what I needed to see.

And I remembered her, out of the blue.

"Oh," I interjected, much too excited for what he had just told me. "She said she would meet us!"

"Where?" he asked instantly, showing little emotion or at least way less than I had expected.

"I didn't mean to change the subject. I'm sorry, but maybe this will help? Penuel. That was all she said."

He looked up toward the sky and let a faint smile creep upon his face. "You just now told me?"

"Sorry, I tried. You left. Then I forgot. You know, with maybe losing my relationship again and all. What is it?" I asked, looking up toward the same sky and his face.

"Hebrew. It means the face of god. It's where Jacob wrestled with the gods and came away with a limp."

"I guess I should have known that," I answered.

"You're not a pastor anymore. Never were that kind of pastor, right?" He laughed.

"So, what's it mean?"

"I don't know. We'll worry about it later."

"Hey," I threw out. "How much time do you have?"

He shook his head. "It doesn't matter."

"Also—" I held out my hand. "Did you have anything to do with this place?" I pointed toward the gas station that had arrived to our quiet little neighborhood. "We had a really good thing going over there." I nodded over to a now-vacant beautiful little spot we had once been able to get local vegetables and fresh milkshakes from before neighbors had complained and it shut down.

He didn't bother answering me.

"Also, I assume things have calmed down enough for you to be with me?" I asked.

Dark clouds suddenly filled the sky—clouds that were beyond storm. The gas station disappeared and we were in the field again. Yellow-gray grasses stretching in every direction as far as I could see. It was a lonely gray scene.

"There are two things the masters spoke the most on. Two things you have completely ignored." A rough, cold breeze blew across the grasses and into my face, sending a shiver through me. "I assume you know them." He was still standing, staring off into the distance, but he did look back, awaiting my answer.

"I feel like there are a lot—"

"Two," he interjected with a sigh. "Two."

"I don't know."

"Money and tribal violence. The two very few pay any attention to."

An arena appeared in the distance, or maybe it had been there and I just hadn't noticed it. It was old, matching almost exactly the architecture of the Coliseum in Rome. Three stories of arched entryways moving up toward the sky with perfection and grandeur.

"Distracted. Numb."

"Money, really?" I muttered while staring at the arena and trying to get a gauge on its size. I stood to my feet.

The arena disappeared, as though taken from me, and we were suddenly back to the gas station. It was recognizable as the gas station but also draped in the sheet of transparent darkness that he had shown me earlier, as though blended with some other world. I could make out vague shapes of cars and people but each shadows of what they normally were. Colors were far less vibrant.

"I suppose we'll begin there, then," Ehs answered, still, thankfully, in the form of James. Just thinking about the mouthless face gave my body another tremor. He pointed.

People were walking to and from their cars, filling up their gas tanks as they normally did, and as I watched, the scene returned to the one I was more used to. Full color. Normalcy. As I always remembered. I looked behind me. The couch was gone.

"Whether you like it or not. Whether you agree or not. Which, judging from your response, you don't like, don't agree, and are generally ignorant."

"Can we be nice?" I asked sincerely.

"Your country was founded on them … gold, silver, and temporal profit. And we crafted a religion that obliged and begged for more. The wise have always known you were weak and susceptible to the destruction these things bring. Yet you enjoy them immensely. And so we took advantage and began our own propaganda of a different nature … of which you are still perpetuating and did moments ago."

"It's not *just* money," I responded.

"Exactly," he answered, as though he'd expected me to say that. "Of course not." His voice became much quieter. "I know of no country where the love of money has taken stronger hold on the affections of men. Love of money is either the chief or secondary motive in everything Americans do." He looked at me, as though waiting for me.

I, in turn, waited for him.

"Close to two hundred years ago Tocqueville said that … can you imagine what he would say now? No, it's not *just* money," he said. I couldn't tell if he was mocking me or not. I figured he was. "Why didn't you give him money?" he asked.

"Who?"

"Who?" He was definitely mocking me. "All of them. Your excuses are endless and yet, not once in your entire life have you held a cardboard sign asking for money. So, again, why do you not give it to every person you see who is?"

"Well," I started to argue. "It's complicated."

"Have you ever begged for food?"

I didn't answer.

"Have you? Answer me," he commanded.

"No."

"Have you ever been so desperate for a drug to escape your hell that you have pretended to ask for food?"

"No."

"Have you felt the humiliation from stares at you through the windshield? Have you ever felt ignored, unseen, invisible?"

"Well …" I had but not like they had … I knew that much. "No."

"Why is it complicated?"

"It's—"

"Can you not afford the ten dollars? Or can you not afford the time to acknowledge a human?" He looked back toward the gas station. "Or can you not afford to waste life on something that won't get you higher in the games?"

I wanted to argue, but I didn't, or couldn't. "Most things are complicated," I decided to argue after all.

"Yes," he answered. "They are. But not this." He pointed. "Do you see that man?"

Once I really started paying attention, I could see about twenty men in front of me, of all different sizes and shapes and, judging from their appearance, financial backgrounds. There was one filling up a rusted-out Chevrolet pickup that had seen better days and another getting out of a Subaru that, if it were a dog, would be put down. Another man was at the Redbox, in a business suit, presumably picking out a movie for the night and another was getting out of an Escalade. One more was filling up a Hummer.

"*That* man?" I asked back with sarcasm.

"You *know* the one I'm talking about."

I looked over the parking lot again. At another man who was talking to a woman in a parking spot and … the guy getting out of the Subaru. I saw him. He looked disheveled to say the least. Whatever he had spent his day doing had been dirty. He wore heavy work boots, khaki pants, and a white T-shirt, all of which were covered in dirt. Not landscaping dirt. Poverty dirt. Dirt that collects from a hard job and after many days of not washing clothes. He practically stumbled into the front doors of the gas station/convenience store.

"Yes …" Ehs whispered, a little dark for my tastes. "That's the one. Do you think he's rich?"

"No," I answered.

"Have you already brushed him aside?"

I was not ready for the comment and, to be honest, I wasn't sure I liked it, in the same way no one likes when someone calls them out. "I mean …"

"Of course you have. I know the thoughts that have gone through your head. Hard worker, at least. Maybe. Either way, poor. Smells. What could he possibly do for you? You maybe thought of all the ways you could help him, but that is the only thing he could offer you. He could make you feel better for helping someone lesser than you, because he is definitely less than you."

I did a terrible job pretending to be offended. "Well …"

"Of course you have. You are always under its spell, as is he. Why do you think he walks as though he doesn't belong in this world?"

I watched another man walk out of the store. His spine was straight, his shoulders were back, and he was talking way too loud on a cell phone. I wanted to punch him suddenly, though I didn't really know why.

"That one is very comfortable with the fact that he belongs in your world." Ehs smiled. "Actually, he makes you feel as though *you* might not."

I didn't return the smile. I keep looking at Escalade guy and Hummer guy and a woman in a Suburban and another teenage girl who pulled up in an older Acura. I just watched myself watch them, judge them, love them or hate them without knowing them, based on something that I could see.

"But he's trying," Ehs whispered while moving closer to me. "Right now."

"Trying for what?" The Escalade drove away and another car was waiting behind it.

"Did you know Americans spend two billions dollars a year on premium gasoline?" Ehs asked.

"Two billion?"

"Two billion," Ehs nodded. "Do you know why?"

"To make their cars run better?" I was no expert on premium gasoline or its benefits. I just didn't buy it.

Ehs laughed. "Of course not! It has nothing to do with engines. That two billion is wasted. It does absolutely nothing."

"Nothing?"

"Nothing." A chair suddenly formed behind Ehs and he sat down on it. We were getting comfortable again apparently. Well, *he* was. "It makes the rich man's brain run better—that's about all. If you can afford premium"—he paused—"then you must be premium. Right?" He laughed. "Ah." He pointed toward the doors. "Here comes our friend."

The doors opened and out walked the man I had seen earlier. I noticed the thick beard the second time around. And the dirty hat. He had a slight limp in his leg and probably a few limps in the more hidden parts of him: soul and self-worth. He was holding a string of tickets. I had played the lottery once, when the jackpot was over a billion. His were the daily kind, with the bad graphics and ultraviolet ink and foil that gets stuck in your fingernails. He moved over to his car, spread them across his rusted-out roof, and started to tear into them like a hungry dog digging for food.

"Good luck," I muttered very sarcastically, trying to bring some humor to the situation and to my own feelings of guilt.

"He's just trying to belong in your world, Seth. Just trying to belong. He knows, better than you, that if he drove in this parking lot in that Hummer you would look at him differently."

"I'd probably hate him. I hate Hummers."

Ehs laughed. The man dropped a couple of tickets to the ground and continued to work on what remained. "Of course. In the same way he probably hates you. He doesn't measure up and he knows it. You don't measure up and you know it."

"It's not why I hate Hummers."

"Why do you?"

"They're stupid. A waste of money. Made to drive in the deserts of Iraq and people drive them around cities as a badge. They're a giant badge that shows you have enough money to waste."

"And …"

"And what?" I looked at Ehs, still sitting in his chair, studying the man with the lottery tickets. He had dropped all but one to the floor now.

"You hate waste?"

"Yeah."

"Yet you waste."

"Well, not like that."

"Yet you waste."

"Okay." I looked over at Ehs again. "Yeah, but I'm not rich like that. I don't waste like that." I stopped. "Jealous probably. Like most of my life."

"Hmm," he hummed. "Fortune is not on his side tonight." The man had dropped all the tickets to the ground and was getting back in his car. "Maybe next time."

"Where are you in this?"

Ehs turned and faced me, looking intrigued for the first time in a while. "Where am I?"

"Yeah. Give him the winning numbers. Ruin him further."

He smiled again as the man started his car. A plume of smoke slipped out of the exhaust and into the air. "I'm afraid luck hands out numbers. But—" Ehs stood from his chair. "Even if I could, there's no need. I'm afraid he's already ruined. He believes he doesn't belong in your world and that money is the best way for him to start to matter."

The car was backing up. One reverse light worked. "We've already sold him a fantasy—that one day he'll belong with his magic ticket. And he will keep playing the ridiculous odds—terrible odds—to belong. There's a reason the poorest third of your country buys half the tickets." He lifted his brows and sighed. "Maybe they can belong someday."

As the man pulled closer to us, I could see him more clearly. His beard resembled steel wool that had been used too many times and his skin was as worn as his clothes. He was in desperate need of some premium gas. I reached out to say something to him, or just to let him know that I could see him but he couldn't see me. He slowly drove away, ushering more darkness into the sky through his muffler and into my heart through his disappointment.

"Hmm," Ehs said again. "Please keep in mind I'm only showing you the most obvious example, of course. Hoping you can, at least, understand this one as you try to match it to the … less obvious."

He really did have a way of making me feel like shit at times.

"Come, we have more to see."

The gas station vanished, only to be replaced with a black box. Attempting to get my bearings, I realized we were in a gray neighborhood of black boxes. The roads were what I was used to, as was the landscaping, but where houses normally stood there were simply boxes with no windows and no doors. Big brick neighborhood.

Ehs was still next to me. "Money, at its base, was just a way to trade, to allow humans to achieve specialization. A good move." His voice seemed cheery for a moment. "But it's turned to so much more. Now it's just the surface expression of hierarchy. Of belonging. Of achieving. Of rising."

A well-built man, fairly young, was walking toward us. As he neared, I could see that he was in bad shape. Cuts marred his face, as though someone had taken a knife to it, and bruises and dark scars were visible all over his body. His clothing—what looked like it had once been a suit—was in tatters and there was blood oozing its way out of numerous cuts and slices of flesh.

He was there, but not. Present in a proud body but nothing other than that. A wounded soldier who no longer knew what he was fighting, but still fighting. With pride.

Some kind of door opened in the cube, revealing more darkness inside. A woman came running out of the house before madly embracing him.

"Oh, honey." She continued to squeeze him. "How are you?"

He halfheartedly lifted his arms. Or maybe whole-heartedly but with no strength left. "Hi, honey."

"How was the day?"

"Good. Good. Fulfilled the quota. Beat it even." He managed to smile while grimacing.

I looked at Ehs who, as usual, was just letting me watch.

"Oh," she said, squeezing him again. "I am so proud of you!" She really was.

"Not bad. Not bad." He winced.

"Well." She let go of him and moved toward their cube. "I have some dinner."

At this point, I wondered if she was looking at the same man I was. He was in terrible condition, the human version of the car I had seen earlier. He could barely stay standing and seemed oblivious to everything in the world—and she was just as oblivious to his condition.

"We'll get the wounds cleaned up as best we can," she said, as though she said it every day. "But, let's eat dinner first."

I looked again at Ehs. Back to the brick.

It was instantly a house. We were fully back in the world I was accustomed to, standing at a nice house in a neighborhood near my own. A Mercedes was in the driveway as was a basketball hoop. The man was on his front porch, wearing a nice suit. He seemed to be in great health and condition, as did the woman who escorted him inside. I heard "Daddy's home!" just before the door closed.

"Money does offer the promise of status. And rules to play by. Always more status to gain and the way to do it."

I looked up toward the sky. Darkness was steadily approaching, in more ways than one.

"Have you ever wondered why your country, the wealthiest to ever exist, resembles a developing nation to the degree it does?"

"Well—" I didn't know my nation did resemble a developing nation, let alone why.

"There is such a gap of status. So far to go no matter where you are." He was nodding, staring at the car, the house, me, lost in his own thoughts, or maybe seeing something I could not.

I did look at the closed door. The basketball hoop. The dining room light inside. I thought of my own family. I thought of Rachel.

"One more," Ehs shouted to me. The shout startled me but not near as much as the bone-chilling call he let out a moment later. I was aware of only the beginning. The noise itself was bloodcurdling but it was the sensation of speed that suddenly pushed on me and the inability to breathe that accompanied it that caused me to pass out.

When consciousness returned, I was drowning in a very dark ocean. I desperately wanted to surface but any surface felt far too distant—maybe gone entirely. Free divers will tell you that around seventy feet below, the pressure in your body equalizes and you no longer have to put near the amount of effort into descent. In fact, you're being pulled down and now have to work to ascend. If you're not ready, it can be very dangerous.

Something was drawing me toward the bottom. I was descending somewhere dark and cold and confusing. I had nowhere near the energy I needed to get to the top.

Ehs had told me I could always rise but I didn't feel it in that moment. At all.

I knew very little except that everything felt very dangerous.

TWENTY NINE

I awoke in a house somewhere. I was sitting at a table and a woman was sitting across from me. Three thoughts initially ran through my head, before wondering where I was or what had happened. First, *This woman is stunning*. Two, *I can't believe I'm sitting at a table with her*. Three, *Are we alone?*

Then came all the more ordinary thoughts as my brain returned to life and started humming again, the first being, *Am I dead?*

The house was equally stunning. It was elegant, modern, clean, and simple. And it smelled tremendous. I could say the same for the woman who was, simply, staring at me with flawless skin, blond hair that just touched her shoulders, and blue eyes that were as capturing as any body of water.

I figured the woman was Swedish. Partly because she was stereotypically Nordic and partly because I'm enthralled with Sweden, so being Swedish makes someone even more magical and enchanting to me. And she was all of that.

The house, as I surveyed it, was also very Scandinavian. Or at least my version of it. I was immediately drawn to it as much as I was drawn to not continuing to stare at the woman.

The floors were light gray marble tiles with streaks of white. Almost concrete but warmer. The walls were white with tasteful splashes of wood on doorways and on open steps that went to a second floor.

On the other side was a wall of windows—more like a wall of glass. There was a rectangular pool outside with water so calm it didn't look real. I wondered if it was. Beyond the pool was an ocean view with a setting sun, whose light shone into the room I was in, reflecting off the white walls and dark floor. Set designers would spent days to get this shot.

I was in my dream house with my dream girl.

Is this heaven?

I stood up from the table to avoid staring at the woman and letting certain thoughts invade and consume my consciousness any more than they already were. This woman was not Gwen. It was all natural and all right.

Shit. Is this hell?

And I saw the kitchen.

Black, shiny countertops touched with silver faucets and rich, custom light wood cabinets to coordinate perfectly. Rachel would have killed for the kitchen. It was *our* dream house.

The thought of her kicked my brain. This was not a dream.

I remembered the man with the lottery tickets, the man coming home, I remembered the chilling scream of Ehs and, for a moment, reliving whatever had happened, I became nauseous even in the house of my dreams.

"Okay." I looked back at the woman, ready to face my trial and temptation. "I get it."

"I'm sorry," she said with an accent I didn't really recognize—probably Swedish. *Damn it.*

"I get it. This is some kind of test." I looked around at the house again. If any scene and person was going to test me, I was living it.

Forty is said to be the number of transformation and change. Forty years in the desert after Egypt. Forty days and nights of rain during the flood. Forty days of continuous meditation for the Buddha to attain enlightenment. Forty days in the desert for Jesus. Transformational myths.

I imagined forty days in the house with the woman. If it was going to be my test I already knew I was going to fail. My transformation and change were going to be for the worse. I was not going to be an inspirational myth unless someone wanted to be inspired in how to fail. I prayed I would not be there for forty days. I felt devastatingly weak. But, on the other hand, if I was going to fail I might as well fail immediately and enjoy the forty days.

"This is not a test," she said with just enough brokenness to not be distracting—only attracting. "Welcome to my house."

"Okay." I suddenly felt sweat forming on those parts of your body that you aren't ever aware of until you start sweating on them. The back of my neck, the inside of my arms, my lower back. "Where am I?"

"Heaven," she replied.

I looked around again. There *was* something ethereal about it all. Otherworldly once I was paying attention. I looked at her. I looked at the windows, the view, the pool, the sunset, and the staircase. "For real?" was all I could muster.

"Is it not right?" she asked. "Not what you expected?"

I'd been asked before, "If heaven exists, what would you like to hear god say when you arrive at the pearly gates?" My answer was always, "Not what you expected."

So maybe …

"No, it's not," I answered.

"Good."

"God?" I asked.

"Freja." She smiled and it melted my defenses. Her teeth were as perfect as everything else. Forty days? Forty seconds? She then stood and I realized I hadn't even looked at her body. She was wearing a tight white dress that hugged her curves as one would expect from a supermodel-goddess meant to tempt someone like me.

Whether she answered my question or not, I couldn't remember. Either way, she walked into the kitchen. Without her saying a thing, I followed, assuming she wanted me to act like a good puppy and follow its master.

As I followed, I was as much drawn to the house as I was to her, which reveals quite a bit about myself. The symmetry, the absence of clutter—in both design and how it was filled—and the views. The pool, the lighting, the dark pillars that rose up into the white walls, outside and in. Outside, I noticed the lounge chairs, the concrete benches, the whole patio bathed in orange sunlight resting next to a thin layer of smooth water with a perfect reflection inside of it. As though one outdoor patio wasn't enough, the shallow pool mirrored it perfectly, making it appear as though there were two.

Sure, we can go outside. I'd love to.

Everything was where it should be. Nothing out of place. Just like her.

There was an immaculately ordered wine rack. A single tree outside on black rock with a light shining up into its branches.

Maybe I had died.

About that time, I started to analyze. I couldn't help it.

Would god be a woman?

Wouldn't that be exactly what I would want?

But why wouldn't god be what I would want?

But god wouldn't be a woman like that? That seems pretty devilish.

What if this is the devil?

The devil would want me in a nice house with a nice woman.

Why doesn't god want that again?

It's material. Isn't everything material?

It's not god. Isn't everything god?

But I shouldn't want to sleep with god? Definitely true.

But if god is everywhere then I have slept with god.

What if it's Ehs acting like a really attractive woman?

Definitely wouldn't want to sleep with her then. True.

Why do I want to sleep with anyone at all who isn't my wife?

Uh, she's maybe the hottest woman to ever exist.

It's natural. It's programmed. You have chemicals in your brain.

No, that response is programmed. No, that response to that is programmed.

Is something wrong with me? I'm as attracted to the house as I am to her.

Well, that's probably not true.

Am I really dead?

Do dead people still have confusion and become paralyzed by trying to figure out situations?

"I want you to taste this hamburger."

Yes, those were the words that snapped me out of my looping and confused brain patterns and overheating brain.

"What?" I stared at her, a little awkwardly. Was this some kind of metaphor?

"Here." She pointed at a burger. I had not seen the burger up to that point, which is odd but also expected, given all the much better things that were there to draw my attention. Her hands were slender, but not too slender, and her fingers capped with black fingernail polish. Normally that would have seemed weird but, on her, it didn't. I imagined nothing would seem weird on her. Or off her, for that matter.

"So …" I moved closer to the island that the burger was sitting on. Black fingernails, white fingers, white plate, black countertop, the images were beautiful in their dualistic beauty. I tried to take it all in before looking at the burger. It looked like any other burger … sesame bun, lettuce, tomato, a little cheese sticking out of the side, and a big fat patty. Thick. Juicy. I started to salivate. The rest of my senses were already salivating and now my tongue and taste buds were joining the party.

Everything in my life was delicious.

I'm hungry. In every way.

She lifted her eyebrows and nodded toward the burger. "Are you going to try it?"

"Right now?"

"Yes."

Maybe she's actually asking if I want to try her?

Too specific for that to be true.

But, a burger?

"Well—" I looked behind me at the pool and the sun, still

setting into oranges and reds that were beaming through the glass and into the house, onto the walls and light woods around us. "I mean, can you answer some questions for me?"

"I'm sorry," she replied with a slight smile. "No."

As disappointing as it was, it made things easier. So much for the asking-god-a-bunch-of-questions-when-you-die theories.

If I was dead.

"I can't ask anything?"

"You can ask," she replied again, pulling on her skirt. "But I will not answer."

The wordplay with the English language was a bit of a buzzkill. I hadn't expected that. It reminded me of a guy I used to work with who would always play games like that.

Is god into silly word games? Or maybe she doesn't understand the language.

Or maybe they aren't word games.

"Will you try the burger?" she asked again.

Does god really want me to eat a burger?

"So, you're not god …" It wasn't really a question, more of a statement that she could respond to if she wanted to.

"What is a god?"

I had this one and I smiled just to let her know. "The metaphor of the mystery that transcends all categories of human thought including being and nonbeing." I was quoting Joseph Campbell to her—to maybe god. "Or the depth and grounding of life." I paraphrased another famous philosopher, just in case. Either answer would work for me.

She nodded, raised her eyebrows a bit, and looked out the windows while biting on her lip. She didn't seem as impressed as I wanted her to be. Then again, it was probably weird to tell god what god was or what I thought god was.

"Does that mean yes?" I asked, taking a breath and holding it.

She looked back at me, her eyes staring deep into my little brain. "Do you want me to be?"

I exhaled slowly. "Good question." It was. A really good question. I hadn't really thought about what I wanted god to be. Not in that sense. But I would have wanted a god that would ask good questions.

Did god want me to acknowledge that it was a good question?

But I didn't want god to be a sexy woman in a nice house. That seemed a) misogynistic, b) insulting to the man I thought I was, and c) a tad on the indulgent side.

"No."

"Why?"

This had gone from me wanting to ask a few questions to me answering a bunch of them. I reminded myself that if I ever went back to normal life, to remember to ask more questions and dish out fewer answers. "I guess it seems a little selfish. A little immoral. A little obvious. A little tricky." I shrugged. "A little misogynistic? I don't know—something seems off."

"Why?" she asked, obviously confused.

"Well, I feel like when it's god I'll know it's god and I won't be wondering if it's the devil."

"Really?" She seemed surprised, which made me question my own logic. And everything I ever thought about god. "Some gods are devils to some. Some devils are gods to some. Of course."

She did have a point. God would. So would the devil.

Damn it.

"I don't know," I answered. "Maybe you are. Can't you just tell me though?"

She smiled. "You should try the burger."

The damn burger. What was with the burger? I sighed, this time a little irritated. I wrapped my fingers around the burger, squished it in order to better fit it in my mouth, watched some grease squeeze out on the white plate—the first unclean thing to appear in the house since I'd been there—and I took a bite.

It was delicious. A great burger. Juicy, tender everything that makes a burger a burger. Not a good fast food burger but a good, organic beef, gourmet burger. "Delicious," I mumbled while chewing it, and wondering why the hell I was eating a burger in heaven and not feeling better about it.

"Have one more bite." Her sexiness was wearing off with the continual orders to eat a burger, I'll admit.

But I obliged. It did taste good. Another bite, same expansive, gorgeous flavors. "Yeah," I mumbled again. "Delicious."

"Is it a burger?" she asked.

I actually rolled my eyes.

"Is it a burger?" she asked again.

If I was in heaven, I wasn't sure I was going to like it. Maybe it was hell. *Shit, hell is real. But it's not like we think. It's everything we think we want in life and we have to live with it forever and learn that it's not what we actually want. Oh no, this is going to be terrible. An eternal lesson in misplaced desires. Shit.*

Wait, I've already been to hell and it's not like this though.

"Is it a burger?" she asked again.

"What do you mean, is it a burger? You just told me to eat a burger," I said, a little frustrated, and already dreading an eternity in my dream house with my dream girl.

"What is a burger?" she asked, smiling. I wondered, for the first time, if she was a robot from the future. Some kind of supermodel robot whose system needed to be rebooted or upgraded.

"What is a burger?" I asked, repeating the question just so she could hear how dumb it sounded coming from someone else's mouth.

"What is a burger?" she repeated, just so I could know she was serious, even if she was malfunctioning.

"Well." I figured I would play along with the game. "An all-beef patty, surrounded by bread, and a host of other condiments and or ingredients. I mean a burger can be all kinds of things. Did you know I used to work at a very nice burger establishment?"

"What about a vegetable burger?" she asked, completely ignoring my questions.

"Like a veggie patty?" I asked, still making sure I was supposed to be playing this game.

"Is it a burger?"

"Okay," I sighed. "Right, I guess it's a patty, surrounded by bread and a host of other things."

"What is a patty?"

"Good Lord …" I mumbled. "Are you serious?"

She smiled.

"I don't know. I guess meat or beans or something all shoved together in some kind of burger-looking thing." *Who the hell knows what the correct definition of a patty is?*

"You don't know?"

"Not technically," I said with a raised voice. "I mean, it's a burger. You know one when you see one."

"Seth," she said, suddenly stern. "This is made from plants. And the humans who made this burger started with a simple question. 'Why does meat taste like meat?'"

I lifted my eyebrows.

"They asked what gives it flavor and aroma and what makes it handle and cook like meat? And they set out to answer this question with science and plant-based ingredients. They ended up with a burger patty that bleeds even though there is no blood."

I looked. It did seem to be bleeding.

"Do you want it to be a burger?" she asked.

I frowned.

"Do you?"

"I guess?" I managed to answer.

"Many people have tried to make plant-based burgers in order to solve the problems of climate change, carbon consumption, and ethics. As a result, they have made something that does help with those problems but will never attract someone who prefers meat."

Yes, I was getting a burger lesson from the model.

"Others, however, set out to make the best burger on the planet. A burger that meat-lovers would prefer over actual meat. And they did."

I nodded and frowned and looked confused.

"They have solved a problem while refusing to compromise what people want."

I nodded slowly.

"They have satisfied the desire in order to satisfy their goal."

"And that's pretty awesome?" I was getting the feeling she was implying that it wasn't. "Wait, is it? What's it mean?" I pointed toward the burger, still sitting on the plate where I had left it with its veggie blood coming out of it.

"Our desires are the gatekeepers." She stopped and looked toward the windows.

I looked outside as well. Still the same perfect sunset.

"There is a bedroom upstairs. Do you desire me?"

The switch of gears was a bit sudden but let's just say I wasn't paying attention to the sunset anymore and I was back to trying to decide what was happening to me or being done to me, or testing me.

She walked closer to me and grabbed my hand. It was warm to the touch, and her touch was evocative in nature, calling me somewhere I wasn't sure I should go. Somewhere I had been called before in life. I could smell it.

But it wasn't nearly as obvious as it had been. This felt better. Much better.

"Am I dead?" It felt like an important question.

"Why does that matter?" She seemed to imply it didn't. She squeezed my hand and put her nose against my cheek. God, it felt good whether it was stereotypical or not. It didn't matter. It never does.

I resisted and started to think.

Why does it matter if I'm dead?

What is life?

What does a burger have to do with any of this?

When is this all going to stop?

Why am I even thinking when there is a Swedish supermodel literally breathing down my neck, ready to take me to some kind of dream bedroom with the sun setting over hills and a pool we could relax in after …

"I mean, if I'm dead, well … it seems like I can't make a mistake?"

I half asked and half told-her-so-that-we-could-get-to-it. I just needed permission.

She smiled without confirming or denying my logic.

I could see her naked body with mine. Her chest against mine. Our skin sliding together thanks to a thin layer of sweat. Her moans and gasps for air. I lifted my hand and touched her soft hair, moving it away from her lips before touching my own lips to hers and opening my mouth passionately and sensually.

She pulled away, apparently to speak. "That is interesting logic you have. Where did you learn that?" she asked. She touched my hand again, lightly, sexually. I could feel the energy pulsating from her touch into my entire body.

Uh, from everyone?

"Wait, so am I dead or not?" I asked again.

Please just give me permission to do this. Hell, I don't need permission. Let's do this.

She didn't answer. Instead, Rachel popped into my mind. She had hurt me. Worse than I had hurt her. Gwen was trash and Jaden wasn't. She had given him lingerie … I had never given Gwen anything close to lingerie.

I deserved this moment. Rachel deserved to feel what I felt and I deserved to feel what she felt.

"Fuck it," I said. "Who cares if I'm dead or not? I can't take this."

Before I could lean in to kiss her again, she was leaning in to kiss me. Before I could wrap my hands around her body, she was wrapping hers around mine and pulling me in tight.

It *was* heaven.

I could breathe again. The rush was sudden and almost caused me to pass out, ironically, as though I was drowning on what I needed to live. I gasped and took in lungfuls of air, like one drinks water when they are desperately thirsty. It's so cold and refreshing and quenching that it hurts. But it's worth it.

"I'm sorry." Ehs spoke from near me. I was lying on short grass and staring up toward a dark night with clouds and moonlight. "I should have warned you."

"Warned me?" I gasped, now trying to recalculate my location and or dimension and or life status. "That would have been nice."

Stars were poking holes in the sky. Closer to ground level were some kind of stadium lights creating daylight in the darkness.

"What the hell was all that?"

"What?" He seemed genuine.

"Why am I lying here?"

"I think you passed out."

I could hear people cheering. There was an announcer of some kind.

"But the woman and house?" *Tell me that wasn't real.*

"You must have been dreaming. Went too long without a breath." He moved closer to me. "There's something else I want to show you." He reached down to pick me up off the ground.

"But …" I didn't want to get up. It felt much better to lie there and reminisce.

He didn't care much about what felt better for me and I didn't have time to think about it either. Instead, Ehs yanked me up to my feet and I tried to stand, dizzy, looking more like a newborn deer than a human.

I gained some semblance of life and immediately noticed a bunch of kids playing soccer nearby. Parents were yelling at them on the sidelines.

A kids' soccer game? Oh no. Can I go back to her?

THIRTY

We watched two teams running away from us on an artificial turf field somewhere in the world. The field was lit nicely and the air was probably cold, but I couldn't feel it.

"Seriously?" I asked, still reeling.

Ehs tilted his head like a lion would at a mouse. A very slight sense of entertainment. "Yes?"

"I've been to enough of these," I nodded, feeling riled up somehow. Probably because I was on a soccer field instead of inside a modern piece of perfect architecture and a modern piece of perfect woman. "I coached football, remember? I don't need to see this one."

"Of course, you know the gods of sport well. No need for apologies," he answered, which had me wondering if I had apologized. "You seem agitated."

I took a deep breath, the kind that makes sure that you can actually fill your entire lungs with oxygen if you want to. I had to do another one, because the first one didn't quite fill them all up. "You know, runs are supposed to be relaxing." I took another breath and closed my eyes, forcing myself to engage with some kind of calm. "Isn't that where I was? I am? For good reason it seems. What are you doing to me?" I inhaled again. Long exhale.

"Me?"

"I've felt like shit for judging some poor dude, wondered why the guy in the suit is all beat up, apparently passed out …" I continued. Inhale. Exhale. "I just hung out with some beautiful woman who tempted me like Delilah in a house that I thought could be heaven and we talked about burgers and now I'm here with you reminding me of the shit that is youth sports."

The lion tilted his head again. "Who was the woman?"

"I don't know!" I yelled, almost as loud as some dad to his kid who was apparently "out of position" on the field. "Did I cheat on Rachel again?" I asked, so quiet it felt like the hum of the big lights was louder.

"Hmm," Ehs nodded.

"Hmm?" I mocked his expression.

"Yes."

"I did?" Confusion was still overpowering me.

"What?" Ehs was locked in some kind of trance and I didn't know for how long.

"Hey!" I yelled. "Do *you* know?" Someone scored a goal and one of the sidelines erupted. We both looked at the fans and players jumping around.

"Know what?" he asked.

"Did I cheat on Rachel?"

He shrugged, indicating he didn't know or care. Or both. I wished I could say the same.

"I'm more intrigued with who she was."

"You don't know?" I pleaded.

"Could have been either side." He looked back at me.

"Either side? Light or dark?"

"There are no other sides that matter." He began to walk away from me.

"So she could have been god or she could have been the devil?"

Ehs stopped walking and turned to face me. "She could have been light or dark."

"Semantics," I said.

"No."

"Fine, which one was she?"

He shrugged. "I don't know. Do you see more or less?"

"I don't know!" I yelled, beyond frustrated, moving into nervous breakdown. "I ate plants that tasted like a burger."

"Then you can't know whether it was illuminating or blinding. But gods and devils have been known to do both, depending on your perspective, of course."

"Once again, thank you for the philosophy lesson. But it seems pretty important that we humans are able to tell which we're dealing with."

"It could be." Ehs started walking again, toward the field where the game had resumed. "But not to me. And not as important as you would think—not in the way you think." He turned around, as though irritated I wasn't following him. "Are you coming?"

I looked away to the side, hoping someone would be there to receive my *can you believe this guy* look. There wasn't. So I, of course, followed him. What else was I going to do? Just like I followed her, I followed him. Just following everyone around.

"Did I cheat on her?" I yelled again at him, some ways in front of me.

He stopped and turned around. "You are on a run," I heard. Then he mumbled something under his breath that probably meant I wasn't on a run. I didn't care.

I felt relief and stopped for a moment to bask in it. *I couldn't have cheated on Rachel then.* And a new wave of anxiety that had me catching up to him as he waited.

"Rome survived on two things." Not the words I had expected from him but we were obviously moving on while we walked.

We arrived at the goals closest to us, and Ehs walked directly through them onto the field. The teams were at the far end, where from what I could tell, most of the game was taking place. I didn't know the score but the red team was definitely controlling the game.

"I didn't know that." I had stopped at a white net, not sure that I could walk through it and still aware that you don't walk on a field when kids are playing.

"You're fine," he argued from farther away. "Follow me."

And so I stepped through the net onto the field, moving very slowly to watch my feet pass through what they should not have been able to pass through. I looked down to watch my legs do the same.

The feeling and sight captured all of my attention. So much, I walked back through it a second time. I thought of my dream girl—or devil—again and tried to remember how far we had taken things and whether I should even carry the experience or not since I was apparently on a run somewhere and none of it had actually happened.

Mu.

"So," Ehs continued, walking toward midfield, ignoring my shenanigans of walking through a net over and over. There were now players getting closer to him but he didn't seem to mind. We were in obvious view of the parents and coaches, if we were able to be viewed by anyone, which we were not. "Rome survived on bread and games," he said, much too loud for how far away he was.

He stopped at midfield and turned to face me. I arrived, eventually, walking slowly like a kid follows a parent to the dentist. The two of us were standing in the middle of kids running, the soccer ball passing all around us and sometimes players running directly through us.

"Food and entertainment. That's all they needed." Ehs smiled as a bunch of hyped-up parents started yelling at their kids to *push the ball* and *center* in case their kids suddenly forgot how to play soccer. "Do you know why Rome fell?"

"Well." I was staring at number 10. She was a good player. Maybe the best on the field. Powerful, confident, smooth, she was dribbling the ball up, controlling the defender, even though the defender didn't know she was being controlled. A sign? "Rome? No." I had some ideas but I wasn't really up for expressing them when I knew he didn't care what my ideas were or that they had probably been taught to me by him, through some kind of transitive property.

"They suffocated themselves, under the weight of their own boredom." Ehs followed the ball as it passed around him and then through him, followed by a few players and more excitement and cheers from the stands. In fact, things were getting crazy.

The black team was actually on a breakaway and setting up a scoring opportunity. This meant that there was a tremendous amount of coaching that needed to happen from parents—from both sides. And they provided it.

"Once they lost the games, they didn't know what to do. There was no Netflix, or television, or kids' soccer then. What were they supposed to do? Just sit and watch the flowers bloom and the water flow? Were they supposed to find the wonder in a field of wheat? Were they supposed to find play at a market? Were they supposed to find life in their life? In living? What fun is that? They needed the fight, the competition, the rising."

The black team had it. Two-on-one. Given my ability to instantly determine which side I was rooting for based on appearance and parents' reactions, I was pulling for the black team. They weren't as good and they needed a goal.

The pass was perfect and the finish was even better. Goal. I found myself smiling for people I didn't know existed five minutes earlier. The sideline erupted with cheers and high fives and proud moms and dads and grandparents.

The players were jumping up and down too and the keeper reluctantly, and angrily, kicked the ball back toward us at the middle. I ducked as it went overhead even though I didn't need to.

"Great shot," I muttered, also out of habit.

"Yes," Ehs responded.

As the teams gathered at midfield, the scene changed.

We were suddenly in a small open space of desaturated grass closer to the arena I had seen earlier. It was almost next to us, making me wonder if we were in Rome, suddenly. Hundreds of arched window ways, huge columns, old stone. The arena, however, was not a relic or ruin. It was well cared for. And there were roars coming from its insides, the sound of cheering and applause, making the noise the parents had been making moments earlier seem like a whisper.

The lawn we were on was surrounded by blocks of buildings that resembled an old missionary compound built in some third world country in the eighties: cinder block, simple, and ugly. Whoever had built it had not thought about aesthetics for even a second. It was not made to look good. It was pure functionality. Although I wasn't quite sure what the functionality was as I looked around. There were no windows or doors, besides one, that I could see.

Whatever was happening in the arena had people going crazy. I assumed it wasn't a goal they were cheering. I looked toward the massive structure towering up toward the sky, built by someone who cared immensely about the way it looked. It was gorgeous. Imposing in scale and detail. I stared for a moment and soon realized that it was connected to the ugly building that was surrounding us. "What is all of this?"

He nodded as though he answered me. "I'd like you to go through that door." He pointed toward a set of metal doors, painted the cinder block color of the other building. "You'll be safe. But you need to see it. It's part of this area."

"Do I have to?" I looked toward the doors and back to Ehs.

"You don't have to do anything," he responded calmly. "But it will benefit you."

"And I'll be safe?"

"Yes," he said with conviction, glancing back toward the arena and back toward me. "I guarantee it. Please." He held his hand out as though he were offering me a bottle of wine.

"Was she a metaphor?" I asked.

He frowned. "I don't know."

"Everything is at some level, right?"

"Please." He pointed toward the door.

I was following a request—not an order, I told myself. That meant something, for some reason. I cautiously took a step toward the doors, remembering that I could leave any time I wanted. Ehs motioned me further with his hands and chin.

With some trepidation, some anxiety, and some curiosity, I entered the building, quickly and with a courage that seemed unlike my normal.

I realized, as the doors shut behind me, that I had entered an insane asylum. Ehs had just coerced me into one of my worst nightmares. As he should have. I belonged there for all kinds of reasons—too many to count in the last few days alone—including trusting him and walking through the doors like he had told me to.

THIRTY ONE

Up to that point, I had falsely believed I had a pretty good grasp on what fear was or was not, given all of my conversations around it. Given my experience with it.

I realized in that moment that I'd never been truly afraid of anything. Along with that came the realization that no cliché or mind trick or self-talk was going to help me in any way.

I simply couldn't breathe.

Literally. I couldn't breathe. The doors shut behind me, I noticed the long, dark hallway lined with black doors and small windows in them, had time to think *This place is not cool*, and then it hit me.

It was almost instant. I fell to the ground grasping at my throat as though that would help. If there is no oxygen, there isn't anything you can do, whether you grasp your throat or not. I might as well have been in outer space.

There was only one thought in my head: death. Whatever death looked like or felt like, I would trade it for what I was feeling at that moment. But it was not only physical pain—there was a sense of suffocation of spirit. Of me. I had never realized, up to that moment, that the deeper me lived on something. It needed interaction with some kind of life, some kind of awareness that something is happening or about to happen in the next ten seconds or ten years that might be worth being around for, and it needs a sense—maybe minute—but a sense of worth of some kind.

As my lungs grasped for oxygen, my identity grasped for what fed it. There was nothing. Whatever sustained my spirit or soul or deeper self was as absent as the air that sustained my body.

Then I remembered love. I remembered what it felt like to love and I wanted to love.

I want to love something. I thought of Rachel.

And I started to breathe.

As a young woman with a severe illness once told me, you can empathize but you can't understand. I learned later that I probably couldn't even empathize, given that I would only put her data on my structure and think I could understand her structure. I don't know if anyone will truly understand what I felt. Some would call it empowerment, some would call it a miracle, and some would call it a different kind of chemical.

Whatever it was, breath came with it. With breath came a desire to live. The room somehow knew it. I had survived its gauntlet and earned its trust somehow.

I was back.

I was shaken and stirred but holding on. Curious enough to continue, hesitantly. Interested and intrigued enough to push fear out of the cockpit. Something told me it wouldn't happen again. I held on to that and began to walk down the very dark hall.

Thrillers get us on that edge. The anticipation of shock. Any … second … it's about to happen. Our pulse races, our knees curl up into our chest. Riding those rails is immensely fun and terrifying in all the right ways.

Walking the hall, I was living that edge. My eyes were darting from spot to spot, my heart pounding, my breathing still heavy, my body trying to get its grip on oxygen reentering my lungs and on life reentering my soul. It was the work of birth: bloody and painful. But I persisted to the first door to see if something new could arrive.

It took every bit of strength I had to peer into the window.

What I saw was not what I was expecting. The room was simple enough. Four walls, a nice window, a couch, all in shades of gray. There was no padding, no chains, and no rusted-out gurneys with spilled blood, like I had been expecting from every horror movie I had seen. In fact, it seemed nice.

A man was sitting on the couch. He was dressed in a suit and holding what looked like an iPad on his lap, sliding his fingers along the screen. He seemed content enough and I pressed my nose up against the glass, trying to figure out why I didn't find the psychopathic murderer I'd expected to be in the room, wearing jagged lipstick, jumping around hysterically and yelling out profanities.

I continued to stare, and he continued to not notice me. There was no bed, no toilet, no other furniture save for the couch. The window had no bars but it was high enough that no man, or woman, or human, could reach it.

In that sense, I suppose, it was a cage.

The man appeared to be my age. He had a slight beard, and his full head of hair was swept backward and short on the sides. His skin, hair, and eyebrows were a rich ebony with a few streaks of gray like thin clouds at twilight. He wore a dark shirt and dark pants with bare feet. It was then I saw the chain. A black chain wrapped around his ankle and laid across the floor before entering the wall. Oddly, it seemed to disappear into the wall instead of being attached to it.

He still had no idea I was watching. I wondered why he needed a chain in a cage. Rabid maybe.

I tapped on the glass with my finger. If I was in a zoo, I could at least let the animal know I was there.

He looked up immediately. It took a moment but his expression went from somewhat normal to deathly frightened—a sporadic change from one panicked expression to another. That was more what I had expected and I backed away from the window, afraid what might come next.

Within seconds he lunged for the glass. His fingers smashed against it, his face staring through the window at me. I could hear the chain rattle against the floor and see his teeth in front of me, on proud display as if he thought of himself as wolf more than human.

"What are you doing?" he yelled frantically. "Are you crazy?" The question was as ironic as they get. "Run!"

He said that last word with such force and opinion and strength that I did. Instantly. I ran to nowhere … just away from him, settling into a space of wall between doors. After staying for a moment, a new grain of courage emerged and I peered into another window.

The room was the same as the previous one in some ways—four walls and a window. But it was larger, maybe twice the size, and there were pews in the room, all facing away from me and the window I was looking through toward the front and a cross. At the foot of the cross was another man, or so I thought. But the more I stared at him, I realized he looked identical to the man I had just seen. I squinted, hard and intentionally, as though that would change things. It didn't. The chain was still there, attached to his leg.

I had only stood at the window a few moments before the man started to look to his side in a way that made me nervous. He was obviously anxious, as though he could feel me watching him, which made me feel like someone was watching me. I looked on all sides of me but there were only more doors and a long empty hallway.

He eventually turned completely around, revealing that he was either an identical twin or the same man. There were no doors in the wall that would have indicated any way to get in and out.

His expression was the same as I'd encountered moments earlier. Fear and panic and outrage in human form. "What are you doing!" he yelled, more of a command than a question. "You're losing your mind!

Get out of there!" He looked back to the cross as though it was about to do something and then back to me. "Run!"

I looked around, still expecting something to jump out of the wall and grab me but it didn't. Still, I left the doorway and moved down the hall to a room opposite the one I had just looked into. Just in case they were all connected.

Another room. Four walls. The window. Smaller and containing an ATM with a man standing in front of it. The man. The same man. Same chain. He looked up instantly at me and I moved away.

Another room with a field in it. And him. And the chain.

Another room with what looked like a pharmacy. Shelves with drugs lining them and the same man behind the counter.

Room after room. Scene after scene. The same man. The same words. "Run!" "You're crazy!" The rattling of the chain.

I kept moving and, as I did, the hallway only stretched further. There was no end that I could see on either side. At one point I returned from the direction I had come only to find that the rooms had changed. They were no longer the field and the pharmacy but a funeral parlor and a cubicle. Then a courtroom. And the man was always there, looking at me with his foreboding dark eyes, now expecting me each time I looked, anticipating the crazy man in the window, just as I waited for him. Obviously, one of us wasn't right?

The more I saw him the more I realized that he was not necessarily afraid—as I had first suspected—but worried. There was fear in him, not for himself but seemingly for me.

"Listen," I said as calmly as I could, looking into another door. The setting was a desk with a laptop on it. He was typing and facing the doorway. "I need to know what this is."

He glanced back and forth, quickly. He slowly got up from the desk and made his way toward me, the rattle of the chain echoing off the walls. He was still checking all around him as though there were countless spies on all sides.

"What are you doing?" he whispered this time. "It's not safe for you. Don't you know that?"

"Why?"

"Why?" he repeated incredulously. "Why?" he repeated again, looking around. "Who are you?" He was confused suddenly.

"I'm a visitor," I answered as calmly as I could. "What is this?"

"It's security," he answered. "And you are crazy to be out there!" He said *out there* like it was some rugged wilderness and not a hallway lined with doors.

"Security?" I repeated this time.

He glanced around nervously again. "Yeah, security. It's safe in here."

"Safe?" I looked at the four walls and the high window.

"Are you …" He leaned in close and his breath stuck to the window between us. "Do you know what lives out there?"

"Out where? In the hallway?" I looked on both sides of me and saw more doors and more windows in the doors. If all of them were this man, what the hell was that supposed to mean? I wondered if the fear was going to return or if I would even get out. Or how long the doors lasted. I looked back into the room. He was right, there *was* a sense of security with the scene.

"The hallway?" he asked, obviously perplexed.

"Yeah." I looked again to make sure it was still a hallway.

"You've lost it, man," he said. "I don't know what to tell you. You can't see the trees?"

"You mean the forest?" I asked, not sure what he was getting at. "I can't see the forest through the trees?"

"No," he yelled, building himself up. "No, there are trees all around you! You're practically in its lair."

"What?" I responded, my energy rising as his did. "I'm in a hallway with thousands of doors!"

"You're surrounded by trees! It's out there!"

"What is?!"

"Her! The beast! The snake! The monster! Kid, you're crazy!" He was screaming now at the top of his lungs and my own heart was pounding.

"Listen, I don't know what you're seeing but I'm not in a forest. I'm in a hallway looking at you in a room with a desk. I've seen you in all kinds of rooms. What are you doing in there? And why are you chained?"

"Chained?" He breathed out a heavy, exasperated breath and closed his eyes, forcefully calming himself and, obviously, at his wits' end as to what to do with me. A feeling I had lots of empathy for. "Listen to me," he said more slowly and with obvious calm intention. "You're in grave danger, man."

"Danger!" I yelled. "You're in a padded cell." I was exaggerating. A little. "You're insane!"

"You're calling me insane?" he yelled back, grabbing at his thick hair and messing up the style job. "Me?" He was looking around, begging for someone to show up to back him up. "Me? Listen, I'm done. I've got nothing left for you. I've got work to do. I've got lots to figure out for tonight. So, if you don't want to listen, just leave me alone. I can't be distracted by you anymore. I don't know what you're talking about or what reality you're seeing … but"—he leaned in close again, his breath fogging up the gray glass—"you had better start moving and stop talking."

"Wait," I said to him. "Wait."

He lifted his chin.

"Where are *you*?"

"What do you mean?" he asked. "Where am I? You have eyes?" He started to walk away.

"Hey!" I shouted. "Wait. Yeah, I have eyes but I'm obviously not seeing what you are. I see a hallway and you see a forest. Where are *you*?"

He frowned as though he hadn't thought of it.

"I need help," I said, just to make sure he knew that I was definitely the one who was wrong.

"That's for sure." He seemed to look around the room, at the desk and at the walls, before looking back at me. "I was just playing with you."

"What?" I returned. "What does that mean?"

"Man—" He shook his head. "You're in a cell. You have a big chain on your ankle and padded walls." I looked again at the hallway I was in. "The walls are padded," he repeated with all seriousness.

I didn't know what to say. I had never spent time with a certifiably insane person but I had seen enough movies and I felt like he was doing whatever mind games the psychopath usually did to the innocent FBI officer.

I just frowned.

"I'm sorry, man." He seemed utterly serious. "I shouldn't have done that to you. You keep looking through that glass like you want out so bad." He stepped away. "I'm sorry. I shouldn't have lied to you."

"But …" I started.

"I know. Again, I'm sorry. I hope you can get out at some point and enjoy life a little. But it's probably best for everyone that you're in there for now." He almost seemed sad, his breath still fogging up the window between us. "I gotta go. I do have work to do. That wasn't a lie."

I backed away from the glass. "What work?"

"Gotta get to heaven …" He smiled.

"Really?"

"Yeah, man. Oh yeah." He smiled again. Such a nice smile for a crazy man.

"So, what's your room look like?"

"I'm not in a room," he answered. "You are. I'm walking down the hallway and leaving this place. I've had enough. I got work to do. But you keep showing up every time I look in a door on my way out."

I stared at him the same way he stared at me: as though I was looking at someone so insane that I could barely believe it—or someone so insane that you began to think you might be just as insane, which might have been worse. Were we making each other insane? What do you do when you both think the other is so misinformed that it's hopeless?

"Good luck," I said and moved away from the door. He did the same and I could hear his chain rattle across the floor, through the door. I wondered if he could hear mine. I looked down at my ankle to see if I had one and I wondered if he did the same.

"Hey," I yelled out. "What's your name?"

"Thunder."

"Thunder?"

"Yeah, that's my name."

"Which way is the door?"

Thunder pointed, not in the direction I had come but in the opposite direction, almost begrudgingly, feeling bad that I couldn't follow him out.

I ran in that direction, passing numerous doorways and not stopping to look. The hallway seemed to stretch forever in the same pattern, no matter how far I went, until I noticed an open door ahead of me. I slowed down and looked in the door next to me. A classroom. One person sitting at a desk. It was him.

I kept going until the doorway was next. The open doorway. I peeked my head around it, more like a kid than a spy, and saw that it was the courtyard I had entered the building in. Or at least it looked identical. I walked through the door and slumped to the ground to sit down, rubbing what felt like sweat and stress off of my forehead, although I don't think either was removed. I massaged my temples for a moment before I heard more loud cheering, the roar of applause and excitement still building in intensity. It seemed massive, as loud as any football game I had been to, coming from the arena.

It was then I noticed a different section of the arena, stretching up toward the sky not too far away. There were markings in its stone in a language I didn't understand. I assumed I had walked around to the other side, which meant the hallways had been rounded. I looked back only to see the still-open door and then looked up at the arena as the cheering continued.

"Hey!"

I recognized Ehs's voice and turned to look.

"Are we done yet?" I asked.

He smiled a big grin. "Not quite. It's time for the real game. And we have good seats."

I reached up and rubbed my neck. I felt like I needed to massage some kind of knot out of it. Actually my whole body felt like one big knot.

"Let's go."

I followed.

THIRTY TWO

We actually didn't have good seats, which surprised me. We were in the nosebleed section of the coliseum-like structure I had only seen from the outside, up to that point.

A massive oval-shaped arena stretched in front of us, with a large field of red dirt in the middle. The stands—stone benches surrounding the field—were packed with people of all shapes and sizes in the fashion and style I was used to. If I was expecting togas and robes there weren't any. It was like any modern-day sporting event without the kiss cam or video screens to show the kisses on. In an ancient structure.

I noticed there was no sunlight of any kind and looked toward the sky above the arena, noticing the wall for the first time. We were back in the shadow of the wall that rose high above us, in the distance, like a god. That I had missed it up to that point irritated me. I was used to it, even when it was visible and towering over me.

Though there was no sunlight, there did have to be light of some kind because it wasn't dark, like night. Ambient light came from the sky but in a way I wasn't used to. I looked up into the muted blue with a few scattered gray clouds in the distance.

"Where does the light come from?" I asked.

"Everywhere," Ehs answered. "You just don't tend to notice it here."

He was right. I hadn't noticed that either, until that moment. Which made me think about all kinds of things in regards to sunlight and light and darkness, but those thoughts couldn't last long because Ehs soon nudged me with his shoulder, indicating I should look at the arena.

"Couldn't you get us better seats?" I asked. "With your connections."

He laughed. "I don't really come to these anymore. No need. But I do miss them," he said, leaning forward in his seat.

In the arena a massive pole had been erected in the middle of the red dirt, rising at least fifty feet into the air. At the top of the pole was a platform of some kind with a chair on it, almost a throne. That was it. There was nothing else.

"Here they come," Ehs said, pointing to a gate on the far side of the arena. "The priests."

A black gate opened and the crowd began to cheer again. People on all sides of us were raising their fists into the air and screaming as the doors opened.

A man appeared in the door. In a suit. I was definitely expecting a man wearing a black cloak with a *Phantom of the Opera* mask holding a blade. But the man looked like half the men around me, aside from the suit.

He walked out into the arena and lifted his hand into the air. The crowd all yelled.

"He's a priest?"

Ehs motioned toward another gate.

Another man came out, dressed similarly. And then another, then a woman, until eventually there were seven of them, all waving to the crowd like some kind of royalty.

"Wait, those are the priests?" I asked, still staring at the very boring men and very boring women waving their hands around.

Ehs smiled, like he tended to do when he loved my ignorance. "The bankers, the priests, the celebrities, the politicians, the CEOs … names don't really matter much, do they? It's all just a label."

"Well, words do matter, actually."

Ehs shrugged. "Fine. Words matter. They are the leaders of an ideology."

The men and women were now walking around the arena, shaking hands with those in attendance who could manage to touch them, who reached out for them as though they were healers. I kept staring, a little amazed at the amazement of everyone else. It should have been boring to everyone around me and I kept trying to understand why it wasn't.

After they had made their way around, they all ended up sitting in seven chairs in the center of the arena on the front row, staring at the platform.

"The emperors, Seth. Those who run the games."

"The games?" I asked as another group of people emerged from another gate. They were the same boring people, waving their hands to the crowds while the crowds went wild.

"Do you have a cell phone?"

"Yeah," I answered, feeling for it in my pocket even though it wasn't there.

"It's not just the fact that you now carry a port into your soul, it's that you pay money to do it."

I closed my eyes and sighed.

"And it's not just that you pay money to do it. It's that you pay enormous amounts of money to do it. And it's not just that you pay enormous amounts of money to do it, it's that you pay enormous amounts of money to companies that constantly dehumanize workers, pay them as little as possible, or hire them illegally, and you don't care. You let them dehumanize you as well."

"I care."

He laughed.

I didn't respond. Who was I kidding?

"But none of this is actually about money, or things, of course. That would be too obvious."

I looked over at him and saw people standing and cheering beyond him, a blur of figures.

He looked back at me.

"This is about the voices who remind you you don't measure up." He nodded toward the arena where some kind of energy was building. "This is about climbing. This is about using whomever you need to use to get higher. Always higher. Higher with your religion, higher with your economy, higher with your relationships, higher, higher, higher …" He looked back toward the arena, and I followed suit. "Money works well, of course, because of its blinding nature. It's such a tangible illustration of hierarchy that it masks actual worth."

"Oh." He looked over me. "Did I tell you I'm actually beginning to think I was wrong about some of your political leaders?" He smiled.

"What?"

"They are perhaps more subtle than I had first thought."

"Really?"

"They dehumanize, sell more dehumanization, and the very people they dehumanize—all of you—follow along." He frowned. "I didn't think things were working that well."

"Yeah, well, I tried—"

"But—" he interrupted. "That is not my main concern. Small potatoes, as you say. They're revealing Insipid, opening up what was once hidden. Many are seeing the Christians' endless support of parties, and realizing the worthlessness of the religion. I had not anticipated that side effect." He seemed to be in honest thought about the entire political spectrum. Pleased and upset.

"If Jesus were a country, he'd be Sweden, right?"

The crowd went wild and, for a second, I thought they had all heard my joke. Turns out more priests were entering the arena. I felt like they had enough but more just kept coming.

Ehs did laugh. "The atheists run countries much more like the great ones than the religious countries—that's for sure. They also die better—understanding it's a natural process and not a twist of fate from the hands of a god."

"But—"

"Don't be deceived though. The region of the north does much well but it is still seduced by the dictatorship of corporation and money. You're all so vulnerable to anything that will give you power. Once you get a taste, you only become more blind to the power you have always had. And still do."

"Are all the priests out here yet?" I motioned toward the arena.

"Just about. Too many, I agree. But they all love them." Ehs looked at me.

"We're fucking idiots," I bemoaned.

"No." He turned back to the crowds. "Never use that excuse. You're just blind to the light. You're addicted to darkness. Your eyes cower in the light and the shadows are where you are comfortable now. Fighting and killing one another to find worth in the darkness while the light shines brighter and bolder than you could ever imagine." He looked toward the wall. "If only you could see it."

"I have."

"I know."

"It wasn't what I expected."

"You're addicted. It takes time to wean yourself. Some will never be able to live in the light and so they can't live in themselves. Advertise. Consume. Narcissism." He pointed toward the arena.

"Narcissism?" I asked. "Indulgent worth? Isn't it because we feel no worth?"

"Hmmm … they are the same."

"What's that supposed to mean?"

"Narcissists are so easily drawn to her lies. Her winsome, seductive, stroking words of praise, of manipulation, of consumption. Your system would never work without its false promise of redemption and salvation through consumption." He paused, distracted by something, before letting a sly smile creep across his face. "Here we go." He pointed.

I looked. The crowd was in a frenzy now, hyped up like it was the Super Bowl. Screaming, yelling, chanting, it was European soccer (or South American soccer) on steroids. The energy was contagious.

I found myself getting excited and I wasn't even sure why.

The suits, now standings, were definitely not why. Although I did notice some had a more unique flavor of fashion, but it was all high class and purposeful. Boring, somehow.

Gates opened, massive gates on the ground floor of the arena that I hadn't seen up to that point, and, as though a hole had just been blown into the side of a dam, thousands of people began to rush out of the gates. If the energy had been a ten, we were now at twenty.

I could barely hear my own thoughts. I stood to my feet, both to get a better look and because everyone else was. I began to yell, unconsciously. I couldn't help it. People talk about peer pressure but this was peer hypnosis and I wasn't sure they were even my peers.

I was yelling in wild rage and slamming my fists into the air.

People continued to flood out of the gates—there were five openings—and into the arena as fast as they could run without stampeding one another. At first.

Ten seconds in, as I was still chanting, I realized there was more than stampeding going on. There was killing. Murder. Bodies were beginning to gather by the gates and paint the floor in red blood and flesh. The dirt had not always been red, I assumed.

The crowd, at the sight of blood, took on the energy of predators, feeding on chaos and death. There was another level of frenetic, pulsating lust rising … for something.

I put my hands down.

Bodies were piling up even as more people were flooding out of the gates, like a massive faucet of dark water rushing toward the center of the arena but also spilling into every corner and crevasse. They were literally beginning to fill the arena from the floor up, dead and alive.

"How …" I uttered.

"Hierarchy leads to superiority, which leads to contempt, which leads to …" He stopped. "Animals."

I looked at Ehs. I was shocked. I was in awe. I was curious. I was humiliated. I was too enticed and dismayed with my reaction to look back.

Ehs didn't even bother to look my way. He just kept staring, expressionless.

I looked back toward the arena and I saw him. The man from the gas station who had come out with the lottery tickets.

Somehow, amidst the flow of humanity, he stood out to me. I was able, even, to zoom in on his shape. He was running fast, over bodies piling up beneath him, and trying not to slip in puddles of blood. The scene was becoming more horrific, in every way, with each passing second. Limbs and corpses scattered everywhere like some hideous medieval war scene. I could see people strangling other people around them, pushing aside others, and some just racing toward the center as fast as their legs would carry them.

My guy was running. He was much faster than I had thought and he was much more agile than I would have expected. I imagined he had been quite an athlete in high school. I was pulling for him like I always did with the underdog. My heart was racing. He reached a clearing of sorts, near the front of the pack, and was suddenly attacked by three other people—they jumped on his back like wolves on a water buffalo and my entire body shuddered with revulsion as they killed him in front of my eyes with their own bare hands and raw, bloodthirsty hearts.

The crowd was going wild.

Tears began to stream from my eyes, like the people still streaming in from the gates. I had never seen such violence and mayhem from my own creatures. I felt cold just watching, colder still that they were me.

Do I have this in me?

Then I saw him. The man in the suit whom I had seen come home to his wife, beaten and bruised but meeting quotas. Again, somehow he stood out to me—I don't know how. He was already lying dead on top of other bodies, smiling, as though he died knowing he had, at least, tried.

And then I saw parents from the soccer game. And then I saw kids and elderly, some dressed in suits and ties and others running in athletic shorts. The entire spectrum of humanity was there, still flooding out of the gates to their deaths.

It was Normandy but there was no enemy to kill, no great cause to die for, no purpose, at least not that I could see. It was simply carnage and chaos, death and destruction on a level that I could not have ever imagined nor did I ever want to.

I looked to Ehs again. He was as stoic as I had ever seen him, like an apathetic carving of stone. He refused to look at me but simply continued to stare straight ahead.

I had no words to speak and even if I had I'm not sure it would have been possible to hear them above the roaring of the crowd.

I looked back to the arena. I couldn't keep my eyes away. Bodies were everywhere, in some cases piling onto one another in ways that reminded me of old footage of concentration camps I had seen. Just bodies, one on top of another, as though they had never been human—and to those that had put them there, they were not.

I fell to my seat and threw up on the ground in front of me. I felt the hand of Ehs on my back, trying to comfort me somehow, and yet insisting that I watch at the same time. His hand felt as cold as the air and the chants that were now making their way from my ears into my heart.

I looked up again.

If the people running had resembled flowing water earlier, their shapes were now a still pool. Bodies were stacked everywhere—in fact, the people that were still alive were now maneuvering the bodies into more piles. There were teams of people, I could see, working together like some kind of maniacal psychopathic gangs with no ability to feel.

The crowd was still enthralled with the entire scene and the "priests" were seated and sipping on some kind of wine while picking at plates of food that had been set before them.

I leaned over and vomited again, hoping that every last element of the scene could leave my body as easy as my digestive juices. But they did not and could not.

I couldn't watch any longer. I sat in my chair and looked toward the ground, trying to recover breath, soul, and my own humanity.

My senses were overwhelmed and began to shut down. The noise began to fade into nothing. My mouth became dry and tasteless and my body felt numb. I closed my eyes as their ability to focus, even on my feet and the ground in front of me, faded.

I held my head to keep it from falling and stayed that way for some amount of time. It could have been three seconds or it could have been three hours. I'm not sure I had the ability to monitor time.

But Ehs nudged me and awoke me from my coma.

The crowd was like a nuclear explosion—it was the calm before the blast that would remove even the oxygen. The air around me was stale, cold, and full of death. I hesitated to even breathe it and join myself to the horror that it enabled. Ehs was pulling me to my feet again and I eventually stood as he asked and opened my eyes.

Time had passed, evidenced by how the arena had changed.

The bodies that had been spread across the floor had now been mostly piled one atop another into a massive pyramid around and below the pole, reaching its way toward the platform. People had moved countless bodies from the bottom toward the top, literally climbing over their fellow humans to get higher and higher before being killed by their fellow humans.

The crowd, in anticipation and eerily quiet, was deafening in its own right.

The pyramid of bodies had reached the platform and there were two people standing on top of it. From what I could see, they were the only two people left alive, staring at one another. I immediately recognized one of them: the man from the rooms I had just been in, chained and locked in his cell, warning me to leave. It was Thunder.

Thunder stared at the other man and nodded. The man dipped his head, almost bowing, before Thunder picked him up like a toy, broke his neck, and threw his body onto the top of countless others they were standing on. He then stepped onto the platform.

As though on cue, the crowd clapped its hands in some kind of strange pattern, creating the sound of thunder on all sides of me, before erupting into the frenzy of celebration and cheering that had been happening earlier. The explosion of celebration.

Thunder waved to the crowd from his platform and looked toward the High Priests who were all standing and applauding along with the stands. I looked at the stacked bodies and instantly remembered the strange section of the wall that I had seen earlier: the less-defined sort of pyramid that had stood out from the rest. I now knew what it was.

We were building our own sections of the wall. I hadn't seen a Shadow anywhere, apart from the still one standing next to me. No need for bricks in many places, just our fellow human beings.

I fell into my chair this time, unable to stand or sit. Ehs picked me up.

The next thing I knew I was sitting in the courtyard I had been in earlier. It was quiet again. Dark, still, in the shadow of the wall, but quiet, and the quiet lulled me back into awareness.

Ehs was nearby, sitting on a bench. He stood to his feet and walked closer to me, lifting me up and helping me to the bench where we both sat.

"I'm sorry," he whispered. "I know it was hard."

"What was that?" I managed.

"The truth."

"Where's Thunder?"

"Back in his cell. Although he gained another room today."

"Another room? What does that mean?"

"You only see your chains when you move, Seth." He nodded toward the arena and piles of bodies that I assumed were inside of it.

"He seemed to be moving pretty well to me," I countered.

Am I missing something?

"Some will call it movement, of course. He'll eventually become a priest if he's lucky." He looked up toward the sky. "Well, lucky is what most of you call it."

I gained energy and straightened my back and thoughts. "Was

that real?"

Ehs lifted his brows. "It was true."

"The truth is real," I shot back.

"No." He stood to his feet. "The truth is truth. Only sometimes is it real."

"I can't handle the games right now, Ehs." What could I handle anymore?

"Hierarchy is addicting. It is true. Your addiction to feeling better by taking someone else down is matched only by your resistance to the power and value you already have, that you cannot accept. Because, that would mean they are all equal to you. When you're striving for privilege, equality feels like oppression." He sighed. "You will die to not feel oppressed, smothered by your addiction to it."

And just like that I was standing in the parking lot of the local gas station again in my shorts, running shoes, and shirt. It was not yet dark, though it felt like it should have been. I walked over to the gas station, slowly, unsteady, and unsure.

Two cars honked at me but no one bothered to hit me and no one bothered to see if I was okay. I can't say I would have stopped for me either.

There was a small bench in front of the gas station that I had never seen before but was glad to find. I sat down on it and tried to catch my sanity, and breath. I eventually keeled over, my head in my hands staring at the concrete sidewalk and my neon green shoes resting on it. The color was abundant compared to where I had been and the air felt good to ingest.

"Hey," a voice said. "Are you alright?" It was a rugged voice, one I didn't recognize. A tired voice but compassionate.

I looked up. What little sanity I had felt like it was fleeing fast. It was the man I had seen buy the lottery tickets, standing there in front of me. I assumed I looked like I was staring at a ghost because that's what I felt like I was doing and because he seemed very concerned with whatever I looked like.

"You don't look so good," he said, with a warmth I didn't feel like I had experienced for a long time or would have always reciprocated.

"Yeah," I sighed. "I don't feel good."

"Well," he nodded, affirming that we were all feeling the same way. "Anything I can do for ya?"

I shook my head, blinked my eyes, and ran through a list of questions to make sure I was not concussed.

What year is it?

Who is the president?

What is 7 x 9?

"Were you here earlier?" I asked, only confirming to him what I'm sure I looked like. I was definitely not doing well.

He did not seem to appreciate the question. "Why the hell you care?" he grunted, suddenly not very warm.

"I'm sorry," I mumbled. "I just thought I had seen you here earlier."

He was even less impressed with that line than the one before it. "I don't know what your deal is man, but I'm gonna assume you're just fine and move on with my life. Fuck you, was trying to help," he mumbled, turning to leave.

"I'm sorry," I said. "I'm really sorry." I stood to my feet and reached out my hand. "Thank you."

"For what?"

I had to think. "I don't know. For asking me, I guess. And all I did was ask if you were here earlier. It was rude. I'm sorry."

"Hey." He reached out his hand and shook mine. "It's good, man. It's good. Hard day at the office will do weird things to you."

"Yeah … I'm sorry."

"Don't be so hard on yourself. Go buy some lotto tickets—big jackpot right now." He pointed toward a sign that had a huge number on it. "Maybe you'll have better luck than me."

"I'm sorry," I repeated again.

He seemed taken aback, not really sure what to do with me. "For what, this time?"

"Just. Everything."

THIRTY THREE

There is a kind of night that comes rarely but when it does, you can feel it. There is a soothing quality on one end and an uncertainty on the other. Paradox in all its glory.

Rain had been falling at a steady pace for hours. With it a thick fog had arrived and when I woke up in the middle of the night to go to the bathroom, I ended up staring out our second-story window, enraptured by the scene. Well, after I had stared at Rachel, sleeping next to me.

We were surviving again.

Outside the window, the streetlight was doing its best to resist the invasion of darkness and mist but was not going to hold out much longer. The rhythm of the rain was soothing and the road was now holding streams of water, glossy, moving into visibility and then disappearing into the gray toward a storm drain somewhere.

There was therapy in the inability to see too far, a comfort, and a hypnotic quality to the elements moving in and out of darkness and light. A hypnotic quality to the smells of unadulterated nature and the rhythm of the universe.

I absorbed the free counseling of the night after absorbing the charged counseling earlier in the day, and tried to lean into the unknown again, along with the now, even if the now felt unknown and the unknown felt unnerving. This felt better than the tossing and turning and trying to get back to sleep in the middle of the night that I had been experiencing moments earlier.

I even smiled.

I felt ready to return to what would hopefully be a more restful sleep. But upon attempting to go back to my bedroom, I found that I couldn't move. The fog was with me, inside the house, holding me, containing me, more like a web than tiny water droplets. I put more effort into taking a step but the resistance just grew stronger. I took a deep breath and watched the substance surround me, swirling, as though I was in the middle of a storm, albeit a peaceful one.

I closed my eyes for a moment, preparing for a forceful attempt at opening them and waking up—in case I was still asleep—when I heard him.

"G'evening, Seth." It was a deep and consoling voice with a strong Southern accent, warm and inviting.

I opened my eyes to a new scene. Rolling hills. A clear, dark sky with more stars than I had seen in years. The air was as warm as the moonlight. I was immersed in the natural therapy of somewhere.

The silhouette of a man was standing on the hill next to me, staring up at the stars, almost appreciating them.

"Ehs?"

"Excuse me?" The man looked toward me and I could make out long, greasy hair on the sides of his drawn-out face. A nicely combed beard covered the bottom of his head and a blue bandana wrapped tight around the top. A leather vest and patterned shirt filled out his torso, and tight blue jeans and cowboy boots rounded off the whole costume.

"Ehs?" I said again.

"'Fraid not, my friend. But … have a seat." The voice was half country singer and half radio host. The bass tones were grooving and friendly. He took a seat.

"Okay." I sat down too and the short grasses felt warm on my hands and butt. "Where am I and who are you?"

"Me," he chuckled. "Just a friend. We go way back." The voice was money. If he wasn't already getting paid for doing voice-over work for commercials, I was willing to be his agent and find him work.

"We do?" I looked closer into his face, which was hard given the faint light of the moon. Deep wrinkles but friendly dark eyes.

"Well, maybe." He took a worn-out hand and rubbed it through his beard, contemplating something. "Now, as to where we're at … well, why don't you take a look and tell me what you see."

I stood back to my feet, as though it helped me think. It did help me see. I noticed, in the distance, trees. It was a forest. Given that it was night, they were devoid of color: black trunks with dark leaves. Still, the forest grabbed my attention in the way the fog had out my window. It was soothing.

"Seth." He motioned toward the forest. "What do you see?"

"Rolling hills. A forest. A moon. A—"

"No, no. I'm asking you what ya really see?"

"Well." I looked toward the man and wondered if I could record his voice for my own meditation sessions. "I mean, I'm not sure what you're asking."

"Patriotism." He said the word almost like a question. "Are you a patriotic man?"

I looked back toward the trees just to confirm there was no patriotism of any kind to see. "Right," I said with a bit of confusion, not sure if I was answering and not sure I was with someone entirely all there, even if his voice was soothing and his look was like someone who had just won a country music lifetime achievement award.

"What is it?" he asked.

"What is patriotism?" I asked. "You're asking me?"

"Sure," he said, laughing again. "Not too hard now, is it?"

"Are you a friend of Ehs?"

"Well, well." His voice went down another octave, almost vibrating the air. "I don't think so. I do know of him, but let's just say I'm … on the other side."

"You're a Ray?" I asked, staring more intently, looking for some kind of sparkle in the skin but just seeing more leather and finding sparkle on a huge silver belt buckle in the shape of a bald eagle instead.

A gentle, rhythmic laugh, followed by a spit. "No, just a human, for the most part." I noticed the big wad of chew in his cheek.

"Okay, okay." There was no way a human was able to transport me to some other land but maybe I was dreaming. Or it was Ehs.

I decided to roll with it.

"So … what are you asking?"

"Patriotism. What is it?" he repeated, slowly, looking up at me. "Take a look out there." He patted the grasses as though they were alive and he were gathering them like hens and calming them down. "C'mon, have a sit down. Relax a little, alright?"

I sighed and sat down again on the warm grasses, still not exactly sure what was happening, but not exactly worried.

"So …" he said slowly, methodically. "You got sumthin' for me?" A light chuckle.

"Dedication to a nation, I guess. Pride and support?"

"In what … did you say?" he asked.

"A nation."

"Well what's that, Seth?" he asked with a smile exaggerated by all the facial hair above his lips.

"A culture. A people. At best. At worst, nothing, really. A pretend line in dirt."

"Pretend, huh? Well …" He looked out over the hills and to the forest. "Where would you say we are right now, just you and me?" he asked.

I shrugged and looked over the scene again. "Texas?"

He chuckled. "Not quite. But it is *your* country, *your* home.

Your place of birth." He touched my chest with each "your."

There was a warmth in my soul. I was sometimes a critic of my country, but whenever I was away from it, I was always proud to return. I nodded, replaying his words, and wondering if we were near the city I had lived in as a kid.

"And now," he asked, "where would you say we are?"

I studied the hills, the sky, the forest again, but nothing perceptible had changed. "Well . . . It's different?"

"Yes, sir."

"I don't know," I answered.

"Russia."

It didn't look different, but I did feel it. It was subtle but it was not as warm. There was something irritating about it.

"Not quite the same, is it now?" He shrugged. "A little colder?"

I nodded, pretty sure my bias was playing a role in my experience. Like always. Maybe that was his point?

"And now?"

Nothing changed that I could see so I didn't comment. I looked over and wondered how he got his mustache to be so thick and straight instead.

"North Korea."

The feeling that had been subtle was no longer. I felt much less warm, almost anxious, looking around nervously. "Are we actually?" I managed to ask, forgetting the mustache.

"Amazing what some words, as you say, will do, isn't it?" he said. "I might say they're a little more than words, my friend." He smiled. "I think there's sumthin' special about an actual place to call home."

"Are we back?"

"Well, does it matter to ya?"

"Maybe."

"Then sure we're back."

I did feel better, even though I knew there was no reason for it.

"Seth, have ya figured out who I am just yet?" Another gentle smile after the smooth, hypnotizing words in that low-level hypnotic voice. Another spit off to the side.

I took one more look in the moonlight. Thick wrinkles and marred skin from years in the sun. Deep, inviting eyes. The thick but nicely trimmed gray beard and the gentle eyebrows, like two storm clouds resting on the weathered forehead. "No."

And with that, the cowboy vanished, only to be replaced by a man in a white robe, with long, straight hair parted down the middle. The same eyes, although much younger and unblemished skin.

"Jesus," I muttered.

"I'll admit. This is not my best look," he answered in a very clear voice, much more refined and much less appealing. A pure American accent, as though he were an actor from Kansas. "But it's how you might recognize me."

"What was the cowboy thing?"

"Oh," he answered with a smile. "Just an image. I mean, I could do this."

The long hair stayed, as did the general features of the face, but the outfit was now camouflage, with an American flag on the sleeve and thick, tan military-style boots.

"What is … I mean?" I stuttered. I stared at the face of Jesus that seemed to match every painting I had seen—which was nothing like the actual face of Jesus, I assumed, but still recognizable. But wearing a military uniform?

"Or maybe this will help you feel comfortable?" he asked with, again, a different voice—a little more rigid and terse. The uniform vanished, only to be replaced by a dark suit with a crisp white shirt. A Rolex watch snuck out from under the sleeve and the same hair brushed across a high-end fabric that hugged the shoulders tightly. A younger face, but still the face of the cowboy Jesus without the weathering. "How's this?" he asked, looking down at himself.

"Well … I mean …" I just stared. It was all like I was witnessing a terrible painting or bad photo editing. It didn't feel right. "I guess I like the cowboy."

The cowboy was back. "Well," he said with his addictive tone and drawl. "That's what I'd figured for ya. Why I showed up as I did the first time."

"Okay." I tried to nod. "Right." The cowboy was the best but that didn't mean I liked him.

"So, tell me, Seth. Why do you think ya felt so different each time?" He looked out at the hills in front of us again. "You say it's just a piece of land. Not to ruffle your feathers but it's never just land."

"Well … I mean … it's home. It's familiar."

"Seth." He chuckled: a very manly and tough chuckle but a chuckle nonetheless. "I think it's more than that. God's Country ain't just two words."

"It's not?" At that point, I was officially confused at Country Jesus and found myself staring at the patterns in his flannel shirt just below his beard.

"The pledge, Seth. Do you know how many other countries include the words 'under god'? Or how many countries include 'in god we trust' on their dollar bills?"

I shook my head. I really didn't.

"Zero."

I went from shaking my head to nodding my head. I'd always imagined a conversation with Jesus as more … enjoyable than the one I was having.

"This place that you call home begun a little differently, Seth. For good reasons. It was started with god at the center. And this place ain't like no other. I'll do whatever it takes to keep god there and to spread that love around the world." He seemed nice but his words were starting to bother me.

"Now I'm no goat. I understand it's not all perfect. But—" He paused and waited for my eyes to leave their investigation of the flannel and look up at his. "It's right. It's good."

I tried to nod, frowning and moving my head very slowly.

"Ya see, I get a bad rap from many. From you." He paused again and probably noticed the flicker in my own eyes. "Humble. Quiet. Meek. Walkin' 'round getting my ass whooped." He paused to spit again. "Well, that ain't the real Jesus, Seth."

"It's not?" I asked.

He chuckled again and looked down at his vest, which he gently pushed aside to reveal two guns on each side of his chest. "This," he said, nodding, "is the real Jesus."

"It is?" I asked. "I mean—"

"Seth!" he said louder, with a bit of force behind it. "Do ya think I don't know?"

"Don't know?" I repeated, a little nervous with Jesus, for the first time.

"The weapons sales. The defense spending. The wars. The power. The collateral damage?" He spoke plainly and his voice made all of it sound more appealing than I wanted it to be. "Do you think I don't know?"

"I guess … no?" I was struggling. "I don't think that?"

Do I?

"God bless America. God bless the troops. God bless." He stared at me with a long, worn-out expression. "Do you think these words are meaningless?"

I no longer knew how to answer Jesus's questions.

You've got me stumped, Jesus. But not for the reasons I had always thought Jesus would stump me. I guess that's good?

"It's an evil world out there, my friend. Have you heard of Hitler? Of Stalin? Of Mussolini? Of Rhodes? Of King Leopold? I could go on and on, Seth."

I nodded, sure that he could.

"I did not come to bring peace." Another spit. "A sword, my friend." He smiled. So nicely. And then looked toward his guns again. "A sword back then, at least. All the same."

I hoped I looked confused and I hoped he would notice.

He seemed to. "I understand this is hard for ya." He reached out and touched my shoulder, like a friend would. "Maybe this will help." He nodded toward the hills and I looked to see why.

It only took a moment.

Night vanished. It was the stunning part of the day when the sky is beginning to show the effects of a sun that has just decided to leave. With dark blues giving way to magical oranges and reds that line the horizon as well as anything that the setting sun touches, including myself and . . . Jesus. His weathered and worn skin looked more weathered and worn in the light. His beard more gray, painted with streaks of pepper. His skin matched the color of desert rocks that surrounded us. He kept staring forward and I soon followed his lead.

In front of us was a massive idol of some kind, made of what appeared to be black stone. It had to be three stories tall. Intimidating as hell. The overwhelming shape, if I had to guess, was a bull, but there were other elements. Huge, massive horns rising up toward the darkening sky. They were more the horns of something evil than the horns of a bull. Purposefully off somehow. Human arms stretched out in front of the bull, with palms facing upward, as though asking for something, or offering praise to something. The hands were higher, making the arms slope toward the bull's belly. In the belly a fire burned. I could smell it quickly: the scorched wood. I could feel it: the waves of heat emanating out even though it was far away from me. It was a good and raging fire inside of it.

The bull's ears were circles of gold. There were silver and gold lines carved into its skin in no recognizable pattern to me.

I was beginning to sweat.

"What is this?" I asked, assuming Jesus the cowboy was next to me.

"You will see," was the answer, but it was not from Jesus. I immediately looked again, only to see Ehs in the shape of James exactly where Jesus had just been. He sensed I was staring at him and he looked away from the idol and toward me with a scheming smile. "Did you enjoy my impersonation?"

I frowned, not sure whether to be comforted or shaken further.

Ehs transformed immediately into the shape of Jesus that I had seen earlier, the same shape that showed up on paintings. Long, parted hair, white skin. "What," he said in his own voice. "You thought this was Jesus?"

Seeing Ehs in fake Swedish Jesus was disconcerting whether I wanted it to be or not. Little did I know what was coming. "What's happening here?"

Ehs gave no answer. His smiled faded and he turned forward again, looking back to the massive cow in front of us, seeming to indicate where the answer would come from.

I heard the chants moments later. They were somewhere close, maybe behind us. Before I could turn, I saw them. An ancient people of some kind, judging from their leather sandals and long cloaks. Those in the lead wore wooden masks that imitated the head of the massive bull they seemed to be walking toward.

My senses were on high alert. Anxious. A dark energy arrived in the air. "I don't like this," I said out loud, in case Ehs wasn't sure.

"Very few do," he said matter-of-factly, still looking forward.

There was some kind of chanting. It didn't take a rocket scientist—or better, an anthropologist—to know what was happening. A primitive sacrifice of some kind to a primitive god of some kind.

I hoped for corn or a goat, but I sensed from the mood and energy of the crowd in front of me that I would not be so lucky. Moments later, I saw the baby and my own energy and mood descended into its own fire.

"No," I said out loud. "I don't want to see this." I suddenly wanted to be with my own children again.

Ehs looked to me slowly with an expression that said more than words ever could. "But you must," he ordered, his words marching in step with the mood of his entire being. "Because it is true."

I willed myself to look forward again.

The chants were getting louder. There were women in the back, and one in particular weeping. I felt tears strolling down my own cheek almost instantly. The tears of her and myself grew larger as the baby moved away from her in the crowd and toward the men up front, wearing the hideous and now, in my mind, evil masks.

"Ehs, I can't do this." I stared at the mother, her arms outstretched and seeming half hopeful her baby would return, half honored it would not. I imagined my own children, which fueled my own sadness.

"Hmm," he uttered, seemingly uninterested in my feelings. "Ironic."

I turned my back as the baby's cries reached my own ears, and the hands of what seemed like the leader of this disgusting group of people. "No. I can't."

Ehs grabbed me by the shoulders and forced me to look. He was not human anymore, somehow. There were too many hands holding me for him to only have two. My shoulders were gripped, my chin was held high, and there was some kind of strange tendrils of fog that began to embrace my body, my eyes even, forcing them open. "You will," he hissed and the words entered into me. I could feel their cold rushing through my blood and somehow overtaking my own conscience.

I would.

And I did. I saw it all. Fortunately, no one wanted to drag it out. Even the priest. There was intense crying and moaning at the pain of such innocence needing to die. I cried at the pain of such ignorance, of humans believing it was necessary.

There were speeches, there were prostrate bodies and open arms to the idol and eventually the baby was placed on the open hands and released. Given the angle of the arms, and whatever substance was placed on them, the baby, quiet suddenly as though even he knew his fate and accepted it, fell into the fire, burned into oblivion along with a portion of innocence I had still had up to that point.

I wanted more than anything to close my eyes but whatever dark wizardry Ehs had over me wouldn't let me and I hated him for it, suddenly, in a way that I had never hated him.

Something held my lips in place as well, preventing me from speaking. I could only cry more tears, their salt reaching my lips.

The group seemed pleased somehow, happy, inside of their grief. I assumed there was more to the show, but almost as though they were performing for me, they left as fast as they had arrived.

As they did, I felt my own ability to control my body return.

"Fuck you!" I yelled out. "Why did you do that?"

"Do what?" he asked with a perplexed expression.

"What are you doing to me?"

"Oh," he smiled. "I'm so sorry, Seth. I didn't make you do anything. This is, I'm afraid, all *your* doing."

"This isn't a game, Ehs."

"Oh," he repeated with an even larger smile. "I don't think it's me who needs that warning."

I wiped away tears and wished I could wipe away the image and the cries and the idol, still sitting in front of me.

"So primitive, isn't it? So barbaric."

"It's fucked up."

"Yes," he hissed suddenly. "Isn't it, though?"

I frowned, still not sure I was supposed to get his point. And then he nodded toward the idol.

I looked and as I did it transformed almost instantly.

Into the shape of a gun. A massive gun, its barrel sticking up toward the sky and made of whatever black and polished stone the bull had been made of. The same arms reached out, nothing changed of them.

And then another group of people came, wearing suits and black dresses. Sunglasses. Modern. I almost recognized them. They were led by more suits, and eventually a child—much older this time—was passed up to the other men in suits who rolled the elementary student into the fire.

Ehs forced me to watch again.

"Hmm," he finally spoke after they left. "So barbaric, isn't it? Feeding the gun god your elementary students."

I said nothing.

Because the altar changed again. It was a massive jet, covered in US Air Force symbols and flags. The same fire. The same hands facing upward. Surrounding it was now a wedding crowd. Wailing, from a different culture.

Then the altar became a flag. Around it was a crowd of soldiers sitting in a circle.

Then it was a cathedral with a crowd of young altar boys surrounding it.

And then it was Ehs, the familiar shape I had come to known, his own arms outstretched, asking for something that I assumed someone was giving him although there was no crowd. And then it was Jesus, in each shape I had just conversed with. And then it was Ehs again.

And then the crowd changed a final time. I was in it. I was a little boy. My mom was dressed in black. It was as though I was watching old footage from my father's funeral that I only remembered through old film footage. Or I had time traveled. Either way I was riveted in repulsion.

I felt a simmer in the bottom of my own blood. "What is this? Why are you showing me this?"

"Who did your father die for?" Ehs asked, back in the form of James sitting next to me.

I stared at him. The simmer getting louder and more violent within me, and more irritating. "Fuck you."

"Hmmm," he nodded. And suddenly he was back to Cowboy Jesus. "For me?" The baritone voice was back but I didn't give a damn.

"Hell no."

"For me?" Ehs asked, suddenly as the traditional Jesus form.

"My dad died for this country!" I yelled, pointing out toward whatever scene was in front of us. "Whatever that meant to him. He left my mom alone and me lonely! For the rest of my life. I never knew him. He died, Ehs! Gone! He believed in equality and justice and fighting evil." More tears. I hadn't thought of my biological dad often but when I did I usually cried for everything I had missed and everything I would never be able to miss because I had never known.

The tips of Ehs's mouth turned into something delicately evil. It was subtle but slimy. "Your father," he hissed, "died for us. For me. For darkness. Don't honor his death by lying to yourself about it."

I lunged at him. I've never lunged at anyone but the smirk on his ugly face was the final straw. I fell into his body and threw him to the ground. I tried to punch at his face but I was not a fighter and he was a warrior. After punching his stomach, fighting against his resistance, and feeling like a little brother fighting a big brother, I found myself facedown in dirt, still tense and with a new pain in my shoulder.

"Violence when nothing else works, right?" he mocked.

"Fuck you! He was my dad! God! My life! My pain! My mother! Let me out. I'm going home."

"I'm sorry," he said with a slow drawl. And his demeanor did change. "I didn't think it would hurt you so much."

"What the hell did you think? You don't care."

"I do," he said quietly. "More than you think."

"Okay, well, I mean … I get it, sort of. But this isn't right. At some point, we have to protect—"

"Protect?" he screamed, almost with a high-pitched ring behind it, sending shivers through me. "Protect?" he asked much more quietly, allowing me breath again.

The rolling moonlit hills returned, basking us in some kind of welcome calm again.

"The end is coming, Seth." The silhouette of James was resting calmly on the hill next to me again. Somehow, there was peace again.

I sat still. Breathing. Trying to calm. I don't know how much time passed as I tried to process and center whatever was happening to me. Within me.

"The end," he eventually repeated.

"End of the world? Now?" After the previous experience, I wasn't sure if he was kidding or not. But, if the world was ending I had to get back to my family.

He laughed and it reminded me of the days when he used to laugh more. I wanted to laugh but couldn't quite let it escape.

"End of the world," he repeated. "I haven't even been able to brag about that one. Rapture is one of my personal favorites. All me. No one believed it would work when I came up with it." He looked off somewhere, reminiscing about some dark world creative meeting, I presumed.

I still couldn't smile.

"Armageddon. Give them an idea and they will make it happen. Look at them lust after war and violence as though it will save them. So, of course they place it as their final hope! You see it, don't you, Seth? Tell me you can't help but see it."

I nodded, not necessarily wanting to agree but trying to understand what I could.

"I'm going to miss you, Seth," he said softly. "I am."

"What was all that? What are you saying? Doing? I … just … Jesus? Did that baby really die? What? I …" Words were not flowing easily.

"Seth, it's my end. I could have shown you more zones, sections, walls, but I figured you have seen enough of piles of darkness and suffering humanity. There's no reason to show the violence and empire of your country that we use to guard it all."

"What?"

"I hoped your American Jesus might make more of an impact," he said in the deep Southern voice that I had grown to like, even if I was still processing what it had said. Or Ehs had said through it.

"I'm not sure I even get it all. Except you shredding my country?" The hills were soft and sweet and I looked out to them again.

"No," he said quickly, holding out his hand. "No. Violence and destruction in the name of empire. Yours just happens to be winning right now and justifying it all in the name of your gods. You are our current favorite, which makes you the worst."

"The worst?"

"Your history is nothing but oppression through force. It continues today. Millions, Seth, if you add them all up. You've killed millions while asking for a blessing that your prophets and teachers already explained has come—mostly to the ones you kill." He looked off into some space ahead of him. "And will never come—to those that do the killing. Don't feel bad. Your country learned well from her mother, who learned from hers, who learned from hers. The ways of violence and empire have been passed down nicely."

"We've done a lot of good."

"Your point?" he asked.

"Well …" I wasn't sure.

"It's never all bad. If it were, no one would trust it. The least amount of light to justify the worst of darkness. That's our goal," he said plainly and without emotion, although it stirred plenty in me. "There is only one thing you need to return with. I will tell you simply. My days of stories and speeches are done." He looked up to the stars again. "You pledge … to me. You fight … for me. You kill … for me. You are *our* army."

The words felt like their own kind of army raping and pillaging my interior. "Ehs … my god, I know people—"

"You cannot serve two masters," he interrupted, and then waited for me to look at him. "We make sure you are not tempted." His form took on that of Jesus in camouflage one last time for me.

"I know good people!" I continued. "Who have …"

"Seth. Stop. We are not talking about people."

"I don't know what you want me to say." I didn't and it was probably best for me to stop trying.

"Preferably nothing." He smiled. "My end is near."

I just continued to look confused. "What end?"

"It happens to us all. Decay. Destruction. Death." He looked down and picked at some stems of grass.

"I'm sorry," I said with as much kindness as I could muster, still feeling emotional whiplash and wondering if we would all be better off with him dead.

"I suppose. This will be my last."

"Last?"

"Seth." Ehs looked with soft eyes. Softer than I had seen in him. "I hope I was able to help her in my final days. I hope I helped you see as well."

"You have." I turned to face him directly. "Thank you," I said sincerely. "Even if I'm still trying to comprehend it."

"Thank you," he returned. "But we are not quite done."

"Good." I wasn't quite ready to say goodbye even if I still was carrying anger at his words, his deception, and everything it was doing to me.

"Penuel. We will meet there."

"We will? The three of us?"

"Yes," he nodded, not as excited as I would have anticipated.

"This is amazing?" I did feel some kind of jolt. "This could be it!"

"It might be," he muttered, still without much energy.

"When?"

"You'll know."

"Okay …"

"Aren't you happier about this?" I asked, trying to find my own well of joy to tap into.

"The Kingdom of Heaven," he said, somewhat out of the blue but with grave sincerity. "The Tribe of Light. The only one that matters to us. Any other is narcissism in group format. Your nation is especially dangerous." He sighed. "Your tribe must die—you must lose your tribe in order to find the tribe of life. You will not find it, clinging to any others."

I closed my eyes, too exhausted to argue.

"Be careful of the nightmares we sell to you as dreams."

"Seth," Rachel said, still half-asleep from the bedroom. "Are you alright?"

"Huh?" I moaned, my breath filling up my bathroom window with steam. "Huh?"

"Are you alright?"

"I don't know if I am, honestly. Can I just hold your hand?"

"Seth ..." Rachel was sitting up. "Of course, come here." Her voice carried such grace I felt tears coming to the surface again.

"I need you, babe."

"We need each other. I think that's why we're fighting like we are." She leaned in to me and I leaned in to her.

I felt like a baby, clinging to Rachel's hand like I had not clung to it in a long while. It was the only anchor I had, as I eventually found sleep again, but not before first getting up to give my daughter a kiss on her sleeping forehead.

PART THREE

THIRTY FOUR

From that day forward I had a nasty kink in my shoulder. If I was driving I would feel pain pulsating down my arm. Sitting at my computer I would contort myself into all kinds of shapes as I tried to relieve the pressure.

It hurt like hell and I complained a lot about it.

Ehs was off the radar and I blamed him for the kink. I blamed him for lots of things but the kink especially. It was a physical reminder of him, my renewed mental images of Jaden and Rachel having fun together, and my regular nightmares of children being burned alive.

Maybe he was busy. Maybe The Seers were watching, maybe he was just giving me time to heal. He had said the end was coming and I knew it wasn't over yet. Everything inside of me told me there was more. That I would see him again. Maybe only one more.

Rachel had been gone on a weeklong trip and the trip contributed to my nightmares, hallucinations, and general discomfort with life. She was leading a yoga training of some kind. Jaden was there, of course. His wife was there as well, whom I had met and been happy to find stunningly attractive—but I still had fitful dreams that clung to me after waking and throughout the day, like my grandmother's terrible perfume used to.

I had a few phone calls with Rachel while she was gone, which never went especially well. Jaden, she had told me, felt terrible and had not expected the reaction. I, in turn, blew up that she was even talking to Jaden about it.

I blew up at everything, all the while with images of that beautiful Swedish woman in my own head. All while wondering if I had actually done to Rachel what I feared she would do to me again.

I was a mess. Rachel knew it, I knew it, and I felt like Rachel was wearing a countdown timer on her head that was slowly ticking off the seconds she was going to put up with me and my vague criticism, lack of empathy, cowardice, and general malaise about life.

The shoulder wasn't helping.

Rachel made an appointment for me to go and see her massage therapist. I don't know why I couldn't make my own appointment but a) I don't like to see doctors and b) Ruby (her massage therapist) and I have not always had the best of experiences.

Ruby is not like most massage therapists. Ruby is the kind of person that massages your calf and says, "I didn't know your father was sick but it's obvious you're carrying it in your calf."

I've come up with all kinds of things I want to call Ruby, usually followed by the realization that my father hasn't been doing well and everything I think seems crazy about her is also usually true. Not to mention, given what my life had consisted of for the past few years, I had about as much right to call someone crazy as the pope does to make fun of someone for being Catholic.

Ruby says she reads energy. Since I had spent a few weeks seeing energy, I believed her. But, if I'm honest, the only thing more vulnerable than having someone put oils on your body while you're in your underwear is having someone do that who can also read your energy.

It takes a lot of energy to hide your energy but my shoulder was really hurting and Rachel made me the appointment and … I was a little curious to see what my energy was saying after hanging out with, and getting to know, a Shadow.

Let's be honest, I knew what my energy was saying, I was curious to know if Ruby was going to pick it up. It was an experiment of my own sanity, my own faith, and maybe she could give me some wisdom on who was winning the battle between light and dark.

Upon arrival, we talked about greens and how healthy they were. We talked about cupping and whether or not I was okay with it.

Hell yes.

We talked about the Olympics and how people freaked out that some of the athletes had been cupped.

Why?

And then I was facedown, feeling good. We talked about yoga, we talked about Buddhism, we talked about the benefits of yoga and yoga for children.

"Did you know that yoga was basically come up with in order to allow people to stay longer in meditation pose?" she said while working on my back.

"I did not," I mumbled with my eyes closed and my head encased in padding while I looked at the floor.

I could probably stay in this pose a lot longer though.

After about an hour, she flipped me over to my back and returned to work on my shoulder. *That* shoulder. The words "hurts so good" were appropriate. I was practically moaning with pain—and delight.

"I'm sure you noticed it a little while ago," she said while massaging the hell out of my arm. "But I can connect with people on an energy level. I can see priorities and what's important sometimes. You might have felt it when I was on your leg."

"Right," I nodded, although I wasn't real sure if I had felt it. I was also a little nervous what priorities I was giving off and how in the world my leg was communicating them.

"I have to tell," she continued, "I was working on a *lama*—teacher—not too long ago. I had to be very careful, he wanted me to just stay in one area. You know," she said while rubbing my thigh. "They aren't as … open as we are."

"Right," I repeated, wondering if she could sense that I was not always that open either. Maybe she was dropping me a clue.

"Well, I was working on his shoulder and the strangest thing happened. I connected with him on an energy level and I saw nothing. There was *nothing* there. We think of nothing as so empty and cold but this wasn't. It was almost indigo and spacious and beautiful. It was clear. He was clear of all distractions."

"Wow," I hummed. "Wow." I wondered for a vague moment what kind of toxic waste dump she was seeing in my energy. It was not spacious and beautiful, I knew that. So far, she had been pretty quiet, probably waiting to find the words for me. I wonder if she could see Freja naked and if she could see how angry I was at Ehs for making me hurt. Could she see jealousy? Could she see affairs that tried to mask weakness and regret with more weakness and regret? Had Rachel told her about us?

I wasn't eager to continue this line of thought, so I started shooting out word flares, hoping to distract her energy sensing. "You know, they say the word *space* is outdated. There is no such thing as a void. There are always particles. There are always things happening."

"Hmm," she nodded, distracted by sending pain through my body.

I continued. "Maybe that god-shaped hole is supposed to stay a hole—of space. For mystery, for paradox, for the unknown. If we fill it, well, there's no room for mystery."

"Hmmm," she said. "Right. There is something about the space that we need and that is beautiful."

"Why are we always trying to fill everything up?" I said, wondering what my answer was and if "god-shaped holes" actually did exist and if they did, if god really wanted to live in a hole inside of a human.

"I know," she said with words much more gentle than her massage.

Minutes later she was on my shoulder again. There was a spot, one specific spot, and she had managed to find it. As she pressed on it, fire shot through my entire body but it was a burning that felt useful. So much pain is useful.

But it felt like it was killing me. "Whoa," I groaned. "That is the spot. Right there. That's the bad boy."

"I know," she answered and began to simply press on it. Consistently and clinically. And with energy.

It hurt even more. I closed my eyes and began to breathe. The hurt was everywhere in my body and in my head, pulsating and growing in its magnitude. If the *lama* had shown her some cool energy, I figured I could at least try to show her some too. I went into my best meditation.

I began to imagine clouds. Dark clouds. White clouds. Dark sky. White sky. The clouds were flowing overhead and I heard her say, "Whoa. Yeah."

Was she talking about the clouds? Either way, I liked where it was going so I continued to breathe big breaths. I began to imagine light and color and beauty coming into my body with each inhale and I imagined dark, cold smoke, that I had gotten fairly comfortable with, leave my body with each exhale.

I kept up the mantra and the clouds disappeared. I was just seeing the color come in and the darkness leave. *Love in. Fear out.*

"Are you trying to get rid of me?" The voice was one I knew well.

"Seriously?" I muttered.

"What?" he asked, as I felt a brush of wind by my face.

"I'm having a massage. Trying to relax."

"Your body will continue to. You'll be fine."

"What?" I opened my eyes and then said "What!" again but with a very different emphasis and dramatic flair.

"Welcome to Penuel."

Rocky desert stretched as far as I could see in every direction. Dried-out grasses decorated rolling hills that were speckled with massive chunks of rocks, like a bad case of acne on a teenage face.

The whole scene seemed one color: burnt orange. Sure, there were light burnt oranges and dark burnt oranges, but it was all similar, except for a few green bushes here and there and a forest, of sorts, in the distance. As I looked at the scene, bathed in a brilliant hot sun, I realized it was the same scene I had visited with Ehs as Cowboy Jesus earlier, only it was day now, not night.

"Different during the day, isn't it?" he asked, standing on top of a massive rock, staring out over the scene. "Although you did see a bit of it at sunset." He was normal James still, wearing dark jeans and a T-shirt, but there was something about the way he stood that reminded me of the crappy *Jesus* films I'd seen growing up. It was, mostly, the landscape, but there was something about him too, standing in this landscape with a certain presence. Maybe bad acting? Maybe I was preparing for Jesus to show up again since he had last time.

"Where are we?" I asked, still squinting in the sunlight and wondering why Ehs wasn't bothered by it.

He turned his back on the scene and took a few steps toward me. "Still asking where … I thought I would have been able to cure you of that habit by now." He seemed jovial, more than I had seen in a while.

"You're in a good mood." I wasn't sure I wanted him in a good mood, considering I still felt like he had offended me on our last visit. Not to mention I was still straining against the brightness and already starting to feel the heat. I instantly looked down and sighed in relief. I was wearing the shorts and T-shirt that I had been wearing before I had gotten in my underwear for the massage.

"I don't have moods. But, there is something about this day: this is it," Ehs said, standing closer to me now. "We've reached the moment we've been waiting for."

"Meeting her?" I asked with skepticism.

He smirked. "That and more. I doubt we will see each other beyond today. There are many variables but our relationship is, most likely, not one of them." He nodded, neither sad nor happy, seemingly not sure what to feel. Or at least how to show it.

"I'm sad," I offered. "I've enjoyed this." I squinted my eyes even tighter. "The last trip was a bit offensive to me, but—"

"You'll get over it," he interjected. "You'll be fine after your ego recovers. I have enjoyed it too." He looked back over the scenery and I noticed sweat dripping down his face. "I suppose we can talk as we wait."

"Can we have a tent or—?" Before I finished, a white tent had formed above us and the shade immediately felt cooler. Plus, I could see much better.

"Good idea."

"And I feel like we need a couch?" A white sofa appeared on the edge of the shade so we could sit and relax and still appreciate the views. "So," I continued, taking a seat. "Did you set up a time with her or something?"

"We don't work like that. She knows I'm here. She will come when she's ready. If she is."

"And why here?" I asked, confused, looking out at the landscape that was not my favorite in all the world. It probably wasn't dead, but it seemed to be. Dry. Hot. Extreme in every sense. I imagined the lizards or beetles waking up every morning, crawling out of their holes and asking the gods why they had not been born in a jungle instead.

"Not my choice," he answered, taking a seat on the couch next to me. "It's your turn."

I frowned.

"You ask the questions and I will answer as best I can." He smiled. "This will most likely be your last chance."

I stared out. The blue sky was empty and a single hue, devoid of anything other than that specific color. It was beautiful against the oranges but it was all so lifeless. "I don't know …" It was an opportunity I had often wanted, and once there, it was tinted with a sadness that wouldn't let me remember the questions.

Ehs waited patiently, enjoying the moment as much as I assumed he could while I waited for my brain to find its questions.

"Why?"

"Why what?" he asked.

"Why do you do it?"

"What?"

"All of it. Hiding light. Blinding. Evil. I don't even know the term anymore but why do you all do it?"

"We know no other way," he answered.

"No." I shook my head, squinting in the light. "I don't buy that. You know another way. You've been talking to me about it."

"Why do people kill? Why do they hate? Why do …"

"Because of you," I answered.

"No," he threw back, almost angry. "Do not blame us for the existence of darkness and give yourselves an excuse for your behavior."

"Where does it go back to? What's the original point?"

"You can't have light without darkness." Ehs looked down. "I'm sorry, there is nothing more to say."

"So there is good in darkness?"

"Of course."

"And bad in light?"

"Of course."

"Then all of this is just … who knows what?"

"Nuance, one could say. It's where the life is found." Ehs nodded, waiting for a moment. "Never let anyone purposefully remove nuance. And never be ignorant of its existence. Both are us. Both are me. Wherever nuance is not, you can assume we are."

I just stared forward at the rocky horizon. I was beginning to appreciate the scene's beauty.

It was quiet for a moment, both of us in our heads.

"Is it America?" I asked—which felt out of place but I didn't feel like there was time to organize my questions into topics.

"No," he answered quickly. "Avoid the surface manifestations. Look to the deeper, root causes. In everything. America is the greatest manifestation of Insipid, yes. But it is not just America. Insipid is spreading across the globe, thanks, in part, to America."

"Seems like it's a lot of America."

He nodded. "Yes, it does." Ehs had rarely answered questions without the games so it felt important to ask more. "It has flourished there."

"Should I move to Sweden?" Like I said, there was no time to organize.

He laughed. I laughed with him.

But I'm being serious.

"You know the statistics better than me."

"Yes, I do," I replied. "If the Scandinavian countries do everything better including sex, healthcare, education, equality, charity, environment, wome—"

"I understand."

"Without god," I added.

"Yes," he sneered. "I doubt it's related." A torrent of sarcasm.

"So I *should* move there?" I chuckled to hide the seriousness.

"No country will heal your consciousness," he answered with a grin. "Help maybe, not heal."

"Yeah," I bemoaned.

"Although, speaking of happiness. They usually lead that category as well." He then smirked. "A country can definitely help ..."

"So I *should* move."

"Happiness is never good for profits," he added, and dollar bills appeared in his hands. He began flipping them in the air. "Materialism depends on you not being happy. Ironically, thinking you will find your happiness in it—again, you know the statistics—makes you less happy. Ironically, that is exactly what the beast wants. You keep believing it will provide the very thing that it takes." A pile of money was at my feet and slowly vanished as I watched it.

"One more time?" I felt like I needed to understand that one. If I wasn't going to move to Sweden.

"Capitalism feeds on a desire that will never be fulfilled. In fact, it will only increase the desire. So it feeds itself." He looked up at a lone bird floating high above us—a black speck against the blue. "On you."

I was staring at him, trying to make it sink in.

"Seth." He looked at me. "You've been told poison will make you feel better. You drink it and wonder why you feel sick. So the system sells you a new poison."

I nodded.

"We're not just talking about this currency." He pointed to the ground and the dollar bills were back. "Church attendance. Patriotism. Sex. Happiness is never good for any profit."

I took a moment to think on his words.

"Stop drinking my poison." He almost pleaded. "It's everywhere, in so many forms. But you know what can be found deep within you. Under the surface. Away from the distractions."

"How?"

"Stop letting yourself be seduced by the lies. The truth is not as intoxicating but it is much more fulfilling." His eyebrows shot up and the bird above us let out a call.

"I'm struggling with Rachel. This whole lingerie thing. I'm acting like … God, I'm just so immature." I shook my head, calling out for help somehow. "I did the same to her. I can't. I just … I feel like—"

"It is your imagination that is responsible for love. Not the person," he whispered. "Your imagination must be tamed."

"How?"

He shrugged. "Be grateful for the moment." He closed his eyes. "Squeeze the most out of every second that is possible. It carries abundance if you will ever see it for what it is and stop worshiping what you want it to be. Stop worshiping what you want your memories to be. Stop worshiping validation from poisonous systems that only seek to destroy you. These are the things you already know."

"Yeah, but I feel like I need to hear it every day." I looked over at him with his eyes still closed. "And you're much more blunt than usual."

"We don't have time for games." His eyes opened again—staring up at the bird.

"This battle. Is this a battle? What are the battles?"

"The same as always. Light against the darkness."

I sighed. "So, are you sorry?"

He looked over at me. "Do you want me to pretend to be or tell you that I have no capacity to be sorry?"

"Neither."

"I'm afraid."

“Of what?”

“Darkness winning.”

“It won’t,” I answered bluntly. “It can’t hold forever. It might for generations but it, eventually, will fall.”

He sighed and looked up toward the tent waving with a slight breeze. “Keep believing that.”

“I’ll try.”

“How did you do it?” I asked. “How do you do it? I mean, I know, but, how? Really?”

“I’ve told you. Every source of wisdom, at its core, has told you. The enlightened, the mystics, the teachers, have told you for generations,” he answered.

“Once more? For old times’ sake?”

“Look.” He pointed out toward the desert and a small wall appeared around a hole in the ground. The wall was made of ancient, rough bricks, still mostly intact but crumbling in sections as though it had been in the heat for millennia. “A well.”

“Right.” I was a little thirsty.

“It all starts with a well.”

A woman appeared from behind a rock outcropping carrying a leather-looking satchel of sorts with a rope attached to it. It occurred to me that I no longer wondered whether she was real or not. She appeared real, even tired, as though she had walked a long way. Her body was fully covered in black cloth, except for her face, where I could see only a set of dark and dry eyes.

“Of course, the well is there to get water.” Ehs leaned back further in the couch.

The woman reached the side of the well and sat down, taking a deep sigh as she did. Eventually, after removing some rope around her shoulder, she began to lower the pitcher or container into the hole slowly, letting out more rope, and peered down into the hole, watching the container move further into the darkness.

“This is where everything goes wrong.” He paused and we both watched the woman. “Everything.”

“Why’s that?”

“That well provides water in a land where there is none. It quenches thirst. It provides life.”

“Right …” I let out slowly, intent on the woman. She had hit water and was now pulling up the container.

“And so the well has value.” Ehs was also watching her. She pulled the container out of the hole, splashing some cold water onto the tops of the bricks and staining them momentarily. I was even more thirsty. "And once something has value, the games begin."

The woman vanished and I was back to deciding whether she had been some kind of hologram or mirage or whether we had seen an actual woman at an actual well someplace on Earth: a woman who had no idea we were sitting in couches watching her and talking about her.

"That well"—Ehs nodded toward it—"is incredibly important. It is vital. It gives life and there is nothing more important than that. Right?"

"Right."

"So, you protect the well." Armed guards appeared around the well. Modern-day soldiers in desert camouflage, helmets, and black rifles. "You protect the well." The armed guards vanished and a group of priests surrounded the well. "You protect the well." The priests disappeared and a group of what looked like protestors appeared. They were holding signs that read JESUS SAVES, YOU'RE GOING TO HELL, NO SHARIA LAW IN AMERICA, and a variety of others that I couldn't read before they too vanished.

I looked over to Ehs sitting back like the producer of an Academy Award winner. He was relishing every moment of entertainment he was providing me as evidenced by the smug smile on his face. I looked back to the well.

"Of course," he continued. "There are other wells. Other ways to find water." The well transformed into something similar but with bricks that were a little smaller and overall in better shape.

"Those too have value. They too give life. And so—" He paused. "They too must be protected."

Six men appeared, soldiers of a different kind. They wore dark pants and shirts and most of them had their heads covered with more black cloth, revealing only eyes. They too held guns. "It must be protected." The soldiers vanished and were replaced by six imams with beards of varying lengths and head coverings of various designs—some white, some red and white turbans, and some with a taqiyah. "It must be protected." The imams vanished and a new group of protestors appeared, this time holding vary different signs. I read ISLAM WILL DOMINATE THE WORLD and BEHEAD THOSE WHO INSULT ISLAM and SHARIA before they too vanished, leaving only the well, the rocks, and the blue sky.

"You understand?"

"I think …"

"There are other wells," he continued, nodding toward the scene. And the well changed again. Newer bricks, again. A similar shape, still wrapping around a hole in the ground—or at least where I assumed the hole to be.

"These too have value. These too give life and access to enlightenment. And so"—he paused—"they too must be protected."

Six more men appeared, soldiers of altogether another kind. They wore white camouflage, white helmets with thick goggles covering their faces, and white boots, as though prepared for snow—oddly out of place in the desert. "It must be protected." The soldiers vanished, replaced by six men and women in white lab coats. Each was talking at the same time and it was hard to hear any of them over the other, but I did hear "stars," "biology," "cultural tendencies toward primitive deities," "evolutionary traits," and "chemically speaking," as though each of them were lecturing somehow. "It must be protected." The scientists, or whatever they were, vanished and a group of protesters appeared, this time holding very different signs. I read GOOD WITHOUT A GOD and FREEDOM FROM RELIGION and RELIGION: BECAUSE THINKING IS HARD before they too vanished, leaving only the well, the rocks, and the blue sky.

"Hmm," I nodded. "Didn't see that one coming."

Ehs continued. "None of this is about wells, of course. Or religion. Or even beliefs. Experience maybe. Worth. Value. Tribes. Identity." He stood to his feet, looking directly at me, still sitting.

"Measuring up. Belonging. Trust they will not leave you empty tomorrow. It's all there is in so many ways. You crave it and you fear you will lose it. We massage the fear. You believe it is the well and you forget about the water. And once you have done that, hell is unleashed." He looked back toward the well.

It was as though a brief history of humanity unfolded before me. It was all so quick that I could barely absorb one scene before another transitioned. But I saw early sapiens. Fire. Rocks carved into strange shapes. I saw temples, mosques, churches, and synagogues from primitive, ancient religions that I did not recognize to cathedrals of religions I was more used to. I saw religious leaders of every kind—or at least I assumed that's what they all were as I recognized some of them. I saw flags—so many flags flailing in the wind and I saw many of those flags burning. I saw soldiers of ancient Rome, of modern-day Russia, warriors of Native American tribes, and men driving pickup trucks with guns in the back. I saw tanks, and German troops, I saw Hummers and divisions of US soldiers. My pride betrayed me in all kinds of ways. The hair on the back of my neck stood tall as my flag waved and I saw jets soar through the air, tingling my nerves. And yet … I saw shopping malls and electric chairs, along with parades and factories. I saw bleached corals and extinct animals, I saw rows of pigs in tiny cages as far as I could see, I saw words being typed, humans having sex, and sermons being preached. The barrage of images was overwhelming, too hard to keep up with. I saw weapons, I saw disease, I saw death and life, businesswomen and politicians, sailors and kings, tractors, and fruit trees. I saw statues and assemblies and museums and labs. With all of it, I saw the well, sitting in the middle.

"The world becomes so consumed with defending and evangelizing their wells, that they forget the water. They die of thirst on the battlegrounds of doctrine, of belief, of legalism. Of any structure."

Ehs stood to his feet, engaged with his own story. "People design cups to hold the water, and they would die for the cup, or the glass, or the clay pot, never having put the lip of the cup to their own and tasted the life inside." He looked down at me. "This was purposeful. That water is a disease to us. If we can give you a bit of the disease, just a taste, then you will be immune to the full experience later. You understand this?"

"Just enough life, to stop us from looking for more? Just enough love. Just enough mystery. Just enough … god?"

He looked back at me. "No one remembers the water. No one remembers the reason the well exists, only that it does. And they steal wells, build their own well, tear down wells, attack wells, defend wells, insist on going to wells, insist that others go, and on and on it goes … the poor water inside. Usually just barely tasted. Never submerged or swam in. Never played in with others."

"Some, right?" I asked, looking at the now lonely well. "Some are finding the water."

"Of course," he nodded. "And those that drink from the water find others and they realize that they all drink from the same underground sources. The divine, some would even dare to call it. The Grand Mystery."

"Yeah." I nodded, looking up at him. "Few will find it."

"It's much easier to tell stories about the well. To memorize them and talk of your great leaders who discovered the wells than it is to drink from the well yourself. It's easier to describe water. To talk endlessly about clean water and bad water, about bad descriptions of water, about good descriptions of water, about great men and women of history who once tasted water. Don't taint the well! Kick them out if they bring bad water. If they drink bad water, even worse. Send them to the desert to die, even while those who defend the well die without knowing. It's easier to read the menu than it is to order and eat. It's easier to believe than to experience. It's easier to attain than to accept. It's easier to never die and never live than it is to rise after death."

The well continued to sit there, lonely, empty, surrounded by sun and heat. "It's always easy to talk. The words promise you a fulfillment that never happens. It's much harder to emulate." He frowned, looking up, again. The bird was still high in the sky. "As we started this discussion with capitalism, I can tell you it's just another surface manifestation."

"Say it again."

He looked deep into my eyes. I could feel the penetration of darkness. "Seth." His voice boomed suddenly. "We want addicts to the poison so we brand the poison as salvation."

"Why?" I sighed.

"There is no Christian way to drink. Or Muslim. Or atheist. Or to love." He sat down again. "Because the light never manipulates. And the darkness does."

"But why are there bad things?" I asked, sensing that if I never asked that question to Ehs or Emonee, I would regret it. It was the universal question.

Ehs laughed in a way that I had not seen him laugh before. "Why are there good things?"

I frowned.

"It's easy to explain bad things. Have you seen what happens to a fetus in utero? Have you seen what happens to the brain of an infant who cries too much? Do you know what trauma does to a human, physically and mentally? Do you know what trauma to the Earth does to its systems and to yours? It's easy to explain bad things … well, most of them. What is hard to explain is why that fetus, that baby, that child, that adult, finds a way to love their children and resist the primal urges that call them to destruction in ways they never experienced themselves." He nodded, slowly, almost processing the question himself. "The darkness prefers you to be caught up wondering why bad things happen. We've done well. The light would prefer you wondering why good things happen. Few do."

"Yeah," I agreed. "You're right."

"Of course I am." He smiled.

As did I. "Okay, what's going to happen?"

Ehs leaned back. "With what?"

"The world."

He laughed. "You determine that. You and the rest of your kind. Love and mystery never manipulate, even the future. Or they would be neither. And both are required for each other and for every moment. You cannot manipulate the present or else it is no longer the present."

"Do we need any well?" I asked, looking back to where I had last seen them.

"Ah." He smiled broadly. "Now you are starting to ask the right question. Those who have truly tasted the water that comes from it, realize they are swimming in an ocean of it."

I looked out expecting to be deep underwater but it was still just the two of us, staring out at what looked like a barren and dry desert, though was probably neither.

There was something solemn about the moment. The anger I had felt at times, the confusion, the frustration—they were as absent as any more questions I had once had. We both remained silent for a while longer, Ehs standing and me sitting, staring out, sensing the majesty and letting any manipulation go.

I don't know how much time passed. Then the bird screamed above us. And Ehs turned quickly and exclaimed, "Go and find her."

"What?" I asked, after jumping to my feet.

"She's out there. Go and find her." He pointed toward the desert and vanished, as did the tent and the couch I had been sitting on. It was not the way I had planned our goodbye but something told me that's what it was. That I wouldn't see him again.

I didn't have much time to think about it—the sun was blaring, the air was dry, the rock was hard, and I was desperately thirsty for water.

THIRTY FIVE

Moments later, I was begging for the heat. It was cold. Frigid cold. The wind was vicious, ripping through my clothes and into my skin. My skin felt like it was tearing. I had to look to make sure it wasn't.

It was dark and thin trees scattered the fairly flat horizon. I was standing on a layer of snow that covered the ground and graced the branches near me. The moon was bright, and the sky seemed to touch everything. Even the snow had a blue tint to it.

It was exquisitely beautiful and brutally harsh at the same time. Like most of life. I pondered for a quick moment, before realizing that my body was starting to violently shiver in an attempt create warmth where there was very little. There was no time to ponder.

I looked behind me, just in case I had been missing something big. I had. And it was big. A massive light-colored tent. It was not a tent you would find at your average store, or a wedding, but more of a thick covering made of skins and hides and fabrics stretched out over wooden poles—I could see their ends rising toward the clear, bitter sky, carved into the shapes of animal heads.

There was a light emanating from inside and an apparent doorway covered with more animal hides. I had no idea what was inside but when you're cold, and there is something that looks like warmth fifty feet away, nothing else much matters.

I made my way through the snow—quickly—and eventually reached the primitive entry, just before my feet felt like they were going to fall off.

"Hello," I said, calmly, but with force. With a tender strength, like the trees that surrounded me.

There was no response.

"Hello, anyone there? Do you mind if I come in?" I asked, again very polite considering the fact that my teeth were knocking around inside of my mouth and the numbness was creeping further toward my ankle.

No answer.

I pushed the thick hide aside and peeked inside.

There were more skins on the floor, and some hanging on wooden poles with carvings of horses and dragon-like creatures. There was a fire providing warmth, and it drew all my attention as I made my way as close to it as I could without burning myself alive. Or maybe even burning myself alive. It didn't matter at that point.

"Hello," she said.

She.

I, of course, turned around instantly, with my back to the fire to see her. Her human form was beautiful. The word has been diluted over the years to mean surface sex appeal but she was far beyond that. So far beyond, I didn't even notice the surface. There was a rarity about her, there was something deeper and innocent and precious. Her blond hair, braided and long, almost glowed and her sapphire eyes were as exquisite as the blue-bathed snow on the branches outside.

I stared for a moment, trying to put all kinds of things together in my mind. "Where am I?" I managed to ask.

She smiled. "Mu. So addicted to the where, the what, the how, the when ..." Her smile warmed me as much as the fire did. "You're *here*."

"Okay," I nodded, still as cold as I had felt in my entire life on one hand, and as warm as I had ever felt on the other.

She reached to the floor and lifted what looked like a grizzly bear off of the floor. "Put this on." It was a massive cloak made of animal fur. Powerful. Rugged. Heavy.

Maybe it's some kind of evolutionary leftover or maybe it's just all the movies we've seen, but you give most of the human species, maybe men especially, a hood and a light overhead to cast their face in shadow and they will stare at themselves in a mirror for a bit and make all kinds of faces, imagining themselves as some fictional character much more powerful than they are. They talk with an accent. They become the myth, the legend, the hero. They become someone else whom they like better.

In the same way that Ruby could feel my energy, I felt energy from whatever cloak or coat or fur she gave me. It was alive and I held it, staring at it for a long moment. It was an intoxicating feeling—contagious.

I wanted more. And it was easy to get more. I pulled the cloak around my body and the hood over my head. Once on, it was surprisingly light. And energizing, like a blood transfusion, pumping some kind of antidote to fear, a value, into me that I rarely felt. I was protected. I knew I could not be harmed. It had my back. And my head, and my chest, and my arms and my legs as it drug across the ground behind me.

I felt warm almost instantly with a gracious and soft power. I lifted out my hand toward the air, looking at the hide hanging from my arms. I was the gladiator. I was a leader. I was in control. But, somehow, without violence.

"Wow," I whispered, looking at myself as best I could and, almost, wishing for a mirror. As I was, I looked at her and realized she was wearing mostly leather, browns and tans formed into a dress of some kind. She seemed much tougher than me, wearing much less, and I suddenly didn't seem as formidable as I had thought.

Still.

"Are you ready?" she asked, throwing me off a little more. She didn't seem especially excited, or nervous, or afraid … but curious.

"Ready?" I removed the hood, sensing that I didn't need to be too badass.

"He's coming."

"So that's a good thing, right?" I asked, smiling.

"Maybe." She sat down on a simple and crude wooden chair with animal skins on it.

"Maybe? I mean—"

"Do you trust him?" she interjected.

I intentionally thought about it for a moment, just to make sure I believed what I was about to vocalize. "Yes."

She nodded, neither affirming nor denying whether or not my trust was a good thing or whether she agreed with it.

"Ehs has talked about a battle …" I added. Fortunately, if a battle was coming, I felt more prepared for it with the cloak on.

"There are always battles, Seth." She answered my lack of question plainly as she had before. "Your own are the most important. Are you ready for *that*?" The question was impactful enough on its own. The gaze of her blue eyes took the words and accelerated their punch on my entire structure. I felt it. The power of love is a cute saying but that's what her gaze, her question, her demeanor emanated. It was powerful but it was not cold. It was intense but it was not overwhelming. It was challenging but it was not discouraging.

Of course I'm ready, in this cloak.

"Yes," I answered, nodding, in case she couldn't tell how confident I was from my voice.

"Good." And she looked toward the tent entrance that I had come through earlier. Moments later two Norsemen rushed into the tent, and I felt a bit smaller, again.

I was the water boy on a football team. The men were rugged and handsome, with long blond hair pulled back tight into braids. The sides of their heads were shaved and they wore heavy animal cloaks similar to the one she had given me. But they also had black leather armor, huge wooden shields, and thick swords hanging from their waists. There was the smell of battle, of dirt, of wilderness and snow, an energy of courage that surrounded them and filled the tent. They were, in fact, the definition of badass. I hugged my own cloak tighter and did manage to stand tall, in the face of jealousy and intimidation.

Completely ignoring me, like a lion would ignore a sandgrouse, they spoke emphatically to her, in a language I did not understand but that sounded as rough and wild as they looked, Germanic with an archaic twist.

She remained steady, unfazed by the storm that was approaching.

"Seth—" She motioned toward something behind me. "Leave that way."

"Leave?" I asked, making sure I had understood properly.

"Now." There was an urgency—still without fear.

Shouts began from outside the tent, followed by some kind of commotion and a rough entrance by a rough-looking man. He was dressed in similar fashion but his hair was long and black and his face painted in some kind of mixture of dark oils. The eyes were wild, rebellious, unhinged and he already had his sword out.

"Now," she said, again, pointing toward the door.

Who was I kidding? If the Norsemen couldn't protect her, if she could not stand for herself, what was I going to do? Still, I tasted shame as I rushed out of the tent with metal swords crashing into each other behind me, and with an idea how the story was going to play out.

"Ehs!" I shouted as the cold night air hit my face, hoping he was there, at least in some form or another. "Wh—"

A hand smothered my mouth before I could finish a word. It smelled like poverty and I could taste salt and dirt.

Words were spoken in a language I didn't exactly understand but that I didn't exactly need to. "Shut up" was the obvious gist. I did just that and eventually, as the hand released from my mouth, I turned around to see who it belonged to.

If youth is a state of mind, then age is not all it seems to be. Some fifteen-year-olds have been through more horrors than some eighty-year-olds and those experiences leave their scars, sometimes visibly and sometimes not, but they affect others' perception of our age. Age is more than years. It is the experiences of those years. The happenings.

The man in front of me was no older than my own son, maybe

twenty. Maybe sixteen. His eyes were vibrant, his skin was fresh, and his movements energetic. Yet there were scars. I could see the old wounds, partially healed, on his face, I could feel the old wounds, not as healed, in his soul. He had seen far more than I had, committed crimes I had only read about, and I couldn't blame him. He was angry and afraid for reasons I could only try to understand. He was simply trying to survive.

"Ehs," I dared to whisper, in disbelief, struggling to put it all into place.

He lifted a dirty finger to his lips and shook his head. His dark hair framed a face that I had never seen before but that I recognized nonetheless. Black fur covered most of his body and his sword was stained with fresh blood that dripped toward his dark boots.

I nodded slowly.

His eyes said it all, but he held up his hand in case I didn't understand. I was to wait outside.

I did.

I stared at the moon. I stared at the trees. I wondered how the air was so cold and yet I felt so warm. I thought back to the delivery man telling me a story that I now seemed to be living and I wondered how and why and where and …

Mu. Un-ask the questions.

I wondered, instead, what I was supposed to learn.

There were the noises of birds. Noises of combat. Noises of silent night snow and darkness. Noises that distracted me as time passed by. I heard her say "Seth" and I entered back into the tent.

It was not the same tent I had left.

THIRTY SIX

There were three dead men with puddles of blood beneath them. The two Norsemen whom I had assumed could not be killed were close to each other, lying on their backs, resembling two dead bears except for the blond hair lying above their heads.

The wild-looking man with the painted face, whom I assumed had killed the Norsemen, was also lying on the ground, on his stomach much closer to me. A blade was protruding out of his back and judging from the growing pond of blood, I assumed the metal went deep.

The boy, Ehs, was holding her. She was looking into his eyes and both of them seemed oblivious to the carnage below them. Both of them also seemed unaware of the fact that I had entered their space. He was holding her cheek with his dirty hands and she was smiling, anxious but calm.

I smiled, until I looked at the man directly below them. A tremble moved through his body, feigning life, and panicking me for a second.

They didn't care. She lifted her hand and opened her palm in front of him, revealing a white stone. He looked down as though the stone meant everything in the world and stared for a moment before wrapping his fist around it.

He leaned forward and gave her a gentle kiss on the forehead. I noticed a lone tear on his cheek. She obviously noticed the tear as well, reaching out to rub it away, with deep comfort and care.

There were no words exchanged but there didn't need to be. I saw something between them, something as tangible and real as I have ever seen or felt or experienced. And then she turned her back on him and walked out of the tent.

"Ehs," I said. "You can't let her leave." I felt like I was speaking to myself as much as him.

He paid no attention to me, as though he couldn't hear me. Maybe he couldn't. He took out the stone, looked at it one more time and another tear streamed down his cheek.

It was something tender and enchanting in all the ways we want those words to matter.

And then it was shattered.

Three men rushed into the room, and the man whom I had assumed to be dead sprouted to his knees, with the blade still sticking from his back, and roared something evil and menacing. In a flash that the boy seemed prepared for, but didn't bother resisting, there was an attack from every angle and before I could even calculate what had happened the man was lying on the ground again with the sword still in his back but now a smile on his face, as his boy's lifeless body was carried out of the tent by the other three men.

I was alone in a tent filled with the signs and scents of death. Confused. Sad. With a moment to think, I tried to put pieces of the puzzle together but the blood kept distracting me. Or maybe the fear the man was going to jump to his knees again. Not to mention the thoughts of what had happened or was happening to Ehs or to her or, for that matter, to me.

My thoughts, or at least my attempts at thinking, were killed by the sudden and jolting noise of the tent I was in being ripped away from the earth and toward the sky. I cowered to the ground as the heavy fabrics and animals skins vanished in the frigid air above me.

Like a field mouse that had just had its home ripped apart by a wolf, I suddenly felt naked and exposed, and terrified of how and what had just taken away my only sense of protection. Of being as weak as a field mouse. And of seeing the wolf.

My eyes were closed, I eventually realized. Feeling warm in the heavy cloak I still wore, I slowly opened them to see what new sights were now before me.

It was still night. Still cold. The moon was still shining and the snow was still glistening in shades of blue on the ground and in the dark tree branches. The night fabric of the sky was bedazzled with stars, glistening like diamonds on a black dress.

And there were birds surrounding me. Black birds. Ravens. I hadn't noticed them, at first, because of their silence. When I did, the silence became eery, almost terrifying. The birds stood on the ground lined up in rows, like soldiers, each of them facing toward me, forming divisions and brigades, all staring forward with their black eyes, as though waiting under order.

The sky filled for a moment with hundreds more who, silently, and abnormally, soared through the air like a cloud before falling to the sky and lining up in spots and formations that were obviously intentional.

I took a deep breath, feeling like I was going to need it.

Something can feel "not right" in a church service and something can feel "not right" in a dark alley at night. Our lives become normative, our rhythms become routines, we are pattern-matching creatures, of whatever patterns we are surrounded by.

I felt "not right."

It wasn't the silence of thousands of crows. It wasn't the fact that I was in an alternative dimension or reality or world or dream of some kind. It was all something else. Carl Jung described intuition as "perception through the unconscious" and numerous philosophers have combined intuition with spirituality and truth and faith. We gain knowledge without knowing we are.

I was gaining knowledge and it was "not right."

I wrapped the cloak tighter around me and stared back at the thousands of eyes looking toward me, just as a light snow began to fall. The more I stared at the birds, I realized they were not entirely opaque shapes. There was a subtle transparency.

Whether the birds were ordered, programmed, or had their own sense of intuition that something was not right, on cue, like well-disciplined troops, they began to rise into the air in front of me. Though their mouths remained closed, the sound of the wings was storm-like. Harsh, and very cold, waves of wind rushed toward me but I couldn't take my eyes off of the flocks as they filled more and more of the air in front of me, with perfection and unity.

Eventually a massive wall formed in front of me and, as I watched, the birds morphed from their bird shape into bricks, each stacked one on another up into the sky and at least one hundred feet on each side of me. I was suddenly standing in front of a massive wall that I could see through partially to the dark trees and fields of snow on the other side.

And a form appeared. A man, walking toward me. Vague in shape but recognizable nonetheless.

It was Ehs, but it was "not right." My intuition was sending out a code red to my entire body and my nerves were responding. The adrenaline factories were running at full speed and my senses were each heightened as though the sentries of my own body were preparing to order the troops into war.

I may not have been a fighter but I was going to have to be.

The wall opened for Ehs, parting down its center, and the boy I had seen earlier walked toward me. He was smiling but the smile was not the smile of friendship or trust that I had grown accustomed to. It was a more subtle and dangerous type.

"Thank you, Seth," he said, his words sharp suddenly.

As he passed through the entrance, the wall sealed again behind him.

I knew better than to ask what was happening or where I was or why in the hell everything was "not right." I just looked at the boy of seventeen or eighteen, his stained skin, oily hair, black leather armor, and dark eyes. The eyes were so dark that looking into them made me feel the same, and I looked away.

"It honestly was a beautiful moment. To *feel* again. To taste again, even if it was for only a moment that cannot stay."

"Where is she?" I asked.

He closed his eyes for a moment and I was able to breathe again. The wall behind him was alive, somehow, and seemed to mock my question with subtle laughter.

"Where," he repeated, shaking his head.

"What happened to you?" As I heard my own words, they carried more courage than I felt. There was something remarkable about them. I could almost see them leave my mouth, slide through the air, and hit his ears. "You're not right."

A glitch shivered through his body and something similar happened to the wall moments later as though it relaxed for a moment and its form started to fall before regaining its composure and strength.

Ehs waited for me to look at him. "I am Ehs, Lord of The Legion, Commander of The Dark, Servant to The Accuser, General of the Insipid Realm." The words hit me like the wind had earlier. I could feel them penetrate through my flesh and organs. There was an inflection and layer to his voice that had remained hidden up to that point. "I am here," he stated with dark power. "I am darkness."

He then spoke in his own language—the one I had heard briefly a few times in my life and it was infinitely terrifying. The sound that came from his mouth thundered across the landscape and slithered its way into my ears at the same time. As he spoke, or manipulated sounds, the wall began to transform back into the shapes of crows that I had seen earlier. They were no longer quiet, each of them calling out with their high-pitched caws, the feathers of their necks extending out with pride in front of them.

The order had left. The birds were swirling throughout the skies, a chaotic tornado of shrieks and laughs, mocking and confident. Another torrent of wind, icy and bitter, blasted across the landscape both from wings and from nature. The sounds were so loud I could hear nothing, the visuals so overwhelming and erratic, I felt blinded.

I pulled the cloak I wore around my head and tightened it so that only my eyes remained visible. I looked toward the ground, trying to steady myself from the turmoil that was twirling around me and beginning to infiltrate me. I took deep breaths, staring down at the snow, recalibrating my senses through my breathing.

You always have your breath. Come back to your breath.

Still, I could not deny that something was happening. Ehs was changing and I knew it. I could sense him morphing into something massive and tall, his shadow overwhelming me and continuing to spread across the snow, removing all sense of color and life as it did.

There was the sensation of something beyond dark. Beyond cold. Beyond terrifying. A nearby shape was absorbing my ability to feel and that prompted in me a new type of fear. A fear coming from somewhere else, somewhere outside, somewhere more evil and destructive.

Ehs was standing over me, far above me. I could feel his eyes. And only after another breath and another tug of the cloak did I slowly tilt my head, daring myself to see what I was standing next to. Or under.

It was the shape I had seen once before. Human, mostly, facing away from me. Arms and legs. A massive cloak hanging over all of him—thick, heavy, dense. I could see nothing in it. A nothingness with form. And power. It was not the absence of something as much as it was the invasion of everything. All in a cloak whose bottom brushed along the white snow next to me, sweeping delicate snowflakes into the night and sending more chilling air across my body.

I looked up as Ehs took another step away from me. He seemed to grow taller as I watched—the back of his head was at least three body lengths above me now. It was pale and deathly white, almost transparent, and clean shaven. On top of his head was a black crown, not ornate or decorative but menacing and painful. Thick, glossy metal bands, braided together, twisted around each other and into the skin on his head. There was an energy to the crown that emanated out from it, through his entire body and cloak, to me. A fog. A shadow. A blindness. Call it what you will but I felt more of it than I had ever consciously felt in my life and it was suffocating.

I stumbled to my knees, still trying to breathe. Ehs heard me and turned, revealing the face I had seen—and partly expected—but could not prepare for.

His eyes were black holes, like those found in deep space. And like those, they seemed to absorb light, trapping it in their pull, and refusing to allow it to escape. Where noses usually were, below the suffocatingly dark eyes, was another hole. There was no mouth, just more white skin, like a massive skull wrapped in extinction's skin.

As devastatingly painful as he was to look at, the energy

emanating from his being was worse. It was the energy of annihilation itself. Ehs lifted the hood of his cloak over his head, masking his face, or lack of one, and covering it all in more shadow. He held up his arms into the air, which made it appear as though he had wings and as if the deep recesses of space were opening and filling the sky above me.

When he dropped his arms, the ravens, which I had forgotten about, fell silent again and began to organize themselves into lines. It was almost instant. Ehs turned to face them.

As he did, the birds morphed again. As hideous and frightening as they had been, I almost immediately wished for them to return. Each of them dissolved and faded into soldiers, from another time. Everything about them was painted in darkness. Black metallic helmets with black feathers rising up toward the sky, black heads with even darker eyes and no mouths, black glossy armor covering their chests and arms and legs. Each of them held a sword and shield, each as dark as night, and wore cloaks laid across their backs, just touching the snow.

The army that had formed in front of me stretched as far as I could see in any direction. I stood to my feet behind Ehs, so I too now faced them directly and I could see nothing but soldiers in front of me. Soldiers of, I assumed, The Legion.

The warriors I was looking at made all others I had ever seen seem as powerless as a child's plastic toy.

Behind us, far away, was the wall. I could see it rising up into the night sky and the darkness of space beyond it. The universe felt accusatory and cold and full of death. Ehs turned again to face me. I felt as small, insignificant, and powerless as I have ever felt in my entire life.

An eerie silence descended over it all. There was not the sound of breathing, the sound of wings, the sound of legion, the sound of chanting, or the sound of air. It was completely silent, as though everything in the world knew what was about to happen. It was the inhale before diving into the water.

Moments later, it happened. It sounded and felt like the Earth was cracking. I looked toward the wall and watched as a mountain-sized piece of it crumbled from high above toward the ground. Sections, the size of houses, tumbled toward snow-covered land and, despite the soft surface, shattered upon hitting.

And that was just the beginning.

Then there was a light.

THIRTY SEVEN

I felt warm … a warmth of my own biology I hadn't realized had vanished. I felt joy … a joy I hadn't realized had been smothered and blanketed by oppression. I felt freedom … a freedom I hadn't realized had been taken by some kind of subtle and slithering chains of the dark.

As though the wall was separating day from night, beams of light, color, and kindness shot through each hole that appeared, causing the darkness, monotone, and cold to flee.

Bricks continued to fall. Rays of light continued to shoot through with some kind of life. Green grass replaced snow, and leaves appeared instantly on the barren branches where the light touched them. Summer replaced winter.

Ehs shot into the sky leaving a trail of clouds in his wake, like some medieval rocket, and The Legion turned all of its attention to the crumbling wall.

I heard a different song in the air and it was coursing through the veins of my soul. I began to run, aware of the smell, the smells of air after a rainfall. Aware of my skin, alive with life. There was flavor to the world again … I could hear it, see it, taste it, absorb it, and enter into it.

Another crack shattered in the distance. Another massive sound hit the air and my body shook as did the ground underneath me. I looked toward the wall and more of it was missing, with bright light now shining through all around me, below me, and to the sides, interrupting the march of the dull and monotone.

But, The Legion began to move. A vast horde of violence hurtled itself toward the wall. If the wall was going to collapse, I had a feeling they were not going to let it go easily. In fact, it had become obvious they were well prepared.

The sky was suddenly filled with shapes, massive ravens, more like pterodactyls than birds. The ground was filled with more shapes, soldiers, marching like ants, pouring across the landscape.

Rays of light would hit and immediately the shapes would vanish but there were too many, and they continued toward the wall, unflinching. There was a seemingly infinite number of bodies coming and I did not know if darkness would be able to overtake the light. But if it could, it was going to happen directly in front of me as I watched, alone and excited, energized and depleted.

As more and more of the wall began to come down, more shadow shapes in the air and on the ground continued to advance toward the ever-widening swaths of light striking through the air. Soon enough there was a black dust floating above the snow and in that dust, more and more rays, literal rays of light, could be seen finding their way toward me. The more the darkness advanced and disappeared, the more visible and stunningly beautiful were the Rays.

The light continued to shine strong. As I assumed it would. But, the darkness continued to march, as though there was no light. As I assumed it would.

Up to that point, everything had been in front of me. I might as well have been in a theater, an audience of one. The wall, the shapes, the soldiers, the light were still all on display but then something drew me to turn around, facing the opposite direction.

I had not noticed the mountains in the distance. I had not noticed that the sky had lightened, either from a rising sun or from whatever daylight was now allowed into the scene from beyond the wall. But now I saw it all, the peaks in the distance, dressed in their finest dresses of snow, and there were forests beneath them, with the trees standing like bridesmaids.

It was beautiful and I found myself smiling. At light. At nature. At change. Most likely because I didn't know what else to do.

There was no time to analyze. I was present, not by choice but because the past and future were not as interesting as the moment. To try and absorb it, to simply be, required all of my focus. I noticed something new amidst all the chaos behind me: a massive storm front.

There were black clouds, almost ethereal in nature, infinite somehow, black holes that erupted with a clash of thunder and flashes of dark lightning—like black fire spewing across the sky.

And the storm began to move. There was what looked like rain pouring out of the clouds but it was black and dark, more blood-like, and formed what looked like a transparent wall of more darkness coming from the clouds above.

Faster than I have ever seen any storm front move, the clouds made their way toward me. As they did, any light that touched it would melt the front edges but quickly be overcome by whatever magic recipe of darkness was brewing inside of them almost like a wave of heat-melting snow.

Behind me there were chants and roars and an energy so palpable I could almost reach out and touch it. A rain began to fall … a dark and lifeless water from the now dreadful sky above.

I could no longer even think of smiling. I turned to face the wall, again.

Already, troops were reaching the base of it. Some vanished amidst the light, and some seemed to be eradicating the light and filling the wall again. And the light was fading. I felt cold again and a sense of dread. The cloud and The Legion continued to move against it, masking its warmth, smothering its life.

I turned around. The mountains were visible again, but another evil was forming. A thick fog was coursing over the ground. At first glance, it looked like a dam had broken but, on second glance, I saw it too was a cloud, moving fast in between the trees, consuming everything in its midst like a black steam from the pits of hell itself. If hell had pits.

It, like everything, moved with urgency and precision. I thought for a moment of trying to run from it but remembered a video I had seen of an attack on three baby eagles. The only one that survived was the one that huddled in and stayed still. So, like with a roaring forest fire, like with The Seers, I hoped and prayed it would move over me and not consume me.

I got down with my back to the sky, clenching my knees, wrapping the skins I wore tight around my body and took a deep breath. Moments later, the fog was surrounding me.

It was silent suddenly. Deathly quiet. I opened my eyes but I was blinded—I could see nothing. I grabbed at my eyes to make sure they were still there and my pulse quickened, absorbing the oxygen I was holding onto.

I began to feel nothing. Nothing was everything.

It was death. Though I was alive, I knew it was death. Maybe we all do. Maybe we recognize it in those times, maybe we've lived it before, maybe it's where we come from but for whatever reason, I simply knew. It was death. I could smell it in emptiness, hear it in nothing and see it in darkness.

I waited for it to come more permanently, almost content in the awareness there was nothing I could do to resist it in those final moments.

I recounted how I had gotten myself here. The blind trust. The faith in false hope. The insistence on the potential for change in those that could not.

To hope that death could bring relief seemed futile and just as stupid but I did it anyway. It was better than whatever hellish present I was existing inside of.

But it did not come.

My eyes were suddenly equally blinded with light. Whatever darkness existed vanished, as though it had never been born, and I stumbled on the ground for a moment, trying to gain my balance and senses on my hands and knees. Finally, I felt firm enough to look up.

The wall had collapsed again and light was shining all around and through me. And this time, it had form. It was her. Massive and angelic and beautiful. Beyond beautiful.

Infinite beauty and bliss. Emonee in all of her glory.

There were other creatures all around her. I call them creatures because it's hard to call them anything else. Almost human, almost bird, almost the sun … they were everywhere, simply being. They had arrived and she was leading them. They didn't carry swords or guns or any weapon of any kind. They didn't ride any kind of creature.

They simply shined.

And the darkness shrieked wherever the light was, which was seemingly everywhere suddenly. It was no longer night. It was no longer cold. The Legion was melting on the ground and in the sky and the wall was crumbling, massive chunks of it falling and colliding with the ground, which struggled to stay together as it felt each impact.

The clouds that had previously consumed everything in their path struggled now against her and her warmth. The fog that had slithered and darted across the snow now stopped at the edges of her iridescence.

I smiled as big of a smile as I had ever smiled even while trying to regain control on the roller coaster of emotions I was still riding.

"Yes!" I yelled out to her. "Yes!"

And then I heard Ehs. His call, even in his own language, was recognizable. I looked back toward the mountains and saw him, ever larger, ever more menacing, walking toward us with an iron sword raised toward the storming clouds above him. They had wilted but now seemed to be gathering their strength again.

I looked back to her, anticipating the light would pull out shields or shoot flaming arrows of white, but they didn't. They simply stretched and grew larger, spreading their warmth to as much of the land as they could and eradicating any darkness of any form that attempted to resist it.

For a moment.

Then The Legion expanded. I assumed the sight of their commander inspired them. The dark fog reappeared and soared into the air, evading light wherever it was, and eventually became one with the storm that had reappeared above.

The dark side had confidence.

Ehs stepped toward her, unafraid of her beams. In fact, his cloak seemed to ingest them whenever they interacted—sending a shiver down my spine. Nothing had been impervious to her up to that point.

He was near her. They looked into one another's eyes. Hers radiant. His sullen. The Legion attacked. The fog and storm enveloped. Then Ehs drew his sword of forged death and, in an instant, slammed it into the center of her very being.

The darkness plowed full force into the light.

The collision was monstrous in every way. The ground shook, the air rattled, and my heart stopped.

Her smile faded.

And, though I had not been killed, my heart felt like it was dead.

It was over. The entire landscape knew the end but it had to play out.

It was like a million bees taking down an antelope. Slowly, with the patience of death and an addiction to violence, the multitudes won. And though she continued to fight in the way that the light always does, as did the others around her, she began to eventually become consumed by the darkness and her light, which I thought could never be masked, slowly began to fade.

She continued to smile, although it was the smile of someone in pain … and still at peace.

It was in that moment that I fully realized my error. Words can only hint at the emotion I felt.

Regret, I realized, was just a taste at the very edge of it. The pit in the stomach. The loss of breath. The longing to undo … at the thought of *those* words, of *that* night, of *him*, of *her*, of *it*, of the *decision*, of the *rage*, of the *lust*, of the *emotion …* little did I know how deep the pit could extend inside of me. It saturated and surrounded me.

I was sick.

I had trusted something I should not have.

I was enraged. I was angry. I was destroyed.

The Legion shouted at her with everything, screaming out obscenities and curses while the fog wrapped around her light and the storm drenched the top of her with inky rains.

And Ehs held the sword fixed and firm until all of her light was extinguished.

The wall was back. The snow had regained its composure. The night reigned again. The Legion, though wounded, filled the sky with ravens once more, somehow celebrating and calling out laughs to one another.

And Ehs turned. To face me.

His weapon of death, in the form of a sword, was held directly at me.

And I, somehow, in that moment, decided I would not wilt in the face of the Lord of The Legion, Commander of The Dark, Servant to The Accuser, General of Insipid.

She was gone, but there is something about cloaks.

It was dark, but there is something about light.

I was blanched and petrified, but there is something about courage.

Maybe she was not gone.

THIRTY EIGHT

Ehs and I faced each other. Nothing else existed.

The Legion had vanished. The snow, the mountains, the trees, the night had all been replaced with a gray, flat landscape and darker gray sky that both stretched as far as I could see. The horizon was a straight line, perfectly level in every direction.

There was nothing to look at to distract myself from him.

For the first time, I did not think about "where."

He stared down at me, his face a shell of what I was used to, and I could not help but imagine that shell in James, in the delivery man, in Elle, the obese woman, in the factory manager, in every shape and voice I had seen. It had always been there, staring at me with the dark void of eyes and the empty face and expressions, hidden by the veil of humanity that I was used to.

There was no denying it now.

There was another shape of some kind moving around inside of him, swirling, almost a physical manifestation of his energy in the shape of long, drawn-out, snakelike clouds slithering in and out of his legs, as though waiting for orders.

I spoke first, staring at the blade still directed toward me and then daring to look into the eyes of the pale face. "Why?"

He laughed in return. It was not the jovial laugh that I had heard so many times. Not even the sarcastic or condescending laugh I had witnessed. It was a laugh that rejoiced in misery. My misery. And it hurt, physically, like the sounds had teeth sinking into my skin and soul.

"Why?" I uttered, exasperated and sad, trying to cling to something.

He continued to laugh and I continued to hurt.

But, there was an anchor somewhere, attaching me, not letting me go.

As though he read my mind, I could hear his whisper, emanating from within his head, deep and dark in structure. "Let them go."

Though the anchor held me, it hurt me. Maybe the anchor was

holding me back?

The smokelike snake that had been weaving in and out of his cloak around his ankles shot straight for me, wrapped around my head, and suffocated me in an instant. I couldn't speak or breathe or feel until it released and returned to him. And left me gasping for air and maybe even an end to it all.

"Your trust in change will kill you," he said in a serrated whisper that felt rough and reckless and all around me.

I shook my head. "Jesus! Jesus Christ. By the blood of Jesus I cast you away." I didn't think it would work but as the whisper ripped and the fog suffocated I was becoming desperate for anything, including words that I had grown up believing had power.

The laugh returned, eradicating the words and making me feel weak and insecure and helpless. Which hurt.

"Words," he said, still laughing. "You and your words. Always words. Words, words, words."

I looked down, clinging to whatever spark was inside of me, that refused to be extinguished if I paid attention to it. "I believed you."

"Most do," he answered with a boom that was precise and succinct and sent a pain that jolted through my entire left side for a moment.

"I thought …" I didn't know what I thought. "I thought you wanted …"

I guess I did know what I thought. I thought demons or Shadows or whatever the hell he was could change, or could want to change, assuming there was even a capability to change.

There was deafening silence from him. Yet the sword did drop slightly.

"What was true?" I asked, feeling defeat push me down.

"All of it." The words crashed like thunder, deafening and disorienting.

Yes, I was holding steady and the fact that I was gave me comfort somehow. "The walls, the shadows, the light, it's all true?"

The expressionless face nodded subtly and the eyes twirled like the deep recesses of the fringes of the universe.

"What was not true?" I asked, as though I could trust his answer.

"Your illusions." The words cracked all around me, disorienting me momentarily.

I could only shake my head and look around to empty spaces as though I would find answers or a respite there. "Why?" I stumbled. "What?" I cracked, not near as powerfully as his words. "What have I done?"

"Evil," he answered, in that rough whisper again. "You will never understand." The words wrapped around my cloak for a moment, looking for a way in, and then fell to the ground.

I looked at him, and it, the smoke slithering within and around his body.

The laugh returned. The hideous laugh that reverberated and fed on terror. I cowered slightly and let it attack me with its many layers.

"You were so desperate to trust," he mocked in a grim voice that seeped out of the ground and the air I breathed. "Desperation. Consumed by what you rejected."

I looked down, trying to solve his riddles. I remained standing. I was standing and continued to find courage in that fact, somehow.

"I am darkness!" The voice exploded and the shape of clouds swirled around his entire body. "I am death." As though the land had not been dark enough, a new layer of despair descended from above me, smothering what little light there was. "I am fear."

The clouds formed into the shape of a snake and slithered through the air. Reeling its head high, as though to gain momentum, it then lunged for my neck. If it had been searching for a weak spot, it found it.

The fangs of fear sunk deep and I could feel its venom spreading like fire through my veins. Everything told me I was a failure. Everything told me I could never again face another human, or speak to another human, but that I should grovel and beg for some degree of worth and merit from whomever would give it. Its poison was shame and it was spreading quickly, heading for the center of my inner being.

Everything told me that god had failed me. Left me to die. That evil was more powerful than good. That hate was more powerful than love. There was nothing to save me.

Every fear reigned, infecting me and hiding me, transforming me into something I did not want to be. *Who was I? What was I? Did I exist? Had I ever?*

Ehs observed, distantly, with no emotion or care. The apathy hurt even worse than hate.

I would have hoped to die, but since the idea of hope was destroyed, I could not even hope for that.

I could only wallow in misery and torture and doubt and rejection and fear. And assume it would last forever.

I no longer could stand. I collapsed to my knees and clutched my legs up into my chest, in an attempt to feel or because I could not feel. It was all the same.

"This is who you want me to be." The words crawled into my

ears, like worms, emanating from a different source than I had expected. I could feel them moving inside of me, forcing me to pay attention to them.

"You ignorant wretch of human flesh. Garbage on the refuse heap of the universe. Love, you will see, does fail. Love, you will see, does not win. Love, you will see, cannot stand against power." It was the snake speaking through its poison and once inside my brain, the words expanded and stretched into something more lethal, filling my skull, mixing with the venom of shame that was already saturating me.

Yet.

The cloak that wrapped around me was alive. I could feel it suddenly. It was moving, there was an energy to it, a life to it, and it was counteracting the poison. As though injected with an antidote, I felt creativity, not war. Love, not violence. It was minuscule but the sliver was all I needed.

I stood to my feet and faced him directly. The eyes revealed a faint surprise. I could sense it. That fed the mustard seed of courage within me.

Ehs lifted his sword again toward me.

"You fool. He still doesn't understand," he thundered.

"No." I held up my hands. "You don't."

There was nothing.

"And you won't kill me."

The sword rose into the air and though everything should have told me that I had lost, nothing did. Something else was pulsing in and through the veins of my true nature.

"I refuse to believe it." The fog reeled at my words, as though it had never heard such a thing. The sword remained where it was. "I refuse to see you as Lord of The Legion, Commander of The Dark, Servant to The Accuser, General of Insipid. I reject it!" I shouted, gaining more and more power from somewhere or something.

His pale head tilted and the fog was reeling, frenetic and stirring around his body. Anxious.

"This"—I pointed directly at him—"is not you. It's me. This is not …" I looked up at his dreadful face staring down at me. "You."

Suddenly it wasn't. He was James again. Normal, nice James wearing a dark cloak.

The shock literally made me stumble backward in our strange, flat gray space that we were standing in. I forgot my cloak was on and tripped over it, literally landing on my back.

I looked to James for a laugh but there was no expression on his face. Void, like his eyes.

"Ehs?" I asked, lifting myself up.

It was James but the closer I looked, it was not. Parts of the other Ehs were more obvious. There was some kind of strange swirling inside of him that I could see. There were the dark eyes and his mouth, though visible, appeared almost sewn shut.

He continued staring forward.

And something inside me made me want to speak. Maybe it was the old pastor in me. Maybe it was my best self. Maybe it was my true self.

"There are lots of things I don't know in this world, Ehs." I started slowly.

Nothing changed, which I took as a sign but I didn't know if it was good or bad. It was like he was blinded suddenly, in the way he had always blinded others.

"There's crazy shit in this world. Ten-year-olds with brain tumors and refugees and waste and executions of innocent people and … fuck, man!" I yelled. The sermon was not as eloquent as I wanted it to be. It was hard with no audience except a lifeless Ehs. "It sucks. Starvation, corruption, pollution, and religion that doesn't give a shit about any of it. Okay, I get it! There is darkness and there is stupidity. I get it."

Some kind of clouds now began to form inside of James. I could see them gathering within his own skin. Preparing? Ehs remained firm, expressionless and vague.

"I don't know anything. I honestly don't. I don't know if god cares, or if god exists, I don't know if god is anything other than the relationships and interactions of the universe. I don't know if there is a heaven or a hell or if the light will win or if the darkness will prevail. I don't even know if I am alive or dead right in this moment."

Again, there was nothing. The clouds had settled out of his body and into a fog at the base of his shoes, and he was now rising out of it.

"But Ehs. I think … no, I know … something.

"When the father runs out to hug his son who has betrayed him. When he embraces him and they stand in the driveway crying and laughing and planning a party. I know it puts a choke hold on me.

"When the grandmother hugs the man who has killed her daughter and grandson. When they write letters for years back and forth and when she loves him, a killer, and makes him believe he is more than a killer.

"When the prisoner is out of jail and smiling in the sunlight once again.

"When the prince of Egypt says I am your brother. I am the one you tried to kill but now I will save you.

"When the woman realizes she is valued and worth something again and she can talk about the assault without that pit in her stomach or that wound in her soul.

"When the white police officer speaks on television to a nation about the atrocities he has done to people of a different color … and he can barely get the words out through tears … apologizing … hoping for a different nation.

"When she walks off the airplane and he is waiting for her.

"When the artist tells it like it is. When I laugh and cry and smile and get angry at the way it is.

"When the man who had been dropped off at the orphanage finds his father years later. The father who had left him to die and rejected him all his life. When he finally has the bravery to call him 'Dad,' as he watches him die.

"When the boy, after searching for years, with every fiber of his being, finds his mother and they embrace in the center of the village.

"When he has the sword drawn, when he is ready to kill the man that has tormented him his entire life—when he has every right and chance and justification to penetrate his heart and take his life. And he chooses not to.

"When men wearing white hats dive into the rubble to risk their own lives and pull out innocent victims.

"When the man who is being killed by an empire of darkness for leading a revolution of light against it, is executed, and he manages to understand and have empathy for those killing him, even while he dies.

"I know that stuff. I know it's real."

I fell silent for a moment, absorbing all that was happening and beginning to realize my own words even as they continued to flow.

"I know this force is strong. It contains those stories. It propels us to create more. Some call it god. Some don't. But whatever that mystery is, that interaction between molecules at their most basic level, that thing … is somehow … some kind of …" I was struggling again. "Love?" Force? Abundance? Worth. I don't know … well yeah, I know, it's all those stories I just told you. I know it's in us. With us. Within us. It is us … at our best. It's you, Ehs."

The fog was drifting upward toward Ehs's shirt and shoulders, masking much of him.

"It's me. I know that. It's us." I felt like I wanted to cry but I couldn't. "It's us, Ehs!" I begged him.

He flinched but I had nothing more to say.

I looked toward the ground, the gray dirt, and took deep breaths of whatever air was in the room. I had said all I could.

I looked into his face, desperate for some hint of emotion, of reaction, of feeling. But there was nothing. I imagined an alternate reality where he was moved, or at least thinking, where my words had some impact.

For a short moment.

"You are almost there," a voice uttered. I immediately looked up. The hideous face had returned. The dark cloak. The bleached flesh over his mouth. The coiled crown. Speaking in a sterile and empty voice devoid of life. "You will need your words to comfort you in the darkness. Goodbye. Your naivety is nothing compared to your arrogance and ignorance."

The fog wrapped around him, hiding his shape completely.

Then, immediately, the fog descended and consumed me, robbing me of any goodness I had managed to build or convince myself of. Rage grew. Utter disbelief flowed. Despair expanded and consumed me.

I was suddenly marinating in one of the most dangerous cocktails in the world.

THIRTY NINE

The walls, if they were walls, felt ... soft? I tried to run in every direction I could and each time I was stopped. What stopped me wasn't hard—in fact it practically enveloped whatever part of my body hit it—but there was no penetrating it, and after five minutes of hitting something on every side, including below and above me, it didn't matter how or what it created it: claustrophobia was setting in fast.

And I was in a state of enraged panic.

It was black in every direction except for a spark of fire hovering in the middle of the room. It was only a spark: a spark that didn't fade or grow, which was disconcerting. It only floated, weakly. And yet, I felt its power—it was the only thing in the room besides myself, I assumed, that was alive in any way. If a spark that doesn't start a fire can be considered alive.

I ran toward an edge again, thinking I could maybe push through or over. But whatever was there was much further out than I remembered and by the time I finally hit it, I was exhausted and fell quickly on my back.

Still nothing but darkness surrounded me in every direction. I stood again and reached above me and felt nothing. I jumped as high as I could and felt a barrier of some kind.

I was able to find the spark again, now much further away than I imagined. There was no set size to the space—one second it was moving in on me and the next it was pulling away. Either way, the spark was all I had in the room to save me from completely losing my mind, especially when the room felt big: it was my compass, my north star, as faint and weak as it was.

At least it was light. And a direction.

I began walking back toward it, quickly, eager for its touch.

And then I quickly turned, as though I would surprise whatever held me in place. I tried to run with all the power I could muster into the strange walls, as though I was running into Ehs. However, they had moved in much closer than I remembered and slammed into me almost immediately. The surprise took away any power I would have had.

As though any of it mattered.

I screamed as loud as I could. Anger, frustration, fear, outrage, revenge, and a lust for violence. And pure hysteria. But, even my scream was empty … it lasted only a second before being absorbed into the darkness. Even the therapy of vocalizing primitive outrage had left me.

I walked back to the spark, the faint spark, frozen as a single splinter of light that erupts when a rock strikes flint … I longed for it to grow into something warm and embracing. Or I wanted it, honestly, to fade and leave me in complete and utter darkness where I could at least die or go blind.

But just sitting there, it too was beginning to contribute to my quickly growing insanity.

It felt like I had only been there a few minutes.

I didn't know. I could have been there for hours. For days. For weeks. For months. For years. My mind started to play tricks on me, or not … How long had I been there? Where was there? Was I still lying on that massage table? Was I alive? Was anyone alive?

I screamed as loud as I could and my throat ached from the intensity I tried to create but couldn't. Everything was absorbed into the nothingness. I pounded my fist into whatever floor held me amidst darkness and began to cry and yell and wonder how long I could cry and yell.

"God!" I yelled. "Fuck you!" I screamed.

"Fuck everything! All of it! Kill me!"

My fits were epic. My tyrannical rages were historical in their hysteria.

And still nothing happened.

I laid down in what felt like a coffin. It was my worst nightmare and I didn't know if I would ever wake up. It's probably most people's worst nightmare.

"Seth." It was a quiet whisper. Generic.

"What?" I instantly sat up and started turning my head in every direction I could to try and find the source of the words. "What?" I tried to yell. "Where are you?"

"Right here." The words were barely louder than my own breathing.

"Where!" I demanded, still panicking at the way the room, or thing I was in, absorbed and transformed my own voice.

"Here."

I stared at the spark.

"You?"

"Yes."

"It only takes a spark to get a fire going," I began to sing, mocking the fact that I was talking to a spark and indicating my growing inability to hold on to reality at the same time. "That's really the only part I know. Does anyone know any other parts?" I laughed, or tried to. "It only takes a spark—" My voice, coming back to me, had a maniacal bend to it, almost turning around to haunt me, even though I had uttered it.

"Seth." The whisper was stronger but still just a whisper—as though it took everything in its power to be that loud. "It is I."

I stopped. I stared. It was just a scratch of light against a canvas of black. A line, but, staring at it more intently than I had, I could see it was slowly pulsing with some kind of quiet life. Somehow. An ember after a deluge.

"Who?" I whispered back, trying to stare at this thing floating in front of me, almost like a glitch, but a glitch I was suddenly clinging to even more than I had been. "Are you okay? What's happened?"

"Thank you," she answered first. "The I."

It seemed like it could be her, though it took everything in me to recognize her and part of me wondered if I was just making myself believe it so I wouldn't be alone. The mind is plenty powerful enough to create our realities. "What? What happened?"

"It doesn't matter." There was little emotion to the voice. There was no expression to read. I didn't know if she meant it or if she was taunting me.

"Where are we?"

"A cage," she answered simply.

"Am I alive?"

"You ask that a lot, don't you?" Somehow she still had some kind of sense of humor or ability to think in the room and that gave me courage that I could too.

"Okay, so I am?"

"Seth."

"What?"

"Space."

I sat down on the floor, next to her, her spark right in front of my face, and even then barely illuminating anything. "I'm sorry," I said mournfully, ignoring what she had said. "What have I done?"

There was no answer.

"Well, what have I done?" I yelled out, reaching for the sky and hitting something instead. Something that felt like nothing.

If it's nothing, it can't feel like anything, you idiot.

Had it lowered? Was it lowering? Was I being squeezed by

whatever cage I was in?

There was no answer. Just her barely visible spark gasping for life and light in front of me.

"I will kill him. I will, if he just lets me," I said.

"No."

"No? No, because I can't? No, because I shouldn't? Don't give me—"

"Stop." She was begging … and so I did.

"Where are we?" I asked, along a different line, my favorite question again.

"What do you want?" the voice asked.

"To get out! And what happens now?" I yelled, pounding my hands into the floor.

There was no answer.

I then remembered Ehs and words that he had spoken to me long ago that I had never recalled, which was shocking in itself. Maybe I had never wanted to recall them. But, I did then. He had told me I could leave whenever I wanted and so I decided, simply, to leave.

But nothing happened.

If something had happened I might have believed in something of life. But, there was nothing. I was convinced I was dead.

Did Ruby know she was working on a dead man? Did my family know yet? Did Rachel—the thought of Rachel killed me, even if I was already dead. I missed her. God, I was in hell. Worse than hell. I hoped the second death, at least, was good theology, because if I was going to sit in that box for eternity …

No, I didn't believe that.

And she was there.

"Why aren't you speaking?" I yelled at the spark.

"Seth," she whispered. "We don't need words."

"Well, do you have a fucking key then?" I screamed, in a demanding tone at a spark hovering in the air in front of me inside of a claustrophobic box of nothing that felt stuffy and heavy and suffocating.

"It will come," she whispered, even softer than usual.

"It?" My heart lifted. God?

There was no answer.

"It?" I repeated. My heart fell. Ehs?

Nothing.

"Hey, who is coming?" I screamed at the top of my lungs, my voice smothered and muted by darkness.

I stood to my feet, a little surprised the room let me, but happy to look down on her lame spark and shout again at the top of my lungs.

"Who is coming!"

No answer.

I began running from one side of the room to the next. Sprinting. Slamming into the wall. Sweating. Dying within death from what felt like heat exhaustion, insanity, and darkness. I turned back to her and yelled again. "Why won't you answer me!"

Suddenly I was dreaming, as though I wasn't dreaming already. Or was I? What was happening shouldn't have happened, even accepting the realities of the world or dimension or whatever it was I was in, so I assumed it was some kind of dream though I was aware of the whole thing. Maybe it was just a new reality that felt like a dream inside of an already altered reality.

In reality, I have no idea.

Dreams within dreams. Or dreams within nightmares. Or possessions within possessions. I suppose we're always possessed by something, no matter where we find ourselves and that possessions can always get darker or lighter.

It was all moving somewhere.

Dear god, what is happening to me?

Whatever it was, I was looking at Ehs. He had returned to a more familiar shape—that of a human. And he was walking around a familiar space: my front yard.

The grass was green. The air was blue. It was a perfect early fall day, which I assumed it was in the normal world. Ehs, in the form of James, walked across the grass and to the front door.

The door opened and my daughter was there. She smiled and gave him a hug and my heart would have ached if it had any more ache left in it. She left him and laughed about something, running back into the house.

Where Ehs soon followed.

My wife was in the kitchen and she smiled at him as well. He walked over to her and kissed her. Seeing Ehs kiss my wife would have made me sick to my stomach. But my stomach and soul and body were already as sick as they could get so there was not much of an effect. Maybe beyond apathy is a deeper pain. The way she smiled at him felt like torturing a dead man. Yet I still felt it somehow.

She said something to him but I couldn't hear. I was there but I was not.

Ehs began to move up the stairs as though he owned the place. That would have bugged me too. Under normal circumstances. But not in that moment.

He eventually reached the bedroom and eventually the bathroom where he decided to stand in front of our mirror. Oddly, I couldn't see his face. I was behind him and he was blocking my own vision. I wanted to see his face desperately so I could imagine it dying, like I was in that moment.

Aware, even in the dream.

Where apathy had reigned there was emotion. Again. A new darkness. Another level as though there could be more levels. I moved and changed my viewpoint but by the time I could see his face, it was not the face I had grown accustomed to seeing on him. It was a face I was much more accustomed to: my own.

It was right there staring back at me. In the mirror was the face I would always see in the mirror, but dark, wispy, and transparent suddenly—almost a shadow.

I didn't know if I was seeing the future, the present, the past, or some kind of insight into what the entire journey had been, but none of the options were good. None of the options were less terrifying and traumatic and I began to try and process all of them.

But our brains don't work in dreams or in states like that. Not reasonably. I just cried. I don't remember starting to cry but then I was doing it—crying, shaking, wailing.

And suddenly I was terrified. The tears had left but I was panicked that something was about to happen to someone in my house. Maybe to me.

I was still in my house with him. Was I processing within the dream? This never happens.

And then I was overcome with sadness and grief and pain.

I went from one emotion to the next with little or no transition—the way we often do in dreams, but I was aware that it was all a dream, in the way we often aren't.

What is any of this?

Then I awoke back to my previous nightmare.

A small flame surrounded by darkness. Emotionless.

There was a small child all over the news that had been pulled from the rubble of Aleppo. The child had experienced pain that no human, let alone one of such beauty and innocence, should ever experience. Yet, in this cruel world, he had. And his response by the time he was filmed was that of nothing. He was numb. He didn't cry. He didn't smile. He didn't love. He didn't hate. He didn't miss. He didn't want vengeance. He didn't hunger.

He simply existed and it seemed worse than death.

Back in the box, I was sure it was worse.

I simply existed.

The flame was there, flickering ever so slowly, and I could do nothing but stare at it.

"Are you afraid?" she asked.

I didn't answer because I had to think about it.

"Of what?" she asked.

"Everything," I answered with more numbness. "That I am empty."

"You are almost there," she whispered.

"What?" I sat up. Had I been lying down? "What did you say?"

She did not repeat it.

"You fear the darkness."

"No shit!" I yelled at the stupid flame that represented everything I had ever believed.

"I love you."

"Well thanks so much," I answered with sarcasm. "As though that matters. We've already learned that's a bunch of shit."

"Even in the darkness, I love."

"That's very nice. I know. But you don't tell a cancer patient they're loved and expect them to feel better. They don't care. They don't want cancer. And I don't want to be in this fucking box and whether you love me in this box or not, again, I don't really care." I was sweating, profusely. Chemicals of every kind filled my body, trying to make sense, trying to take control, trying to get me out, trying to die.

"Fine."

"Fine?" I asked, incredulous.

"Fine."

"What's that mean?"

"If you want to live in the darkness, you are welcome to. If you want to live in the fear, go right ahead."

"Well, I don't see whatever you're doing getting *you* out of here."

"I don't need to."

And she vanished.

She was gone. Everything was gone. My point of reference was gone and the walls were now within inches of my body on every side. I could feel them.

I *was* buried alive. Or buried dead. Or just buried. Either way I knew I wasn't going to last much longer.

I screamed until I could no more. I shouted every obscenity I had ever learned until I could no more. I gave into anger as much as I ever had until I could no more. I cried out for every god I knew of. I threw curses at every god I was aware of.

I begged for help, but none came.

I tried to lean into the emptiness for some kind of hollow relief that would last only for a passing moment that could have been any length of time—I had no gauge, no direction, no way to measure, nothing but nothing.

I did remember she said she loved.

I did remember she said she loved me.

I did remember she said she loved me.

The walls collapsed. They were gone.

I was free? I tried to smile but it felt like I had forgotten what a smile felt like or how to make one appear.

Then I realized I was in hell, but only because I had been there before.

THIRTY NINE POINT FIVE

I recognized her immediately. Knowing it was her made it not nearly as enjoyable as the first time. I hadn't known what I was dealing with then. I hadn't known what to be afraid of. They say ignorance is bliss … I say ignorance is not being terrified of something that you haven't learned to be terrified of, yet.

Knowledge is a fucking burden sometimes.

I was in front of Lucy again. She was beautiful. Beyond measure. More than I remembered, but, at that point I didn't remember what I remembered.

She simply stared. As did I.

In any other situation the stare would have gotten extremely awkward. But, in that situation, it was hypnotizing. I liked it. I loved it. I was also terrified of it because I knew that I was not supposed to like it or love it. Yet, I couldn't stop liking it and loving it as though those portions of my self-control were no longer under my reign, but something else.

I began to spiral again and I looked out toward the beach scene that was all around me—the same I had seen years earlier—to calm myself. The waves were gently crashing with a rhythmic sound and motion. The sun was setting in cliché majesty and beauty. The air was tender and warm on my skin. The fall leaves were there, in some other direction, as were the snow-capped mountains and whatever else I wanted.

I realized the scenes became whatever I desired as soon as I desired them. Almost before I did.

Infinite choice was driving me as infinitely mad as no choices.

"You're okay," she said plainly, as though it were impossible to imagine a reason I wouldn't be. "Settle down."

"Okay," I responded, wanting to be okay and wanting to settle down.

"There's nothing to worry about," she said, taking a few steps closer, holding out her hands as though I was a rabid beast, about to attack her. Which made me wonder if I could, or should.

"Well, I could argue with that," I responded, half myself and half-possessed by confusion and delirium and god knows what else.

"Like what, Seth?" Her voice *was* soothing.

"Like you being the devil. Like me being in hell. Like me believing a demon and finding out I shouldn't have. Shocking, by the way. I shouldn't have believed a demon." I laughed, except my laugh didn't even sound like me.

Did I laugh? Am I laughing?

"Am I even laughing right now?" I heard a laugh again and tried to look at my own mouth to see if it was making the sounds.

Lucy smiled. I assumed she enjoyed watching someone officially lose their mind.

"I don't know if I'm dead, insane, plugged into some kind of virtual reality experimental experience, or if all of this is actually happening." I began rubbing my own arms. It somehow connected me to something.

She smiled again but in a way I never expected the devil to smile, because the smile made me feel better. She then shook her head, almost disappointed, almost proud. I couldn't really tell. "I don't know where to begin," she said.

"I know the feeling," I answered, which was very true.

She laughed. Gently. "Where should I?"

She's laughing?

"Anywhere," I answered. It wouldn't be the first time I would listen to darkness and play along with it.

"Who told you the devil was bad?"

A real softball of a question. "Everyone."

"And you believe everyone?" she asked, still staying far enough away to not make me feel afraid she would turn into a red-horned beast and stab me but close enough that I felt like she cared.

"Sometimes."

"Even when ..." She took a step closer. "... the truth is based in myth, fantasy, and religious teachers who have never met the devil—you still believe everyone?"

"I think plenty have met you. Practically are you."

"True," she smiled.

"And you're in the bible?"

"That's funny," she smirked.

She should have. We both knew no devil was spelled out in any bibles.

"Well." I figured I would try again, a little less reactionary and rote. "I, honestly, don't believe in a devil. Or didn't. But I do think there is something evil and there's …" I looked her up and down. "You. So, what am I supposed to believe? You're standing in front of me."

"Fair enough," she nodded.

"Okay," I nodded in return.

"Who told you the devil was bad?"

"No one," I responded, differently this time. "No one that matters. I've seen it. Experienced it. Your boy Ehs is." I looked down, almost ashamed to say it to her face. "Evil."

She didn't hesitate. "Why?"

I looked back up at her. "Why?" I yelled. Then louder. "Why?" And even louder. "How many times do you want me to yell *why*?"

She said nothing.

"He lied to me."

"When did he lie to you?"

"He's a narcissist. He's out to destroy whatever he can. Including me."

She waited.

"He said he wanted to change," I uttered, feeling stupid again for believing him and answering both of her questions.

"And how do you know he didn't?" she asked.

"He told me I was an idiot for believing him."

"Is that true?" she asked.

"Of course it's true," I answered a little rough, quickly forgetting who I was talking to.

"So," she said, smiling. "He wasn't lying."

"No," I responded, a little agitated. "He told me I could trust him. He told me I could help him. He told me— What's your point? What do you want from me? What does any of this matter?"

"What do *you* want?" she returned, taking another step closer and looking me up and down as I had her a minute ago.

"Well, that's a good question …" Looking at the beach again, feeling the weather, looking at her … I wasn't entirely sure.

"Are you afraid?" she asked, throwing me off a bit.

"Why does everyone ask me if I'm afraid?" I responded. "Of course I am!"

"Of Ehs?" she asked.

I thought back to his mouthless face. The darkness that surrounded him and had suffocated me. The lies, the deception, the stories, the trust. The power. The apathy. "Sure."

She smirked. "Not enough."

"Okay," I said. "Cute, yeah, yeah. You already had me in a

fucking coffin. What else is there?"

Her smile told me that there were all kinds of things and I needed to watch my words and attitude carefully.

I decided to do both.

"I never said you were wrong, Seth, I was just curious." The way the words slid off of her tongue and into the air instantly made me more nervous. "But—" She stopped.

"But?" I asked, cautiously.

She smiled and "hell" changed rather dramatically and quickly. Wherever or whatever I had been looking at—the beach, the mountains—began to slide away, as though I were riding an elevator and the scenes I had been living in were simply a nice wallpaper. As we continued to rise up, where I had been went down, and since it was not wallpaper but still a three-dimensional world, the whole visual was very disorienting and nausea-inducing. Seconds before I puked all over the floor of whatever was lifting me up, we stopped and I found myself high in a sky I recognized.

It was my sky. My city. My country. My world. And the wall was in the distance, not too far away. Actually, when I looked at the wall it was close, as though whatever perspective I was looking at the world from was able to draw everything closer than it actually was.

A giant observation deck that seemed to know where my eyes were focused and drew it closer. It didn't magnify it, it simply drew it closer. Or maybe it drew me closer. The whole effect made me sick and nauseous almost instantly. I felt the same way I had when I used to watch someone play a first person video game. The world was not matching with my brain in a way that my brain wanted it to.

"You're strong," she said.

I wasn't quite sure what to do with that statement.

"I have a gift for you."

Cliché overload.

You know I was once a pastor, right?

I had preached on the story back in the day. Jesus was brought up to a high place and offered the world—by the devil. As we stood together in our own high place, I didn't want her offers. To be fair, I didn't even know what it was, but I figured I shouldn't, even if I wanted to.

She waited for me to look at her.

I did, but she didn't do anything.

I waited.

Again, a long pause.

"Okay, I get it. You going to tell me to turn stones into bread or something?" My humor surprised even me as it left my mouth. Humor takes arrogance, or at least confidence, and I wasn't sure I had either. Yet somehow I was cracking jokes.

She didn't laugh. Or do anything.

So, I looked back to the world.

And I saw Rachel. It was quite strange. I could see her clearly performing some kind of yoga routine on a beach in front of about twenty-five people. She was strong, powerful … a leader. I desperately missed her and the tremors started deep in my belly. The quakes of sadness. I could feel them erupting. *Rachel!*

I saw my kids. Each of them. As though in three different frames. My son was running on a city sidewalk. My oldest daughter was drinking coffee in a shop somewhere. My youngest daughter was doing flips in a gym. I reached out my hand to touch them but I could not. Tears were forming behind my eyes. God I missed them so much.

My whole body was shaking now with the tremors of sadness and loss.

I saw Jaden. He was also on a beach, walking hand in hand with his wife, their bare feet tickled by the waves and the smiles on their faces proudly displaying the fact that they were enjoying it. More tears. I missed even Jaden.

I saw Leo, sitting in a cell. Alone. Empty. Shoulders slumped, staring at the floor as he sat on the side of an empty bed in an empty room. I wanted to hug him and tell him he was going to be okay. I wanted to hug myself.

I was bawling now, my vision clouded by sadness expressing itself.

I saw Gwen. She was lying on a bed with her husband lying next to her. He was wearing his flight uniform and she was wearing a nightgown of some kind—her preferred fashion statement. She was leaning in to him, smiling.

I saw Richard. He was sitting at a night stand reading a bible, with glasses on, staring intently.

I saw the rest of the board, the man from the beach at Priest, my extended family, Aubrey, Lemi in some kind of warehouse, and the Swedish supermodel Freja sitting by her modern pool. Kids were playing soccer, the man from the gas station was hammering nails outside, and Elle was watching television on a couch, alone in a dirty apartment. The coffee shop owner was smoking a joint. The delivery man was driving his truck and James, I saw James for the first time … not with Ehs inside of him and he looked … a lot like me.

I turned to face her again, wiping away tears and mad that she could see me cry. "What do you want?"

She wore a grin with a perfect curve. "What do *you* want?"

I looked back to my world. "That."

She observed my tears. "That?" she asked quite simply, although with a hint of disappointment. I felt like the kid who wanted to play with the three-dollar yo-yo on Christmas instead of the eight-hundred-dollar toy car and she was my parent. "That?" she repeated, looking out at my yo-yo and shaking her head, believing there to be so much more I would want.

Maybe I did?

Tears erupted from the fire of my gut, again. Seeing them all out there, so close and yet in some other place that I could not get to … I was covered in deep longing and sadness. I don't know if Jesus cried in his story but I didn't care much either way. I sobbed and let the tears roll down my face onto the platform below me.

She continued to just observe my sadness, saying nothing throughout it.

I eventually stopped, having emptied whatever lake the dam was holding back. And because her intent stare began to remove emotion from the space around us.

"What would you give for that?" she repeated.

I closed my eyes to better think about the question. "What do you want?"

"To make you happy," she said.

"Then, that's easy. You can let me go."

Slowly, and with a smile that dripped something ugly, she began to shake her head. "It's not me that is holding you here."

I frowned, not sure if she was lying or telling the truth or how I was ever to know the difference between the two ever again. "Then who?"

"Where is your god? Do you even believe anymore?" she asked instead.

I had to close my eyes again, not sure how to exactly answer that question.

"Maybe," I answered.

"Maybe?" she asked. "What does that mean?"

"It means I might."

"I'm afraid," she slithered suddenly, in a voice that made me shudder. "You will need to find your answers quickly."

For a split second, I saw it.

It was cold, empty, and terrifying. It was not horns, it was not red, and it was not holding a pitchfork. It was an accusation. It was pedophilia, racism, assault, greed, slavery, and genocide. It was fear, shame, and violence. Visible, felt and seen, somehow.

It was an instant and I fell to the ground from the immense pain it caused me.

And then everything changed. Again. Of course, because everything always changed.

FORTY

I was suddenly aware of my breathing. It was loud enough that I couldn't miss it. Not an ominous volume but a noticeable volume, an awareness like in snorkeling or scuba diving. When you're underwater you become immediately conscious of the thing that keeps you alive because that thing is suddenly not surrounding you. It's much more precious.

As I became more accustomed to where I was, I noticed many similarities between being underwater and what I felt. Things were slower, as though I was floating in something, or always had been and was finally aware of it.

My movement had a slight resistance and it was hard to see too far, as though whatever substance I was surrounded by diffused and constrained vision. There was a dark shade to perception: a shadow over everything.

After registering the what of the environment, I realized the where. I was on the ground of the arena I had been in earlier. I could see the stained red dirt. The tall platform in the middle. The gates. The seats where thousands had cheered, including me. The ancient architecture. I looked down and felt ill at the carnage and chaos I had witnessed, at the death that had filled whatever space I was standing in.

I was alone.

It was only me in the entire ocean of an arena. Me and my breathing. Me and my almost floating. The absence of anything was both calming somehow and electrifying in another sense. I found myself hyperaware—like when swimming in an ocean. Every fish, every rock, every piece of coral, every movement of sand and vague blur in peripheral vision is seen and noticed and reacted to, because the environment is not the one we live in. I felt the same there. Ready for something to appear.

And, of course, it did.

A gate opened and I saw Ehs. Not the friendly Ehs of James, but the despicable and ruthless Lord of Darkness Ehs. The long, black cloak, almost alive in the way it moved and absorbed light and floated in the dark air like long hair underwater. The ashen skin. The absent mouth and eyes. The coiled dark crown of metal.

The eyes penetrated me with nothingness and stopped my breathing for a moment.

Worse than Ehs were five shapes that walked or swam or floated in after him, imposing on their own, together dreadful. A disgust welled up inside of me at more of the blank, expressionless faces with their dark crowns and cloaks swimming against the thick air. I assumed they were the other Lords … Ehs had been kind using words like war, security, labor, and education for me. I could see then they were all Lords of Darkness and each commanded legions of their own. I felt smaller and smaller, beyond insignificant, with each infinitely empty gaze turned toward me.

I looked down toward the blood-stained ground, still foggy like the sandy bottom of an ocean, wondering if I would be next to soak the dirt, and realizing that I was almost hovering above it.

Another gate opened—the sound echoing and muffled—and I immediately recognized The Seers, swimming across the ground toward me in their chaotic organization. The thousands of small spherical shapes formed into a similar shape as the other Lords, walking as some kind of collective mass of darkness, which forced me again to look away.

There were fewer and fewer safe places for my eyes to land.

A sound of chanting reached my ears and forced me to, again, look up in dread of whatever was coming next. It was emanating from an opposite tunnel and eventually revealed itself to be six of the soldiers I had watched earlier.

They were covered in matte black armor now, with heavy shields and swords hanging off of their chests. Together they carried a massive throne above their shoulders. The throne was confusing in its own right—almost metal, almost dark cloud, almost the ink of a squid swirling amidst the currents of whatever contained us. Its inability to form a shape made it frustrating to look at. Whatever sat or floated on it was even more disconcerting to see. At times it was snake, at times it was a soldier, at times it was everything wrong with the world, and at times it was Lucy.

I immediately looked away, unable to handle the onslaught of injustice, abuse, and torture I felt from it, as though it was shark and I was prey and everything around me was closing in. Whatever ocean I was in was not the tropical and warm one I had always enjoyed but the deadly and cold instead that I had once experienced with Ehs.

A blood-stained bottom of packed dirt was my only solace. I stared at it, floating above it and noticing movement all around me but afraid to look. Eventually I dared and I saw her again. She had been placed in the middle of the group of Lords and Seers, which now included six smaller Lords. Nothing was settled. Everything was constantly moving and flowing and swirling and murky.

The sound of ravens sent my eyes upward.

Thousands appeared almost instantly in the gray ocean above me, circling, calling out all at once. The sheer volume was overwhelming and I fell to my knees, covering my ears, wishing the sound would go away and curious as to how there was sky underwater and how birds were flying. I looked up and saw them continuing to move, darting back and forth like schools of flying fish or flocks of swimming birds. They were all the same. I wondered if they took my movements as some kind of bowing to their power, which in the moment made me feel sick but I could do nothing else.

Eventually it all stopped and when I looked again the ravens had lined up across the entire floor of the arena. Thousands of them. Thousands more lined the arena and still more moved around above me, circling and gliding and leaving small black wakes behind them: miniature contrails filled the air and made it all the darker. Those on the ground and in the stands transformed into soldiers, like those I had seen earlier and similar to the six who had carried her in. Almost transparent and empty, but also devastatingly strong. Swords. Shields. Black armor. Ethereal power and arrogance.

I managed to stand to my feet again, somehow.

Before I could spend too much time considering my predicament, my place in it all, my future, or what the hell kind of environment I was in—it was still confusing—two people appeared directly in front of me. Their presence was a surprise to say the least.

On my left was the beautiful woman from the modern house. Freja. The sight of her did help me smile, her blond hair flowing in the air like a mermaid's. She was as stunning as I remembered. She floated me a smile back, warm and sensuous, inviting and welcoming. There were no hamburgers with her.

On my right was someone I could only assume was Jesus. He was not the Jesus I had seen earlier, but the Jesus I would have expected to match the man that had lived in the Middle East a couple of thousand years earlier. Dark skin, wavy black hair just long enough to swim around his cheeks, and a thick black beard. There was a gentle strength to him that made me smile. A rawness. An imposing kindness. He returned to me a smile.

"Jesus?" I vocalized, though it was hard to speak, as if something rushed into my mouth when I opened it.

He nodded.

“These are your choices,” Lucy said, her words sailing on a current to my ears. Her voice was familiar but her shape was still far away and slithering and sliding around her throne, which was doing the same, as though it was all agitated and anxious. I felt pain just looking at her. Not productive pain. Not even fearful pain. Just pain. I felt fear looking at her. Not fear of what might happen—which fear usually is—but fear of what *was* happening. She was somehow a present pain, a present fear, incarnate, and accusatory that I was not enough … of anything. The experience of that was enough to blow me backward, gently and carefully, still contained, but to my knees again, this time covering my eyes.

I hoped Jesus or Freja would come to help me, but neither did.

“Your choice. Which will die and which will live,” Lucy said, this time much easier to understand, as though standing next to me. I did not look to see if she was, but instead stared at Freja and Jesus, back and forth, and trying to decide what Lucy meant. “Which one is worthless and which one will save you.”

“I’m afraid I don’t understand,” I said, carefully and cautiously and still with effort, while standing again to my feet, feeling resistance and containment with every movement.

A mocking chuckle rippled through the arena, through the soldiers, and eventually to the Lords and Lucy herself. “These are your gods,” she repeated. “You will choose the one that lives and the one that dies.”

Something—maybe a wave or current or Lucy herself—forced my head down and then my hands open. Two stones appeared, one in each hand. As I held them I could see them switch from white to black and from black to white and I realized I could decide what color they were. As I thought it, either stone would turn. It was a grain of magic and light-heartedness in the midst of a sea of danger.

I felt brave somehow. I noticed it in the deep recesses of my mind. Maybe it was Jesus standing next to me, maybe it was what I had already been through, maybe it was the idea that if they were going to kill me, they already would have. Maybe it was the stones themselves. But something birthed strength in me.

I returned to watching the stones flash back and forth, and managed to wonder if my antics were driving everyone crazy. I hoped—for a flash—they were.

“Enough,” I heard from her in a voice I never wanted to hear again. It was like the jolt from an electric eel and the sting of a jellyfish to my internal organs. I immediately stopped and stared toward the ground, closing my hands, seeing my feet levitate off the ground as the air held me. "You will choose. Her. Or him. And your choice, if correct, will free you. If wrong, your choice will destroy you along with your god."

It was then, with her words, that my processing centers burned up. They say in war that soldiers lose their frontal cortex—their ability to reason. If my brain was a computer, those chips officially went offline too. I felt them frying. I entered some other realm of human experience in that moment, with little ability to process much of anything. The scene itself was too much, let alone the stakes at play.

Even death felt like something I couldn't understand.

I frowned and looked up at Jesus. The robe he wore was dirty and torn, floating lightly around his body and lifting away from the soil. His dark leather sandals were bathed with red dust even though it felt like dust couldn't live in whatever we were swimming in. I looked at Freja. She was dressed immaculately and none of the dust or dirt floating in the air seemed to touch her white dress or flowing blond hair. Or perfect curves.

Mu. Illusion. Symbol. Metaphor.

She was the dark. I could feel it. She was "the world." The cars, houses, and raw infatuation for more.

He was the light. I could feel it. He was the "sacred." The faith, love, and hope for more.

The stones were, I assumed, guideposts to the paths of life.

I felt the dark tomb again. The one I had come from. I threw up onto the ground just thinking about it. If that were my death and I would be forced back in there, forever … or even for a day …

My own vomit swirled around at my feet. There were muffled cackles from somewhere around me and smothered calls of birds from somewhere above me.

Jesus. Of course, right?

I looked again at the woman in white.

Why is she wearing white?

She didn't seem evil and tempting and all of the things wrong with the world. In fact, as I stared at her I remembered our conversation. Processing centers were slowly coming back on. I remembered the false Jesus on the hills, the cowboy, the trickster, the disguise.

Is this all a trick?

Fuck.

"They both live," I said out loud.

If it had been a ripple of a laugh earlier, it was now a roar, like a massive stroke of thunder or a wave crashing into the shoreline. Not comedic laughter but biting, acidulous laughter. It was a felt energy surrounding me and moving away from me, and the dark shapes seemed to respond to it, like underwater flora responds to the waves: a ripple flowed through each of them.

Under normal circumstances I may have crumbled, but I was still not close to functioning normally. I reached to rub my head and noticed that my hands were shaking so hard I could barely make them move where I wanted. I would have cried but it felt like I was surrounded by tears.

Leo appeared in front of me, shocking me back into reality or whatever simulation I was in. His expression was not nearly as perplexed as I would have expected it to be nor as flabbergasted as mine was.

"Leo?" I asked. "What?" I reached out to grab him but he made his way to stand next to Jesus. Jesus wrapped his arm around him instead and the two smiled at each other, almost ignoring me.

Others began to appear faster than I could even count. Bob. Aubrey. The delivery man, Nate. Elle. Gwen. Gwen's husband. Jaden. Jaden's wife. My children. Marie, our therapist. Richard. The entire board of the church. The owner of the coffee shop. The man from the gas station. The pastor. The man in the BMW. Parents from the soccer game. Gwen's son. The wedding party. The man in the wheelchair from the hospital. The tourist from Hawaii with her big hair. The man from the lake with his grunge metal shirt. James. Normal, nice James was there staring at me and he slowly waved.

It was all still slow, still maintained, still resisted, as though time was under the same spell I was. My breath became loud again. I could hear it pulsing through me, faster than it had been when I had last noticed.

Emotions fled once more. Reasoning followed them, away from me, again. I was only surviving, barely.

There were groups crowding around Jesus. And there were others crowding around Freja. And the entire choosing of teams made me feel unsteady and uncertain about anything that was happening or was about to happen.

My kids were standing with Freja in her white dress. Richard was with Jesus. The man from the gas station stood next to Freja and could not stop looking her up and down. I didn't really blame him. The tourist was with Jesus. In fact, as it played out I began to see that most of the people I liked were with the very nice woman from Sweden who had shown me a fake hamburger and most of the people I did not were with Jesus.

What ability I had left to panic kicked in.

I was a demon myself.

Or possessed.

Or a maniac with no capacity to engage his mind anymore.

Or a possessed maniacal demon—maybe Jesus was going to have to save me? Could I even be saved? In that moment, I felt I was beyond redemption and hope and swimming in accusation.

I stared at my children, hoping to find human emotion of some kind but they were almost … empty. Robotic. As though present in form only. The sight of everyone from my life began to make me cry again as I had earlier. Tears of outrage, confusion, and loss more than sadness. Crying underwater in a sea of tears. My whole body was shaking, stumbling, barely able to hold on any longer. "Stop this!" I yelled. "Please. I'll do what you want."

"Choose one group to destroy. The other group to live. If you refuse altogether, all of the humans will die."

Group?

The. Humans. Will. Die.

Five words that took me by the throat and started squeezing. I only continued to cry, my tears staining the red ground and making it seem like my own blood. It might as well have been. There was a power in the arena that I understood could follow through on whatever command she wished for. It reigned in this reality.

Death was my only decision? I was not only choosing a god but people I loved. To live or die.

"What kind of sick game is this?" I managed to ask, only to be answered by an ocean of laughter and humiliation.

The humans. I looked to them again: the eyes, the ears, the hair, the lips, the shoulders, the feet, the teeth, the hands, the fingernails. I stared at each of them. Humans. Whether it's the story we have told ourselves or the reality of the universe, we have some foundational element to us all. It's very deep and often buried with lifetimes of layers that prevent us from accessing it. But, in that moment, it made its presence known to me.

Something strong in the midst of so much that felt weak.

I looked at the group again. "Where is Rachel?"

There was an odd pause in the arena. I felt it. A doubt of something. In the same way the laughter had been felt, I felt the pause. The unknown. My own courage grew a bit more.

We all floated there for a moment, everything moving slowly but nothing happening.

Then she spoke. Rachel. My wife. "Seth," she said plainly. She was standing next to me with her arm on my shoulder. I doubted my own experience, for fear it was an oasis in the midst of a parched desert.

I hugged her as tight as I had ever hugged anything, squeezing, feeling, holding on to what was real. Or, at least, felt.

"Seth," she said. "It's okay."

There was some kind of rumble of anxiety through the arena. A pessimistic curiosity and unnerving. I looked to Ehs and watched his shoulders drop.

Emonee appeared next, not as the ray of light I had last seen and not as the spark in the darkness and not as the old lady at my house. Just a woman. About Rachel's age. Oddly normal, when standing next to Rachel. Not a twin but everything felt comfortable with her. I felt as though I had known her all my life though I had never seen her in that form. She wore a black, free-flowing dress that danced around the air, merging into her dark hair that did the same.

The good thing growing in the recesses of me was moving upward, to my mind, my heart, my soul.

"Rachel?" I looked at Emonee and back to Rachel. My tears had vanished only to be replaced with more curiosity and bewilderment—which was an emotion I felt rippling beyond me and into the crowds. There was no light to Emonee, eradicating darkness, but there was a presence of liberation amidst chains.

"Emonee and I have been hanging out for a while," Rachel said, as powerful as I had ever heard her voice. "I'm sorry I couldn't tell you."

I said nothing with words but everything with my furled forehead and searching eyes. There was confusion, bordering on betrayal, but also a comforting sensation that was filling me up.

"Seth." Rachel grabbed my hand. "Kill him." She pointed toward Jesus with a cold finger. I saw his eyes grow sad and hurt. "Trust me."

"Jesus?" Chaos reigned inside me again. Utter inability to decide anything, again. Stress was the king of every inch of my body and I was its servant. I was floating in stress, contained and resisted by it. "Trust? But, that's Jesus. Now? You know her? Are you real? Are you sure? Are you … I don't understand."

"We both had to learn things," she said quietly and walked next to our children. She hugged them and then hugged Freja with a casual give and take of smiles that made me think it was not the first time Rachel had met her, which only sent more cortisol through my body—as though it could handle any more. But if she was with my children, I would have to take out Jesus. At least my family would live.

If anyone comes to me and does not hate his father, his mother, his wife, Jesus apparently once said … fuck.

The nice normal lady in the form of Emonee moved and stood

by Jesus, inviting more chaos, just when I thought my decision had been made. Rachel then moved from Freja to the side of Jesus, next to Emonee.

I could only keep staring back and forth. "Rachel? What?" I looked up to Lucy. "I don't understand!"

"Choose!" echoed through the room. There was no option inside of it and the arena erupted with the calls of the birds, the soldiers who sounded like birds—and the people who surrounded me and had for years.

Everyone was awake suddenly. Present. Aware. Screaming and shouting at me every kind of piece of advice possible.

"Do not be deceived!"

"Trust your heart!"

"Save us!"

"Trust Jesus!"

"Systems!"

"Pastor Seth, you know what to do."

"That's not Jesus!"

"Make up for your mistakes now!"

"This is life or death!"

"Play!"

I heard some and I didn't hear others.

I was floating in a cacophony of words and the chaos of the birds and the overall blinding emotions and energies of the entire arena.

The decision weighed down on me, like some force driving me into the red soil, as though gravity had been turned on directly above my head. It drove me lower and deeper until my knees and hands were aching from the pressure driving them down. My face was going to be next.

That thing in us as humans though.

I thought of Ehs, oddly, and managed to look toward him. Far away, through the distractions, I saw him. Foggy and murky but I could see that he was looking at me. And, somehow, I trusted him. In that moment, I trusted him almost more than anyone else.

Or maybe I trusted myself.

Something began to make sense.

We can't make you do anything.

Release valves.

Knowledge!

Abraham.

Fear.

The Separated.

Not far enough.
You're almost there.
So close.
Scared of something that doesn't even exist.
Light.
Darkness.
Don't weigh yourself down.
The light only reveals.
We hide.
I'm dying.
You were the perfect choice.
Don't ask where.
Nuance.
Wells.
God bless.
Space.
All of it.
Let them go.

And confidence was born. That thing in us humans was giving birth to an ability to live. A dark liquid surrounded me, as though it had come from me. It swirled for a moment and eventually swam away into the distance toward Lucy. A passion was there to find a way. An instinct to forge ahead.

I found the ability to speak. "Can I ask each of the gods one question?"

"One," she answered from her toxic brew of ink and tar.

I paused to think. I *could* think.

"What must I know?" I said as loud as my courage would allow me to, staring Freja in the eyes. "What must I know?" I said equally as loud, directly into the eyes of Jesus. "Tell me the one thing."

There was another pause within the space. A silent contraction.

"You must know who you want to be," she said plainly, with her nice accent.

"You must know what's in your heart," he said gently.

It was finished.

There was no longer a need to deliberate, except to create drama, which I was present enough to know I wanted to do. I held up my hands and watched the rocks turn black and white, almost like flashing dualistic traffic signals. I chose my color for each before closing my fist and lifting them into the sky, holding them there and waiting for her to say something. I was making her speak.

"Your choice," she uttered. "Now."

Soldiers moved in on both the woman and Jesus, drawing out their swords, holding them to their chests. The guards surrounded me as well. They surrounded the people I loved and had known throughout my life that was about to end.

I saw flashes of the darkness, of Ehs, of shame, of confusion, of fear inside of their transparent shapes.

My fists began to shake, representing what was happening all over my body. Floating in fear I felt okay. I stared directly at her, my eyes peering into her swirling confusion on her dark throne of lies. I faced her directly. I almost dared her.

I opened both of my hands to reveal two black stones.

"Kill them both," I shouted. "The gods can all fucking die."

Spears plunged into Freja's chest and the side of Jesus, spilling blood into the air and ground and both collapsed to the floor, struggling to breathe.

I had a momentary sliver of doubt that I had made the correct decision watching them both go down.

But it was only a moment.

I saw Lucy and her throne immediately vanish.

The Lords were gone too, except for Ehs, who was back in the form of James, with his hands lifted high, celebratory somehow.

The soldiers disappeared and the water that held it all vanished too. The birds and The Seers went with their environment.

As though some massive veil was lifted from the arena, I saw light. Everywhere. In fact it was all I could see but it was not light of white but light of color. I was the mantis shrimp hero but I understood it all. The light moved within and around us all, through us, containing, propelling, moving, creating.

We were floating in light, not in whatever had been masking it.

I could see it all. I could breathe like I had never breathed before. I could hear. I could taste. Light.

The shapes of my family and friends melted away only to be replaced by something more true.

The form of Jesus melted away only to be replaced by something more vibrant.

The form of Freja melted away only to be replaced by something more dark, and yet, necessary.

It was good in every way, even if it was not perfect.

And I said these words to whomever was listening. Or to myself. "What is."

Whatever form was where Jesus had been emanated love and

mystery. As did the woman. As did James. As did Ehs. As did Rachel.

As did I, because we were all one somehow. Connected, united and light. There were no differences, there were no memories, and there was no future. It was all just there.

Present. Being. Together.

Words are too weak to describe the whole of the experience but that is all that anyone needs to know.

And then I saw nothing but black. It was dark again. Quiet and silent.

I once heard a free diver talk about what it was like to be hundreds of feet underwater without any kind of breathing apparatus. To be at the bottom. She talked of taking a moment to absorb it, to even wave to the ocean because, she said, that darkness and quiet are peaceful when you have won a battle with yourself.

Whatever darkness I found myself in was peaceful.

I even waved before opening my eyes.

And I woke up on a massage table.

"Wow," Ruby said out loud. "Did you feel that? I felt that. That was—" She paused for a long time, still working on my shoulder. "That was something."

"Yes," I cracked, barely able to get a word out. Could I possibly have any more tears to cry?

I did. They burst forth from a dam of emotions. They were a different kind of tear. There was so much emotion I didn't know if my body could express it and stay functioning. I was crying uncontrollably—joy and peace and light and pain flooding out of every pore.

I wanted to see Rachel.

I wanted to see Emonee.

I wanted to see Ehs.

I wanted to see myself.

I wanted to see.

EPILOGUE SIX MONTHS LATER

Food has never tasted so good. Hugs have never felt so warm. Smiles have never sent such happiness through my cells.

I've had plenty of nightmares but there has also been bliss.

Hours have passed into days, which have passed into months.

At times it has felt dark with all of my gods dead but with gods dead, there is space for something greater than mere idols. It's in the darkness that we find the strength to destroy walls and let in more light, to the system and our hearts.

I have wished I could go back to the images, the metaphors, the games, the temples, the cold emptiness even, but I can't. He is gone. I go on the same runs, I've had the same massage, and I've done more yoga, expecting my world to change at any moment.

It hasn't. Not like it once did.

Rachel and I have spent hours exchanging our stories. I have heard more than I imagined I could. Her stories are hers to share but they are just as mind-boggling and necessary as my own.

The more time passes the more I wonder what *it* actually was. The more I don't see him, the more I wonder if I made the whole thing up. The more I don't see the wall, the more I wonder if it was all in my imagination. The further the memories recede into my brain, the greater the chances that they were never real to begin with.

The more I internalize them, I wonder if they were internal to begin with. The more I think about them, the less I know.

Of course, that always seemed to be the point in some sense.

Two days ago, just after Christmas, our family was out for breakfast. After a couple cups of coffee and before the meal came out, Rachel remembered that she left her phone in the car. I, of course, offered to go and get it.

I gave her a gentle kiss before I did because I could not give her enough kisses if I kissed her every moment of every day.

The restaurant was on the same street as the local courthouse, a big piece of old architecture that stands out in many ways, especially for its artistry. I crossed the street to our car and found myself staring up at the sky, at its towering peaks, before grabbing the phone.

"Seth?" the voice sounded familiar but distant, like an old high school friend.

Two people were walking away from the courthouse. He was wearing an oversized suit and she was wearing a simple dress. They looked nice, on purpose.

"James?" I stared at the face I had first met years earlier in a coffee shop. The normal face that I had gotten to know very well. There was something abnormal about it and I realized it was finally human again. Mostly. As much as any of us ever are.

"How are you?" he asked, running up to me and embracing me. I squeezed him back although I wasn't quite sure why.

"You remembered my name?" I asked, a little surprised.

"Are you kidding?" His smile was a thing of perfection on a level beyond the physical. "How could I not? You changed my life!"

I smiled too, just because his was too contagious not to. "I did?"

"Are you kidding? I wasn't doing well. At all. Felt trapped. Going through the motions. Making bricks, right?"

"Right," I repeated, with an odd stare.

"Dark," he said slowly. "Gray." Another pause. "Monotone." He smiled. "Insipid."

"Insipid?" I uttered.

"What kind of life is that? Walls and chains. Prisons, right?"

"Right."

"I mean, you got me out, man. You got me out. Your words. Your love. Your support. Your grace. Your trust." He smiled again, with vivid color and joy. "I mean, man." He reached out and embraced me again. "I can't thank you enough. Even after all that I did to you. I know life was hard for you too but you stuck with me all that time. What can I say?"

"But—" I mouthed, still embracing him. "But…"

"Hey," he pushed me back and looked me directly in the eyes. I had looked in the eyes many times. "I love you. Thanks for doing what I needed. You made it real, my friend."

"But—" It was the only response I could give.

"But, nothing. I just left the courthouse. Things are looking better. Wrapped up some loose ends and I'm ready for a different, more vibrant life. There's a lot to fight out there."

"Right…" I was apparently only able to say two words. "But…"

That was the other one.

"Jeez, Seth." He patted me on the shoulder. "It's like you're seeing a ghost."

"Right."

"Well, keep up the good work, man. One hole at a time." He laughed.

I laughed. In awe and confusion.

"Oh, crap," he shouted. "I can't believe it. This is my wife. Mary."

I actually looked at her, surprised that I hadn't already but James had fully captured my senses. She was dressed simply but beautifully. There was something about her that I immediately recognized. Calm and peaceful. I had seen her in the arena. And Rachel had mentioned something about meeting a Mary …

"Nice to meet you." She held out her hand and I shook it. I just smiled. Melting in her gaze.

"Nice to meet you," I answered more truthfully than I've ever meant.

"Been trying to hook this one for a long time, man. A long time. Feels like years in the making." He laughed. "But, you know some things take a lot of time and change." James laughed and laughed and Mary laughed and they leaned in and kissed each other with a kiss I recognized well.

It was a kiss whose image I never want to leave my mind. My eyes grew misty with joy.

"Oh." Mary reached into a pocket and pulled out a rock, a simple white stone. "I wanted to give this to you. It's not much but it has always meant something to us."

"But …" I turned it over and felt the texture.

"Oh," James said, reaching into his own pocket. "Yeah, here. Take this one too." It was a simple black stone.

"Yeah, kinda strange something so simple means so much. But a lot of metaphor in that stone. Right?" She smiled.

"Right …"

"Hey." James lifted a hand as though he was toasting. "To light. And life. And the fight. And. You know. The Great Mystery?"

I lifted my hand as well but James and Mary were too busy staring at each other to notice. They leaned in for another kiss and I made sure to sear it on my mind along with their smiles.

I haven't stopped smiling, or seeing and feeling them in everything outside and inside of me, since that moment.

Two stones sit on my desk as I type these final words.

One is black and one is white, although I will say, there is a lot of gray between them.

And the rocks smile with me.

AUTHOR GRATITUDE AND PROPS

Heidi!
You won't have to hear me talk about this book anymore! Okay, you probably will. The number of drafts you have read, the number of times you have pulled me out of the dip of writing hell, and the number of times you have pulled me down from the arrogance of writing heaven, are too many to count. Thank you for making me, and this story, what we are, and for always smiling when I need it and kicking me in the ass when I need it, no matter where we are in life. You are the absolute greatest partner a human could ask for and an even better marriage partner. I freaking love you.

Isaac and Abbey.
Thank you for reading multiple drafts of your "dad's book" and not rolling your eyes but dishing out amazing words of encouragement and insight instead. You two are way too smart and I'm way too proud of you.

Anna.
You haven't even read this thing but you probably know more about it than anyone because you've been forced to listen to your dad talk about it incessantly for hours upon hours. You are such a star and such a light and well ... now you have to read it?

Robin.
Will you be my editor forever? Please. Thank you for your time and passion, your dedication, and for smoothing out all the rough edges, shining all the dull spots, and making this baby hum. And thank you for caring, more than a job, for it.

Greg.
I don't know how you do what you do but thank you. Grammar and sentence structure are not my forté — as you know — and I'm so glad they are yours. (Also, I'll be calling you for the next book.)

Pasma.

There has not been a bigger fan or master of encouragement for this. From the first time you read it, you haven't stopped pushing, loving, and insisting on its worth. Every creative and project needs a creative sidekick — thanks for being mine!

Robyn.

Your pile of notes and comments were invaluable, even if I knew how much work they meant was coming and hated them a little at first.

Sarah C.

Thank you for the time and energy you put into reading drafts and all of your comments. Again, priceless.

Rand, Kari, Jeff L.

Thank you for reading early drafts, all the way through, and telling me what you thought! I so appreciate the effort and feedback.

Branches.

If you ever went to Branches, or knew me as your pastor, you'll recognize pieces of the stories, the experiences, and some of me. Though I'm no longer a part of your community on Sunday mornings, thank you for your grace, your support, and your love for all of those years. Most of this story was written during that time and I hope you feel nothing but love for it, and maybe a spur to keep moving, changing, searching, and finding The Great Mystery. I know I do.

And Jesse Mac.

Thanks for being a college freshman at the coffee bar and telling me to write this book. It's those little things that kick off big ones.

Finally.

Though I've never met most of the people on the list below, I have had the pleasure of surrounding myself with their writings, their speeches, their podcasts, their conferences, and whatever else I could get my hands on from them. They have tremendously affected how I see the world, people, and my own self. It's ironic that many on this list have been labeled as dangerous and heretical. I'm sure Ehs would be proud. If you like anything in this book, make sure and find anything created by any of the following people and dive in. You won't be disappointed. So much of what makes this book great is owed to these amazing, enlightened, creative, and free human beings.

(in alphabetical order)

James Altucher
Kurt Andersen
Reza Aslan
Rob Bell
Cynthia Bourgeault
Gregory Boyle
Russell Brand
Brené Brown
Joseph Campbell
Sean Carroll
Ron Chernow
Paul Coutinho
Alain de Botton
Anthony de Mello
Jacques Ellul
Pete Enns
Viktor Frankl
Daniel Gardner
Elizabeth Gilbert
Jack Gilbert
Malcolm Gladwell
Seth Godin
Hafiz
Tomáš Halík
Yuval Noah Harari
Johann Hari
Sam Harris
Kent Hoffman
Catherine Hoke
Pete Holmes
Aldous Huxley
Amy-Jill Levine
Carl Jung
Sebastian Junger
David Kastan and Stephen Farthing
Harold Kushner
Dalai Lama
David Leddick and Shawn Coyne
Mario Livio
Mark Manson
Kyriacos C Markides
Raoul Martinez
Thomas Merton
Friedrich Nietzsche
Keith Payne
Esther Perel
Daniel Pink
Steven Pressfield
Richard Rohr
Peter Rollins
Hans Rosling
Carlo Rovelli
Rumi
Leonard Scovens and Agnes Fury
Alexander Shaia
Dax Shepard
Michael Singer
Alix Spiegel, Hanna Rosin, Lulu Miller
Spinoza
Bryan Stevenson
Andrew Sullivan
Cheryl Strayed
Pierre Teilhard de Chardin
Pádraig Ó Tuama
Desmond Tutu
Jessica Valenti
Sarah Vowell
Alan Watts
Richard Wilkinson and Kate Pickett
Tripp York

One more list. Thank you to each of the following people/families for the extra trust, support, and excitement for this book!

The VIP's.

Kari and Jason Cardon
Landon and Sarah Crecelius
Dana and Tony Fryman
Hannah and Lauren
Melanie and Jeff Hart
Jessica and Nathan Henry
Nancy Janzen
Tyler Lafferty
Jeff Lanctot
Janice and Fred Leaf
Aaron and Leith McHugh
Aaron and Darcy McMurray
Rand and Robin Miller
Ron and Barbara Miller
Jeff and Jenny Oswalt
Jonathan and Michelle Pasma
Whitney and Jordan Tampien
Sheli Williams
Jesse Aldulaimi and Marina
Matthew Beever
Jason Bilyeu
Katie and Luke Clum
Tom Davis
Colleen and Don Ellwanger
Danny and Lisa Leaf
Jennifer and Adam Little
James Fisher
Ryan and Janny Kiely
Kris and Alexa Mayhew
Menley Neitzel
Krystyn Satko
Sean Tyson

Visit insipidbook.com for ways to keep the story going including book club questions, marketing materials, merchandise, and more.

Ryan has always been in love with story and its power over society. He spent 12 years creating stories and design for the best-selling Myst video game franchise. He spent 10 years telling stories every Sunday as the pastor of Branches—a church he started—before leaving religion altogether. He has started two companies to share stories through art, authored four books and a blog, hosted two podcats, and is currently creating a story for an upcoming video game as well as a screenplay for an upcoming television show.

Ryan loves to travel, to see and hear the stories of different cultures and peoples around the world. He lives in the Pacific Northwest with his wife of over 25 years and three kids, and thinks it's all a pretty fantastic and fortunate story to be living.

rsjmiller.com
(podcast) lightslikeus.com

www.ingramcontent.com/pod-product-compliance
Lightning Source LLC
Chambersburg PA
CBHW060818310726
48980CB00002B/335
* 9 7 8 0 9 8 9 5 4 5 4 6 4 *